The
MX Book
of
New
Sherlock
Holmes
Stories

Part XLIII
2024 Annual
(1874-1888)

THE MX BOOK OF NEW SHERLOCK HOLMES STORIES

STORIES

PART XLIII
2024 ANNUAL
(1874-1888)

SOUTHAMPTON STREET

359

EDITED
BY
David
Marcum

OFFICES

TRADITIONAL HOLMES
ADVENTURES
COMPILED FOR THE
BENEFIT OF THE
RESTORATION OF
UNDERSHAW

ISBN Hardback 978-1-80424-478-4
ISBN Paperback 978-1-80424-479-1
AUK ePub ISBN 978-1-80424-480-7
AUK PDF ISBN 978-1-80424-481-4

Published in the UK by
MX Publishing
335 Princess Park Manor, Royal Drive,
London, N11 3GX
www.mxpublishing.co.uk

David Marcum can be reached at:
thepapersofsherlockholmes@gmail.com

Cover design by Brian Belanger
www.belangerbooks.com and *www.redbubble.com/people/zhahadun*

Internal Illustrations by Sidney Paget

CONTENTS

Forewords

Adventures

(Continued on the next page . . .)

(Continued on the next page . . .)

(Continued on the next page . . . .)

**These additional Sherlock Holmes adventures
can be found in the previous volumes of**
The MX Book of New Sherlock Holmes Stories

(Continued on the next page . . . .)

(Continued on the next page . . . .)

PART V – Christmas Adventures

(Continued on the next page . . . .)

(Continued on the next page . . . .)

PART VII – Eliminate the Impossible: 1880-1891

PART VIII – Eliminate the Impossible: 1892-1905

(Continued on the next page . . . .)

Part IX – 2018 Annual (1879-1895)

(Continued on the next page . . . .)

(Continued on the next page . . . .)

(Continued on the next page . . . .)

PART XIV: 2019 Annual (1891 -1897)

(Continued on the next page . . . .)

The Poisoned Regiment – Carl Heifetz
The Case of the Persecuted Poacher – Gayle Lange Puhl
It's Time – Harry DeMaio
The Case of the Fourpenny Coffin – I.A. Watson
The Horror in King Street – Thomas A. Burns, Jr.

PART XV: 2019 Annual (1898-1917)
Foreword – Will Thomas
Foreword – Roger Johnson
Foreword – Melissa Grigsby
Foreword – Steve Emecz
Foreword – David Marcum
Two Poems – Christopher James
The Whitechapel Butcher – Mark Mower
The Incomparable Miss Incognita – Thomas Fortenberry
The Adventure of the Twofold Purpose – Robert Perret
The Adventure of the Green Gifts – Tracy J. Revels
The Turk's Head – Robert Stapleton
A Ghost in the Mirror – Peter Coe Verbica
The Mysterious Mr. Rim – Maurice Barkley
The Adventure of the Fatal Jewel-Box – Edwin A. Enstrom
Mass Murder – William Todd
The Notable Musician – Roger Riccard
The Devil's Painting – Kelvin I. Jones
The Adventure of the Silent Sister – Arthur Hall
A Skeleton's Sorry Story – Jack Grochot
An Actor and a Rare One – David Marcum
The Silver Bullet – Dick Gillman
The Adventure at Throne of Gilt – Will Murray
"The Boy Who Would Be King – Dick Gillman
The Case of the Seventeenth Monk – Tim Symonds
Alas, Poor Will – Mike Hogan
The Case of the Haunted Chateau – Leslie Charteris and Denis Green
        (Introduction by Ian Dickerson)
The Adventure of the Weeping Stone – Nick Cardillo
The Adventure of the Three Telegrams – Darryl Webber

Part XVI – Whatever Remains . . . Must Be the Truth (1881-1890)
Foreword – Kareem Abdul-Jabbar
Foreword – Roger Johnson
Foreword – Steve Emecz
Foreword – David Marcum
The Hound of the Baskervilles (Retold) (*A Poem*) – Josh Pachter
The Wylington Lake Monster – Derrick Belanger
The *Juju* Men of Richmond – Mark Sohn

(Continued on the next page . . . .)

Part XVII – Whatever Remains . . . Must Be the Truth (1891-1898)

Part XVIII – Whatever Remains . . . Must Be the Truth (1899-1925)

(Continued on the next page . . . .)

Part XIX: 2020 Annual (1882-1890)

(Continued on the next page . . . .)

The Adventure of the Matched Set – Peter Coe Verbica
When the Prince First Dined at the Diogenes Club – Sean M. Wright
The Sweetenbury Safe Affair – Tim Gambrell

Part XX: 2020 Annual (1891-1897)
Foreword – John Lescroart
Foreword – Roger Johnson
Foreword – Lizzy Butler
Foreword – Steve Emecz
Foreword – David Marcum
The Sibling (*A Poem*) – Jacquelynn Morris
Blood and Gunpowder – Thomas A. Burns, Jr.
The Atelier of Death – Harry DeMaio
The Adventure of the Beauty Trap – Tracy Revels
A Case of Unfinished Business – Steven Philip Jones
The Case of the S.S. Bokhara – Mark Mower
The Adventure of the American Opera Singer – Deanna Baran
The Keadby Cross – David Marcum
The Adventure at Dead Man's Hole – Stephen Herczeg
The Elusive Mr. Chester – Arthur Hall
The Adventure of Old Black Duffel – Will Murray
The Blood-Spattered Bridge – Gayle Lange Puhl
The Tomorrow Man – S.F. Bennett
The Sweet Science of Bruising – Kevin P. Thornton
The Mystery of Sherlock Holmes – Christopher Todd
The Elusive Mr. Phillimore – Matthew J. Elliott
The Murders in the Maharajah's Railway Carriage – Charles Veley and Anna Elliott
The Ransomed Miracle – I.A. Watson
The Adventure of the Unkind Turn – Robert Perret
The Perplexing X'ing – Sonia Fetherston
The Case of the Short-Sighted Clown – Susan Knight

Part XXI: 2020 Annual (1898-1923)
Foreword – John Lescroart
Foreword – Roger Johnson
Foreword – Lizzy Butler
Foreword – Steve Emecz
Foreword – David Marcum
The Case of the Missing Rhyme (*A Poem*) – Joseph W. Svec III
The Problem of the St. Francis Parish Robbery – R.K. Radek
The Adventure of the Grand Vizier – Arthur Hall
The Mummy's Curse – DJ Tyrer
The Fractured Freemason of Fitzrovia – David L. Leal
The Bleeding Heart – Paula Hammond
The Secret Admirer – Jayantika Ganguly

(Continued on the next page . . . .)

Part XXII: Some More Untold Cases (1877-1887)

(Continued on the next page . . . .)

The Dundas Separation Case – Kevin P. Thornton
The Broken Glass – Denis O. Smith

Part XXIII: Some More Untold Cases (1888-1894)

Part XXIV: Some More Untold Cases (1895-1903)

(Continued on the next page . . . .)

Part XXV: 2021 Annual (1881-1888)

(Continued on the next page . . . .)

The Switched String – Chris Chan
The Case of the Secret Samaritan – Jane Rubino
The Bishopsgate Jewel Case – Stephen Gaspar

Part XXVI: 2021 Annual (1889-1897)

Part XXVII: 2021 Annual (1898-1928)

(Continued on the next page . . . .)

Mrs. Crichton's Ledger – Tim Gambrell
The Adventure of the Not-Very-Merry Widows – Craig Stephen Copland
The Son of God – Jeremy Branton Holstein
The Adventure of the Disgraced Captain – Thomas A. Turley
The Woman Who Returned From the Dead – Arthur Hall
The Farraway Street Lodger – David Marcum
The Mystery of Foxglove Lodge – S.C. Toft
The Strange Adventure of Murder by Remote Control – Leslie Charteris and Denis Green
(Introduction by Ian Dickerson)
The Case of The Blue Parrot – Roger Riccard
The Adventure of the Expelled Master – Will Murray
The Case of the Suicidal Suffragist – John Lawrence
The Welbeck Abbey Shooting Party – Thomas A. Turley
Case No. 358 – Marcia Wilson

Part XXVIII: More Christmas Adventures (1869-1888)
Foreword – Nancy Holder
Foreword – Roger Johnson
Foreword – Steve Emecz
Foreword – Emma West
Foreword – David Marcum
A Sherlockian Christmas (A Poem) – Joseph W. Svec III
No Malice Intended – Deanna Baran
The Yuletide Heist – Mark Mower
A Yuletide Tragedy – Thomas A. Turley
The Adventure of the Christmas Lesson – Will Murray
The Christmas Card Case – Brenda Seabrooke
The Chatterton-Smythe Affair – Tim Gambrell
Christmas at the Red Lion – Thomas A. Burns, Jr.
A Study in Murder – Amy Thomas
The Christmas Ghost of Crailloch Taigh – David Marcum
The Six-Fingered Scoundrel – Jeffrey A. Lockwood
The Case of the Duplicitous Suitor – John Lawrence
The Sebastopol Clasp – Martin Daley
The Silent Brotherhood – Dick Gillman
The Case of the Christmas Pudding – Liz Hedgecock
The St. Stephen's Day Mystery – Paul Hiscock
A Fine Kettle of Fish – Mike Hogan
The Case of the Left Foot – Stephen Herczeg
The Case of the Golden Grail – Roger Riccard

(Continued on the next page . . . .)

Part XXIX: More Christmas Adventures (1889-1896)

Part XXX: More Christmas Adventures (1897-1928)

(Continued on the next page . . . .)

(Continued on the next page . . . .)

Part XXXIII: 2022 Annual (1896-1919)

(Continued on the next page . . . .)

(Continued on the next page . . . .)

Part XXXVI: "However Improbable . . . ." (1897-1919)

(Continued on the next page . . . .)

The Case of the Missing Minute – Dan Rowley
The Peacock Arrow – Chris Chan
The Spy on the Western Front – Tim Symonds

Part XXXVII: 2023 Annual (1875-1889)
Foreword – Michael Sims
Foreword – Roger Johnson
Foreword Steve Emecz
Foreword – Emma West
Foreword – David Marcum
The Adventure of the Improbable American – Will Murray
The Return of Springheeled Jack – Brenda Seagrove
The Incident of the Pointless Abduction – Arthur Hall
The Adventure of the Absent Crossing Sweeper – Steven Philip Jones
The Adventure of the Disappearing – Dan Rowley and Don Baxter
The Abridge Disappearance – David Marcum
The Adventure of the Green Horse – Hugh Ashton
The Adventure of Woodgate Manor – Sonya Kudei
The Incident of the Mangled Rose Buses – Barry Clay
The Sandwich Murder – DJ Tyrer
The Adventure of the Wandering Stones – Mark Wardecker
The Charity Collection – Paul Hiscock
The Catastrophic Cyclist – Tom Turley
The Adventure of the Sketched Bride – James Gelter
The Adventure of the Downing Street Demise – Brett Fawcett
The Continental Conspiracy – Martin Daley
The Belmore Street Museum Affair – Bob Byrne
The Adventure of the Furniture Collector – Tracy J. Revels
The Serpent's Tooth – Matthew White

Part XXXVIII: 2023 Annual (1889-1896)
Foreword – Michael Sims
Foreword – Roger Johnson
Foreword Steve Emecz
Foreword – Emma West
Foreword – David Marcum
The Muddled Monologue – Ian Ableson
Bad Timing – Gordon Linzner
The Adventure of the Living Terror – Craig Janacek
The Adventure of the Predatory Philanthropist – I.A. Watson
The Affair of the Addleton Giant – Margaret Walsh
The Adventure of the Faithful Wolfhound – Tracy J. Revels
The Texas Legation Business – David Marcum
Death at Simpsons – David MacGregor
The Adventure of the Reluctant Executioner – Arthur Hall

(Continued on the next page . . . .)

(Continued on the next page . . . .)

Part XLI: Further Untold Cases (1877-1892)

Part XLII: Further Untold Cases (1894-1922)

(Continued on the next page . . . .)

The following contributors appear in these companion volumes:
Part XLIV – 2024 Annual (1889-1897)
Part XLV – 2024 Annual (1898-1917)

Editor's Foreword:
"A fake, is it? Well, strike me!"
by David Marcum

Once upon a time, in long-ago days that are receding inexorably away from us into the misty past, the opportunities for admirers of Mr. Sherlock Holmes to enjoy his adventures were quite thin on the ground. For the first six years between late 1887 and late 1893, there were only twenty-six published Holmes narratives – *Twenty-six!* – with the last of those telling of Holmes's supposed death at the Reichenbach Falls. Then there was nothing – officially and Canonically, that is – until *The Hound of the Baskervilles* was serially released in 1901-1902. The next thirty-three Canonical tales appeared over the following twenty-five years, with more than one-third of those appearing as *The Return of Sherlock Holmes* (1903-1904), while publication of the others were sometimes separated from one another by years.

And then, the well might have dried up. At the end of the 1920's, both Watson and then the First Literary Agent had died, and Holmes was long removed to Sussex. He wasn't exactly retired from detection, but the majority of his time was then more involved in his apiaristic studies, and also working on his *magnum opus*, *The Whole Art of Detection*. For the admirers of Mr. Sherlock Holmes, there was a vast Holmesian vacuum.

Of course, there were other detectives who had filled the void when Holmes left Baker Street, although their arrivals didn't occur overnight. Dr. John Thorndyke was accepting clients at 5A King's Bench Walk in the late 1890's, so he overlapped Holmes's London practice by a few years. Solar Pons went into private practice in 1907 – possibly at 7B Praed Street, or perhaps somewhere else in those early days before moving so close to Paddington Station. Sometime after arriving in England as a war refugee in 1916, Hercule Poirot made his way to London and set up a consulting practice at No. 14 Farraway Street. The 1920's welcomed Lord Peter Wimsey to 110A Piccadilly Street and Albert Campion at 17A Bottle Street, with plenty of work for both. Their various biographers and literary agents provided information when news of Holmes was lacking, but what was needed – then and now and always – were more of Holmes's cases. *Lots more.*

In the early days, there were many Holmes parodies, but they're bogus and forgettable wastes of time. Seeing the supposedly "clever" and "humorous" ways that Holmes and Watson's names were misspelled and distorted is now quite painful. Why go down those dead-end rabbit holes if stories about the True Holmes can be obtained?

The earliest extra-Canonical adventure was William Gillette's 1899 play (and later film and radio show) *Sherlock Holmes*. It had some painful inaccuracies – that bizarre romance that Gillette awkwardly jammed onto the conclusion, and ignorantly naming Professor Moriarty *Robert* instead of *James* – but it helped to fill the chasm. Then, decades later, Edith Meiser brilliantly realized that Holmes's adventures would be perfect when dramatized for the young radio medium. After multiple broadcasts of many of the pitifully few sixty Canonical stories, she brought forth additional previously unrevealed adventures – "The Hindoo in the Wicker Basket", "The Haunted Clock", and possibly the first explanation behind the events of "The Giant Rat of Sumatra". After Meiser's association with the radio show ended, other chroniclers – like Denis Green, Leslie Charteris, and Anthony Boucher – carried on her important work.

Although many details of these early extra-Canonical adventures ended up being incorrect, courtesy of script writers adding their own poorly informed touches to Watson's notes, it was still good news when a number of new stories also appeared in the 1930's and 1940's by way of films starring Clive Brook, Arthur Wontner, and Basil Rathbone. In the 1950's, Adrian Conan Doyle, son of the First Literary Agent, and John Dickson Carr revealed *The Exploits of Sherlock Holmes*. While Adrian, along with his brother Denis, had made many enemies within the Sherlockian community that resulted in attacks on this particular Holmesian volume, it's actually an excellent collection of stories about the *True Holmes* – set in the correct period, and with no non-Sherlockian aspects and agendas awkwardly grafted on.

1959's Hammer version of *The Hound* was notable for several reasons: The first time Holmes was excellently acted by Peter Cushing. The first Holmes film in color. But also because it had a vastly altered and fictional ending. (This wasn't the first time that *The Hound* had been violated. Several German versions leapt in entirely absurd directions, and even Rathbone's version added a séance and left out Lestrade.)

The 1960's gave us, in addition to the Canonical offerings of Peter Cushing and Douglas Wilmer, the first film encounter between Holmes and Jack the Ripper, *A Study in Terror* (1965 – although the first print encounter was *Wie Jack, der Aufschlitzer Gefast Wurde* [How Jack the Ripper Was Caught] in 1907). The book version of *A Study in Terror* contains extended alternating chapters of both Holmes's investigation and Ellery Queen's contemporary follow-up as he's reading Watson's account – and along the way, it happily provides another book in the Queen Canon.

The parodies had continued all along, of course. All sorts of films over the years indirectly referenced Holmes when they placed characters in deerstalkers – Laurel and Hardy, The Three Stooges, The Marx Brothers, Abbott and Costello, and even The Little Rascals (a.k.a. Our Gang, depending on your generation). 1956 brought the brilliant *Deduce, You Say,* starring Daffy Duck and Porky Pig as Dorlock Homes and Dr. Watkins. Throughout, no one ever said that Daffy Duck or Harpo Marx or Lou Costello had actually *played* Sherlock Holmes. People had enough sense to realize that Holmes was *Holmes* – separate from these completely different characters displaying Sherlockian aspects. But in 1971, the shift between harmless Holmesian parody and more detrimental Holmesian replacement began to occur with *They Might Be Giants* starring George C. Scott. He portrayed a modern-day judge, Justin Playfair, who slides into mental illness after the death of his wife. He believes he's Holmes, and those around him seem to believe it, but there is never any question – Scott is playing *Justin Playfair*, a man with a debilitating delusion, and he is *not* ever actually *Sherlock Holmes*.

And yet . . . when people now make lists of Holmes on screen, they list George C. Scott as Holmes – *although he never actually played Sherlock Holmes!*

This terrible trend of slapping Holmes's name on any character and then asserting that this *was* Holmes, as if Holmes was some body-and-time hopping Time Lord, began to gain traction. In *The Return of the World's Greatest Detective*, Larry Hagman plays *Sherman* Holmes, a modern-day policeman whose motorcycle falls on him – and he wakes up believing that's he's *Sherlock* Holmes – and now some people think that Larry Hagman played Holmes. 1984's *The Return of Sherlock Holmes* was a new twist – Sherlock Holmes had been frozen in the 1890's and was thawed out in the 1980's. The same sad gimmick was repeated in *1994: Baker Street.* In neither case did the actors actually play Holmes, as Holmes was *not* frozen and thawed out in the latter Twentieth Century – but people still credit these as actual Holmes films, and indicate that these actors played Holmes – which they did not. These films eroded the actual facts about Holmes in people's minds, wherein they forget or willfully ignore that Holmes was a man born in 1854, and not a thawed-out Holmesicle in modern times. Nor was he a mentally ill judge or brain-damaged motorcycle cop.

In between these two frozen films, Michael Caine played Reginald Kincaid – and not Sherlock Holmes – in *Without a Clue* (1988). This is another parody Holmes film, and not a legitimate post-Canonical work – and yet, lists and artwork regularly include Caine as "Sherlock Holmes", despite the fact that he never played him.

Meanwhile, the idea of using Holmes in non-Holmes ways continued to grow as well. There have been more versions of Sherlock Holmes-versus-Dracula than I care to list here, and sadly, in almost every case the authors forget Holmes's dictum of "No ghosts [*or vampires*] need apply,", and they essentially and simply re-tell Bram Stoker's *Dracula* with Holmes replacing Van Helsing. This opened the door to all kinds of other Holmes-as-Van Helsing encounters with Frankenstein, the Wolfman, demons and devils (including Satan himself), mummies, Lovecraftian Gods, steam-punk monstrosities, dinosaurs, sea monsters, space aliens, brain-eating spoors, brain-eating space-alien spoors, and just about any other supernatural critter imaginable. *No ghosts need apply? Pfui!* In these cases, no normal client need apply, because Holmes is too busy looking for his cross and his garlic and his holy water and his silver bullets for the next monster encounter.

And as *Fake Holmes* became even more un-moored from *True Holmes*, it was easier to graft on various other aspects – taking him from the person described in the Canon to a various levels of dysfunctional brokenness, to the point that certain television shows presented him as a full-on sociopathic murderer or a tattooed New York drug addict paying off a prostitute at the exact moment he meets his new Watson (and that we, the viewer, first meet him too).

But thankfully, the *True Holmes* has *not* been lost in this red tide of Holmes-in-name-only.

In 1974, Nicholas Meyer inaugurated the new (and still ongoing) Sherlockian Golden Age with his discovery of *The Seven-Per-Cent Solution*. The story is flawed, of course – the parts about Moriarty being a victim, for instance, and that the Great Hiatus never occurred, were apparently grafted onto the manuscript by Moriarty's heirs in an effort to rehabilitate his reputation. Still, the world was electrified when this book was released, for it became apparent that there were unknown Watsonian manuscripts out there in the world, waiting to be discovered – in scattered Tin Dispatch Boxes (for there were apparently more than one of those,) and hidden in people's attics and buried in their grandparent's papers. In 1975, *The Seven-Per-Cent Solution* became a major film, further pouring gas on the previously smoldering *True Holmes* fire. Stories began to trickle forth from authors like Sean Wright and Nick Utechin and Daniel Stashower – slowly at first, and then more and more and more. That particular genie, thank God, was out of the bottle for good.

But imagine a world where Nicholas Meyer and the rest *didn't* discover Watson's manuscripts – first *The Seven-Per-Cent Solution*, and then others. Would the misdirection taken by George C. Scott's *They Might Be Giants* have become more influential? Would the parodies and

4

subversive versions of *Fake Holmes* have become even more established with no Sherlockian Golden Age to hold them in check? Would Holmes as Van Helsing become the new norm, replacing in people's mind the Canonical Holmes, and making the latter original adventures no more than footnotes or a jumping-off place? Or would Holmes have irrevocably become the poster child for murderous sociopaths, as almost became the case in the early 2000's after the frantic and urgent efforts of that television show's producers to permanently hijack him that way?

In 2015, *The MX Book of New Sherlock Holmes Stories* was specifically created to remind people of the *True Holmes* – a hero and not a villain. A consulting detective, and not a monster hunter. Someone to be admired and taken seriously, and not a subject of comedy and ridicule. A champion born in 1854 and set in a specific era, and not a Doctor Who wanna-be who can be dropped into any timeline.

Now, nearly ten years later, with 45 volumes (and more in preparation) and over 920 stories, more weight has been added to the scales on the side of the *True Holmes*. But *Fake Holmes* is still sitting over there, grinning and gibbering on the other side of the see-saw, and the work isn't done.

We can but try.

* * * * *

"Of course, I could only stammer out my thanks."
– *The unhappy John Hector McFarlane, "The Norwood Builder"*

As always when one of these collections is finished, I want to thank with all my heart my incredible, patient, brilliant, kind, and beautiful wife of nearly thirty-six years, Rebecca – Every day I count my blessings and realize how lucky I am, for she is the finest and fairest of them all!!! – and our amazing, funny, creative, talented, and wonderful son, and my friend, Dan. I love you both, and you are everything to me!

With each new set of the MX anthologies, some things get easier, and there are also new challenges. For several years, the stresses of real life have been much greater than when this series started. Through all of this, the amazing contributors have once again pulled some amazing works from The Tin Dispatch Box. I'm more grateful than I can express to every contributor who has donated both time and royalties to this ongoing project – both for the current set, and also the 200+ contributors from around the world since the beginning. It's amazing what we've accomplished – as just mentioned, over 920 new Holmes adventures in 45 volumes (so far), and over $120,000 raised for the Undershaw school for special needs children!

I also want to give special recognition to the multiple contributors of this set: Arthur Hall, Tracy Revels, Marcia Wilson, Daniel D. Victor, Susan Knight, Alan Dimes, Paula Hammond, Mike Adamson, Jonathan Schneer, and Daniel Lenois.

Additionally, I cannot express how thankful I am to all of those who keep buying these books and making them the largest and most popular Sherlockian anthology ever.

I'm so glad to have gotten to know so many of you through this process – both contributors and readers. It's an undeniable fact that Sherlock Holmes people are the *best* people!

I wish especially thank the following:

- *Daniel Stashower* – I first became aware of Mr. Stashower in 1985, when his Holmes adventure *The Adventure of the Ectoplasmic Man* was first published. That was during those dark days when only one or two good traditional Canonical Holmes pastiches were published per year – and that's if it was a good year! I was halfway through college, and bought it and devoured it, impressed at the meeting between Holmes and Watson and Houdini, and also learning a lot more about Houdini than I'd previously known.

  From there, Mr. Stashower went on to write and edit a number of other works, including several volumes about the First Literary Agent (*Teller of Tales: The Life of Arthur Conan Doyle* and *Arthur Conan Doyle: A Life in Letters*, both multiple winners of the Agatha, the Edgar, and the Anthony awards, and *Dangerous Work: Diary of an Arctic Adventure*) and co-editing four Holmes anthologies (with Martin H. Greenberg): *Murder in Baker Street, Murder, My Dear Watson, Ghosts in Baker Street*, and *Sherlock Holmes in America*.

  I was thrilled to finally meet him in 2020 when I attended the Sherlock Holmes Birthday Weekend in New York, when he signed for me another volume he'd co-edited, *The Worst Man in London* (containing the facsimile manuscript of "Charles Augustus Milverton", along with a number of related essays). His work has been important and impressive, but personally I'm most grateful for what he's done to bring more Holmes adventures to light. Having admired his Sherlockian work for nearly forty years, I'm thrilled that he's a part of these books.

6

- *Steve Emecz* – From my first association with MX in 2013, I observed that MX (under Steve Emecz's leadership) was *the* fast-rising superstar of the Sherlockian publishing world – and more than ten years later, that has not changed. Connecting with MX and Steve Emecz was personally an amazing life-changing event for me, as it has been for countless other Sherlockian authors. It has led me to write many more stories, and then to edit books, along with unexpected additional Holmes Pilgrimages to England – none of which might have happened otherwise. By way of my first email with Steve, I've had the chance to make some incredible Sherlockian friends and play in the Holmesian Sandbox in ways that I would have never dreamed possible.

  MX has become *the* powerhouse premiere Sherlockian Publisher, providing new stories for those (like me) who need them, and writing and editing opportunities for those (like me) who might not otherwise have had the chance.

  Through it all, Steve has been one of the most positive and supportive people that I've ever known.

  From the beginning, Steve has let me explore various Sherlockian projects and open up my own personal possibilities in ways that otherwise would have never happened. Thank you, Steve, for every opportunity!

- *Roger Johnson* – From his immediate support at the time of the first volumes in this series to the present, I can't imagine Roger not being part of these books, and once again he has heeded the call. His Sherlockian knowledge is exceptional, as is the work that he does to further the cause of The Master. But even more than that, both Roger and his wife, Jean Upton, are simply the finest and best of people, and I'm very lucky to know both of them. Many many thanks for being part of this.

- *Brian Belanger* – I initially became acquainted with Brian when he took over the duties of creating the covers for MX Books, and I found him to be a great collaborator, and wonderfully creative too. I've worked with him on many projects with MX and Belanger Books, which he co-founded with his brother Derrick Belanger, also a good friend. Along with MX Publishing, Derrick and Brian have absolutely locked up the Sherlockian publishing field with a vast amount of amazing material. It's very gratifying to see the old dinosaurs trembling with every new and worthy Sherlockian project, one after another after another, that these two companies create. Luckily MX and Belanger Books work closely with one another, and I'm thrilled to be associated with both of them. Many thanks to Brian for all he does for both publishers, and for all he's done for me personally.

And finally, last but certainly *not* least, thanks to **Sir Arthur Conan Doyle**: Author, doctor, adventurer, and the Founder of the Sherlockian Feast. Honored, and present in spirit.

As I always note when putting together an anthology of Holmes stories, the effort has been a labor of love. These adventures are just more tiny threads woven into the ongoing Great Holmes Tapestry, continuing to grow and grow, for there can *never* be enough stories about the man whom Watson described as *"the best and wisest . . . whom I have ever known."*

David Marcum
April 6th*, 2024*
The 141st *Anniversary of*
the first day of
"The Speckled Band"

Foreword
by Daniel Stashower

"*This I am sure of,*" Arthur Conan Doyle once declared, "*that there are far fewer supremely good short stories than there are supremely good long books. It takes more exquisite skill to carve the cameo than the statue.*"

The comment reflected hard-won experience. Early in his career, while practicing medicine in Southsea, Conan Doyle seemed on occasion to begrudge the time he spent pursuing the short story form. "*I realized that I could go on doing short stories forever and never make headway,*" he would recall. "*What is necessary is that your name should be on the back of a volume. Only so do you assert your individuality, and get the full credit or discredit of your achievement.*"

He soon reversed course. In April of 1891, even as his novel *The White Company* was enjoying notable success, Conan Doyle's career as a medical practitioner reached a turning point. Having recently abandoned his practice in Southsea to study diseases of the eye, the thirty-one-year-old physician moved his family to London and declared himself ready to "*put up my plate as an oculist*", setting up a consulting room at 2 Upper Wimpole Street. His lease entitled him to a consulting room and a share of a waiting room, but, as Conan Doyle ruefully admitted, "*I was soon to find that they were both waiting rooms.*"

His thoughts naturally turned to literature, and he now approached the subject of short stories in a more congenial spirit. It struck him that there might be some benefit in writing a series of stories featuring a single, continuing character. This offered an advantage over the more conventional serialized novel, because the reader would not lose interest if one installment or another was missed. "*Looking round for my central character,*" he wrote, "*I felt that Sherlock Holmes, whom I had already handled in two little books, would easily lend himself to a succession of short stories.*"

This proved to be a life-changing decision. Not only had Conan Doyle made a canny marketing decision, but he had also found the natural showcase for the talents of Sherlock Holmes. In the two previously published Holmes novellas – *A Study in Scarlet* and *The Sign of the Four* – the detective had been obliged to trundle offstage for long patches of exposition. The short story format offered a compact execution and brisk pace, and highlighted Conan Doyle's singular talent for puzzle plots.

9

Within weeks, Conan Doyle began sending the first of his Sherlock Holmes short stories to a new magazine called *The Strand*, and the rest – in a cliché he would have abhorred – is history.

"*I've written a good deal more about him than I ever intended to do,*" Conan Doyle would observe in 1927, forty years after Holmes first saw print, "*but my hand has been rather forced by kind friends who continually wanted to know more. And so it is that this monstrous growth has come out, out of what was really a comparatively small seed.*"

The phrase "*monstrous growth*" admits a number of interpretations, with a heavy suggestion of Conan Doyle's ambivalence towards his famous creation. One naturally wonders what he would have made of the present volumes, the latest in a series of forty-five – *Forty-five!* – collections of short stories, all contributed by kind friends continually wanting to know more. Even so, I feel confident that Conan Doyle would look upon the MX book series with a kindly eye. "*If every man who receives a cheque for a story which owes its springs to Poe were to pay a tithe to a monument for the master,*" he once declared, "*he would have a pyramid as big as that of Cheops.*" Each of the stories in this series owes its springs to Conan Doyle – unabashedly so. As yet there is no Egyptian pyramid dedicated in Conan Doyle's name, but at last count these books had raised some $120,000 for the Undershaw school, which provides a specialist setting for children with learning difficulties and additional needs, under the banner of "*eliminating the impossible*". It is difficult to imagine a more fitting monument to the master; one that preserves the legacy of his Hindhead home even as it helps to insure – as someone once remarked – that education never ends.

Daniel Stashower, BSI
January 2024

A Letter From Scotland Yard
Discovered by Roger Johnson

My dear Dr. Watson,

Further to our correspondence of the 15th *ult* . . . .

No, scrub that. This is strictly unofficial and off the record, and if you so much as think of publishing any part of it, *I will have you, sunshine*, good and proper.

Right. Where was I? Oh, yes . . . .

I see that Mr. Sherlock Holmes has decided to pack in the detective business and retire to the south coast. Very nice, too! I also am about to become a gentleman of leisure, having been detecting, I may say, for quite a few years more than Mr. H, but I don't expect to be moving from my little house in Camberwell – not till they carry me out feet first, anyway.

Well, well! I can't say I begrudge Mr. Holmes his retirement. Goodness knows he's earned it, and I'm not too proud to admit that he was a great help to me on many occasions, and to some of my colleagues as well. Toby Gregson – He hates being called that! – *Tobias* Gregson is probably indebted to Mr. H. for his promotion. Did you know that? At all events, he became an Inspector shortly after the successful conclusion of the Arnsworth Castle affair.

Come to think of it, I may even owe *my* rise in the force to Mr. Holmes, though I like to think that my own good qualities had something to do with it. If I remember correctly, Mr. H. once said I was the best of the professionals, and I've always taken that as a high compliment, even if he did also call me "that imbecile Lestrade"!

Dear me, but we've seen some times, haven't we, Doctor – You, me and Mr. Sherlock Holmes! "We have heard the chimes at midnight, Master Shallow."

Hah! That surprised you, I'll bet: *Me* quoting the Bard! The fact is that I once saw Beerbohm Tree play Falstaff, and I've never forgotten his performance. I couldn't tell you which play it was – "The Merry Wives of Whatsit" or "Henry Ivy" – but it was the best evening I ever had in the theatre, outside of the Drury Lane pantomimes, of course. (I say, can you imagine Herbert Campbell as the fat knight and Dan Leno as Justice Shallow? That *would* be something, now, wouldn't it?)

We have seen some times, though, haven't we? That Norwood affair, the business out in Herefordshire, the Black Pearl of the Borgias . . . Great days, Doctor, great days! And, you know, I was right about that last case: The Mafia *was* involved, after all, even if its involvement did turn out to be a bit of a red herring.

Do you recall our first proper meeting? Well, of course you do. It was at an empty house in Lauriston Gardens, Brixton – empty, that is, apart from Toby Gregson and a *very* ugly corpse. Gregson was at his most pompous, I remember, and Mr. Holmes was at his most superior. I don't need to tell you that he was always keen to prove himself a better detective than any of us, and in those early days, I sometimes suspected that that outweighed his wish to see justice done. Later, of course, I discovered that I was mistaken, but it was a close-run thing on occasion.

That, as I say, was our first *proper* meeting, though we had seen each other a few times before then, without either of us knowing just who the other one was. I quickly realised that you were sharing digs with Mr. H., and in time he told you that I was – Let me see – "*a well-known detective, who got himself into a fog recently over a forgery case*". Yes, well . . . it's true enough, as far as it goes, though the case was a good deal more complicated than Mr. H. would admit.

You weren't exactly complimentary about me yourself, were you? A "*little sallow, rat-faced, dark-eyed fellow*" you called me then, and not so long after, you said I was "*lean and ferret-like*". Well, I suppose a ferret is a more useful creature than a rat! I rather like ferrets, as it happens. My old dad used to breed them – lithe, handsome things they were, very cat-like in their ways, wonderful for getting in and out of tight corners, absolutely fearless, and unbeatable for rabbiting. You know, I really don't mind being called ferret-like! A ferret's as good a model for a detective as any sort of *dog*.

Come to think of it, you've compared me to a dog on occasion as well. Not a hound – I think you kept that particular simile for Mr. Sherlock Holmes – but a "*small wiry bulldog*". That made my wife sit up, I can tell you! She's always the first to admit that yours truly is no oil painting, but even she couldn't work out how the same person can resemble both a *ferret* and a *bulldog*!

Let's see. That was the Dartmoor business, wasn't it? Why I ever let Mr. Holmes talk me into these things I shall never know. You wouldn't *believe* the trouble I had with my own Superintendent and the Deputy C. C. of the Devonshire Constabulary! I'm sure it put my career back two years. Ah, well, it's all water under the bridge, and I wouldn't have missed it for the world, though I don't know whether Sir Henry would agree. Still, he seems to be getting on all right these days, thank goodness.

What was that stuff about an *unsigned warrant*, though? *"Coming down with* unsigned warrant." I can only imagine that you had lost the telegram I sent and wrote the first thing that came into your head. After all this time I can't remember just what I did say, but I'm certain I never mentioned an *unsigned warrant*! What's the use of a warrant if it isn't *signed*?

And while I think of it, I've often wondered why you described me as *little* and *small*. I'm *thin* – always have been, eat like a horse and never put a pound on – and I'll grant you that I'm shorter than Mr. H. Well, most people are, aren't they? He's a fraction over six foot, I think, and, as you said yourself, he's so *very* lean that he seems to be considerably taller. (It's odd, but *my* leanness seems to have the opposite effect!) I'm shorter than *you*, if it comes to that, but only by half-an-inch. In fact I stand – or did, in my prime – exactly five-foot-ten, the absolute minimum height for an officer in the good old Metropolitan Police.

I hope you don't mind me letting off a bit of steam. It's not really anything personal, you know. Only things are rather slow here at the moment. If I weren't writing to you, I'd just be tidying up my desk and clearing out my cupboard, getting ready to leave the Yard.

I'll miss the old place, of course I will. Old, did I say? This is *New* Scotland Yard, mate, and they don't let you forget it, especially if you've been around as long as I have, and remember working at *Great* Scotland Yard, the other end of Whitehall! Well, you'll remember what that was like. We occupied half-a-dozen buildings around Whitehall Place and Great Scotland Yard. It was dark, poky, and uncomfortable. This place is like the Langham Hotel by comparison, but that's not why I'll miss it.

It's the *people*, the fact that every day is different, the knowledge that you're helping to keep London safe . . . but there's more to it than that. We work hard here, you know (and it is mostly brainwork, whatever Mr. Holmes may say to the contrary). Sometimes it can be dull, but *most* of the time – Well, you've written about the "Adventures" of Sherlock Holmes. I can assure you that the adventures of G. Lestrade have been no less exciting!

Still, I can't deny that the best of them have been the ones I shared with you and Mr. Holmes. The Baskerville case really was a corker, and it would have been hard to top that business of the stolen submarine plans. Police work isn't always appreciated, despite what you may read in the papers, so it's nice to get a bit of public recognition – Ah! I know what you're thinking, but you're wrong. True, there was no public recognition in *that* case: You said yourself that it was part of "*that secret history of a nation which is often so much more intimate and interesting than its public chronicles*". But we all knew, didn't we, that we'd done the country good service, and that we had the approval of the people who matter.

If anyone should ask me, though, what was the most memorable adventure in my forty years with the force, I'd have to say the arrest of Sebastian Moran. Not just because it cleared up a particularly baffling murder case. Not even because it put an end to the Moriarty gang at last, but because it rather gloriously confirmed my suspicions that Mr. Sherlock Holmes *was* still alive and that he would eventually come back to London. You know, Doctor, I was never so glad in my life as when I got his message asking me to be in Baker Street that night!

And now, even though only one of us has reached what I'd call retirement age, we're both packing it in. Goodness knows what Mr. Holmes will find to do down there in Sussex, but I intend to spend my time in the garden. Mrs. L has made it very clear that she doesn't want me in the house all day, getting under her feet!

You've got yourself a good practice now, haven't you, just off Harley Street, and I can't somehow see you retiring for a good many years. Well, if anyone deserves success, Doctor, I reckon it's you. You've said a lot in your memoirs about the remarkable qualities of Mr. Sherlock Holmes, and you've even come to appreciate that we in the C.I.D. aren't lacking in skill and intelligence! But you've rather tended to hide your own light under a bushel. On occasion, you've made yourself out to be a bit of a booby, which is something you're definitely *not*!

Your military service may have been fairly short, but it was by no means ignominious. You're intelligent, skilful and courageous. Unlike Mr. H, you have a gift for making friends – and you're a better shot than he is, for all his fancy pistol-work indoors. (My word, wasn't Mrs. Hudson's face a picture when she saw what he'd done to the wall of your sitting-room!)

Above all, Doctor, you're honest and straightforward. It's been a pleasure and a privilege to know you. If I may adopt the language of the streets for a moment, and use a phrase that I'm sure Mr. Holmes would recognise, you, Dr. John H. Watson, are a *Diamond Geezer*!

Please give my best regards to Mrs. Watson, and believe me to be,

Yours very sincerely,
G. Lestrade . . .

. . . by way of Roger Johnson, BSI, ASH
Editor: *The Sherlock Holmes Journal*
February 2024

An Ongoing Legacy
for Sherlock Holmes
by Steve Emecz

Undershaw
Circa 1900

With over six-hundred Sherlock Holmes books in print, we continue to have lots of fun publishing Holmes stories. *The MX Book of New Sherlock Holmes Stories* is by some way our largest and most successful project.

Since 2023, every book bought on our website means we donate a meal to a family in need through ShareTheMeal from The World Food Programme (WFP). I am proud to have been a member of the external advisory council and a mentor with the WFP for several years, and part of the team in 2020 that was awarded the Nobel Peace Prize. You can find links to all our projects on our website:

https://mxpublishing.com/pages/about-us

Coming into 2024, it is audio that has been the fastest growing segment – though we do see some fans still wanting print, so we will continue to produce paperback and hardcover versions – especially of this series.

Steve Emecz
March 2024

The Doyle Room at Undershaw
Partially funded through royalties from
The MX Book of New Sherlock Holmes Stories

A Word from Undershaw
by Emma West

Undershaw
September 9, 2016
Grand Opening of the Stepping Stones School
(Now *Undershaw*)
(Photograph courtesy of Roger Johnson)

"Until you spread your wings, you'll have no idea how far you can fly."
– Napoleon Bonaparte

There are so many attributes to an Undershaw education, both within the classroom and in the world beyond. Who we are and the strong Undershaw character we show to the world are as real on the outside as they are on the inside. We are who we say we are. Our sense of community, our strong culture, and the values which shape our behaviour all become the very tangible qualities of an Undershaw student.

We have had such a wonderful start to 2024, and at this juncture of being halfway through our school year, it's such a pleasure to recount some of our achievements that go so far in illustrating the cultural fabric of our school.

Under the leadership of Will Milner-Smith, Undershaw's Physical Education Lead, we have seen an exponential increase in participation in sports, particularly football. We have four teams across the school, all of

17

which compete across the county in accessible leagues. Our girls' team has just returned from a tournament hosted by Fulham FC (London's oldest professional football club, established in 1879) where they were not only triumphant, but congratulated for their 'tournament values' by the staff and students from the opposing teams. Illustrating their football skills alongside their inter-personal skills has been the focus of our physical education curriculum, and it was wonderful to see these skills shining through.

To continue the theme of resilience, a group of students have just completed their Duke of Edinburgh Award Bronze Expedition, which involved two days of walking and an overnight camp. The technical skills on show (map reading, setting up camp, fire lighting, and campfire cooking) were balanced beautifully by their life skills and school values of respect, kindness, and resilience – and obviously a huge dose of teamwork.

We are also excited to bring you news of our first collaboration with an international school: Kampinda School in Zambia. PEAS (Promoting Equality in African Schools) is one of our partner charities supported by the Leo Lion Foundation. This is the first of many opportunities of this type for Undershaw, and we're excited for the future of this partnership where we can share best practice and get to know more about the world, our friends in other geographies and cultures, and shape a new way of working.

Undershaw continues to recruit and retain the very best talent, and to that end, all our Teaching Assistants have just been awarded the Open University qualification in 'Understanding Autism'. Not only does this illustrate their significant passion and commitment to our students at Undershaw, but also Undershaw's belief and investment in our staff. Careers at Undershaw are sought after, and working at a Centre of Excellence for SEND education is an enviable role.

We are so proud of our school, and of the staff and students who showcase our vision every day. I continue to be proud of our relationships outside the gates too, some with people who have never set foot in the school but know from our reputation of the abundance of good that we do here. I thank you for sharing your talent with us and for your keen commitment to us and to our remarkable students. Thank you for being by our side as we look forward to end of the academic year, awash with all its celebrations, fun to be had, and the promise of the new beginnings in the year beyond. I look forward to writing again in the Autumn with more news from Undershaw.

Emma West
Headteacher, Undershaw
March 2024

"Undershaw." Hindhead Conan Doyle's House.

Editor's *Caveats*

When these anthologies first began back in 2015, I noted that the authors were from all over the world – and thus, there would be British spelling and American spelling. As I explained then, I didn't want to take the responsibility of changing American spelling to British and vice-versa. I would undoubtedly miss something, leading to inconsistencies, or I'd change something incorrectly.

Some readers are bothered by this, made nervous and irate when encountering American spelling as written by Watson, and in stories set in England. However, here in America, the versions of The Canon that we read have long-ago has their spelling Americanized, so it isn't quite as shocking for us.

Additionally, I offer my apologies up front for any typographical errors that have slipped through. As a print-on-demand publisher, MX does not have squadrons of editors as some readers believe. The business consists of three part-time people who also have busy lives elsewhere – Steve Emecz, Sharon Emecz, and Timi Emecz – so the editing effort largely falls on the contributors. Some readers and consumers out there in the world are unhappy with this – apparently forgetting about all of those self-produced Holmes stories and volumes from decades ago (typed and Xeroxed) with awkward self-published formatting and loads of errors that are now prized as very expensive collector's items.

I'm personally mortified when errors slip through – ironically, there will probably be errors in these *caveats* – and I apologize now, but without a regiment of professional full-time editors looking over my shoulder, this is as good as it gets. Real life is more important than writing and editing – even in such a good cause as promoting the True and Traditional Canonical Holmes – and only so much time can be spent preparing these books before they're released into the wild. I hope that you can look past any errors, small or huge, and simply enjoy these stories, and appreciate the efforts of everyone involved, and the sincere desire to add to The Great Holmes Tapestry.

And in spite of any errors here, there are more Sherlock Holmes stories in the world than there were before, and that's a good thing.

David Marcum
Editor

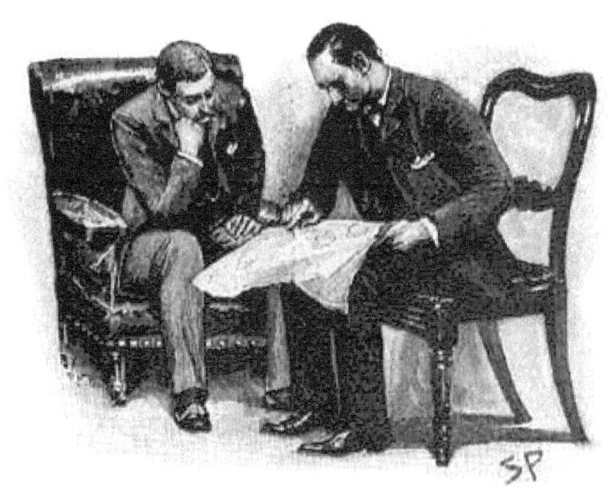

Sherlock Holmes (1854-1957) was born in Yorkshire, England, on 6 January, 1854. In the mid-1870's, he moved to 24 Montague Street, London, where he established himself as the world's first Consulting Detective. After meeting Dr. John H. Watson in early 1881, he and Watson moved to rooms at 221b Baker Street, where his reputation as the world's greatest detective grew for several decades. He was presumed to have died battling noted criminal Professor James Moriarty on 4 May, 1891, but he returned to London on 5 April, 1894, resuming his consulting practice in Baker Street. Retiring to the Sussex coast near Beachy Head in October 1903, he continued to be associated in various private and government investigations while giving the impression of being a reclusive apiarist. He was very involved in the events encompassing World War I, and to a lesser degree those of World War II. He passed away peacefully upon the cliffs above his Sussex home on his 103rd birthday, 6 January, 1957.

Dr. John Hamish Watson (1852-1929) was born in Stranraer, Scotland on 7 August, 1852. In 1878, he took his Doctor of Medicine Degree from the University of London, and later joined the army as a surgeon. Wounded at the Battle of Maiwand in Afghanistan (27 July, 1880), he returned to London late that same year. On New Year's Day, 1881, he was introduced to Sherlock Holmes in the chemical laboratory at Barts. Agreeing to share rooms with Holmes in Baker Street, Watson became invaluable to Holmes's consulting detective practice. Watson was married and widowed three times, and from the late 1880's onward, in addition to his participation in Holmes's investigations and his medical practice, he chronicled Holmes's adventures, with the assistance of his literary agent, Sir Arthur Conan Doyle, in a series of popular narratives, most of which were first published in *The Strand* magazine. Watson's later years were spent preparing a vast number of his notes of Holmes's cases for future publication. Following a final important investigation with Holmes, Watson contracted pneumonia and passed away on 24 July, 1929.

Photos of Sherlock Holmes and Dr. John H. Watson courtesy of Roger Johnson

The
MX Book
of
New
Sherlock
Holmes
Stories
Part XLIII
2024 Annual
(1874-1888)

"Dr. Roylott, I Presume?"
by Kelvin I. Jones

Doctor Grimesby Roylott
Never seemed to laugh a lot,
And neither was he kind,
nor especially
Very grand.

But of this you could be sure;
Of Roylott's dark and sullen side
Nobody could be sure,

As his wife found out,
To her regret,
Though, on first meeting him
Amid an audience
Of officers' wives in the Mess,

She'd found him
Charming and disarming,
Quoting her favourite author,
Rudyard Kipling,
Telling tales of Ganga Din,
And plying her with glasses
of Empire gin.

He'd seemed to her
So awfully nice.

But the tales she later told of Roylott
Soon after she married him
Were of a different order,
For then she discovered
Roylott was steeped in debauchery,
Violence and sin.

On their return to Blighty
Later that same summer,

She'd heard the rumour
From her maid,
How, when in the village inn,

Roylott had supped deep
From his glass,
And a foul, dark mood
Then stole upon him,

And those pitiless eyes
Chanced upon another
Loitering there at the bar;

Then the room drained empty.
Locals were seen, with trembling hands,
Packing away their darts.

For, so went the tale,
When in the grip
Of that brooding fury
And charged with hale,
No wise man might could stand against
This monstrous genie of a human being
 From the safety of the saloon bar,
As Roylott, with quick, deft jabs
Of his spatulate, and warty hands,
Hands which could bend a steel poker,
Or might break a man in two,

Now, with a rain of blows,
Drove the object of his contempt
To the unyielding ground,
Then twisted his steel-capped boot
Into the man's face,
And remained standing, content,
To finish his pint,
His dark face awry,
Watching his witless
Victim's blood slowly dry.

Here then, Roylott lived,
In darkling and oppressive gloom,

Amid the shadowed silences
Of his upper storey rooms
At Stoke Moran,

A cursed, unhappy dwelling,
Grey and mullion – windowed,
Which had lain for centuries
Like a festering sore,
Deep in the sunless vale
Of this vast and barren
Wilderness of land.

Roylott was the grim
Stone-faced master 0f this soulless place,
Here with step – daughters Julia and Helen,

And so merciless was he,
That not long after their mother died,
In a train crash at Crewe
He beat those daughters'
Naked bottoms

With his pandy bat
Or hard-slippered shoe,
Informing each
That their discourtesy to him
Would never be forgotten,
Until their virgin bottoms
turned black and blue
As they lay, defenceless,
There upon his lap.

For Roylott was no ordinary man.
His lip were always scarlet red.
stiff was his back as hardened steel;

Here, to and fro,
He walked the tracks of Birlstone land,
Like some fierce and deadly despot,
Lashing out at gypsies
Who dared to settle in the woods nearby.

On these poor folk
He set his cheetah and his tiger,
And here with his savage companions
They wandered both night and day,

Midst crenellated Gothic towers grey,
Until the travelling folk disappeared
Fearing they might be torn or ripped,
Limb from limb.

Knowing that
If he schemed and plotted right,
Each step-daughter would die a hideous death
One cold and harrowing night;
And that their deaths
would follow soon,
A snake he trained
to his sole command thereafter,

A swamp adder, some said
Was the deadliest snake
In all of India
Which might strike a man dead
In thirty minutes.

A vicious, spiteful thing it ever was.
Each evening when
The girls retired to bed,
Roylott would feed and beat it,

And when the doctor spat
Upon this venomous

Serpent's head,
And the odious thing twisted and bent
Under the cruel and repeated blows
Of his malign
Master's leather whip,
Or lay, bruised by his Penang Lawyer
Walking stick,
Roylott's savage voice bent the snake
To his tyrant's fixed and merciless will.

The swamp adder learned rapidly,
Soon getting the hang of it,
And he would reward it
With headless mouse or mincemeat,
Sliced from rat.

Then the doctor would, each night,
Stand upon his wicker chair,
Cooing gently to his deadly
And unearthly messenger of death,
His much adored 'Speckled Band'.

For Roylott
Was dark. His hair was black, his thoughts
Were dark as an ink stain blot.
He was a man who did not talk a lot.

When he'd lived in India.
He'd heard his servant swear
Under his breath. Roylott took a club
And beat him hard, using all his force,
Showing the man no remorse,
And thus consigned him to an early death.

The servants found Roylott late that morn,
Standing steadfast in the hall.
His shirt was stained with blood and gore.
He stood there like
A bleached and alabaster statue,
Cursing and castigating them all.

Each evening now

After sun went down,
You would find him almost naked,
Standing on that battered wicker chair.

His strength and purpose never faltered;
The daughters would be doomed to a tragic fate.
His grim intent was cunning, measured.

Each would grant him
Two things he desired;
His incestuous pleasure
And the sole contents
Of their combined estates.

No one would hear them scream for mercy,
As each then fell to the viper's bite.

He stood upon that battered chair,
Night after night
Indulging his vision
Of those soft white limbs,
Naked in the pale moonlight.

But he had not heard them coming back,
That smart detective and his friend, the quack.
Nor did he hear that whipping cane
As Sherlock drove the angry reptile
Back to its Master's cold, dark domain.

So he who digs a pit for his neighbour
Is doomed by the plan which he devised,

And falls into the pit himself,

Trapped by his own dark enterprise.

In Stoke Moran, his ghost
So villagers do still say,

At fall of dusk
Still may be seen lingering
By edge of wood or towers grim.

But Roylott,
That creature of the dark
With long black side whiskers
And riding crop

No longer threatens
His step-daughter's life.

Here in the churchyard
Of the quiet village
Still stands the tomb
Of Roylott, late of Stoke Moran.

Wreathed by ivy.
No trace may be seen
On the mildewed tomb
Of this dangerous doctor or his devious plan.

But on many a frosty winter's night.
When all is cold and quiet,
And though fires are lit in every room,
Still can be seen that hardened face;

His skin reptilian,
Those cursed bile-shot eyes
Ever watchful,
Black with venom,
Peering out
From his Black Widow gloom.

NOTE:

This poem is based on the character of Dr. Grimesby Roylott in "The Adventure of The Speckled Band" by Sir Arthur Conan Doyle, in *The Strand Magazine*. This dark Gothic tale by Doyle was his favourite of the Holmes tales, as it is also mine.

– KJ

Devil's Milk
by Marcia Wilson

It might have been the lateness of the hour, but just then, Montague Street looked . . . *faded*.

Lestrade paused underneath the watery light of the street-lamp and ignored the faint rumble of carts behind his back. Somewhere in the grey-green buildings, a man and woman were screaming it out over something that had to do with the Regent's Canal – of which one could still get a healthy whiff whenever the wind shifted from the north side.

The inspector listened with half-an-ear. Were it a domestic dispute, he would be more concerned with homicide. Even in London, it didn't seem likely that someone would stick a person over the smell coming into the open window. It wasn't as if a shut window would be able to keep the wind out . . . .

Montague Street was full of moments like this – and considering the sheer unfashionable reputation of the surrounding areas, that was almost a compliment.

A man like Bob Cratchit wouldn't have been able to afford better. Times had slipped to a poorer state even since *A Christmas Carol* – Lestrade couldn't possibly imagine the Cratchit family being so cheerful and fearless in this day and age. Now one's worries would be much much worse than an ailing Tiny Tim and a daughter who couldn't get home to spend the holiday with her parents. They'd be worried about that same daughter getting home safely, or what their children might be doing to bring home survival money. The fifteen bob-a-week . . . .

In the darkness, a huddled man was coughing the last of his days out with emphysema. The sounds were clarion-clear. The fog was rolling slowly in. The night would be another battle for this man in the open air, against the dampness of the stinking puddles.

Lestrade picked his way across the gleaming black pot-holes. Rheumy red and blue eyes stared back at him, defiant and silent. The inspector courteously avoided eye contact. It would neither be appreciated nor wanted. The wind blew up a terrible reek: Rotting garbage and offal and human wastes . . . they all moved quickly. Lestrade stepped to the other side of the street, and the homeless man to the dubious shelter of the snicket between a small shop and the very building Lestrade was about to enter.

Fruit, the small man realized. There must be a fruit-monger's stall and he threw the spoilt parts in the street. It did occur to him that perhaps the poverty wasn't so dire here, for in some parts of the city, even a stinking-rotten cabbage would be ripped apart and eaten by a man hungry enough. He'd seen it too many times. He'd seen two men nearly kill themselves with their knives over a rotten cabbage. And yet they had fought the policeman, for better they starve than shame themselves at being put in gaol.

A small black shape flitted across his path. Its mate ran directly over his shoe. He swallowed an oath. Rats were a part of London, although more so the closer to the water. He didn't miss that part of his early days along the banks, where the feel of those tiny paws was a regular occurrence.

He was never partial to animals . . . but to rats he was the least attached.

High time he got this over with.

He took a deep breath. The door-knocker was of the old-fashioned, solid sort, a conglomeration of iron and brass, and it was of such an unpleasant mien he doubted even a starving man would nick it for the metal. Jacob Marley's ghost supplanting the ring wouldn't have been as unsettling as this contraption meant to resemble a Chinese dog with an African lion in its ancestry.

I haven't read any sort of Dickens in years. Something must be the matter with me.

And in the meantime, the fog was rolling its way to him. Lestrade grimaced at the enemy's latest approach and lifted the knocker, glad for his gloves. Through the thin leather, he felt the clammy chill of weeping metal.

The landlady who answered was a frightening sort. The stamp of womanhood that sought control as a right of her station. The hard, small eyes scoured him like carbolic acid once, twice, even three times before pausing to think that he might desire admittance.

His badge, Lestrade was strangely amused to note, took no more than a moment's consideration.

"He's inside tonight," the old dragon said of the hand-drawn image in his hand. "Has he done something, then?"

Lestrade caught the underlying eagerness in the dirty woman, and something contrary and obstinate rose to the challenge. "Not at all. An assistant to a case, if you get my meaning."

Oh, she loved the implication that one of her lodgers in this dirty town and filthy street might have seen something. With a grin shy of three teeth (all on the bottom), she paid a huge kick to one of the doors in the hallway, and she stood aside when that same door was torn open with enough force to send its hinge shrieking.

"I trust you have a reason for this interruption?" The high voice belonged to a man who was either upset beyond all comprehension, or hadn't finished settling his vocal gifts. Lestrade's hopes sank as he watched the drama unfold: A dismayingly young-looking man bent over the landlady like a serpent over a bird.

"Not I, Mr. Holmes!" The sniff was fantastic. "Your *guest*."

"Guest?"

Lestrade's heart had still been in the process of sinking at the proof of youth upon that lean face. Then the head with black hair turned, and eyes grey as a spring cloud fastened upon him. Not so young, then. Just moves like a young man does still.

"Mr. Lestrade," a voice came forth. That swiftly, the impression of youth and inexperience had rolled away like a holed carpet. "You haven't yet recovered from your duties upon the London Particular."

Something about that voice – or perhaps the way he was being looked at, up and down like something that was on the other side of the zoo-bars – hackled. "If someone's been telling stories about my competency, sir, I would like to know about it."

The young man chuckled as if Lestrade had said something amusing. "Not at all," he responded with a swiftness that made the other's head spin. "You are underweight – else your clothing is cut slightly too large for your form, and with your eye to dress that would be most unlikely. A man who spends his limited pay on the better footwear would hardly ignore the cut of his coat when a tailor charges by how much cloth he must provide." A long, nearly skeletal finger dipped in the air between them, and before Lestrade could finish enduring the unpleasantness of his face warming under embarrassment –

"You are a most unhealthy colour, even for someone who serves his life among the streets of London. A yellowish tinge such as that would suggest a blow to the liver, but you are obviously not of that sort. Nor do you reek of the noxious chemicals that labouring in a factory would bring." With complete unconsciousness, the other hand waved at the startled detective – it still had a battered pipe between the fingers. "You may have a jaundiced view, Inspector, but you are certainly not jaundiced of the liver."

"I beg your pardon?" Lestrade protested hastily.

"So. We have a man that, for some reason, has been putting his health at risk by spending far too much time in London when he should be resting in the countryside away from the fogs. Why is he not? Smoke is a common cause – possibly the leading such cause – for such a dry, sallow complexion . . . but he can hardly separate himself from the cause of his illness if he leaves the city, for that is his livelihood." The stem of the awful-looking pipe went to those thin lips. Smoke poured out. "Poor diet, exhaustion, stress, and one's blood line are the leading causes of sallow skin. Despite your efforts to be discreet, Inspector, you have a truncheon at your waist underneath your coat. However, it isn't of the usual and more commonplace oaken-colour model the average constable clips to his belt. It's a much older style, unique to the Special Constables appointed to deal with the many regrettable riots during the early portion of the Queen's reign – which, if I may, was before you were even born.

"Your truncheon was smoothed down and painted black. A very simple crown is scratched into the paint, along with two interesting initials: *CID* which might in itself mean *Criminal Investigations Department*, but for the *GL* beneath. There was a rather famous example of the Metropolitan Police by the title of Chief Constable Davids, '*the Wonderful Welshman*', who personally appointed a Constable G. Lestrade from his beat along the Thames to the offices of Scotland Yard. He died without heirs, I am told, but he must have meant something to you, for he passed along his truncheon."

The air seemed thin . . . or Lestrade's lungs had shrunk in the hallway. The man was standing there, smoking, and that damned smile was still hovering over his face. Lestrade struggled to breathe in a way that wouldn't be any worse than it was now.

"Really, Hiatt needs to rethink the pattern of the single-locking handcuffs." The young man wasn't finished. "The non-adjustable grips can cause more problems than they solve."

Lestrade had one of the least-proudest moments in his life: He'd forgotten why he'd come to see this lunatic.

"Have a drink."

That quickly, Holmes turned his back and went inside his room. The door was left open. Lestrade took a step inside, not being told otherwise.

Books littered the walls and floor in stacks, piles, and almost-neat shelving construed of whatever furniture would do the service. Lestrade had the feeling that were it only possible, Mr. Holmes would have put his books on the ceiling in a similar fashion and then completely ignored the danger to his head.

Books weren't the half of it in the dirty-looking light. Glass chemistry bits speckled here and there like discarded Christmas ornaments. A few of them Lestrade was positive he had never seen before, and he'd been haunting the laboratories of late. The largest piece was a glass cone with the tip missing . . . he was almost certain it was some sort of condensing extractor, but he'd never seen one that size before.

The little man felt positively dwarfed in the face of this disaster. While he hadn't expected it, a flicker of sympathy for the man's landlady stubbornly showed itself.

"Whisky and soda," Holmes was saying, "on the shelf. I did have cigars, but I fear they didn't survive my latest guest." He gave a sniff that somehow made Lestrade completely forget about the mess. "Aesthetics who smoke to curb their appetite are a strange lot." He turned swift as a dancer, bent over a glass bowl, and struck the bottom of his pipe so the unused dottle popped out like a cork. There appeared to be a collection of them already. "One ought to smoke for better reasons." The last was said under his breath.

Lestrade was wondering what madhouse he had been sent to . . . and who could he blame for this sort of joke? Someone must have set Dr. Roanoke up to this.

"Why *Lestrade*?"

Lestrade nearly jumped out of his skin, caught guilty in having a thought. Holmes was standing up against the undersized and pitifully small fireplace, a freshly-loaded pipe for disaster already lighting in his fingers.

"I beg your pardon?"

"Why *Lestrade*?"

"I . . . that is . . . my name is Lestrade." Lestrade stammered. At least his back was to the door if this turned into a case for the Black Maria. The possibility of this being a joke was swelling like dough on a warm day.

"No, no." Holmes waved his hand so quickly the smoke went flying in all directions. He really is lean as a scarecrow, the detective realised. "You failed to react when I mis-pronounced your surname, my good fellow. Thus you are either so used to the common pronunciation, or you chose that form deliberately. I was merely curious as to its motive." He paused and added swiftly, "Although I have encountered a family of Basques who place the emphasis on the second syllable, you haven't the look of that particular branch of Iberian bloodstock. Western Peninsula for you, with your small stature and rounded eyes, in which case one might argue you merely returned to the land of your forefathers. Still, the matter of the surname is only for my personal curiosity."

Lestrade grimaced. This man appeared to take all forms of curiosity as personal! "How someone uses my name isn't a thing I can easily control."

"You could correct someone as soon as they made their error."

"Harming a person's pride isn't a good idea."

"So you allow them to attack yours? There is a price in that form of courtesy."

Had he just been scolded? Lestrade fought for control again. Want to ensure a short, interesting, and ugly career in the Met? Tell your Chief he's got your name wrong. "My name is mis-pronounced, perhaps, to you. It isn't to me."

"Ha!" The bark of laughter was short and sharp . . . and loud as a gunpowder snapper. "Better the Cockney form than the French? You are in a large company. The drinks are below the glasses."

"Thank you, but no. I am not here to drink." At least, he wasn't before he came here . . . .

Mr. Holmes tilted his head to one side like a curious parrot. The nose only helped that impression.

"Dr. Roanoke, of Scotland Yard, requested me to detain you with what he called a 'pretty problem'."

The reaction was so extreme Lestrade nearly took a step backwards. The grey eyes went silver as mercury, and a flush traveled up that bony face. Lestrade was shocked that this took some illusion of years off the man – he was in his third decade, surely, but his sheer thinness and the impression that his brow was overgrowing his head made one think he was much taller and older than he really was.

Just how old is this boy? Does his mother know he's spending his college education on squalid rooms in Montague Street?

"By all means, present the problem to me, and I shall see if I can assist."

Relieved that this part was over with, Lestrade pulled out the tiny money-bag and placed it on the table. Neither man looked at it, for the move would have given deep offense and created a heavy pall upon the negotiations about to start.

"A dead man under Dr. Roanoke's attention was a suspected poisoner. When the investigation grew too close, it would appear that he took his own wares to prevent the hands of British Law."

"Ah, so you've finally caught up with the good Mr. Frogge." Holmes responded with a touch of sarcasm. "I warned the Yard some time ago that his life was drawing to the end of the circle."

"That may be, but I wasn't made aware of that, Mr. Holmes."

"Continue."

"Very well." Lestrade ignored the slight slur against his profession. "Dr. Roanoke is stumped at a piece of paper found in his pockets. It would appear to be from a diary, but the wording is peculiar. Three words in particular are puzzling him: '*Milk*' goes the first word, and then beneath it, under an indention, are two more words separated by a comma: '*Devil's*' and '*Wolf's*'."

46

Holmes threw himself backwards into a chair (ignoring a book in the back), his eyes glowing like unholy little lamps as he pressed his fingertips together. Lestrade encountered his most unsettling sensation yet, for the man was thinking, to the point that Lestrade could *feel* him thinking. Just a bit harder, and he would be able to hear those cogs grinding.

"Mr. Frogge, for all his commonality, was a Continental of the first water," Holmes mused. "And he came from a most distinguished family of chemists, some of whom developed or assisted in the development of many drugs we use today." His thin lips twitched. "My expertise comes from my natural interest in organic chemistry, you see. It was inevitable that we would meet one day on the battlefield."

"I take it there was no love lost." Lestrade guessed with no effort.

"Perhaps in a way." Holmes' smile grew wider, and it resembled a silent snigger. "He did feel flattered enough at my attention that he promised to find a way to poison me personally. I'm sure he would have, were he not so caught up in a contract with Merck."

"Did you speak to the Yard over that?" Lestrade was shocked.

"No proof, Mr. Lestrade. No proof – no bother."

Lestrade stared as the threat of premature death merely washed over the young man.

"Back to your strange paper . . . It was most likely a diary page. The man kept a log of his more interesting compounds. But as to what the substances were . . . ." He pursed his lips together thoughtfully. "Frogge kept to the German standards of extracts. *Wolf's Milk* is merely the English translation for *Solomon's Seal*. The plant is graceful, yet otherwise unremarkable, but the small rhizomes have a sweetish flavour when tasted, and the German peasant holds the belief that a wolf will dig up the root and eat it when he suffers damage in battle."

"*Solomon's . . . Seal?*" Lestrade pulled out his notebook and wrote it down, thinking that he had earned his own fee for tonight.

"*Devil's Milk*, I fear, you will have a greater trouble with. It is a generic word for several different plants in the *Euphorbia* name, commonly known as *spurge*, all marked with the ability to leak an acrid and thick white sap or latex when wounded. What the Devil has to do with it, I'm certain I have no idea, but I should like to find out some day." He puffed slightly, remembering he had a pipe. "None of the plants that I know of that description are meant to be taken internally. Dandelion has been called '*Devil's Milk*' on occasion, but no one hears of a dandelion poisoning. No, if this is a case for poisoning, look to the bottle of Euphorbia on his cabinet. If it is a case of a general tonic, I would say go no further than the patch of dandelion in his salad-bed. Either way, you shall come to a conclusion."

His pipe recalled, Mr. Holmes regarded its stem. "Frogge was attached to the plants that could kill as easily as they could heal. If he was using Euphorbia, then I would suggest one should look at the clients who were being treated for skin-cancers. The sap's use in dissolving such marks are well known. He may have even treated them successfully, assuming they never roused his strange temper and led him to throw his terrible additives into his potions." Grey eyes flitted over Lestrade again. "He was a man of his pride, our late Mr. Frogge. To his peculiar way of thinking, death by using a man's own medicine against him was in truth The Hand of Justice."

Dazed beyond the grip of speech, Lestrade found himself standing under a street-lamp like a common loiterer.

He was actually sweating.

What had just happened? He was a policeman – an *Inspector* – and if anyone was supposed to be upset and off-balance, it shouldn't be him!

No wonder Roanoke sent him in his place. This Holmes character – and a man who was overly blessed with character if there ever was one – was like no one in his life. He flushed again to remember the little ways he'd been embarrassed by the man. His clothing, his ill appearance, his own name.

And yet the man – or boy, or some strange combination of the two – had figured out what had taken Roanoke hours. That quickly he'd put it in his mind, and his mind had tossed out the answers.

"Take this to Mr. Sherlock Holmes of Montague Street, but don't tell him what I suspect. If he comes to the same conclusion, then we'll know I'm right."

Lestrade rubbed the back of his neck, thinking. They had all sorts of consultants working for the Yard, but damned if he'd ever seen one like this.

Well, he was rude and crass, even if he was smart, but Lestrade could notice things too. All that mental showing-off had to have been from all that reading scattered about the room . . . and it was clear that, given a choice between a book and a meal, the book would win.

Aesthetic, was it? People starved themselves for different reasons. He didn't completely respect those who had the means for food and didn't take care of themselves. But the way that man nipped about – there was a chance he actually forgot to eat once that brain took over.

Plants that heal, plants that kill. He wasn't so unfamiliar with them. Good Lord! England was crawling with poisonous plants. But that idea that something that could kill could also heal was familiar too.

Something bitter could be something sweet in the long run, if it helped cure an unpleasant condition.

The thought came to him then, in that weak puddle of light, and he started laughing while the homeless man in the gutter wondered if he should call for a bobby.

A bitter substance for a sweet outcome.

One might as well describe Mr. Sherlock Holmes.

The Mystery of the
Extraneous Cadaver
by Mike Adamson

Thursday, the 10th of March, 1881, was the day upon which Mr. Sherlock Holmes and I were due to give testimony in the case of Mr. Jefferson Hope, murderer of Mr. Enoch Drebber and Mr. Joseph Stangerson, and would indeed have appeared before a magistrate at the Old Bailey but for the passing upon the Saturday night of Mr. Hope due to the rupture of his aortic aneurism. Thus did the case reported in *The Echo* and other papers as *"the Lauriston Gardens affair"* draw to a close, leaving me, John Watson, damaged soldier late of the Afghan wars, to ponder the particulars of my desire to commit to paper the peculiar intellectual practices of my co-lodger.

We had been rooming at Baker Street since the January of the year, as Britain suffered a spell of exceptionally bitter weather, lingering in March with hard frosts and fresh snow on some evenings. The conditions conspired to keep us by our fire much of the time, but I was to learn that very little could keep Sherlock Holmes from a case. Thus, when our Thursday morning was punctuated by an unexpected pull upon the bell below, I sensed some new diversion placed fatefully before us.

Our landlady, Mrs. Hudson, showed a gentleman up and presented his card, and when she had departed, Holmes inspected the proffered identification.

"Dr. Hargreaves, do make yourself comfortable and explain in what way I might be of service."

Dr. Eustace Hargreaves was in late middle age, and had a comfortable, fatherly sort of face with silvering hair and moustaches. He carried himself as a professional man, and I was delighted to discover a fellow practitioner of the healing trade – an assumption dashed a moment later as he spoke.

"Mr. Holmes? The detective who assisted the gentlemen from Scotland Yard in the recent business over Lambeth-way?"

"I have the honour to be such. And this is Dr. Watson, also of your profession."

"Delighted," he returned, offering his hand. "Gentlemen, I am a forensic pathologist."

My good humour collapsed somewhat as I realised that he dealt exclusively with the recently deceased, but I covered my momentary professional distaste as he pressed on,

"I serve as an assistant divisional surgeon to the Buckinghamshire Constabulary, working out of the police station in Trinity Road, Marlow. I provide forensic services in the southern part of the county and neighbouring areas, and report to my senior in Aylesbury." He paused a little self-consciously. "I have something of a tale to tell. I hope you will be favourably disposed to assist me, gentlemen, as after long and exacting service, I feel I have been failed by the higher-ups of my own institution."

"What has happened, Dr. Hargreaves?" Holmes asked with an anticipatory tightening of his keen, fresh features, and a moment later we settled into chairs around the fire to receive his tale . . . .

"January's blizzard was the worst in living memory," Dr. Hargreaves began, as Holmes stuffed his pipe and arranged himself like a praying mantis in his armchair, long legs outstretched. "Here in London, I understand snow drifted three foot deep, but in the country, things were even more dire."

"A great many lives were lost," Holmes murmured.

"Some hundred, across the southern counties. Anywhere south of the Humber, the British Isles were savaged by wind and snow of truly Biblical proportions. Marlow lies just below the rise of the Chiltern Hills, and we experienced conditions such as these eyes had never beheld before. From the 17th to the 20th of January, we had a veritable national emergency, and many people died when they were caught outside upon some errand. There were many broken bones due to falls upon ice and, in the days afterward, as the worst of the snow melted off, bodies were discovered where they had fallen. As Divisional Surgeon, it was my job to register these unfortunates, take down their particulars, and make some inferences upon the circumstances of their deaths – looking for foul play as a matter of course, but in such a disaster it was sheerest formality – before they could be released for proper burial."

Our guest seemed sorely troubled now, and I poured us port all around. With the warmth of the wine, he pressed on. "As soon as conditions allowed, I travelled to Beaconsfield to register their deceased. Those found abroad from their homes but not yet identified had been gathered together at a hall in the village of Flackwell Heath, about midway between the towns. I was there over the night of the 24th to the 25th of January. And something strange happened." The note in his voice sent a shiver up my spine, and I gulped my port. "On the 24th, I examined and registered four victims of the storm. But on the next day there were *five* in the hall."

"Five?" Holmes asked in a monotone, sitting forward a little.

"It's hardly something one could be in error about, Mr. Holmes. In all my career in pathology, I have never miscounted the cadavers in my care. The fifth body was unidentified. Certainly no one came forward, though his description was circulated to the nearby towns, and when the rest had been released to their families for decent burial, we were left with one, supernumerary to the original, official count. There is no paperwork for who delivered the body, no record of where he was found, or the circumstances of his demise."

"Your examination?" Holmes asked in the same flat voice.

"The body was in a bad state, but there was no frostbite, as would set in had his *pre-mortem* exposure been lengthy. There were some abrasions, typical enough when falls are involved, and several heavy contusions, as if he had fallen into a woody bush or shrub. It was my opinion one of these blows, received to the cranium, may have rendered the fellow unconscious, and he simply froze to death before he could ever be found."

"But you have suspicions – ?" Holmes was less asking than stating, and I was by now taking notes as fast as I could write.

"I drew the matter to the attention of the Coroner's Court but, overworked as they were, they considered it only briefly. As for the issue of the body's sudden appearance in the hall . . . ." He paused, finished his port at a sip, and shook his head. "I was censured for incompetence." Dr. Hargreaves couldn't go on for a long moment. "Me! A London Hospital graduate with an impeccable record over thirty years of service!" He scowled. "The Chairman was Justice Sir Cyril Alcott, and my heart rather sank to find him in charge. You see, we had sharp words, years back, when I felt he was setting aside my medical testimony in order to obtain the conviction he preferred. To suggest any such thing is of course legal heresy, but what else could I do? This left me obliged to bring the circumstances to the attention of a court which would find in me a handy scapegoat.

"My own superiors weren't happy, but could do nothing, and I fully expect to be dismissed, but to their credit they are taking the matter of my replacement as slowly as they may." He frowned darkly. "The body was assigned a pauper's grave at Council expense and the matter shelved, tied up as neat as you like by the assertion that I am too far into my dotage to perform my job!" He balled a fist and seemed about to slam it into the opposite palm.

"Clearly, you have an alternate explanation in mind," Holmes added in a measured tone, the ghost of a smile at his lips.

"Of that you may rest assured, Mr. Holmes. I have had a month and more to think over this matter, and the more I dwell upon it, the more sure

I am. I did *not* make a mistake. The hall was gloomy, certainly, and matters hurried, but the difference between four bodies and five is a whole human being, and I shall never be old enough to miscount so. My assistants – that's Mr. Cantwell and a relative of his from High Wycombe, whom he dragooned into lending a hand to shovel snow and such – could likewise not account for the extra cadaver, and were inclined to dismiss it as a delivery that went unrecorded due to the general confusion of the moment. But the mere fact the fellow couldn't be identified is enough to suggest to me that the cranial contusion wasn't the result of a fall. Mr. Holmes, I believe that man may have been murdered."

"And where better to hide a tree than in a forest?" Holmes smiled with the thrill of the chase and bounded from his seat. "Dr. Hargreaves, I'll take your case."

With Holmes, as I found over the years, inactivity was to him a slow death, and the promise of intellectual stimulation the spice of life. Mystery waited for no man, it seemed, and no sooner the decision than we were on our way. I found myself swiftly packing a travelling case with the few necessities of a day or two away. Then I gave Mrs. Hudson a knock to let her know we were bound for parts westward as Holmes placed our cases by the front door and found us a passing cab.

Ten minutes saw us in the familiar vastness of Paddington Station, and we had time for a morsel at the buffet before boarding the 12:10 Great Western service. The green locomotive eased forth on time and the drab countryside flowed by as we left London's precincts behind. Meltwaters stood in bright runnels and ponds in fields, and a white scattering of frost still clung to existence in the shadows of copse and wood, where new leaves were yet to take on their spring character.

The train took the single track northward from Bourne End and had us in Marlow at twenty-minutes-to-two. Marlow is an ancient town dating to Saxon times, nestled against the rolling sweep of the Chiltern Hills and fronting upon the Thames, and a more picturesque place one couldn't imagine. But the blizzard some seven weeks earlier had drifted snow twelve feet deep in places, great walls of whiteness that had closed railways and imprisoned thousands in their homes. None would soon forget the roar of hurricane-force winds, or the terror of conditions which had reduced visibility to nil from one day into the next.

From Marlow's quiet station, a cab took us the bare half-mile to Dr. Hargreaves's home on York Road, around the corner from the Duke of Cambridge public house. We were invited to board with the doctor and his good lady, though the latter was busy with civic duties as a member of the Parish Auxiliary, still looking after those maleffected by the disaster.

Dr. Hargreaves had the day away from his duties at the police station a quarter-mile east, and escorted us to the bar of the Duke of Cambridge, where he was well known, and ordered up a light meal and mulled wine. We found ourselves in a quiet corner by a crackling hearth, with just one or two patrons drifting through to escape the still-raw weather.

As we waited on our meals, Holmes drew off his gloves and folded his fine musician's hands on the table before him. "Now, Dr. Hargreaves, let us identify your enemy."

"My . . . enemy?"

"Indeed. It is self-evident that concealing the murder would have been best served by merely abandoning the body at the site of the assault, to go unnoticed perhaps for days. Instead, it was found quite promptly – Deliberately? – and brought to the attention of regional authorities, packaged in a shroud and delivered to you. The assailant seems to have pushed his luck in a profound way, and would only do so to make a very particular point. If its object was to bring about disrepute, it has succeeded. However, we cannot ignore the possibility that the act was of manifold purpose. After all, the blow disposed of the man. Then *his* disposal compromised the pathologist. They seem two neat parts to a single vendetta."

"Two birds with one stone, you mean?" I asked, jotting quickly.

"The possibility exists. To resolve the matter one way or another, we must identify the victim."

"There has been no response to our circulated description," the pathologist replied. "We expanded the area, but still no luck. The conventional wisdom in this situation is that he was of no fixed abode, a tramp or traveller. He was evidently no gypsy. For one thing, they look after their own, and there were no gypsy bands in the area at the time."

Our meals arrived and we busied ourselves for a while, but eventually Holmes returned to his first point. "The clue is in the method. You must cast your mind back, Doctor: Who might perceive himself – or indeed *her*self? Crime knows no boundary at the gender divide – slighted or wronged by you, perhaps even many years ago?"

Our host gave a very genuine shrug of perplexity. "I have endeavoured to treat fairly at all times. To the best of my knowledge, I haven't stepped upon any toes professionally, I have had no acrimonious exchanges with others in my field, and I can hardly think a student would hold so visceral a grudge for some bad mark."

I coughed softly. "Were you a general practitioner or even a specialist, I would suggest a disgruntled patient. But those already departed rarely complain about the service."

A momentary cloud crossed Dr. Hargreaves's features, but he

shrugged and concentrated on his plate, and a faint chill went up my spine. Did our client know something germane to the investigation, but with which he was unwilling, as yet, to part? Holmes, I was sure, also registered the moment of discomfort in our host, but kept it to himself, and we didn't speak of it during the afternoon. Indeed, I quite forgot about it as the events of the day unfolded.

After lunch, Dr. Hargreaves found us a cab and journeyed with us to Marlow Police Station, in Trinity Road, where, though off-duty that day, he made us at home in the room set aside as his laboratory.

"Murder and fatal accident are rarities hereabouts, Mr. Holmes," he explained, showing us the neat, white chamber with its benches, examination table, and locker for the deceased. "We were fortunate the disaster incurred such cold, as there was simply nowhere to put the victims in our usual facilities." He gestured at the station about us. "A small country police station with a small force, a small lockup . . . . This room is the only one of its kind for miles around, which tells you something of the rate of violent crime in this area. Locally, my services are required comparatively infrequently, for which I am very glad, though I travel as called upon by the Buckinghamshire Constabulary."

"Describe the events surrounding the discovery of the extra body," Holmes prompted, easing his spare frame onto the hard, cold dissection table. I shuddered silently to watch him seat himself comfortably upon the slab.

"Well, the storm was still blowing fiercely hard by the 20th of January, but by then we were getting reports of those who had gone missing or were known to have perished. The storm blew out by the next day, but left prodigious quantities of snow to be fought through, which meant days more went by before we began to get accurate figures. On the 23rd, I was asked to travel east to Beaconsfield – about three miles – where I duly processed three unfortunates laid out at their police station. The following day, we journeyed back to Flackwell Heath, where the village hall had been taken over as a temporary morgue, gathering victims from Bourne End, Wooburn Green, Loudwater, and such.

"I had taken along my orderly, Mr. Henry Cantwell – keen chap, excellent worker, graduate of Barts. He asked to work here with me last year, rather a compliment, I thought. Anyway, a police coach got us there and back through still pretty-severe conditions. In Flackwell, the secretary of the hall had taken delivery of three bodies by that point, which I duly examined and recorded my impressions. A fourth came in that afternoon. We returned to the hall on the morning of the 25th to complete the paperwork, whereupon the secretary drew my attention to a fifth body."

Holmes nodded as he absorbed the information. "How were the

deliveries recorded? How exactly?"

"Each body was accompanied by an official manifest signed by the local authority where it was discovered. Entries in the laboratory ledger acknowledge receipt of each and acceptance of them into my custody. This is standard practice." He drew down a leather-bound volume from a shelf and opened it for our consideration, along with a manila folder which contained the collected manifests of the episode. Four were clipped together, and he placed them by the open volume. "These are the delivery papers for the four official bodies at the hall in Flackwell."

Holmes let up a window blind for best illumination and took out his magnifying glass to study the papers. "Might some tea be possible, Doctor? This place is devilish cold." He spoke with a quiet distraction, as though all his attention were now consumed by the matter before him, and I quietly ushered the pathologist away in search of the station's tea urn and biscuit box, to allow Holmes his undivided attention.

An hour and two rounds of tea later, during which time Dr. Hargreaves and I had chatted upon matters medical in the station's common room, Holmes appeared at the door and called us back. "I believe I have some progress," he stated simply, and I knew by his tone the scope of his understatement.

In the laboratory, he showed us one of the delivery slips, laid over a book so the afternoon light slanted across it at an acute angle. He had borrowed Dr. Hargreaves's five-inch magnifying glass on its stand, and he gestured for us to scrutinise the document afresh. After a long moment for each of us, I frowned. "Whatever you've spotted, Holmes, I'm not seeing it."

"The slip is signed by a Constable Jenkins, village bobby in Loudwater, dated noon on the 23rd of January. He would have organised the transport to Flackwell. Observe closely: The description of the load."

I squinted, stared at the silvery pencil strokes, taking in each. *"1 deceased body"* I read in a whisper. Then I caught my breath and glanced up. "Holmes! There's been an erasure here – I see an impression of other pencil strokes."

"Had the paper been a heavier stock, it would have resisted the pressure of the pencil. As it is, you'll note that a *2* has been erased and a *1* substituted. Likewise, *bodies* has had its last three letters removed and a *y* added."

"Well, blow me down!" Hargreaves murmured, nodding as he also saw what Holmes's keen eyes had discovered. "It was in front of me the whole time!"

"We often see what we expect to," Holmes said simply. "The human brain has a faculty for filtering out anything at variance with our

56

expectations."

"So," I huffed, "the question becomes: Who made this change? The dispatching constable, the carter, or the receivers?"

Holmes raised a brow at Hargreaves. "The time of departure as noted would indicate this was the delivery recorded in your ledger as the fourth *single* body. Was there only one body in the cart when you accepted it?"

Now Hargreaves frowned, clearly thinking back. "I wasn't there when the delivery came in, Mr. Holmes. I was taking coffee at the public house, and was called over by the Flackwell bobby. A single body was laid out when I arrived. Mr. Cantwell had logged it in, and the carter was already gone."

"And where might we find Mr. Cantwell?"

"He's visiting family up in High Wycombe, not due back 'til next Monday. I can give you his address there, if questions won't wait."

Holmes made a face, frustrated that the next obvious question was put on hold, then nodded with a smile. "Appreciated, Dr. Hargreaves. It seems we must first locate the carter and speak to Constable Jenkins. Are you up for a journey?"

Life was largely back to normal now, and finding transport wasn't difficult. A coach was procured for the next morning, and we retired to the Hargreaves' home as early dusk stole over the picturesque hills, their shadow swallowing up the town. We had found Mrs. Hargreaves a most personable sort of keen mind, and most interested in our description of the case just gone by. We dined upon roast pork, and took port by the parlour fire until mid-evening, whereupon we were ready to retire, having been billeted in the rooms of the Hargreaves's grown family – one son taught classics at Harrow, another served in the Navy.

However, before we could suggest calling it a day, Dr. Hargreaves took his lady's hand and they shared a silent nod. "Mr. Holmes, Dr. Watson . . . . Earlier, you asked me if I could recall anyone who might bear me ill will. The answer is no. However, that doesn't mean that such a person may not exist." He sipped his port and took a moment to find his voice. "The truth is that there is a shadow in my life, a very old one, and I cannot discount the possibility it has risen to do me harm. Professional disgrace is one thing, but an unidentified, and likely murdered man is very much another, and they can hardly be separate events."

Holmes folded his hands calmly. "Whatever you have to tell us, sir, rest assured it shall be treated in strictest confidence, insofar as matters permit."

He hesitated, and his wife squeezed his hand. "I can ask no more than that. Very well. Let me take you back many years. Nothing I am about to say will be of any surprise to Dr. Watson, but the events have haunted me. My dear lady has long known, but our sons have never been aware of these things, and I pray they never shall. But with my decision to speak, that's in the lap of the gods."

"Tell me," Holmes whispered.

"It was in 1849. Thirty-two years ago, I was a senior student at London Hospital, in Whitechapel. At that time, the transition to anaesthetic surgery was underway but by no means complete, and one of the popular parlour games of British society – American too – was the so-called "chloroform party". Guests sniffed chloroform for its intoxicating effects. They stumbled around, drunk as lords, and felt little or nothing when they inevitably injured themselves. That's how the anaesthetic effects of the substance were first discovered – it was a source of entertainment long before it was of practical value." He drank again, composed himself, and I jotted quietly, notebook upon the arm of my chair.

"One evening, a group of students, myself and three others, held a late-night chloroform party. We used hospital supplies in a basement storeroom. This was right against the rules and would have earned us all a whipping were it known, but headstrong young men run such risks merely to prove their worth to each other. Well, things were most jolly. After all, we were going to be medical professionals, we knew the stuff and how to handle it. But the fact remains that in the early days it was imperfectly known, and the trade of the anaesthetist was in its infancy. Accidents happened."

The hairs stood up on the back of my neck, and I had an awful premonition of what Dr. Hargreaves was about to relate.

"We each invited a friend, young women out for a dare, and all was going swimmingly – until one of us made a mistake."

"Overdose?" I whispered, and he nodded gravely.

"My friend Tommy Beal was a promising doctor, and I have always believed it was pure error. We had all used a little but not so much as to relinquish our judgement. But three of our guests had succumbed to the effects and finally gone to sleep, while Tommy's girl, a young lady by the name of Emma Davies, was still playing. He gave her one last drop and, however it happened, she went down and her vitals slipped. Before we knew it, she was gone." He set aside his empty glass, his face pale and haunted. "A life lost for no reason at all. A stupid, stupid game. Well, what were we to do? We panicked, as one does, and only Roger Bates was thinking clearly enough to act. The other three girls were asleep, and next day agreed that discretion was the better part of valour. All we need do was swear secrecy among ourselves, conceal that the party ever occurred, and disavow all knowledge of what happened then."

58

"What *did* happen?" Holmes whispered.

"Roger and Tommy carried her out, and then the rest of us got our friends away to somewhere safe to wake and recover. Emma was reported missing the next day, and her body was eventually found by the river." He put his head in his hands for a long moment. "The matter was never tied back to us, but we knew – Oh, we knew, Mr. Holmes, Dr. Watson! We knew we had been instrumental in that young girl losing her life. An accident! But to reveal all would have served none, least of all her. Her family is another matter, of course, and my heart has always gone out to them." Mrs. Hargreaves placed a hand on her husband's arm. "When questions were asked of her friends, I provided Tommy with an alibi. That was perhaps my gravest sin – indeed the only actual lie I have perhaps ever told."

Holmes cleared his throat as he strove for words. "A foolish youngsters' game resulting in the loss of a life is nothing new in the world. To strive to avoid the consequences, before society and the law, is also commonplace. No harm was intended, and many lives were indeed lost to the capriciousness of the substance in those early days, so it is hardly for me to cast any moral judgement upon the events of thirty-two years ago. Had you spoken, you would doubtless have been expelled, your career stillborn, and the world would have been deprived of the great good you have done since that day.

"Nevertheless, the family has remained without a factual account of their loss, and the law was deprived of the opportunity to consider a matter which would otherwise be recorded as death by misadventure – Correct, as it happens, but a conclusion without context." He shrugged his thin shoulders. "Thank you for admitting this, Dr. Hargreaves. It cannot have been easy for you. With regard to the current situation, the obvious connotation is that revenge is being exacted upon you for your part in the event. Tell me – what about the other students?"

"Over the years, they've faded away. Roger had a surgical accident and died of hospital gangrene. Tommy became a military doctor and was killed on active service in India. The last, William Dowty, went overseas and we lost track of him twenty years ago. To all intents and purposes, only I remain."

After a long moment, Holmes rose slowly and gave a simple nod. "Thank you, Dr. Hargreaves. I shall concentrate on the case before us, and follow wherever it may lead. Should it occasion some revelation regarding your past reaching wider notice . . . Matters must take their natural course."

"This is understood," the doctor whispered, and I saw his hand clasped white in his wife's.

The following morning we spoke no more of his dire commentary, but set out as planned. After a breakfast of steaming porridge and plenty of tea, Dr. Hargreaves bade us farewell, for he was on duty that day, and presented us a note of introduction to the officer in question. Our coach arrived at nine sharp. Matched greys drew a comfortable brougham, and we had engaged the driver for as long as necessary. In topcoats, boots, scarves, and hats, we embarked and watched the scenery as we followed the roads eastward by Wells End and Bourne End, then turned north past Wooburn Green and Dunelm to Loudwater, in a swayback valley of the hills. Three-and-a-half miles as the crow flies was over five by road, and the season's mud was no impediment to the tractive power of two horses.

Constable Jenkins operated his service from his home in the tiny village, there being too little business to warrant a police station as such. He was a bluff and friendly sort, a big lad who looked handy in a scrap, and had probably taken police training as an alternative to the inevitable farm labour of rural parts.

"Aye, gents, I remember the day. I got old Horace to do the run over to Flackwell. Cost me half-a-crown, though it be just half-a-mile there and the same back. But he was happy with the beer money."

Holmes smiled genially. "Can you tell us about the, *erm*, cargo?"

Jenkins nodded sadly. "Right tragedy, it was. A lady from one of the farms disappeared on the first day of the big blow, and wasn't seen again. Apparently she'd gone out to try to bring her sheep in, and things were too much for her . . . . The other we found on our side of Fennel Wood."

"There were two bodies in the delivery?" I asked with an air of innocence.

"Yes, sir. The lady and the old tramp, whoever he was." He turned and gestured to an Ordnance Survey map of the district on his study wall. "Fennel Wood lies in between Loudwater and Flackwell Heath, you see."

"And this fellow, Horace," Holmes went on. "What can you tell us about him?"

"Nothing to tell, sir – honest as the day's long. He's a jack-of-all-trades – has turned his hand to just about everything in his time, from knife grinder to carpenter. He's sheared sheep, mucked out stables, hauled loads, and drunk his weight in gin twice over."

"Salt of the earth, then?" I put in with a smile.

"That's him to a *T*, sir. He can do just about anything, 'cept read or write."

A quick glance with Holmes confirmed the obvious, and we excused ourselves from the officer's study to step out into the bracing morning air.

"Well, that scuttles two possibilities," I remarked flatly. "The carter was illiterate, so couldn't have doctored the manifest, and the dispatching

60

officer sighted and recorded both bodies."

"Something of a slipshod inquest, as Dr. Hargreaves intimated might be possible," Holmes remarked, stuffing his pipe as we stood upon a street corner. "Discovering that the missing body had definitely left Loudwater wasn't difficult. It would seem undue attention was focused upon Dr. Hargreaves for not knowing it was present. We may fairly discern Justice Alcott's hand in this."

"Neither did Mr. Cantwell know of the body, by his own testimony."

"Ah yes, the errant Mr. Cantwell. The one who actually received the delivery and logged it into the ledger as one body, and who is clearly literate, and therefore capable of changing the manifest."

"So it points to him now?"

"He is the obvious next link to be explored."

"High Wycombe, Dr. Hargreaves said. Do we press on?"

"I would like to know more about Mr. Cantwell before we show our hand." Holmes checked his watch. "A quarter-after-ten . . . Plenty of time." He ignited his pipe and waved for the coachman to draw our carriage up to us. "Back to Marlow first. I want to beg a glance at Mr. Cantwell's employment file, which I'm sure Dr. Hargreaves can obtain for us. Then I shall be taking the next train back to London. I must visit Somerset House."

With that cryptic reference to the great records depository, Holmes was content to meditate upon matters as we made our way back, and after a brief stopover at the police station, the coach delivered Holmes to the railway platform, and myself to the house on York Road. I no doubt had several hours to while away, and spent a few in the comfort of The Duke of Cambridge, or walking in the foothills of the Chilterns behind the town. I was still very much at the beginning with regard to learning Holmes's ways, and his peripatetics often left me rather in the dark. I simply trusted that all would become clear in due course, and ensured my notes were legible and orderly.

Holmes was back on a late service, and walked up to York Road in the evening chill. He smiled quietly but kept the details to himself, as he was often wont to, and over dinner remarked simply that he anticipated an early closure of the matter. He asked Dr. Hargreaves if, first thing in the morning, he would be so kind as to telegraph his orderly in High Wycombe with an urgent request to meet at the constable's house in Loudwater, intimating that a further victim had been discovered. From that moment he wore a somewhat seraphic expression, which reassured me he had worked out the particulars, and I turned in with confidence that our hunt wouldn't be prolonged.

We met at Constable Jenkins's house at ten the next morning. The weather had cleared, and we had a pale blue sky over the spring buds that fought valiantly into leaf. Mr. Cantwell appeared on the road from the north, having come down by pony trap. He parked by the kerb and was welcomed by his superior. Drawing off his gloves, he stepped into the parlour.

Cantwell was a round-faced chap with a widow's peak and high colour, about my height and weight, and all business – quite brusque in fact. He looked around the convivial sitting room, dominated by Constable Jenkins's desk, and raised a brow at Dr. Hargreaves. "Your message said something about a body, sir."

"Indeed," Hargreaves said heavily as Jenkins closed the door and put his back to it, and we settled into seats. "But not a fresh one, Henry. One a couple of months old, and long since buried."

Cantwell squinted with a sudden apprehension, but covered it well enough as he took a seat by the cheerful flames. "What is it, sir? An exhumation job?"

"Unnecessary." He indicated Holmes and myself, and introduced us. "These gentlemen have been looking into the business of the fifth cadaver."

Now his eyes narrowed again and I observed a tenseness come over him. "Has light been shed upon all that, sir?"

"You could say that." He took his seat as Holmes rose, and I licked my pencil afresh.

"Thank you, Dr. Hargreaves." Holmes took a long pause. "Let me take us back to the dire last week of January, when the snows were deep and temperatures cruel. After a visit to Beaconsfield on the 24th, Dr. Hargreaves and Mr. Cantwell journeyed to Flackwell Heath, there to review cases from the surrounding area. Three bodies were laid out in the hall – which we visited this morning – and a further delivery occurred in the afternoon. Dr. Hargreaves was in the public house when it arrived, and was called over. We have an affidavit from the Flackwell village bobby confirming this. When he arrived, an extra body was laid out with the prior three. Are we correct so far, Mr. Cantwell?"

"Perfectly, sir. What's this all about – ?"

"I shall get to that in a moment. The problem, you see, is that Jenkins consigned *two* bodies for delivery to your makeshift morgue that day. And the cart driver, whom we interviewed earlier, also remembers two, and will swear to it. The mystery is how two were delivered but one vanished, only reappearing the next morning."

"It's a head-scratcher all right, sir."

Holmes studied the man for a long moment, then spoke very

precisely. "You recorded in the official ledger the delivery of only one body."

"Correct again, sir. There was just the one when I entered the room."

"You weren't present when the delivery was actually made?"

"That's right, sir."

"Then who helped the driver lift out the body? He is an elderly man, and certainly unable to lift the dead weight of a deceased human being."

Cantwell gave the ghost of a shrug. "That would be my cousin Stan, who came down to help out with the fetching and carrying. He brought it in. I sighted one body and recorded it in the ledger."

Holmes drew a deep breath and let it sigh away. "We will of course need to speak to this cousin to get his side of things, but I put it to you, Mr. Cantwell, that you're lying through your teeth."

He bristled at that and looked around sharply for his superior. "Dr. Hargreaves, sir, I must protest!"

His reply was chill. "If I were you, Cantwell, I would save your protestations until we've heard out Mr. Holmes."

I glanced up from my record and found Constable Jenkins like a statue, blocking the door, tensed like a fighter, ready to spring should the need arise. Holmes paused, glancing at the senior pathologist. "Dr. Hargreaves, at this point I will ask if you prefer that I should ask Constable Jenkins to step out while these matters are discussed."

After a long moment, Hargreaves shook his silver head. "My good lady and I talked about it last night, and have decided there is no way to keep old secrets any longer. The music must at last be faced." He was subdued, but resolute. "Ask your questions, Mr. Holmes."

With a nod of acceptance, Holmes steepled his fingers and pressed on in a tone devoid of emotion.

"I visited the national records office at Somerset House yesterday, Mr. Cantwell. All births, deaths, and marriages are to be found there. You were born in 1856 in Camden, son of John and Alice Cantwell. But your mother's maiden name was *Davies*."

A silence fell over the room, disturbed only by the crackle of the fire, and Cantwell swallowed hard. His face became a mask, as if he knew he was undone.

"Alice was the sister of Emma Davies, who died seven years before you were born, in a misadventure with chloroform."

"'Misadventure'?" he hissed, a spite suddenly rising in him. "'*Misadventure*'? It was downright criminal negligence, and those responsible got away with it! My family has always known that they covered for one another. Oh yes, very tight they were. Even the other girls there on the night wouldn't say a word because they knew how much trouble they'd be in just for being there."

"Then if none would speak, on what did you base your belief that a crime occurred?"

Holmes's question struck him speechless. He stammered for a moment, then swallowed hard again. "My Aunt Emma lost her life. There was chloroform on her breath when they looked at her body. Some cock-and-bull was talked about footpads using chloroform to keep their victims quiet, but she was neither robbed nor molested. Everyone knew she was going out with a medical student, one of a group of friends, and a right band of brothers they were. But they just 'happened' to be elsewhere. Their identities were protected at the time – something superior about their profession, the good name of the hospital, or some such nonsense. I saw the police report. It took years to get it. I had to *qualify in the profession* to get into the archives unsupervised! That's when I found out who those other students were. By then, her friend Tommy Beal had died, with the army in India. But the man who assured the police he was drinking with Tommy Beal when Emma Davies went missing turned out to be alive and well, and working in Marlow." His eyes went accusingly to Dr. Hargreaves.

"That explains your request to be posted to the Buckinghamshire Constabulary."

"Easily done. The great man was dead well-pleased to have a promising junior the trade eager to work in his shadow." Hargreaves looked daggers at the younger man. "Come off it, Guv. You enjoyed having your vanity appealed to."

"So it was all about revenge," Jenkins put in gruffly. "How does the old tramp fit in? What could he possibly have to do with what happened in 1849?"

"Tramp?" Cantwell asked, attempting an innocent face.

"The tramp," Holmes repeated firmly. "The second body in the delivery – the one your cousin conveniently missed, and which magically reappeared the next day."

"How should I know?"

"Mr. Cantwell," Holmes said acidly, "I would advise you that, should you try these innocence games before a jury, a judge will remember them – in time served, or strokes received. Fact: The manifest for the delivery was changed. Fact: The carter is illiterate, so could not have done so. Fact: You were in the hall, are literate, and had already set in motion a scheme to disgrace Dr. Hargreaves. Do you intend to implicate your cousin? It's a very minor stretch to also infer that the tramp was made available quite deliberately for the purpose." Holmes's unblinking eyes bored into Cantwell. "Did you or your cousin murder the old man?"

64

"No," Cantwell replied sullenly, but at once squeezed his eyes closed with an air of some impasse being reached in the workings of his own conscience, after which words tumbled quickly. "He was nobody, but he ended up being useful. He'd made a nuisance of himself as far north as Holmer Green, I heard about him when the Guv'nor and I went up there in December. He was hanging around, begging food and shelter, and would turn nasty when he was moved on. The bobby up there will tell you as much. He kept coming back. Women in the village were feeling uneasy. Then he wandered down here and tried it on with Stan's missus!"

He raised a hand sharply. "No, Stan had nothing to do with it. I was coming back from High Wycombe on the first day of the blow and met the old tramp by the roadside. He tried to beg a lift and when I told him to be off, he took a swing at me. I *swear* I struck out in the heat of the moment. I never meant to do him in. Next I knew, he'd gone down among rocks and bushes with a mighty thump. So, yes, I saw off the old pest, but given the way he was behaving . . . There's a fair chance a jury might see it my way. The worst thing I did was to leave him where he lay."

"Because by that time he offered you a possibility to prosecute your wider agenda," Holmes went on in a dour tone. "You had a ready-made corpse, which you knew would find its way to Dr. Hargreaves's attention sooner or later and, being unknown in the district, would present a puzzle. Were you by any chance responsible for circulating the appeal to anyone who might know him?"

"I made sure of it. Anything coming back from Holmer Green, I conveniently lost."

"Obstructing an investigation," Jenkins said heavily, ticking points off on his fingers. "Interfering with the course of justice, concealing evidence . . . ."

"Then it was a matter of ensuring it was your cousin, Stan, who received the bodies," Holmes went on.

"I left the room the moment I saw the cart coming."

"And what did he do with the tramp's body?"

"Put it in the hall's storeroom for the night, under a tarpaulin. Temperatures were freezing. Nobody would smell anything. He never looked in the bag – it was just an object to him, and he did as I asked."

"Then how did he know which body to lay out and which to conceal?"

"It made no difference. Either would suit the purpose, so long as there were *two* that day."

"You realise you have incriminated your cousin? You have made him a distant accessory to some degree of murder, and a conspirator to both slander and the intent to pervert the course of justice."

"He was ready enough. He's family, and the grudge is his to bear as well."

Holmes huffed a short-tempered sigh. "So the scene was set for the mysterious appearance of an extra body, which neatly called Dr. Hargreaves's competence into question – especially with the attitude of the presiding judge – as the system assumes all subordinates work under direct supervision. It worked well-enough for his dismissal to now be a matter before the Buckinghamshire Constabulary." He sat forward. "Let's say you successfully cost him his position and his reputation. *Then* what?"

"Oh, no, Mr. Holmes. Not one more word will I say, and especially not about the future."

Now he was tight-lipped, and we saw we would get no more from him. Holmes nodded to Jenkins, who produced his cuffs and shackled Cantwell's wrists with the admonishment: "Mr. Henry Cantwell, you are under arrest for the murder of the old man, for the slandering of Dr. Hargreaves, for conspiracy, and anything else that comes to the surface in due course."

"We should take him back to the lockup in Marlow," Dr. Hargreaves said with a grunt of displeasure, and Constable Jenkins drew on his topcoat to accompany us into the street. The police coach was waiting, and the driver stepped out from where he had been sheltering to mount the box and take the reins as we five boarded up and squeezed in.

The coach moved out with a crack of the whip, taking the main road south through the gentle valley, often following the course of the River Wye, which tumbled down from the higher country on its way to join the Thames below Bourne End. Cantwell was sullen, silent now he had said his piece, unable to meet his superior's eyes any more than Hargreaves could look upon the man he had mentored. Holmes and I kept silence too, aware we were in cramped proximity to one guilty of at least manslaughter. We would be in Marlow again soon enough, and the sordid business of bringing this matter to trial would begin.

But Cantwell had other ideas. Perhaps his hope that a jury would forgive both his striking out and abandonment of his victim to the elements was mere bravado and, given time to reflect, he saw only a noose awaiting him. His hate was such, ingrained over two generations of family tradition, that he would want to take Dr. Hargreaves with him. But the odds of his achieving a conviction for Emma Davies's death after so very long, as well as Hargreaves' lifetime spent in service, must have seemed abruptly remote to him. Cantwell awaited his chance, then moved like lightning.

Hands still shackled, he rose in a blur, had the door open, and leapt for the verge as the coach passed the lower parts of Fennel Wood, by the village of Dunelm. He rolled in the damp grass, and was up and into the trees in a trice as Holmes rapped on the ceiling and called out. Moments later, the four of us spilled out upon the chill and muddy lane. Holmes led the way, with Jenkins on his heels, and I followed a little more sedately with the pathologist, my walking stick very much my extra limb on such ground.

I heard their calls from the dense shadow of the trees ahead. In the dappled light of the pale spring morning the chuckle and spill of the Wye filled my ears, underlying the sigh of the wind in the new green. I hurried as best I could, my shoulder aching like a nagging tooth at the cold and the demands upon it, but I was determined not to let Holmes down. I saw him ahead, bent to inspect prints, then straightened and listened intently before beckoning, and we set off down a shallow embankment where the snow had given way to new grass.

These woods were old, had crowded upon this river since time immemorial, and though they would one day likely be cut back for new development, they yet preserved a sense of the ancient. A cold stillness filled them, broken by the flutter of a bird's wing or the scurry of a rodent in the spring growth. A man might go to ground here as surely as a fox, and Holmes tracked him like one.

Five minutes went by as we quartered the woods above the swiftly flowing river, where it hurried by in its bed among rocks polished slick, and Constable Jenkins ranged near and far in case we missed our man and he doubled back. I began to feel we had indeed lost touch with him when Holmes shouted and we raced downstream a way, to find my colleague on the near bank, his revolver in hand to fire a warning shot.

Below, Cantwell was making his way across the rushing stream at a series of stepping stones. Yet they were meant for use in the lazy days of summer, not the urgency of spring when meltwaters from the hills drained to the sea through innumerable waterways, swelling and urging them to a cataract in places. "Cantwell! Give yourself up! There's no sense in this!" Holmes fired the shot, but the fugitive had no intention of returning to custody, and pressed on.

I have learned that one develops an extra sense when matters are dire, and I felt it for perhaps the first time on that riverbank in the Chilterns, as every faculty I had told me Cantwell couldn't possibly make it – not because his hands were still handcuffed, but because the rocks were too slimed with algae for him to keep his balance. Two rocks further toward the opposite bank, his feet went out from under him, and he plunged into the racing swirl, went under, and vanished.

Now we pelted along the high, grassy bank as he was swept down, saw him reappear, turn over, lift his hands as if in supplication, then he was driven under again by the current, launched between rocks, and tumbled headlong into broken water.

We found him lodged among rocks and fallen branches a few hundred yards on, and Holmes and Jenkins braved the slick rocks and tormenting flow to grab him up and drag him onto the bank, but when I went to my knees to examine him I could only shake my head. A terrible contusion bled from his scalp, and in moments I found the evidence of a broken neck. "He must have struck his head on an underwater rock," I murmured, rising to lean upon my stick. "He wouldn't have known anything after that point."

We four looked down at the sad remains among the spring woods – the end of one life amidst the bursting forth of others. Holmes, soaked to knees and elbows, controlled his shivers masterfully and spoke for our ears alone. "Dr. Hargreaves, only we present know what happened, it is in our testimony of Cantwell's confession that an inquiry will be able to reach an accurate conclusion. Are you fully prepared for your own past to come to the attention of others?"

"I am without a choice," Hargreaves said simply. "Perhaps I have hidden from reality far too long, and the time has at last come for me to tell the story of that terrible night in '49, as it now forms part of the narrative we have just seen unfold."

Jenkins and I nodded quietly, and Holmes managed a smile. "It may be possible for the hearing – under *any* judge but Alcott – to be held *in camera*. Such an application would, I think, be granted."

Now Hargreaves drew himself up with an air of facing his fate and making the best of it, come what may. "We can leave Cantwell here for the moment. The constables from Marlow can be back for him in an hour. At the moment, we need to get you fellows somewhere warm and dry."

We trudged back up toward the road and waved to the coachman to pull up to us. I could only feel the senseless tragedy of it all – a student silliness, families torn with grief and anger, a cascade of criminal acts pouring down from that point. Perhaps Dr. Hargreaves hadn't administered the fatal drop to Emma Davies, but he had kept faith with his friends in concealing the misdeed, and some measure of blame must, inevitably, attach – and he knew it.

We headed off toward warmth at Marlow Police Station, and I looked back once to where we had left a man, alive moments earlier, and wondered how different matters had really been the night this all began. A mistake, passions inflamed, desperate measures, twisting the law for personal ends – in these things the story seemed to have ended as it began, with tragedy. The animal need to escape had robbed the vigilante of his remaining days, as surely as a mistake had ended a young woman's, when, beyond all question of student irresponsibility, incompletely understood science itself had played a part in the loss of a life.

Holmes and I stood a little apart from travellers on the platform at Marlow Station as we waited on the ten-to-eight Saturday train. The day had brightened, and the promise of spring seemed at last with us, but the sun was now two hours set and my thoughts were sombre.

"To live so many years with such a weight upon one's conscience," I murmured. "A terrible burden, which I hope higher authority will grant due weight."

"A fair court should do so," Holmes replied, finishing a small cigar. "It will mean Dr. Hargreaves's quiet retirement, of course, but let us be clear: Although the death of Emma Davies was regrettable in the extreme, chloroform parties weren't *illegal*, and she actively requested the additional dose which did the damage. This constitutes misadventure, not murder. The crime lay in concealing the circumstances of her passing, and Dr. Hargreaves's provision of an alibi to his friend."

"I can understand the bitterness of the Davies and Cantwell family branches," I said with a thoughtful nod, "but to weave fresh murder into a plot to seek justice for another seems chaotic at best, and insane otherwise."

"Such is the nature of chance. Had the tramp not crossed paths with Cantwell that day, matters would have unfolded differently. And I do believe Dr. Hargreaves has paid for his part in that sorry escapade in '49, in both personal guilt and sterling public service ever after. I will offer such advice to the court of inquiry, should my opinion be valued thereby."

A whistle shrilled from up the track, and I saw smoke and steam over the trees. "My second case with you, Holmes, and a very different matter from the last . . . Do they all have their own distinct flavour?"

"Each and every one, Watson," Holmes returned with a smile as the train pulled in with a wheezing of brakes. "But the details *can* sometimes haunt one." He boarded the train without further care, but I couldn't help glancing back into Marlow town and thinking of the drama which had just unfolded. It was worth committing to narrative form, I thought, that one day – perhaps after Dr. Hargreaves had passed on – a wider audience might come to appreciate the delicacies at play here.

The Adventure of the
Doubtful Conviction
by Arthur Hall

Of all the adventures that I have been privileged to share with my friend, the consulting detective Mr. Sherlock Holmes, there is one which is always uppermost in my memory from our early days together. His deductions and conclusions, I knew, were always founded on inescapable truth, so that the many guilty parties who attempted to trivialise or deny his evidence did so in vain. The official detectives of Scotland Yard, who had once looked upon Holmes's methods with the greatest disapproval, came to understand that his peerless logic was invariably immune to a defence based on lies or false witness. Only once was this brought into question by some who, after some experience of my friend's abilities, had every reason to know better.

I recall gazing from our sitting room window one evening in late spring, watching the glow of the sunlight disappear from the street, when my attention was drawn to a cab as it came to rest below. In the fading light, I recognised the passenger, who emerged and strode purposefully to our door.

"We are about to receive a visit from Inspector Lestrade." I told my friend.

Holmes looked out from behind the evening edition of *The Standard* and replied in a voice that betrayed his boredom of recent days. "Let us hope he brings something of interest. I was beginning to suspect that all of London's criminals had either been incarcerated or decided to retire."

I said nothing, but hoped that his black mood would lighten as we learned the purpose of the inspector's visit. We heard our landlady answer the summons of the doorbell, and then came the heavy but familiar tread upon the stairs as we waited.

"Come in, Lestrade", Holmes called in response to the knock on our sitting room door. As our visitor was now so familiar to us, Mrs. Hudson had not troubled to accompany or announce him.

The little detective entered and I knew at once that something was amiss. His expression was grave, and his voice cold as he refused Holmes's invitation to sit with us.

"Clearly, something is causing you great concern," my friend observed. "Pray tell us what has occurred."

"Lester Rawe has passed away."

Holmes looked mildly puzzled. "When was this?"

"Two days past."

"In his own bed?"

"In the hovel in Limehouse where he has lived ever since he came to our attention, and probably long before."

"Lestrade, I am aware that Rawe was a burglar of long standing, one of the few who repeatedly foiled all attempts of the Yard's finest to halt his career, but I am at a loss to deduce why you should come here to announce his demise in such an accusatory tone."

The official detective hesitated, and I wondered if he regretted his attitude, but when he replied his voice was unaltered.

"On his deathbed, he admitted to entering the house of Miss Annie Kearn and murdering her."

All was silent for a few moments. Holmes's expression deepened, not unexpectedly, for I was aware of the implications that this news presented.

"That was five years ago," he said. "One Gerald Quince was convicted of the crime and has resided in Newgate ever since. He escaped the hangman because there were doubts about his sanity, and Miss Kearn's set of four antique diamond brooches were never recovered."

"Precisely," Lestrade retorted. "And now, Lester Rawe admits – on his deathbed, mark you – that *he* was her murderer. As I recall, Mr. Holmes, it was largely on *your* evidence that Quince's guilt was established. Your deductions – the smudged footprint, the hair impaled upon the broken window-pane – that robbed that man of five years of his life. Why, I remember my extreme doubts about your methods at the time, and those of my colleagues at the Yard, but it pleased the court to accept your testimony."

"The conclusion was inescapable. Quince was Miss Kearn's killer. How is it that, after the many times I have aided the Yard since, it takes no more than a doubtful statement by a professional burglar of long standing to bring my methods into question?"

"I hesitate to believe that Rawe would have made a false confession as he faced death. You may recall that he was a profoundly religious man."

Holmes nodded. "A contradictory trait for a criminal, but far from unique. Come, Lestrade, there is more to this, is there not? You would not practically accuse me of negligence on such an insubstantial basis."

"Well, yes," the inspector fiddled with the brim of his hat which he held before him. "There have been questions in the House. My superiors are very displeased."

"Ah, now we get to the root of it. And who, may I ask, has been asking such questions, as if I cannot deduce it from reports in the dailies?"

"It was Mr. Patrick Ribbert, M.P."

"That well-meaning champion of the convicted prisoner. How many robbers and murderers has he sought privileges and sympathy for during his career of the past two years? The man is deluded, and easily convinced by a smooth-talking solicitor of his client's innocence or remorse."

"Nevertheless, the situation is as I have described. There are still those at the Yard, some far above my level, who have always harboured doubts regarding your procedures. I fear that they cannot be ignored."

Holmes looked up suddenly from his contemplatory position, but spoke calmly.

"What then do you or your principals propose to do?"

"There will be an investigation, of course. The case of Gerald Quince will be reviewed. Doubtless some of my superiors will wish to return to other occasions where you have been involved with us."

"That is what I would have expected, under the circumstances. Very well. Conduct your enquiries into my methods, and even my past behaviour if you must, and I also will conduct my own investigation into the veracity of the confession of Lester Rawe." He rose to his feet. "Now, if there is nothing else, we wish you good evening, Lestrade."

After the inspector's departure Holmes said little, but from his expression I could tell that he was considering the possibilities and probabilities of the problem that had been set before him. Only once did I attempt to intrude upon his chain of thought, remarking that the scant evidence presented stood little chance against his already established reputation.

"That is perhaps true," he replied distantly, "but I will not see this agency brought into disrepute, even in the slightest. If this matter is not corrected, there will always be those who doubt our accuracy and integrity, and who knows how many crimes will succeed that I could otherwise have prevented?"

We retired shortly afterwards, with Holmes still in a pensive mood. The following morning, I approached our breakfast table to find him already surrounded by papers discarded as he searched his index.

After greetings had been exchanged our landlady entered, and it was after our bacon and eggs were consumed that he enlightened me.

"I have made some progress. It seems that Miss Annie Kearn inherited her brooches, and was known to have allowed sight of them to only one person: The Mayfair jeweller, Saul Brunstein, was reported to have taken charge of them to ascertain whether their aging settings remained secure. I propose to pay Mr. Brunstein a visit this morning. If you have nothing better to do, Watson, perhaps you would care to accompany me?"

"If I can be of any service, I would be delighted."

Mr. Saul Brunstein's shop proved to be less elaborate than I had expected, and was situated between a milliners and a purveyor of exclusive fragrances in the heart of Mayfair. Our cab having departed, we entered the premises and waited while a young woman selected her engagement ring, with her intended looking on. Holmes examined the display cases with some impatience, but I used the brief interval to study the man who was the object of our visit.

Mr. Brunstein was tall, though not as tall as Holmes, and had the grey pallor of one who spends little time out of doors. A sombre dark suit was draped around his spare form, and he wore a winged collar and black tie with an enormous knot. I noticed that his body was held slightly bent as he moved, as if from long toil in that position. His age, I estimated, would be about fifty-five years.

Presently the couple left the shop, appearing delighted with their purchase. Holmes stepped forward instantly to the counter.

"Am I addressing Mr. Saul Brunstein?" he asked pleasantly.

At once the proprietor's eyes narrowed.

"You are indeed, sir. How may I assist you?"

"My name is Sherlock Holmes. I am conducting an enquiry at the behest of Scotland Yard concerning a set of antique brooches that I understand you once repaired or examined for their owner, Miss Annie Kearn."

Mr. Brunstein didn't relax his expression, but replied slowly and carefully after a moment had passed. "I had formed the opinion, Mr. Holmes, that you are a private agent who is unconnected with the official force."

"That is certainly the case, although I have aided their investigations to their satisfaction on a number of occasions. The matter I wish to discuss was presented to me by Inspector Lestrade, so I would appreciate your co-operation."

The proprietor paused for an instant, which seemed to be his habit. Then his face adopted a look better described as a grimace, rather than the smile that may have been intended.

"Very well. The brooches were quite unique in my experience. That is why I remember the transaction, although it took place five or more years ago. I recall reading that the items were subsequently stolen and the poor lady was killed."

"She was murdered," Holmes confirmed, "but it has now arisen that the man imprisoned for the crime may after all be innocent, since another

73

has confessed. That is the situation from which I am attempting to extract the truth."

Mr. Brunstein considered, then nodded slowly.

"There is perhaps a way that I could help. During my conversation with Miss Kearn, she spoke several times of Mr. Jake Weller, who was apparently a confidant of hers. I formed the impression that they enjoyed a close relationship, and so he may have information that could be valuable to your enquiry."

"You believe that he may know something of the crime?" I interjected.

"That is doubtful, but he certainly is conversant with both the history of the brooches and the day-to-day life of Miss Kearn. I think that you might find some sort of direction from him." Mr. Brunstein tore a scrap of paper from a pad on the counter, scribbled an address on it, and handed it to my friend.

"We are obliged to you, sir," Holmes said. "Can you bring to mind anything more?"

As Mr. Brunstein shook his head, I was aware of the door opening behind us. His face lit up as he saw a new customer.

"I regret that I cannot, gentlemen."

"Then we will bid you good morning."

Holmes wore a smile of satisfaction as he raised his stick to hail a passing hansom, but after giving the driver our destination we rode in silence.

"Aren't we returning to Baker Street?" I enquired presently.

He turned to me from observing our changing surroundings. "Try to curb your desire to fill your stomach, Watson. There is, I think, sufficient time to visit Mr. Jake Weller before luncheon."

"You aren't anticipating that this interview will take long, then?"

"Perhaps not. Are you armed?"

"I have my service revolver," was my surprised answer, "but I hadn't realised that it would be needed."

"It is likely. I know of Jake Weller. He is a killer for hire. I marvel that he has eluded the attention of Scotland Yard for so long."

"But Mr. Brunstein sent us to him," I said incredulously. "Surely he cannot be aware of Weller's history?"

The smile returned to Holmes's face. "I am quite certain that he is. There is little mystery here, I think."

We left Mayfair and Knightsbridge behind and came upon the Kensington Road. The cab came to rest near a short street of terraced dwellings that led off the main thoroughfare. This place was new to me, but Holmes seemed to be familiar with it, for he paid our driver without asking further directions. The cab left as we stood on the corner, and he glanced from house to house. As we watched, a telegraph boy mounted his bicycle and departed. He passed us by without a glance, but Holmes's gaze was fixed on the house he had just visited.

"As I suspected," he murmured.

"You expected Weller to receive a telegram?"

"I am not surprised to see it at about this time. How else would Mr. Brunstein warn him of our impending arrival?"

"You had misgivings about the jeweller, from the moment you saw him," I concluded, remembering Holmes's demeanour during and after the interview.

"Even before that," he said as we strode towards the house. "Consider the facts as we know them: Miss Kearn was reported to be of a secretive nature, was she not? Who, then, knew that she possessed antique brooches of considerable value? I would wager that no one knew, until she entrusted them to Mr. Brunstein for examination and repair. As he alone knew of their existence, the possibility is that he hired Gerald Quince to steal the brooches, but the crime was discovered. I imagine that Quince hid them in some place as yet undisclosed, and this affair is an attempt to secure his release from prison so that he can recover them."

"But Holmes," I objected, "five years has passed since the robbery and the murder of Miss Kearn. Why would Mr. Brunstein, or anyone else, wait for so long?"

"My index indicates that the insanity that has plagued Quince since his incarceration has retreated somewhat of late. It is likely that he was not capable of recollection until now."

We paused, now only yards from our destination.

"So the confession of Lester Rawe was somehow forced?" I ventured.

"Undoubtedly, unless he was a willing conspirator who saw himself as having nothing to lose. Hopefully we will discover all shortly, but now I see that the door is ajar, which suggests that our approach hasn't gone unobserved." He produced his weapon from his pocket. "Stand back, away from the line of fire."

I drew my own firearm and took up the position that he had recommended. From an oblique angle, he stretched out an arm and pushed open the door fully.

"Mr. Weller," he shouted into a room that appeared empty. "We wish to question you about Miss Kearn. There is nothing more against you, as yet."

His words echoed slightly, but were followed by silence. We waited for some minutes, but there was no change or sign of life.

"Very well," Holmes said then, and entered the house.

At once I heard violent movement, and my friend slammed the door back on its hinges. A cry of pain was followed by a heavy revolver skidding across the floor, and then a small man in a collarless shirt with a hand pressed against his bruised face was revealed. He staggered towards us, but then saw our weapons and stopped abruptly.

"You were lucky, Mister," he growled. "Another moment and I would have shot you both dead."

"I have no doubt of it," Holmes answered. "I am aware of your reputation, although it is apparently unproven."

"The law isn't smart enough for that."

I saw his eyes flicker towards his lost weapon, which had come to rest a few feet from me.

"I strongly recommend that you abandon all thoughts of retrieving your revolver. Be in no doubt that we will fire instantly, should you make any attempt." Holmes kept his own weapon pointed at Weller's heart. "Watson, be so good as to remove the temptation, and to pick up that telegram form that I see crumpled upon the floor."

I transferred Weller's revolver to my pocket, and opened the screwed-up ball of paper:

> *Two are coming to you. Be ready. You know what you must do.*

I relayed the unsigned contents to Holmes, who nodded.

"How were you intending to dispose of our bodies, Mr. Weller?"

"There are ways."

"Of that I'm sure, as I am that you have used them before now. Tell me: Was it you or Mr. Saul Brunstein who induced Lester Rawe to confess to the murder of Miss Kearn?"

Weller scratched his unshaven face, and I saw Holmes's weapon move slightly in response.

"Why should I tell you anything, Mr. Sherlock Holmes?"

"Ah," said my friend, "so you recognise me. It would be as well for you to talk to us, I think, unless you are prepared to pay the penalty for attempting to kill us, and for whatever means that was used to cause Lester Rawe to falsely confess on his deathbed. That is without mentioning your possible involvement in the robbery and subsequent murder of Miss Kearn. All this you will face alone, for your accomplice will certainly deny his connection. Scotland Yard will, I am sure, be glad to see this crime taken off their books."

Weller stood very still, then seemed to recognise the impossibility of his position. Fear crept into his eyes.

"It isn't true!" he cried. "I had nothing to do with that robbery and murder, I swear! I never met the lady, and I didn't know Brunstein in those days. I didn't know Quince either."

"It may be that we, and the official force, can accept your assurance," Holmes said. "But as it is, we would need to have more facts in our possession in order to form an opinion."

"It's like this, see." With the prospect of taking the entire blame, Weller was suddenly eager to talk. "Brunstein knew about the brooches and wanted them. He said they were worth thousands, and the lady didn't fully realise their value. He paid Quince to lift them, but it all went wrong. The coppers caught him, but not before he'd hidden the brooches away somewhere. Brunstein went to see him in prison once or twice, but he seemed to be out of his mind and couldn't tell him where the goods were, although he could have been faking it. Once he knew it wasn't the rope for him, he might have decided to keep the brooches for himself, if he got out one day."

"So you, together with Brunstein, set about somehow causing the dying Lester Rawe to confess to a murder which he hadn't committed, in order to get Quince released. After that, he would quietly disappear until he divulged, voluntarily or otherwise, the hiding-place of Miss Kearn's property. Is that what was intended?"

"No, not by me!" Weller exclaimed frantically. "It was Brunstein, all of it. I tell you, he's capable of anything. He told me of his earlier life, full of stealing and killings it was, he isn't as respectable as you might think. It was his idea to threaten Rawe – to tell him his daughter would be found with her throat cut if he didn't confess as he was told. Brunstein hired me to persuade Quince to talk, after we'd got him away, and then to get rid of him."

"I can promise you," Holmes assured him, "that before long, Mr. Brunstein will receive what is due to him. As for you, your fate will be decided in court. Not that you deserve it, but you may take comfort from the fact that you have escaped the rope yet again – although I think it likely that you will end your life in prison."

Weller scowled, bowed his head, and said nothing more.

"Shall I seek a cab for our return," I asked Holmes, "or a Post Office to telegraph the Yard?"

"A Post Office, if you would be so good, Watson, my revolver and I will keep our friend here company until you get back, and then we'll await Lestrade. I'm rather looking forward to explaining the truth of this little affair to him, and to hearing him pronounce that my reputation, which was affected as a side-issue, is restored."

The real ending of this affair which, as Holmes described, had little mystery about it, came several months later when both Brunstein and Weller were hanged. Holmes's report to Inspector Lestrade caused the official detective to look into the archives and discover that both men had committed capital crimes in the past, using assumed names.

The antique brooches belonging to Miss Annie Kearn were never recovered.

The Case at
The Turkish Bath
by Brenda Seabrooke

"Watson, you've been favoring your injured leg of late. Instead of improving, you're backsliding, no doubt caused by using the stairs too frequently. I believe it's time you betook yourself to a spa for some treatments."

I looked at Holmes in amazement. Why would he think so? Just the previous day, I'd congratulated myself on my progress after taking a Jezail bullet in the Battle of Maiwand not quite two years earlier and recovering from the ensuing enteric fever which, in my personal and medical opinion, was far worse than the bullet. I was lucky to escape septicemia from that piece of metal, but I was in more danger of dying from the fever than the bullet.

He didn't notice my glance as he rifled through the morning post. We'd finished breakfast and were enjoying coffee by the fire. Spring was not yet aware the weather was supposed to warm up for Easter.

"I hardly think I'm an invalid, and using the stairs has aided my recovery. I no longer need to use the stick, though I take it along to beat off the things your stick uncovers in your cases."

"*Touché*, Watson. You are feisty this morning. Late night?"

"No more than usual. If you noticed I ate a hearty breakfast. I feel fit as a fiddle, though I daresay yours isn't as fit after last night's concert. Why do you want me to go to a spa?"

"To give *me* a reason to go to a spa – looking after my charge. Your war wounds are giving you pain and rendering you almost helpless. Someone recommended the salt cure at The Turkish Bath in Selwyche. I'll wheel you around in a bath chair, and you can indulge your love of food. I hear the cuisine is quite good at spas."

"Why do you really want to go to a spa? And don't tell me it's for my health. Why do you need an excuse? Is it a case?"

"Eliminate the impossible, Watson."

"You never go on pleasure trips, so you must have a case."

"Correct." He smiled. "You will make a detective yet."

I snorted audibly. "Is it a murder?"

"No."

"Espionage?"

"Not this time."

When had it been espionage?

"A directive from Downing Street?"

"No, indeed, but I'll spare you the more mundane guesses. We are to observe and report. Nothing more."

"Report on what?"

"Some untoward occurrences that occurred at a spa owned by – let's say a family connection, and leave it at that."

Holmes had his secrets. I had yet to find out about his family life since we met in 1881. I looked out the window and thought about a warm salt pool as sleet tattooed the windows and wind moaned around the eaves. "Where is Selwyche?"

"Near Worcester. I believe the weather in the Severn Valley will be an improvement over London's present arctic state."

"I wouldn't count on it, but at least it's south of Scotland." I knew how cold that was, as I spent my first dozen or so odd years there.

I went to my room to pack my warmest wearables. The next morning, bundled up, we traveled by train to Worcester, where a conveyance waited to take us to the town of Selwyche, as no railroad lines yet connected with the small spa town. It was indeed small, with only two salt baths available, and one of those so small it had no inn attached like the Turkish one where we were booked for a week – or longer, depending on the progress of my treatments and Holmes's case.

The walls of the spa loomed in the dark night like a white crenellated Turkish castle – or perhaps it was Egyptian in design. I haven't been to Turkey, and had stopped only in Cairo on my way to India. On my return, I was unable to leave the ship or my bed, save for short halting walks in the corridors when we sailed through calm waters in order to keep myself somewhat in working order.

A pair of torches lit the entry. Holmes helped me down as I leaned on my stick more than I ever had since my return from the subcontinent. We slowly made our way inside where David Anderson, the proprietor of The Turkish Bath, awaited us. Holmes introduced us and we signed the register. I used my own name, but we decided Holmes should be Roderick Moore. Anderson and Holmes acted as if they'd never known of each other until now.

"Roderick, I need a rest, dinner, and early retirement in that order," I said in a voice I hoped sounded like I was about to collapse.

"And so you shall, Doctor. Take my arm."

"Is there not a bath chair available?"

"Indeed – " Anderson began, but Holmes interrupted him. "We've been sitting all day on the train, and you need to walk to the room to get your blood circulating."

I did as he said, and we followed Anderson at a slow pace in the event we were being watched.

Our valises preceded us to the ground-floor rooms, to the right of the entry tower. The two guest room wings radiated out from the tower to embrace the common rooms. The baths had a salt pool in each, one for ladies and one for gentlemen. When the door closed behind us, I let go of Holmes's arm and stood straight. I leaned my stick against the door frame.

David Anderson was tall with springy brown hair, lively brown eyes, and energetic in his thirties. He handed Holmes a folded sheet of paper. "Here is the list of the guests and staff. Only my co-owner, Gerald Ellis, and I live in. The rest of the staff come in the morning and leave at night. April isn't the best month with Easter falling on the ninth this year, but we have eight guests at present. Three of them are military, survivors of the Crimean War and Indian uprising: Colonel Maybry, Major Banks, and Major Dalton. Lady Faradene is a widow of good age with her young companion, Edith Browne. Phillip Willowby is a vicar, apparently with some wasting malaise. Lord and Lady Penhurst are a May-December couple. She is, I believe, his second or third wife. No children except from the first wife."

He handed over another folded sheet of paper. "This is the list of recent occurrences. I don't suspect any of the staff. They've been with me since the spa opened."

Holmes glanced at the last list. "Money stolen from the office desk. A box of candy Lord Penhurst bought in Selwyche disappeared. Lady Penhurst's fan – lost. Lady Faradene's peacock brooch containing diamonds, sapphires, turquoise, and pearls – disappeared." Holmes raised his eyebrows. "Small things, and then something valuable."

"Yes. I was prepared to overlook the small things. Money can be misplaced. A fan can be dropped anywhere. Candy left behind somewhere when carrying several packages. But a brooch with jewels cannot be overlooked. So far no one has left, and Lady Penhurst said she may have mislaid the fan, but if this continues, the bath will acquire an unsavory reputation and guests will stop coming. I cannot afford to lose a single guest.

"I don't know this, but I suspect it may be sabotage by someone from the outside who wants to force me into a sale – quite possibly the owner of the competing spa. These springs are valuable. I have two of them, side-by-side, which can accommodate more guests than my rival across town. He may want to drive us out of business. We're beginning to gain a reputation among spa visitors, and The Turkish Bath has a certain cachet. More than one guest has exclaimed over the décor, and how that itself takes them away from their pains and the dreary weather."

He was telling us more about the spa and the staff when we were interrupted by a knock on the door. I quickly threw myself on the bed and Holmes laid a plaid over me as Anderson answered the door. A stocky youngish man with dark brown hair and a pink complexion entered with a laden tray.

"It's cold, I'm afraid," he said in a pleasant voice, "except for the soup. Warmed it myself."

Anderson introduced us. "Gerald is an investor in the bath." A sturdy chap also in his thirties. I wondered if he and Anderson had been at school together.

"You have a third investor?" Holmes asked.

"Yes, a silent partner. I believe your family knows him."

Holmes nodded. "Indeed."

Ah. Holmes's family. *He has one then*, I thought. That connection, no doubt, was the reason we were here. I waited for more information, but none was forthcoming. "I'll leave you to your meal. Holmes – er, *Roderick*, come down to the office after you've eaten, and I'll show you about the place."

"Enjoy your stay," Ellis said with a grin, "and good hunting."

I thought Holmes would go with them then, but he played the part of the attendant to the infirm and stayed with me. He even ate his cold beef and salad and hot barley soup, followed by a pear tart.

Our rooms connected by a door in case the invalid that I was supposed to be needed help at any time. Anderson and Ellis had thought of everything, but as proprietors, they were accustomed to accommodating guests and their various infirmities and problems. Holmes went off to survey the facility. I changed into my nightclothes and settled down under covers with a yellow book that I'd picked up at the train station. When Holmes didn't return right away, I felt a nap coming on, and woke up the next morning to find the book under the covers with me, as was often the case.

Holmes brought my breakfast on another tray, as befitted a semi-invalid. I was hungry, so I partook of my second meal in bed, which I hadn't done since I was returned to England. I dressed quickly and met Holmes in the hall outside our rooms. I eschewed the bath chair left outside my door and leaned on my stick as he escorted me to the men's bath for my first session in the warm water.

"I have great hopes for these baths to amend your infirmities," Holmes explained. "Though the salt is in the spring, the water has been

82

pumped into the pool and allowed to evaporate after each use until the salt lies thick as white sand in the shallow pool. Warmed water is then pumped in for the treatment baths."

"I won't actually be in the spring itself?"

"No." He opened a door and we entered a small anteroom with another chamber off to the side for changing and introduced me to Carl, the employee in charge of the men's bath. I studied him as he opened a cabinet. He was muscular, mid-thirties with blond hair, bright blue eyes, and a trace of an accent. Anderson had mentioned he left Germany to escape conscription in the constant wars in that part of the world. His wife Greta was the attendant in the women's bath.

He took a white garment out of the cabinet and handed it to me and another to Holmes, and showed us cubicles where we could change. The establishment supplied muslin suits modified from bathing costumes which we donned. Holmes, it seemed, was to take the baths as well.

I have been in a few bizarre occasions with Holmes on his cases. This was merely one more. I felt rather silly in the flimsy one-piece garment, but Holmes looked as silly as I felt.

"Some *chentlemens* don't like the nude baths," Carl said with a smile, "so to oblige them we provide the bath suits."

Holmes helped me into the pool. Away from the steps, the sides slanted to allow bathers to lie back if they so desired and stare at the ceiling, which was partially glassed in to allow maximum light, highlighting décor which was meant to be Turkish. Two large brass lanterns held candles against the dark of this sunless day. They flung patterned shadows on the walls. I hobbled obligingly on Holmes's arm and took my place staring upward. The warm salty water felt amazingly soothing. "Roderick," I drawled, "we must add The Turkish Bath to our schedule for the year. Perhaps every other month in winter?"

"I will make a note."

We were soon joined by the three military men, all on the far side of fifty, the single Mr. Willowby (who looked to be about mid-forties or more), and Lord Penhurst, close to (if not over) sixty. We military men did the usual "Where did you serve?", and "Wasn't it beastly?" downplaying the horrors of battles, bugs, and climates. Holmes and his Lordship listened as we told our tales. Willowby kept his head down and didn't contribute more than an occasional yes or no in a low voice to the conversation.

At most, we spent a comfortable hour in the salt. Holmes and I were the first to leave, to great hilarity about becoming brined. After sluicing the salt away with tepid water, we dressed and returned to my room.

"What do you think of the male guests," Holmes asked me as he closed the door.

"They seemed jolly enough – Well, perhaps not Mr. Willowby – and harmless, and I cannot imagine them stealing or sabotaging anything."

"Do not be deceived. As we know from past experiences, the most innocent-seeming can be the deadliest."

"Surely not a peer of the realm."

"Perhaps not. Willowby seems the most infirm of the lot, with possibly the exception of Lord Penhurst."

"Yes, he didn't have much to say for himself."

"As a non-military man myself, I daresay he couldn't get a word in with all those stories you were telling of tropical derring-do."

"'Derring-do' indeed. Staying alive is as close as we came to any of that."

I pushed away my memories and leaned on my stick as we strolled to a large room, located off the hall on the right side of the men's bath, where a cheerful fire warmed and welcomed us. Our morning's companions joined us one at a time, with the two majors last. We were to discover they were always together. They both leaned as heavily on their sticks as I pretended to do. Lady Faradene and her companion, Edith Browne, entered about two minutes after the Penhursts. Why, I wondered, could they not enter together? I soon had my answer: Lady Penhurst, widow of a marquess, outranked a mere baron.

A teacart held pots of tea with all the accompanying *accoutrements* and a plate piled with biscuits. We would not go hungry in this spa.

Holmes took a long time to drink his tea and nibble his two lemon biscuits. Mrs. Hudson would be glad if he gained a little weight here. He sat to the side of the company and didn't seem to be watching them, but I knew he was. I followed his lead. As newcomers, we needed to test the waters, so to speak.

Only one incident marred the morning. Lady Faradene picked up the box of comfits she'd been nibbling. "It's empty, Browne."

Miss Browne jumped up, nervously scattering her own food. She rushed to the teacart and picked up the plate of assorted biscuits. "Would you care for one? It's almost time for luncheon. The lemon wafers are especially delectable."

"I would not. Go immediately and purchase bonbons at that shop."

Miss Browne cast a longing look at the delectables as she hurried away to don a cloak and run to the town shop. After a few minutes, Mr. Willowby arose and tottered out, mumbling he needed to rest for the afternoon and would see us at luncheon.

When the meal was announced, the remainder of the guests rose and adjourned to the dining room. I wasn't hungry, but I managed the excellent cuisine, and Holmes did the same. Conversation was desultory, centering on the morning's baths. I noticed Mr. Willowby was still absent. Too much food for some, I surmised. The guests retired for a little nap. Holmes and I pretended to do the same, but instead took the opportunity to survey the town. We stopped at the post office for him to send telegrams.

"It isn't outside the realm of possibilities," I remarked when we resumed our stroll, "for someone from the town to be slipping into the baths and pilfering, just as Anderson suspected."

"A few pounds," Holmes mused as though the objects had some connection to one another. "Candy. A fan. Possibly a brooch."

"Sounds like things that might appeal to a female. Perhaps the same person took all of them."

"Indeed." Holmes was noncommittal.

The town proved to be larger than a village, no doubt due to the two baths. Salt Spring Spa had no guest facilities beyond the baths themselves. The building was utilitarian, sparse on decoration. Its clientele weren't as well-heeled as those of The Turkish Bath. Holmes talked with the manager, but he wasn't the owner as Anderson and Ellis and their partner were of The Turkish Bath. He wasn't aware of any plans for expanding the facilities. The absentee owner was a large land-holder with no commercial interests.

We inspected the town's three inns, one Spartan for travelers, one slightly more elevated, and one of considerably more comfort, but not up to the décor and facilities at The Turkish Bath. We strolled the High Street, noting the shops clustered there. Holmes made a few enquiries. No goods missing since before Christmas. The proprietors had to watch pilfering during the holiday season, but otherwise all had been quiet. The jeweler remembered he made a sale just that week of an engagement ring, a heart-shaped red garnet with pinpoint diamonds around it. "Very romantic, but not ruinously priced." He described the buyer as a nice fellow. "He quoted the Bible."

"Indeed. Do you remember what verse?" Holmes asked.

"It was from *Proverbs*, I think it was – something about a virtuous woman being above the price of rubies, and all he could afford was a garnet."

"Was he grey-bearded and whiskered?" Holmes asked.

"And hunched over?" I added.

"No indeed. He was tall, clean-shaven, and his hair was dark chestnut. Not thirty yet, I'd say. He wore spectacles."

The description didn't fit any of the guests.

We walked to the candy shop where Holmes bought a box of chocolate-covered bonbons. "These are, I believe, a favorite of Lady Faradene."

"They are indeed," the proprietor said, affecting a French accent through his thin moustache. "The ladies like them. Lady Penhurst sent her companion to buy a box just today."

Outside I said, "Holmes, you never eat candy."

"I have been known to taste a bite of Turkish Delight, but I shall take these to Mrs. Hudson."

We stopped by the post office to check for messages. There was only one, and Holmes slipped it unopened into his pocket.

"Aren't you going to read it now?"

"In good time," was his inscrutable reply.

We returned to The Turkish Bath. In the light of day, it resembled a Moorish fortification I'd seen in books, even more than it had the previous night.

After their naps, the guests returned to the common room, as Holmes referred to it privately. "It's as if I were back in school."

The guests seemed to be a homogenous group as they paired off for two tables of whist, and I heard someone mutter about Russian whist, while one of the ladies said, "We're decidedly English here."

"We need two more players for a third table," Lady Penhurst said. "Perhaps Mr. Anderson and Mr. Ellis would make up another table."

"Indeed not," Lady Faradene said in ringing tones.

She clearly meant one doesn't socialize with the hired help – never mind they were two of the owners. I wondered if that included the pair of us, a doctor and his valet.

"We're quite comfortable watching," I said. "I'm still a little tired from the long trip and wouldn't be at my best, I fear."

Remarks were made about how quickly the baths would cure my ailments, though Mr. Willowby didn't look as if he'd benefited much. He was bent over in an upholstered chair with a high back, his head tilted downward. I studied him undetected and noted his grey facial hair almost formed a cloud, obscuring his features as much as I'd ever seen. Had he received wounds to his face that needed covering?

I haven't played a lot of whist. I learned on the ship going out to India, but on my return, I was too feeble to sit for very long. These were avid players. The ladies as well as the men played as if on a battlefield. The colonel was particularly aggressive, while the majors were more cautious. Perhaps their whist styles could be attributed to their rank – but if that were so, I would expect them to be reversed with the colonel more careful.

"Do you play?" I asked Holmes.

"Not if I can help it."

I swallowed a laugh. "It is a pleasant way to pass time, usually, but I fear some of these players, if not all, are ruthless in pursuit of tricks."

"We know at least one of them certainly is."

"You know who is behind the thefts?"

"Not entirely," he said, "but somewhat."

After tea, everyone repaired to their rooms, perhaps for another kip. Holmes and I took the opportunity to examine the ladies' bath, which proved to be identical to the gentlemen's, the corners of the room squared, high windows giving the illusion of a temple. The walls were stuccoed a pale restful peach color, and here, too, brass Moorish lanterns hung on long chains. Holmes felt the water.

"Still warm?"

"Indeed." He raked his fingers through the salty sand, clouding the water until it was too murky to see through. "Hmm . . . ."

"Nothing here." I turned and started for the door. Presently Holmes followed, and we resumed my invalid walk, leaning on my stick with him holding my other arm. "I day, Roderick, I have no need of aid. The morning treatment has done wonders."

He didn't let go of my arm. "Let's not overdo it on the very first day. A fall would undo all of your progress."

I wondered if anyone was listening. Holmes seemed to enjoy treating me as an invalid, something I had never allowed from the first day we moved into the Baker Street flat.

We returned to the common room where the whist games had resumed. Holmes walked me to a chair. "I believe I could do with a spot of tea," I said. "All that walking has made me thirsty."

A smile flashed across his face as he went to the teacart and poured a cup of Darjeeling. He offered biscuits, and then partook of his own tea and lemon *bikkies* as we watched the whist players.

The winners of the afternoon games were Lady Farradene at the ladies' table and the colonel at the other. "What opinions have you formed about the guests?" Holmes asked me when we next returned to our rooms.

"The three military men are compatible. The difference in rank matters little, because their battle experiences and infirmities override rank. Mr. Willowby is so infirm that I expect my services may be needed at any moment. The ladies, with the exception of Miss Browne, are sharp-tongued. Lady Penhurst is of, shall we say, *lesser breeding* than Lady Farradene, who lets her know it in little remarks that stop just short of rudeness. Miss Browne is thoroughly cowed by her employer. She appears to be a gentlewoman of little means. Perhaps a vicar's daughter."

"Astute of you, Watson." He offered nothing of his own opinion. Perhaps it was compatible with mine. One could never tell with Holmes. He dropped no clues.

After an excellent evening repast, we adjourned to the common room where Lady Penhurst, in her rose-colored silk gown, set off by a fine ruby and diamond necklace, treated us to a medley of songs, including her husband's favourite, "Drink to Me with Thine Eyes", during which he gazed at her with love in his eyes. Major Banks read a long poem in which he spoke, rather facilely, as different characters. At Lady Farradene's prodding, Miss Browne, neatly attired in brown silk, recited an amusing monologue pertaining more to the seaside than a mineral spa. Colonel Maybry was persuaded by the two majors to contribute.

"Well," he said, smiling behind his walrus mustache, his eyes lost in folds of pinkish flesh, "I was considered of good voice in my younger days. I could manage a small contribution." Whereupon he stood up and *a capella* sang a wee ditty about a lion catching a camel. The camel challenged the lion to a race to see who was faster. The lion knew he was, and thought it would be amusing to prove this and then eat the camel. Of course, the lion was faster, but the camel kept going for days, leaving the lion behind to ponder how he'd been tricked. "Rather Aesopian, I'm afraid," he said at the finish.

In a carrying voice, Lady Farradene said, "I do hope that is the end of tonight's entertainment."

She drawled her last word out so long we were all in danger of falling under a spell, but her words were broken by a scream issued from Lady Penhurst.

"My necklace!" With her hand at her bare throat, none of us could fail to notice the winking diamonds and sparkling rubies were missing. "My necklace is gone!"

Everyone jumped up to see and crowded closer. All began to talk at once.

"Quiet, please." It was Anderson. In two strides he was at her Ladyship's side. "Where were you when you missed it?"

"I was there." She pointed to a yellow brocade chair in a corner, but pulled away from the wall with a bookcase behind it.

"A light, please," Anderson said.

Normally at this point, Holmes would take charge, but he stayed by my side. Major Dalton picked up one of the lamps and gave it to Anderson, who used it to light the floor in back of the chair, underneath and on the sides.

"Anything?" Lord Penhurst asked.

Anderson next examined behind the bookcase, but found nothing there either. He handed the lamp back to the major. "Hold this if you please."

I kept to my role of invalid as Holmes remained my attendant. He watched the search intently. Anderson slid his hands between the cushion and sides and back of the chair where her Ladyship had been sitting. I tried to remember if any other guests had been in that vicinity, but couldn't recollect. I wondered if Holmes could.

Anderson removed the cushion, and there lay the necklace coiled like a jeweled snake. He scooped it up and gave it to her Ladyship. "I suggest having the clasp seen to before you wear it again," he advised.

"But we just got it back from the jeweler's for cleaning," she said, holding it in one hand and almost caressing it with the other. "If the clasp was loose, I'm sure he would have repaired it

Ellis joined us then, having heard the commotion. "Let me lock it in the safe for you," Anderson said.

"Oh, that isn't necessary," she said.

I couldn't resist taking the part that Holmes would normally play. "Where do you keep your jewels?" I asked her.

"In a locked case in our rooms."

"I've had experience on long voyages where jewels were locked in the captain's safe," I said. "Think of this as a ship and allow Mr. Anderson to lock them up."

"Well, if you think so, Doctor," she said.

"I must insist on it," Anderson said. She and his Lordship left with him to collect her valuables. "Lady Farradene?"

"I have a dragon to protect my jewels."

I assumed she meant Miss Browne. I wasn't sure how far that dainty dragon would go to protect her Ladyship. She sat in the far corner without speaking. She, of everyone else in the room, could have glided like a shadow behind the yellow chair and opened the clasp. The necklace might have slipped out of her grasp, but why would she do it? On orders from her employer?

"I think not," Holmes said later. "She wouldn't risk prison for her employer's spite."

I was inclined to agree.

The evening entertainment over, the party dispersed.

I'd half-expected the guests to resume their cutthroat card games, but they appeared too tired after all that food and napping and excitement. I felt exhausted myself and ready for an evening of quiet reading, but that wasn't our purpose in coming here.

Our rooms were across the hall from the commons, three other rooms on our side and five on the other side of the spa. The ten upstairs rooms, unneeded, were closed off. Entrance stairs led to that floor where Anderson's and Gerald's quarters were located above the lobby and office. Holmes's was the outside room. Mine was next. The three officers' rooms followed and then the office and stairway. I tended to think of the two majors and colonel as a set, though I daresay that they possessed unique personalities as different from each other as coffee from tea. On the other side, the rooms began with Lady Farradene, Miss Browne, two rooms for Lord and Lady Penhurst, and finally Mr. Willowby.

Holmes joined me in my room. With the door closed, I flung my stick away and sank into a wicker chair that reminded me of home. "What do you think of the missing necklace? Was it an attempt at theft or something else?" I told him of my thoughts about Miss Browne.

"Three possibilities: One – The clasp is faulty and it slid down behind the cushion. Two – The thief could have walked behind the chair and loosened the clasp, but he or she would need a practiced hand to carry it off."

He paused and rubbed his chin.

"You said three."

"The third: Lady Penhurst did it herself to stir things up."

"Indeed. I would attribute that more to Lady Farradene than Lady Penhurst. In fact, though, Lady Penhurst may have felt left out with only the loss of a fan, whereas Lady Farradene lost a valuable brooch."

Holmes sat down and looked at me with amusement. "Very good, Watson."

"Did you read the telegram?"

"Yes. It wasn't of interest – just verifying the colonel's existence and mentioning he'd not had a happy life, burying two wives and all of his young children from disease in India."

"Yes, I'm a walking example of that. I ascribe my survival to the sea air on the voyage home."

"You were remarkably lucky after your wounding."

"Are we remaining awake for the night?" I asked, ready to try to find some coffee if the answer were affirmative.

"Not for the entire night, no. We'll just listen for an hour or two."

We listened, but heard nothing save the footfalls of first Ellis, then Anderson checking the exterior doors, locking the front door, and walking the halls before retiring.

I looked at my timepiece. "It's midnight, and a drowsy numbness is upon me," I told Holmes who was reading some scientific tract while he kept watch. Still reading, he arose and went to his room, while I retired to my bed as he, no doubt, did the same.

More telegrams arrived for Holmes the next morning, which he read in the hall as we walked to the breakfast area. He stuffed them into a pocket. "Later, Watson."

The two majors were having a jolly breakfast when we entered the dining room after a restful, albeit short, night. "Is the colonel still abed?" I asked.

"Not seen him this morning," Banks said.

"We were up late last night in his room," Dalton added, "and he was still going when we retired around half-two."

The dining room filled as the guests involved themselves with breaking their fast. Mr. Willowby sat alone in a corner, reading a newspaper as he ate. I noticed he surreptitiously glanced up from time to time at the Faradene table, which was in his line of sight. The majors were in conversation with Lady Farradene and Miss Browne when we left for the bath. The Penhursts elected to breakfast in their room.

I went ahead to the bath, not limping or leaning on my stick as much as the day before, alleging only one bath had vastly improved my infirmity. Holmes stopped by the office to see if there were any more replies to the telegrams he sent the day before.

The bath chair was left, not by my door, but at the door of the changing room. Was someone else expecting difficulties today? Carl arrived with a load of bathing costumes at the door to the spring at the same time I did. "*Goot* morning, sir. The delivery was *zomewhat* late this morning. I'll have these ready for you before you *haff* your shoes off."

He was as good as his word. I entered the salt pool room only to be met by a strange sight: Colonel Maybry floated in the center of the heavily salted water. That seemed more enjoyable than lying still at the edge of the pool. I decided to try it. I flipped onto my back and instantly floated as if I were on a cloud.

I propelled myself out into the middle of the pool, bumping the colonel slightly. "Excuse me, Colonel. Been here long?"

He didn't reply and appeared to be asleep. I lay back and soon drowsed as I floated on the surface of the pool. Holmes joined me and even floated for a while, but soon became bored. "Are you awake, Watson?"

"Mmm. Barely."

"Was the colonel awake when you came in?"

"Umm, don't think so."

"Would you look at him? Professionally? I don't think he's sleeping. I think he's dead."

I drifted a bit and suddenly his words sank in. "Dead?" I sat up and discovered one could almost sit on thickly brined water. I maneuvered myself over to the colonel and felt for a pulse. Nothing. The man was dead, and not only dead, but in the warmth of the water, may have been dead for some time.

We exited the pool and quickly redressed. When Carl returned with a load of folded towels. We broke the news to him. He paled under his natural rosiness and looked for himself. Holmes left to find Anderson and returned with him a few minutes later.

"Was it his heart? He mentioned his heart was dicky last time he came – in October, I believe."

"He's a regular then?" I asked.

"Oh yes. He's been coming here since we opened three years ago."

"What about the two majors?" Holmes asked.

"This is their first visit."

"But they say it won't be their last," Carl said, as one who is anxious for his job.

Holmes sent one of the waiters to fetch the police constable while Carl, Holmes, and I removed the colonel from the pool and laid him on the floor. On the other side of his face, I saw salty water dribble out of his mouth. Only one reason for that, unless he tried to drink the water: He had drowned.

"That's impossible," Anderson said when we broke the news to him. "Water with the degree of saltiness in the spring will not allow one to go under."

"Afraid he's right, sor," Constable Dobbs said. "Nobody can drown in these salty springs."

"I wouldn't be surprised if he didn't suffer from *angina pectoris*," I said, "that led to a heart attack."

"When do you think it happened, sor?" the constable asked, taking out a pencil and pad.

"That will be impossible to determine," I said. "The warmth of the water would delay *rigor mortis*. Sometime late last night, he appears to have changed for the bath and entered the pool. The two majors left him around half-two, so sometime after that, according to their earlier comments. Maybe he felt discomfort as many heart patients do and attributed it to indigestion. A walk would have been more efficacious in either case, but he may have thought the warmth of the water would restore him. He could've suffered the attack and fallen back onto the side of the pool. He then could've slid down into the water. Your coroner may confirm my findings."

"Then t'was a natural death?" Constable Dobbs asked, pencil poised.

92

"Given the information here, I would say so," I said. He seemed relieved, as did Anderson who'd joined us.

With the constable satisfied the death was natural, they left to make arrangements for the mortuary to collect the deceased and, no doubt, to perform the autopsy.

When we were alone, I showed Holmes the bruises on the colonel, one on the back of each shoulder. "He may have suffered the heart attack, fallen backward into the pool, hitting his shoulders on the edge and sliding on the incline. The salt water could have splashed into his mouth, which most likely was open at that point."

"Hmm," was Holmes's only comment.

"I sense you have questions," I said.

"Indeed."

"If he was in the throes of a coronary, how was he able to turn the sluice wheel to heat up the pool? It was still steamy when I arrived."

"A very good question, Watson. I think we can assume his needs gave him strength, or else the murderers did it."

"Murderers?"

He would say nothing further, but he made no more pretense of being at the spa for my health. To the guests gathered in the commons, he announced himself. "I am Sherlock Holmes, a consulting detective from London."

The group seemed amazed. And entertained. Lady Penhurst applauded.

Both Penhursts looked excited, as if this were a play they were watching at the Criterion Theater. The two majors seemed wary, as if the enemy, Death, might be lurking not on the battlefield, but here instead, around a corner or behind a potted palm.

"He seemed all right last night when we left him," Banks said.

Dalton nodded in agreement. "He might've been in more pain than usual, but he didn't comment. We left his room at about half-two. We assumed he would turn in then as well."

Mr. Willowby sat with his head sunk to his chest as usual. Surely the current event should have awakened some curiosity in his deepest soul. Might his mind be affected by his infirmity? Lady Faradene appeared eager to get on with the play. Miss Browne, hesitant and uncertain what her role was, attended her Ladyship's needs, supplying her with a fresh box of bonbons and a frothy lace handkerchief.

"Is this for our amusement?" her Ladyship asked.

"It is not," Holmes said. "The colonel's death is real. We believe he had a heart attack and fell into the pool."

"Is Doctor Watson not a doctor then?" Lady Faradene enquired.

"I am a physician, late of the army surgical corps, invalided out after injuries at the Battle of Maiwand."

"Where did you obtain your medical degree?" Lady Faradene asked.

"The University of London, with later work at St. Bartholomew's Hospital."

"Are you a detective now, too?" Miss Browne asked.

"I assist Mr. Holmes on his cases from time to time."

"Dr. Watson helps me with my cases while he is recuperating," Holmes added. "Now I shall need to interview each of you separately."

"Why, if it was a heart attack?" Lord Penshurst asked.

"For the record," I said. There really was no need for further looking into the matter. The colonel was overweight, in poor health, ate badly, didn't exercise, and possibly suffered from angina. If the coronary hadn't happened here, it was bound to happen elsewhere, and fairly soon, but Holmes, no doubt, wanted to clear up the rash of petty crimes that occurred at the spa, and I suspected to deduce they were random and not the work of some diabolic agency.

"What a lark!" Lady Penhurst said. Everyone turned to look at her and she, perceiving their disapproval, had the grace to turn slightly red and add, "If he weren't, of course, really deceased."

Anderson lent his office for use as the interview room. Lady Faradene, as the ranking member of the company, was first. No one disputed that. Anderson moved up teatime to be served earlier in the commons since they would not be playing whist this morning. Lady Penhurst arranged herself on the most comfortable chair. I sat to one side with my notebook and pencil at the ready.

"Thank you, your Ladyship," Holmes said.

"Whatever for?" She lifted her lorgnette hanging from a gold chain around her neck and stared at him through it. The diamonds around the rim winked in the utilitarian office light.

"For setting an example, of course," Holmes said.

She preened a little, but her slightly extruded pale blue eyes still watched him. "What is he doing?" She pointed her lorgnette at me.

"Taking notes. Now tell us, please, what your actions were after dinner."

"You were there. You know what we did. We listened to dreadful musical pieces, followed by recitations and readings. The major was mildly amusing. The one who read in voices. I can't tell the two apart."

He had actually been very funny. I'd noted she had laughed as much as the rest of the company.

"And then there was the excitement of the lost necklace," she added.

"Yes. What time did you retire?"

94

"At ten of the clock. Browne brought me my usual cup of hot milk. I drank it. Browne then read aloud for half-an-hour."

"You heard nothing unexpected?"

"I did not hear a man having a heart attack, if that's what you mean. I don't believe that requires any noise. The colonel was probably tipsy, as usual, and lost his balance."

"Was he often tipsy?"

"I said 'as usual'." She stared through the lorgnette.

"Miss Browne occupies the room next to yours. Is there a connecting door?"

"Yes, certainly. She has to be able to come to me when I need her."

"Was it open or closed last night."

"Closed, of course. Poor girl snores. Why all these questions for a heart eruption?"

"I'm just satisfying the constabulary." Holmes gave her the briefest of smiles.

"I need to talk to him. I have a complaint about my stolen brooch."

Holmes picked up an object under a paper on the desktop. It was a peacock glittering with opals, sapphires, turquoise, and pearls. "Would this be the brooch you lost?"

"Why, yes! Where did you find it? In that colonel's pockets, I suppose. I never did trust colonels. All wanting to be generals, but they can't quite climb that high."

"Indeed, not amongst the colonel's things. The brooch was found by myself in the lady's pool. I searched it while we waited for the constable."

She held out her hand, but Holmes continued to hold the brooch.

"There's the matter of the missing fan that belonged to Lady Penhurst."

"Oh, I wondered whose that was. I found it this morning on the path." She pulled the missing fan out of the folds of her voluminous claret woolen dress and dropped it as if it were a dead mouse on the desk. She snatched her brooch and stood up. "Are you finished with your impertinent questions?"

Holmes inclined his head and she swept out of the room.

Anderson escorted her Ladyship to the commons while Ellis brought in Miss Browne, who confirmed everything her Ladyship said – except the snoring. "I most certainly do *not* snore! The first night, she wanted the door open. I entertained her with my snoring ability while fully awake and, within minutes, she closed the door. She even did it herself without ringing for me. '*I never want to hear those fearful eruptions again!*'" she added in perfect imitation of her Ladyship.

Holmes suppressed a smile.

"The truth is, she snores most horribly." She smiled, and her plain face suddenly was no longer plain. Her eyes were a cornflower blue, unlike her employer's pale watery ones, and her fair hair was agreeable. She wore a plain grey gown as befits a companion.

"Did you go out after you left the countess to her snores?"

"I may have." She looked down at the handkerchief her fingers twisted in her lap.

"May we see the ring, Miss Browne?"

"How – how did you know?"

"I am a detective, remember? I have seen you fingering your handkerchief without using it for handkerchief duties, and I've had some intelligence about a ring purchased yesterday."

"You won't tell?"

"Of course not."

She untied the end of her handkerchief and held out a small gold ring set with a heart-shaped garnet encircled by tiny diamonds.

He handed it back. "Very handsome indeed. I believe you were receiving this ring sometime after ten last night, after her Ladyship fell asleep."

She blushed, but looked straight at Holmes. "And if I did? A proposal is not a crime."

"It is not. Did you see or hear anything out of the ordinary?"

"We did not. We were in the garden. It was quite cold."

I doubted they noticed the temperature.

"You have my best wishes. Both of you. You may go."

I waited for his explanation, but he merely smiled briefly and called for the next interviewees.

"To whom is she engaged?"

"Oh come, Watson, it's as obvious as the nose on your face."

The Penhursts came in together. Holmes questioned her Ladyship first. She was a woman of ample figure in a pleasing way. Her brown eyes were warm and her hair was russet. Her gown, too, was woolen, but the color of topaz. Holmes returned her fan and said it had been found in the shrubbery where she must have dropped it. After a short discussion concerning which shrubbery, he assured her he didn't know the particular bush. He went through the questions because she seemed to be enjoying being in a "playlet", as she called it.

"We retired after the performances finished, but did not go directly to sleep. I read to my husband – for awhile."

"What did you read?"

"Oh – Ah, Miss Austen's *Pride and Prejudice*."

"If we searched your room would we find that book?"

"Yes indeed," she said with confidence. "After about half-ten, we went to sleep. Well, his Lordship had already fallen asleep. Reading does that to him."

"Did you hear any noises in the hall?"

"I may have heard Mr. Ellis making his rounds, but I hear him every night. I heard nothing untoward."

His Lordship confirmed everything she said, including *Pride and Prejudice*. "Never seem to get past the first chapter. My wife has a soothing reading voice."

"Indeed," Holmes said, managing not to smile.

His Lordship was short and rotund with pale blue eyes. He'd buried his first wife. Holmes's telegrams had revealed that he already had his heir and two more sons. This wife was taking the best of care of him. "She doesn't want to move to the dower house if she can help it," Holmes commented later.

Willowby came next, bent over as he shuffled down the hall, with Anderson hovering to prevent a fall.

"You may sit up straight Mr. Willowby," Holmes said after Anderson had departed. "Your secrets are safe."

Willowby did so and transformed before our eyes. He still wore the whiskers and grey hair, but he took a deep breath and straightened his body into that of a much younger man, and a healthy one as well.

"How did you know?"

"I saw through your disguise from the beginning. You bought a ring at the jeweler's. You bought it in the guise of yourself rather than your invalid disguise, except for your spectacles. The jeweler remembered you. What is your real name?"

Willowby looked surprised. "It's Adams – albeit John Phillip Adams-Willowby. Quite a mouthful. I shortened it for obvious reasons."

"Are you really a vicar?" I asked.

Willowby nodded, and Holmes said, "He is. I conformed it with a telegram." He looked at Willowby and asked, "What did you hear last night?

"Nothing of interest. The usual sounds of the day ending. People walking in the hall."

"Where did you divest yourself of your heart?"

"In the back garden. I go out for a smoke around eleven every night."

"You have my congratulations."

"Thank you." Adams-Willowby's eyes were a bright steady healthy blue. He walked out as himself.

A few minutes later, Gerald Ellis confirmed the vicar's night smokes.

"I'd no idea so much went on late of night at The Turkish Bath," I said when we had a break. "You must enlighten me further"

Holmes's look was inscrutable. He asked for the two majors to come in together, in order to speed up the interviewing before luncheon was served.

"Tell me about your actions after everyone retired for the night," he told them.

"We sat up drinking rather late," Banks said.

Dalton nodded. "In the colonel's room. Then we took ourselves off about two, wasn't it?"

"More like half-two," I believe," Banks said. "Maybry said he felt poorly and wanted to sit in the bath awhile. We thought we had dissuaded him. Last we saw of him he was pouring another glassful."

"Was he?" Dalton said. "I didn't notice. Haven't been that squiffed in a while."

I'd been quiet during all these questions, but now I asked one. "Why were you so quiet? I didn't hear a sound last night. Squiffed soldiers – including majors in my experience – are anything but quiet."

"We've had good practice in our time sneaking into quarters."

"No doubt," Holmes said, "but now you will return to your former quiet retirement."

Both majors stared at him, and I had the sudden feeling they were trying to assess how much he knew. Finally Banks nodded. "Yes, we will."

Dalton agreed.

"And do tell everyone how much The Turkish Bath at Selwyche helped your injuries," Holmes added.

The majors left by cart to Worcester as soon as they were packed. By then, the day was so far gone we decided to stay until the next day. All was calm and pleasant. Mr. Willowby, as we continued to address him, declared that the salt spring improved his infirmity so much he could walk upright again. To celebrate, he removed the beard, though he pretended to have shaved it off.

With the military cleared out, only seven of us were left. Not enough for two whist tables, but even if we had one more, I doubted Holmes would play. That suited me. The Penhursts were jovial, but overly-so at times. Lady Faradene was barely civil as usual. Miss Browne and Mr. Willowby could only send glances to each other, but more openly now. Lady Penhurst sniffed a romance in the air and cosied up to Edith Browne and the formerly old young man. Soon, I suspected, the vicar might be offered a living on the Penhurst Manor, and in that case, the vicar and the companion could marry. Lady Penhurst would enjoy that. She would enjoy even more putting Lady Faradene out of a companion.

Constable Dobbs brought over the results of the autopsy performed by the coroner who officially ruled the colonel's death a natural one, a coronary.

Holmes and I had time for two more soaks in the salt baths. I felt almost back to normal. Maybe I should return in the future, with or without my valet.

When our carriage arrived soon after breakfast the next day, Holmes assured Anderson that the owner of the rival bath at the present time had no designs on his baths. "You're quite safe. I can't speak for the future, but nothing that happened here was in any way connected to an attempt to drive you out of business. The majors, I feel certain, will recommend your establishment to all of their army friends. The colonel's death was most unfortunate, but as far as we could ascertain, it was natural."

"Holmes, I can't thank you enough." Anderson wrung our hands until we had to remove ourselves and climb into the trap with our luggage. Ellis ran out with a packet of comestibles for our journey. "Lemon *bikkies*, I hope," I said as we drove away.

The Severn Valley was preparing for spring, with buds beginning to show on the trees as we drove from Selwyche to the train station. Holmes smoked his pipe and said not a word. We didn't talk until we were in our compartment.

"All right, Holmes, out with it. Do you still think the Colonel was murdered, and if so, why didn't you tell the constable?"

"Three reasons: First, proving murder might be difficult. As you yourself noted, it is entirely possible the man suffered a heart attack, fell against the side of the pool, rolled into the water, and swallowed some in his death throes. He'd been up late drinking. That and his age contributed to his unsteadiness."

"I'll grant you that. What are the other reasons?"

"A murder at the spa might mean the death of the spa. Anderson and his partners are planning to expand, to compete with other springs and baths around the country. No need to mention murder if it's one we can't with certainty prove."

"And the third?"

"I wasn't hired to solve a murder. I was hired to find out who was doing the pilfering, and to find out if the rival spa owner was trying to give The Turkish Bath a bad name in order to force a sale."

"What made you suspect murder?"

"The bath chair had been moved to the spa. A good explanation might have been available, but when we retired for the night, it was outside your door. That is most definitely not proof, but it might signify."

"If the Colonel didn't have a coronary," I asked, "what do you think was the cause of death? He wasn't asphyxiated or throttled or stabbed or shot. All of those would've been found at autopsy."

"Both majors served in tropical countries where many exotic poisons exist," he said. "No doubt some cannot be detected, and mimic the effects of a coronary."

"Indeed, there are," I agreed, "and some might not be found during an autopsy either, but I can think of another less messy way. A hypodermic filled with air to cause an embolism."

Holmes nodded. "Possibly someday a hypodermic needle will be found deep in one of the potted palms. By then, the thinking will be that one of the guests discarded it there."

"Why would someone murder the colonel anyway? And who might have done it?"

"The two majors, of course."

"Why 'of course'? What reason could they have to murder him?"

"They were seconded to the same regiment as the colonel in India after theirs had been cut off, leaving them stranded. The colonel ordered a sortie. It was a suicide mission that didn't come from higher up. The colonel wanted glory for himself in order to strike for general. The two majors received grievous wounds while more than half of the men were killed, and many wounded. The colonel himself wasn't wounded since he remained safely in the rear. He later received a slight wound and used that as an excuse to retire."

"Those telegrams told you this?"

"They did, but they also confirmed what I already had surmised. I thought it odd that they had similar service histories in the same location, but didn't seem to know one another. The colonel may not have remembered the majors, but they would never forget him. They're the only guests who would have had reason to murder the colonel. Or they could have stood by and watched it happen naturally."

"It was one of three then: An accident, a watched accident, or a murder."

"Succinctly put. And none could be proved or disproved, though somewhere I suspect a pinprick might be found from an injection site, but who could prove the colonel hadn't received it from a physician?"

"What about the lesser crimes?"

"I found the peacock brooch in the men's pool. No telling how it got there. Possibly the colonel found it or stole it and it fell out of his pocket."

"But you told Lady Faradene you found it in the ladies' pool."

"I suspect she may have worn it on her bathing costume to show off her jewels to Lady Penhurst whom she disdained as common. She didn't question me about it. I also suspect she may have snooped in the men's bath when it was empty, but I do not care to attempt to know why."

"The candy?"

"Stolen by the colonel. I found the box under his bed. He stole the money as well."

"How do you know?"

"He wasn't a wealthy man due to his profligate life, and he was an opportunist. He apparently hid it in a leather army pouch, again under his bed. Or perhaps the murderer staged it. Either way, it wasn't done by someone seeking to discredit the spa."

"I thought perhaps Willowby found or took it to buy the ring for Miss Browne. When will their wedding be, I wonder – a poor vicar without connections?"

"Perhaps he has made connections here."

"All the loose ends neatly tied up. Well done."

"Except for finding the brooch, the money bag, and the empty candy box, I did nothing but watch and let the play continue."

I suspected he'd done more, but, like the murder, I couldn't prove it.

"'*All's well that ends well*,'" he said.

"I thought you weren't literary."

"What schoolboy doesn't know the names of the Great Bard's plays?"

Mrs. Hudson was delighted with the box of bonbons and the packet of scented bath salts we had brought her from the spa.

Within a fortnight, we received an invitation to the marriage of Miss Edith Browne to Mr. Arthur Adams, the new Rector of Penhurst.

101

The Silent Prisoner
by Ember Pepper

"But its effects are so deleterious, Holmes!" I declared, fighting the urge to toss my morning paper aside in anger. "I don't care if it is legal or not. I would say the same if someone engaged in an excess of alcohol."

"Mmm, understandable," my flatmate murmured from his spot reclining on the divan in his blue dressing-gown. His sleeve was still rolled up, and the syringe lay discarded carelessly next to his open morocco case.

"Holmes, you aren't listening to me!"

"I am, Doctor. I merely disagree."

"As a medical man, I think I would know more than you on the topic."

"Is that what you would think?"

The words were spoken with such amused condescension that I threw my paper down onto the breakfast table in a fit of exasperation.

It was the warm summer of 1882. At the time, this personal habit of his was new to me. In the first year of our living arrangement, I had described my fellow lodger as possessing a "temperance and cleanliness" that forbid the notion of narcotic usage. As we settled more comfortably in our lives together, I had recently discovered I was regrettably mistaken. Evidently, the man had simply been on his best behavior to avoid losing out on an agreeable arrangement with someone willing to split rent with him.

He looked at me through narrow eyes and sighed. "I assure you, Watson, I am fully in control of the dosage."

"I simply don't understand you, Holmes. Cocaine and morphine affect the mind – that great brain you take such pride in. It simply seems uncharacteristically foolhardy for you to dabble in such dangerous hobbies, at the risk of your carefully honed skills."

He let his head fall back and his eyes close. "That is exactly the point. At times, it is pleasant *not* to think."

That gave me pause. I tried to place myself in my friend's shoes. I tried to imagine what it was like to see every small detail of the world as glaringly as I might see a glob of jam on a companion's face. It sounded tiring, but Holmes carried such pride in his deductive abilities that I found it surprising he would express such a feeling.

"I'm a thoroughbred quivering at a gate that never opens," he continued, "There is no noteworthy crime to be seen. The lack of creativity in the criminal classes should, in and of itself, be a crime. Give me something worthy to occupy my mind, and the need for distraction vanishes." He waved his hand airily. I could see faded puncture marks on the pale underside of his arm.

I cast a dismayed glance around at the multitude of ruffled newspapers that dotted the sitting room. I fought with the urge to scour the pages for something to divert him, but I knew he had already gone over every word himself and found nothing to pique his interest.

We were saved by Mrs. Hudson's announcement that a young woman was waiting to see us. I sprang up, accepting the meeting before Holmes could respond, and hastily cleared up the paraphernalia scattered on the table.

Holmes, to his credit, stood, straightened his dressing gown, and sat in his chair, attempting to look presentable.

A diminutive woman roughly our age entered timidly. From the modest design of her dress, I gathered she was of the working class, perhaps a servant. She wasn't particularly pretty, but her face held a wide openness and an artistic scattering of freckles that was pleasing.

She waited for us to bid her to sit and did so as if commanded, solidifying my theory that she was employed in a household staff.

"I beg your pardons, sirs," she started, "I know I came without an appointment."

Holmes waved the apology aside. "I see that you are a parlor maid, and you arrived using your last coin on a carriage that you were obliged to disembark from some streets away. You are recently engaged, but you have not yet informed your employers."

The woman glanced downwards at herself in surprise. After a moment, she frowned. "I can see how you might've guessed about the walking, as I have some mud on my shoes, but I cannot see how you came about the rest, sir."

"Not just any mud, but the specific color and consistency near the renovations of the apothecary nearby. The rest was similarly easy to deduce. The direction you came from – as evidenced by the soil on your boots – would put you in the direction of Belgrave and Grosvenor Square. From the sturdiness of your boots, the slight fading of your well-mended bodice where your apron ties have rubbed over a period of time, and the slight wear at the knees of your skirt, I can easily deduce that you are a maid, specifically at one of the wealthier households, as your clothes are of higher quality to reflect the station of your employers. I know you hired a carriage for at least part of your journey because your shoes hold traces of only one soil. Your coin purse is now empty, save for the faint impression of a ring inside that you wish to keep with you, but secret."

She smiled with unabashed joy. "That's astonishing, sir! A few months ago, you helped the Newgates in a small matter. The lady's maid there spoke highly of you. I'm glad she wasn't making up stories."

A slight flush crept up Holmes's cheeks at the praise. "A small matter, indeed. But I suspect something important weighs on you, dear."

"Well, yes. My name is Lucille, and I work as a parlor maid for a home on Chester Street. My employer, Mr. Philips, was murdered the day before last. It was in the papers." At this, she glanced around confusedly at the chaos of newsprint surrounding us.

"Yes, I recall it," Holmes answered. "His throat was slit in his parlor. They arrested the gardener."

"Asa," she clarified with some emotion in her voice. "His name is Asa, and I am sure he did not do it."

At the beat of silence and the quick glance Holmes and I shared, she frowned and shook her head vehemently. "I know what you think, sir, but this is not sentiment. As you said, I am spoken for. I've known Asa for years. His father was the gardener before he died, and Asa stayed on to take over his duties. I know him. What's more, there is no reason for him to kill Mr. Philips at all!"

Holmes sucked on the inside of his cheek for a moment before deciding to continue. "As of now, Miss Lucille, I'm not sure if your story merits further investigation, but I don't want to be hasty. Can you tell me exactly what events took place?"

"Of course. I was there when it happened. I didn't see the killing, thank God, but I saw his body." Here, her pleasant face was marred by the memory. "There was blood everywhere."

Holmes held up a hand. "A moment. I know it is tempting to jump straight away to the *plat de résistance*, but let's step back. Before that unpleasant event, what took place?"

"I was tending to the fireplace in the sitting room when I heard the dogs barking. The master has two Irish Setters that he dotes upon. *Doted upon*, rather," she corrected with a wince. "A few moments later, I heard some crashing and thudding noises from the parlor. I went to the door and called through, but there was no answer. I had no key, so I summoned the butler who was in the kitchen, and he unlocked the door." She took a moment to compose herself, as if she were entering the room once more and needed to steel herself for the sight.

"Inside," she continued, "Mr. Philips was in his chair by the hearth with his throat slit. There was blood all down his front. Asa was standing next to him, and the patio door stood open."

"And his proximity to the body is what led to his arrest?"

"You mean was he collared only because he was near Mr. Philips' body? Yes, I think so. He even claimed he saw no one else enter or exit the parlor through the patio door."

"What doorways lead to the parlor?"

"Three, sir. The one I stood at opening to the hallway, the patio door leading to the backyard, and the door to the right to his study."

"Was the study searched?"

"Yes. No one else was there."

"Is there an exit from the study to the hallway?"

"Yes, but to flee out the front door, someone would have passed me and no one did. I am sure of it."

"The hallway provides no other means of egress?"

She faltered, clearly at a loss.

In a softer voice, Holmes rephrased, "There are no other doors connected to the hallway besides the study and parlor?"

"Oh! Well, the other wall of the hallway is shorter because the sitting room takes up the main space in the front. The parlor door is across that room under the stairway. The only other room opposite the parlor and connected study is the kitchen and servants' quarters."

"Is there a backdoor in the kitchen?"

"Of course, sir, but it has a basic latch that can only be locked from inside and the door was locked, so no one could have escaped through that way and secured the door behind them."

"Why is there only a latch?"

"There has always been an old latch, but the newer lock that we used to use broke a few months ago, and the master had yet to arrange for it to be fixed."

"What was the state of the parlor?"

"Some items on the master's desk were thrown about as if there was a struggle. The round table next to his chair where he put his teapot and cup were knocked over. That must have been the sounds I heard that so alarmed me."

"But he was in his chair by the fireplace?"

"Yes."

Holmes fell deep in thought for a long while as we waited patiently for him to reemerge. When he did, he leaned back and tapped his chin.

"Tell me about the family," he requested.

"Mr. Philips is a widower twice over. I only knew his last wife, a French woman by the name of Villiers, who died about seven years ago of something with her breathing." She struggled a bit to recall the name. "She got filled with water."

"Pneumonia," I supplied gently.

105

"Yes, I think that was it. She left behind a daughter named Adelaide. She is about twenty now. Mr. Philips also has an older son named Grant. He treated them both well, and he took care of Adelaide as if she was his own. He made his money making parts of steam engines, but he retired a few years ago."

"What is Adelaide like?"

"Very nice. Smart too. She never acts like she's better than us. Though I realize she is, of course," she corrected quickly. "In any case, she is a good person, and she has taken his death badly. I see her crying."

"And his son?"

"He keeps more of a distance but has never been unkind. To be honest, I do not know much about him."

"Do they both live in the house?"

"Yes."

"Where were they during the murder?"

"I don't really know where Adelaide was. After the chaos of finding Mr. Philips, she appeared. I guessed she came down from her room on the first floor. The other Mr. Philips – Grant, that is – had left for a play at the Princess Theater and didn't return until later that night. Asa had been arrested, but the police were still there, looking around when he returned."

"Who was the policeman in charge?"

She pulled her face in strained recollection. "Gregory, I believe."

"Gregson, you mean?"

"Yes, that was it. He was nice. I don't think he really wanted to arrest Asa, but the boy was the only one there, so it looks bad for him."

Holmes stood with a sudden burst of energy. "I'll look into this for you."

A huge sense of relief washed over me. I tried my best not to show it, but the young lady gave me a curious look. She stood as well. "Thank you so much, Mr. Holmes. I can't pay you much . . . ."

"You needn't pay me at all," Holmes said brusquely. "If this proves interesting, that will be enough recompense. And I have no need to burden you with financial worries, as I am aware of your situation. Now, here is some coin for your return. No, no, please take it. I cannot in good conscience send a lady off to make that journey by foot. I will arrange to meet Gregson at the house later today."

As soon as the brisk rustle of our charming guest's skirt had faded down the stairs, Holmes fetched the page, sent off a short telegram to Gregson at Scotland Yard, and then retreated to his room, emerging half-of-an-hour later fully dressed and immaculately groomed.

"Will you join me, Watson? I'm off to the Philips' to look around. We're meeting Gregson there."

106

"We haven't yet received a reply from him."

"I did not request one." He smoothed his hair in the looking glass above the mantel. "I directed him to meet us forthwith."

"And you simply assume that he will drop his other duties and responsibilities to obey your every whim?" I asked with amusement.

He lifted a dismissive shoulder. "Gregson is brighter than most of the other Yard members combined. He won't choose to ignore further insights on a case."

Holmes was correct, of course. Gregson had preceded us there, and the alacrity with which he must have done so belied the annoyed protestation he greeted us with when we met him at the gate of the Philips' ornate, two-story Georgian home.

The blonde inspector tutted at us as he unlocked the wrought-iron gate and led us up the steps to the entrance.

"I'll never quite understand you, Mr. Holmes," said he. "You read a little entry in the newspaper about a murder and somehow see the complex mystery at the heart of it."

"While I would delight in permitting you to believe that of my powers of deduction, in this particular case, it isn't true. A servant requested my help. You believe it is a complex case?" Holmes probed.

"Its complexity lies in its lack of complexity, sir," the inspector sighed, unlocking the door and entering without knocking.

"Is the house empty, Inspector?" I asked.

"No. The son and step-daughter are still in residence, but the parlor and study are cordoned off and being watched by one of my men for the time being."

"May I ask why?" Holmes inquired with a certain amount of satisfaction in his voice. "I was under the impression that you had arrested the man?"

"I have arrested *a* man," Gregson corrected.

"Yes, a gardener by the name of Asa."

"Asa Andrews."

"Yet you seemed unconvinced of the rightness of this?"

We followed him into the foyer that branched off, on the right, to the spacious sitting room. Opposite, curved a beautiful wooden staircase, and under this was an asymmetrical hallway with three doors dotting the longer side and one door at the end of the short wall.

A young officer, who I vaguely remembered was called something like Williams or Willis, was leaning carelessly against the parlor door, straightening to attention as we entered.

"Well, Mr. Holmes," Gregson started, "the thing is, there really isn't any other answer for it. The young man was standing over the dead body seconds after he was killed. There was no one else about."

"However?"

"I cannot figure the point. I've talked to the young man. He claims his innocence, of course, and seems sincere. He gains nothing from his employer's death."

"Nothing that we are aware of, at least," Holmes suggested. "What story does he give?"

"He claims he heard the struggle as well and came in through the unlocked patio from the back garden. He says Mr. Philips was already dead."

"What was he doing outside?"

"Well, he's a gardener."

"Yes, but it was after dark."

The inspector shrugged. "I'm not a gardener, Mr. Holmes."

Holmes gestured to the parlor door. "May I?"

Gregson opened the door. The parlor was dimly lit area with a desk cluttered with papers. These were strewn about as if disturbed by a struggle. To the right, near the entrance to what I assumed was the study, was a small fireplace bracketed by two comfortable armchairs. The table next to it was toppled, and the tray of tea and one lone teacup was scattered on the stone of the hearth.

The inspector apologized. "Of course, the body is gone and my men have been in and out of here. I haven't moved anything else. I wasn't expecting you to come along," he added ruefully.

"Yes, yes, why preserve clues if I'm not here?" Holmes murmured sardonically, already examining the bloodstains on the armchair near the cold fireplace. "Ah, I assume this knife here is the murder weapon?" he pointed to a small porcelain-handled blade lying on the desk.

"Yes. I looked for finger marks. There were none."

Holmes frowned at that, gently picking the weapon up with a gloved hand and analyzing it up close. He glanced back at the desk. "You observed, I'm sure, that this comes from Philips' set there?"

He pointed to a small glass case hanging open near the edge of the cabinet near the door.

"Of course." Gregson sighed. "At least that indicates a crime of passion. If this were planned, the murderer wouldn't have needed to improvise in such a way."

"Hmm," Holmes murmured with evident doubt. "The data could support multiple theories. It's always a mistake to become attached to one without properly excluding the others."

Properly chastened, Gregson quickly turned up the gaslight to allow Holmes to move about the space. We both stood and watched as he peered at almost every inch of the room with his magnifying glass and crawled around the carpet methodically, and with complete disregard to the state of his own trousers.

When he was finished, he slipped his tool into his coat pocket and stood in the middle of the parlor, gazing around contemplatively.

"Was the gardener wearing gloves when you arrested him?"

Gregson's face filled with bright realization. "By Jove! He was not, Mr. Holmes."

"Then you're correct, Gregson. As is our bright parlor maid. There are multiple issues with the idea that Asa Andrews killed this man. One," he ticked off with long, scarred fingers, "there were sounds of a struggle, yet Philips seemed to be sitting in his chair when he died, his throat slit quickly. Two, as you said, he had no gloves on, so why would the knife be bare of all finger marks? And three, all Mr. Andrews would accomplish, as far as we know, by killing Mr. Philips is potentially making himself jobless. I assume this door leads to the patio and the back yard?" He pointed to the French doors and then strode through them without waiting for confirmation.

The patio was a midsized but elegant design of wood and awning. Three steps led down into the grassy yard lined with trees and meticulously maintained flowers. It wasn't large, but was sufficient enough for some cozy benches and a gazebo nestled in the corner.

"The patio doors aren't the only way to access the yard," Holmes noted, pointing at the narrow stone pathway that snaked beside one side of the house to a small gate opening to the shady alleyway.

"Correct," confirmed Gregson. "That's where the kitchen door opens as well."

We followed Holmes as he sidled around the house and walked up and down the narrow path, pressing on the kitchen door and examining the gate. He followed the pathway back to the yard, bent low to the ground, and peered for some time at the grass surrounding the stepping stones that made a dotted line from the patio to the gazebo.

"Did you examine the summer house?" he asked, stepping inside the round little building.

"We didn't," the inspector admitted. "I don't see how it would be important. If another intruder were here, Asa Andrews would have seen him, but the young man hasn't made any such claim."

"Where does Andrews sleep?"

109

Gregson pointed to the entrance of the food cellar. "He sleeps down there. The female servants sleep off the kitchen, and the butler has a small sitting room cordoned off by a curtain in the wine room."

"Cozy," Holmes commented wryly. "Look here." He pointed to one of the sills circling the gazebo. We stepped close and saw that he was looking at the remains of a cigarette.

"Recently smoked," he observed. "Also, and I'm sure you'll agree, Inspector, that this is noteworthy. There are two cigarette ends here, and they are of different brands. One is a Churchman's, and then one is Sobranie . . . ." He trailed off thoughtfully at this.

At last, Gregson seemed compelled to push the discussion onwards. "So two people were in the gazebo. Are you sure they must have been here last night?"

Holmes picked up the spent smoke and sniffed it delicately. "I'm fairly certain that these are recently smoked. We know it wasn't yesterday, as your men would have noticed. Why would Andrews not mention others in the yard? He can see clearly into the gazebo when he exits the cellar."

"Maybe he came from around the side," I suggested.

"That may be true, but that brings up another question: Where was he coming from? Besides, I see clear evidence in the footprints that someone, a male, exited the gazebo hastily – I can see because he didn't bother to stay on the stones – and entered the patio. This could only have been Andrews."

"So our gardener was in the gazebo?" Gregson murmured. "That isn't what he told us. He said he had just transplanted a potted plant to the flower bed when he heard the commotion."

Holmes stepped smoothly to the rows of flowers. "There is no pot here and no evidence that any of these plants have recently been transplanted, so we know he is lying about this, at least. But does that mean he's the killer?"

The question seemed to be rhetorical, so Gregson and I stayed quiet as the detective made a few more careful laps around the yard.

A thought struck me. "If there was another occupant in the gazebo, did you track any of the footprints to see how he or she escaped notice? If someone slipped around to the alley, it must have been by running across the grass."

Holmes worried his lip, staring so intently at the ground that I wondered if he had heard me. I was certain he had, but he seemed strangely disinclined to answer. I got the impression he was perturbed that I had brought the idea up.

"Let's take a look at the study," he said finally, ignoring my query, and we returned to the house. The study was accessible, as Miss Lucille

110

had said, from both the hall and the parlor. We entered through the parlor and Holmes gave the room a cursory examination, focusing primarily on the carpet, before following its exit to the hall. Exactly opposite was the doorway to the kitchen.

Holmes entered. The room was spacious with a modern range and ample room for food preparation. To the side was a good-sized room, half-blocked by curtains, where our maid Lucille and the cook slept.

Holmes went straight to the faded green backdoor and put his face very close to the hasp latch above the doorknob. He made a little hum of excitement and quickly withdrew his little lockpick case which also housed a small assortment of tweezers. He used one of these to carefully remove something from the latch, holding it up to the light for us to see.

Gregson squinted at it, struggling. "Is that part of a string, Mr. Holmes?"

"Indeed. This casts new light on the assumption that no one could have fled from this exit and secured it behind them."

"Curiouser and curiouser," the inspector murmured.

"Clearer and clearer," Holmes corrected. "Are the son and daughter home?"

As Gregson led us upstairs, he wondered, "If we know Andrews came from the gazebo to the study, and there was another person in the gazebo with him, could this mysterious visitor be the murderer who then fled through the study and out of the back entrance? Could Andrews be covering for this person?"

Holmes made a non-committal noise in the back of his throat. "This would have to be someone he cares enough about to face the noose alone to shield him or her. But we don't yet have enough data to know, so there is no use speculating."

Miss Philips, formerly Villiers, permitted us into her chambers with polite grace. She was an exceptionally pretty girl with rounded cheeks and large dark eyes. Her face was marked with clear signs of grief. Dark smudges marred the delicate skin around her eyes, and they were red from weeping. Despite this, she held her composure admirably and bid us to sit. Holmes, who had already begun quite impertinently perusing her room, sat last.

Two beautiful Irish Setters lay at her feet, looking melancholy. I wondered how aware they were of their master's death. It seemed to me that we often underestimate animals and their capacity to feel. They whined softly.

"I don't have much to tell you, gentleman," she began as she sat, petting the head of one of the pups absently. "I was up here in my room when I heard Lucille scream. I rushed downstairs to find her at the doorway to my step-father's parlor. Inside – " Here her voice broke. " – I saw Asa standing next to him. Waterhouse, the butler, was speaking loudly to Asa, asking him what he had done, I think. I can't really remember. I couldn't really focus on anything else but the sight – " She choked off and took a moment to control herself. "Someone fetched the police, and I was led to the sitting room, where I remained until they arrived."

"Who led you to the sitting room?" Holmes asked.

Her face frowned in concentration. "I'm not sure. I think it was Lucille. I apologize. I remember as if through a fog." She took a deep breath. "What will happen to Asa? Surely, he cannot be condemned simply from being in the room?"

Gregson cringed. "That would depend on the jury, Miss."

She paled even more. "Oh, dear Lord! That cannot be."

"You don't believe he is guilty?" Holmes asked. "Even if there seems to be no one else who could have committed this crime?"

She shook her head. "No, sir. I know he didn't do it."

"How do you know?"

She struggled for an answer before reasserting feebly, "I just know it, sir."

"When you have eliminated all other possibilities, whatever remains must be the truth."

She leveled a determined and confident look at the detective. "Have you eliminated all else? I know you haven't, since Asa didn't kill my father."

I could tell Holmes was impressed by her demeanor. He gave her one of his all-encompassing quick glances and then stood. "You may very well be right, Miss. By the by, did you hear the dogs barking before the tragedy?"

She hesitated, then responded with certainty, "Yes, a little before we heard the clashing and clanging."

"How long a pause was between the barking and the commotion?"

"Oh, about five minutes, sir."

"Do your dogs normally bark?"

"As you can see, no. Only if they feel threatened."

Holmes gazed at her for a long moment, a twinkle of satisfaction in his eyes. Finally, he dipped his chin at her, and we politely excused ourselves.

The son wasn't much help. With a restless and preoccupied wiggle of his knees, he told us he had gone to the Princess Theater at eight o'clock by way of the family driver before disembarking a few streets away, choosing to walk to take in the pleasant evening air. He returned a little past eleven to find the police in his home and his father murdered.

112

The driver in the small carriage house attached to the east side of the home confirmed this tale. He had driven the young man about halfway to the theater, let him out, and then retrieved him from the theater at eleven. They had made haste to return, as the driver had informed the son that something terrible had happened at home.

"Why do people kill, Watson?" Holmes asked as we three were back on the pavement outside the quiet house.

Gregson and I glanced at each other. "As you have often said," I answered. "Money, love, revenge, or self-preservation."

"Correct. I believe narrowing down motive will provide us with the answer."

"Several more recent theories suggest that some may be prone to violence with no motive," Gregson supplied.

Holmes frowned, "While I applaud you keeping abreast of current ideas, and I don't disagree, I believe this is rare. Madmen surely exist, but they are usually easily recognizable and lack the foresight to plan their crimes. Besides, if you're right and this is simply a well-functioning madman who committed this crime for the thrill of it, then I have no power to track him down. A motiveless crime is one of the hardest to investigate."

"So," Gregson continued, taking the rebuff with aplomb, "you believe the killer came through the patio from the alley, killed Philips, and to avoid the gardener coming from the gazebo (doing Lord knows what) he slips through the study, across the hall while the maid's back is turned, and exits the backdoor, securing it behind him with – "

"String," Holmes finished. He made a quick pulling motion with his hand, as if mimicking the jerk of the string to force the latch closed. "Child's play, really."

"So, Asa Andrews was simply a casualty?"

Holmes looked thoughtful. "I'm reserving judgment on that point, Gregson. Where is the young man being kept?"

"You can see him at the Old Bailey."

"And did Mr. Philips have a personal secretary?"

"Yes, a Mr. Evans. I haven't spoken to him."

He provided us with the address, and we bid him *adieu*, fetching a cab to visit the secretary near Shepard's Street.

"Where there's a will, there is a way," Holmes quipped as we settled ourselves in the cramped seat. "There's a banality to it, but it often proves true that a will sheds light on why a murder occurs. Philips was a wealthy man. It would be naïve of us to fail to look into how all that wealth is going to be dispersed."

Holmes surprised me by ordering the driver to stop near a carriage depot. He hopped out and disappeared inside for a few moments before returning with an air of satisfaction. He wouldn't tell me what the detour was about, no matter how I pressed him.

"Surely it's all clear to you, Watson," he responded obliquely.

"Not at all," I confessed.

He shrugged and would say no more until we reached Shepard's Street. We were allowed into the small flat by a servant who clearly thought we were official police, and Holmes did nothing to dissuade her of that belief, much to my silent chagrin.

Mr. Evans had evidently heard the news of his employer's death. He held himself with professionalism, but I could tell that Phillips' death had affected him. He told us he had very little time, but permitted us to sit down at his small desk in the office off his sitting room.

"I assume you're curious about the status of the family's inheritance? I don't believe in coincidences," he stated matter-of-factly, "so I feel obligated to tell you that there have been some recent alterations to the will."

Holmes lifted a surprised eyebrow. "'*Have been*'? Past tense?"

"Just yesterday, in fact."

"That's curious. Usually one is killed to *prevent* possible alterations. What was changed?"

"Mr. Philips made most of his money in engines. He sold his business about five years ago to his business partner. He was a good man and wished his estate to be split evenly between his son and step-daughter, with a small amount given to certain charities."

"And now?"

"That all remains. You see, in the original will, he had stipulated – much to the step-daughter's consternation – that she only be given her portion once she married a man named Elms – a gentleman old enough to be her father," he ended meaningfully.

"Why ever for?" I exclaimed.

Mr. Evans sighed. "Mr. Philips was a good man, but old-fashioned. He worried that his step-daughter wouldn't be taken care of if she weren't married well. Mr. Elms was his good friend."

"And, as you said, she wasn't pleased with this?" Holmes asked.

"Not at all. It was a source of tension between them. She declared that she wouldn't marry anyone she did not wish to, no matter the financial repercussions."

"If she believed that was the state of the will, this would mean she would have no motive to kill the old man," I commented.

"Miss Adelaide couldn't murder anyone," Evans asserted firmly. "For money or any other reason. However, that stipulation is exactly what Mr. Philips removed. He had come to his senses that it was unfair to put

114

such requirements on her, even in an effort to protect her. It was removed yesterday."

"Did she know he was going to remove that condition?"

"I'm not sure. He indicated to me that he hadn't spoken of it to his children, but one of them may have figured it out in some other way."

"You said you didn't believe Adelaide capable of murder, but what of the son?"

Evans leaned back, taking a deep breath. "I don't see him doing something so extreme, but he had some resentment toward his father over Adelaide. He insisted she wasn't really family, so no inheritance should go to her, whether she were married or not. Of course, he was aware that Adelaide was refusing her stepfather's arranged betrothal, so he really had nothing to fear on that point."

"Until yesterday."

Evans nodded. "Until yesterday."

"What do you think of the gardener?"

The man across from us frowned in confusion. "I hardly know the boy. Our paths don't have many reasons to cross."

"Did you know he was arrested for the murder?"

"That is surprising. What possible reason could he have to want to see the old man dead?"

Holmes rose. "That's what we are hoping to discover when we speak with him."

Asa Andrews was a fair-haired, handsome young man whose face, while lined with stress, was refreshingly open. He sat on the other side of the old dilapidated table secured in cuffs. He seemed suspicious of us until Holmes introduced himself. He, like Lucille, had been made aware of Holmes's reputation through an apparently healthy line of communication between the neighborhood's servants.

He leaned his head back and closed his eyes in relief. "Oh, thank the Heavens. If anyone can prove I'm innocent, it's you."

"A minute," Holmes forestalled, clasping his hands on the table. "Much of what I am able to do for you depends upon you, young man, and how honest you are with us. Tell us what happened the night of the murder."

"I was in the yard, transplanting some plants from their pots – "

"Were you?" Holmes interrupted.

Perhaps I imagined it, but the boy's face paled. He pushed bravely on though, stubborn in this lie. "Yes. It's best to transplant at night to avoid stressing the plant." He paused, obviously expecting Holmes to contradict him, but the detective remained silent, staring expectantly at him. "I heard the dogs barking near the patio door, which was odd because they don't bark often."

"Could you see the patio door?"

"Not where I was sitting. It was blocked by some trees. In any case, it never occurred to me that something terrible was happening, so I continued my work. Then I heard some commotion, like clattering – as if something had been knocked over."

"How long between the barking and the clattering?"

"About five minutes."

Holmes nodded, clearly pleased that this aligned with the daughter's remembrance.

"At that," the boy continued, "I went to see what was going on. The patio door was ajar, and the dogs were whining as if they were scared to go inside. I called out to Mr. Philips and entered carefully. I saw him sitting at his chair and the table with his teapot and cup lying on its side. I had the thought that he must have dozed off and accidentally hit the thing with his elbow, but I was worried that the sound hadn't wakened him. He is an older man, you know. *Was* an older man," he amended softly. "Someone began knocking on the hall door, but I had touched his shoulder and realized there was blood everywhere, so I didn't answer. I felt too shocked to speak. Before I knew it, Waterhouse was inside yelling at me and Miss Lucille was screaming. After that, it becomes a bit of a blur, but no matter what I told the police, they seemed to believe I had killed him. And they brought me here." He lifted his shackled hands in helplessness.

Holmes considered him for a long while. The boy held fast for an admirable amount of time before he began to shift uncomfortably in his seat.

"What were you really doing in the yard?" he asked the prisoner quietly.

"As I said, I was tending to the flower pots."

"You were not. Don't insult us by continuing to insist on this."

"What does it matter?" the boy asked, clearly frustrated. "I could have been practicing the waltz, and it means nothing of significance to what happened."

"You were not alone."

At this, Andrews' face went very white. "I'm not sure how you came to that conclusion, sir. I was outside by myself."

"We found two types of cigarettes discarded in the gazebo, where your footsteps emerge."

The boy clutched compulsively at his own fingers. "They must have been there before, sir. I was alone in the garden, as I said."

Holmes leaned back, running a tired hand across his face. "You realize, young man," he began wearily, "that if you weren't alone, there is a witness who can corroborate your story and prove that you were in the gazebo at the time your late employer was being murdered? This minor point, as you seem Hell-bent on framing it, may make the difference between your freedom and a noose?"

The boy looked down at his lap in defeat. "And you believe there is no way to prove my innocence outside of that?"

"There may not be."

There was a protracted silence. We could hear the muted jingle of the guard's keychain on the other side of the door.

"I was alone," he finally said, his voice so soft that I hardly heard him.

Holmes looked dismayed by this, but he nodded and stood. "So be it. I'll do what I can for you."

"Mr. Andrews," I leaned forward across the desk imploringly, "All you have to do is provide the name of your companion and we can prove your alibi."

He said nothing and I, begrudgingly, rose and followed Holmes outside to the pleasant air of the descending evening, so at contrast to the grim reality of the silent prisoner inside the bars of the building.

Holmes looked upwards at the pink-and-orange dusk and let out a long breath.

"I don't understand, Holmes."

"You don't?" he asked in surprise. "You see but you do not observe. The parts are all here. If you could make the connections, it would all be clear to you."

I struggled. It was like peering into the darkness to make the details of a shape visible.

He jerked his head and bid me to walk with him. "I see the chain of events as if I witnessed them myself. The issue is proving it."

"Can you lower yourself to explain it all to me?" I asked with some irritation.

"Of the two children, who had more reason to kill their father?"

"The son," I answered confidently. "He was likely trying to do so before he amended his will, but wasn't aware that he had already done so. But he was at the theater."

"Was he?"

"The driver said – "

"That he had taken him halfway and then let him out."

"You believed he doubled back?"

"It would be easy to do. Perhaps a bit of a walk, but he is young. And, in fact, when I stopped by the depot, I was able to learn that a man bearing his features rented a cab to the theater a little after nine."

"So he doubled back through the alley, entered the patio – which Andrews couldn't see from the gazebo – and killed the old man, exiting through the study and the kitchen. Following that, he rushed to the carriage depot and paid for a ride to the theater."

"He attempted to create an alibi – more than our man Andrews has done – but no alibi is perfect unless it is authentic."

"But why would the dogs bark at him? And why did there seem to be a struggle when Philips was evidently killed in his chair?"

"As to the dogs, they are excellent judges of character, so that's a point that is possibly testable. The façade of a struggle is vitally important and illuminates the heart of this case."

He fell silent, and I understood that he was hoping I could draw the same conclusions he had. I ruminated on it until I came to the only answer I could think of.

"Staging a struggle, a loud one, would insure that the body was found. He wanted to draw attention to it. But why? Why would he run that risk when he could have slipped out without notice?"

"What end did it accomplish?" Holmes asked simply.

"It led to Asa's arrest. You mean to say that he was meant to be framed for this?"

"I believe so. Further – " We were approaching Scotland Yard. " – I believe that both occupants of the gazebo were meant to be framed, but the mystery guest instead slipped around to the front of the house."

Realization dawned on me. "And seemed, from Lucille's perspective, to be coming down the stairs from her room," I finished. "So it was Adelaide in the gazebo with Andrews. Whatever were they doing?" I wondered.

Holmes made a full stop and turned to stare at me with an expression equal mix of disbelief and amusement.

"Oh," I realized, flushing a bit, "Of course."

"I thought that would be immediate to you. After all, you are '*Three-Continent Watson*'," he remarked with an aggravating smirk.

"That was a jest, Holmes," I growled.

"Mmm. In any case, you can understand why the young man seems adamant to keep her presence out of it."

"How do we prove this?"

"That is what I'm working on," he tapped his head.

"The string," I pointed out.

"What of it?"

118

"He doesn't know you removed it."

Holmes frowned and then he beamed with pride. "Good man! That is brilliant! The servant's area in the kitchen would be sufficient . . ." he murmured thoughtfully. "Let's gather our friend, Gregson, for the *denouement*."

We arrived back at the Philips' house when it was well after nightfall. Waterhouse answered and was more than amenable to our little plan.

Holmes and I were waiting comfortably in the sitting room when Adelaide and Grant came in to see us. Holmes stood and shook the son's hand.

"Forgive our intrusion at this difficult time. Inspector Gregson has removed his men and considers this a resolved case, but I have my reservations. May we have your permission to continue our investigation? I'm particularly interested in your kitchen and that hasp lock. I have some theories as to how it was secured from the outside, and I am hoping that there may be some evidence remaining."

"I have no objection," Adelaide said.

At the same time, her stepbrother frowned. "Whatever for? It seems you're grasping at straws, sir. I can't fathom why you are going so far as to protect that little traitor."

Adelaide looked supremely uncomfortable while I tried desperately to appear as if I did not notice.

"It has nothing to do with protection," Holmes answered brusquely. "There are inexcusable unanswered questions in relation to this murder that seriously cast doubt on Mr. Andrews' guilt. I cannot believe you would tolerate an innocent man going to the gallows for something he did not do."

"He was the only one there. He was standing over the body mere seconds after the murder occurred. I don't see what is unanswered."

Holmes nodded and stood. "Very well then."

Adelaide rose quickly, her face flush with panic. "Sir!"

Holmes waved her off. "There is nothing I can do without permission to examine the house."

"I give you permission!" she declared.

"You speak out of turn, Adelaide!" her stepbrother barked. "This isn't your house."

She looked at Holmes with a desperation that was difficult to endure, and even more difficult to ignore as we must. Holmes shook his head in defeat and moved from the room as the two siblings began arguing behind us.

On the front porch, Waterhouse was waiting with the two Irish Setters. He passed them to us dutifully, and I held their leashes as we circled to the tree-covered dirt alleyway that led to the gate and kitchen door. The gate opened with a low creak, and we stood at the kitchen door for a moment, waiting.

The silence stretched on and I began to feel my heart sink. Perhaps we had misjudged what he would do –

Something banged against the door. We could hear the sounds of a brief struggle and Gregson's recognizable voice ordering someone to sit.

The latch made no sound as it was drawn back, and the green door swung open silently to the kitchen. Grant Philips was sitting at the table, Gregson's cuffs secured around his wrists. The door to the hall opened at the same time that I stepped in with the dogs who began to bark in earnest at the young man.

He hissed and shoved at them with his foot. "Get those mangy dogs away from me!" he spat.

"See?" said Holmes. "What did I say, Watson? Excellent judges of character."

I managed to get them outside, wrapping their leashes around one of the gate's bars.

When I stepped back into the kitchen, Adelaide stood at the other door, framed by the gaslight flooding the hall, her mouth open in shock. "What is happening, sirs?" she demanded.

"I caught your brother red-handed removing key evidence," Gregson accused.

"What exactly did you see?" Holmes pressed.

"He came in here and dug out the string you had Waterhouse wrap around the hasp latch and put it into his pocket."

At this revelation, young Mr. Philips paled and slumped in his chair.

"Capital!" Holmes declared. "I trust this, along with the information from the carriage depot, will be enough to get Andrews out of gaol?"

"I'll drag the dogs up for testimony if I have to, Mr. Holmes," Gregson declared.

"Someone tell me exactly what is going on!" Adelaide insisted.

"Your brother here savagely murdered your father because he knew he was intending to change his will to allow you equal inheritance with no stipulations regarded your marital arrangements," Holmes explained. "A change that was made yesterday, unbeknownst to Grant."

At this news, the scoundrel chuckled darkly under his breath and closed his eyes in resignation.

"He intended to implicate not only Asa, but Asa's mystery guest as well – but that didn't quite go as planned."

120

Holmes did not specify, but he gave Adelaide a meaningful look that spoke volumes. Her face turned red, and she dashed from the room in distress.

"It doesn't matter," Grant commented idly. "I can still ruin her when I confess to the whole thing at the trial."

"And then you'll hang," Holmes snapped.

Gregson pulled him up roughly. "Quite a mouth you have on you, for someone whose days are numbered. Come along."

He was roughly bustled out of the house and into the street, where more of Gregson's men were now waiting, but we did not follow. We ascended the stairs, and Holmes knocked softly on the open door to Adelaide's chamber.

We entered without being bid to. The young lady was standing at the window, looking out into the distance. When she turned, she pressed a hand to her stomach and wiped wayward strands of hair from her face, clearly attempting to gather herself.

"I'm sorry," she said with wavering voice, "I shouldn't have behaved in such a manner. I simply cannot believe Grant would do such a thing for money. It's only money."

Holmes cleared his throat. "We do not believe it was simply for money."

Her eyes filled with tears. "I see." She vacillated and then asked, "How did you know? That I was in the summer house with Asa?"

"The particular citric scent of one of the cigarettes left there was present in your room. Distinctly feminine footprints were clearly visible in the grass fleeing towards the alley and turning back towards the front of the house," Holmes explained gently. "For what it may be worth, Mr. Andrews said nothing of his relationship with you. I believe he would have gone to his execution protecting you. He clearly loves you very much."

She swiped at the moisture on her cheeks. "I would not have allowed him to. I was hoping you could save him before I had to say anything."

"You needn't say anything now. It isn't necessary. And anything your darling brother feels compelled to announce will be quickly disregarded as the anger of a bitter man."

"You are a wealthy woman, Miss Adelaide," I said softly, "and while it may be unorthodox, I imagine this will allow you the freedom to choose the husband you desire."

"I lose one man I care deeply for and gain another," she observed. "My feelings are understandably conflicted."

Holmes nodded, and we left her there to come to terms with them in her own time.

The Predilections of a
Pious Poisoner
by Mike Adamson

The sheer number of cases that have passed before the keen eyes of my friend, Mr. Sherlock Holmes, has never ceased to amaze me. Investigations crowded upon each other, and at times, especially in the early days of our acquaintance, I was hard put to know how Holmes kept the details of each straight in his own mind. It was all I could do to maintain a semblance of order on paper, for he would grasshopper from case to case as details presented themselves. Sometimes, when cases were bogged down or awaiting some epiphany, another matter would raise its head and consume his attention in a brief burst of focused cognition

One such case took us away from the mill of minor matters in London to the sunny farmlands of Kent in the mid-September of 1883 – a rum business by all accounts, and one in which Holmes had the opportunity to exercise some of his more arcane skills. Indeed, it wouldn't be overstating matters to say that our very lives came to depend on the acuity of those faculties.

The affair began, as did so many, with a visitor at Baker Street. Mrs. Millie Hazel was a fine, strong countrywoman with bright eyes, a forthright demeanour, and sandy hair pinned up under a wide-brimmed hat. She wore a floral dress, as became the late summer season. We had received a letter foretelling her visit, and Holmes had attempted to project the nature of her business. A lost possession? A missing entanglement of the heart? A family matter? His suppositions couldn't have been wider of the mark.

Our windows were open to the breeze from Baker Street, the air sweet with the smell of fresh-mown grass from Regent's Park. I showed the lady to a chair in our sitting room and served lemonade – such was the warmth of the day.

She smiled guardedly. "I hope I'm not wasting you gentlemen's time, but I'd not come if I thought it any less than crucial."

"In your own words, Madam," Holmes replied evenly, steepling his fingers and adopting the expression that told me he would accord her thoughts every concentration.

"I'm the midwife from the village of Kingston Cray, in Kent. That's in the Sevenoaks area. I've noticed something odd in the village these past eighteen months or so. People keep dying."

"People do," Holmes interjected with a smile. "It's a consequence of their mortality." I cleared my throat as a subtle caution for my friend not to be clever at the expense of a lady, and he moved on at once. "How were these deaths significant, Mrs. Hazel?"

"The manner. Poison. Four in a year-and-a-half. Now, the police say they're satisfied that there was no funny business, but it's starting to worry a lot of folks. One was food poisoning – a bit of bad fish, they said. Another was an accidental eating of the wrong mushroom. A third swelled up something horrible. A reaction, the doctor said. But by then he – old Dr. Tanner – was getting a bit concerned himself. The fourth was heart failure, and we know that can be brought on deliberately."

"What did Dr. Tanner say about that one?"

"Nothing, Mr. Holmes. It *was* Dr. Tanner."

Now, Holmes sat forward with a blossoming of interest. "Do these four victims have anything else in common?"

"Yes, Mr. Holmes. They were all members of the local Catholic parish, and they had all annoyed their priest on religious grounds. Except perhaps Dr. Tanner, and his passing seems awfully convenient if there *is* anything amiss with the others, as he was in the best position to know."

Holmes nodded with a pensive look, and his eyes met my own. "Watson, your impressions as a medical man?"

"Each of these manners of death is quite common, especially in the country. Food poisoning can happen anywhere the hygiene of preparation falls short. Getting the wrong mushroom is a hazard of gathering from the wild, though country folk, as a rule, know their fungus. Swelling up – that's an acute reaction to something in the immediate vicinity. It can cause airway obstruction, with predictable results. Heart failure?" Now I could only manage a mild shrug. "Doctors are as mortal as any and *might* miss their own symptoms . . . but I honestly doubt it. If we're on the theme of poison, here, then an overdose of foxglove might very well induce heart failure."

"Eighteen months," Holmes mused. "That's long enough to lull coroners from seeing any pattern, given how overworked they are." He regarded Mrs. Hazel with a steady gaze. "You feel these events are connected? That they are the result of deliberate misdeed?"

"I do, sir. And others have such fears too. Even Sergeant Dawkins at our little police station says he isn't comfortable with the way things were left, but who's he to go against the findings of the county coroner? Why, people have moved away from homes they've known for generations in order that the next one not be themselves."

"And only their religion unites them? No other characteristic?"

"They weren't even very keen churchgoers." Our guest could only give a charming, feminine shrug of her shoulders. "Do say you'll help, Mr. Holmes! I've not much to recompense you with, but I know many a villager who would contribute a handsome sum to be free of this fear and worry."

Holmes rose and gave her a shallow bow. "How could I decline such an invitation? I shall look into the matter. Now, Mrs. Hazel, are you staying in London any length of time?" At her negative, he went on. "I would ask you to return to Kent directly. We shall follow tomorrow, arriving unannounced, apparently as summer visitors escaping the smoke of the city."

"Thank you, Mr. Holmes, Dr. Watson," she said with a most genuine smile as she rose. "It'll mean a lot to the people of Kingston Cray."

For Mrs. Hazel's safety, we wouldn't approach her again until the matter was resolved. We packed, and in the morning rode the London, Chatham, and Dover Railway as far as the station serving the village of Longfield, where we obtained the hire of a carriage to take us the two-and-a-half miles south-by-west to Kingston Cray, which nestled among its yellow, reaped farmlands.

We took lodging at The Tottenham Inn in Maidstone Road, finding the landlord, James Colville, Esq., a personable and friendly chap. We were vague as to our reasons for visiting a rural village at late harvest time, and soon walked out in the glorious sunshine for a stroll along the main street of the village to a cottage bearing the blue lamp at its gate, which proclaimed it the Kingston Cray Police Station.

Sergeant Peter Dawkins was a bluff and genial sort, a big-enough lad to dissuade farmhands who had had a pot or two of cider too many, but we doubted there would be much in the way of criminal enterprise in a place so small and quiet. He sat in his front room with a newspaper, his desk a mess of forms and a logbook. His jacket and helmet hung on the back of his door, and he came to his feet rather quickly when his lady announced visitors.

"Sherlock Holmes?" he began, as if the name were familiar but just out of reach. "From London, you say?"

"Indeed, my good man." Holmes was succinct, not relishing bringing a slow country copper up to speed on his own case. "I engage in private investigations, and have been approached by an interested party to look into the matter of four deaths in this village over the last eighteen months."

"Oh – oh, I see." Sergeant Dawkins drew on his jacket as he spoke. "Pardon me bein' out of uniform, an' all. Things are quiet as a tomb hereabouts." He broke off for a moment. "Mr. Holmes – of the Lauriston Gardens business?" Now he was all smiles. "We get the London papers through of a weekend. I remember reading all about that affair. Well, Mr. Holmes, if you've come to look into our mysterious string of 'tragic accidents', you're more than welcome."

"Excellent. I would like to review any paperwork you have relating to the incidents, and would be interested in your personal recollections and impressions."

"More than happy to help, Mr. Holmes." Dawkins called through to his good lady for tea, and then opened a drawer in his cabinet and rummaged through the papers. "I held onto the files. We don't get much in the way of mystery out here, sir. Nothing more puzzling than front-bar affrays at closing time. To have members of the community poppin' off in their prime is well out of the ordinary." He closed the drawer and waved us into seats before his desk as he sank into his leather chair. "Let me give you some background. There have been four to date.

"The first was Henry Twyville, on – " He looked and consulted the first folder. " – the first of April, 1882. He was a cobbler by trade. He'd nailed just about every pair of boots between here and Eynesford. Nice enough chap, never any trouble. He'd had dinner with his family one Sunday evening and collapsed with pain and sweats. Old Doctor Tanner came quick and gave him an emetic and plenty of water, but whatever the bad stuff was, it acted fast. The strange thing is, though it certainly looked like food poisoning, the fish was fresh-caught in the River Darent that morning, and no other member of his family was ill, though they all had the same. The coroner put it down to plain bad luck that he'd got a piece tainted in some way."

"That seemed too great a stretch to you?"

"It did, sir. Why, I'd have expected at least one other to suffer, given as there were five in the family and odds workin' the way they do." He shook his whiskery head. "They took a terrible shock by it, as you'd expect. They'd not been big churchgoers before, but they felt the need for the comforts of faith after Mr. Twyville was taken from them so abruptly."

Mrs. Dawkins brought in a tea tray and poured for us as her husband shuffled his files. When we had the sweet and fragrant brew before us, he went on smoothly.

"Then there was Arthur Fielding. The dreadful case of the wrong mushroom. It was very odd, because Arthur was a botanist by training, retired down here from London, and knew the wild mushrooms of these parts like the back of his hand. He faded quickly, and though they got him to hospital in Sevenoaks, there was nothing they could do. He died on the third day. They called it *Destroying Angel,* and the coroner said it was – " Here he read from a file. " – '*a mistake even an expert could make*'." He sighed once more.

I nodded silently to Holmes. I'd heard of that one.

"Third was Ted Holliday. He was a shop assistant at the grocers along the way. He went into the most frightful reaction to something – swelled up so his eyes wouldn't open, and he was wheezing for breath. Doctor Tanner came at once, but there was nothing he could do. It was awful, and just like Mr. Twyville, his family witnessed it. That was in May last." He squinted and tapped the file. "It had happened to him once before – years and years back – but that time he got away with it. Nobody knew why then, either." He opened the next file.

"Then we lost Dr. Tanner himself, just back in July. Hale and hearty, if no longer young . . . Heart failure in his surgery. Another doctor was sent for, who pronounced death and gave the coroner his opinion of heart failure. There it is, Mr. Holmes." He closed the folders and passed them across. "You're welcome to borrow those."

"Thank you, Constable. Now, I gather you are dissatisfied on each count. Are there specific circumstances that make you doubt the official verdict?"

Dawkins counted them off on his fingers. "The odds of one out of five pieces of fresh-caught fish being bad? They lay in the same basket till they were filleted. If there was taint in one, it would have at least travelled to the next, if you follow. The chances of a genuine expert mistaking his mushroom – they just seem long to me. Ted Holliday had never had a reaction to anything present in his shop before, nor has anyone else since. What could it have been? I'm not saying it wasn't natural causes, but maybe those causes had a helping hand? Same with the doc." He took a long pull at his tea. "We're a small community, Mr. Holmes, so we know each other pretty well, and Dr. Tanner was the sort you thought would go on for many a year yet. I'd not have been surprised if he'd seen the next century."

I made notes the whole time, my hurried scrawl filling pages as the impressions flowed. At last, Holmes asked one final question. "I apologise if this information is already to be found in the files, but . . . were there any other circumstances, coincidences, surrounding these passings? People in unusual places, where they shouldn't be, gifts, visitations . . . ?"

"None where they had no business being." The constable thought back with effort. "There was some talk at the time, just silly superstitious stuff, and I'm sure there's nothing to it."

"What about?" Holmes whispered.

126

"Wrath of God," Dawkins replied in similar volume. "Each of them had made some remark about the church. The Church of St. Genevieve serves Catholics in this area, and there are times you'd be forgiven for thinking the Reformation was still on. Not that there's any open hostility between Anglicans and Catholics – of course there isn't, but there is tension. Most view it as good-natured rivalry between the faiths, and when it comes to things that really matter, we're all on the same side. But the remarks were passed."

"Yes?" Holmes pressed gently.

"Mr. Twyville was a recent convert, certainly after the birth of their children, and had decided to bring the family into the Catholic fold. His reasons were his own and no one's to question, but after joining the congregation, he apparently made a few disparaging comments about the disposition of moneys within the parish – the priorities of the clergy and so forth – suggesting that while the faith may have been to his liking, the *priesthood* was not."

"And the others?"

"Professor Fielding was both a religious man and a scientist. He balanced those things as people have learned to. But he had no time for fools, and when he heard how tradesmen had been waiting two years for payment for their repairs to the church roof after the blizzard of '81, he wasn't shy about calling it a scandal. He enjoyed a drink a bit more than the local clergy liked, too, and they had words once in public on that score – Arthur Fielding and the curate, Father William, in The Tottenham one Friday night. Just as he went at the whole theological debate with Father Danielson another time. Tom Holliday? He was the odd one out, really. Had a reputation as a wild one 'round the village. The sort who was too fond of the cider and – How shall I put it? – pestered other men's wives? He'd had two black eyes on account of it. When reproached for his behaviour by Father Danielson, he was less than repentant, I've heard. Took his penance, but was back with a vengeance the next week."

"And the doctor?"

"He's the mystery. Catholic all his life but didn't really practice. He minded his *P*'s and *Q*'s, as any public servant should, and there's nothing to suggest he ever said a word against anyone."

Holmes set aside his empty cup and rose to offer his hand for a firm shake. "Thank you, Constable Dawkins. You have been of inestimable assistance. We shall return these files in due course. Now, we must be away to arrange a delicate meeting of an entirely different sort . . . for which you might oblige us with certain names and addresses."

Constable Dawkins checked his files and a local map and wrote out the information Holmes required, and then escorted us to his gate. "Good hunting, sirs, and I look forward to your discoveries." As we were about to step into the street, a bicycle bell warned us against that intention, and a lady swathed in dark blue nodded a greeting as she swept by. "Got to mind your toes when Mrs. Carmichael is out and about," Dawkins added with a smile. "Fair owns these streets when she's doing Father Danielson's many good works. You'll meet him in due course, I've no doubt."

The constable's wry expression forewarned us of the nature of the clergyman, and we sallied forth with a sense of starting to come to grips with matters.

A quiet meal at the pub gave us time to consider the information we had been provided, and over a nice ploughman's lunch, accompanied by a local cider, I perused the reports from the medical perspective. Holmes cogitated on matters his own way, but, when I had finished my cheddar cheese and fresh-baked bread, he inclined his head at the paperwork between us.

I dusted my hands with a frank nod. "We're playing the Devil's Advocate here, questioning the county coroners in every instance." I caught his eye. "They won't appreciate this, Holmes."

"An irrelevant consideration if they were, in fact, wrong. Do continue."

"Well, in none of these events does the evidence, as summarised by the police, *forbid* the act being deliberate, and therefore not misadventure but murder." I took a long draft of cider with relish. "The tainted fish – certainly food poisoning, but of a particularly swift sort. It normally takes many hours for the effects to set in, allowing at least some time for a competent doctor to head off the worst of it. We aren't always successful, true, but the emetic Dr. Tanner administered should have cleared residual toxin from the patient's system and given him a fighting chance."

"Your conclusions, then?"

I felt rather on the spot, as Holmes was the one who drew the conclusions, but he was asking, and this is my profession, so I took a deep breath and applied the sort of logic Holmes had striven to impart to me these past years. "*If* the meal were tainted, it was with a toxin of uncommon rapidity. Other possibilities circulate around this one, though."

"Yes?" Holmes asked with a tight smile.

"Given that no one else suffered the slightest effect, the meal might not have been tainted at all. Mr. Twyville may have been poisoned somewhat earlier, in an entirely different way, by someone who knew the standard diagnosis would be food poisoning and that the automatic prescription would be an emetic to get the toxin out as soon as possible. If the poison were orally administered, the emetic would certainly re-emit the residue thereof, but its exact nature would be masked by the regurgitated food." I tapped the folders. "There's no record here of Dr. Tanner taking a sample for culturing, though any London hospital should have been able to provide him that analysis without difficulty."

"So, the event was swiftly fatal, and the regurgitation was, of course, disposed of at once. Dr. Tanner was of considerable years. Much of his career took place before germ theory became the accepted norm. Perhaps, in the heat of the moment, he forgot the analytical approach and let the evidence be lost. Once again, there is no suggestion in the *post mortem* report that it was anything other than natural causes."

"Then Fielding. Destroying Angel, *Amanita virosa,* is a pure white mushroom related to the 'deathcaps', whose various species are found around the northern temperate regions of the world. It generates a virulent toxin that sets up a chain reaction in the human body. It follows a predictable cycle of events, from severe illness to the amelioration of symptoms and then their return, before the patient's gradual fade to mortality. There's no question that this was how Professor Fielding died. The only question is whether we accept that the toxin got into his system accidentally, or in accordance with someone's agenda."

"And if we said someone had managed to infect Mr. Twyville, why not Professor Fielding? And Mr. Holliday?"

"He worked in a greengrocer's shop. There are dozens of different plant- or soil-based microbes present at any time. Normally, they are of no consequence. To have such a profound reaction meant he was expressly susceptible to something – his own unique quality that would tend to ensure no one else was caught in the trap. This means someone knew Mr. Holliday had an Achilles's heel and exploited it."

"By bringing him into contact with that substance at some point." Holmes nodded. "And the doctor?"

"The notes all point to classic heart failure. It's a shame no blood was drawn for a closer look, as I'd be willing to entertain there being a rather large amount of foxglove in his system. He was seventy-six years old, carrying more weight than was healthy, and it may be assumed that he was inherently stressed by his profession. The coroner comments that Tanner should perhaps have relinquished his position to a younger man long since. But that's assuming a lot. I know many a doctor who is perfectly competent to work into advanced age. Indeed, their experience alone is worth its weight in gold. None can tell a man to put himself out to grass until he's good and ready, and Dr. Tanner had no history of cardiac trouble. My impression is that he was a good-enough doctor to look after himself."

I buried my nose in my glass while Holmes arranged the files in a stack, laid a hand on them, and spoke in summary. "Individually, the cases were perhaps reviewed without benefit of wider context, allowing assumptions to be made that favoured the easiest answer – natural causes. Collectively, however, they form a pattern that supports quite the opposite." He attracted the attention of the landlord, and when Mr. Colville came over to collect our plates, he put the question of the publican's impressions of the deceased.

Colville was a tall, rather rotund, jovial-faced chap in a striped apron and sleeve garters, and he took a conspiratorial interest when he knew we were here to look into the village's lost citizens. He came back from the kitchen and drew a chair up, straddled it, and spoke quietly, though we were the only ones in the bar at that hour.

"Well, they were all Catholics – I'm Anglican myself, as are the majority here – but I'd have to say they were what you'd call *characters*. The old professor, with his tweeds and his collecting bag – you'd see him going off in the early morning, and he might not be back 'til sundown. He used to walk miles, knew every tree and field. I heard he was considering writing a book on the nature of these parts as his retiring gift to science. I often wondered what he might have seen in the mist of a morn, whether of this world or another."

"Mr. Twyville, the cobbler. Was he also a 'character'?"

"He could be. Grand hand at skittles. Played for the pub team against sides as far off as Sevenoaks. Handy at cards, too. Learned his trade in a factory making boots for the army, always had a story to tell from those days." Now Colville scowled. "Holliday – now there was trouble. A character of a different sort. When I heard he'd dropped off the perch, I assumed some husband had curtailed his philandering permanently. He was a pathetic womaniser. I saw him try his luck with two, three women a night in here – until the village got wise to him, and pretty soon womenfolk would have nothing to do with him in public. His manager cautioned him to keep things professional in the shop, too." He gave a sigh. "The doctor? George Tanner was a regular for as long as I've been keeping this inn, and I never heard a word against him." He raised a finger. "Except, oddly enough, from their own priest. *He* was on the outs with them all at one time or another. There again, Father Danielson never has a good word to say about anything or anyone."

My brows must have risen, though I didn't take my eyes off my notebook.

"Oh, yes, Dr. Watson. He's the fire-and-brimstone type, never winds down when the subject is Hell and Damnation, and guides his flock less by leading from the front than by prodding from the rear. He was at odds with the doctor over the whole matter of – What do they call it these days? 'Voluntary motherhood'? The Church is against it, but George saw the medical value, and they had many a lively debate. It came down to the reverend making it an Ecclesiastical order, and he found out he couldn't order George Tanner to do one damn thing. Father Danielson threatened to have him excommunicated if he defied the Church. George told him to get on with it – at his age, he was in no fear for his soul."

Holmes wore an expression of the most fascinated absorption. "Do tell us more, Mr. Colville."

"Ted Holliday – the whole matter of his wild oats, of course. Father Danielson actually took him aside for a talking-to. I hear there were references in sermons that could only be about him. But it seemed our amorous grocer was the sort who didn't listen well to anything that went against his personal grain, no matter how loud it was shouted. So, chalk up a failure there to the persuasive powers of the clergy."

I flipped a page and massaged my hand, finishing my cider in a welcome lull.

"Henry Twyville, now, he ran afoul of his preacher on account of that business with the gypsies. It was early last year. We had a whole party of travelling folk here in the late winter and early spring period, and things had been hard. They were scrounging for work, anything to make a few pennies, and Henry saw the priests turn away the travellers when there was plenty they could have done around the church and grounds. Father Danielson denounced them as criminals to a man, who would likely be off with the altar pieces if he let them anywhere near. It was bad form, to say the least, and when tackled about it by concerned folk later, he claimed he was only doing what majority feeling demanded."

Colville rolled his eyes. "Odd, when Catholics are in the minority in this town, and the Anglican Church hadn't a wink of trouble when they found the gypsies work for a couple of weeks. Well, Henry was one of those who took up the matter before the parish council – called the priests penny-pinching misers and was quite strident in his belief that the travelling folk had been wronged."

"And what did Father Danielson have against the professor?"

"Oh, leaving aside the rather public business of those unpaid tradesmen, theirs was the usual old grievance: Faith or science. They sparred a few times, even in public. It was a lively debate and seemed in good nature. But one day, tempers frayed. Father Danielson took to task anyone's ability to embrace both camps, declaring such an outlook flawed at best and hypocritical at worst, and anyone who held it was certainly bound for infernal regions. That was too much for Arthur Fielding. Apparently, using his Royal Society credentials, he wrote to the bishop with a strong complaint against the clergy assigned to Kingston Cray. We never heard any more about it, but the unfortunate encounter with the wrong mushroom was just a few months later."

Holmes steepled his fingers and concentrated for a few moments, almost like a man at prayer. When he looked up, he had a calm smile for the landlord. "We have a small social gathering to organise. If our guests care to attend, may we use the snug for an hour or so tomorrow?"

Colville glanced over at the neat, cosy annex off the end of the bar, traditionally the place where lady patrons gathered to be away from "men's talk".

"By all means."

Holmes rose, and I joined him, glad to be done recording for the moment. "Come along. We have some letters to write."

In Holmes's room upstairs, I glanced across at my friend as his pen raced along lines at a small writing bureau by the window. "Are we making any progress?" I asked. "I seem to have taken an ocean of notes, but besides the general conclusion that the different poisons were very possibly administered deliberately, there doesn't seem much to go on. Certainly, those priests aren't the most popular people, but argumentative, opinionated men *don't* make many friends. It could be that they argued with all four victims because they argued with more or less everyone."

"Well noted, Watson. We will, of course, look farther than the existing body of information. But to answer your question: Yes, we are making progress. The next step is to speak with great delicacy to the families of the victims. Remember, we're looking for patterns of commonality, a thread that links them. I am positive such a thread exists, and when we find it – we tug it and see what unravels."

Notwithstanding a further encounter with Mrs. Carmichael's flashing pedals on the way to the post office, the village postal system was quite efficient, and we had all our replies in the positive over breakfast next day. Mr. Colville's cook laid on a nice morning tea for our guests, who were expected at eleven. A table had been set with a bright cloth, a huge earthenware teapot, and a tray of sandwiches and cake. Constable Dawkins was there to make the introductions, and we found ourselves facing a small gathering of people who had clearly weathered bereavement. Some were still dealing with it in their own ways.

Small, dark-haired Mary Twyville knew first about this meeting, as she had become the village postmistress to see her three children through school. Gladys Tanner was the doctor's elderly widow. Silver-haired and a little hard of hearing, she walked with a stick and was very quiet in her bearing. Tony Holliday was brother to the greengrocer, a sharp-faced young man who worked on nearby Nott's Farm and seemed as unlike his brother, as far as demeanour was concerned, as could be imagined. Professor Fielding had no family locally, but Mrs. Jones, his housekeeper, had agreed to speak for him.

"Thank you all for coming, especially at short notice." Holmes stood with hands behind his back, wearing a most diplomatic smile. "As I outlined in my letters, I have the honour to privately investigate mysterious issues, and have assisted Scotland Yard on a number of occasions. I was asked by one of your fellow villagers to consider the passings of your family members, and at this point, I can say with some certainty that the coronial verdicts might have been rushed, or based on incomplete information."

Mary Twyville stirred her tea and took a cucumber sandwich before looking up with a quiet, guarded expression. "Are you saying you have reason to believe that my Henry was taken from us deliberately?"

"It is too early to say, Madam, but the possibility exists."

Mrs. Tanner crossed herself. "If there is even the ghost of a chance that someone has got away with the most grievous sin of them all, Mr. Holmes, I'm sure we'll do everything we can to help. What do you need to know?"

"Quite simply this: Did any of you see or hear anything out of the ordinary – at that time, or earlier or after. Someone where they shouldn't have been. A visitor. An unexpected gift, a letter – anything."

The four took tea and thought back, chatted among themselves on this and that, and I saw Holmes's eyes darting like a snake from one to another as he seized on each passing comment. They spoke of their difficult days in commendable detail, thinking back with all their might.

"Henry had visited The Tottenham in the afternoon," Mary Twyville said, nodding over the memory. "A quick cider with friends. He told me the professor had shown him some samples he had collected. When he got home, Mrs. Carmichael had come to visit with a batch of baking – dear soul, always so kind. She stayed for some tea and helped me with dinner." She looked at her hands with a faraway expression. "To think, these hands prepared the very fish that took Henry's life. I remember it – the largest, choicest piece. I knew he loved his trout, so I set that one aside, special."

Such memories flowed, and there was little specific for me to record save general impressions of the scene, until Mrs. Twyville spoke of *the figure in the mist.*

"From time to time, I'd see someone out walking at first light," she mused. "I just thought it was Professor Fielding on his rambles, but I've seen whoever it is *since* he passed away."

"Whereabouts?" Holmes asked softly.

"I live by the meadows backing onto Church Wood, and sometimes at sunrise I see the walker up by the tree line. I can't make anything out. The person is always in simple, dark clothes and carries a bag or basket. As I say, I always thought it was our scientific gentleman out studying his butterflies and wildflowers when the first dew was on the world."

Tony Holliday sat forward with a thoughtful look. "Now you mention it . . . I've seen the walker too. Up by the Crowhurst copses, or near the old mill."

Mrs. Jones, who somehow reminded me so strongly of our own dear Mrs. Hudson, nodded over her tea. "I remember the professor saying he had seen an elusive rambler on his dawn excursions. Just now and then. A figure he saw from a distance, but who could always manage to melt into the trees and disappear. He paid it no mind but assumed he had a fellow naturalist in the village. He kept an eye out for the rare orchids in the spring and birds' eggs in season, in case the walker was actually an unscrupulous character collecting them for buyers in the city."

Mrs. Tanner gave an apologetic smile. "I'm afraid I'm of no use on this point, as I don't get out much, and never before ten of a morn."

"Think carefully," Holmes returned, a hand upraised to underline the importance. "*When* did you each see this mysterious walker? Was it before or after the tragic events that befell this village?"

"My Henry was still with us," Mrs. Twyville replied at once. "I remember mentioning 'the man in the mist' to him just a few days before . . . before it happened."

"Thank you, Mrs. Twyville," Holmes added softly. "I know it cannot be easy to speak of matters surrounding your husband's passing, but I assure you it is of the most crucial importance."

Now, Mrs. Jones also nodded over her recollections. "And the professor last commented on having spotted the phantom walker – up towards Westfield Wood, not long before his accident with the mushroom."

"A pattern emerges," Holmes whispered. Then, "Mr. Holliday, can you remember when you encountered this ghost of the dawn hour?" The fellow squinted in thought but shook his head. "No matter. Two out of four is enough to work with. Now, would you all please think carefully once more. Have you a particular person, a friend or acquaintance, whom you all might share?"

The question took them by surprise, and eyebrows were raised. Mrs. Jones answered for them. "In a village this small, Mr. Holmes, everyone more or less knows everyone else. It would be difficult to point to a particular person ahead of any other." She frowned. "If you're implying what I *think* you might be – "

Holmes had no chance to reply, as the door to the bar was thrust back with a rattle of its bell and a draft of sweet summer air, and a sudden shadow fell over the proceedings. Something dark hovered in the corner of my eye, and I looked up to find two clergymen in the black suits and white dog collars of the Catholic Church. One was a bulldog of a man in late middle age with a grizzled beard decorating his jutting jaw. A pugnacious arch of brow sent his stare over us all. His silvering hair was drawn back severely, and big, hard hands matched the wide girth of a man of apparent strengths. At his side hovered a taller, thinner, younger man, clean-shaven, with cropped dark curls and a narrow, reserved expression upon lips that were set in a seemingly disapproving line.

Constable Dawkins rose stiffly and nodded to the newcomers. "Mr. Holmes, Dr. Watson, let me introduce the reverend gentlemen from St. Genevieve's. Father Charles Danielson, and his curate, Father William Stride."

As Holmes turned to him, Father Danielson offered his hand with an air of touching something he would rather not. "Forgive the interruption, but it's a rare event for four members of my parish to be meeting with strangers to the village."

"Merely a casual gathering," Holmes replied evenly.

"Mr. Holmes is here to look into our spate of unfortunate passings," Dawkins added gruffly, and I was unsure, for a moment, if Holmes had wanted the priests to know that at this point.

Danielson raised a straggling brow, fists on his hips, presenting the very image of the protector of his people. "What's that you say? What is there to reexamine?"

Holmes was smoothly evasive. "Perhaps little, perhaps much."

"I doubt you'll find any stone left unturned by the police and coroner's office," Danielson said bluntly. "They were most thorough."

"I'm sure they were. But I shall satisfy my own curiosity all the same. A professional interest."

"Every man has a right to his trade, but I would ask you not to reopen old wounds. I saw the grief in my parishioners, Mr. Holmes, and I wouldn't have them face such upset again if it can be helped."

"I shall step with the greatest care, Father Danielson. I assure you of that."

"Be all this as it may be," Constable Dawkins added. "Mr. Holmes has been invited to this village to address the concerns some people feel over these passings. And I, for one, am very happy to have him here. Look at it this way, Father: If there's nothing to worry about, Mr. Holmes will surely reach that conclusion. But if there is . . . He'll get to the bottom of it."

135

Father William was about to remonstrate, but his elder shushed him with a gesture. Danielson smiled indulgently. "Well, I'm sure matters will work themselves out. But I already rest entirely assured – in God, if nothing else – that affairs reached the ends intended by the highest judge of all, and that is a *final* judgement."

The air was rather brittle, and I cleared my throat softly to remind the gentlemen that we had the company of the gentler sex.

"Perhaps we could resume this in a more appropriate venue," Holmes asked calmly, his eyes never leaving Danielson's.

"You're welcome at the rectory," Danielson fired back. "I would entertain any debate you may care to bring."

"This afternoon, perhaps," Holmes replied, and the tensions faded as the priests nodded to the ladies and absented themselves in a flurry of black cloth.

The late summer sun was warm on our necks as we walked up the few hundred yards towards Church Wood. Insects rose at our approach from the dry grass, and it seemed the countryside drowsed in its rest before the return of harsher weather.

We looked back at the village, its buildings strung out along Maidstone Road like gems upon a thread, and I could easily imagine an early riser glancing from a window and seeing a figure, indistinct with distance, against the dark background of the wood.

"Our working hypothesis is that the mysterious rambler might be our man," Holmes mused as we neared the rise of oak and beech. "At the very least, this person knows the area intimately, and we are assuming some specific knowledge of mycology. It takes an expert to tell one type from another – and to prepare out a toxin without incurring a dangerous exposure in turn."

"Those credentials should be on record," I replied, leaning on my stick for a moment. "We're postulating a university-level education. I imagine few in this village have ever even seen the inside of an institution of higher learning."

"Of course," Holmes added as he pressed on, "it could be just the opposite. Old country knowledge, passed down for generations. That calls for no credentials but the school of life itself, and is recorded by none."

We entered the welcome shade of the green wood, with its merry birdsong, and passed a pleasant hour inspecting the moist leaf litter around great trunks or studying what grew upon dead bark and fallen branches. We easily found many species that would become prolific as the autumn progressed – some dangerous, most not. Holmes had brought along a textbook, Ackerman's 1879 work *Fungi of the British Woodlands*, through which we paged as new specimens came to light, and soon he was quite satisfied that we had our method of murder.

"An adept in toxins would have a natural pharmacy right here. It isn't always appreciated by modern medicine – to which knowledge of herbs and such is tantamount to witchcraft – but in these woods is a veritable cornucopia of medicaments. Willow bark for headaches and inflammation, digitalis from foxglove to calm an arrhythmic heart. Half the mushrooms in these glades have therapeutic value. But along with the beneficial sorts are those that are decidedly not. There are kinds that bring on hallucinations, for instance. And those that simply kill, unsubtly and awfully."

We sat down in a patch of dappled sun to look out through the trunks across the meadows and indulged in a pipe.

"What do we really have?" I asked. "It would take an expert in poisons derived from nature to use this method, but we have no candidate who displays any adequate reason, or can be demonstrated to have known all four victims."

Holmes blew a smoke ring before responding. "Let us be absolutely dispassionate, Watson. Remember, murder isn't the act of a sane mind, and to go about it in the way we are postulating places it firmly in the realm of cold and calculating premeditation. It is absolutely deliberate, and always carried through effectively. So perhaps we should be asking ourselves: Who benefitted from the demise of those four individuals?"

I blinked for a moment. "You mean motive?"

"Precisely. Whom did they offend? There seems no suggestion of any connection between the victims – a cobbler, a grocer, a doctor, and a retired academician – to make them, as a group, special. They must have been *individually* special to their killer." Holmes puffed distractedly as he thought. "The womaniser *might* have attracted the wrath of some cuckolded party, but the black eyes he had already enjoyed would seem to have effectively replied to that matter. What offence a cobbler could have committed beyond an inadvertent overcharging, I cannot imagine. The doctor? A badly misjudged diagnosis resulting in someone's suffering or death would be a motive for the ultimate sanction. But a complaint to the General Medical Board is the far more likely action of any ordinary person, no matter how aggrieved they may be. And what might a retired scientist have done to provoke his own slaying?" He shrugged his bony shoulders.

"Assuming there's a reason at all," I commented softly.

Holmes shot me a glance and took his pipe from between his teeth. "There must be a reason. Behaviour at odds with the norms of a society *must* be driven by some overriding purpose, obscure as it may be.

Otherwise, we would live in a world where nothing made sense and nothing could ever be relied upon."

"I hate to come back to the obvious," I murmured.

"Please, be obvious," Holmes invited.

"The church is the only discernible connection. The fact that they were members of the same parish. That's it."

Holmes frowned. "I wonder precisely how large Father Danielson's congregation is."

"It can't be much. The Anglicans are the larger group, and the entire population of the village and its outlying farms can't be more than a few hundred."

Holmes *harumphed* in his frustration. "Those priests are unpleasant, but I can spare precious little credence for them deliberately reducing their own congregation. In and of itself, it makes no sense." He squinted into the dappled light. "Unless they have some other secret, something they perhaps brought with them to this parish. A secret a few of their parishioners might stumble upon, and which they are willing to kill to keep quiet." A shiver went up my spine at his tone. "The first death wasn't long *after* their arrival. That much is a matter of record."

We rose and dusted leaves from our trousers. "This has more than usually sordid overtones," I murmured. "One tends to think of clergy as being, well, *better* than such things."

"None is above crime, Watson," Holmes whispered, tapping out his pipe. "Time we bearded the dragon in his den."

The Church of St. Genevieve was a fairly recent construction, a late eighteenth-century rebuilding of a ruin from centuries past. Nevertheless, its square, Saxon design melded with the green oaks and seemed an eternal part of the landscape, while the graveyard in its care was lined with the modest stones of a bare century of the faithful. Beyond its moss-grown bounding walls, the rectory was a comfortable two-storey cottage nestled among the eternal forest, where songbirds and the rustling breeze complemented a scene as peaceful as could be imagined.

We walked up the gravel path, and the lacquered timber door opened before us. Father William stood framed in its arch for long moments. He stared with some unspoken accusation, as if we were the embodiment of presumptuousness – that to question the priest was to question God, and we thus, to him, defined ourselves as wrongdoers from the start.

But he stepped back and showed us in, and we found ourselves in the wood-panelled study of Father Danielson. Against a floor-to-ceiling bookcase of ancient volumes, the formidable priest sat behind his desk, paperwork spread before him, and he concentrated on a document without looking up, writing, reading back, at last signing. After a pointedly rude interlude, his gaze came up to us. "Now, gentlemen, we had something of a disagreement earlier. You must forgive my protectiveness towards my flock. If we got off on the wrong foot, I apologise." He gestured at the plain, hard wooden chairs before his desk. "What is it you wish to discuss?"

I took out my notebook and pencil as we sat, and Holmes launched into his inquiry with the greatest tact I had ever seen. He was like a surgeon working around a particularly difficult excision, taking every pain not to disturb the tissues until he fully understood their disposition.

"As I explained, Father Danielson, I have been asked to bring my skills of detection to bear upon the series of unfortunate passings since 1882, in the hopes that I might spot some connection missed by those who have previously considered the matters. I have spoken to Constable Dawkins, who kindly loaned me the official files, and I have interviewed the next of kin, as you saw this morning. In each case, death was attributed to natural causes, but I find nothing in the events to prevent those causes having been deliberately induced."

"Murder?" Danielson's brows rose, and his defensiveness flared. "Have a care, Mr. Holmes. This community is a family, of which I have the honour to be head, and I would take grave exception to any of its members being accused of the ultimate sin against his brothers."

"I didn't say I suspected a Catholic," Holmes replied quietly. A silence followed, in which the priest seemed to fight for meaning, and Holmes went on, "Given the antipathy towards Catholics and their history of persecution, it would at first seem more logical to look to the Anglican community for a likely suspect."

Now Danielson regained his composure. "And have you found anything yet?"

"No. The only factor uniting the victims is their membership in this church, so that relationship is the only ground, fertile or otherwise, to be examined."

The priest steepled his fingers and shook his wild head slowly. "But there have been only good relations between the faiths in long and long. Oh, across the water, they fight like cat and dog, but that's *there*, not here. Never here."

"I understand that the four men who passed away weren't what you would call staunch churchgoers. Their relationship with their faith was a less-demanding one than for many."

Danielson made a noise in his throat, and Father William poured a glass of water from a silver jug on the side table. A few sips seemed to cover the time he needed to think about a reply. "It's true that their commitment to the faith wasn't the profound thing it should be and *is* for most. Henry Twyville was a recent convert – he and his family had been made welcome here a bare six months before his untimely end. Yet, once he was in the Church, it didn't seem to inspire him quite as it did before he joined. Church seemed a duty rather than a joy. Young Mr. Holiday, well . . . I think he was a Catholic for no other reason than that he was born one. I think he found the tenets of his religion more hindrance than boon. Had he not passed away when he did, I had half-made up my mind to ask him if he wouldn't be happier trying the *other* crowd."

"Excommunication?"

"No, no, nothing so formal, nothing so harsh. But he was a bad example. He made people uncomfortable, and my best efforts to reclaim his soul were like wind in the trees compared to the voice of his baser needs."

"What of the others?"

"Professor Fielding. Now, there was a hard man to understand. A churchgoer from birth, but when *Darwinism –*" He almost spat the word. "– triumphed in the public consciousness, he opened his arms to it. Maybe I'm an old man and set in my ways, but nothing about it makes sense to me, even now. I almost envied his ability to balance the two sides of life – to see God's hand in the universe as revealed by science and yet somehow set aside its contradiction of the Bible, which is something that is otherwise held beyond question. Be that as it may, we never shared a common viewpoint. I always felt that he judged me for my faith, and that he felt my sermons never applied to him. Perhaps I do him a disservice, but there it is. His learning placed him upon a different level, and it wasn't a comfortable way to be. For either of us."

"The doctor?"

"Old George Tanner was as fine a man as you could hope to meet. He had a compassion and humanity that frankly dwarfed my own. He learned his medicine in the bad old days, and squared his conscience with cutting people limb from limb while they were wide awake and suffering to rectify their problems. I don't know if I have ever had such fortitude, no matter what depth of prayer and meditation I might reach. I respected him very much."

I noted all this in quick-fire strokes of my pencil and sensed that Holmes was at a cusp in his questioning.

"Forgive me the indelicacy of the next point, Father Danielson, but I have been told by others that each of the four had had quite public disagreements with you. Tempers had flared. Things were said. Letters were written to bishops."

Father William stirred in discomfort, where he stood to one side like a black pillar. "Whatever are you suggesting, Mr. Holmes? Father Danielson is the lynchpin of this community. A parish priest must be all things to his people – a father, a leader, a protector, a guide, a confidant. To let down his community in any way is a black mark against his very soul, and I assure you, that trumps any wrongdoing before merely mortal law."

The young man's attitude was almost surly in its self-absorption, the certainty of his belief that his position was unassailable. Holmes took the statement in his stride and, I was positive, read the curate's character in an instant. "I state my observations, sir, and request information pertaining thereto. Am I to assume that police officers didn't ask this question previously?"

"They most certainly did not," Father William replied.

"Then their investigation leaves something to be desired." Holmes's eyes swivelled back to the senior priest. "I'm waiting, sir."

Father Danielson cleared his throat and raised a hand to his assistant. "It's a fair question, Father William. Half the village was witness to our moments of disagreement, so it's hardly a secret." He took a sip from the glass. "Yes, we had our outs. With Henry Twyville, it was over those blasted gypsies. I didn't care to have them around. Maybe it was my failure of Christian charity to send them packing, and at the time I was sure the fact they were accommodated by our Anglican fellows had more to do with them thumbing their noses at *us* than any greater tolerance for the travelling folk. It got a bit out of hand. We had a real barney before the parish council, over at the hall." He spread his hands with a wide shrug. "I regret it, but what's done is done, and there's no taking it back."

"And the professor?"

"Again, much regretted. What can I say? He challenged my faith, and the *way* of faith, and I rose to its defence. Things got heated, but who am I if not a spokesman for God upon Earth? I have taken my vows, Mr. Holmes, and I will defend my position to my last breath. I believe in Heaven and Hell, and in both salvation and damnation. The moral course we chart through life between these extremes is very much the business of priests. I said that when the day came when I told him how to categorise his butterflies, he might *then* inform me of the eternal verities." He sighed. "Unfortunately, our exchange was in a public house, and therefore a source of entertainment to all and sundry. It was hardly the Huxley Debates, but there were those with pints in their fists who scored our discussion like tennis and seemed to take a delight in favouring the *rationalist* position." He spat the word, and I could see the matter rankled badly. Tough fingers drummed at his blotter in a moment's distraction.

141

"There were other issues, too, though." Holmes looked sidelong at Father William. "A set-to with regard to Arthur Fielding's consumption of alcohol, another very public dispute. And also in a public house." No comment was forthcoming, and he ploughed on. "And the matter of the unpaid tradesmen. I understand he was most vocal and public in his criticism of the Church on that score."

"Making the parish's books balance is no easy task," Father Danielson growled. "Yes, the roofing people had to wait for their money. They aren't the only ones." A shutter seemed to slam up, and he would say no more on the point.

"Mr. Holliday," Holmes prompted. "In what way was your cautioning of him public?"

"He was a predator, Mr. Holmes. And when it came to him staring indelicately at the ladies in church, I took it upon myself to correct him. I didn't taint the sanctity of the Church itself, but had it out with him on the village green, and I didn't care who witnessed it. The more, the better, I felt, for it was his shaming I was after. Yes, it was public, and I took a few verbal cuffs myself in the process." He paused, then forced out the next words in a stiff way. "He had some very hurtful things to say about the nature of celibate priests and the things we might get up to due to the unnaturalness of our occupation's demands. He implied that his lechery was wholesome by comparison, and that was when – God forgive me – I struck him." The older priest sat back and shook his head. "Letters to bishops? I can assure you, I've had a few back."

After a long pause, Holmes moved on from the point. "That leaves only Dr. Tanner. I understand the root of your disagreement concerned 'voluntary motherhood'."

"It did. The Catholic Church forbids it. We view the gift of new life as coming direct from God, in His good time, and at His divine discretion. Children are a blessing, Mr. Holmes, and interfering with that process so as to enjoy the carnal pleasures yet avoid the duties of family consequent upon them, we view as very much a sin. How George Tanner could feel differently, I didn't understand, and I charged him with the duty of his faith. He rejected that duty. Technically, that was grounds for excommunication, and in some parts of the world he *would* have been. We argued at his home surgery, and voices were raised. We were overheard from the waiting room, and the matter went round the village like hay fever. It's been no simple matter standing up of a Sunday morning and talking to my congregation when every last one of them knows my feet of clay." He breathed a long sigh. "That's it. My soul is bare. What penance do you assign, Mr. Holmes?"

"I shall think upon these matters, Father Danielson," was all he would say, and a moment later a soft knock heralded the housekeeper.

Mrs. Carmichael, we had as yet encountered only from afar. She was a small, mousy woman of middle years, in rather old-fashioned attire, the very image of propriety. She announced afternoon tea and propelled in a serving trolley. As she poured, the priests excused themselves – stepping out, I was sure, for a private consultation as to where they stood on all this.

"You mustn't judge the fathers too harshly," Mrs. Carmichael murmured as she presented us with best china and a sweet brew. "They have a difficult job, being the leaders of a minority faith in a land where the Church itself was denied so roundly."

"What's that?" I asked as I accepted my cup.

"Oh, yes, there was a time when to be a Catholic was to be shunned. Why, in the census of 1676, not a single soul would admit to the faith in this area, so afraid were they of persecution. If Father Danielson seems harsh in his ways, he is defending us from such harm ever returning." The little woman seemed absorbed by her faith, her hands clasped before a large cross at her breast. "He is a soldier of God who marches between us and any harm the mortal world might do. And I'm not shy about saying I have the greatest respect for him."

She bowed herself out, and Holmes and I had a moment's privacy. Before I could speak, Holmes's eyes lit upon something, and he crossed to the bookcase, silently tapping a spine. Among a row of textbooks on matters that seemed quite tangential to the religious position, I recognised Ackerman, 1879. We shared a glance filled with meaning before the priests returned.

"I see you've met our housekeeper," Father Danielson said with a pleasantness I was sure was in defiance of the confessions he had made. "I don't know where we'd be without her. She takes care of the day-to-day matters, leaving us free to focus upon the spiritual."

"The very backbone of the parish?" I asked with a forced smile.

"More than you might guess," Father William replied, taking a cup. "She was housekeeper to clergy in the next parish over – Farningham – for many years, but moved to Kingsford Cray to work. She came to us in the July of '81, arranged by the Bishop when we took over from old Father Mulgrave. He went in-harness, and his curate became a missionary. She is the very soul of Christian charity – I've never known a harder worker. Besides keeping house for us, she is very active on the parish committee, takes part in the village ladies' society, runs every errand under the sun, even cooks for the underprivileged. She says her energy comes from God, and I, for one, can believe it."

"You were very lucky to receive her services," Holmes observed. "Organised by the Bishop, you say?"

"Indeed." Father Danielson set down his cup, and opened a desk drawer, sorted papers, and drew out a letter. "This was his recommendation." He read: "'*I have known Mrs. Carmichael since 1868 as a devout and active woman. She did missionary service in the 1850's, with experience in India, and I had the honour of performing her marriage to the late Benjamin Carmichael. I commend her to you with a full heart, sure that she will bring her own energy to every task and confident of her boundless ability to carry out the good works of the faith in whatever way might be required.*'" He laid aside the letter. "No man could ask for better."

I was taking this down as fast as my hand would move, as some sixth sense told me there were priceless nuggets among the flotsam, so I was somewhat nonplussed when Holmes finished his tea and rose to go. I followed suit, finishing mine in a hurry, before handshakes were offered all around. "Thank you for your time, gentlemen," Holmes said simply. "I'm sure our paths will cross once more."

At that moment, I believe he was still gathering information, but when I saw him pause with a sudden flinch of his bony shoulders as we passed through the hall towards the front door, I knew some connection, some profound association, had made itself apparent to him. When we stepped out into the afternoon sun, I hurried to keep up as he led us briskly back towards Maidstone Road. All he would say was that he had a suspicion, which must be explored before he could make progress, and left me sitting in the sun on the green as he hurried on to Constable Dawkins's house.

During the evening, Holmes sat by the hearth in The Tottenham, smoked his pipe, and nursed a whisky-and-soda. He stared into the flames, quite withdrawn, such that he was poor company. I put my nose in a yellowback I had picked up at the station before leaving London, sure he would confide in me when the time came. We retired around ten, an hour after the last gold-and-mauve flushes of twilight had left us, and I contented myself to know our efforts here were a game still in play.

However, when we descended for breakfast next morning, Holmes had mail – a telegram, which he opened and read at once – and I saw a certain brittleness in his features as connections fell into place. When he folded the slip into his inside pocket and smiled thinly, I knew we were entering the final quarter of this particular match.

"And now," he murmured as I poured us coffee, "we bait our trap."

I was taken somewhat aback by his technique, for his rhetoric, in public hearing, took on a barbed character directed at the Catholic Church, and the Church of St. Genevieve in particular. I knew Holmes wasn't a religious man and had no specific prejudice – for him, *all* religion fell short of his worship of logic and rationality. Thus, his comments I took to be deliberate in the extreme, and while they weren't expressly distasteful to the Anglican majority, I observed a growing discomfort among other patrons of the inn. I was more than a little uncomfortable myself, and glad when Holmes excused himself to spread his ill-feeling further afield – the shops along Maidstone Road, in the post office, and another public house.

I understood that he was recreating the situation we believed to have existed between the Church of St. Genevieve and the previous four victims, and I trusted him to play with fire, but I could only stand back and take no part. Nor did he ask me to contribute to his amassing of ill will.

All during the day, he made such remarks, finding himself in debate with villagers here and there – a philosophical discussion on the village green, for instance, in which a number of elderly residents applauded his denigration of Catholics in a truly distasteful exhibition of prejudice that might otherwise never have emerged from behind closed doors.

By evening, when we took our meal at The Tottenham, the village was quite abuzz with it all, and the landlord had taken on a distinctly cool attitude towards us. Before we retired, Holmes assured me quietly that he knew what he was doing – he wasn't a man who hated in the plural, to use the polite term, and that I should put my faith in the trust I had developed for his methods and instincts these years past.

Next morning, Holmes had mail – a hurt letter from Mary Twyville, lamenting that one who had come seemingly with an open heart should turn on her community so vilely. Holmes squared his shoulders and nodded with thinned lips. "All shall be revealed," he whispered, pocketing the missive. The next envelope was hand-addressed from St. Genevieve's. "Ah. And the bait is swiftly taken." He opened it, and his eyes raced along the lines. "We are invited to afternoon tea at the rectory to '*further discuss the matters so challenging the harmony of this village.*'" He nodded with stern satisfaction. "I assure you, the exercise has afforded me no pleasure, Watson. I have never sought to add to the burden of my fellow human being. But it was necessary to provoke the right response."

"Which is?"

He patted his pocket. "Why, we are once more to enter the rectory. But this time, with very different intentions. On *someone's* part."

We had been invited to visit at three o'clock and were punctual. What our hosts didn't know was that Constable Dawkins was following at a distance and would be waiting, silent and unnoticed, outside the front door, within reach of an urgent shout. Holmes was very certain his assistance would be required, and I went into this interview with a tight feeling in the pit of my stomach.

Mrs. Carmichael opened the door to us and relieved us of our hats in the hall. She seemed decidedly cool today. A tightness of her mouth betrayed all the things unsaid. I had to admit, Holmes had done a wonderful job of assassinating his own character, and regretted that my own had obviously suffered by association.

Father Danielson received us with a stern face, his curate likewise, and we found the parlour prepared with a coffee table set for pleasant refreshments. We were ushered into seats to one side while the clergymen took the other, the table forming some neutral space between opposing factions. For a long moment, the older priest held his silence, then gestured with an open hand. "Why, Mr. Holmes? When we spoke before, I sensed no antipathy in you towards the faith in general or ourselves in particular, beyond the natural distancing of the investigator's profession. But yesterday, you spent many hours in a verbal assault upon this community, its tenets, its leadership . . . I must ask you, *why?*"

Holmes was icily reserved. "Father Danielson, in London, those who know me will tell you that I never do anything without reason. As you correctly observed, my manner underwent a shift yesterday. You may infer that I was exposed to information that changed my outlook."

"What revelation could so swiftly and totally poison a reasonable man against an entire community?"

"What indeed? Is such a thing even possible?"

"Mr. Holmes, you confuse me. You evidently spoke ill yesterday. I asked you here in the hopes there would be discussion. Have you come here to defend your position, to explain it in some way – or merely to deny it?"

"None of these. As I say, I came into possession of information that set me upon a train of reasoning. I was able to further support that reasoning with a simple inquiry. As for my disparagement of this particular church, I assure you, it served its purpose. We are here, after all."

The priests shared a glance filled with perplexity. "Mr. Holmes, you have always been welcome here, so long as you come to speak constructively and in amity."

At a soft knock, the parlour door opened, and Mrs. Carmichael brought in the tea trolley. All comment was withheld as she prepared the beverage. She poured the tea with great care, added sugar as requested, and when a fine porcelain cup and saucer had been presented to each of us, she gave a small bow to the priests and turned to go.

"Do stay, Mrs. Carmichael," Holmes said at once. "I'm sure you'll find these proceedings of great interest. No, no, I insist."

With that, his eyes travelled among our group, and he raised the cup to his lips – but paused before drinking.

For a long moment, I saw from the corner of my eye the intensity of his concentration, and in the social awkwardness, I began to sip to occupy the moment. But Holmes's right hand shot out to my left wrist, arresting the motion of cup and saucer. The priests had also not yet drunk, and the very air seemed charged with tension.

"A sign of good faith," Holmes said evenly, his eyes cold and unreadable. "Exchange cups with me, Father Danielson. And Father William with Dr. Watson." He smiled thinly. "We are dealing with four unexplained deaths, each from apparently natural causes, yet all of which can be accounted for with reference to toxic substances. And St. Genevieve's is central to the affair. As I say, a sign of good faith."

The older priest's eyes narrowed, and for a difficult moment I thought he would explode with outrage. I was poised for him to hurl the china and exert his obvious strength, but he simply extended his cup and saucer and took Holmes's instead. "As you say, good faith. Faith is what this is all about, and if there is a gesture to be made, then let me be the one to make it." He raised the cup in salute. "To your good health, Mr. Holmes."

Silence – an electric feeling in the air – all cups were raised towards lips.

"No!" was the banshee wail, and the cup was struck from Father Danielson's hand. Tea splashed the tablecloth. China broke with a sharp crackle, and I came involuntarily to my feet. Mrs. Carmichael stood by the end of the table, her eyes wide and wild, hands white-knuckled with fear, knotted into fists as she fought for breath. As a doctor, my first thought was that she was on the verge of some seizure, such was the extremity of her emotional turmoil.

But eventually, all things fall into place of their own accord. Father Danielson looked from his empty hands to his housekeeper, and an expression of the most profound anguish filled his features. "Oh, dear God, no!" he wailed. "Not under my very own roof. Please – *No!*"

In another moment, the small, unobtrusive woman gave a convulsive gasp and turned to flee, and Holmes went after her, shouting for the constable. Dawkins came in with a wash of sunlight along the hall, and the housekeeper tugged over an ornamental planter to spill soil and a potted palm that impeded Holmes for the crucial seconds she needed to reach her kitchen. The stout old door slammed, and we heard a key turn in the lock.

"Around the back!" Holmes cried, and they exited the front door, tearing around by the parlour windows. I followed in their wake and found them trying their strength against the rear kitchen door, also apparently locked.

I stepped up on the edge of a garden bed to put my eye to the kitchen window, peered through the mesh curtains, and was greeted by a terrible sight. "We may be too late," I said tightly.

Holmes put his elbow through the stained glass of a lozenge-shaped window in the door, broke out the razor-pointed fragments, then reached through with care, found the bolt and worked it free. In moments we were in, and I went to the woman at once. She was hunched over the stone sink, unmoving, and a shocking redness made her solution obvious. I could have bound the slashed wrists and confidently expected her to pull through, but a slashed throat was beyond anyone's ministration. The sink was painted with flowing blood, a carving knife abandoned among it all, and Constable Dawkins could only cross himself, then turn to block the door as the priests tried to enter.

Young Doctor Bailey, who looked after the village now, pronounced death within the hour, and a wagon came up from Sevenoaks to take Mrs. Carmichael's body into care. She would be held during the inquest, and the future of the parish was in this moment uncertain. Both priests were very much in a state of shock, and Doctor Bailey administered a sedative so that they might sleep the clock round.

The village as a whole mourned without knowing all the details, and Holmes asked for a public meeting at the church hall the next day, where he promised all would be revealed and he would beg their understanding for his boorish and offensive behaviour.

Constable Dawkins, Mary Twyville, Millie Hazel, Mr. Colville, and so many others gathered in the hall, and Holmes took his oration with all gravity. One Inspector Melville had come up from Sevenoaks to take charge of the case, and Holmes laid out the general strokes for the benefit of the people of Kingston Cray. He explained his actions and apologised profoundly to the community, saying only that the killer of the four villagers had been revealed, none should now go in fear, and a normal village life should be possible hereafter.

But there was much more to say, and afterward, he and I walked up to the rectory with Constable Dawkins and Inspector Melville. There we met with Fathers Danielson and Stride, who had slept deeply and spent the morning in prayer. They were heavy-eyed, and sat in their dressing gowns in the parlour when we arrived. Mrs. Jones had looked in to get them breakfast, for they were hardly able to look after themselves. Nevertheless, they made us welcome, and Inspector Melville, a tow-haired chap with a face sunburnt from too much enjoyment of the season, took out his notebook. He preferred to stand, along with the constable, but I took a seat, knowing Holmes often paced as he made his summations.

"Would you guide us through all this, Mr. Holmes?" the inspector began, and I licked my pencil in preparation to keep pace.

"My pleasure." Holmes put his hands behind his back and composed himself. "The four deaths were each due to natural – biological – causes, but each could be forced if one chose. Food poisoning, an acute reaction, a mistaken mushroom, heart failure. It took someone with specific knowledge to do these things, but also someone who could move unnoticed throughout the community – hiding in plain sight, if you like. When I began this investigation, I asked if people remembered anyone where they should *not* be. An element out of place. But the correct question would have been, who was *always* there? Who could pass unnoticed among this community, taint a fish, leave a dangerous substance, introduce a poisonous mushroom to a basket of edible ones, administer a drug . . . ."

The priests sat with stony faces, still almost uncomprehending of the magnitude of what had happened. They had my sympathy, not simply for the shock they had been dealt, but for the challenge to their faith posed by such an event unfolding in what should have been sacrosanct precincts.

"At first, there seemed no solution, and I could see why the initial investigations had reached a verdict of misadventure in two cases and natural causes in the others. But then the families of the deceased remembered 'the walker in the mists', and that suggested a gatherer of medicaments from nature – in this case, the harmful rather than the beneficial. A casual reconnaissance of the nearby woodlands revealed a mixture of hallucinogens and poisons, should one have the skill to extract and prepare them. Mrs. Carmichael was a missionary in India in her younger days, and a telegram to her superiors quickly revealed that her specialty was the preparation of medicines from their natural form. Thus, she had the requisite skills.

"The whole matter was focused upon the Catholic community, so Catholicism was involved. Religion is a strong motivating factor, and all four deceased had drawn the ire of their clergy. Ironically, it was nothing so dire as to provoke these gentlemen to overstep the bounds of their vows, with the possible exception of Mr. Holliday's comments upon the Green, which earned him a frankly well-deserved rebuff. But they were sufficient to incense and provoke another. Still, the pieces didn't match up – until, as we were leaving some days ago, I noticed a framed certificate in the hall. It is a recognition of Mrs. Carmichael's years of valuable service – as Dr. Tanner's secretary. That was the job she came here to take. As it was

Dr. Tanner who treated Tom Holliday's chronic reaction years ago, his fatal weakness was there in the medical files to be found."

"Circumstantial," Inspector Melville murmured.

"I would not have gone into court with it," Holmes agreed with a nod. "Also circumstantial is the fact there were two deaths under mysterious circumstances in the Farningham Parish while Mrs. Carmichael kept house for the clergy there in the 1870's. These pieces weren't going to fit together any better: Mrs. Carmichael had the run of the community, was known to all, cooked for many, was never out of place, and always on the move.

"I have had the opportunity to speak to others in the last twenty-four hours, and she was well-known for walking in the countryside, gathering wild flowers for the altar, and many another of nature's provisions. Her kitchen is well stocked with dried, prepared herbs from the forest. Were she not devoutly religious, I would have called it a witch's apothecary. Foxglove is in ample supply – its container is out of place with the rest, as if it were the last used.

"I submit that this was to be her method of disposing of me, paying me out for my offence to the community. I would remind Dr. Watson and the good fathers that the milk was already in the cups when Mrs. Carmichael brought in the tea trolley. She made up each cup and presented it to us individually. The milk disguised the fact that one cup already contained a quantity of foxglove, sufficient to bring on cardiac symptoms within two hours of ingestion. My impression is that she expected Father Danielson to respond to my disparagement with a thundering sermon, and my subsequent illness could be put down to the effects of force of personality – thin at best, I grant you. The dried herb doesn't have the bad, pungent odour of the fresh plant, but it isn't without scent altogether, and I was able to detect its taint over the fragrance of the tea."

"One cup?" I asked, pencil upraised. "Holmes, you stopped me from drinking too."

"Dramatic effect. It made no sense for both cups to be doctored. At that moment, Mrs. Carmichael was still trying to pass it off as natural causes, her usual way of working. *Two* men falling dead with heart failure more or less simultaneously in the same place would surely be enough to alert even the most overworked coroner to the likelihood of foul play."

Father Danielson stirred in his seat and posed a point. "This was all assumption, until you smelt the herb. What if you had been wrong? What if she hadn't reacted?"

"If I had been wrong? We would have swapped cups, drunk in trust, exchanged some conciliatory dialogue, and my investigation would have been confounded. But I *invited* the attempt on my life, Father Danielson.

Just as I was certain Mrs. Carmichael wouldn't allow harm to come to you, even at cost of her own life. If the cup were poisoned, she *had* to move."

"Taking her own life," Inspector Melville murmured. "I know there have been Acts of Parliament on the subject, but within the Church, suicide remains a grave sin. Is this the act of one so very devout?"

Father William nodded at this point, though he could find no words, and his senior gave voice to their feelings. "It really is a matter that cannot be set aside. None who believed so fiercely would do such a thing willingly."

"Yet she did. And correct me if I am wrong, but suicide isn't an *unforgivable* sin. It is a contentious philosophic issue, but there remains latitude for believing that one may indeed be forgiven at the court of final judgement, should one's reasons be pure enough. And was she not already imbued with certain *latitude?* She was assigned here by a bishop whose recommendation runs – " Here, he took out a transcript from my notes and read: "'*I commend her to you with a full heart, sure that she will bring her own energy to every task and confident of her boundless ability to carry out the good works of the faith in whatever way may be required.*' I submit that she did so with full vigour, making certain excisions that were necessary to restore to the church the measure of respect she believed it was due.

"Moreover, I suspect that your bishop knew full well the mission he was entrusting to Mrs. Carmichael. She spoke of soldiers of God in the abstract, but seems to have believed any could fit that description."

"This is monstrous!" Father Danielson exclaimed, thumping the arm of his chair with a balled fist. "None of this can possibly be true!"

"Come now, Father. Mrs. Carmichael's suicide constitutes a confession!"

A difficult silence followed. Then Inspector Melville cleared his throat. "There's a lot of assumption here. Can you tie her movements to the four individual deaths?"

"Not with certainty, after so long. We have established that she personally knew and was frequently in the company of the whole congregation. That she had been employed by Dr. Tanner would enable her to drop by for a visit and surreptitiously administer the foxglove that triggered his heart failure. Similarly, she could locate Destroying Angel in the woods, prepare it, visit Professor Fielding when she knew he had been out collecting mushrooms, and introduce just a single piece. Nature would take its course from there. Neither Dr. Tanner's widow nor Professor Fielding's housekeeper recall a visit immediately prior to the events, which introduces the element of circumstantiality.

"Mr. Holliday? She knew the nature of his fatal sensitivity from his files and could have identified the correct toxin by trial and error. All she needed to do was surreptitiously leave a fine dusting of some powdered mushroom or herb around the shop where he would come into contact with it, and his susceptibility meant only he would be affected. However, she, like so many others, was in the shop frequently, so tying her presence to the event explicitly isn't possible.

"That leaves only Mr. Twyville. Mrs. Twyville has confirmed that Mrs. Carmichael visited their home that afternoon. The piece of fish to be served to Mr. Twyville was distinct from the others, so mere slight-of-hand would be required to introduce a biological poison to that one piece." Holmes sighed through flared nostrils. "None of this is as precise as I usually prefer to be, but at such a removal from the events, time tends to erode the resolution with which we view those events."

Inspector Melville made a few last notes and closed his book with a regretful expression. "Obviously, we'll reopen inquiry into the two deaths in Farningham in light of all this. But the scandalous nature of what's been going on guarantees the case will be held *in camera*. There's no call to have the papers blowing up the sensational aspects and bringing the Church into disrepute. There'd be no justice in the Catholic community being victimised by others, as would, of course, happen. People would be assaulted, shopkeepers would be burnt out – it would be an utter mess, and for what? The actions of one insane zealot."

We shared a glance filled with meaning, and I closed my own notebook. We were done here, and after suitable farewells, including a visit to Millie Hazel, who had first set us upon this course, we were on our way that afternoon northward to Longfield to catch the westbound train back to London. But all the way home to Baker Street, I felt that Holmes had uncovered some particularly unpalatable truths this time, and the odds of an account of these matters being deemed suitable for publication were correspondingly slight.

Nevertheless, my notes stand in testimony of one of Holmes's more obscure cases, and I hope they are read and appreciated one day, if for no other reason than that I saw him thwart death itself on no more than the acuteness of his sense of smell.

The Devil's Snare
by Paula Hammond

Holmes was lounging in his armchair, busily packing his before-breakfast pipe with all the dottles left from the previous day's smokes. I had just rung for breakfast and was contemplating my own pipe of Ship's when Mrs. Hudson materialized at the door.

Our landlady was an eminently practical woman who had come to accept her home being invaded by all manner of strange characters with almost saint-like serenity. That morning, however, she looked so sorely tested that both myself and Holmes immediately leapt to our feet. "Why," I asked, "whatever is it?"

"You'd best come see for yourselves," she answered, "and, Doctor, bring your bag, I'm afraid you may have need of it."

Although it was still early, that morning was one of those bright days when summer hadn't yet given way to autumn. The hallway was illuminated by a shaft of sunlight streaming through the fanlight, and it was this which made the figure lying on the floor look as though he was carved in marble.

On closer examination, the prone youth was revealed to be dressed entirely in white. A mane of black hair framed his face, which looked curiously flushed. His body was rigid, his hands tightly clenched, and while he was fair-faced, he had a pinched and terrible expression, which was made all the more horrifying for way his eyes stared, unblinking, at the ceiling.

His pulse was fast and irregular, his pupils dilated, and it was these final details which gave me my diagnosis: *Epilepsy*. Fortunately, I was familiar with Trousseau's work and, while medicine is still woefully uninformed as to the causes of the *grand mal*, I was relieved that I could at least treat its symptoms.

I loosened the poor fellow's tie, removed his collar, and tried my best to make him comfortable, placing my own jacket beneath his head as a makeshift pillow.

For a moment, it seemed that the catatonia would pass. Then the youth's body began to shake and spasm with such fearful violence that I feared he would injure himself. Thankfully, the epileptic paroxysmal didn't last, and Holmes and I were soon able carry him up to our rooms. There, we drew the blinds and lay him on his side, on Holmes's bed, to recover.

Holmes had often spoken dismissively of the fairer sex, but he always exhibited a great courtesy to them in person. "My dear Mrs. Hudson," he said, in the gentlest of tones, "you've had quite the shock. Please, do sit down and tell us everything."

Our redoubtable landlady would only acquiesce once she had furnished us with that great British cure-all – a pot of tea – after which she settled into Holmes's favourite chair to relate the morning's events.

"I was preparing rashers and eggs for yourself and the Good Doctor when I heard someone at the door," she related. "The bell rang in a series of quick, sharp *dings*, so urgent-seeming that I dropped what I was doing and fairly ran to the door. When I opened it, there was a young man standing there, a cigarette in one hand, the other still on the bell pull.

"I don't think he saw me at all – his attention was quite elsewhere. He was straining to look at someone or something over his shoulder, so that when I asked if I could be of assistance, he almost jumped out of his skin.

"He spoke quickly, in a breathless tone that spoke of great urgency. He asked if this was the residence of Mr. Sherlock Holmes, and when I said that it was, he asked to be admitted.

"All the while we spoke, he continued glancing over his shoulder, as though there was someone he wished to avoid – someone who was fast on his heels . . . ."

"Did you see anyone?" Holmes interrupted.

"No, but the young man was on the step, which quite obscured my view of the pavement below."

"Excellent, Mrs. Hudson. Please, continue."

"He was nervous – jumpy I'd say. I felt sure he must be in grave danger, so I wasted no time in asking him to step inside.

"He was almost in the hallway, still glancing back, when he threw up his arms and let out the most horrifying cry. His head spun 'round and he fixed me with the most awful stare. Oh, Mr. Holmes, what a look he had! As though he had seen the Devil himself.

"I can tell you, I closed that door as fast as I could, throwing the bolt for good measure. I was just turning to speak to him again when I saw him shudder, then topple over. He dropped like a stone, and with such force that I heard an almighty crack as he hit the tiles. He looked so pale, I was convinced he had done himself a serious injury. He will be all right won't he, Doctor?"

I was reassuring the dear woman when, as if on cue, Holmes's bedroom door opened and out walked our visitor, looking a little ragged, but considerably less wan than he had half-an-hour earlier.

In another life, Mrs. Hudson would have made an excellent nurse. Within ten minutes, all three of us were seated around a roaring fire with a fresh pot of coffee and plates piled high with those neglected eggs and rashers. Within fifteen minutes more, we were replete – our visitor sore-headed and a little embarrassed, but otherwise well, and keen to relate his tale.

"My name," he began, in a soft voice, softened further by a gentle Cornish burr, "is Christopher Angove. I was orphaned when I was five and raised by my maternal uncle, Captain Pengellys.

"My Genni is soon to come into her majority, and we are planning to marry." Here Angove paused, and added in a defiant whisper, "Oh, the doctors have quite different ideas about that, of course! They would have me dosed on bromide and heading for a life of lonely solitude. But my uncle has always wanted the best for me – and my fiancé is quite prepared to take the risks of an epileptic for a husband.

"No, Mr. Holmes, despite the rather sad spectacle I've presented this morning, my life isn't that of the invalid. It is as rich as any young man could hope for – and about to be enriched further by the addition of a loving wife and, if the Lord blesses us, a family.

"However, the reason for consulting you has nothing to do with any of these things . . . . ." Here Angove faltered. "Before I go further, Mr. Holmes, I must ask you something. It will no doubt seem curious, and it may color your perception of me in the asking of it. But ask it I must, for the events I am about to relate occasion a certain flexibility of mind that isn't usual. My question is this: Do you believe in *devils*?"

"I have met real, flesh-and-blood men to whom I would happily apply the epithet '*devil*'."

"I mean Biblical devils, Mr. Holmes. Physical incarnations of evil."

If Holmes thought any less of our visitor for his question, he didn't show it. Instead, he answered in the same measured tone he often used with clients. "Why do you ask?"

"Because I am bedeviled, Mr. Holmes! Even now, even here, on the streets of this great metropolis, I am not safe. I'm being hunted, Mr. Holmes! Hunted!"

"I believe in *facts*, Mr. Angove" he answered. "Eliminate the impossible, and whatever remains, no matter how incredible it may appear, will be the truth."

"So, you admit the possibility?"

"I have no evidence to either prove or disprove the existence of what people call devils. So, yes, I would admit the possibility."

"And have you, Mr. Holmes, ever seen a devil?"

Holmes paused, his eyes twinkling mischievously. "If you mean a creature from the fiery pits – You would not credit it, but in my youth, I actually went in search of such a being."

Angove looked sufficiently intrigued for Holmes to elaborate.

"When I was a boy, it was rumored that a creature of great age and malevolence roamed the grounds of the school. It was said to walk the dormitories every evening, and if you weren't a-bed by lights out, it would appear and drag you off."

"Heavens!" I said, momentarily entranced by the unexpected revelation from Holmes's past. "What a tale to tell to young boys!"

"Indeed," Holmes smiled demurely. "The story was well established by the time I started as a boarder and, like all good stories, it was based on verifiable truths.

"The school was once a monastery which had been gifted an area of woodland by the King in the Twelfth Century. The land was said to be the abode of a demonic beast, whose lust for blood was so fierce that the King believed only God's influence would calm it. Apparently it failed, for the woods took on an ominous reputation. It was claimed that those who entered them would surely die.

"By the time the monastery became a school, there had been enough unexplained deaths in and around the area to make the woods off-limits – but that didn't stop boys from daring each other to spend the night there. The year before my arrival, two boys had gone missing. When they were found, they were quite out of their minds . . . ."

"Holmes!" I cut in, shooting a glance at our ashen-faced guest.

Holmes gave me the whisper of a smile before replying, "Oh, I think the young man is quite recovered, but you're right. That is a story for another time. Please, Mr. Angove . . . ." Holmes waved a hand airily, for our visitor to continue.

"Kit," Angove said. "Call me Kit. Everyone does."

"Well then, Kit, tell us about your devil."

"It isn't so much my devil, as St. Mawr's. The legend goes back centuries – although I hadn't heard it until Skipper Williams told it to me."

"And who is Skipper Williams?"

"Genni – my fiancé's – father. He's in the same line as my uncle."

"Fishing?"

Kit raised an eyebrow, quizzically.

"I recognize a fisherman's calluses when I see them" Holmes explained.

Angove was tall and well-built, and now that Holmes had identified him as a fisherman, it was easy to see how the work and the elements had fashioned him into the fine young man he was.

"My uncle has a small fishing fleet" Kit continued. "Nothing too grand, you understand. Six boats, which has given him income enough to school me and make me an allowance – which I rather waste on clothes!" He blushed, chuckling at his own expense.

"Uncle still thinks of himself as a humble fisherman, but he spends as much time behind a desk these days as he does at sea. I help him when I can, as he intends for me to take over the running of things, in time. As I say, he has never considered me an invalid. 'Fresh air and exercise – that's the ticket!' he's always said."

"If I may," I interjected, "how long have you been afflicted by these seizures?"

"Since I was a boy. My uncle believes they stem from my parents' accident. They died when their carriage overturned. I remember nothing of the tragedy but, since then, the fits have come on me in times of distress, so my uncle may have the truth of it."

"When your parents died," Holmes asked, "were you left anything in trust?"

"I see where you are going, Mr. Holmes," Kit replied, with an fresh edge to his voice. "No. My parents were barely starting out in life. All they had was each other. And all my uncle had was his beloved little sister. He's always cared for me as if I were his own."

"And this devil?"

Kit took a deep breath, steadying himself it seemed, before replying. "They call it 'Old Tebel'. He's said to haunt the hills around St. Mawr's. He latches onto young men and carries them away on their wedding night."

"For what possible reason?" I asked.

"To protect Cornish maidens from unsuitable beaus!"

Holmes barked out a laugh.

"I agree, Mr. Holmes," Kit said, quietly – as though somehow the creature he spoke of could be conjured just by the saying of its name. "Any other time, I would have been laughing along with you. But this thing is real. You must believe me!"

"It followed you here?" Holmes asked, leaning out of his seat, in an attitude of intense concern.

"The truth, Mr. Holmes? I've begun to see him everywhere. Never fully, you understand. Just glimpses. A shimmering shape, something in the mist, half-formed, half-seen. But so unnerving that terror has begun to weigh upon me like an anchor. I fear I am losing my mind."

I had a sinking premonition that the young man's nervous system wouldn't stand up to a recitation of his encounters with this mysterious creature, but Kit was determined to persevere.

157

"I'm fine, honestly, Doctor," he said to my expressions of concern. "Let me tell you what I came to relate. Then, you and Mr. Holmes can decide if my troubles are worthy of your attentions."

Holmes pushed a glass of brandy into Angove's hand. The young man took it gratefully, downed it in one swallow before closing his eyes, and continued.

"I've known Genni since we were children. Her father used to work a lugger on the Atlantic Fleet out of Falmouth. He would be away for weeks at a time, and Genni's mother would send her out to ramble the hills to get her from under foot. We spent many-a-summer together climbing trees, fishing, and paddling – and had plighted our troth to each other long before we knew what the words meant.

"Genni's mother died before we reached adolescence, and my Uncle Jacob offered her father a job, so that he could be closer to home.

"Over time, our friendship grew into something more significant and, when I finished school, I didn't think it forward to ask for her hand in marriage.

"Genni isn't yet twenty-one. We cannot marry without her father's permission. Alas, he will not give it – feeling that a young man like myself, with little experience of life, may come to regret marrying so young. 'A childhood companion,' he says, 'is quite a different thing to a wife. And what you take for love may be nothing more than the natural affection that children, raised almost as siblings, have for each other.'

"In faith, I cannot be angry at his decision. Genni is his only child. His caution is natural. And he hasn't been unfriendly. Ordinarily, he's a quiet sort. Keeps himself to himself. Genni is his cook and housekeeper, and the two of them live very simply in his little cottage by the bluff. Yet, he has thrown open his home to me – and I have become a regular at his table.

"It was one evening, a week after my proposal, that it happened. I had been invited for supper. After, as Genni busied herself in the kitchen, her father and I took a circuit of the garden. The skipper passed me his cigarettes, and we talked of the future, with me I impressing upon him my good prospects, in the hope that he might relent and agree to our marriage sooner rather than later.

"After a while, the evening turned cold – a storm was coming and I had already begun to shiver – so we retired to the sitting room to warm ourselves in front of the fire. The weather quickly turned from bad to worse. Soon, the wind was howling down the chimney and rattling the casement windows so that, even in the cozy room, we felt its effects.

"I remember, as the evening grew darker, I found myself feeling strangely detached. The lights from the lamps and fire seemed too bright.

I sunk back into the chair, into the dark, pulling a blanket around my knees. It was while I was in this queer frame of mind that Mr. Williams suggested a round of storytelling – the storm seeming to lend itself to tales of weird and wild things.

"I should, perhaps, have cried off, but he was in a rare good humor and I was keen to spend as much time in Genni's company as I could."

"'Here's tale you should appreciate, young buck,' he said, laughing, 'though mayhap you won't appreciate it quite so much once I'm done! Old Tebel has lived in these hills for longer than there have been people to tell of it,' he commenced.

"'*Tebel* is a Cornish word for the Devil – at least that's what my old Ma told me, for that's what the monster is said to look like: Tall, red-skinned, with clawed hands, and hoofs where its feet should be. His head is wreathed in fire, and he has a set of large, milky eyes – for he lives in the dark places and, like all creatures of the night, has great, saucer-like eyes with which to pierce the veil.

"'Now, the Tebel has a fancy for young girls, and it's his greatest joy to watch them. He never reveals himself to them but, oh, they feel his regard, of that you can be sure. He's there when they walk the wooded vales, there when they splash across the brooks and streams, there whenever they're out, in the lonely places. It's the Tebel who makes the young girls uneasy as day turns to night. It's the Tebel who makes them jump at shadows. It's the Tebel that makes them speed up their tread, although there's nothing to be seen beyond the gloom which grows ever thicker, ever darker.

"'In all of its unnaturally long life, the Tebel has never harmed a girl or a woman. No. You might say he feels proprietorial about them. As though these beautiful young creatures are his, and his alone. And it's there that the danger lies.

"'For while Old Tebel is content to creep and peep, to watch and lurk, should one of his young maidens appear with a beau, then bloody murder is the result.'

"While the tale was harmless enough, the more the skipper spoke, the more uncomfortable I began to feel. The light still hurt my eyes, and swaddled in my nook, I began to imagine that I was, in fact, ensconced in some deep cave, and instead of Williams sitting across from me, there was Old Tebel. I do not lie when I say that I saw the skipper's face begin to shift and remold itself into the form of a hideous demon. So strong was the vision that, in the grip of it, I unknowingly, cried out."

"'Oh, now Tás!' Genni jumped up. 'Enough of that!'

"Her father – *Tás* is her pet name for him – looked unchastened. Indeed, he seemed delighted at how well his ghost story had been received."

"'The Tebel is neither fast nor stealthy,' he resumed with a chuckle. 'You will hear him come for you. You will hear his hooves on the road, behind you. You will hear the *snicker-snick*, as he sharpens his claws. You will feel his fiery breath on your neck, and when you turn around, you will see him in all his demonic glory. Redder than arterial blood, burning with an unholy fire, and in his huge eyes, you will see your own reflection. You will see how you blanch as he moves towards you, and you will watch, paralyzed, unmoving, unable to cry out, as he hoists you onto his shoulder and carries you away!'

"I should, perhaps, have recognized the signs of an oncoming seizure, but it came upon me so quickly I barely knew what was happening.

"When I awoke, I was back home with my uncle. Beyond a dreadful thirst, I was well, yet I could remember nothing of what had happened – and I haven't felt at ease since."

"Have you seen this Tebel again?"

"Many times, Mr. Holmes. At first, whenever I visited my dear Genni, but increasingly, he seems to haunt my every movement. Why, this morning, as I was walking from the station – enjoying the sights of the city – I suddenly felt his baleful gaze. By the time I reached your door, I was convinced that I was about spirited away!

"Yet what is worse, Mr. Holmes, is that every time the old devil appears, the *grand mal* assails me. Each fit is more terrifying, more violent. After the last attack, I was insensible for many days. It was then that I determined to break it off with Genni. But oh, Mr. Holmes, if you have ever been in love, you will know that the heart and the head aren't always in accord. Instead, I have chosen the path of the coward. For this past month, I have kept my distance. We write to each other three times a day and, this morning, came the most wonderful missive. She declares that her love for me has only grown in intensity and, when she comes of age, nothing will stop her. We will marry – devil or no!"

"If I may ask, Kit, why did you think to consult Mr. Holmes? Forgive me, but demons are hardly his usual stock-in-trade."

"It was at my uncle's insistence. I had set out yesterday to speak to the skipper. Going against her father's wishes doesn't sit well with me. I still believed I could persuade him – and I wasn't disappointed. He said that time had proved me faithful and, seeing how miserable his Genni had been, he no longer has any wish to keep us apart. He gave us his blessing, although he wouldn't let me speak to Genni then – He wanted to give her

160

the good news, and claim a little credit back for himself after being cast as the villain for so long.

"I was so giddy that I immediately went to tell my uncle the news. To my surprise, instead of sharing my joy, he insisted instead that I set out for London – there to see you out and engage your help."

"He's clearly a perceptive man" replied Holmes in that quiet, intense way he has when a case begins to consume him. "Very perceptive. Now, Kit, I think Doctor Watson would prescribe bed rest – and plenty of it."

Angove didn't take much persuading. Holmes led him back to his own snug, little bedroom, leaving the two of us alone to plan.

"What do you think?" I asked. "Do you think there's a case here buried under all the monsters and myths?"

"I do. So far, everything I've heard screams foul play. I've no doubt that Mr. Angove is in deadly peril. But I must not ignore the possibility that this devil – for want of a better word – is *psychosomatic*. What do you think, Watson? Is he a reliable witness?"

"Is Christopher Angove really seeing devils, or merely imagining them, you mean?"

"Quite."

"It's hard to say. Throughout history, epileptics have been regarded as insane, half-witted, possessed. The Romans believed the illness was contagious. Until recently, it was said to be caused by sexual excesses. Many of those attitudes persist. Even in England, in the enlightened nineteenth century, you will find epileptics refused work, condemned to the work-house, or worse, to an asylum, because of a misunderstanding of the illness. Those who enter such institutions rarely leave. All I can say with any surety is that we have no idea what we're dealing with."

"Perhaps a better question, then, would be: Could his visions be caused by the epilepsy, or should we seek some outside force?"

"The mind is a curious thing, but from what little I know of epilepsy, if visual or auditory hallucinations occur – and it is rare – then they occur *during* the seizure, not before."

Holmes stoked the fire and, for a while, we sat in silence. Then he finished his abandoned before-breakfast pipe, fixed his cool, grey eyes on mine, and said "What we have heard is very suggestive, but we must step cautiously. Watson, I have never needed you more. I will be relying on your knowledge and good sense to guide me."

With those words, I suddenly felt a great weight fall upon me. I only hoped that I was equal to the confidence Holmes placed upon me.

St. Mawr's nestles on the southern coast of Cornwall, looking for all the world like a picture book painting of how an English fishing village

161

should be. A long, straggling street fronts the sea and, along it, runs a row of picturesque cottages, painted in breezy blues, pretty pinks, and sunny yellows.

A pier stretches out from the sea wall, affording a fine view of the remains of a medieval castle on the peninsula. The castle itself is a surprisingly squat and ugly thing – which, as many visitors have commented – quite spoils the otherwise idyllic scene.

The region owes its prosperity to a flooded valley which was carved out during the Ice Age and now forms one of England's largest natural harbors. It is in this harbor that St. Mawr's fishermen ply their trade. And it is in the wooded hills above the village that those who have made their money in that most perilous of occupations build the homes.

Cornwall may be known as the English Riviera, but the journey to Saint-Tropez is considerably easier than the one we took from London to St. Mawr's. A hansom, a sleeper-train, and a steam ferry were necessary to reach the village itself. An open carriage was awaiting us on arrival and, after a long and weary journey, it was a delightful to have the fresh sea-breeze on our faces as we were whisked through the village and up, into the hills, beyond.

Captain Pengellys's home is known as *Dowr Carrek*, which is Cornish for *Rock Anchorage* – and the age-worn, angular grange turned out to be a wonderfully suitable place for the square, much-weathered sea captain.

The driver had barely brought the horses to a halt when a berry-faced hulk of a man appeared. He lolloped, ape-like, towards the vehicle and, before we could protest, he'd taken our bags and was heading back towards the grange, calling for us to follow.

Pengellys may have been a man of some standing locally, but his home was a place of domestic simplicity. There were no armies of servants – just a cook and a maid who came from the village "to do for the captain". They shared his table and his confidences as though they were family.

Holmes, whose Bohemian soul railed at the straight-jacket of society, was quite charmed.

As soon as we had refreshed ourselves from the journey, we were invited into what the captain called the back parlor for a glass of mead and some saffron cake.

A pair of French windows opened out from the parlor into a walled garden and, while Pengellys attended to some household duties, we took the opportunity to explore. The garden was a sprawling affair, filled with all sorts of nooks and hideaways that would have been delightful in the summer. This late in the year, it was sorely overgrown, with only the hardiest of plants still in bloom.

Holmes made a beeline for a foul-smelling broadleaf, with striking, trumpet-shaped flowers.

"Look here, Watson," he said, in a tone of suppressed excitement.

"Interesting?"

"Very. This, my dear Doctor, is the infamous *jimson weed*. A poisonous plant from the nightshade family, it's more commonly known as *The Devil's Snare*. It's found far and wide – often in coastal areas. Its seed pods get scooped up with ship's ballast, or washed and blown onto foreign shores. It's also become a popular curio with travelers who bring it home, intrigued by the tales they hear of the plants more unusual qualities."

"Oh?"

"Oh, indeed! Originally, shaman used the flowers to induce visions. Ingested, they cause delirium. In large doses, they bring on fits, madness. Even death . . . ."

Before I could question Holmes further, we heard Pengellys's voice from the parlor, calling us in. Kit had been instructed to help Mrs. Harris in the kitchen, allowing us to talk freely with him while his young ward was otherwise occupied.

"I asked Kit to engage you because I know that something is still very amiss," he began. "It seems to me that someone has it in for my boy. I can see no rhyme nor reason for it but, in the last year, Kit has become a shadow of himself. I begin to fear for his life, Mr. Holmes, and that's no lie."

The big man's keen, dark eyes traveled from Holmes to me, and back again – and my companion appeared to be appraising the captain in much the same way.

"You don't believe in this Old Tebel, then?"

"It's rot, Mr. Holmes. All this talk of devils and demons! I'm a Christian man, so perhaps I shouldn't be so quick to dismiss the possibilities, but I can think of better things for one of Old Nick's creatures to do than haunt lovestruck young men."

"Tell me about his epilepsy" I interjected.

"We have never hidden Kit's illness. On the contrary, I've been sure that it was known so that should he be taken bad, those around him would know what the trouble was and how best to care for him."

"And generally, how often do the fits come upon him?"

"Why, never Doctor."

"Never?"

"When he first came to me, he had a very hard time of it. But good Cornish air, and the feeling of being useful – that's all a man needs to grow up strong. Until this Tebel business, he hadn't had an attack for seven, eight years – more even. It was my belief that he had outgrown it."

"Is that possible, Watson?"

"It's widely held that fresh air and hard work is beneficial. And those who are stricken as children do sometimes recover as adults," I affirmed, not feeling anywhere near as confident as I sounded.

"Has he ever had hallucinations – visions – before?" I continued, trying to get a feel for Kit's symptoms.

"When he was a child, he swore for months that his mother was watching over him. But I couldn't tell you if it was the grief or the illness at work."

"And when the fits resumed, did you notice anything different about them?"

"They appear with no warning, are more violent, and take a greater toll." The captain sighed sadly.

"Mmm." Holmes steepled his fingers together and regarded Pengellys intently. "You said that you felt someone might 'have it in' for Kit. Has he any enemies?"

"Hardly! I may be partial, but the boy hasn't a bad bone in his body. Why would anyone take against him?"

"What about yourself, Mr. Pengellys? Any business rivals?"

"Psh! This isn't London, Mr. Holmes. I'm a fisherman. My neighbor's a fisherman, my neighbor's neighbor is a fisherman, my housekeeper's husband is a fisherman. The only thing anyone gets hot under the collar about here is the size of their catch. Besides, at sea, your life may depend on the man next to you. Grudges get themselves worked out pretty fast in those situations."

"Your domestics?"

"Mrs. Harris and Elowen, you mean? They've been with me this past year, since my old housekeeper retired. Came with good references from Falmouth."

"Didn't Williams used to ship out of Falmouth?"

"He did. What of it?"

"Just following a train of thought, Mr. Pengellys. Do they tend the garden?"

"I do it myself. I rarely have the time to keep on top of the weeds, these days – though why you should be asking about that, I'm sure I don't know," he added, sounding irritated at what he must have taken for random queries.

"What about Williams?"

"Man's an odd fish, but he owes me his livelihood. His daughter is about to become my daughter. What grievance could he have?"

"Indeed." Holmes said, his eyes glinting. "Do you have any suspicions?"

"Nothing more than my guts telling me Kit is in terrible danger. But look, I've been speaking to Mrs. Harris about supper this evening. I haven't sent out the invites yet, but I was thinking of asking Williams, Genni, and some of the other skippers. Give the dog chance to see the rabbits?"

"That sounds ideal, Mr. Pengellys. Now, if you'll excuse me, I'm of a mind to take a little constitutional. Tell me, are the boats back yet?"

The captain glanced at the clock on the mantel. "Not for a couple of hours. They'll come in with the tide."

"Excellent! Perhaps I can take that invitation round to Miss Williams, then?"

The captain gave Holmes a sly, knowing smile, looking considerably warmer towards him than he had a few moments earlier.

"Watson?"

"Yes?"

"You don't mind staying here?"

"Not at all. Truth be told, I'm still a little fatigued by the journey."

"Then look to Kit, and ensure he isn't left alone with anyone outside of the family."

"Lord!" Pengellys exclaimed. "Is it that bad then?"

"It may be nothing at all," Holmes said. "Time will tell, Captain. Only time will tell."

Pengellys may have considered himself a humble fisherman, but he certainly knew how to host a splendid supper.

Holmes and I were to be guests of honor, and it appeared that everyone who was anyone had come out to give the "gentlemen from London" a good looking at.

Despite that fact that Pengellys employed at least half of the twenty people seated around the table, the conversation was refreshingly free of attempts at affectation or flattery. The captain often found himself the butt of the joke – and gave as good as he got, with no indication of bad blood.

The young lovers spent much of the evening glancing at each other, clearly oblivious to anything else.

The captain kept the drink and conversation flowing with an enviable ease, although it didn't escape Holmes's notice that his glance was often towards the couple.

Most of the talk was, as the captain had warned us, about catch sizes, which appeared to be a topic of endless fascination. Only once were voices raised. Yet even then, it seemed like the rehashing of age-old grievances, rather than real malice.

"Any minute now," Kit, said to me, conspiratorially, nodding towards a jowly, blancmange of a fellow, busy filling his face, at the end of the table. "Three glasses down, and he's about to start at it."

"You're a good man, Jacob" the florid-faced skipper suddenly said, raising his voice to be heard over the general murmur of table-talk. "God knows, I don't begrudge you your success, but how can one man, with one boat, hope to compete with you and your six? Should I come home empty handed, I can't send out another boat to try their luck elsewhere. Should I hit a good patch, I can only take what will fill my hold."

Kit leant over and whispered, "He does this every time, Doctor!" The complaint seemed so well-known, it was followed by a chorus of, "Hush, Lowen!" and groans of, "Not this again!"

"I won't be silenced! Lowen barked back, waving a fork piled high with slices of roast beef, like some ancient battle standard. "You can fill six holds, while I go hungry!"

"*You* go hungry?" a voice chipped in from the end of the table, which occasioned much laughter. "That's a new one!"

"So, that's how it is?" Lowan cried, his face, purpling even more. "You invite me here to be mocked!"

"Come now," the captain said placatingly. "Five times in the last month, my fleet has turned home empty, while you've hit gold. Luck is either with you or not. My offer still stands. You can come out with my boats – we'll work the fields together."

"I'd rather be my own boss, thank you," was the sullen reply.

"You know full well that Cadan often puts out with us. He's still his own boss."

"Psh! For now. But I know what you're about, Jacob. You want to buy up every boat out of St. Mawr's."

"Rot! Seas are rich enough for us all to share! Come, fill your re-glass, refresh your plate. We're all friends here."

Lowen did, indeed, return his attentions to his plate, after which the table returned to its good-humored chat.

I was seated beside Kit and Genni, who seemed well-suited in every respect. Kit was tall and broad-shouldered. Genni was almost as tall, and brown as a berry. Where Kit was dapper in his choice of fashion, Genni's clothes were simple but tasteful, her long, black hair worn down and unadorned. When she spoke, it was in a sing-song voice, full of joy, and free of artifice. London society would have had no time for her, but I was quite enchanted.

166

Skipper Williams had been placed beside Holmes, allowing my companion to easily get the measure of the man without seeming to pry.

Williams proved to be taciturn, initially speaking only when spoken to. It took all of Holmes's considerable charm to thaw him out at all.

"You must be looking forward to the wedding, then?" I heard Holmes occasion.

"As much any father looks forward to losing a daughter," was Williams's morose reply.

"Surely, you aren't so much losing a daughter as gaining a son?" Holmes teased.

"Oh, you must take no notice of an old man, set in his ways, Mr. Holmes," Williams said, lightening his tone. "Genni is my only family. Of course, Kit would be a fine catch for any young woman."

The evening progressed in much the same way, with neither Holmes nor myself hearing anything that pointed at deeper resentments towards the captain or the young lovers.

Within a few hours, the party began to break up, the fisherman being keen to get some rest before the early tide drew them back to their boats.

Holmes and I had retired for a glass of port with the rest of the stragglers, and were exchanging notes on the evening, when Holmes suddenly grasped me by shoulder.

"With me, now, Watson! If I'm not mistaken, we are about to reach the end of the game."

Despite the evening chill, it appeared that some brave souls had ventured outside, for the French doors were now ajar.

I followed Holmes outside where I saw Kit and Skipper Williams, walking towards an ornamental gazebo, deep in conversation.

I took Holmes's lead, moving cautiously along the wall, using the shadows and soft grass to mask our approach.

"Well, then, my lad, it's all agreed," I head Williams say. I saw him reach into his pocket to pull out what appeared to be a cigarette case, which he offered to Kit. "I think we've time for a celebratory smoke before we head indoors, don't you?"

Williams struck a Lucifer. As the match caught, its phosphorous glow illuminated both men in a blaze of white light and I was momentarily transfixed by the look of utter hatred emblazoned across Williams's face.

I didn't hear Kit's reply for, in a flash, Holmes was beside him, with myself practically falling over my own feet to catch up.

"Ah, there you are, Kit!" Holmes said nonchalantly. "The young lady sent me out to find you. I'm sure the skipper won't mind if I share a cigarette with him instead?

167

Without waiting for a reply, Holmes whipped the cigarette out of Kit's hand, and leant forwards to light it on Williams's match.

If Angove was bemused by Holmes's rudeness, he didn't stay around to comment, for the news that his lady had requested his presence was enough to send him rushing indoors.

"Interesting," Holmes said, regarding Williams cooly. "Can't quite place the blend."

"I really couldn't tell you," Williams responded, sounding uneasy. "Picked them up at the port. They aren't my usual."

"Really? They look home-rolled." Holmes pulled enthusiastically on the cigarette, blowing little smoke rings in the skipper's face. "It has a strange scent, but I'd warrant Watson would find it less noxious than my usual mix."

The fisherman coughed and began to back away. "Well, I must be going," he stammered and, with that, he hurried for the French windows. "It's getting late."

"Why don't you see our new friend out, Watson," Holmes said airily, still drawing on the cigarette with an attitude of beatific calm.

I did as asked, recalling Holmes's insistence on not leaving Kit alone.

By the time I reached the parlor, Williams and Genni were the only remaining guests.

If the skipper had seemed self-conscious during supper, he was now in a state of intense agitation. Without a word, he grasped Genni by the elbow and fairly dragged her from the room. I watched them leave and, with a nagging but undefined sense of foreboding, I raced back to the garden.

I was at the windows when I heard a dreadful cry – so loud and tortured that my skin went cold and the hair on my arms began to bristle. I ran then as I had never run before, stumbling in the dark over penchants, fountains, bell jars, and all sorts of garden ornaments, in my eagerness to aid my friend.

The garden seemed impossible to navigate. In the gloom, I found walls where there should have been none. Bushes seemed to throw themselves under my feet. Rose thorns became barbed wire enclosures that plucked at my flesh and tugged at my clothes. And through it all, I could hear Holmes howling, like a man possessed.

Almost as suddenly as they began, the cries stopped, and I felt my blood run cold. I staggered on, feeling dreadfully afraid, until finally, my outstretched hand found the cold metal of the gazebo. Remembering the last time we were here, I fumbled in my jacket for my matches and, after several attempts, one ignited.

Holmes lay no more than a few feet from me – his long frame curled into a fetal ball, his breath coming in rapid gasps.

As I got nearer, I could see his flushed cheeks, mouth twitching, his pupils, so large and dark, that they quite consumed his face. He threw up his hands, coving his eyes against the flare of the match, with an audible groan. "Holmes, what is it, man?" I asked. "Can you speak?"

For a moment he seemed to shake off whatever had him in its grip. I saw a flash of recognition blaze in his eyes, and raising one hand like a twisted claw, he motioned me to come closer.

I knelt beside him, placing my ear to his mouth. He made a sound somewhere between a sob and a choke, then speaking with a feverish energy, he said "Red as a beet, dry as a bone, blind as a bat, mad as a hatter."

He shuddered again, his long hands, grasping at the night air, his eyes frantic. "Red as a beet, dry as a bone, blind as a bat, mad as a hatter," he repeated. The delirious refrain went on for many minutes, and with such intensity, that I began to fear for my friend's sanity. Then, I reminded myself that this was Sherlock Holmes. Regardless of appearances, there was some part of his remarkable mind that was trying to tell me what had happened.

I tried to question him once more, but it was clear that Holmes had quite exhausted what reserves he had. He let out one more heart-rending groan and, pointing to some horror which only his own disordered mind could see, he slipped into unconsciousness.

With the captain's aid, I made Holmes as comfortable as I could. Beyond that, there was nothing else to be done – and I fell back into anguished watchfulness.

It seemed increasingly clear to me that Williams was to blame for whatever had befallen Holmes. I kept re-playing that scene in the garden, over and over, in my mind. The cigarette – it had to be that. Yes! When we had first met Angove, Mrs. Hudson had said he was smoking. Holmes had been unable to find the cigarette. Then, I had wondered why he'd looked for it. It now seemed beyond doubt that there had been some toxin in it – and in the one Holmes had ingested the previous night that had been intended for Kit.

The Captain shared my instincts, along with a burning need for action. So it was, with Kit watching over my friend, that we headed out into the early morning to confront the skipper.

When we reached the bluff, we discovered a small crowd gathered around the little cottage. A pall of smoke hung in the air. With it came a cloying, fetid odor, that caught in the throat and made the eyes sting.

The captain jumped down from the trap, with a look of thunder on his face. "Williams?" he demanded. "Where the devil is Williams?" Pengellys buttonholed one of the bystanders. "You! What goes on here?"

"Seems the skipper lit a bonfire in the garden before he sailed," the man replied. "Damn fool left it smoldering. Would have had the whole house aflame if it wasn't for the neighbors raising the alarm."

The captain was in no mood for small talk, and neither was I. What was left of the cottage door lay on its hinges and the burly man pushed his way into the house, following the tracks of water and footprints left by the impromptu firefighters.

Apart from some smoke, the cottage was undamaged, but the small garden was a blackened mass of tangled and half-burnt foliage.

"What the Hell do you think was he about, Doctor?"

"Covering his tracks" I hazarded.

Pengellys bounded upstairs, calling for Genni, but found the place deserted.

"He could have taken her with him?" I suggested.

The captain ran his hands through his thick hair, tugging at his curly locks in frustration. "Damn it, Doctor, I've known this man for decades!"

We appeared to be at an impasse when a cry from outside sent us rushing for the door.

Genni, barefooted and soaked to the skin, was running across the road. The captain took flight toward her and, before long, he had swept the young girl off her feet and into his arms, holding her with all the protective instincts of a papa bear with its cub.

"Calm yourself, girl, calm yourself!" he said to the sobbing woman, but she was quite overwhelmed.

"Come, Doctor!" Captain Pengellys cried, carrying her to the trap. "Let's go home. It looks like we have another patient for you to care for."

The events of the last few hours had clearly taken their toll. On the trap, Genni fell asleep in my arms. It was fully twenty-four hours before either she or Holmes awoke – thankfully, both very much recovered.

We were gathered in the parlor, with the blinds drawn at Holmes's request, and it was there, in the unnatural gloom, that he related a tale whose details were as dark as the room itself.

"It was the story of Old Tebel that sparked my interest," he said, his voice cracking. "Was Kit such an invalid that a ghost story would send him into a fit? I didn't think so. Indeed, I tried one of my own, and even in his weakened state, Kit showed no signs of alarm at it. No, the story of Old Tebel was intended to create mischief. Or sew the seeds of some.

"Still, Watson had told me that epilepsy was poorly understood – and I felt on unsteady ground. Then, I learned from the captain that Kit had quite outgrown his illness . . . and that changed everything.

"Let us imagine that someone wishes to do harm, using a toxin that will induce hallucinations and bring about fits, safe in the knowledge that the effects will be taken for epilepsy. Let's imagine they throw in a tale of devils for the disordered mind to feed on. Very quickly, the *who* and the *how* becomes clear.

"There are many toxins that cause fever, delirium, tachycardia, mydriasis – a dilation of the pupils – even hallucinations. Only one, to my knowledge, causes all of these, plus a dreadful thirst and pronounced photophobia – *Datura stramonium*. The symptoms can be summed up by this jolly little ditty: "*Red as a beet, dry as a bone, blind as a bat, mad as a hatter.*"

Holmes rummaged in his jacket pocket and pulled out a handkerchief. Inside was a crushed, white bloom which I recognized immediately.

"Jimson weed!"

"Quite."

"Why, Mr. Holmes," the captain stated, "I have some of that in my own garden. It grows wild over these parts. It's an insidious weed. I've spent many a day trying to eradicate it."

"I had noticed," Holmes smiled. "As you say, it's common enough. My visit to Williams's cottage revealed that he had his own quite-splendid jimson weed plant – Only, unlike yours, his was well cultivated, with signs of regular clipping. The plant blooms late in the year, but his plant's flower heads were already quite gone."

"But good Lord!" Pengellys cried. "Why!"

"I kept asking myself the same question. What good is the *who* and the *how*, without the *why*? The only possibility was the marriage. So determined was Williams to prevent it that when the young couple vowed that they would press ahead regardless of obstacles, he set out to put an end to it once and for all."

"You mean – ?" I asked, aghast.

Holmes nodded grimly. "The cigarette I ingested was enough to lay me out for twenty-four hours – "

"You knew!" I cried.

Holmes held up a hand, placatingly. "The flowers could have been placed in Kit's food or drink, but that wouldn't explain his fit in Baker Street. The more I heard, the more I believed that the cigarettes Williams had been giving him held the secret. Nothing was certain, beyond the fact that, if I was correct, the risks to me were minimal. But to Kit? After months of being dosed with cigarettes, Kit was already, as the captain

171

noted, a shadow of himself. I believe had he ingested that last dose, then madness or death would have been the final result."

"But why?" asked Kit, horrified.

"I think" Holmes said gently, "that Genni can tell us that."

The young girl sat on the floor beside Kit, looking so unlike the happy, confident young woman of the party that my heart went out to her.

"Mr. Holmes is right," she said. "I always knew that Tás was reluctant for me to marry. It is the way of fathers, I think. No man is ever good enough. Not even – " She glanced at Kit sadly. " – the boss's son. But it wasn't until last night that I realized the hatred he bore for Kit.

"After we returned home, he was like a man possessed! He swore that no daughter of his would be 'sullied by a union with a mentally deficient'! I've never seen him like that. The way he snarled, the way his face twisted – it was as though I was looking at Old Tebel himself!

"Then he began pulling up the plants and building that terrible pyre. I was so fearfully afraid of what he might be about that I ran to the one place I knew he would never find me – the sea caves. You remember them, Kit? How we played there as children?

"He was so wild, so crazed, that he didn't see me leave, but later, I saw him, running along the sand, calling my name. I have never been so afraid. He railed and screamed and cursed, pounding through the surf until I became convinced that he would wake the whole village with his ravings. Indeed, a couple of fisherman, readying their boats for the tide, accosted him and asked him what he was about. For a moment, I thought he would recruit them to his cause, but instead he headed off, towards the cove where our own boat is anchored."

To hear such a story, to learn how one man had been twisted by hate until all reason was gone, shocked me to my core. Williams had lost everything – family, home, livelihood – and he was now a fugitive. And why? Ignorance, half-truths, and fear. "Good Lord!" I cried, feeling a deep despair creep upon me. "So that's it? He's slipped away then?"

"Don't worry, Watson. We can inform the authorities. Put the word out at the ports."

"Oh, I don't think that's necessary" the captain avowed. "If he went out with his crew, it won't be long before they'll be chomping at the bit to come home. If he didn't . . . Well, he'll soon have to put in. No skipper, no matter how skilled, can navigate Cornish seas on his own. It's just a matter of time."

"But what if he gets away?" I cried, feeling that some redress was necessary.

"What if he does?" Captain Pengellys proclaimed. "Good riddance! At the end of days, there'll be a devil waiting for him right enough – but it won't be Old Tebel. For now, I can consider myself doubly blessed. I already have the son of my heart – and now I have the daughter too. This is your home now, Genni, and as soon as we can arrange a priest, we will make that official."

At that moment, I looked from Genni to Kit, and suddenly I felt a flush of hope. These young people had endured so much, yet their love had remained strong.

"This is what it's all about, aye, Doctor?" said the captain, beaming with fatherly joy. "We cannot stop the hate, but we can counter it with love."

"Indeed, Mr. Pengellys," I said. "Indeed."

NOTES

- Trousseau is Armand Trousseau, whose work covered what modern medicine would term neurological diseases, such as apoplexy, epilepsy, and Parkinson's Disease. He was one of the earliest physicians to describe *grand mal* seizures in detail.
- Bromide was an early treatment for the symptoms of epilepsy, and it is still used today. In the Victorian era, side effects could be severe, including skin blisters that could cause permanent scars, lethargy, slurred speech, uncontrolled body movements, and sexual disfunction. In Holmes's era, many of those with mild epilepsy preferred the fits to the cure.
- There is no St. Mawr's in Cornwall. We can only assume that Watson has changed the names to preserve the privacy of those involved in the events.
- Cornish folklore doesn't have any reference to an *Old Tebel*, although the word *Tebel* does mean *evil*. It is likely that Williams made up the story specifically to target Kit.

Umbrella Trouble
by Robert Stapleton

The month of October can often be one of the most depressing periods of the year – at least as far I am concerned. Especially when the weather is wet. That day, a gloom hung over our shared rooms in 221b Baker Street. The rain outside continued with a persistent intensity which seemed to allow for no respite.

My friend Sherlock Holmes was sitting much agitated, glaring toward the drawer which housed his syringe and supply of cocaine. I recognized the expression on his face. He was resisting temptation with practically the same intensity that Odysseus must have used when he resisted the death-call of the Sirens. And gradually losing the struggle.

I picked up my copy of the local morning newspaper and scanned the advertisements.

"I see an exhibition is being held at the Town Hall in Camberwell," I said.

No reaction whatsoever came from Holmes.

"Quite apposite to the day," I continued, trusting that my friend was indeed listening. "The exhibition concerns wet weather gear." I put down my newspaper. "Which reminds me: You really must purchase another umbrella."

"An umbrella?" Holmes sounded horrified as he looked round at me with irritation evident in his eyes.

"Certainly. In order to protect you against this insufferable downpour."

"Watson," he said in a tone which suggested disapproval, "the very idea of going outside in this weather, merely in order to purchase such a protective contraption, is totally illogical. The most appropriate time to purchase an umbrella, if indeed such a time ever does exist, has to be when it is, in fact, not raining outside."

"But everyone is carrying an umbrella nowadays," I replied. "Come rain or shine."

"Everybody? Surely you exaggerate."

"Not by much."

My friend's face now took on a defiant expression – which, in contrast to his former appearance, made a refreshing change.

"I bought an umbrella not long ago," he said. "A matter of a couple of months, in fact."

"Yes, I remember. And you left it on a Fulham omnibus – or so you informed me later. You never did find it again."

"It is all a matter of habit," said Holmes as he continued to fix me with his thoughtful gaze. "If my mind is engaged with other more important matters, I can hardly be expected to pay much attention to what other items of apparel I'm supposed to be carrying with me. It's rather like having a child with you and having the responsibility of keeping an eye on him or her. While I cannot speak for others, an umbrella, as far as I am concerned, is a sheer waste of time, and of good money."

"But you never forget your hat."

"Now that is a different matter altogether," he said. "I hardly need to think twice about what is on my head. My fore-and-aft hunting cap is quite sufficient for me, thank you very much. After all, it has a peak at the back as well as at the front. And that keeps the rain from dripping down the back of my neck."

"As you say," I retorted, "it is all a matter of lifestyle familiarity. Habit. In which case, I hardly think that I, myself, could ever become used to wearing such a cap on a regular basis."

"Which is why you own an umbrella, while I, at the moment, do not."

"*Touché.*"

"And besides, the first gust of wind would inevitably turn the thing inside out and force its owner to engage in a jolly dance. Comical, but hardly practical – at least in fulfilling my chosen profession."

He chuckled for a moment at the image he had conjured up. Then he turned to look out of the window and gave a long, heartfelt sigh.

"You certainly cannot stay in here all day long," I told him. "It's already been raining for the last two days, and shows little sign of ending just at the moment."

"If Scotland Yard could come up with some case worthy of my intellectual talents," said Holmes, "that might prove to be a better reason for venturing outdoors than going in search of an umbrella."

I stood up and reached for my coat, hat, and cane.

"Are you coming?" I asked.

"For what purpose? In order to purchase an umbrella?" He sighed and forced himself to rise from his chair.

"We can at the very least take a look at what the shops have on sale."

"Very well," he said with a sigh. "If I must. But I insist that we take a cab."

We alighted from the hansom in the middle of Regent Street and immediately ducked under the arcading, in search of shelter from the unrelenting downpour.

176

As fortune would have it, we had arrived directly outside the premised of Messrs Baldersby and Jones, Milliners, being the precise establishment we were seeking. They claimed to sell, and even rent, hats and other items of clothing and goods to the more discerning of customers, and we had both been patrons of the place during recent months.

"I suppose there is no escaping the fact that you wish to visit this establishment," sighed Holmes. "But I enter without any obligation or intention to purchasing anything."

Immediately inside the front entrance, a display of umbrellas and parasols attracted our attention.

"I see the proprietors are enjoying a brisk trade in these protectors from the present spell of weather," I said.

Holmes remained stubbornly silent.

As we were entering the shop, a young woman in a dark coat burst out through the front entrance, pushed past us, and unfurled her newly purchased umbrella above her head. She then scurried across the road, narrowly dodging an omnibus and a brace of cabs.

In her wake, both Holmes and I heard something fall to the ground.

On closer investigation, we noticed that an item of jewellery had fallen onto the roadway directly in front of us.

Holmes bent down to retrieve the article.

"It appears to be a woman's diamond bracelet," he said as he looked carefully at the object. "Expensive."

"The bracelet must belong to that young woman," I concluded, nodding in her direction. "There is nobody else around us who might have dropped it."

I then raised my arm and waved and shouted to the young woman. But she had already gone, and my words were drowned out amidst the cacophony of the morning traffic.

As he continued to examine the bracelet with great care, Holmes ventured with me into the milliner's shop, almost colliding with one of the sales staff.

"Good morning," said the man in a smart suit. "It must be Dr. Watson and Mr. Sherlock Holmes."

"Ah, good morning, Mr. Baldersby," said Holmes, suddenly taking an interest in the events taking place around him, and brightening up considerably.

"I recognize the deerstalker cap," said the shop owner. "Purchased from here, no doubt."

"No doubt."

"There you are, Watson," said Holmes as he turned to me. "Yet another reason to celebrate my sartorial individuality."

I chuckled.

Baldersby nodded, and the matter was dropped. "How may I help you, gentlemen?" asked the shop owner.

"The young woman who just left these premises in such a hurry," said Holmes. "It seems that she has dropped an item of jewellery into the roadway. This bracelet, in fact. We picked it up immediately outside your front door."

"Oh dear," said Baldersby, furrowing his forehead. "I have no recollection of having seen it before, and it was certainly not on her wrist when she purchased the umbrella. Otherwise, she would have made a noise by rattling it as she opened and closed her purse. I notice these things."

"I happen to know that you are assiduous at keeping records of those who purchase items from your establishment," said Holmes.

"That is quite right, Mr. Holmes. It really is important to us to record the contact details for each of our customers – if only to provide the patron with a proper receipt."

"In that case, you must have been particularly busy this morning."

"Run off our feet, I am pleased to say."

"Then you might be able to help us communicate with the young lady, in order to find out if the bracelet really does belong to her."

"I fully understand," said the man in the suit, "but it is our policy never to reveal details of our customers to any third party."

"Then you must also understand," said Holmes, "that in this particular case, the alternatives are either for us to notify the police, or for yourself to visit the young lady instead."

"On a day as hectic as this, that would be impossible," said Baldersby. "And it would be against our professional interests to be seen to have a policeman calling here."

"As we picked the bracelet up outside in the street," mused Holmes, "it is possible that it really has nothing to do with your business here."

"True. Well, if there is no alternative, and if it really is a matter of returning lost property, then providing you with her name and address would perhaps be an act of public service."

"Precisely."

Armed with the name and address supplied by Mr. Baldersby, Holmes and I took a cab to Cumberland Court, a suite of townhouses some half-a-mile away from Regent Street.

In answer to our knock, using a large and impressive brass knocker, the front door was opened by a young woman in a maid's uniform.

"How may I help you, gentlemen?" she asked. "I am sorry to have to tell you that the family are out for the day."

Holmes touched his hat. "We are looking for a young woman by the name of Agnes Smithercote."

The maid appeared surprised by this news. "Well, if you have any business with Agnes, then you'd better go round the back, to the servants' and tradesmen's entrance."

"Is she is a member of staff here, then?"

"She certainly is. Senior housemaid, in fact. A bit above her proper station if you ask me. This morning has been her half-day off, so she will probably be back again by now."

The same maid answered the back door when we knocked there a moment later and called upon us to step inside.

"You will find Agnes Smithercote in the servants' quarters," the maid told us. "Down the corridor, and first door on the right."

We knocked upon the door she had indicated, and a female voice from inside invited us to enter. There we found Agnes, a tall, slim, fair-haired young woman sitting in a corner of the room, reading a daily newspaper.

"Miss Smithercote?" inquired Holmes.

She looked up. "Yes?"

"My name is Sherlock Holmes, I am a private consulting detective, and this is my friend and colleague, Dr. John Watson."

"How may I help you, gentlemen?"

"Less than an hour ago, you visited a shop in Regent Street."

"Indeed I did. You might perhaps consider it inappropriate for a mere housemaid to be doing her shopping in such a thoroughfare."

"That is your business entirely," countered Holmes.

"I was there in order to purchase an umbrella."

"From Baldersby and Jones?"

"That's right. I like to purchase top quality goods whenever I can."

"Indeed. You hurried out, pushed passed us, and rushed across the road."

"Did I?"

"And, as you unfurled your newly purchased umbrella, something fell to the ground. Do you remember that?"

"I seem to recall feeling something brush past my shoulder, but I was running late and had no time to stop and look around me. I didn't consider the matter particularly important at the time."

"It seems that the item which fell to the ground was an item of jewellery."

Agnes laughed. "I can assure you, Mr. Holmes, that I am not wealthy enough to own any jewellery."

"But you could afford to buy a new umbrella."

"I have been saving up my money for many month in order to buy one. While we as a family were never well off, my mother always insisted that we purchase goods of the highest possible quality."

"Which you did."

She nodded. "I am convinced that my new purchase will serve me well for many years to come."

"So, you are not missing any pieces of jewellery."

"That is what I have already told you."

He held out the bracelet for the young woman to see. "Have you ever seen this before?"

"Certainly not! Is this the item you found fallen onto the ground?"

"Yes."

"Then I think, if I owned such an item, I would treat it with much greater respect and care than the person who lost it."

"I too should hope so," continued Holmes, "but it seems that the bracelet must have fallen to the ground when you raised the umbrella in order to open it against the rain."

"So it seems."

"Did you not think of opening it while you were still inside the shop, before parting with your hard-earned money for it?"

She laughed.

"Mr. Holmes, you obviously do not yourself own an umbrella. Are you not aware that it is commonly believed that opening an umbrella inside a house is risking bad luck?"

"Of course. I had it had slipped my mind for a moment. But how do you imagine the bracelet might have found its way into the folds of your umbrella?"

"I imagine somebody must have dropped it in there."

"On purpose, or by accident?"

"You're a detective, Mr. Holmes, and a good one – or so I have heard. What do you think happened?"

"It is far too early in our investigations to determine that." He stood up. "Well, thank you for answering my questions, Miss Smithercote. If a reward is offered for the return of this bracelet, then I shall certainly put your name forward to receive it."

She smiled. "That is very kind of you. Even in my present job, life can be somewhat limited by the price of everyday expenses."

Once outside, Holmes and I consulted on our next step.

"I have a number of errands to run," I told him. "One or two elderly ladies require my professional attention from time to time, and today is my day for visiting them. Although one particular old lady is now confined to

180

her own home, she is well known among the privileged classes of London. If I could take the bracelet along with me, she might be able to help identify its owner."

"Splendid," replied Holmes, handing it to me. "Meanwhile, I shall have to call into the offices of *The Evening News*, and then return to Regent Street, in the hope that I can persuade Baldersby and Jones to let me have a list of all of their customers during the past week or so."

My old ladies always looked forward to my visits, and loved to have somebody there with whom they could chat. The lady I had in mind was surprised when I showed her the bracelet.

"That is a most beautiful piece of jewellery," she told me. "Wherever did you get hold of it, Dr. Watson?"

I told her the truth: That we had found it dropped in the street and were now looking for the owner.

"Then I hope you manage to find her. I am quite sure that the owner would be delighted to have it returned to her again."

"Have you ever seen it before?" I asked.

"You know," she told me, looking more closely at the bracelet, "I think I have . . . ."

When I returned to Baker Street later that afternoon, the rain was still torrential. As I loitered on the opposite side of the street from our rooms, waiting for the late afternoon traffic to clear sufficiently for me to cross in safety, I felt a hand touch my arm. I turned and found myself facing Sherlock Holmes.

"I believe we have visitors," said Holmes as he looked up at the windows of our apartment.

"So I see," I replied as I observed a police four-wheeler waiting outside our front door, and two silhouettes passing in front of the window – both men.

"How did your afternoon progress?" he asked me.

"Productive, I hope," I told him. "That old lady I was telling you about did remember the bracelet. She had seen it before, at an evening gathering some months ago. She is convinced that it belongs to Lady Leonora, the wife of Sir James Bullingworth-Webb, the Member of Parliament."

"Interesting."

"That's what I thought, but how it connects with the present investigation, I really have no idea."

"Perhaps we shall find out within the next few minutes. Come, Watson. It's time for us to discover exactly who has pressing business with us, and what that business might be."

Now heedless of the traffic, we both ran across the road, in through the front door, and up the stairs in double-quick time.

Without knocking, Holmes burst in, turning the heads of both of our visitors abruptly in our direction.

"Ah, Lestrade!" said Holmes in a tone which appeared brighter than the weather.

"There you are, Mr. Holmes," said the inspector. "I'm glad you have finally arrived."

"I was hardly expecting you."

"But you did put that enigmatic notice in the evening newspaper reporting that a certain item of ladies jewellery had been found."

"Ah, yes. The first edition seems to come out earlier every day. Still, I'm glad you're here in response to it."

"We are here also because we're engaged in a rather delicate business, and we are in need of your assistance. That entry in *The Evening News* shows us that we're certainly on the right track."

"Indeed?" said Holmes, as he invited us all to take seats around the room.

"This gentleman," continued Lestrade, "is Mr. Hamilton Bullingworth."

"The brother of Lady Leonora Bullingworth-Webb," added Holmes.

"That's quite right!" said Mr. Bullingworth, rather surprised. "Inspector, I can see now why you told me that this gentleman was exceptional."

"Purely elementary, I assure you," replied Holmes, with a smile.

"But now to business," said Lestrade.

"And it has something to do with Mr. Hamilton's sister."

"Correct."

"Kindly elaborate."

"It seems that on the night before last, the Bullingworth-Webb household suffered a burglary. A break-in, during which a certain item belonging to Lady Leonora was stolen from her jewel box."

"A certain item? A diamond bracelet, perhaps?"

"Precisely."

"Watson."

Taking my cue from Holmes, I reached into my inner coat pocket and brought out the bracelet which had been at the heart of our investigation.

"Great Scott!" exclaimed Bullingworth. "You've found it!"

"But how?" demanded the inspector.

"It fell from a newly purchased umbrella in the middle of Regent Street earlier today," replied Holmes. "I feel that, if any reward were to be offered for finding it, then the money should go to the young lady who purchased the umbrella in which it had been concealed."

"Certainly, certainly," agreed Bullingworth.

"I shall provide you with her name and address later, but first I should like to hear a detailed description of what occurred."

"Correct me if I'm wrong, Mr. Bullingworth," said Lestrade. "But it seems that during the evening, a man climbed up the outside wall of the house, broke in through the upstairs window, entered the lady's boudoir, opened her jewel case, removed that bracelet, and left by the same method."

"And how do you know that it was a man?"

"A large sized muddy footprint was found on the carpet flooring of the bedroom. It was larger than that of any normal woman."

"Or perhaps of any medium-sized man."

"That was our conclusion."

Holmes allowed a pensive expression to spread across his face.

"During the following day," said Holmes, "the thief obviously found the bracelet to be a little too hot to handle. Indeed, he tried his best to lose it by pushing it down into the folds of an umbrella which was being offered for sale in a certain shop in Regent Street."

"And you have been trying to return it to its rightful owner throughout the day."

"Indeed. But that was yesterday's crime," said Holmes. "Why have you come to visit me today?"

"A second break-in, almost exactly the same in every respect as the first, took place only yesterday evening."

"And what was taken this time?"

"Forty pounds in cash," said Hamilton Bullingworth. "Eight five-pound notes."

"And how do you know that it was the same thief as on the previous occasion?"

"Another footprint was discovered."

"Exactly the same as before?"

"That is the way it appears."

"An oversized boot, leaving a muddy footmark?"

"Yes. Precisely that."

Holmes tried hard to suppress the guffaw of laughter which was welling up inside him, but he failed, and let out the sort of laugh which might have been heard as far away as Whitehall.

"Forgive me, gentlemen," he said a moment later, "but this all sounds somewhat farcical to me."

"Farcical! Do you have an idea who the thief is, then?"

"I have a good idea. But first I would need to examine the scene of the break-ins."

"Of course," said the policeman.

"Very well, Lestrade. Kindly take us there."

Crammed together into the police vehicle we had passed earlier, the four of us rattled through the streets until we entered a gateway which led up along a gravel pathway to the front entrance of a particularly fashionable upper-class house on the north-eastern edge of London.

One of the maids answered our knock upon the front door and ushered us all into one of the front reception rooms. There we met Lady Leonora, a middle-aged woman, whose extraordinary personality filled the entire room with the sense of her presence.

"This is Mr. Sherlock Holmes," Inspector Lestrade explained to the lady, "and Dr. Watson."

"They are here to assist with the investigation into the theft of your diamond bracelet," added Hamilton Bullingworth. "And I am delighted to say that they have already managed to retrieve it."

"That is excellent work," declared Lady Leonora. "Who was the thief?"

"So far," said Lestrade, "he has not been identified."

"That is extremely unfortunate," she replied. "And what about the theft of the money?"

"We assume it was the same person who broke in on both occasions," said Lestrade, "but we're still in the dark as to the identity of that culprit as well."

"On the other hand," explained Mr. Bullingworth, "Mr. Holmes thinks he might know the name of the thief."

"Then who is it?"

"It would be a grave error to jump to such conclusions before examining all of the evidence at first hand," added Holmes. "I think we should like to begin by visiting the location of the crime – or crimes."

Lady Leonora, together with her brother, Mrs. Williams the middle-aged housekeeper, Lestrade, and myself all stood in the doorway to her inner bedroom – watching – while Holmes examined the room where the robbery had taken place.

As he examined the carpeted floor, Holmes complained that he would have also liked to examine the scene of the first break-in. "It is a great shame, but you assure me that it is much the same as the second."

"And the carpet had been brushed and cleaned after the police had examined the scene on that first occasion?"

"That is correct," said the lady of the house.

184

"That's right," said the housekeeper. "We are proud of the way we keep a clean and tidy house."

"As far as you are concerned, Lestrade," asked Holmes, "can you confirm that?"

"I can indeed, Mr. Holmes."

"And I understand that a large muddy footprint was discovered on the carpet in the middle of the room."

"Yes, sir. The chambermaid spent a great deal of time scrubbing it away."

"But the same footprint, or a similar one, has appeared during last night, and is here before us now."

The housekeeper nodded.

"Can you confirm that it is the same or similar imprint, Mrs. Williams?"

"As far as I can tell, yes," replied the housekeeper. "You'd have to speak to the chambermaid about that."

"I intend to do that as soon as I have finished here," replied Holmes.

He next stepped over to the window and examined it carefully. He discovered that it was currently unlocked and standing slightly open to the outside atmosphere. He pushed open the window and looked outside. Then, with a grunt, he closed it again and returned to continue his examination of the floor area. Finally, he declared that he was satisfied and invited those of us standing in the doorway to come inside the room.

"Lady Leonora," he said, "I would be grateful if you could please show me exactly where the bracelet was kept before it was stolen from this room."

"Certainly," she replied, as she wandered over to where her personal items were positioned beside her bed. "I have always kept it in this small wooden box. It was kept locked at all times, and remained in the drawer beside my bed."

"But it is no longer in that drawer."

"That is evident."

"And where do you keep the key?"

"Oh, the key has always remained on the chatelaine which I keep in the same drawer."

"So that if anyone knew where to find the bracelet, they would have no difficulty in locating the key. All they would need is a knowledge of your personal habits."

"I suppose you are correct, but where I kept my jewels was never any secret. I expect everyone in the household knows about it. I merely expected everyone to respect my privacy."

"But that has been returned to its rightful place," Lestrade said.

"Thank you for your help, Lady Leonora."

"So," said Mr. Bullingworth, "the culprit could have been anybody."

"I hardly think so," replied Holmes. "But I think the time has come for us to have a conference of everyone in the household."

"We could meet in the drawing room," said Hamilton Bullingworth.

"That would be ideal," replied Holmes.

"The evening meal will be served at seven o'clock," said Lady Leonora. "Immediately after that would seem to be a suitable time for the meeting."

Everyone nodded.

"And I trust that our visitors will join us for our meal," added Lady Leonora.

"Splendid," replied Holmes. "But first I need to confer with the chambermaid."

I sat with Holmes as he interviewed Annie Longtown, the chambermaid.

"I have a few questions to put to you," he began. "If you're willing to help me out, that is."

"Certainly, Mr. Holmes," said the pretty auburn-haired young woman. "What would you like to know?"

"I'm referring to the two break-ins that took place in Lady Leonora's rooms recently."

"Yes?"

"I understand that you were the one who cleaned up the bedroom after the first burglary. Is that so?"

"Presumably you mean the muddy footprint. Yes sir, I cleaned that up the first time. After all, it is part of my job. It took a great deal of effort to make it clean again, I can tell you. And I shall no doubt be the one to clean up this time as well – now that you have finished examining the place."

"Quite. In which case, can you tell me about the window? Is it always kept shut, or is it sometimes left unlocked, or even left open?"

"The window, sir? No. Her Ladyship always insists that it is kept shut at all times, except perhaps in the middle of summer, when the heat is oppressive. But the window doesn't have a working lock, so it wouldn't be very difficult for somebody to open it, even from the outside."

"What you are saying is that both last night and the night before, the window was shut. Is that right?"

"Probably, sir. At least as far as I am aware."

"But you say it could have been opened from the outside."

"Yes, sir."

"Now, I want you to tell me about the first footprint – the one you had to clean up yesterday, apparently identical to the one you will be required to clean up today. What can you tell me about them?"

"What sort of thing do you want to know?"

"Was the footprint large or small?"

"It was big, sir, very big – just like the second footprint. It must have been made by somebody with an extremely large foot."

"Or perhaps a rubber waterproof boot."

"Yes. I suppose so."

"That is very interesting, Annie. Thank you."

The young chambermaid seemed relieved. "I'm glad that was helpful to you, sir."

"Now, tell me, who has the largest feet in the entire household?"

The girl giggled. "Well, I suppose it has to be Isaac Sudbury, the gardener. Although what he might have been doing inside the house, wearing those big boots, I really cannot say."

"Might he have been breaking in?"

"To steal her Ladyship's jewels? It is just possible, but I hardly think so. I can hardly imagine him climbing up the foliage outside and then climbing in through the window. Have you met our gardener?"

"Not yet. Why? Is he getting on in age?"

"He must be at least a hundred years old if he's a day."

"And have you any idea who has the smallest feet in the household?"

"The smallest? Of the men, I would imagine it would be Ambrose Bullingworth, Lady Leonora's nephew. She has quite a large family of siblings, you know. Down in the servants' quarters we often joke about how small his feet are. Almost like those of a woman. He also has a slight gap between his front teeth. Otherwise, he's quite attractive."

"Does he know that you talk about him?"

"No. But if he has any understanding of the life of servants, he will have a good idea that we do."

"Is he intelligent?"

Annie pulled a face. "Not really. His main interest is in gambling. The horses, you know."

"And does he get himself into debt?"

"Oh, yes, sir. I happen to know that a couple of bookmakers are pressing him for payment at this very moment."

"And one more thing."

"Yes?"

"Do you know if anybody in the household has purchased a new pair of cuff-links recently?"

She thought for a few seconds. "I'm not sure, but I think Ambrose has been talking about getting a new pair. Though how he could manage to afford them, I really couldn't say."

"Thank you, Annie," said Holmes. "Now, where might I be able to find Isaac Sudbury at this hour of the day?"

"He'll be in or near his potting shed, I should imagine."

Isaac Sudbury was sitting in his potting shed when Holmes and I arrived there. He was drinking a large mug of tea. He did appear to be somewhat elderly, perhaps well over the age of sixty, but looking vigorous for his many years.

"I am Sherlock Holmes," said my companion. "And this is my friend and colleague, Dr. John Watson."

"Well, good afternoon, gentlemen," he began. "Would you care to join me in a cup of tea?"

"Thank you," replied Holmes. "It might help warm me up on such a depressing day.

"And you, Dr. Watson?"

"Yes," I replied. "I think we all need cheering up today."

A moment later, we were all sitting together in the shed, looking out at the rain.

"I heard you were in the house," said Sudbury. "News travels quickly in a small community like this. They're all a load of nosy-parkers around here."

"I can imagine," replied Holmes.

"Now, gentlemen, how can I, in particular, help you?"

"We're here concerning the theft of Lady Leonora's bracelet," replied Holmes.

"I had no doubt about that. And am I one of the suspects in this case, Mr. Holmes?"

"Certainly not in my mind," replied Holmes, warming up his hands by wrapping them around the hot mug. "But a large footprint was discovered at the scene."

"Is that so? And it's well known that I have the largest feet of anyone on the property. Are those the grounds for any suspicion?"

"Not your feet, but perhaps your waterproof boots."

The gardener reached over to a corner of the shed, which was obscured in shade, and brought out a pair of rubber boots. "As you can see, these are impressively large, but when I'm working outside, I need them to be both waterproof and capable of taking a pair of thick woollen stockings."

"Indeed."

188

We sat together in silence for a moment. Then Isaac Sudbury looked Holmes square in the face. "Go ahead, Mr. Holmes. Ask the question you seem so eager to put to me."

"Very well," said Holmes. "On the evening before last, did you discover that one of your boots was missing?"

Isaac nodded. "I certainly did. One of them, at least. I thought that was a bit odd. If somebody was trying to steal my boots, why would they not take both of them?"

"Indeed. Was it the right foot or the left foot?"

"The right foot only."

"And when was it returned to you?"

"That's rather difficult to say exactly, but it was in its proper place the very next time I looked in here. Certainly by the following morning."

"That's all very useful information," said Holmes. "Thank you. But then there occurred a second break-in – yesterday evening, in fact – when somebody entered the same room, employing the same method of entry, and this time removed a certain quantity of cash."

"So I heard."

"A second footprint was discovered on that occasion. Much like the first time, or so I am told. Did you find your boot missing again last night?"

"Indeed I did. I thought it was extremely impertinent to violate a man's possessions for a second time."

"I think I'd feel exactly the same," said Holmes.

"But we both know the identity of the culprit – isn't that so, Mr. Holmes?"

"I'm still in the process of amassing information," replied Holmes. He rose to his feet. "Come, Watson. We must prepare for the family meeting later this evening."

The evening meal was generous and enjoyable, but a nervous tension remained in the air throughout. It felt as though some people would have liked to have the serious business of the evening dealt with as quickly as possible, while others wanted to delay it for as long as they were able. For some reason, Ambrose Bullingworth, Lady Leonora's nephew, needed to leave the table part-way through the meal, and was absent for quite some time. However, no one seemed to notice this, let alone show any concern over his absence.

The gathering of the household, immediately after the meal, involved just about everyone. Lady Leonora, her brother Hamilton Bullingworth, his son Ambrose, Annie Longtown the chambermaid, the housekeeper, and even Sudbury the gardener, now wearing a respectful pair of shoes.

With the evening lights now lit, and with the odours of the meal still lingering in the air, the room now held an air of expectation.

Holmes stood up in the middle of the gathering.

"Ladies and gentlemen," he began. "I hope not to detain you here very long, but this business needs to be dealt with before the end of this evening."

Most of those present appeared to agree – or at the very least, they remained silent.

"The theft of the bracelet, and then of the money, would seem to have been perpetrated by someone in the household. Someone here now."

A low muttering of surprise ran around the gathering.

"But who is it, Mr. Holmes?" demanded Lady Leonora.

"Let us clear one thing up immediately," said Holmes. "There was no break-in. When I examined it, the window showed no sign of having been forced open, and the foliage outside showed no indication whatsoever of having been disturbed by somebody climbing up. That means that the intruder entered the bedroom from the hallway, simply by the use of a key. In which case, I need to ask: Who had access to a key to your bedroom, Lady Leonora?"

"I suppose just about anybody could find a key if they really wanted to," replied Lady Leonora.

"Hmm. We must leave that for the moment. Let us now reconstruct in our imagination exactly what must have happened during the theft. Late on the first evening, the thief took one of the gardener's boots, dirty from his working outside, opened the door to the bedroom, and entered – and all of this during the hours of darkness."

"I have to admit," said Lady Leonora, "I heard nothing at all, even though I was asleep in the same room. The very thought that someone was there makes my blood run cold."

Holmes continued. "The thief then placed the muddy boot onto the carpet, where it left a soil-stained impression. Next, the thief took out the box of jewels, extracted the key, and used it to open the box. Then, having taken the bracelet out of the box and replaced it, the thief opened the window, in order to suggest that a burglary had occurred and that the thief had left that way. That person then left the room by the door, in order to return the boot to its owner."

"Diabolical," declared Hamilton Bullingworth.

"Later that following morning," continued Holmes, "the same thief took the bracelet along to the shop of Baldersby and Jones, the milliners in Regent Street. There, unobserved by the management, the burglar dropped it into the folds of an umbrella set amongst those being offered for sale."

190

"Who do we know who was in Regent Street that morning?" demanded Hamilton Bullingworth.

Holmes took a sheet of paper out of his inside pocket and opened it up.

"I have here a list of all the people who purchased items from Baldersby and Jones on that day."

"And?"

"The name of Ambrose Bullingworth is on the list."

All eyes turned to Lady Leonora's young nephew.

Ambrose seemed to turn a more ghastly shade of white.

"I didn't steal that bracelet!" he declared with passion. "I swear it!"

"Let us continue," said Holmes. "The second break-in, which again, as we have seen, wasn't a break-in at all, followed the pattern of the first. Once more, the thief had ready access to the bedroom, although this time her Ladyship had taken the precaution to sleep in one of the guest bedrooms. It seems that the burglar knew exactly where her Ladyship kept her cash, and removed forty pounds from her wallet."

"Forty?" demanded the chambermaid, before she could stop herself.

"It was your plan all along to take cash from her Ladyship," Holmes said, with his eyes fixing the chambermaid as with a gimlet. "Is that not so? You took the bracelet purely in order to distract attention away from your intended theft, which was that of taking the money the following night. You knew that Ambrose had gone to the milliner's shop in Regent Street, in order to purchase a pair of cufflinks, so you followed him shortly afterwards and dropped the bracelet into its hiding place, precisely in order to point the accusing finger at him. Your name is also on the list of clients given to me by the shop's owners, so there is no point in you trying to deny it."

"But I do deny it!" said the girl. "At least, I deny being the thief."

"No. This entire farrago has been your doing."

It was now girl's turn to grow unnaturally pale. With all eyes now riveted upon her, Annie Longtown found that her legs would no longer support her, and she slipped to her knees, covered her face with her hands, and began to sob.

"So," said Lady Leonora, her voice now turned cold as ice, "it really was you, Longtown."

"You knew that your privileged position would keep you quite safe from suspicion," said Holmes. "But as chambermaid, you had ready access to her Ladyship's jewels and cash anytime you wanted. The rest was simply drama, in order to cast suspicion onto other people. The muddy boot, which suggested the gardener was responsible, was ridiculous. You had probably already taken the bracelet earlier on the day of the first supposed burglary, and the money on the second occasion, so on neither night would you have had to risk alerting the sleeping Lady Leonora."

"I needed the money!" sobbed the girl desperately. "I needed it in order to pay for my mother's medical care! She is dreadfully sick."

"You could have come to me," said her Ladyship. "I would have helped you. You didn't have to steal my money."

"I wasn't thinking!"

"I imagine you were indeed thinking, Longtown," said Holmes in a tone which implied grave accusation. "The plan was well considered, though somewhat amateur in nature."

"But I took only *twenty* pounds," she said between sniffles.

The tense atmosphere remained, until Hamilton Bullingworth broke it with a cough.

"I think that is enough for one evening," he declared. "We all need to take this matter away, and think carefully about it."

"The facts are clear enough to me," said Lady Leonora. "But I suppose you're right. We will need a level head in order to decide what to do with this young woman. I suggest that we adjourn this meeting until tomorrow, immediately after luncheon. In the meantime, Inspector Lestrade, I would be obliged if you would take this young woman into custody and bring her back here tomorrow in order to learn my considered decision about her fate."

Holmes and I found a cabbie who knew us and was quite accustomed to our returning home at such an hour, and had become something of a friend to both of us.

The moment the cab stopped in Baker Street, Holmes and I disembarked, and immediately noticed a group of three thugs emerge from the shadows. They were brandishing heavy sticks as they slouched toward us.

During my time in the army, I had been trained in effective methods of self-protection, and I held my stick so as to be ready to fend off any attack. Holmes, I already knew, could prove himself to be an effective street-fighter, and held his own cane ready to defend himself. As we waited for the thugs to begin their assault, the cabbie joined us, holding a heavy stick. We were ready.

"What do you want?" demanded Holmes, as he addressed the thugs.

"We have a message for you, Mr. Holmes," said the leader of the gang.

"What is your message?"

"Tomorrow, you must remain at home, and spend your time nursing the bruises we're about to give you."

192

"Very well, do your worst," Holmes challenged him. "If you can."

This seemed to provoke the thugs into aggressive action. They stepped menacingly forward in order to confront us as we took up our position beneath a street gas-lamp.

Three against three. That seemed fair enough. And as we continued to exchange blows for several minutes, it was the thugs who seemed to fare the worst of any of us.

But one thing tipped the balance decisively to our advantage. The door to number 221b opened, and Mrs. Hudson emerged. Silhouetted against the inside light, she brandished her broom-handle and launched her own assault against our three attackers.

They hardly stood a chance, and one by one, they slunk away, snarling like wolves – until just one remained, pushed up against a wall by Holmes, who held his cane pressed up against the man's throat.

"I thought I recognized you," growled Holmes. "You are the one they call 'Green Harry'."

"So?" the man croaked.

"Now," growled Holmes, "tell us who sent you."

He relaxed the pressure on the man's windpipe, sufficiently to allow him to answer.

"It was this young toff," said the thug.

"Young toff?"

The man nodded.

"Do you know his name?"

"No."

"Did this young toff have a gap between his front teeth?"

"Yeah, that's him."

"Very well," said Holmes. "Now, take yourself away from here, if you wish to avoid something worse happening to you."

"Then I shall bid you a good night, Mr. Holmes," said Green Harry. "And if you come across that young toff, tell him the fee he offered to pay us was far too small to guarantee success."

"Or was it the appearance of our landlady? I admit she can be a bit fierce at times."

The following morning, with our few bruises bathed but still painful, we discovered that the rain had dried up and the clouds were dissipating.

Holmes set out early, on his own. His mission, or so he told me, was to consult with Lady Leonora ahead of the gathering there after luncheon. Exactly what he did that morning, he didn't confide to me, even when he returned, excited but in time to enjoy a rather frugal lunch.

It was with some reluctance on my part, but with a sparkle of expectation in Holmes's eyes, that we returned to the townhouse of the Bullingworth-Webb household early that afternoon. We found the same room somewhat more crowded than on the previous occasion.

Holmes took a centrally positioned chair while I stood in one corner, from where I had an excellent view of everyone present.

The miscreant chambermaid, Annie Longtown, who was now looking unkempt and crestfallen, was seated in the far corner, attended by a robust-looking uniformed policeman. Lady Leonora was seated in her upright but well-upholstered chair, clearly the one in charge of the proceedings which were to follow. Beside her stood a man in a black frock coat, whom I recognized as her husband, the Right Honorable Sir James Bullingworth-Webb. Hamilton Bullingworth stood beside him, with a face like thunder. Other members of the household had gathered as well. Many of the servants had come to either support or to gloat over Annie Longtown's predicament. Lestrade sat in a comfortable seat beside the window, looking impatient to be about his other work. And beside the doorway stood a man who was new to me. He was thick-set in body and, beneath his grizzled beard, his face displayed the ravages of all kinds of weather. A seafarer, beyond doubt.

Having satisfied himself that everyone had now assembled, Sir James drew the gathering to order.

"Ladies and gentlemen, thank you for coming together here this afternoon. Although I wasn't at the meeting yesterday, having had business at the House, I am cognisant of the matters which were discussed here. I think I had better hand things over to my wife, who has something to say concerning the so-called break-ins that have taken place here in recent days."

Lady Leonora looked around at the gathering.

"We need not go over the details of the events which discussed here yesterday evening," said Lady Leonora, "except to say that Mr. Holmes explained to us how the theft was made of my diamond bracelet, and of forty pounds, both from my own bedroom – a violation which I find it difficult to forgive. This criminal behaviour was perpetrated by a member of my own household: My personal chambermaid, Annie Longtown."

"She is here at your request, ma'am," said Lestrade, "awaiting your decision about prosecution."

"And that brings us to the next point in our investigation," said Holmes.

"Which is?"

"Since the chambermaid denied taking the full forty pounds, but admitted to taking only half of that amount, who was it that took the other twenty pounds?"

All eyes once more returned to Ambrose, who glanced from one face to another, and saw nothing in them to offer him any consolation. Then he turned back to Holmes and waited to hear what he had to tell the gathering."

Facing Ambrose, Holmes said, "Hiring those thugs to attack us last night was tantamount to a confession. They complained that you short-changed them for the job. No doubt they will want to talk the matter over with you – not that you were short of money," continued Holmes. "But you were hard-up earlier in the day. The cufflinks you bought from the shop in Regent Street were put onto your account, and not paid for immediately. You were perhaps anticipating a windfall in order to pay for them. Also, it is well known that you engage in betting on the outcome of horse races. You are in debt. When the opportunity arose, you took it. You were one of the first people to enter her Ladyship's room after the theft had been discovered. You saw the money lying there, and you imagined that when the thief was found, that person would pay the penalty for the full amount taken."

"This is a rum business, Mr. Holmes," said Lady Leonora.

"Indeed it is, ma'am," said Holmes. "Annie Longtown attempted to incriminate Ambrose, and Ambrose, in his turn, although he didn't know the identity of the thief at the time, tried to incriminate the chambermaid."

As Holmes sat back, his story told, a great sigh ran around all gathered there.

"So," concluded Hamilton Bullingworth, "both are guilty."

"That is evident," said Holmes.

"In which case," declared Lady Leonora, "I have now reached my decision."

Not a sound could be heard from anyone present, as the expectant pause appeared to foretell doom for the two young people now accused of theft.

Lady Leonora turned her acerbic stare onto the chambermaid. "I have decided that you, Longtown, will be dismissed from my service immediately. I shall not provide you with a reference, since that would require me to include mention of you as a thief. On the other hand, I will attempt to find you some kind of employment, however menial, through my own various contacts. I shall do this in order to allow you time to repay me the money you took. You will have twelve months in which to repay that twenty pounds you stole from me. If you fail to do that within the calendar year, then you will go to prison."

Annie blinked. "How can I raise that amount of money in so short a period of time?"

"Genuine hard work," replied Lady Leonora.

Annie hung her head and stuttered a muted word of gratitude.

"Now to Ambrose: You need to grow up, young man."

"Yes, Aunt Leonora."

"This man," she indicated the seafarer, "is Captain Kilberry. He is master of a steamship which plies between Southampton and the Far East. He is known to Mr. Holmes, who recommend him to me when we talked the matter through earlier today. I have decided that you will sign up to be a member of his ship's crew, for the next twelve months. During that time, you will save up as much as you can and, at the end of a year, you will return to me that twenty pounds you stole. Succeed, and the slate will be wiped clean, so to speak. Fail, and I shall ask that your case be brought to trial, and insist that you go straight to prison. Do you understand?"

"I understand," Ambrose croaked.

Captain Kilberry's face showed that he was looking forward to knocking this young man into shape.

"Very well," declared Sir James. "The matter is now settled. Is there any further business we need to deal with at the moment?"

Holmes spoke up. "Only that I shall shortly present you with a bill for my fees, together with expenses incurred during the conducting of this case. Also, that the young lady who was responsible for discovering your bracelet should receive a reward. I can give you her name and address."

Lady Leonora looked at her husband, who nodded his agreement.

"Very well, Mr. Holmes," she told him. "And thank you for your professional assistance in resolving this case."

With that, Sir James dismissed the gathering.

Lady Leonora's chambermaid, now discharged from her position, and her nephew, now thoroughly disgraced, both left in order to collect their personal effects in preparation for leaving the house – one to return home to face the endless struggle to pay her way in life and return the money she had stolen, the other to be taken in hand by Captain Kilberry. Which of the two I pitied the most, it was difficult to decide.

"I have to say," declared Holmes as the two of us ventured out into the fresh air, with the October sunshine lighting up the western sky, "that I am glad to be out of that place. What a household, eh? Hardly a brain cell among the entire family."

"I tend to agree with you," I told him.

"Now you can perhaps see the sort of trouble that purchasing one of those contraptions can bring you."

"An umbrella?"

"Certainly. In this case, it turned out to be a veritable Pandora's Box."

"Now it's your turn to exaggerate, Holmes."

He laughed.

"Just deserts for Ambrose, perhaps," I continued.

"Oh, Ambrose is just a young fool who needs to grow up."

"And what of Annie Longtown?"

"Now there is a woman with poison in her heart, Watson," said Holmes. "I'm quite sure she has stolen from her mistress before this occasion."

"Really? She seemed such in innocent young thing."

"You are easily taken in by female beauty."

"But concern about her sick mother must have been playing on her mind," I told him. "I would dearly like to offer her family the benefit of my medical assistance."

"Watson, my dear fellow," continued Holmes. "Spare her your sympathy. A reply to a telegram I sent to the Essex Police, near to where she lives, this morning elicited the information that that young woman's mother is both alive and in a healthy condition. At this moment, she is preparing to have a severe word with her daughter."

"Then she was lying in order to gain our pity, and to soften the pain of her retribution."

"I can assure that this present situation is nemesis as far as she is concerned. She is now reaping the consequences of her duplicity – not once, but on many occasions."

"On the other hand, it all seems to have worked out well for Agnes Smithercote," I said. "The young woman who found the bracelet in the first place."

"Or who unwittingly dropped it into the road."

"She is now in possession of a smart new umbrella, and is in line to receive a reward for discovering the diamond bracelet."

"And good luck to her," replied Holmes. "I hope that Fortune and her umbrella will keep her safe from the severest downpours for the rest of her life."

"I agree with that sentiment," I replied.

A moment later, Holmes brightened up as a thought occurred to him. "A concert of chamber music is being performed this evening at Covent Garden.," he declared. "Are you free to join me there?"

"It would certainly be a much-needed refreshment," I told him. "After all we've seen during the past day or two."

"Capital!" said Holmes. "But no more mention of umbrellas."

I smiled and kept my own counsel on the matter.

The Adventure of the
Siren's Tower
by Tracy J. Revels

The newspaper headline read *"Siren's Call Lures Boy to Fatal Plunge"*.

In breathless prose, the reporter told the tragic story of the death of Anthony Hudson, the young ward of Mr. Howard Walsh of Seaview House in Cornwall. On the first night of September, Walsh, a widower, was attending a wake while the other residents of his domicile – Young Hudson, along with Miss Sarah Walsh, and a small staff of servants – passed the evening in their usual occupations. Everyone retired between ten and eleven, with the master of the house returning at around two. No one was awakened during the night, but when the young man didn't come down for breakfast the following morning, a search commenced.

When Hudson wasn't found in the house or the stables, the alarm was raised, and neighbors were called upon to assist. The Reverend Mr. Alexander Honeydale, vicar of the parish, made the sad discovery at mid-morning. The boy's corpse was laid upon the rocks beneath an ancient structure known as the "Siren's Tower". There were no clues as to when or why Hudson had abandoned his room to go to the tower, and as the youngster had no enemies, his demise was ruled a death by misadventure. The report concluded with a legend that the tower was haunted by the ghost of a siren who had been captured by a sea captain and confined to the structure until she died. Her singing is heard on certain evenings, and many of the locals attributed the death to being enchanted by her melodies.

"What utter nonsense," Holmes said, and I realized, to my embarrassment, that I had been reading the story aloud as our train rattled across the countryside. "Tales of vindictive sirens may suffice to entertain the credulous, or the tourist, but I am neither."

"Then it is nothing more than it seems. The lad died by accident."

Holmes lit his pipe. "Perhaps. Let me provide you with more of the facts of the case, some of which were supplied to me by Inspector Banks."

I had met Inspector Charles Banks once before. A thin, wiry, nervous man, he had moved from the city to take up a more relaxed life in the Cornish countryside. I could only imagine how distressed he was to find a mystery on his doorstep.

"Walsh, as you know, was a textile magnate in Manchester until his retirement some ten years ago. Anthony Hudson was raised beside

Walsh's daughter, though never adopted. Mrs. Walsh died early this year, just as plans were being made for Miss Sarah's London debut. The girl is described as winsome, charming, and flirtatious, as well as an heiress of no small means. Banks describes Walsh as something of a domestic tyrant, though well-respected by the small staff of the house and viewed with deference in the village."

"Did Hudson attend boarding school?"

"He did until his foster mother died. He took her death very hard and wanted to remain with his family during the time of mourning. Banks summed him up as a proverbial bookworm, fond of fantasies and ancient legends. Hudson informed Banks he planned a career as an author, something his guardian clearly hoped to discourage." Holmes offered a sly smile. "Surely you understand Walsh's concern."

I snorted, ignoring the playful jab. "An imaginative chap like that might have been attracted to a tower with a legend," I said instead.

"Yes, but why in the depths of the night?"

"The headline refers to Hudson as a 'boy', but he was almost of age to depart for the university, not a child to be going out on foolish adventures."

Holmes puffed on his pipe. "Based on Banks' information, Anthony Hudson was smaller and slower than other lads his age – in many ways still a child despite his years. Still, one might concede a dare, or a prank, if the boy had brothers or friends. But Hudson was quiet and solitary, almost a hermit who rarely emerged from the family's library."

"You mentioned his grief over his foster mother's death. Has self-destruction been considered?"

Holmes reached into his coat and drew out an envelope, and from this he removed a cabinet-sized photograph.

"Considered, yes, but certain factors argue against it. The first is that no one in the household observed the boy to be exceptionally downcast or morbid in his mind in the days preceding his death. The second is this image." He passed it to me with a sharp nod. "Banks may be nervous and unfit for many aspects of detective work, but he has always been interested in the newest scientific methods of investigation. He had the presence of mind to send for a local with photographic equipment. Tell me what you make of this image."

I grimaced. I had attended Holmes at numerous murder scenes. Indeed, the very first case upon which I accompanied him began with a dead body. Enoch Drebber had died with twisted limbs and an animalistic grimace on his features. His horrible face still haunted me in my dreams. But to see a body preserved forever by the combination of light and shadow was somehow even more horrible. Though I understood its necessity, and the great advantage it provided to investigators like Holmes, it seemed a gruesome violation, an eternal indignity.

Anthony Hudson was lying upon his back, his arms and legs splayed widely, his eyes open yet glazed. He rested upon a rocky bed, and it was certain that the back of his skull had been shattered. I muttered that a fall was clearly the cause of death.

"The tower is perched on a cliff, looming some two-hundred feet above the rocks," Holmes stated. "It is unlikely that anyone could survive a fall. The highest tide that morning occurred at nine, but the rocks rise above the water, and the position of the body was such that it wasn't washed from the stones but only dampened by the spray. Tell me, Watson, what else do you observe?"

I forced myself to reconsider the unpleasant image. "The boy is rather small of frame, but doesn't seem to be malnourished. He is dressed in shirt, belt, trousers, and a short jacket. He appears to be barefoot and – What is this dangling from one ear?"

"Spectacles," Holmes said. "The youth was almost blind without them."

"So, what is it in this image that argues against suicide?"

"Several details, but I am drawn especially to the glasses. It is well known that most individuals who jump from great heights, if they wear spectacles, remove them before committing to the abyss. Ah, we seem to be arriving."

Indeed, the train was pulling into the station. We disembarked and were greeted on the platform by Holmes's friend. Banks was a tall, thin man who seemed to sway and bend in the breeze like a willow. The hand I shook was skeletal, but his dark eyes were bright and quick.

"So good of you to come," Banks said, as we moved to our carriage. "How I wished you had been here on that tragic morning a week ago. The poor boy is buried, the family has all been questioned, and Walsh has accepted the verdict that it was a terrible accident brought about by his curiosity. But I am unsatisfied. I feel there is something that I have missed."

"And you don't believe in a siren's song?" I asked. Banks barked a laugh.

"It is amazing what some of the locals will accept. Let us go to Seaview House first. I'll warn you that Walsh will not be enthusiastic about the interview. He feels enough has been done, and we should allow the boy to rest in peace. However, I must put an uncomfortable question to him."

"What is that?" Holmes asked. Banks replied with a cheeky grin.

200

"You aren't the only detective to have secrets, Mr. Holmes. But you shall see! And to be frank, I am glad to have both of you along, as Walsh's temper is formidable."

I struggled not to allow Holmes to witness my amusement, and my friend took the inspector's comments in stride. An hour later, we reached a manorial pile that looked over the turbulent ocean. As we approached, Banks pointed out the Siren's Tower, a circular construct of rough gray stones only a quarter-mile south of the family home, and easily accessible by a graveled path.

"Was it used by the children?' Holmes asked. "It seems an ideal spot for watching ships or playing pirate games."

"Walsh told me that his youngsters were forbidden to go there. The tower has but one chamber at the top, and the wooden stairs inside are old and rotting. There was an accident some years ago – Miss Sarah's leg was broken – and the children haven't been there since."

"That Walsh is aware of," Holmes said.

"He keeps the door to the tower locked."

Holmes lifted a brow. "Does he wear the key on his belt? Otherwise, I would wager that his children have been inside. Was the door found locked on the morning Hudson's body was discovered?"

Banks looked embarrassed. "No, come to think of it, the door was open. I climbed the stairs and investigated the little room at the top, but there was no blood or any clue besides some old blankets and a half-emptied bottle of wine. We have many tramps this time of year. I'm sure one of them left the items behind."

Holmes could no longer bury his smile. "A half-emptied bottle is also a half-filled one, Banks. You have exceptional transients in your neighborhood, to abandon a bottle that isn't drained of its contents!"

Our conveyance drew up at the door of a great red-brick house, some three stories tall and thickly covered with creeping vines that gave it a charming, rustic look. Just as we descended from the carriage, the building's portal flew open and a silk hat went flying, followed by a leather satchel, which spilled papers onto the ground. A moment later, the chapeau's owner was similarly ejected, shoved onto the portico to the sound of a deep voice shouting, "And stay out!"

"We seem to have fortuitous timing," Holmes whispered to me as the young man straightened his attire. He wore a checkered coat along with dark, wine-colored trousers, and carried a heavy walking stick with a polished silver griffon's head for a knob. He was perhaps twenty-five years of age, broad-shouldered and handsome, though the web of broken vessels in his nose hinted at an unhealthy fondness for drink. He gathered up his hat, clearly embarrassed to have his rough dismissal witnessed.

201

"Good morning, Freddy," Banks said. "I take it Mr. Walsh isn't in the mood for company?"

"Indeed not, Inspector." The young man straightened the crushed brim of his hat. "I was merely paying a social call, to see how he and Miss Sarah were faring in their sad bereavement. Please don't bother yourself, sir," he said, as Holmes stooped to gather up the papers, before the wind could whisk them away. "I shall not delay you – but do consider yourself warned."

"How goes the insurance business?" Holmes asked. The young man took a startled step backwards. Holmes merely motioned to the papers in his hand.

"Oh. Oh, yes! You seem rather a wizard, sir, to draw a stranger's employment out of thin air like that. Frederick Phillips, of the Great Northumberland Agency, at your service. All of Cornwall is my territory, and business isn't booming. Well, good luck, and I hope I shall see you at the pub soon, Inspector."

"Finest darts player I've ever met," Banks said, as the young man strolled down the lane. "Quite companionable. He visits the village twice a month, is popular with the lads. Well, now, let us beard the grouchy old lion in his den."

A grim, elderly butler admitted us to his master's study, where the walls were covered with industrial drawings. Walsh was a stout, balding man with double chin and a pair of piggish eyes. He grunted at Bank's attempts at pleasantries.

"I tell you, the matter is settled, and we shall grieve for Anthony in our own way. Banks, you shouldn't have bothered these gentlemen."

Holmes's gaze fell upon a portrait over a small fireplace. It showed Walsh, a lovely woman in a summer's dress, and a small, golden-haired girl. Holmes gestured to it as he spoke.

"At what age did young Hudson become your ward?"

"When he was ten. His parents were both killed in a house fire, but Anthony was visiting a chum that night, and thus escaped. James Hudson had served me faithfully as my chief bookkeeper, and Margaret Hudson was a distant cousin of mine. There being no other family to claim Anthony, I took the child in."

"Your wife was agreeable to the arrangement?"

"What does it matter?" the man spat. "She was my wife, she had to obey me, and of course Anthony spent most of his time at school. Agnes had her hands full, planning things for Sarah." Walsh abruptly slammed his hand to the blotter. "That is all you need to know. I dislike personal questions."

202

"But I must put another one to you," Banks said. "Where were you on the night Anthony Hudson died? Please don't insult me by repeating your lie of being at Edgar Sullivan's wake all night, for I have spoken with his widow."

"She is a grief-stricken woman!" Walsh snapped. "Her mind is addled!"

"What of the minds of five men who sat with the corpse, and said you left at eleven, before the final round of drinks were served?"

Walsh had risen from behind his desk, his fat hand clutching the top of a marble bust of Henry VIII. I felt certain he would fling it at the inspector, but at the mention of other witnesses, he abruptly dropped back into his chair.

"I would prefer not to say."

Holmes turned from where he had been walking around the room, studying the various decorations. "I would recommend you make a clean breast of it, Mr. Walsh. Otherwise, one might suspect you climbed the tower and pushed your ward from its window."

"That's absurd!"

"Think of the scandal," Holmes added, "when the inspector is obliged to bring you in publicly for further questioning."

Banks struck an almost comically resolute pose and removed a pair of handcuffs from his pocket. Walsh threw out his arms.

"No. No, by God. I'll tell you but . . . Please, this must remain between us. As gentlemen."

"Mrs. Cleeves is a notorious widow," Banks said as we exited the study. "Said to have been the keeper of – Ah – Ahem! – *disreputable* house in Manchester, near the factory where Walsh's fortune was made. Moved here the same year that he did. Most curious!"

"Interview her immediately," Holmes advised, "before Walsh has time to send a message. She will dissemble, perhaps, but I'm certain you can find a method for encouraging veracity."

"Well, there is that matter of her bulldog, which bit an elderly neighbor. I think a promise of no prosecution for her canine would guarantee the truth from her lips." Banks rubbed his hands together eagerly. "I shall return as quickly as possible. You're in no danger here, I think. Talley-ho!"

Banks galloped away. Holmes consulted with the butler, who showed us to Hudson's bedroom. The chamber was small, but every shelf was lined with books, and more volumes were stacked in the corners and about the bed. A small desk was covered with notebooks and crude drawings. At Holmes's request, I looked through them, taking in their gist.

"He was writing a fantastic story," I said. "All about knights, maidens, and dragons." I nodded at an outline of an adventure and a family tree which included elves, ogres, and fairies. "How sad to think this fable will never be shared with the world. Holmes – What's wrong?"

My friend rose from his prone position, where he had been looking under the bed. He returned to the single armoire, scowling down at the bottom.

"Where are his boots?" Holmes muttered. "Anthony Hudson was barefoot when he was discovered. The path to the tower is graveled and harsh and – " Here he removed the photograph, considering it again. "There are no stockings. It is true that when a body falls from a height, its attire is often startlingly disarrayed, but for both shoes and stockings to vanish seems impossible. I wish I had been there to examine the soles of his feet and his toenails."

"Toenails?"

"They would have told us a great deal. Come, Watson, let us have a few words with the staff."

The servants – the cook, housekeeper, butler, and two maids – were soon gathered into the kitchen. It was a small household for such a wealthy man, and I quickly drew the impression that Walsh was something of a miser. It was also clear that the staff genuinely grieved for their lost boy.

"He was no trouble," the housekeeper proclaimed. "Why, my Johnny at that age was the Devil's own imp! But Master Anthony preferred to keep at his books, and he never so much as broke a vase or stole a cookie."

"He lived in a dream world," the solemn butler intoned. "He imaged himself as a Percival or Lancelot reborn. He once told me he hoped to grow into a perfect knight."

Holmes thanked the servants and dismissed them. But as they filed past, he tapped the arm of the youngest maid, asking her to remain.

"What is your name?" Holmes asked, his voice taking on the kind, soft whisper of a priest.

"Havers, sir. Louise Havers."

"You are of an age with Master Anthony, are you not? Perhaps you can prove insight that your elders lack."

He gestured for her to be seated. I noticed how she shivered as she perched upon the wooden bench. She had remained silent while the others described the boy, but now I noted the shiny quality of her face and understood that she had been wiping away tears.

"I don't know what I can add, sir."

"Was he your friend?"

"I – I . . . ." She was clearly struggling with her words, weighing sentiment against the demands of propriety. "He was kind to me. He would

204

read his stories aloud, and he promised that he would name a princess for me when he wrote his epic."

Holmes smiled gently. "It sounds as if the boy was perhaps a bit in love with you."

The girl blushed. "Oh, no, sir! That wouldn't be proper. But he was always eager to protect me, especially when Edgar, the stableboy, was forward. I will never forget when Edgar tried to steal a kiss from me and Anthony set upon him with a thin little stick, as if it were a mighty sword. Edgar trounced him, but Master Anthony wore his black eye like a badge of honor."

"And what became of Edgar after the affair?"

"He was sent away, sir. I believe he works for Mr. McGruder now."

"And when was this fight?"

"Just a month after the mistress was buried."

Holmes thanked the girl and dismissed her. He rose, frowning.

"Let us venture to the scene of the tragedy, Watson, and see what it has to tell us."

Collecting our coats from the butler, we started down the gravel path. The sky had grown cloudy, and the wind was rising. We noted that two travelers were coming abreast along the narrow lane. Walsh was driving away from the house in a dogcart, no doubt heading to the village. He was met by a beautiful girl riding sidesaddle on a spotted pony. The wind and the roar of the ocean prevented us from hearing their words, but we paused to watch an intriguing pantomime.

Walsh halted his nag and hopped down from the cart, waddling like a drunken toad. He waved his fist as he approached the lady, who was clad in a frothy blue-and-silver frock and crowned with a roguish bonnet. The girl counted his anger with a show of her own displeasure, waving her riding crop in Walsh's face. At last, with a great flailing of arms, he seemed to win the day, and the girl whipped her pony into a gallop toward the house. Walsh climbed back into the dogcart. With a savage snap of the reins, he drove on.

"His daughter?" I asked.

"It could be no other," Holmes said. "Did you note her attire?"

"It appeared to be quite the smart ensemble."

Holmes lifted one eyebrow. "Indeed, it is very fashionable – but not for a young lady still in deep mourning for two members of her immediate family. It appears that neither her mother nor her foster brother's death has affected her to any degree. But let us file that observation away for the moment."

We resumed our stroll and in a matter of minutes reached the infamous tower. The antique door remained unlocked. A wooden staircase twirled upward along the wall.

"Dare we risk the ascent?" Holmes asked. "Ah – What is this?"

"Footprints?" I asked.

"No." Holmes struck a match and held it close to the wall, plucking an object free from the masonry. "Something more intriguing."

He held out a black ribbon.

"Neither faded nor soiled by the elements. I doubt it belongs to the ghost of the siren."

Cautiously, we began to climb the stairs. More than once my stomach sank when I heard an ominous creak. Fortunately, we reached a landing, and a door that opened into a small chamber. Perhaps it had once been a medieval lady's solar, for the long, high, glass-less window gave a fine view of the sea beyond. Several old blankets were piled against the opposite wall, as well as a half-consumed bottle of wine.

"Clearly this is a place of rendezvous," Holmes said. He took out his lens and examined the ledge of the window, then leaned through it, looking down toward the rocks where the boy had met his demise. He reached out, feeling the uneven stones of the tower's construction. "Much becomes clear. You see it, of course?"

I sighed. "I fear that I do. What a shame. I thought she was such a nice girl."

Holmes turned. "You did?"

"Yes. The maid seemed quite sincere in her affection for the boy."

"Ah. And what do you believe happened here?"

I pointed toward the blanket and the bottle. "Isn't it obvious? Anthony Hudson was lured here with romantic promises and then – Holmes?"

My friend had hurried past me to leave the room. Shaking my head at this sudden, baffling action, I followed him, fighting alarm when he bolted down the stairs. He raced through the door while I was still gingerly plucking my way along the aged boards. By the time I exited the tower, Holmes was deep in conversation with a scrawny, red-faced lad who was herding sheep with the assistance of a black-and-white dog.

"Yes, sir, I used to work for Mr. Walsh," the boy was saying as I approached. "But I got in trouble for fighting with his ward. It was a silly thing, sir. He thought I had no right to kiss Miss Louise, after I'd decided to make her my sweetheart. Gave him a shiner, I did, but I got sacked for it."

"And how do you like your new situation?" Holmes asked, as seriously as if he was addressing a Lord or M.P.

"I like it fine, though I wish Mr. McGruder would give me new a new coat." The boy shivered, drawing his canvas jacket closer on his chest. He had clearly outgrown it. His boney wrists protruded from the worn cuffs. "It gets cold out here, taking care of the sheep."

"But I see your master has given you a fine pair of boots," Holmes noted.

"Ha! I found these."

"Indeed? Where?"

The boy pointed to some bushes, across the lane and a quarter-mile down from the tower.

"I found them when everyone else was out looking for Anthony."

"They appear too tight and uncomfortable. Would you exchange them for a sovereign to purchase a better pair?"

"And how!" The lad ran off barefoot with his dog and his sheep. I took the boots that Holmes held out to me.

"These are surely Hudson's."

"Indeed. But does it seem likely that the boy, even if he intended a daring climb of the tower, would have abandoned his shoes so far from it, on the other side of the structure, instead of closer to his dwelling?"

"But . . . Our theory – "

"*Your* theory, Watson. I didn't claim it was a valid one. Let us return to Seaview House and see what Inspector Banks has learned. I see by the fresh ruts in the lane that he has arrived in our absence."

I confess that I followed Holmes with less than my usual enthusiasm. I am a patient man, and aware that my intellectual abilities paled in comparison to his. Yet we had heard the same things – the maid's confession of Hudson's attraction to her, her admission of the stableboy's jealous rage, and even the lad's boast of injuring Hudson. Clearly there had been an arrangement of sorts between the stable boy and the maid, and to get revenge for the boy's sacking, she had lured young Hudson to the tower with the promise of a reward for his gallantry – the black ribbon confirmed her status as an accomplice. The stableboy had been waiting in the chamber, perhaps hidden in the blankets, and he had thrust young Hudson from the window to his death, then claimed Hudson's boots as a perverse trophy.

Inspector Banks was indeed waiting for us in the parlor, where the duplicitous maid was laying out afternoon tea. I found it difficult to look at her without feeling enraged. Holmes, however, spoke gently to her and inquired whether Miss Sarah might join us for refreshments. She nodded and hurried off to fetch her mistress.

"Quickly, Banks, before the lady arrives – What did you find?"

"Mrs. Cleves confirmed that Mr. Walsh spent the late evening with her, departing for Seaview House around one-thirty in the morning. She also claims that they spent most of that time engaged in – Ahem! – *Bible study.*"

Holmes laughed. "I think we may discount the second claim and focus upon the first."

Banks waved a hand. "She did tell me one interesting bit of gossip: She said that Walsh was quite wroth with his daughter, who is reluctant to go through with her society debut."

"Did she say why?" I asked, but before Banks could answer, Holmes shushed us. A moment later, Miss Walsh entered the room.

I noted immediately that she had changed from her fashionable riding attire into a day dress of black crepe, dull and lifeless, as befitted the deep stage of mourning. Its only ornamentation was a cameo brooch of Aphrodite, which had been pinned-on upside down. The girl's splendid blonde hair likewise seemed hastily and incompletely arranged, leaking pins, with tendrils slipping free from the coiled braids about her head.

"I am sorry Father isn't here," she said, her voice cold and formal. "I understand, Inspector, that you are unsatisfied that Anthony met his end by an accident."

The girl's icy demeanor clearly rattled the former Scotland Yard man. Holmes stepped forward and took charge.

"There are a few aspects that trouble us, Miss Walsh. Once they are made clear, your beloved brother will surely rest in peace."

"He wasn't my brother," the girl corrected as she took a seat, her proud head held high. "He was merely Father's ward. Father only took him in because his parents died and Father had always hoped for a boy, but there was only me." She bit her lip suddenly, but she couldn't prevent the sudden stain of anger and resentment that colored her cheeks. "Anthony spent most of his time at school, and he was only fifteen, whereas I am nineteen. We were never particularly close."

"But surely you knew something of his character?"

Miss Walsh drew her arms tightly around her. "I knew that he was silly and fanciful, obsessed with stories of knights and dragons. Why, one evening he came down to the table all dressed in a surcoat and cape that Louise had crafted for him, like he was going to a fancy-dress ball. There was a row that night. Father marched him upstairs and thrashed him – told him to get it out of his head that he would be an author. Father told Anthony he would go to Oxford and become a lawyer, or Father would disinherit him."

208

"Yet your father valued him enough to take out a large life insurance policy on him, one that should go quite a way to financing your London debut," Holmes said.

This revelation crashed like a thunderbolt. Banks dropped his teacup onto the floor, and the girl shot from the chair, her little hands clenched into fists.

"That is a lie! Father would never do such a thing. And Freddy would have told me if he had!"

"But surely your debut – !"

"I don't care about it! I never have! Mother was forcing it on me and that is why I – " She caught her breath, then gathered her skirts, and fled the room. Banks retrieved his teacup and grimaced.

"Was it really necessary to upset the girl, Holmes?"

"I fear that it was."

"How did you know about the insurance policy?" I asked.

"There is no policy, at least to my knowledge. I lied."

"Why?" Banks asked.

"To test a theory. Inspector, if you would be so kind, I am famished, and these teacakes are hardly more than a cookie's worth of nourishment. Perhaps you will be so good to join Watson and myself for an early supper in the village?'

Banks – like most lean men – was enthusiastic about the prospect of food. We abandoned Seaview House and set out for the village. Holmes edged forward, tapping Banks on the shoulder as he drove.

"Which pub does Mr. Phillips favor?"

"That would be The Hart and Hare."

"Excellent. Let us eat there, and perhaps, if the young man is still in the village, he will join us. He appears to be a delightful fellow, and excellent company."

By good fortune, we found Phillips at the pub, surrounded by several local lads, and with a commanding lead in his game of darts. As the loser bought Phillips a pint, Holmes drew Banks off to one side and whispered in his ear. The inspector quivered and shook his head, but Holmes nodded sternly. At last, Banks went to the bartender and made a request. A minute later, we were shown to a private room, and soon afterward, Phillips joined us.

"Inspector! And I see you've brought you friends. I hope old Walsh wasn't as rude to you as he was to me."

Holmes pushed out a chair with his foot. "Join us. Banks tells me this establishment makes the best pasty in all of Cornwall."

"Ah, that is true. And you must try some *yarg* as well! But nothing is better than the beer."

The cheerful chap settled in, and for almost an hour he regaled us with amusing stories and local gossip. Then, just as we finished our meal, he looked to his watch.

"Ah, I must be going. If I miss my train, there shall be Hell to pay with my – *What?*"

This exclamation was inspired by the clicking of a handcuff to his right wrist. The mate to the cuff was attached to Bank's left arm.

"I'm sorry, Freddy . . . but you are under arrest for the murder of Anthony Hudson."

At first, I thought the larger man might bolt for the door, dragging Banks' willowy frame behind him. But our friend seized Phillips's shoulder and held him in place with surprising firmness.

"Surely you're joking?" the young man croaked.

"No, Freddy," Banks said. "Mr. Holmes has told me what happened, as if he were there watching it. How you and Miss Walsh were in the tower, and you threw Anthony Hudson through the window."

"No, that isn't how it happened! Anthony was on the other side of the open window. He spied on us! It was – !"

A sudden silence fell over the table. Phillips, once so merry, appeared shattered. Holmes leaned forward.

"If you tell the truth, we can help you. But if you lie, or feign ignorance, it will not go well, and we cannot advocate on your behalf."

"You know so much already, if you know about *her*," Phillips sighed. "Very well, I shall tell you the thing we promised to keep secret, to take to our graves. But you must believe me that it was an accident. I never meant the poor lad any harm, and neither did Sarah. It was horrible when it happened. Sarah fainted right away, and I thought I would have to carry her down the stairs. But then I slipped more wine over her lips, and she revived. It was she who said I must throw the boots away and never tell anyone but . . . No, no, I'm getting ahead of myself.

"I've loved Sarah from the first time I saw her, on the day of her sixteenth birthday. I visited Seaview House often, always on the pretense of some policy or investment, but once the old man began to understand that my interest was in his daughter, he became curt with me. Mrs. Walsh was worse. She was determined that Sarah would attend all the balls and parties in London and marry some lord or earl. How could a poor man like me compete with that?

"But Sarah loved me. She followed me out to the stable and kissed me on the lips and pledged herself to me – that she would never allow any of those fancy toffs to turn her head, and that even if her parents threw her out without a penny, she would marry me when she came of age. That thought kept me warm on many a cold night, and I even refused commissions that might have advanced me in my field, so that I could always return to Seaview House and pay my compliments to my darling.

"It was the week after New Year's when Mrs. Walsh met me in the foyer. She was a proud and haughty woman, sirs, as cold as ice in her ways. She warned that if I ever crossed the threshold of Seaview House again, she would set the mastiff on me. I caught a glimpse of Sarah in the hallway behind her mother, her face all swollen from weeping. Anthony, home on a school holiday, was lurking on the staircase with a paper sword in his hands. I begged to put my case before Mr. Walsh, but the lady had the butler toss me out. It would have been enough to deter any other man . . . and I admit that as I travelled back to London, I pondered whether it might be better just to break it off with Sarah. Her parents clearly had plans for her. But a few days later, a telegram arrived for me, sent by one of my friends in the village. Mrs. Walsh had perished from apoplexy, only hours after my departure!

"With her mother dead, Sarah assured me we had only to wait until the year of mourning had passed before we could wed. Mr. Walsh had concerns of his own and he was often away from home. Sarah and I began to meet secretly, in the stables and, more often, at the tower, for she had acquired a copy of its key. But it was hard to even steal a kiss, for that wretched Anthony followed her, often muttering about how no 'fair maiden' should keep company with a 'rogue'. Once I tried to silence him with shillings, but he threw the 'filthy loot' back at me.

"It was a week ago that Sarah wrote to me in a panic. Her Father was determined to move forward with her debut. She would be sent to spend the season with a maiden aunt in London, a chaperone who would watch her like the proverbial hawk. Sarah begged me to come to the Siren's Tower the next night, to bring wine and warm blankets, and then she would . . . ."

The man's face turned crimson.

"She promised she would give herself to me. She swore that only by getting her with child could we prevent her being sold off like cattle to some nobleman. She no longer cared for her reputation or her father's love. She only wanted me.

"And so, at midnight, I waited in the upper room of the tower. She came as promised, clad in the mourning dress that she hated, but which made her almost invisible on that moonless, rainy night. We lit a lantern and drank together, and she had just loosened her dress and then – She screamed! I swung around. There was Anthony, perched in the window. I can still see his bare toes gripping the ledge, and the wind whipping his hair. The moon came out at just that moment, and the light on his spectacles made him look like a monstrous owl. I yelled an oath at him, and was climbing up on my knees, when – Sir, you must believe me, I never laid a hand on him! But my shout startled Anthony, and he lost his grip and toppled backwards! I ran to the window and looked down and found his lifeless body on the rocks, with the sea spreading out just below him. Sarah flew up next to me, and when she saw it, she fainted."

Holmes had listened with rapt attention. Now he tapped a finger on the table.

"Yet you were able to quickly revive her. What happened next?"

"We came down from the tower room, praying that maybe we were wrong, that he had only been injured. I climbed out onto the rocks with my lantern and saw that he was dead. When I came back, Sarah had found his boots and stockings, where he had taken them off beside the door. We had locked the door behind us, so the only way he could spy was to climb the tower. You've seen it, sir. It wouldn't be a hard thing for an agile little fellow to do, though he shouldn't have done it at night, in the wind and rain. Sarah bid me to get rid of his boots and socks, and to say nothing. She knew she could return home without incident, and no one had known that I was on the property. She kissed me and ran away. I thought to go up and get the wine and the blankets, but the rain was falling harder, and the thunder had begun to rumble, so I lost my nerve. There was nothing on either the blankets or the bottle to identify us. I carried the boots to a thicket, almost a quarter-mile away, and cast them into the bushes. It was only after I returned to my hotel room that I found Anthony's stockings wadded in my pocket. I burned them in the grate."

"You would have done better to have come to me from the start," Banks scolded. Phillips dropped his head.

"Yes, but Sarah's honor was at stake. And I swear upon all that is holy, it was an accident."

Banks scowled, then looked to Holmes, clearly hoping for instruction. My friend remained thoughtful for some moments. At last, he removed his watch from his pocket and opened it.

"I believe you still have ten minutes to make your train, Mr. Phillips. However, before Inspector Banks removes the handcuffs, I would like to offer you some advice."

"Sir?" the young man breathed, his eyes going wide with astonishment.

"You could be remanded to custody for failure to report a death. It was cruel and callous of you to abandon that boy on the rocks, knowing full well it would be hours before any search would commence, and that his body lay exposed to the elements. Even if you cared nothing for him, there were others who did, very deeply."

Phillips hung his head and nodded, shame was obvious upon his features.

"However, as you have told me the truth, I am urging Inspector Banks to say no more, and not to pursue a prosecution which would only serve to ruin your future, as well as bring disgrace upon the young lady. I doubt that her foster brother, who put so much stock in defending her honor – however misguided his efforts – would want her to suffer for a foolish decision."

Banks began to fish the key from his pocket. Holmes leaned over, placing his hand on Phillips's sleeve.

"Miss Sarah is best forgotten. Leave her to God and heed this warning: Death has been a far too convenient visitor in her home. I am further advising Inspector Banks to seek a warrant to have the body of Mrs. Walsh exhumed and tested for poison. Even if it is found that the lady perished of perfectly natural causes, you would do better not to tie yourself to a woman incapable of tears and sorrow upon the loss of a parent, and who thinks immediately of how to hide an accidental death rather than report it. The most beautiful snakes are often the most venomous."

Phillips turned ashen. Banks unlocked the handcuffs and the young man departed with a tearful, whispered thanks. Banks looked back to Holmes.

"What makes you so certain he was telling the truth?"

"The boots," Holmes said. "If Hudson had merely followed them up the stairs, and been hurled from the window, his boots would have been on his feet. Their absence proved he climbed the tower of his own volition. Oh course, it is possible that he entered the chamber after his successful climb and was purposefully cast out the window, but Phillips's entire character argues against it. Had the young lady been alone, however, I have no doubt she would have murdered the boy in cold blood."

Banks turned even paler. "You truly believe Sarah Walsh killed her own mother, to retain Freddy?"

"I do. Unfortunately, the passage of a year would make finding proof difficult, and obviously the family will object to such a procedure. Perhaps the threat of it will provoke a confession, though I wouldn't hold out much hope. From what I have seen, the young woman is made of much sterner stuff than her lover."

There was a strange epilogue to the story. Banks' request for an exhumation was denied. Miss Walsh went to London, where her debut was delayed due to the death of her aunt. We learned through Banks that Miss

Walsh returned to Cornwall after her father married Mrs. Cleeves, the "notorious" widow who had provided his alibi. Banks wrote that the two women bitterly despised each other, and the house was so unpleasant all the servants had departed.

Holmes shook his head as he read the letter. "At least Phillips had the good sense to take my advice."

Five years afterward, Inspector Banks retired, and Holmes and I travelled to Cornwall to join the little jollification held at The Hart and Hare in his honor. Midway through the raucous toasts and loud laughter, I noticed my friend had disappeared. I slipped through the back door of the pub and spotted him walking down the lane. Intrigued, I followed him to the graveyard of the small church and saw him pause to place a flower upon a stone. After a respectful moment, I joined him.

"There was nothing but a wooden cross here before," Holmes whispered. "I doubt the Walsh family has even noticed the addition. It was Banks's idea, and, I think, a good one."

On the marble was a simple inscription:

Anthony Hudson
Rest well, Little Knight

Lightning Strikes Once
by Kevin P. Thornton

It was a Saturday in early spring, the last one of April, as I recall. I used to think of Saturday as the finest day of the week, the glorious first day of a weekend that, in my younger days, would have involved all manner of sports, adventure, and carousing. I had none of those planned for today, save maybe a walk to Lord's Cricket Ground to see how Middlesex was faring against the visitors from Gloucestershire. There were some promising young bats in the local XI and, with the Australians landing in a month, it would be nice to get an early look at the new talent. I went to the table to refresh my cup of tea, stepping over and around Sherlock Holmes, his armchair, and his extended legs.

"On your way back from the cricket, Watson, would you stop at the news agency and see if any of the Glasgow dailies are in? There's a story about a Highland theft ring upon which I was recently consulted, and I expect imminent arrests and a substantial reward."

I stopped and looked at him, then around me. There wasn't any form of appreciable clue as to what I had been thinking as to where I was going. "Devil take it, Holmes! How on earth could you possibly have known what I was planning for the day? I said nothing and did nothing, yet it is as if you read my mind!"

"You are right in that you said nothing, but as to your actions, they were enough to confirm what would have been an educated deduction anyway. First it is the weekend. You have your less-grumpy look about you, and I know, because your medical bag isn't ready at the door, that you aren't seeing patients today, so you are free to indulge your whims. It is April, always a time when that ridiculous sport occupies much of your waking thoughts. It puts a skip in your step, and there are times when you are so giddy with the Rites of Spring that you swing a pretend bat in your hand, just like you did as you went to fetch your tea. Even one such as I, with no interest in the game, could easily conclude that you were walking down the road to the grounds to watch grown men play at a ridiculous pastime."

"'Ridiculous'? Come, come! It is the grandest game in the world – the one that makes us English."

"Then why do the Australians seem to have the upper hand most of the time in this most-English of pastimes? Did you know that Wellington defeated Napoleon in one day at the Battle of Waterloo, setting the course of European history for the next fifty years. *One* day, Watson. Your feeble MCC can't even select an Eleven to beat the Antipodean colonials over *three*? It is a ridiculous sport, and the country would be better off if we taught logic in the schools instead of timewasters."

I wasn't permitted a riposte, as there was a loud "*Ahem!*" from the door.

"Begging your respective pardons," said Mrs. Hudson, "but there is a gentleman who wonders if he could take some of your time, Mister Holmes." She handed over a business card to Holmes, and I glanced over his shoulder:

Tobias Blythe, Esquire,
Solicitor
Blythe, Blythe, and Blythe
Number 17, The High Street
Guildford, Surrey

I welcomed him across our threshold. He was a short, spare man who seemed very precise in his movements and his dress. "And which Blythe are you?" I asked in an attempt at levity that fell flat, somewhere between Holmes's impatience and the legal man's insipidity.

"I am the middle Blythe," he said, *sans* irony. "The first one is my father, Sir Babbington Blythe, and the last named is my son."

"Tobias Babbington Blythe, mayhap?" speculated Holmes.

"That is correct. You have heard of him, Mister Holmes?"

"I have not, Mister Blythe, but I am a detective. It wasn't hard to deduce that such an honourable traditionalist such as yourself wouldn't stray too far in your first-born's Christian names."

Blythe seemed pleased by this.

"Now," said Holmes, "please explain what is so urgent that a man such as yourself would chance upon my offices unannounced. You don't seem to be one to act on whim. What is the urgency in your need to consult with me?"

Blythe paused and looked around as if in a foreign land. I doubt if he had done four spontaneous things in his entire life, and for a moment he looked like someone who might bolt at the slightest sound. But the Blythe line was made of sterner stuff, and the moment passed. He gathered himself, looked Holmes in the eye, and said, "Mister Holmes, I am here to ask you to stop a murder."

"Well, Mister Blythe, you certainly have my attention."

"Most of my work," Blythe began, "is in wills, codicils, landholdings, and inheritances. Even though I come to you with such a weighty matter, I don't normally involve myself in criminal law."

"I harboured no such thought," said Holmes.

"I am not ashamed to tell you that I make a good living. I work hard, and I do diligent, scrupulous work for my clients. *Scrupulous*," he repeated. "One of my clients is a landowner of some means who, for various reasons unimportant to this tale, has farmlands in Surrey that he has allowed to lie fallow. I was tasked some time ago to find tenants if I could, and make some profit from the land. Not knowing all I now know, I thought it would be an easy task. It appeared to be good land. Two farms of equivalent size with buildings for grain and farm animals, and sufficient cottages for farmhands. Yet no one responded to my advertisements in *The Surrey Gazette*, and of the several farmers I knew, none were interested in any offer I made. One went so far as to say that the farms, which sat on and about Hantwich Hill, were cursed, and no good for farming."

Blythe paused, as if this revelation was deserving of some reaction. Sherlock Holmes was made of sterner stuff.

"Pray continue," he said.

"Having ascertained that, for whatever superstition, the land was unlikely to rent to local farmers, I advertised farther afield. After some weeks I had one response. I will admit that I was perturbed I hadn't fulfilled my client's wishes. Nevertheless, the man who came to see me, Mister Shadrach Hananiah Enios, had good references from respectable people, and a promissory note from the bank declaring him to be in sufficient funds, even though he didn't wish to farm. In all fairness to him, I mentioned the rumours, as scurrilous as they were, that the land was cursed. He seemed unperturbed – Nay, I would say he even seemed delighted. I drew up an agreement, and a short time later, Mister Enios and his followers moved out to Hantwich Leeside Farm."

"Followers?" I asked.

"I would hesitate to call them a sect or a religion," said Blythe, "as they didn't seem to be either structured or strictured sufficiently to be so classified. They said they were *The Brethren of Fire and Light*, and claimed to be able to harness the power of the earth. Enios is definitely the leader of his group, and they follow his words slavishly, even though they claimed to be a group of free thinkers. Still, they paid on time, and caused no harm to the land or property. I inspected several times, Mister Holmes. I am a dedicated agent of my clients, and I am diligent."

"Scrupulous," murmured Holmes.

"Indeed," said Blythe. "Moreover, if the current *status* of the agreement between my client and Enios had remained *quo*, I would have had no need to visit you in such a rush." Again he paused, like an inebriated comedian with bad timing.

"What of the *status quo* has changed?" I questioned.

"Ah, yes," said Blythe. "About a week ago, there came to the village a most disagreeable man. He was heard to be casting aspersions on Enios in a way that was most ungentlemanly. Matters came to a head last evening at an open meeting of the Science Institution in the school hall. The topic was 'Lightning and Electricity' – how to gather one from the other. It promised to be a riveting lecture. Mrs. Blythe and I were among those in attendance, along with the Deputy Mayor, and my client, the owner of the aforementioned land. About half of Enios' Brethren were in the audience, ten or more, and Enios himself was the presenting lecturer. He had barely started when the ungentlemanly gentleman, he of the aspersion-casting, stood up in the back row and shouted over Mister Enios.

"'You are a liar and a blaggard, Shadrach Enios!' he shouted. 'You tell your Brethren that you have the power to harness lightning, but you are nothing more than thunder – a big noise with no effect on the universe!'

"'Ladies and gentleman,' replied Enios, 'please allow me to introduce my brother, Meshach. If you are aware of a place anywhere in need of a town drunk, please consider him for the position. He is well qualified – overly so in fact.'

"With a cry of rage, Meshach ran down the aisle, intent I am sure on attacking his brother. Members of the Brethren, with whom he seemed familiar, managed to stop him before he reached the stage, but he wasn't done with his shouting. 'You climb that hill, Shadrach, and I will show you which of us can harness the storms of the gods. Climb it, I dare you, and I will bring down the power of the skies, which are at my command, and strike you down!' There was more of similar ventation as he was finally led away, ranting like the lunatic he surely presented himself to be.

"In conversation with my client after this event, he expressed his disappointment in the tenants I had found for him, even though they were faultless at the breaking up of the lecture. Or so I thought. I had business in London this morning, and on my way to the station, I couldn't help but notice that there were posters all over the town where none had been before. Here," he said holding out one. "I asked my driver to stop and procure this for me." He handed it to Holmes.

"Does this mean this poster is stolen property," I said, "and we are aiding and abetting a criminal act?" Even Holmes thought that a little bit comical, as his frown of disapproval was less pronounced. Blythe however did not.

"I am a servant of the law, Doctor Watson, in much the same way you are a servant to the Oath of Hippocrates. I can assure you I asked him to stop at a point where the sign said, '*Bill posters will be prosecuted*'. Thus, I was within my rights to remove an illegal document."

"Sorry," I said, as contritely as I could manage. "Pardon."

Holmes, having read the document, passed it over to me.

Witness the Power of the Future

Shadrach Enios, Clairvoyant Scientist and Master of Electrical Mystery, will demonstrate, during the next storm, how to harness the spark of the future.

Electricity can be taken from the skies and used to power anything the coming Twentieth Century may hold, in a safe and convenient manner.

Watch *as lightning is stolen from the heavens and used to boil water in a steam engine.* See *the wizardry that can start a fire, and maybe in the future, power flying machines to the moon and beyond!* Gasp *in amazement as Master Shadrach confounds you with his skill at taking the energy of the cosmos and turning it into the energy to run your home.*

All Naysayers, Doubting Thomases, and Unbelievers, even those related to the Master, are welcome to the event, on Hantwich Hill, during the next rainstorm.

When shall we meet again?
In thunder, lightning, or in rain.
When the storm has set upon us.
When the rain falls sideways on us.
Called by Crier to come and join us.
Where the place?
On Hantwich Hill.
To see the power of the gods' own will.

I had barely finished when Holmes, quoting from the poster, added, "'*All Naysayers, Doubting Thomases, and Unbelievers, even those related to the master, are welcome to the event, on Hantwich Hill, during the next rainstorm*' – where no doubt a hat will be passed round after the show and the viewers will be encouraged to part with their hard-earned coin."

Blythe seemed shocked. "Surely there is more to it than that, Mister Holmes?"

"Apart from the egregious misuse of Shakespeare? I fear not. I suspect that you have been played by a master. Tell me, Blythe, about the supposed curse on the farms. Does it involve dead animals in the field with

219

burn marks, as if by the Devil? Maybe occasional fires with no known explanation?"

"Mister Holmes, sir, you are most remarkable! That is exactly what people have said! How could you possibly know that?"

Holmes ignored the question. "And is Hantwich Hill, to which Hantwich Leeside Farm is no doubt attached on the one side, the tallest hill in the vicinity?"

"I would have to check the Ordnance Survey, but I suspect you are right."

"Access to the top of the hill is through the Leeside Farm then."

"It is through both," said Blythe.

"Hmm," said Holmes. "He didn't need to rent both farms then, for his purposes. I presume the other property is called the Hantwich Windside Farm?"

"It is, indeed, Mister Holmes, but this time I can see how you calculated that. You extrapolated the information from the idea of a leeward and windward side to a mountain, and you are correct. My client's grandfather was at Trafalgar with Nelson, and he was given the land by a grateful nation. He named it in honour of the nautical terms, and because he noted that the prevailing winds across Hantwich Hill were similar to what he had observed on duty with the Royal Navy in the Caribbean, albeit with less ferocity."

"You are too clever for me, Blythe," said Holmes. "You saw through my calculations. What is more to the point though is that Shadrach Enios also saw what was for him the perfect piece of land. I suspect if we check on his whereabout, we will find he has been on the road perfecting his show, for a show is almost certainly what it is, for some time. It will be a good show, and it may even have some scientific relevance, but in order to make money, he needed a permanent home near the population of a large city, to draw on the crowds he needs. The names of the two farms, surrounding a hill as they do, would have suggested the very thing he needed most: Winds bringing tempestuous weather."

"What of the curse?" I asked.

"Ah," said Holmes, "that would have been the final proof. The fires and the dead animals are no more the signs of a curse than they are the signs of a summer's day. They are most likely to have been caused by lightning. If Shadrach Hananiah Enios is mystifying the gathering hordes with a light show, he will need the probability of lightning. Hantwich Hill would seem to be the eye of the storm, so to speak."

"But what of his brother? My client is most perturbed at the untowardliness of Enios' brother's drunken behaviour, and doesn't wish to see his family's good name besmirched."

"There will be no besmirching," said Holmes. "Meshach was a plant, and his behaviour and interruption was expected. If you have a look at the poster, you will see it says, "'*All Naysayers, Doubting Thomases, and Unbelievers, even those related to the Master, are welcome to the event, on Hantwich Hill, during the next rainstorm.*' Enios knew his brother would be his naysayer, because he arranged it. Moreover, he had it printed on the poster. That was hardly done at the last minute."

"Then I have troubled you for naught," said Blythe. "I apologize for the inconvenience. Please bill my office for your valuable time."

"There will be no billing," said Holmes. "Your story was interesting enough. I ask only that you tell us by return post how the event goes this evening. I suspect that Meshach Enios will arrive to create more drama, attempt to bring down the fires of Hell on Shadrach Enios, and fail dismally, all to the accompaniment of some flash-bangs akin to those seem on a magician's stage. If you go, and you should, it will no doubt be a spectacle."

"Thank you for your time, Mister Holmes, Doctor Watson," said Blythe somewhat primly. "I may go to the event, or send someone in my stead, but only in service of my client and his familial name. Good day to both of you, and I shall indeed report on the event." And then he left.

Holmes glanced at the newspaper. There are reports of rain to the west of us. "It should be a good show this evening, with the only dry part being Solicitor Blythe and his sense of humour." He must have seen me smiling and he continued. "I am glad you are amused. What part of Blythe's presentation caught your fancy?"

"Nothing much, I'm afraid. I was wondering if there was a third brother ready to make his presence known?" Holmes's puzzlement was real. I had encountered this before – the specificity of his knowledge, and his ability to avoid all he found irrelevant."

"Abednego Enios maybe,? From *The Book of Daniel*? Shadrach, Meshach, and Abednego?"

"I'm sure I have no idea what you are on about."

The next morning, I was awakened by the sound of the door to our rooms opening at an early hour, much too early for the day of rest. In a minute, Holmes came upstairs to my room, knocked, and said, "Watson, there is news from Guildford. Do you wish to come with me? There's an early train in thirty minutes that we can make if we hurry."

I was dressed and down the stairs in ten, and in the hackney with Holmes on our way to Waterloo Station. Holmes was silent – sullen even. I knew him well enough not to ask questions. He would speak eventually.

We had the carriage to ourselves, and were less than a minute out of the train station when Holmes handed me the telegram:

Meshach Enios arrested for murder of Shadrach Enios. Stop. Lightning strike. Stop.

Blythe

"That's impossible!" I stated. "He can't control the elements, can he?"

"I would say not, but I don't know enough about thunder and lightning, save the basics. Thunder is the sound of lightning, and the narrower the gap betwixt the two, the closer the lightning strike. There is an electrical element to it – Benjamin Franklin proved so, I believe – but other than that I am in the dark. I have never had a need to consider it as a means to murder. Do you know anything at all about it?"

"Folklore, mostly. It has been said lightning never strikes the same place twice."

"Bunkum," said Holmes. "That would imply it has a memory, which is nonsense. Also, if it never struck the same place twice, why do tall buildings have lightning rods? Surely the first ones were installed after a lightning strike. If there was no danger from a second strike, why fit them in the first place."

"Indeed. There is also the theory that a body struck by lightning is electrified and can transmit a shock. I can tell you from a medical point of view that is impossible. I know little enough about lightning, but of all the things a human body can do, storing electricity isn't one. What happens when a body is wearing jewellery or other metal adornments, though?"

"We are treading into the unknown, Watson. I have rarely been so ill-prepared for an investigation. We must overcome the lack of science by the strictest of logic, and interview as many of the witnesses as we can. Only then will we know what took place."

"What if you don't find out?" I said.

"Impossible," he said. "I am Sherlock Holmes."

We were met by Blythe *fils*. "Tobias two, Babbington two, Blythe three," he said cheerfully, "but you may call me Toby if you wish." He was of a much sunnier disposition than his father, hardly a difficult task, and he met us in a carriage of substance, as if made to convey both people and status. It didn't suit him, and I suspected it belonged to Blythe *père*. As we climbed into an interior of brocade, velvet, and old wood, I estimated young Blythe's age at no more than twenty-five – young to be a solicitor, but with the advantage of two generations before him to guide the way.

"Our firm has been retained to represent Meshach Enios. He is currently held by the local constabulary, and their investigation, such as it was, is complete. Man threatens to kill brother with lightning, brother dies of lightning strike in presence of accused brother, case closed."

"Has any other brother come forward?" I asked, ever hopeful.

"As far as we know, there were only the two of them. Do you know of more?"

Holmes replied before I could explain. "Watson believes their first names are two of a Biblical trio."

Toby looked puzzled so I clarified. "I thought there may also have possibly been an 'Abednego' Enios, from *The Book of Daniel*? Shadrach, Meshach, and *Abednego*?"

"I'm sure I have never heard of them," said the junior solicitor. "Fascinating. In any event, the crowd that gathered on top of Hantwich Hill last night numbered no more than thirty of so – hardly a successful demonstration, although I suspect they build by word of mouth. They have all disappeared, all except the few from The Brethren, who are all still accommodated at Hantwich Leeside. My father assumed you would like to talk to actual witnesses, so he is there now, ostensibly representing the accused – his client, but in truth he is ensuring the followers don't disappear until you have had your chance.

"You father is most thorough," said Holmes.

"He would call it being scrupulous."

"A splendid word indeed."

The farm was very quiet that morning. There were no livestock to be tended, no smell of animals. It had the look of a farm without the feel of one, as if someone had turned it off at the tap until such time as the farmers returned.

The Brethren of Fire and Light were gathered in the barn. The elder Blythe had demonstrated his organizational skills, arranging them all in the only place they could all fit into. He stood by the hay loft ladder, and before he had a chance to speak to us, Holmes had projected himself into the gathering, in such a manner that all eyes were on him. He stood for about thirty seconds, looking at the whole of the room, seeing everything. He had an ability to sort the wheat from the chaff in such a situation, and he avoided the two men who had taken up strong positions in the gathering as if jockeying for place as the next leader. Instead, he pointed to a middle-aged woman to one side, wearing clothes hard-worn from work, and hair already going grey.

"What is your name?" he said.

"Now see here," one of the men said. "I'll answer any questions you have. You leave her be."

"Sit down," said Holmes, "or your next stop will be the local constabulary to answer questions about being an accessory to what they believe to be a murder." He returned to the woman.

"I am Susan Newton," she said.

"Show me the apparatus you used up on the hill, and explain to me how the game is played."

"Don't tell him now't, Sue!" said the same man.

Holmes ignored him and continued speaking to the woman. "Your leader is dead, his brother is accused of murder, and by the time the police discover this is a con, if they ever do, Meshach Enios will have been hanged. I know that Meshach went to the science gathering to generate interest in last night's show. He has done it before, wherever you have been. What went wrong?"

Susan Newton looked at Holmes for a minute. "So you worked that part out already? I'll tell you the rest then. Meshach doesn't deserve to hang, not anymore than the rest of us." The annoying man tried to interfere again until Susan Newton said to him, "You keeps your mouth shut, David Newton, or else the only thing you'll be getting tonight is the back of my hand." She said to me, "Let's go up to the farmhouse. The equipment is there, and it will be easier if I showed you."

Blythe Senior came with us, leaving his son to keep the other members gathered.

There was a large winder of steel cable outside the farmhouse, with two handles. Susan pointed at it as we walked into the main room. "That's part of the trick," she said as she walked past it. "My husband, David, and that other lummox, Cousin Bob, have to take it up, and then bring it back afterwards. I sent them up to fetch everything this morning. It's heavy, which is why we keep them around." She had a wry smile as she said this, her north country accent adding to her brief smile.

"Now this is the rest of the game," she said, pointing at what looked like a model of a steam engine. "This is the proof that The Brethren of Fire and Light can harness the heavens. Except we can't, of course. It looks like we can, and we tell the punters we can, but this is what really happens." She pulled back the material surrounding the table the engine was on and showed us the array of jars underneath.

"Leyden jars." I said. "I've seen them used in electrotherapy. They are electrical storage devices."

"Hmm," said Holmes. "Nowadays, they're called *batteries*." He turned to Mrs. Newton. "These aren't charged from the sky, are they?"

224

"I should think not. Back at the beginning, Shadrach and Meshach thought it was possible, and one time they managed to get the lightning to flow down the cable towards the jars. It blew them to Hell and gone, damaged the steam engine, and took the eyebrows of the Enios boys, and they were standing twenty feet away. Nay, that plan never worked, but it gave rise to the idea. What we do is set up a steel cable, attached to a wooden pole, far enough away on t' top of the hill that it will get hit by lightning most times, but not hit anything else. We run that cable to earth so the lightning dissipates. At the same time, Shadrach hits a switch, and the steam turbine turns over, looking like it was powered by lightning, but in fact it was run off the Leyden jars. Then we go round with a hat."

"Where does the electricity inside the Leyden jars come from?" I asked.

"We charge those from a static generator we have," she said. "They hold a fair charge, and that's important for the nights when there's a silent strike."

"A silent strike?"

"That's what Shadrach called it. Sometimes the lightning doesn't cooperate, so Shadrach had an act he did so the punters still had a show. He'd reverse the Leyden jars and send a charge out on the cable that looks like it's connected to the lightning rod. He would hold the cable and pretend to be shocked as the charge from the Leyden jars ran out the cable, running the steam engine at the same time. It was a far better show, I'll give thee that, and the takings were often double. Shadrach could ham it up all right, and when the charge shot out along the cable, he really acted as if he was being shocked. But we all knew he'd been holding a part of the cable that was insulated, and the punters couldn't tell if the charge came from above, like they believed, or from under the table, as was. Electricity is pretty fast."

"Indeed," said Holmes. "I'd like to see that cable."

"It's heavy," said Susan Newton, "I'll need some help."

Blythe, who had been standing, staring, imitative of a goldfish in a bowl, seemed bewildered at the speed of Holmes's investigation, He was unhappy to be despatched to fetch David Newton and Cousin Bob. For a second, he appeared to be rebellious and told Holmes to send me, but I gave him my sternest look, the one reserved for patients withholding information pertinent to a diagnosis, and he quailed under the pressure. Some moments later, the two men brought in a length of cable from the spool outside.

"Now that piece is attached to the lightning cable to appear as if it is getting a charge," said Mrs. Newton, "but it is insulated at the join. The other end goes under the table to attach to the batteries, which then

225

connects to the engine on top of the table. When the weather isn't cooperating, one charge goes up the cable creating the illusion of a lightning strike, the other to the engine. Sparks at one end, power at t'other, and there's no sound from the sky, so we called it the silent strike. With the show that Shadrach put on, the punters lapped it up."

"Was that what happened last night?"

"You mean up until the moment Shadrach collapsed, and the rest of us legged it back to the farmhouse? Yes, it was a night with little lightning about. I always hated it when he pulled the silent strike routine. It always felt dishonest – more dishonest than actually getting a strike."

"Even though the entire show was a sham," I said.

"It isn't," she said. "We can get lightning to come down from a storm and land on a spot we choose. That is science. We are just not capable, yet, of capturing it. What we do most of the time is show the possibilities of electricity harnessed from lightning." She paused for a moment. "That part is real. It was the silent strike show that made a mockery of what we were trying to do. I never liked it."

"What of Meshach Enios?" said Holmes. "Surely he tired of his part in the act – causing a fuss, threatening to kill his brother with a lightning strike, acting as a drunk." He stopped, watching Mrs. Newton's face. "Ah," he said. "The drinking wasn't an act, was it? It was a problem. Meshach wasn't happy, was he Mrs. Newton?"

But to that there was no reply.

Blythe Junior had been at the show and confirmed the substance of Susan Newton's story. He was surprised to hear the electricity had come from under the table, "Is that so? I couldn't tell. Electricity is rather quick, don't you know? It looked to me as if it came from the skies, and was a silent strike."

"There is no such thing as a silent strike," said Holmes.

"But I saw it happen," he replied, with all the blind certainty of a junior officer charging the guns at Balaclava.

Several other members of The Brethren also confirmed the story as Susan Newton had related it, most expressing surprise it had gone so wrong. They were unwilling to point a finger at Meshach, although it seemed they all knew of his drinking.

Blythe, meanwhile, having been reduced to a fetch-and-carry man, was unhappy and impatient, and said as much.

"Is Meshach Enios innocent?" he asked Holmes. "And can you prove it?"

"I will have your answer shortly. I need to see that cable again."

226

We left Blythe with more questions than answers. I had one of my own.

"How did you know to ask her your questions?" I asked Holmes.

"You know I have spent much of my life observing human behaviour. The people in the room had divided itself in the way they stood, relative to each other, leaning towards their leader and away from those they didn't trust. Most looked to Susan Newton, as if waiting for answers. No one looked anywhere else. Whether she knew it or not, she was the one everyone listened to, which is why I wanted to listen to her as well."

The trick cable was about sixty feet long. "Long enough to connect to the lightning cable," said Holmes, "without endangering the show." Unlike the longer cable still on the spool, which was bare, this one was covered in cloth. "Hardly an adequate insulation," he said, "but what is?" He ran his hands gently down the cable almost all the way, down to the end that connected under the table to the batteries. "Here, Watson – feel these ridges. What do they suggest to you?"

"I'm sure I have no idea."

"It feels as if something has been here, and is no longer." He dropped the cable as if he himself had been shocked and walked back inside to where Mrs. Newton was sitting.

"Who are the Enios Brothers to you?" He said it in such a harsh manner that a lesser person would have told him everything. Susan Newton wasn't a lesser person.

"We are all members of The Brethren of Fire and Light," she said.

"Do you not think the police will trace you? Birth certificates, family members, friends. Are Shadrach and Meshach your cousins? Nephews?"

Even I saw the change in her demeanour, as if there was a burden to offload. She believed Holmes's prevarication about the police and their abilities. Had she but known the truth, that Holmes had no respect for most constabularies, she might have held out longer.

"I am their sister," she said. "I was born when our parents were very young, and out of wedlock. It was a scandal in the village, and I was placed in the care of a convent."

"So when young Blythe told us there were only the two of them, that was because you weren't a child of record."

"A child of record, Doctor Watson? What a delightfully detached way of putting it. I didn't exist, and when our parents did the right thing and married, they couldn't find me, as I had been adopted, and the convent would say no more on the matter."

"You found them though."

"I did. Out father was on his death-bed, but he confirmed my story to my brothers almost with his dying breath."

227

"And your mother?" I asked.

"She died giving birth," said Susan Newton. "I never met her."

"Abednego," I said, so softly that only Holmes heard me, and ignored my discovery.

"How long did you think you could hide the truth," said Holmes, "that Meshach hated Shadrach. That the show they created to bring in the spectators was based on *two* truths, not one. Yes, Meshach portrayed such a splendid drunk because it was hardly acting. He was a longstanding sot, but when he threatened to kill his brother, it rang true, because it *was* true. Why was that, Mrs. Newton? Why did he hate his brother so much he removed the extra insulation from the cable – the insulation that stopped Shadrach from getting killed on the silent strike nights? And why didn't you say anything?"

"Because I only found out afterwards!" she shouted. "Because I didn't want to believe it. Because I had just lost one brother, and I didn't wish to lose the other. Our father – *their* father – was a bitter man, and when his wife died, he favoured Shadrach over Meshach. At least that's what Meshach always said. He claimed his life was Hell, that his father beat him and hurt him, and that Shadrach did nothing to try and stop him."

"You knew," I said, "and you did nothing."

"What could I do? I wasn't there when they grew up, and Shadrach always denied it. Was Meshach's story true, or the ravings of a drunk?" She looked at me and her question pierced deep. "What could I do, Doctor Watson? How do you stop a murder you don't even know is going to happen?"

I had no answer.

Blythe had many questions. Holmes's answers were curt.

"Your client wanted to kill his brother, and he had the knowledge to do so," he said to the solicitor. "However, he claimed he could do it at will, by lightning, whereas Meshach Enios didn't actually kill his brother. He merely made it possible. Shadrach Enios flipped the switch that caused his own death, and I doubt if you get a jury to understand the significance of the loss of insulation on the cable, or even be able to prove who actually removed it. It is my suspicion that Susan Newton will not testify against Meshach Enios, nor will the rest of The Brethren. Thus, Mister Blythe, you may instruct a barrister to perform a vigourous defence of your client, expecting success, but hardly justice. Now, if we may trouble you for a ride to the station, there is a milk-run train that leaves in forty minutes, and Doctor Watson and I have business to be about in London."

It had been an unsatisfying day. What had promised to have been a mystery of note and intrigue, a death at the top of a hill by powerful yet natural forces, had instead ended up as a grubby little family killing, hard to even define as a murder of premeditation. Not all of Holmes's cases were scintillating works of detection. At least I still had my one little victory.

"I was right about Abednego," I said to Holmes. "There was to have been a third brother, but their mother died in childbirth."

Holmes smiled patiently. It was a smile I knew so well, but this time there was a hint of commiseration instead of his normal condescension.

"You came close, Watson, and there certainly might have been the *wish* for a third brother, but the hatred that the father had for Meshach posits another more likely possibility: That their mother died giving birth to the younger son, and the father blamed Meshach for the loss of his wife."

And then the old Holmes was back. "You may count this as a victory of sorts, if you wish. A rare one, given your ability in the main to draw the most illogical conclusions from the simplest of facts."

Like the rest of the tale, Holmes's words were also unsatisfying.

Plus ça change.

The Missing Calabash
by P.C. Shumway

"**J**udge Hartcliffe was brutally murdered last night," stated Inspector Bradstreet of the Metropolitan Police as he stepped into our Baker Street rooms. The Honorable George Benjamin Hartcliffe III of the House of Lords was an experienced and admired Appellate Court Judge. He was known for his strong-minded decisions.

"Brutal, you say," Holmes said, as he took another bite of his toast.

"I haven't yet been to the location of the crime, but I heard it's a bloody mess. The judge had his throat slit ear to ear."

Fortunately, I had finished my eggs before the inspector threw open our door.

"I have a police carriage waiting outside if you would be so kind as to join the investigation."

Holmes tossed the remains of his toast onto his plate and stood up.

"What can you tell us about the judge?" he asked as he strode over to the Persian slipper and filled his tobacco pouch.

"To my knowledge, Judge Hartcliffe never married. He had a house in Kensington High Street, with a view of the park. He lived a private life and confined his associations to The House of Lords, bishops, appellate court judges, prominent society, and royalty."

"Which explains your soliciting our assistance," Holmes said with a wry smile.

"We have our orders from the highest quarters. Inspector Gregson is in command of the case and is at the scene now."

I sensed a little resentment in the tone of Bradstreet's voice and with the formality of his bearing. He had more years of experience on the force than Tobias Gregson. However, the latter was often assigned the high-profile cases where jurisdiction mattered little. The preference may have been because of Gregson's sharper intellect and more aggressive approach to investigations.

"We know Gregson well," Holmes said as he grabbed his pipe, walked over to the chemical table, and picked up his lens.

The tall, bearded Inspector Bradstreet turned to me and said, "You are most welcome to come along, Doctor."

"If I can be of any help," I replied.

"Your presence is always helpful," Holmes said as he shoved his lens and pipe into his pocket and grabbed his coat and hat.

I donned mine as well and followed my companions out the door.

A brief early-morning May shower wetted the cobblestone streets, from which a light mist arose in the sunlight. There were several uniformed policemen positioned up and down High Street, and one officer standing guard at the front door of Judge Hartcliffe's residence. It was a two-story, grey stone house with large pillars and a narrow balcony-style porch on each side of the front steps. The uniformed officer at the door saluted as we approached.

"Good morning, sir," he said. "Inspector Gregson is inside."

"Very good, Dawson."

The officer opened the door and we stepped into a large entrance hall featuring a marble floor. There were doors left and right of us, and a wide marble staircase facing us which led to the first floor. Holmes stopped at the cupboard immediately to our right and examined the coats and boots. He found a tobacco pouch in the pocket of an overcoat. Opening the pouch, he took a pinch of the tobacco and held it to his nose. "Burley," he remarked, replacing the pouch.

Officer Dawson led us across the hall to the right. He opened the door to the study and stepped aside for us to enter.

"I must resume my post, sir," Dawson said.

"Certainly," replied Bradstreet, who was used to less formality. The officer turned and left us.

The study was a long, well-lit room with a fine-loomed carpet. A writing desk stood left of the door, beside a large side filer. Past the desk was a walnut bridge table with four chairs. The wall beyond the table was shelved with books. Across the room stood a marble side table with two bottles of good scotch, a set of glasses, and a tobacco canister. To our right sat two plush sitting chairs facing a fireplace. A small marble-topped stand was positioned between them. On the stand sat a reading lamp, a large ashtray, and two half-full whisky glasses.

Judge Hartcliffe's body lay face down in front of the fireplace. Beyond the fireplace, a set of French doors led to the narrow front porch. Inspector Gregson was examining the lock and bolt on the doors when we stepped in. He turned to us in greeting.

"Bradstreet. I see you have collected our recruits."

"Good morning, Inspector," he replied.

"We are hobnobbing with high society this morning, Gregson," Holmes said. "What can you tell us thus far?"

"Not much, I'm afraid. The judge lived alone and employed a head-housekeeper, a maid, a cook, and a butler who served as his valet. Except for the maid, they all have been with him for many years. He engaged a private secretary by the name of Thomas Fletcher of Chelsea who attends duties six days a week."

Inspector Gregson glanced at his notepad.

"I spoke with the housekeeper, Miss Alice Reed, who said the secretary has been with the judge for almost two years. The regular staff have rooms in the back of the house on the first floor. Neither she nor the others heard anything last night. The cook has the nearest room, but she is old and hard of hearing."

"I also spoke with the butler, Mr. Walter Evans, who recalled that the judge was sitting by the fire here in the ground floor study, smoking his pipe last night, when he bade him a goodnight at ten o'clock. I asked about the locks and he said he checks the windows and doors every evening before retiring. All were locked and bolted. The judge was afraid of vengeful ex-convicts, so he had bolts installed on all the windows and doors."

"My officers checked the entire house this morning and reported no sign of forced entry. These French doors were bolted and locked last night, but were found unbolted and unlocked this morning."

"That indicates the judge let the murderer in," Bradstreet said.

"Obviously," Gregson said, with a hint of impatience.

"Which also implies the judge knew his murderer," Holmes remarked. "One does not install bolts on the windows and doors and then receive a stranger late at night."

"Perhaps, Mr. Holmes," Gregson said, "but let's not make that deduction yet. Maybe the judge thought he recognized the murderer, but was mistaken."

"I suppose that is a possibility," said Holmes, who understood that Gregson wanted to score all the points.

"The two whisky glasses on the table by the fireplace surely support Holmes's suggestion," I said.

"We shall see."

Gregson looked at his notebook again.

"Miss Reed discovered the body shortly after six o'clock this morning when she entered the study, as she does first thing every morning to tidy up. She sent the maid to fetch the police and to send a telegram to Charles Hartcliffe, the judge's brother and only living relative. Women are always eager to spread bad news. Evans, the butler, was displeased with her."

Gregson glanced at his notebook again.

"Charles Edward Hartcliffe lives in Berkshire, in the town of Slough. From Miss Reed's blushing, I'd say she is quite fond of Charles. The brothers had a falling out three years ago, after their father passed away. They haven't corresponded since."

Holmes walked over to Judge Hartcliffe's body. He lay in a pool of blood, and the scarlet had splashed over the chairs and carpet.

"There is a pattern here on the carpet where blood spattered over the toe of a boot."

"Yes, I noticed that," Gregson said, as if stating the obvious.

"Hand me a sheet of blotting paper, Watson."

I took a sheet from the desk and gave it to Holmes, who laid it down on the pattern of blood where the boot toe was outlined and gently pressed on it. He lifted the paper and handed it back to me. I set it on the bridge table to dry.

Holmes glanced at the body. Judge Hartcliffe was a big man, nearing fifty years in age, of average height, and at least fifty pounds overweight. His balding head was bashed in, and his throat was slit. Holmes examined the ghastly indentation on the top of the skull and then surveyed the blood spatter around the body.

"From the pattern of the blood," Holmes stated, "it appears the murderer is right-handed."

"And how do you deduce that?" asked Gregson.

"The murderer stood behind the body, bent over, and cut the victim's throat from left to right. It is nearly impossible to cut a man from ear to ear while facing him. One's wrist doesn't bend that way."

I pantomimed the action using my right hand while wielding an imaginary knife. I looked over to Inspector Bradstreet and, he, too, was assaulting an invisible victim. He caught my glance and silently chuckled.

"There is blood on the poker," Gregson stated. "It appears the murderer first struck the judge on the top of his head with such force to knock him unconscious before cutting the man's throat."

"I agree," Holmes stated as he retrieved the bent poker from the fireplace stand and examined the blood stain. "Was the poker on the stand when you arrived?" he asked.

"Yes. Everything is exactly as I found it."

"Except for the carpet," said Holmes. "It's difficult to walk near the body without stepping in blood and tracking it all over the room. Officer Dawson need not have ushered us to the study. All we needed to do was follow the trail of bloody footprints across the marble floor."

I stood by the desk while Holmes replaced the poker and began his examination of the room. He produced his lens from his pocket and examined the edge of the mantelpiece. Using a pair of surgical tweezers, he lifted a hair from the face of the mantel and placed it in an envelope. Gregson watched the operation over my friend's shoulder. Holmes examined the collection of expensive curios on the mantel and checked the ashes in the fireplace before walking over to the side table. Gregson followed him around like a puppy. As I've described earlier, there were two bottles of scotch and a set of beautiful gold rimmed whisky glasses on the marble-topped table.

"The judge had good taste in scotch," remarked the inspector. Holmes ignored Gregson and lifted the lid of the tobacco canister, finding the same Burley mix that was in the pouch he'd examined earlier. Holmes walked to the far end of the room, past the bridge table, with Gregson on his heels, and examined the bookcase. Many of the volumes contained legal statutes. He made his way around to the writing desk and side filer. It was locked.

"We haven't found a key yet," Gregson remarked over Holmes's shoulder.

Holmes turned his attentions to the desk and examined the papers. The drawer of the desk was unlocked, but contained nothing of interest. He made his way back to the body and checked the judge's pockets. He found a box of matches, a thin identification wallet with a security pass, several five-pound notes, three gold sovereigns, six shillings, a gold pocket watch, and a small penknife. The dull and blackened blade on the knife showed it was used to clean out a pipe bowl. Inspector Bradstreet collected the items to catalogue. Holmes stood up and walked over to the wall by the door. He kneeled twice to examine the blood stains leading to the French doors and took several measurements using his small pocket tape measure. After examining the lock, he dropped on all fours and reached under a small chair in the corner of the room.

"Halloa! This is interesting." Holmes held up a small jacket potato. He retrieved his lens from his pocket and examined the spud. Curiously, it was covered with dozens of tiny holes. Gregson snatched it out of Holmes's hand.

"This is certainly a strange thing to find in a judge's study." Gregson turned to Bradstreet and tossed him the spud. "What do you make of that?"

Bradstreet was alert and caught the little wrinkled potato. "Strange enough," said the inspector, turning the perforated thing over in his hands. "We can ask the staff if they've seen it before. Perhaps the murderer dropped it."

"It is unlikely to have been accidentally dropped from a pocket," Holmes remarked. "It could have been left here intentionally to throw us off."

"It certainly could have fallen out of the murderer's pocket, Mr. Holmes," countered Gregson.

"I said it was unlikely. Put the ugly spud in any of your pockets, Inspector, then jump up and down and run around the room and see if it dislodges," Holmes said with a smile.

I walked over to Bradstreet and looked at the little brown potato.

"Why it's a dart spud!" I said. "Serious dart players often carry a raw potato in their pocket, just as a billiard player will carry a piece of chalk. Dart throwers stab it occasionally to help their darts stay in the cork dartboard. I believe it has something to do with the starch."

"Bravo, Watson!" said Holmes. "That is certainly what it is. Now that you mention it, I have seen the use of potatoes by dart players in pubs. The question is: What is it doing on the study floor of a wealthy appellate court judge? Did the murderer drop it, or intentionally leave it behind? Was the potato on the floor before the murder was committed? Did someone else enter the study after the murder and leave the potato as a false clue?"

I returned the little spud to Bradstreet.

"Are you inferring one of the household staff?" he asked Holmes as he tossed the potato back to Gregson. Gregson slipped it into his pocket and said, "We'll set the mystery of the potato aside for the time being. You're certainly full of questions this morning, Mr. Holmes. We have more questions than answers. What else can you tell us?"

"The murderer is likely a right-handed man, between six-foot-one and six-foot-two-inches tall, with black hair and in good physical shape." In answer to our raised eyebrows, he added, "The murderer slit the judge's throat from left to right, and left a strand of hair when he banged his head on the fireplace mantel. I calculated his height from the length of his stride marked by his bloody footprints. Only someone in fair physical shape could knock out a man the size of the judge."

"Why, that could be a description of yourself," Bradstreet said with a smile.

"I suppose it could," Holmes admitted.

Gregson asked, "Did you find any other clues?"

"I'm afraid not. The murderer, after slitting the judge's throat, stepped in blood and walked out of the room. There is, however, one clue I didn't find."

We all gave him puzzled looks.

"Where is the judge's pipe? I see an ashtray containing pipe ash, a tobacco pouch, and a penknife in his overcoat, a canister of pipe tobacco on the side table, a box of matches in his pocket, but no pipe."

"There's nothing to that, Mr. Holmes," Gregson snorted. "He could have left it anywhere."

"The butler Evans said he saw the judge smoking his pipe last night," I reminded him.

"Right," Gregson said, with a brief glance in my direction. "The butler could be mistaken."

"Are you suggesting the murderer took the pipe?" Bradstreet asked Holmes.

"It is the logical deduction. But why on earth would he take a pipe?"

"Perhaps the murderer is a mere common thief," Gregson suggested.

"This isn't a case of robbery, Inspector," Holmes said. "The judge has a gold Patek Philippe watch in his pocket, a Fabergé jeweled egg on the mantel, and a Rembrandt hanging on the wall opposite the fireplace. I suspect even the dullest robber would choose something more valuable than a used pipe."

"I agree, Mr. Holmes," Gregson said. "I was just thinking out loud."

"Which brings me back to the question of *why*? Why would the murderer take the pipe, if not to steal it?"

"You get a bit too far into the fog at times, Mr. Holmes," said Bradstreet.

"I agree with my colleague," Gregson said. "The pipe was worth little, and I suspect it is unimportant."

"I'll fetch the butler and the housekeeper so we can ask about the potato," Bradstreet said. He turned and walked out of the study, only to return in less than a minute. He had apparently found the entire staff seated in the parlor at the other end of the hall discussing their futures. They said they would rather not come into the study until the body was removed. Gregson couldn't order removal until the Kensington coroner came on site and pronounced death. The coroner was overdue.

"We can certainly understand their apprehensions," Bradstreet remarked.

"By all means," Gregson said, as he led us out the study door. We walked the length of the wide entrance hall and over to the parlor. I noticed the trail of faint bloody footprints on the marble floor which Holmes had referred to. Stepping into the parlor was like entering a fresh new world. It was an open, cheery room which, like the study, faced the street with a set of French doors. Pink sofas and pillowed chairs were plopped around a low, round coffee table made of solid white marble. The butler, housekeeper, maid, and cook were seated around the table.

"Please excuse the interruption," Bradstreet said.

Gregson nudged the inspector aside and produced the potato from his pocket.

"We found this under a chair in the study. Have any of you seen it before?"

Gregson set the little brown spud in the centre of the white marble coffee table and stepped back to see their reactions.

"On the floor of the study, you say?" said Miss Reed, the housekeeper. She turned and glared at the maid.

"Don't look at me, Ma'am. I never seen it before."

Miss Reed turned back to Gregson.

"Well," she stated, "there was no potato on the floor of the study yesterday."

The cook wrinkled her nose and said, "It isn't the quality of potato I use in my kitchen."

"I am afraid we cannot help you, Inspector," said the butler, Evans, as he gingerly picked up the spud with his fingertips, holding it at arm's length as if it were a dead mouse, and handed it back to Gregson.

Holmes stepped into the room a little further and asked, "Have any of you, by chance, seen the judge's pipe?"

"Good Heavens, Mr. Holmes," Gregson muttered. "Must we go on about that pipe?

The staff all looked at each other and shook their heads.

Holmes said, "The pipe has gone missing. Could one of you describe it to me?"

"It was one of those big, curvy gourd pipes," the maid said. "Imagine smoking a gourd."

Miss Reed looked at her and said, "They put a plaster bowl in the gourd, Ellie."

"The bowl is meerschaum, Madam," Evens stated. "The pipe is a Calabash."

"That's right," said Miss Reed. Turning to Holmes she repeated, "It's a Calabash."

"It was a gift from his deceased father, I believe," Evans said. "His father carved the Judge's initials on the gourd before gifting it to him."

"Please inform one of us if found," Holmes said.

Just then, the front door opened, and Officer Dawson stepped into the entrance hall followed by Dr. Palmer, the Kensington coroner.

Gregson walked quickly over to the new arrival.

"Morning, Palmer. You're a little overdue," he said. "Thank you, Dawson. I'll show Dr. Palmer the body."

"Gregson," Dr. Palmer said in greeting and without enthusiasm. "I was detained by the missus."

I had met the Kensington coroner on several occasions and had dinner with him once. I walked over and greeted him. He was melancholy, yet glad to see me.

"Dr. Watson. It's good to see a friendly face on such a dark day."

"Dark it is," I replied.

He nodded to Holmes and Bradstreet and turned to Gregson.

"Show me, Inspector."

Gregson led the coroner to the study as the rest of us followed. Dr. Palmer stood over the body for a few moments, shook his head, and sighed. He mechanically put on a pair of surgical gloves and briefly

237

examined the body. Looking at his watch, he said, "Time of death between ten o'clock and midnight." He peeled off his gloves and tossed them into his Gladstone bag.

"It's a nasty business, Tobias. I hope you catch the scoundrel. George Hartcliffe was a friend of mine."

The doctor took a black notebook from his bag, glanced at his watch again, and jotted down some details before signing it, tearing the page out, and handing it to Gregson.

"I need a drink," he said, as he grabbed his bag and walked out the door. He bumped into a man who was just coming into the room. The fellow was in his mid-twenties, of medium height and very thin. He had sandy hair, wore spectacles, and carried a brown leather valise. Having just been told of the murder, the young man was in an agitated state.

"Hello. I am Thomas Fletcher, Judge Hartcliffe's personal secretary," he said, stepping into the room. When he saw the judge lying on the floor, he turned pale, reeled backwards, and collapsed in a faint. I was unable to reach him before he knocked into the desk chair and landed on the carpet.

"Bring me some of that Scotch, Inspector," I said to Bradstreet as I loosened the man's collar and checked his pulse. I poured a little into his mouth, which revived him, and I helped him up to the chair.

"Take it easy, Mr. Fletcher," Bradstreet advised him.

The color came back into his cheeks as he looked around and blinked. I made our introductions, and he became cognizant.

"Can you tell us where you were between ten o'clock and midnight, Mr. Fletcher?" Gregson asked.

"You don't think I had anything to do with that!" he said, nodding his head towards the body lying next to the fireplace.

"We need to know everyone's whereabouts at the time of the murder. You understand."

"Of course. I was at home with my wife. She can vouch for that."

"What is your address, sir?"

"We have a flat in Chelsea. Caversham Street. Apartment 14A."

He turned around in the desk chair, opened the ink well, took a note-sized slip of paper from a cubbyhole, wrote his name and address using his left hand and handed it to Gregson. His movements were quick and precise. I could see how he would be an efficient secretary.

"Do you perhaps have the key to this side file?" Gregson asked.

"It is concealed here in the desk." Fletcher slid open a secret compartment in the desk, retrieved the key, and handed it to the inspector.

"We didn't want the staff to pry," he said.

Gregson unlocked the cabinet and opened the top drawer. It was full of file folders containing records of past cases.

"They are in order by offender's last name, and not by court date," Fletcher said. "Judge Hartcliffe and I disagreed on that point. I wanted to file by date, but he wanted to lay his hands on a case quickly and could remember names better than dates."

"We will need to go through these and list criminals who may have wanted to take revenge on the judge," Gregson stated.

"I can assist with that," the young man said. "I'm feeling better now."

He stood up and began rifling through the folders. "Unfortunately, any criminal in any of these cases could want revenge."

Holmes and the two inspectors walked over to the bridge table and sat down. They turned their chairs to face the side file as Fletcher worked with his back to them. Holmes lit his pipe. I returned the glass of scotch I'd used to revive Fletcher to the side table and poured myself a drink.

Gregson suggested to Fletcher that he limit the list to violent crimes and pay special attention to murders.

I joined the others at the round table just as Fletcher turned to us and held up a folder. "Mrs. Beatrice Abernathy. Sentenced to thirty years for poisoning her husband and then stabbing his corpse seventy-five times."

"She's violent enough," remarked Holmes. "Is she still incarcerated?"

"Yes. She has twenty-three years left on her sentence."

"Perhaps we should limit our search to those not currently in prison," suggested Bradstreet.

"Anyone in the gaol can hire someone to take revenge," Gregson said. "However, I agree that for now we need to limit our suspects to persons not currently serving time."

The secretary turned around and continued his search.

There was a courtesy knock at the door as two large men from the coroner, dressed in blues, entered the room with a stretcher. Gregson nodded in the direction of the fireplace. There was, again, a gentle knock at the open door and three ladies followed in the wake of the men. The women brought with them linen, sponges, bottles of cleaning solutions, brushes, buckets, and mops. They discussed a plan of attack while the men rolled the judge onto the stretcher, covered him with a sheet, and strenuously carried him out the door. The women began busily cleaning.

"David Beaumont," announced Fletcher. "Just over ten years ago, when the judge was presiding over the Crown Court. He sentenced Beaumont to ten years for trespassing and attempted murder. Beaumont served his sentence and was released two months ago. The police have lost all track of him."

"He sounds like a candidate," Bradstreet said. "What was his profession?"

"Let me see," Fletcher said as he turned another page. "Here it is. It says he was a theatrical agent."

Gregson rolled his eyes. "Not very promising. Add him to the list and keep searching."

The women had the blood sopped up, the chairs and rug cleaned, and the fireplace scrubbed and dried before Fletcher reached the *D*'s. The atmosphere of the room was greatly improved.

"Thank you, ladies," Bradstreet said as he helped them out the study door.

"We'll be back after everyone has cleared out so we can do a proper job," one lady said as they headed for the front door.

Two more unlikely but possible suspects were added to the list from the *C*'s before the women had finished cleaning. Samuel Cartwright, who wounded a police officer during a robbery, and Archie Clark, who kidnapped and tortured a young girl.

"John Davenport would be a likely candidate if he weren't sitting in Dartmoor Prison," Fletcher said as he stuffed a folder back into the drawer.

Gregson and Bradstreet looked at each other before the former spoke.

"Davenport escaped three weeks ago. Scotland Yard has kept it out of the papers for fear of creating a public panic."

I asked Fletcher why he favored Davenport.

"He murdered his father by clubbing him over the head with a cricket bat and then slitting his throat. The judge sentenced the man to life imprisonment. As Davenport was led out of the courtroom, he shouted an oath of revenge at the judge."

"What was Davenport's profession?" Bradstreet asked.

Fletcher retrieved the folder and opened the file. "It says here he was unemployed, but made his money playing darts."

"Seems to be a fit," Gregson exclaimed. "I think we have our man! What do you say to that, Mr. Holmes?"

"Curious," Holmes replied. "How tall is he?"

Gregson grabbed the file before it was handed it Holmes. "According to this, he's twenty-seven years old, five-foot-four-inches tall, and weighs a hundred-and-forty pounds."

"He's too short for my liking," said Holmes. "Do you really think the judge would open the door to a man he had sentenced to life imprisonment?"

"Facts are facts, Mr. Holmes. The dart potato with all those little holes is hard evidence. Your missing pipe is pure theory. I say we have our man." Turning to Fletcher he said, "When you finish the alphabet, give the list to Bradstreet here."

"I'll certainly return to the task after lunch, Inspector. I must now be on my way to an important appointment."

Fletcher picked up his brown leather case and stepped towards the door.

Holmes leaped from his chair and blocked the door.

"I am afraid we cannot let you go until we have a look in your bag. When you thought no one was watching, you slipped a folder into your valise."

Fletcher turned white, and I thought he was going to faint again.

"Really, Mr. Holmes. I must protest!"

"Protest all you want, my good fellow," Holmes replied.

Gregson walked over and took the valise from the young man. The inspector reached in and pulled out a folder. "*Oliver Fairchild*," he read. "From two years ago. Age fifty-one."

"It was about the time you were hired on as secretary, was it not?" asked Holmes.

"Yes."

Gregson continued reading. "Fairchild was convicted of forgery, sentenced to ten years, and is incarcerated at Pentonville."

The inspector handed the folder to Holmes, since it wasn't of any interest to him. Holmes looked through the folder and selected a letter from Judge Hartcliffe to the Pentonville Prison gaoler, requesting that Fairchild be moved to the modern wing where conditions were better. Holmes found another letter signed by the judge warning the kitchen staff at Pentonville of legal action if foods were not prepared properly.

"Your Judge Hartcliffe signature is an excellent forgery, Mr. Fletcher. However, you drop your crossing of the '*t*' and the '*f*'s. The transfer from the '*a*' to the '*r*' in Hartcliffe is a bit weak. There are four other inconsistencies I could mention. However, my point is made. It appears you secured the position as Judge Hartcliffe's secretary to affect the penal sentence of Oliver Fairchild. May I assume your name is not Fletcher but *Fairchild*?"

Fletcher looked down at his feet. "Oliver is my father."

Inspector Bradstreet sat up in his chair. "This is a serious offence, young man," he said.

"I suspect it's more serious than forgery," Gregson said. Turning to the secretary, he said, "I suggest the judge discovered your dishonesty and threatened to have you arrested. You panicked and struck him with the poker."

"I certainly did not!" the young man objected.

"You knew John Davenport had recently escaped from prison since the police had warned the judge. You recalled what you had read in the

241

case file, so you cut the judge's throat to make it look like Davenport's work. You knew his profession of darts from his file, so you ran to the nearest pub, grabbed a dart spud, returned here, and tossed the potato under the chair."

"None of that is true!" Fairchild cried. "I was home last night!"

"And then you offer to assist us to make sure we find the case file to incriminate Davenport."

Bradstreet slapped his colleague on the back.

"I think you have hit upon it, Gregson!"

"It is a convincing case, Inspector," Holmes stated. "Too bad he's left-handed."

Gregson scoffed. "Left-handed or right-handed matters little to me."

"It accounts for the spud," I said.

Holmes rubbed his chin. "Yes, it does. However, it doesn't account for the missing pipe."

Inspector Gregson shot a look of frustration at Holmes, walked over to the front door, and asked officer Dawson to handcuff the secretary. Gregson then informed us he would step outside to see about arranging transport for the murderer of Judge Hartcliffe to Scotland Yard.

After they had left, I refreshed my drink and poured glasses for Bradstreet and Holmes.

We were enjoying the judge's excellent scotch and discussing the case when Officer Franklin, who was covering for Dawson, stepped in with a tall man in his mid-forties wearing workman's clothing and square-toed boots.

"This is the judge's brother, Charles Hartcliffe of Berkshire, Inspector."

"Thank you, Franklin," Bradstreet said.

The uniformed officer had the good sense not to ask the inspector about drinking scotch while on duty. Franklin walked out of the study and returned to his post.

"I am Inspector Bradstreet, and this is Mr. Sherlock Holmes and his colleague, Dr. Watson."

The judge's brother glanced around the room and gave the fireplace an extended look. "I came as soon as I could. I had to wait for my relief."

Holmes arranged the desk chair for Mr. Hartcliffe as Bradstreet, and I grabbed three of the bridge table chairs and set them facing the newcomer. I could see Holmes's keen eye make a quick study of the man as we sat down.

"I see you're employed as a foreman at the Gas Works."

Charles Hartcliffe looked at my companion. "How do you know that, Mr. Holmes? I suppose Miss Reed told you."

242

"She only mentioned you live in Slough. The gas works is the largest industry there. The coal-tar dust on your boots, the smell of gas, the grime and wear of your clothes places you at the Works. Yet the lack of calluses on your hands makes the deduction of foreman an obvious one," Holmes explained.

Hartcliffe seemed disinterested in Holmes's methods and asked how his brother was murdered.

"He was killed with a knife in this very room," Bradstreet said, sparing the man the bloody details.

"Do you have any suspects? I imagine there are ex-convicts who would want revenge."

"That was our first thought as well, Mr. Hartcliffe," said Bradstreet. "However, we have arrested Mr. Fairchild, your brother's secretary, for the murder."

The news startled Hartcliffe. He regained his composure and said, "I never met him. You see, I haven't spoken with my brother in three years. George is . . . was . . . my senior by six years. We were the only children of wealthy aristocrats. Our mother died giving birth to me."

Charles Harctliffe sighed. "My father and brother blamed me for her death. It wasn't a pleasant way to grow up. George got everything he wanted all his life – nice clothes, expensive gifts, and the best education money could buy. But that is all in the past." He reached into his pocket and produced a Calabash pipe and began filling it. I noticed Holmes give a start as the man continued his narrative.

"George and I had a row three years ago when our father died and bequeathed the entire family fortune to George. We argued about the money, but he refused to give me a shilling."

Just before Hartcliffe put a match to his pipe, Holmes said, "I notice you smoke a Calabash. It isn't a common pipe because of its size."

"The men at the Works are always giving me a hard time about this pipe. It's the only gift my father ever gave me. It was a week before he died. I suppose he was feeling guilty about his shoddy treatment of me. He carved my initials *CEH* into the side. I thought it was quite touching."

He handed the pipe to Holmes. who examined the small initials at the bottom of the gourd's bend. Hartcliffe continued, "Then I discovered he gave an identical pipe with GBH engraved on it to my brother."

Holmes showed the initials to me and handed the pipe back. Hartcliffe lit his Calabash and said, "It smokes a little cooler than other pipes."

Holmes stood up, walked over to the lamp table by the fireplace, picked up the ashtray and set it on the desk by the judge's brother. Hartcliffe took a draw on his pipe and said, "George got everything."

"I know firsthand how it can be with older brothers," Holmes said.

Bradstreet explained how the judge's secretary used his position to forge documents and, when confronted, lashed out at the judge.

"Well, now that I'm here, I suppose I should speak with the staff."

"I would be in your debt, Mr. Hartcliffe, if you could first inspect your brother's rooms upstairs to secure any personal belongings you find before anyone disturbs them. Inspector Bradstreet here can show you up."

Bradstreet gave Holmes a quizzical look and Holmes motioned with his eyes that it was part of some plan. The inspector played along and stood up.

Holmes said, "You can leave that excellent pipe in the ashtray."

Hartcliffe laid his Calabash down and followed Bradstreet out the door.

"Quick, Watson! The door! Keep watch and let me know when you see them returning." Holmes sprang from his chair and grabbed Hartcliffe's pipe. I stood by the door as Holmes fished his penknife from his pocket and started carving on the gourd.

"What on earth are you doing?" I asked.

"His boots Watson. I am always emphasizing the importance of observing a man's boots."

I didn't understand that explanation, and said as much to him as he intently worked on the pipe.

"I kept asking myself why a man would take another man's pipe after murdering him. When I saw this Calabash, it occurred to me a murderer might take a pipe if he thought it was his own."

"Someone is coming. Wait – it's only Gregson."

Inspector Gregson entered the room and saw Holmes busily carving upon the pipe.

"I thought you would have cleared out by now. What are you doing?"

Holmes stood up and said, "Turn around and lift your shoe, Gregson. Quick. We don't have much time. Trust me."

Gregson shook his head, turned around, put his hands on the desk chair, and lifted his right foot behind him.

"I need a little dirt," Holmes said. "Watson and I have been scuffing our feet on this rug all morning but you just came in from outside." Holmes used his knife and collected some dirt off the bottom of Gregson's shoe like he was trimming the hoof of a mule.

"You are a strange bird, Mr. Holmes," the inspector remarked.

Holmes ran over to the fireplace and added a little ash to the dirt before rubbing it on the fresh scratches on the pipe. After rubbing the gourd with his hand and then cleaning it off with his shirt, he held it up to the light.

"This will do nicely," he said as he showed me the initials. He had changed the *C* to a *G* and the *E* to a *B*.

"Now we will have a little fun," he said. I looked out the door and saw Bradstreet and Hartcliffe coming down the stairs.

"Here they come," I said.

Holmes set the pipe back in the ashtray and sat back down in his chair. "Not a word about the pipe, Gregson. I implore you."

I sat back in my seat as Bradstreet and Hartcliffe stepped into the room.

"Gregson – back already?" asked Bradstreet. "This is Charles Hartcliffe, the judge's brother." Turning to Hartcliffe, he explained that Inspector Gregson was overseeing the case.

"We have our suspect in custody," Gregson said to Hartcliffe.

"I am in your debt, Inspector," Hartcliffe said as he retrieved his Calabash from the ashtray and sat down. As the man put a match to the pipe, Holmes said, "It is fortunate that you came by today. I wouldn't want to see an innocent man hanged."

"What do you mean?" he asked.

"It's no use Hartcliffe. Your boots have given you away. The toe of your right boot is clean, yet the left boot is dirty. Why does a man clean only one boot? Because there is something on it that needs immediate attention. A woman will often wipe off both boots even if only one needs attention. However, a man will invariably just wipe off the one dirty boot. You wiped your right boot when you discovered blood had spattered on it when you sliced your brother's throat."

"This is outrageous!" Hartcliffe exclaimed.

"Your square-toed boot matches the blotting I made of the blood spatter. I am sure a microscopic examination of your boot will reveal particles of your brother's blood."

"You're insane."

"After smashing your brother's skull with the poker, you noticed a Calabash in the ashtray. In your excited state, you picked it up, thinking it was your pipe."

"This is absurd!" Hartcliffe exclaimed as he stood up.

"Then tell me how it is that you're smoking your brother's pipe?"

Hartcliffe looked at his pipe and his face turned white. "I can't believe I picked up the wrong pipe again – " Realizing what he had just said, he sat back down and looked at the floor.

"George got everything," he said.

Gregson was speechless.

Hartcliffe sat for a moment in silence. He knew he was defeated, so he began his narrative. "I was shooting darts and having a few pints of

245

bitter at the pub down the street when it occurred to me that my brother was nearby and I could ask him for some money. My rent is due, and I have nothing in the bank. I walked here and saw the light on in the study. I tapped on the French doors and George let me in. He was cordial at first and poured me a drink. We sat talking for a few minutes. When I asked for money, he became angry and said I was drunk and a fool. I don't know what came over me. All those years of abuse from him and from my father filled my head with rage. I grabbed the poker. He lunged at me, and I struck him down hard. He fell to the floor."

Hartcliffe paused to take a deep breath.

"I put the poker back and noticed my pipe in the ashtray. I didn't remember laying it there, but I wasn't thinking straight. I didn't know father had given him an identical pipe. I shoved it into my pocket and felt the dart spud I carry. Then an idea occurred to me. I had heard that John Davenport had escaped Dartmoor a couple of weeks ago and I could make it look like his handiwork. I don't know the man personally, but I saw him play darts once a few years back."

Hartcliffe smiled at the thought of his own cleverness. "I tossed my spud on the floor and took a knife to George. He deserved no better. Then I left and walked back to the pub. I noticed the blood on the toe of my boot, wiped it off, and washed my hands, which were covered in blood."

Hartcliffe paused for a moment, then he looked up and said, "When I got the telegram this morning, I figured I had better show up or it would cause suspicion."

Gregson grunted, walked out of the room, and returned with Officer Franklin.

"Hartcliffe here is under arrest for murder," Gregson ordered. "Handcuff him and take him in."

Bradstreet turned to my friend and said, "I don't know how you do it, Mr. Holmes."

The Burning Heart
by MJH Simmonds

Chapter I

Spring 1885 saw the first public exhibition of the largest flawless ruby ever discovered. Unearthed in India some ten years previously, the "Burning Heart" was put on limited display within the armoured strongroom of a renowned London jeweller. Hundreds flocked daily to view its dark red heart and marvel at the scattered rose-tinted light that danced magically around the room. Day and night, the gem was kept under heavy guard. The newspapers stated, boastfully, that Scotland Yard themselves had tested and approved the security measures surrounding the priceless artefact.

Friday, the thirteenth of March, had seen a dramatic improvement in the weather. Previous weeks had felt distinctly wintry. However, the sun rose high and bright that morning and London basked in its warmth for the first time in some four months. I spent the morning walking in Regent's Park before joining Holmes in town for coffee and a light lunch. It was a joy to again sit at an outside table after so long spent eating and smoking indoors. Holmes was in surprisingly good form, having solved a particularly difficult case just the previous day.

"The new screws were the giveaway, you see," he explained happily. "The whole front section of the balcony rail had been removed, altered, and then refitted. All of the screws were removed except those at the bottom. These were replaced with smooth bolts which allowed the whole barrier to tilt forward if the slightest pressure was applied."

"How fiendish," I commented.

"The poor victim arrived home, lit a cigarette and went out onto the balcony to smoke, as was his habit. He stuck out a hand to lean upon the balcony rail and – Well, you can imagine, Doctor."

"Third-floor apartment, so roughly thirty feet, head first onto the paved inner courtyard. The injuries must have been horrific. At least he would have died instantly." I sighed at man's continued ingenuity and appetite for slaughtering his fellow being.

"The valet then pulled the barrier back into position and quickly re-fitted the four screws, which made the whole frame appear solid. However, the original fixings had scraped out a considerable amount of old paint and rusted metal as they were removed. This meant that he had to replace the

247

original screws with ones of a larger diameter. This would not have been an issue if he'd taken the trouble to age the screw-heads to match the originals. A cursory examination was all that was required to be certain that foul play had occurred."

"So you proved that the poor old Baron did not commit suicide, after all. Bravo. Did you establish a motive?"

"I left that to Gregson. He was off to search the home of the valet's lady friend as I left. I wouldn't be at all surprised if several of the Baron's more valuable possessions are discovered to have mysteriously found their way to that location."

Holmes casually blew cigar smoke into the warm air. With the technical problems solved, he had completely lost interest in the case, leaving the official force to complete the more-pedestrian tasks and, of course, take the credit. If my writings were ever to achieve anything, I hoped that they might at least go some way to redress the balance and reveal the identity of who had, in actuality, solved most of these crimes.

We enjoyed a final coffee and left the cafe just as the afternoon sun began to wane. We took a cab back to Baker Street and there settled down for a quiet evening of reading and reflection. I managed to hold on for a couple of hours before giving in to the lure of the brandy decanter. I poured two glasses and placed them upon the small lacquered ebony table that sat between our respective armchairs. Holmes looked up from his scientific journal and glanced towards the window.

"Someone approaches," he announced. "A telegram, I believe. Hobnail boots, badly repaired, far more prominence to the right foot. Old Bob Roberts, if I'm not mistaken."

The doorbell rang, right on cue. We didn't hear Mrs. Hudson open the door or address our visitor, but we couldn't miss the muffled sound of the voice that replied. Bob Roberts was rather hard of hearing and had developed a tendency to speak at a volume rather more suited to a Sergeant Major on the parade ground.

A minute later there was a knock on the door as Mrs. Hudson brought up the message. Holmes leapt up, swung open the door, and accepted the note, graciously thanking our landlady with a dramatic bow. He stood, silently reading the missive before thrusting it into my fingers.

"Watson," he declared, "unhand the brandy. We have work this evening."

We took a cab to Knightsbridge, the twenty-minute drive passing quickly and pleasantly in the newly arrived spring evening air. Simonicz and Sons was one of London's finest jewellers, regular suppliers of bespoke finery to the great monarchies of Europe. Their London showroom was a cleverly designed combination of elegant wood and glass display rooms, and also a virtual fortress.

I still held the telegram in my hand. *"Burning Heart stolen. Come to S. and S. Lestrade."* Just a few simple words but their meaning was clear. We had a new case.

Chapter II

Inspector Lestrade greeted us as we stepped out of our cab. Several black police wagons were set in a line in front of the esteemed jewellers, and more than a dozen constables were positioned before these, to prevent any over-eager onlookers from approaching the building.

"Good evening, gentlemen." Lestrade appeared even more than usually agitated. "Thank you for coming at such short notice."

"I take it from your demeanour that this affair isn't entirely straightforward," declared Holmes.

"Please come inside," replied the inspector, keen to lead us quickly out of public view. "I will explain all."

Although Lestrade was one of Scotland Yard's more able investigators, and a trusted friend, his first loyalty remained with the Metropolitan Police. The theft of the ruby, after such a public endorsement of the security measures put in place, would, at best, be a cause of extreme embarrassment. At worst, it would make the police appear utterly incompetent.

We passed through the open doorway and into the primary showroom. This was currently bare, all of the stock having been placed into the company safe overnight for safekeeping. Empty mahogany and walnut cabinets lined the walls, the red baize within giving the space an infernal glow. Lestrade gestured us through and into a short hallway. At the far end was an open door, iron-clad, and at least four inches thick. Hanging on massive steel hinges was the entrance into the armoured showroom.

This room was about seven or eight yards square. Ebony display cases filled with precious artefacts lined three of the walls, and in the centre was a large glass cabinet. This was around five feet in height, the first three being simply a wooden base. The upper part was steel bound, with thick glass windows on all four sides. One of these panes was shattered. Glass lay both on the floor and inside the cabinet which was, quite clearly, empty.

"Stay here, both of you," Holmes ordered as he moved forward, as stealthy as a mountain leopard.

For about five minutes, Holmes examined the case and surrounding area in complete silence. Once apparently satisfied, he looked up and addressed Lestrade.

"Tell me all," he demanded. "Spare no detail."

Lestrade sighed. It clearly wasn't the first time he had been forced to recount the story.

"We received the call at around seven o'clock. We were here within twenty minutes, but to be honest, we could have taken our time. The guards had already caught the villains. They were locked up here in this very room."

"Your narrative is about as tidy as your suit, Inspector. Please, remember to whom you are speaking. Try again – or if you cannot, then please bring us the witnesses, these guards of which you speak." Holmes's irritation was palpable.

"I'm afraid that they have already been taken away, back to the Yard. Along with those arrested, they have each been prescribed an 'accelerant', and will be watched for twenty-four hours, just in case one of them has – How can I put it – ?"

Holmes stared at Lestrade, awaiting an explanation.

"I think the inspector is referring to the possibility of ingestion," I explained.

Holmes raised an eyebrow.

"Very good, Lestrade. Although," he added, "I believe this will prove to be fruitless."

"I am sure you are right," agreed Lestrade, reluctantly, before taking a deep breath and beginning his full account.

"The building is guarded by three men. There is only one entrance, which is always within the view of at least one guard. The guards rotate positions every half-hour. One is watching the front, one walking the hall between the front and the armoured showroom, and the other resting in a small area, between the two, just off the hall. As you can see, no guard can ever be more than a few seconds from the front door or the secure room,"

"What exactly happened?" I asked.

"At just before seven, the guards heard the sound of breaking glass coming from the strongroom. They rushed to the door, unlocked it, and ran inside to find two men standing before the cabinet, one side of which was smashed open."

"They apprehended the miscreants and awaited the police?" I concluded.

"Oh no. They pulled back and slammed the door shut, trapping the thieves inside. Then they alerted the authorities."

"Most logical, in the circumstances," agreed Holmes. "Preserve the scene and reduce risk of injury."

"We arrived shortly after and the guards opened up the room. The two men were still there, they had made no effort to escape. We searched them, once, twice, over and over again, but we found nothing. They didn't have the ruby."

"And then you searched the cabinet, base and display, by the look of it." Holmes pointed at the smashed display stand. "Your attempts to rebuild it have been only moderately successful."

"Then you searched the room and the other displays and found nothing," I added.

"Every single inch. We searched each cabinet, tapped every wall and skirting board, examined the floor, and even the brickwork. The jewel isn't here. Unless it does truly lie in the guts of one of the men we have arrested, then I have no clue as to where it could have gone." Lestrade was exasperated.

"I entertained twenty-four possibilities when I entered this room, said Holmes. "Seven remain. What do we know of these guards?"

Lestrade took out his leather-bound notebook and thumbed through the pages.

"Harry Samuel is a former guardsman: Impeccable service record, two medals for bravery, and numerous mentions in dispatches. The owner, Mr. Simonicz, Junior, says he trusts him as well as one of his own sons. He was resting when the sound of breaking glass was heard. Brinwood Gaymes has worked as a security guard for over twenty years without a single incident. Gaymes was watching the door. Young master Kier Lucas was in the hallway. He rushed back to alert Samuel, who had the only key to the door."

Holmes again raised an eyebrow.

"The only key? I find that rather hard to believe."

"I forget, once again, to whom I am speaking," Lestrade sighed rather dramatically. "You are quite right. Mr. Simonicz also has a key, but before you get into one of your wild speculations, Mr. Simonicz was at a function attended by more than fifty people all evening. He had his key upon his person at all times."

"Did he indeed?" whispered Holmes, just loud enough to be certain that I would hear.

"So against all logic and reason, you don't suspect those who were actually here, present?" announced Holmes, unexpectedly. "Those who had the means and opportunity to commit the crime?"

"But the guards have also been thoroughly searched," argued Lestrade. "No one left the building before the police arrived. Two of the three are held in the highest standing, and the boy has never before been in trouble."

"I see it, Holmes," I interjected. "A conspiracy! The guards let the men inside to remove the gem. They then passed it to one of the guards, who hid it carefully before the police were alerted. That would explain everything," I finished confidently.

"Except for one thing, Doctor," Holmes stated. "Where is the ruby? The entire building has been searched by dozens of constables. They have taken up the floorboards and examined every inch of the place. Were it here, I am certain that Lestrade's men would have discovered the jewel."

"Indeed," agreed the inspector. "I even thought I had it at one point – the solution, that is. You see the display stand upon which the ruby was placed? Well, the velvet-covered blocks inside are all hollow. After breaking the glass, it would have been easy to slip the ruby inside one of them, even in the short time that they had before they were discovered. Sadly, after taking them all to pieces, we found nothing."

"What was to stop them simply opening the door and passing it to an associate?" I suggested, irritably.

"The same reason that we know that nobody left the building," Holmes said. "Lestrade has omitted a very important detail here. If I were Simonicz, I would have employed additional security to guard such an important and valuable item. A man or two, stationed outside, watching the only means of entry or exit, would have been my first choice."

Lestrade shook his head in astonished admiration.

"Quite right, Mr. Holmes. I was going to keep that little nugget of information to myself for a while, especially after you had so quickly dismissed my belief in the guards' innocence."

"Oh, Inspector, let me apologise, for I hadn't quite finished my statement. When I asked why you didn't suspect the guards, I was genuinely asking for your reasoning to compare it with my own. You see, I am also confident that these three men had nothing to do with the theft of the ruby."

Momentarily stunned by this exceedingly rare example of humility from Holmes, Lestrade struggled to find words to respond.

"Maybe we should move on," I suggested. "How, then, did these men gain entry?" I asked. "Was anything found on their person?"

The inspector quickly recovered once back on firmer ground.

"Valid questions, Doctor. And here we come to one of the most unusual aspects of this affair: Neither man had *anything* on his person. No tools, lockpicks, or jemmies. Not even a farthing. The glass appears to have been broken by force of hand, a fist wrapped in one of the men's shirts, or possibly a boot."

"Wait a minute," I asked, struggling to understand. "This makes no sense whatsoever. Are you suggesting that somehow they gained entry and then simply smashed the cabinet open and took the jewel? They must have known that they would never escape past the three guards."

"And there we have it. It appears to be a total farce – except for one thing: The Burning Heart is nowhere to be seen. It has been stolen, and we have no idea how, or where it might now be."

Holmes had begun to examine the door to the strongroom and appeared to be paying us no attention. He suddenly spun round to face us.

"The men you arrested," he demanded. "What do you know of them? What are their names?"

Again, Lestrade licked his thumb and leafed through his notebook.

"Brothers. Henry and Edward – "

"Huckle!" shouted Holmes, before Lestrade could finish.

"You know of them, then?" asked a wide-eyed Lestrade.

"Career criminals, excellent locksmiths, and the best safe-crackers in London. I thought they had retired after that Gloomfield Bank business. But this just furthers the Good Doctor's opinion: These men don't smash open cabinets to retrieve jewels. They are *artists*. They come and go, leaving no trace of their presence. Something here is very wrong."

"You can see our dilemma," replied Lestrade. "Wait a moment – what Gloomfield Bank business? Do you mean that robbery last year? Are you saying that you knew who was responsible? Why the devil didn't you share this information with me?"

Holmes looked genuinely surprised.

"Why on earth should I? I wasn't engaged in the case, and neither am I an agent of Scotland Yard. I rather assumed that you had men capable of solving such an elementary problem."

Lestrade shook his head. "Look," he said, "let us just concentrate on the matter at hand for now. Yes, it's strange that such accomplished thieves were so easily caught in the act of committing such an unsophisticated crime."

"And there is your answer, Inspector," Holmes declared. "Part of it, at least, if you are prepared to look."

"Do you have the solution?" I asked, eagerly.

"Not entirely, but I do now know that neither the guards nor the two bank-robbing brothers are responsible for the actual theft of the ruby. The men you have in custody are complicit, for certain, but I believe that they may have been bought."

"Paid to take the blame for a robbery of this scale?" Lestrade asked. "They're looking at twenty years apiece, at least. I cannot see either of them leaving gaol alive."

"Are you sure?" Holmes replied. "What will you be charging them with, exactly?"

"He is right," I agreed, realisation dawning. "This is fiendishly clever. Without having the gem itself, can you prove that they stole it? They could claim that it was already gone when they broke in and they smashed the glass out of frustration. A good brief may well succeed in arguing the case down merely to trespass and criminal damage. They may serve barely a year inside. That is a scenario which might be bought."

"Distraction," Lestrade stated firmly. "We have been deliberately led away from investigating what really happened here."

"Well done, Inspector. Everything from the moment the glass was smashed has been a blind, designed to keep us from seeing what genuinely occurred. I believe that the theft was, in reality, a very simple affair. It just didn't happen *when* we thought it did."

"What do you mean?" asked Lestrade, his frustration growing palpably. "When did it take place?"

"I have a good idea of when and how. I just need to confirm the identity of the real perpetrator. I need to interview the Brothers Huckle. Please arrange this. In the meantime, Watson and shall speak to Mr. Simonicz."

Chapter III

We found the owner in his office on the first floor. As befits the heart of such a business, the room was sumptuously decorated and furnished. Fine watercolours lined the wall, the carpets were Persian, with complex geometric patterns, woven in the finest silk thread. The chairs were fashioned from exotic hardwoods, their seats beautifully embroidered in velvet, satin, and silk. Simonicz's desk was large, hewn from darkly-hued mahogany and exotically carved. Sensuous, organic shapes ran up and down its legs.

Behind this desk stood a small man of about fifty years. The second-generation Simonicz had a kind, gentle face. His lips had a natural upturned tilt, giving him a natural resting smile. Gold-rimmed *pince-nez* sat upon a small nub of a nose. His snow-white hair was swept back and matched a small moustache, carefully trimmed upon his otherwise soft, clean-shaven, face.

"Good evening, gentlemen," he greeted us, warmly. "I hope that you can make some sense of these matters. I fear that it may be a little too much for the inspector."

"Lestrade is one of Scotland Yard's finest investigators," countered Holmes, surprisingly. "He will not rest until the jewel is recovered. You can depend on him. In the meantime, I hope I can trouble you to answer a few simple questions. It would be of tremendous assistance to the investigation."

"Why, of course." Simonicz leaned in closer. "I have read of your exploits in the newspapers, Mr. Holmes," he revealed quietly. "I'm extremely keen to witness how you approach this matter."

"My methods are simple: Reasoning, observation, and research. But today my questions are simply for clarification – to complete the picture, so to speak.

"What is the procedure for the completion of the business day?" Holmes continued. "I know that it's longer and more complicated in the jewellery trade than, perhaps, any other. Who is involved, and in what order do they perform their tasks?"

Holmes smiled benignly, but I had already recognised that these questions weren't mere bookkeeping. They were, in fact, of vital importance to the case.

"Well, it isn't that complicated a procedure," replied Simonicz. "There are three staff present at the end of the day, plus the security guards. The day security is relieved half-an-hour before we close up. Under the watchful eye of the guards, the two salesmen remove the more valuable pieces from display and deposit them inside the safe. This takes about twenty minutes to half-of-an-hour. Visitors are politely requested to make their way to the exit and the manager locks the front door at five. He, or one of the salesmen, checks the strongroom, then closes and locks the door. The three men leave together, and the senior security guard bolts the front door closed behind them. As for myself, I am now resolutely part-time, and if I do venture into the office, I rarely stay beyond four o'clock. I was not present today – Well, not until I was summoned by a most unwelcome telegram."

"Do you happen to know who locked the strongroom door this evening?" Holmes asked casually.

Simonicz thought for a moment, then an expression of realisation appeared on his face.

"Yes, actually I do. Normally, I would have no idea, but I was present downstairs when the inspector asked the same question of Samuel. He said that the manager, Mr. Wise, usually locks the strongroom door himself. However, on this occasion, one of the salesmen offered to do the task for him. 'Insisted upon it' were his words. Now, which one was it?"

Simonicz's face screwed up in concentration as he tried to recall.

"Ah, yes, I have it!" he announced. "Samuel stated that young Tipton was eager to leave and meet up with his fiancée for dinner, and was waiting at the front door. It was Halford who offered to lock the inner door."

"What can you tell me about Halford?" Holmes asked, feigning indifference.

"Robert Halford had been with us for about three months. He arrived with excellent references and has always been conscientious and scrupulously honest. A fine young man. I believe he lives with his family somewhere in the new suburbs."

"I would be eternally grateful if you could provide us with contact details for all three of the staff present this evening," asked Holmes.

"Of course. I'll have the requested information ready for you before you leave."

We bade farewell to the amiable jeweller and returned downstairs.

"The exhibition was announced just over three months ago," I rasped, excitedly. "Surely not a coincidence?"

Holmes almost let a smile slip across his face.

"I knew it!" I declared. "Halford is our man. We may now have the '*who*' and '*when*', but I still have no idea of the '*how*'.

"Patience, Watson. Why, here comes the inspector."

Lestrade was strolling back towards the building just as we exited by the front door.

"I've spoken to the Yard and they're happy for you to interview the Huckles", announced the inspector, but without enthusiasm.

"Chin up!" Holmes encouraged. "I have a name for you to search with your men."

Lestrade's entire demeanour immediately changed. His shoulders rose and life returned to his tired eyes.

"You have the man? Well done, Mr. Holmes!" he declared. "I knew you could crack this."

"We aren't over the finishing line quite yet. The jewel may have already been passed on. You must leave immediately if we are to have any chance of apprehending the thief and recovering the ruby."

Holmes handed the inspector a note with Halford's name. Lestrade left at pace to speak with several constables.

"Do you think that they'll catch Halford with the gem?" I asked.

"Perhaps," muttered Holmes. "If they're quick. Chances are favourable that Halford wouldn't have expected us to have identified him so soon as the thief."

A large, red-bearded sergeant approached us and handed Holmes a folded page of notepaper.

"From Mr. Simonicz," he announced.

Holmes nodded in acknowledgement before proceeding to scribble a short missive onto a leaf of his notepad. He swiftly tore this off and handed it, along with Simonicz's note, to the rather bemused-looking policeman.

"Please take these to the inspector and have him carry out my instructions," he ordered before briskly striding away.

"Are you finally going to share with me exactly how this robbery was achieved?" I asked, with little hope, almost running to keep up with my long, lean friend.

"Of course. Once we have spoken to the Huckles, all will be clear."

Chapter IV

The cab ride to Scotland Yard took no longer than usual but the journey was improved infinitely by the feel of the warm evening air caressing our faces. Free of fog and mist, London's night-time streets were beautiful, the stone and brick buildings illuminated in soft yellows and browns by the light of countless gas lamps.

Once we reached our destination, hard reality quickly returned. As we moved deeper into the labyrinthine depths of the Yard, the temperature seemed to drop, and when we finally reached the cells where the Huckle brothers were being held, I was buttoning up my overcoat against the chill.

"Here you go, gents," announced the old, white-haired sergeant who had shown us inside. "The inspector said that you could have ten minutes with each of them, but when I heard it was for you, Mr. Holmes, I put them in here together so you can have a full twenty minutes with both."

He tapped his nose conspiratorially and unlocked the metal-bound door. Holmes smiled briefly in return and strode confidently into the cell.

I followed Holmes inside while the sergeant remained outside. He seemed to have no interest in our conversation. The cell was small, the walls washed a dull white. Sat side by side on a single bunk were the Huckle brothers.

"A pleasure to see you again, Mr. Holmes," spoke the brother to our left.

"And you, Henry," replied Holmes, helpfully identifying the older of the two brothers.

Henry Huckle was certainly closer to sixty than fifty. He had a halo of thick white hair around an otherwise bald red pate. His eyes were the brightest blue, keen and intelligent. A wide, puckered nose dominated his face, the result of much drinking, I suspected. His brother was perhaps five years younger but far leaner. His hair still had streaks of black among the white hairs and covered his head to such a degree that his eyes were almost hidden beneath the long fringe.

"I speak to you in complete confidence," began Holmes. "I am not employed by the police in this matter, and intend to act in the interests of justice rather than those of Scotland Yard."

The Huckles didn't reply, so Holmes continued.

"I know who really stole the ruby. Inspector Lestrade is currently in the process of arresting Robert Halford and recovering the jewel."

Holmes watched the brothers carefully, waiting for their reaction. To my amazement, they said nothing. Henry folded his arms and Edward took to whistling softly and glancing around the small room.

"I see. You do realise that once we have Halford and the Burning Heart, the charges against you will certainly increase to conspiracy at the very least? At best, you will still receive ten years. What was promised to you before will now not be possible. It's time to tell us all that you know. You may still have a chance of a retirement of sorts if you now cooperate."

The Huckle brothers remained silent.

"Your loyalty will not be rewarded," Holmes warned. "I expect Halford to sing like the proverbial canary once Lestrade gets him back here."

"If he does, he will be dead within a week."

I was surprised to hear Edward Huckle's voice for the first time. His brother hissed at him to cease and remain silent.

"Edward, please continue," encouraged Holmes. "We hear so little from you, but when we do it is always gold."

Henry attempted to stop his brother from speaking, but the younger Huckle pushed him easily away.

"I know you, Mr. Holmes. And I know that you know what was done. But what you don't know is that we done a deal with the Devil. He may have a silver tongue, but his heart is black. We couldn't say no. He would have hurt our families. He is cunning as a snake but much more venomous. Leave us be now, Mr. Holmes. We must do our time."

Holmes's face was dark and he appeared to be fighting an inner battle. Finally, he spoke.

"I understand. I have your confirmation of my theory, and you have my promise that I will not reveal what I suspect to the authorities. It will remain a conspiracy between Halford and yourselves."

"Thank you, Mr. Holmes," replied Henry, clear relief painted across his face.

Holmes turned and departed the cell without another word. I followed him back through the corridors and hallways until we finally exited the building.

"The Huckle brothers will never leave gaol alive," Holmes announced, as we settled down into a Hansom.

"What do you mean?" I replied.

"If they cooperate with the authorities, they will receive lighter sentences. However, their families will be targeted and they will have a price put on their heads. They will not last long in prison. If they refuse to help us, they will be given long terms inside. They aren't young men. A ten-year stretch may already be beyond them. These aren't evil men. They steal from rich men and banks, but they aren't killers – unlike whoever is behind this whole scheme."

"I am not at all certain of what you fear. Surely all involved should be arrested and tried in a fair court of law."

"A presence has been growing in London, dear Doctor. What was but recently shadow and reflection, whisper and rumour, is now becoming corporeal. For the first time, we may have an advantage over them. However, I cannot risk the brothers' lives for merely a confirmation of their involvement."

"Whose involvement? What are you suggesting? That we should deliberately not solve this case?" I was astonished by what Holmes seemed to be proposing.

"Perhaps. If we are lucky, Halford may have already passed on the infernal rock. Why are men so addicted to these useless baubles? They perform no function. They reflect and refract light. They have no practical use whatsoever. Even gold can be fashioned into something useful. I even hear that it is fast becoming essential in the field of electrical sciences."

Holmes appeared unusually uncertain, an image that I can rarely recall.

"If you truly believe that lives are at stake," I stated, "I will support any decision that you make that would remedy this situation, including giving up the ruby. I am a doctor, remember? Life, to me, is sacrosanct, I hold my oath far above any sparkling trinkets," I declared.

Holmes smiled. "I never doubted that for a single moment," he replied.

Chapter V

We returned to Baker Street to await news from Lestrade. We took a late supper of ham, eggs, and bread, and settled down in our armchairs with a glass of brandy and Holmes's seemingly bottomless supply of Havana cigars.

"I would ask the identity of your supplier," I laughed, "but as you have never ventured the information, I presume that it is proscribed knowledge."

Holmes thought for a moment before replying.

"Not quite, Watson, but it is a tale not yet ready to be told, even to you, my dear friend. Please, simply enjoy the spoils of a difficult, but ultimately righteous, conclusion to a particularly delicate case."

We talked further on several subjects. Science and the latest medical advances seemed to be of most interest to Holmes, along with, conversely, the kind of idle, puerile gossip that I always believed to be beneath him. He, however, insisted that, if properly filtered, this was of more practical use to an investigator, such as himself, than any article published in *The Times*.

Just after midnight, we heard the doorbell ring. After a minute or so, there came footsteps on the stairs and a knocking on the door to our rooms. As Holmes appeared uninterested, I rose slowly, padded over to the door and pulled it open.

"Good evening, gentlemen," announced Inspector Lestrade. "Apologies for the lateness of the hour, but I was certain that you would still be awake."

"Quite right, Inspector," I replied. I waved him inside and towards a vacant armchair.

A generous measure of brandy was offered, and a fine Montecristo Number Three cigar was quickly lit.

I eagerly awaited Lestrade's report while Holmes appeared more interested in the length of ash he could form on his cigar.

"We apprehended Halford just before nine this evening. We searched his house and garden for hours. I still have men there, taking up floorboards and digging up the back yard. We will continue tomorrow at first light, of course, but I'm already resigned to the fact that the jewel is there no longer. I knew it as soon as laid eyes on him, Mr. Holmes. His face – he couldn't hide a smirk. That's when I knew we were too late."

Holmes's face remained placid, while I was struggling to contain my delight.

"I see," he replied without feeling. "I will admit that I fear you're correct. The man's reactions do seem to indicate that the gem is long gone."

Lestrade nodded and took a long draught on his cigar. The police and Scotland Yard, in particular, would certainly face some criticism over this affair, but the inspector wasn't directly involved, and the force would soon recover. After all, the police merely acted as advisors. They were not responsible for the actual security. They could simply claim that their advice was incorrectly followed.

Lestrade suddenly appeared very serious indeed.

"Mr. Holmes. I know that you have information vital to this case that you haven't shared. I also believe that you know, or at least suspect, who might be responsible for the planning and execution of this crime, and it wasn't a shop assistant."

Lestrade then sank back into his chair and took a large swig of brandy.

"However, I am also a patient man," he continued. "I do believe that you did everything within your powers to solve this case, but we were unlucky at the end. Now I feel that something has changed. I also know that the reason you are keeping the truth from me must be an exceedingly good one. Share this with me and I swear that I will not take the information outside this room."

Silence followed, and for several tense minutes. I didn't know how Holmes would respond.

"What I am about to share with you, gentlemen," announced Holmes, unexpectedly and rather dramatically, "is mere supposition, you understand."

"Good enough for me," replied Lestrade, raising his glass.

"As we discussed previously," Holmes began, "this whole affair hinges on one thing. Distraction.

"The solution is remarkably simple if you ignore the existing flowery statements and simply follow the timeline." Holmes took a deep puff on his cigar. "Timing?" he asked, now wreathed in grey ribbons of smoke. "When did the theft take place?"

"I'm not sure," I replied uncertainly. "Sometime before seven, of course, for that's when the police were called, just after the cabinet was smashed."

"Not even close," Holmes declared. "The theft occurred within a few minutes of five o'clock at the very latest."

"How can that be?" I asked, incredulously.

"I think we'd better let Mr. Holmes explain," advised Lestrade, puffing contentedly upon his cigar.

I shrugged and urged Holmes to continue.

"The art of distraction works best when the plan is a simple one. The observer concentrates on one thing while the perpetrator acts elsewhere. In this case, the two events are separated not by *space*, but by *time*."

Holmes, without looking, casually reached out his arm towards the glass ashtray sitting on the small lacquered ebony table that sat between our armchairs. His cigar ash, now over three inches in length, chose that exact moment to collapse and fall gracefully into the receptacle below.

"*Time*, gentlemen, is the key. The guards, hearing the smashing of glass, rushed to the locked strongroom and there inside discovered a terrible equation: Plus two intruders and minus one gemstone!"

Holmes was clearly enjoying himself, gradually revealing the solution at his own deliberate pace.

"The guards then acted exactly as they had been ordered. They slammed the door shut and contacted the authorities. This aided both themselves and the real criminal. The actions of the guards were confirmed by an outside agent, one employed independently by Simonicz himself. We can therefore be certain that no one left the building until the arrival of the police."

"But," he exclaimed, a long, marble-hued finger pointing to the heavens, "where was the ruby? The men and the room were searched thoroughly for hours. I presume that the possibility of ingestion has now passed?" Holmes asked, leaning towards the inspector.

As Lestrade nodded, I shuddered at the thought of the poor officers who would have been tasked with this duty.

"The Huckle brothers didn't have the ruby because they did not steal it," continued Holmes, his eyes alight. "At least not then."

Holmes noticed my face of complete incomprehension.

"Try to keep up for now, Watson," he advised. "It will all resolve itself, I promise."

"Of that, I have no doubt," I replied, with as much sincerity as I could manage.

Holmes ignored me and continued his explanation.

"When examined logically, there can be only one reason why the jewel wasn't found: It must have been taken earlier. The entire situation, all of the events from the sound of breaking glass onwards, were a blind, a distraction to hide the mechanics of the real crime."

"When and how was the real crime committed?" demanded Lestrade, completely enthralled.

"The '*how*' is, of course, very simple, but it depended entirely upon the '*when*'. By the way, Lestrade: Did your men find an answer to the question which I wrote down and handed to a passing sergeant?"

Lestrade looked momentarily surprised, then rummaged in his pockets and finally withdrew a crumpled piece of notepaper.

"Do you mean this? It's a note asking for an officer to question Tipton, the second salesman, regarding his dinner plans for that evening. I must admit that I was surprised that it was taken seriously, but now I see what Inspector Downing has written on the reverse, it takes on a new meaning."

Holmes smiled encouragingly.

"Please read what the inspector has written," he asked.

"'*Tipton wanted to leave promptly, as he had arranged a dinner with his fiancée. A friend had secured for them a special bargain deal at a popular restaurant in town. However, the one condition was that they had to arrive early.*'"

"I think I can guess the identity of this friend," I commented.

"Of course it was Halford," confirmed Holmes. "This was the first step of the plan, ensuring that Halford would be the one to perform the final check upon the strongroom."

"The timeline is thus: At half-past-four, the daytime security guards are relieved by the three night-time guards. The two salesmen, under supervision, place the valuable items from the front showroom into the safe. Once this is completed, Halford proceeds to the strongroom and announces to any remaining visitors that it is time to leave. He ushers these out and, once all have left, he closes and locks the door. The manager then lets Tipton leave, slightly early as he had requested, before performing the last few tasks of the day. Finally, Halford and the manager leave the shop and the door is bolted behind them by Harry Samuel."

"Sorry," I admitted. "I still don't see it."

Lestrade hummed, he appeared to have noticed something that I had missed.

"Yes, Lestrade." Holmes smiled. "I can see that you're beginning to understand."

I took the opportunity to refill our glasses and reached for my pipe as Holmes continued.

"Imagine that you are in the strongroom, a few minutes before five, viewing the precious red bauble. A man enters and announces that the store is closing and that it's time to leave. What do you do? Do you wait until you are the absolute last person before leaving? Of course not, you leave along with everyone else there present. If two men waited behind you and then tucked themselves into the dark corners on either side of the door, would you really notice?"

"Good Lord," I exclaimed, "I think I have it now!"

Holmes's withering glance shamed me back into silence.

"This was the crucial moment. Once the last genuine customer had left the strongroom, the Huckle brothers had to act. Halford could remain at the doorway, blocking the view inside for, perhaps, a minute without raising suspicion. This was all the time the brothers had to pick the lock and steal the Burning Heart. But for two such accomplished safecrackers, a mere lock was child's play. They would have had it open in seconds."

"But what about the tools?" I asked, already knowing that the answer would be painfully delivered. "They must have used lockpicks, where did they hide these?"

"Oh, Watson, did you not hear me when I said that the best plans are always the simplest? Once the cabinet was open, the Huckles simply reached inside, took the ruby and handed it to Halford. They also gave him all of their tools before he closed and locked the door behind him."

263

"They then waited until the agreed time," Lestrade added, shaking his head in disbelief. "Seven as it happens, and just as planned, smashed the case and waited for the guards to arrive."

"Exactly, Inspector," confirmed Holmes. "They also knew, from Halford, that once discovered, the guards would lock them inside and await the authorities. The plan played out perfectly. Halford left with the jewel and the tools. He probably passed the ruby on shortly after he left. We never really had a chance of recovering it. The tools are probably now at the bottom of the Thames."

"Well, I never," was all that I could manage.

"So is it case closed?" asked Lestrade.

"I can see no obvious lines of further inquiry," admitted Holmes, unexpectedly.

"In that case," announced Lestrade, rising somewhat uncertainly to his feet, "as it is now drawing closer to the time when it will cease to be late and start to be early, I will take my leave."

I guided Lestrade to the door and wished him a good night. The inspector tipped his hat, turned to depart, and then spun back around.

"Let me know when you are ready to act, won't you, Mr. Holmes? I think it is past time we put an end to these games, don't you?"

I closed the door behind Lestrade and returned, perplexed, to my armchair.

"What the devil was that? It sounds as if the Lestrade isn't only fully aware that you kept much of the case from him, but also suspects that you know the identity of the man behind this whole affair."

"Lestrade has many faults, but stupidity isn't one of them. He has recognised a pattern – the signature, if you will – of this crime. We have witnessed it before."

I rose, shakily, and refilled my glass, Holmes's remained untouched. The thought that an anonymous figure was, somehow, influencing our lives from afar was shocking and unacceptable.

"Do not fret, Watson," replied Holmes, slowly and carefully, "for this time we may, for once, have the advantage of him."

"How so?" I asked, eagerly.

"He believes that he has been successful. The crime has been executed successfully. He has the jewel, and nobody suspects that he is responsible."

"How does that aid us?" I asked, uncertainly, the brandy beginning to take effect.

"There is much still to discover. We will revisit the Huckles once the case is cooler, and there is still more that Halford can provide us, I am sure. The important thing is that he will be off his guard."

I finished my brandy, shared a final smoke with Holmes, and finally took myself off to my room. I still felt the lagging weight of failure as I crawled into bed. Our shadowy adversary might well now be staring into the hypnotic reflections of the ruby and laughing at his success.

I sat up and shook my head. I would not succumb to such negative thoughts. The battle may have been lost, but I believed, with all my heart, that, with the help of Sherlock Holmes, and indeed Inspector Lestrade, we could conquer this villain and be rid of his malign influence forever.

The Curious Case
of the Transmuting Tome
by Daniel Lenois

In selecting which, among those near countless accounts I have made some private note of throughout the years spent working alongside my friend, Mr. Sherlock Holmes, should, by their very nature, be ideally suited for the public record, I must plead guilty at times to having favoured those more spectacular engagements which commend themselves so naturally to literary form. However, of those perhaps less outwardly extravagant examples I have yet to set to print, which nevertheless demonstrate with readiness the evident intellectual dexterity of my companion, few share more intrinsically curious properties than that case brought to our door on that singular Monday in June of the year 1885.

Holmes and I were at breakfast in our rooms when we were suddenly interrupted by the sound of hurried sharp tapping at the front door, so pronounced that it reached us clearly from where we sat. Moments later, our landlady brought us the visitor's card. Holmes took and glanced at it.

"A Mr. Henry Davis," read Holmes. "Very good. Do see him in. I do believe, Watson," he remarked to me, "that our day is about to become of notably greater interest."

Moments later, an elderly man strode into the room, with a purposeful gait that contrasted his frail appearance. He was clean-shaven, the snowy hair atop his head was neatly parted, and the suit he wore was of fine quality. In one hand he clutched a walking cane, upon whose head bore the carved likeness of a raven. As he came within sight of us, Henry Davis looked at us both with that momentary uncertainty that bespoke, louder than words, that he was not entirely sure which of us to address.

"I wish to speak with the Mr. Sherlock Holmes," he declared.

"Your wish is easily granted," Holmes responded good-naturedly.

"You are he?" Davis asked sharply, his eyes trained on Holmes with the unbreakable zeal of a diving falcon in lockstep with its unwary prey.

"I am."

"I have business with you, Mr. Holmes," said he, in the sharp, impersonal tone of the German who took to English at some later date in life. "A personal matter, and one of business also, whose meaning is lost upon me entirely."

"I am at your immediate disposal, Mr. Davis." Holmes gestured to me. "This is my friend, Dr. John Watson. You may rest assured he can be trusted with whatever you wish to say. Please do take a seat, and tell us everything. Spare no detail."

Mr. Davis nodded curtly and sat.

"It is this, Mr. Holmes: In my youth, I attended the University of Rostock, and intended to one day take up a position as a scholar in Germany. In the course of my studies, I was invited to travel, in order to attend prominent lectures given at various foreign universities. It was during one such expedition, in the year 1832, that I first travelled to your country. The lecture itself is of little relevance to this conversation.

"However, it was there that I met the woman that was to soon become the love of my life. With my semester near at an end, I soon returned to England for the duration of that summer, where I could be closer to my Amelia. We married the following spring, and my modest successes in literary publication, along with my duties as a librarian, has seen more than satisfactorily to our needs. It was just prior to my marriage that I changed my name, so as to better integrate into British society. Soon thereafter, I found myself a position as a librarian in a private academic library. In the years since, my life has been pleasurably unremarkable in almost every aspect."

Davis smiled to himself, then paused for a moment, as if to gather his thoughts.

"I suppose I should speak something of the library itself. It is a fairly large building, containing two upper floors in addition to the ground floor. The latter is fairly open in its design, resembling in its composition something of a museum. Aside from our own most prized texts and relics, we occasionally also receive the honour of displaying certain literary objects on loan from other institutions or private estates. Public exhibits are conducted regularly, although our grandeur is as nothing when compared to the university libraries, of which you are no doubt familiar."

Davis laughed harshly. "A reality that has not as of yet become apparent to our director." He grimaced and continued with his narrative:

"The ground floor connects to the one directly above through the use of an elaborate staircase, which splits midway up into two opposing directions, one facing the left wing, the other facing the right. Smaller individual spiral staircases go to the second floor above."

Davis smiled apologetically. "I apologise should my narrative try your patience, Mr. Holmes. I merely strive to be precise in every detail, great or inconsequential. Should any point I have raised appear as unclear to your mind, pray correct me, and I shall make all efforts to elucidate."

Holmes nodded and waved him on.

"The library of which I speak is not one intended for public consumption. Rather, it is most commonly frequented by lawyers, doctors, and even textual scholars from Oxford, Cambridge, and others whose careers align closely with our particular and, dare I say it, rather extensive trove of human knowledge. In more recent years, we have opened our doors to any student, faculty, author, or other relevant person or persons whose research coincides with the contents of our archives."

He cleared his throat and continued.

"The life of a librarian is, I need hardly tell you, hardly an exciting one. Indeed, excitement is oftentimes perhaps to the detriment of our efforts. Our library is open from Monday through Friday, with reduced hours on Saturday and Sunday. The majority of our visitors consist of students and faculty consulting our archives for the purposes of academic study. I am at my station every day from when the library opens its doors at nine a.m. to when it closes at the same time that evening. However, the duties of the librarian do not end merely when the last remaining student is escorted to the door. I often spend an additional quarter-hour or so seeing to it that all is neat and orderly before my departure.

"It was then, last Monday, as part of my regular patrol of the aisles, that I observed that one of the books, a distinctly unremarkable tome on the practical implications of common law, stuck out roughly from the shelf – a shelf upon which it most certainly didn't belong. It is not uncommon for a visiting student, in some urgent rush, to misfile a book, and so I thought little of it. I picked up the book and, upon some sudden impulse, I opened it and ran through its first few pages. To my surprise, I observed that its original table of contents had been cut neatly from its front, and in its place, that of a distinctly different book glued in its place. Utterly baffled by this, I took the book and stored it away in a drawer under my desk, so that I might take the matter up with my superiors in the morning. However, when I returned the following morning and opened my drawer, letting my fingers fall upon the same spot, I was shocked to discover that the original table of contents had been restored, glued back in, and its haphazard replacement nowhere to be found."

"Was the drawer locked?" Holmes inquired from his languid position upon the opposing chair.

"Yes." Our visitor reached into one pocket and pulled out a chain of keys, holding one particularly unremarkable silver key above the rest. "This is the key to my desk."

"Who else has a copy?"

"My assistant, Mr. Edward Williams. It is he that works the shorter weekend shifts. The director of the library, I am sure, has his own key to every lock within the library itself."

"Very good. Pray, continue."

"Well, Mr. Holmes, I tried to put the matter out of my mind. After all, I could no longer prove any harm had been done. Perhaps it had been a meaningless jest between classmates. Who was I to say for certain? The rest of that day passed without note. However, it was Wednesday night, when I was again on my route, that I discovered the volume had been moved again, and the table of contents had once more been torn out and yet another, different to the first replacement, lay in front of me. I again took it to my desk, and again the following morning, all was made well again."

Our visitor took an exasperated breath and then resumed his narrative.

"Nothing of significance occurred Thursday, although now I had a strong inclination that whoever was behind this unruly business would inevitably return. However, I made particular note of the book's designated position on its shelf, so I would know with certainty when it was next moved. Then, Friday evening, having once more passed by that shelf for the third time in the past hour, I noticed that telltale empty space in between the other books that told me quite clearly that the book I sought was once again on the move. I sent for a constable who I knew commonly patrolled the road just outside at that particular time of night, and we scoured the library row by row. No crevice was excluded from our search. No intruder was found. It was then that I decided the matter had gone far beyond what I could hope to resolve. So I look to you, Mr. Holmes, for I have heard it said that you are a man who specialises in wringing meaning from the inexplicable."

A momentary flush of pleasure coloured Holmes's face in response to the compliment. Holmes had ever been a particularly easy mark for flattery, as he himself has admitted to me on any number of occasions.

"There is a certain original quality about your dilemma, Mr. Davis, and I should be happy to avail you of any answers I can uncover. Tell me," he added, "if you normally work Mondays, who is stationing your post at present?"

"Williams," Davis stated simply.

Holmes nodded crisply and turned to me.

"Watson," said he, "if you would be so good as to open your paper and tell me the departure time of the next train to Northampton, I would be eternally grateful."

I did so.

"There is an eleven o'clock from King's Cross," I read aloud.

"Very good," Holmes responded. "Then, I believe, we should have enough time to finish our breakfast. Mr. Davis, if you should be so inclined, I believe our landlady would be more than delighted to furnish you with a plate as well. There are few better remedies for an uneasy mind than a filling meal."

It was near upon two o'clock when we finally stepped off the train and subsequently took a carriage to the aforementioned library. The sky was clear, and the temperature was comfortably warm.

The library was a large building, containing three separate floors: The ground floor and two uppers. It became immediately apparent to me why a singular librarian might have experienced some difficulty in detecting the presence of another person in the complex, multi-layered space.

"Quite remarkable, is it not, Dr. Watson?" Davis commented, perhaps reading my expression.

"Indeed," said I. The word was admittedly paltry in its description, but I could find little else to say in its place, for such was the evident mark of history within these walls that it felt as if we had stepped from the modern day, with all its meaningless noise, into a time long since dissipated into the annals of long-forgotten history. That inevitable and certain sense of physical permanence, contrasted against our own otherwise transient lives, impressed itself most clearly in my mind. I could tell Holmes was similarly moved.

"It is a curious thing, Watson," Holmes remarked. "Within these walls contains an amalgamation of accrued knowledge so vast that entire generations would find themselves unequal to it, and yet, none but a handful at a time commit themselves to taking advantage of such abundant resources. A book is a tool, only useful so far as it is applied to bettering the muscles of the mind. Were more to seize such opportunities as is at their disposal, the world might indeed change for the better." He sighed.

Davis nodded in agreement, then led us down the corridor, up a flight of stairs, and into a smaller reading room, surrounded on all sides by heavy volumes. He pulled a particularly heavy volume from one shelf. The book was a dull crimson, with fine gold lettering upon its cover, spelling it out as a singular volume in a larger numbered collection on the topic of common law and its practical implications. Davis brought the book over to a table and placed it down. I picked it up and flipped through its pages idly. Without another word, he strode out of the room, returning some minutes later with two ordinary brown leather-bound volumes.

"I recognized these as being the two books whose table of contents had been placed so crudely in the book you now hold in your hands," Davis informed us excitedly. "I'll continue to search for further information, when time allows. As you will see – "

He was cut off as a tall, leanly muscular man, whose neatly trimmed silver beard gleamed in the sunlight pouring in from the nearby window, walked into the room. The man's suit was of the highest quality. His grey

270

colourless eyes bore down mercilessly upon any within range. His head was bare, and his movements formal and stately, as bespeaks one of high station.

"I believe, Mr. Davis, now that you have seen fit to return from your trip to London, your time would be best spent attending to your assigned duties," the imposing figure declared sternly.

Davis bowed submissively and exited the room.

The stranger considered Holmes and me coolly as Davis's footsteps echoed down the corridor.

Holmes inclined his head. "I was wondering whether we might cross paths at some point. My name is – "

"I know who you are, Mr. Holmes," the other man responded curtly, his lip twisting into a poorly concealed sneer, "and more to the point, I know *what* you are."

"I see my reputation has once more preceded me."

"Indeed it has, Mr. Holmes, indeed it has! That of an interfering busybody – a meddler! One who consults with criminals, street beggars, and other riffraff. One who, with his every breath and deed, makes a mockery of our law-abiding constables. Well let me tell you plainly, sir: This is a respectable institution. We pride ourselves as being one of the finest collections of legal texts that this country – this world – has ever known, and in shaping generations of future respectable leaders in both industry and in government. I will not have you, or your lackey – " He nodded dismissively to me. " – besmirching the reputation I and my predecessors have dedicated our lives, our very souls, to cultivate. So be you careful, for, unlike your betters at Scotland Yard, I will tolerate no foolishness from the likes of you. Good day, sir." He punctuated his closing remark by rapping his gold-handled walking stick smartly against the floor. Turning sharply, he departed.

My face must have betrayed my evident dislike for this arrogant display of conduct, for Holmes laughed quietly as we heard our new friend stomping away back down the hall.

"You have had the distinct pleasure of meeting the inestimable Lord William Grey, distant descendent of that remarkable baron of the same name, and sometime-cousin to – Well, I suppose it doesn't matter. We have other, more pressing things to consider."

"He bears quite a commanding presence," I grudgingly conceded, still not particularly inclined to extend even the faintest compliment toward the man.

"He does," Holmes agreed readily. "However, at least we cannot fault him for any lack of honesty."

"Did you not take offence at his words?"

"My dear Watson, why ever should I? I should be far more inclined toward irritation at a man who withholds his tongue when I know him to have more to say. It is better to have it all in the clear, where there can be no misunderstanding in either action or intention."

"But the vehemence behind it!" I protested. "What is the cause behind it? Have you some long-standing rivalry or rancour of which you have neglected to inform me?"

"I tell you truly, Watson," Holmes declared, his eyes twinkling, "it is only now that he and I have come face-to-face. I knew of the man by name and reputation alone. I day say he no doubt feels he knows me and my intentions far more intimately than ever I would presume to claim such of him. Much of what we have just heard is as genuine as it is bluster. By virtue of his station and rank, his honour is impugned by the merest implication of any devilry in connection to that over which he governs. To expect him to behave in any manner but that we just beheld with our own eyes would be presumptuous on our part."

"Hullo," I remarked, as my fingers found a place in the book that parted slightly, as if something small and thin divided said pages from its brethren. I flicked to the spot in question. There I found a singular scrap of paper, with an intriguing set of numbers hurriedly scrawled in horizontal rows of three. They ran like so:

7b, 1, 4d.
3, 5a, 2,
8b, 6, 5c

The inexplicable combination of numbers and letters continued on for some additional rows. I flipped the paper over and found a second set.

"I pray you find some meaning in this," said I, "for it is lost upon me."

Holmes took the paper eagerly and, upon reading it, let out an exalted cry of vindication.

"It is just as I had hoped!" he declared triumphantly. "I suspected as much, but without corroborating evidence, I feared we would ever remain several steps behind."

"The meaning," I insisted impatiently. "What is it?"

"It is this, Watson," said he. "Our elusive book vandalist, or his conspirator, has made one crucial error: He left us the key by which to crack the code."

He took a breath and, in that single move, adopted the all-too familiar posture of the professor, expounding on elementary subjects for the benefit of his inexperienced and ofttimes inattentive student.

"Cryptography, my dear Watson, is the practice by which one may readily pass information of high, even critical importance, with the minimal necessary risk of outside exposure through encryption, and conversely, by the same techniques, break the aforementioned cipher in order to divulge the conveyed information. It is a field I have viewed with some curiosity, as I believe it will very well soon prove of great criminal use in obfuscating the efforts of our own law enforcement. Indeed, this is one instance where that theoretical principle demonstrates a practical example."

As he spoke, he pulled a pen from one pocket and, opening the book I had just set down, began repeatedly to glance between it and the scrap of paper, the latter of which he reutilized for his own neatly printed writing.

"If we assume the ever-changing table of contents to be the key, as evidence currently suggests, then the first number likely indicates the chapter number, the second being the indicated word within its title, and the third being the letter."

"What of the letters? Why do they border certain numbers and not others?"

"There, Watson, we must delve further into guesswork, but the explanation that seems most applicable is that the letters indicate that we must look a corresponding number of letters to the right of the one we initially land upon. For instance, the '*D*' that follows the four indicates another four spaces to the right. Someone has made a curious, if perhaps disappointingly unoriginal, effort to disguise what is frankly an unremarkable cipher."

Holmes was silent for some time as he worked. Finally, he thrust the paper under my eyes. I took it and read the following:

> *Saturday, midnight. Carriage waiting in street. Payment upon delivery of goods indicated.*

"There is something very strange about all this," Holmes mused. "There are any number of places one might easily exchange messages with an external agent without any fear of unwanted discovery. Instead, they elect to deliberately communicate in a specific place, at a regularly agreed upon time in the middle of the night, where one might leave the message, and the other receive it, without either seemingly coming face-to-face."

"Perhaps the buyer fears being turned over to the police, should the seller be caught red-handed in some other mischief, and seeks to lessen his own sentence by conveying another to his own well-deserved end," I suggested.

Holmes shook his head.

"While that might indeed have occurred to such men as a secondary consideration, I don't believe it to be the primary incentive in this particular instance."

"Then what was?"

"That the location of the messages itself was of some relevance to the criminal act. However, without further data, we have no basis on which to extrapolate specifics."

Leaving the book on the table, Holmes swept out of the room, with me following in his wake.

As we approached Mr. Davis' desk, we observed that he was already occupied. Before him stood a middle-aged man of medium height and a slightly stocky build, possessing a head of closely cut fine blonde hair which was just beginning to whiten.

At the sound of our footsteps, the figure turned, revealing a face that appeared far younger than his other features had previously indicated. He smiled in a friendly fashion.

"Good day!" he greeted us, inclining his head. "I would surmise you, sir, are Mr. Holmes," he continued, indicating my friend. When Holmes inclined his head politely in turn, the other man clarified. "I cannot take credit for any astute deduction on my part, for I heard your name in passing some minutes ago, when the Chancellor revealed your identity." He winked. "Lord Grey has ever possessed a strong voice, so one can hardly call it eavesdropping when one overhears, even without outward intent."

He gestured to himself.

"My name is Albert Warren. I am one among the faculty of the History Department, specialising in Tenth to Fourteenth Century European affairs."

Holmes and he shook hands. The professor then turned to me.

"Forgive me. I had not the pleasure of acquiring your name earlier."

"This is my friend, Dr. John Watson."

"Very good to meet you, Doctor." Warren smiled and shook my hand.

"You should know," he said to both of us, "you have come on a very auspicious day."

"Oh?" said I.

"Yes, indeed." Warren responded, indicating that we should both follow him.

He led us to one side and a singular encased display, within which lay open an age-stained book, transcribed with careful detail in that singular mother language of Latin.

"Before you," Warren continued energetically, "you behold the *Textus Roffensis*."

"Ah, yes," Holmes remarked introspectively.

274

"It is very pretty," I observed, betraying my own ignorance.

"Pretty?" cried Warren. "Why, man, it is *invaluable*! Simply *invaluable*! It is the paramount document of early English law. It predates the *Magna Carta* by over a hundred years, and is the only one left of its kind! We are fortunate beyond reason that this facility should once more be chosen to display it to the general public! The Rochester Cathedral only rarely lends it to universities, and even then, for very brief periods. On Monday, we shall formally announce its addition here, but I couldn't resist giving you an early preview of what is to come."

He withdrew a silver pocket watch and glanced at it.

"Ah, I must be off. I have but half-an-hour until my next class."

He shook our hands again. "A pleasure, to be sure."

Nodding to Davis, Warren turned to the door.

"He seems quite a passionate sort," I remarked.

"Yes, quite," Davis responded, bemused. "Professor Warren takes his responsibilities quite seriously. A great number of European faculty of the historical discipline, coordinating with our own library director, have taken to certain preparations in advance of the exhibition, Warren chiefly among them."

"How many among the faculty are involved in this enterprise?" Holmes asked.

"Oh, a good twenty or so."

"Is there a visitor's record?" Holmes inquired, with deliberate carelessness. "I would be curious which among them likewise have paid their respects to said display."

"Of course." Davis nodded and called over a younger man, whose light-brown hair had begun to escape its original parting, and spoke to him. Disappearing for a moment, the young man returned moments later, placing upon Davis' desk a large ebony book, which Davis now opened for us.

"Mr. Holmes, this is my assistant, Mr. Williams. He is the one who was good enough to cover for me this morning. Williams, this is Mr. Sherlock Holmes, and his friend, Dr. Watson. They have come at my request to see to a personal matter."

Williams nodded politely, a shy smile crossing his face.

"How do you do, sir?" he proffered his hand to Holmes, and then to me. Then, at a motion from Davis, he returned to his own duties some distance away.

"You don't trust him?" I asked Davis.

Davis shook his head. "At this moment, I do not know who to trust, and who not. Williams will not be the worse for having not been taken into my confidence in this particular affair. It strikes me that one with near-unrestricted access to the contents of this literary vault would be well-positioned to act in a manner consistent with what I have seen." He shrugged. "However, it seems most unlikely in my mind that Williams would go so far as to deface any singular property of these archives."

As we spoke, Holmes was already preoccupied thoroughly examining the entries provided in the book Williams had brought forth. With Davis' assistance, we identified a total of seven professors who had so far entered the library, with Davis assuring us that yet more would likely take time later that evening, after their final classes for the day. Holmes took careful record of the names present, and requested that Davis do the same for the remainder of that day.

"I fear we can do nothing more, Watson," Holmes reflected. "At least not for the time being, and with the eye of our new acquaintance, the Chancellor, heavy upon us, I see no disadvantage in setting aside our current endeavour for the moment, and exploring what other more innocent secrets we can extract from both these magnificent specimens of architecture and any interior galleries they may contain."

Following an early supper, Holmes departed for some time, leaving me to my own devices, with the understanding that we would meet once more at a quarter-past-nine. When I arrived promptly in front of the library at the appointed time, Holmes was nowhere to be found. On a sudden impulse, I strode to the door, intending to knock, thinking perhaps that Davis yet remained inside. No sooner had I raised my hand then the door opened, a hand grabbed me by the arm, and I found myself pulled sharply inside. There was a heavy click as the door swung shut after me.

Save for a few distant flickering candles, all was darkness, such that I couldn't see more than shadows in front of me.

"Forgive me any inconvenience or alarm I might have caused you, Watson," Holmes's voice quietly reached my ear. "For tonight is the hunt, and our prey has yet to arrive." Holmes lit a match and lowered it to what I now saw was a lantern held in his hand. As the flame caught, I could now see Holmes was accompanied by both Davis and Inspector Gregson of Scotland Yard.

"Yes," Holmes observed dryly, "at the risk of further offending our sensible Lord Grey, I thought it best to send for some official assistance, to further hasten a satisfactory conclusion to this little problem."

"A pleasure as always, Dr. Watson," Gregson remarked, shaking my hand.

He turned to Holmes. "My men are in position and awaiting my whistle."

"Excellent, Gregson. And now, for that most trying step of tonight's procedure."

Davis led us all upstairs to the same reading room he had shown us earlier that very day. Holmes immediately extinguished the lamp, and we were all plunged once more into relative darkness.

The minutes crept past inexorably. It wasn't long before I felt we surely must have remained seated thus for hours. However, it couldn't have been much longer than an hour following our arrival when we were interrupted by the unmistakable sound of someone moving about directly below the window. For close to a minute, we heard the shaking of what sounded like a large tree branch. Just then, we heard breaking glass. We were jolted to our feet as the heavy slam of a body landing against the side of the building resonated clearly in our ears, confirmed by the sudden appearance of two arms reaching through the window, with the rest of the man's body awkwardly emerging a moment later. Finally, he collapsed onto the floor.

It was then that we fell upon him. The man bellowed at our unexpected appearance and, turning, struck one of us with a mighty blow, sending the figure crashing back, and tumbling over a number of books. I had seized the man by one ankle but he tore free, sprinting for the door. I ran after him. However, neither speed nor endurance had ever been among my most prominent features, doubly so after my experiences in the war.

Ahead of me I heard the sound of breaking glass. By the time I made my way onto the ground floor, the figure ahead of me had flung open the front door. My heart pounded with both exhilaration at the encounter, and incandescent frustration at having so poorly matched my more athletic rival.

The sound of raised voices and subsequently heavy blows emanating from the doorway interrupted me from my reverie, as so too the hurried footsteps of my companions closed in behind me. "Your enthusiasm does you credit, Watson," Holmes remarked. "However, it was, at present, unnecessary."

Two constables dragged in the still-writhing form of the man they had so directly apprehended, while a third held a large book in his hands. One of the two constables clubbed the intruder again for good measure, and the man collapsed limp, but still demonstrating his consciousness with low groans of pain. At a gesture from Gregson, they released the man, allowing him to drop to the ground.

"Really, Professor," Holmes said sternly. "This behaviour is quite undignified for a respectable gentleman of your station. May we not dispense with these theatricalities?"

By the quivering flickers of nearby candlelight, we could well make out the face of Professor Albert Warren.

Our captive laughed harshly as he spat out a mouthful of blood and saliva.

"What gave me away, Mr. Holmes?" he asked with cold amusement, getting to his feet.

"You overdid your part, my good sir," Holmes informed him. "Of all the descriptors to have chosen, 'invaluable' was perhaps more than a little suggestive."

Warren shrugged.

"I was never much of an actor. Perhaps it's just as well I went into History, and not Drama, as a profession. When I overheard your name mentioned earlier today, I thought the best thing I could do was to put myself front and centre, so much so that none would think to connect me to anything that might come after."

"A commonplace solution," Holmes replied, "but one that perhaps might have shielded you, at least from immediate identification. How came you to obtain a key to Davis' desk?"

Warren snorted. "I've been here long enough to watch everyone at their little rituals. You spend enough time in here, Mr. Holmes, with naught else but the books and the walls to keep you company, and it becomes easy enough to find yourself lost within yourself. The world on a stage around you, and yourself just mindlessly going through the same motions at approximately the same exact times you had yesterday, and the month before that, and the year before that. I knew that once Davis had settled into his routine, I could take the key. As long as it was back before he had begun to close up that evening, I knew I was safe."

"So you took it to a locksmith so as to have its twin forged," Holmes asserted.

"As you say. He wanted to hold onto it for a day or two, and he argued with me, but for every complaint he raised, so too I raised my price for his services. So over the course of several days, we worked out the exact measurements. It seemed a reasonable enough investment at the time."

"What was the meaning behind this plot?" Gregson interjected.

Holmes shot Gregson a look of some annoyance at the interruption, but made no immediate move to contradict him.

"What else?" Warren replied. "Money. I ran up some debts among the kinds of people one ought not aggrieve, and then I found, no matter how much I paid down, they were always coming back for more, bleeding me of everything I had. I had to do something that would pay off all my balances, each with so much interest that none of them would bother further with me. One of them suggested a means by which I could do just

278

so. 'I have already consolidated your debts,' said he. 'Oh?' said I. "Yes,' he continued, 'you need not fear any future reprisal, for so long as you keep faith with me, and me alone.' Oh, what a clever man he was, too! The kind who could look at you with the most earnest friendship, and yet, in those calculating eyes, you see clearly the baleful eyes of death himself staring back at you. It was he who connected me with a certain dealer who traded in works of art and other eccentricities."

"Does he have a name, this man?" Gregson asked pointedly. "The one you spoke with?"

Warren went pale. "I'll not answer that."

"Then it may go the worse for you at the station," Gregson warned him. "You have broken into a building, attempted to steal a priceless treasure, attacked an officer of Scotland Yard, and resisted arrest. Any magistrate would have you sent away for more years than you'd like to count."

Warren's face was set. "I will take my chances."

"Very well," Gregson motioned to his fellow officers.

However, we were all immediately transfixed by the sound of a familiar quarrelsome voice echoing as it neared us. In strode Lord William Grey, waving away with one arm the restraining efforts of the officers guarding the front. "Out of my way!"

He whipped forward his walking stick until it pointed directly forward like a rapier. His face glowed crimson with the clarity of an ember taken straight from the fire. "By all the angels and demons above and below, what is the meaning of this devilry? I will have answers from you, Mr. Holmes, or by Jove, I will see to it you are clapped in irons for this effrontery!"

"Good evening, my Lord. I hope you weren't greatly disturbed by my summons."

"You?" Shock, almost immediately curdling to renewed intensified rage, crossed his face. "You have the audacity to summon me from my bed at such an hour?" He looked as if he was about to say more, but was cut short as his eyes fell upon the array of broken glass. The colour drained from his face just as quickly as it had appeared.

Inspector Gregson at that moment stepped in.

"Mr. Holmes was the one who tipped us off, Chancellor," Gregson said smoothly. "It is thanks to him we were able to apprehend the culprit before he was able to abscond with the book."

Lord Grey's eyes narrowed. "Well? Who is it then? Arrive at the point, man!"

Then his gaze fell upon Warren.

"Do you – mean – to tell me – ?" Lord Grey said thickly, his jaw clenched, "the actions which have brought me here tonight, the perpetrator behind them was one of whom I have had the responsibility to hire?"

No one chose to respond.

Lord Grey stepped forward until he was directly in front of Warren.

"Professor Warren," said he, "your position at this institution has been terminated, effective immediately! As you are no longer a member of staff, your presence on these premises is no longer required."

Once more, his proclamation was handed down like a pronouncement of doom, as his stick struck the ground, producing a cascading series of echoes. He turned.

Warren spat on the ground behind him.

Lord Grey stopped.

In a sudden fluid burst of movement borne of an agility of far younger men, Lord Grey spun on the spot and struck Warren across the face with the protruding domed metallic handle of his stick. Warren collapsed unconscious to the floor.

Lord Grey straightened his suit and, raising one eyebrow, turned to Holmes.

"It might be unbecoming of me to admit it," he observed, glancing at his cane, "but I do feel much the better for having responded so."

He glanced at Inspector Gregson, then back at Holmes.

"I care neither for you nor your methods, sir," said he, "and I shall be the happier for having seen the back of you. However, it must be said that you have rendered some minor service this night, and I shall remember it." He nodded abruptly. "Good night to you."

It was as he strode away toward the door that we heard the redoubled moans that informed us that Warren was once more conscious. Holmes waited until Warren had raised himself up again before he continued his interview.

"Why was this library chosen as the central point for your communications? Why not some other place far away from here?"

Warren shrugged again. "At first, it was a test. Were I to prove myself able to get into the library, undetected, in order to obtain the cipher, obtaining the book itself would prove of little additional challenge. The book selected for the task was fairly commonplace, so it wasn't particularly difficult to swap the pages. As I repeated the exercise, it allowed me to better plan out for myself the route I would need to take to avoid detection." He winced. "At least, that had been the idea."

"What was to be your reward for this undertaking?" Holmes asked mildly.

"A cheque for three-thousand pounds, upon delivery," the man replied. "Near a thousand to clear my debt, and another two for my silence."

"You are then a traitor twice over," Holmes told him coldly. "You have betrayed not only this library and the general public, but yourself as well. A history professor who would abscond with historical documents of such priceless value for his own personal gain has disparaged and dishonoured the academic ideals which he, by virtue of his profession, swore to lifelong allegiance."

With a word from Gregson, Warren was taken away into custody by Scotland Yard.

Following a closing interview with the inspector, informing him as to what remaining details would most aid in his formal report, Holmes and I departed upon the earliest train back to London.

It was some days later, when we were in our rooms in Baker Street, that Holmes received a dispatch from Scotland Yard. He read it, then handed it to me. It was a short letter from Inspector Gregson, informing us that the newly unemployed Professor Warren had been found dead in his cell, having seemingly taken his own life in the night.

"Perhaps his guilt has caught up with him," I remarked, with perhaps just a touch of insensitivity colouring my satisfaction.

"I wouldn't be so quick to assume so," Holmes responded thoughtfully. "Whatever other faults he very well does possess, nothing in our interview with him indicated the remotest remorse for his actions, let alone to the point where the mind rationalises the taking of one's life. Gregson sent over a full copy of his report, which of course was also made available to his superiors, in which he accounts for the man's full story. I believe our late Professor erred in one singular regard, and may perhaps have well earned a different reward than he had originally sought at the outset."

"It is murder, you say?"

"It is difficult to say. If it is so, it was very cleverly and efficiently managed. There is an evil wind stirring, Watson. From where it arises, we cannot yet determine. But I will be much mistaken if we don't see or hear telltale sign of its passage again soon."

The Adventure of the
Restless Knight
by Will Murray

Sherlock Holmes was in a peculiar mood that night late in August of the year 1885 when I tripped up the stairs to our shared Baker Street apartments, shook the rain from my umbrella, and placed it in the stand before entering.

"Good evening," I greeted as I removed my waterproof.

"And a good evening to you as well, Watson."

Holmes had been smoking his cherry-wood pipe, and I noticed that he had set this aside and had replaced the briar with a cigarette. While Holmes preferred the pipe to cigarettes, it was most often his mood that governed his selection of tobacco and how he took it.

Although he sat in his comfortable velvet-lined chair by the cold hearth in a manner that suggested relaxed repose, the burning cigarette told me otherwise. Often I had seen him pace this very floor, smoking cigarette after cigarette as he wrestled with a mental problem whose outcome was almost always decisive. And correct to a fault, I might add.

The evidence of the set-aside pipe suggested that Holmes had begun his present mental exercise in a rather mellow mood, and had now become increasingly agitated.

One wouldn't suspect agitation, however, looking at his graven profile. He seemed awkwardly calm. There was a certain fixity in his grey eyes, and in the poise of his otherwise-relaxed body. Also, I could tell by the way his mouth was firmed up into a rather bloodless line that he had fallen into a difficult problem.

"A new client, I presume?" I inquired as I took my preferred seat.

"Lestrade has unburdened himself of a vexing one. And he appears to expect me to solve it for him. Hence, I find myself the burdened party."

"I'm keen to hear about it."

"But I'm not so keen to relate it to you. With all due apologies, I rather wish I hadn't accepted the challenge. There is no coin in it. No recognition – for Scotland Yard will undoubtedly take all of the latter for themselves."

"I've never known you to be concerned about credit."

282

"I am not," snapped Holmes. "I'm merely listing grievances because I'm at an impasse and wish to unblock the dam of my frustrated thoughts through diversion."

"That is too bad, my dear Holmes, but you forever seek such challenges, and so regularly, that upon occasion you'll inevitably confront a stone wall."

"I would like to demolish this particular stone wall," he declared.

"Well, you may tell me about it at your convenience – or not at all, if that's what you prefer."

"What I would prefer, friend Watson, is that Scotland Yard do their own work. This particular matter is vexing, but is otherwise inconsequential. It doesn't rise to the degree where it is a satisfying challenge. It is simply a stubborn puzzle of a handful of pieces."

"I've known you to solve many puzzles with no more than three pieces," I remarked.

"True, but the problem with puzzles is the proportion of pieces available, as opposed to the number of pieces that exist, of which one may be ignorant. Three pieces of a twelve-piece puzzle might be sufficient for someone equipped with a brain such as I own, but twelve pieces comprising a puzzle of one-hundred elements is much more daunting."

"I take it you don't know, nor can you accurately guess, as to how many pieces this particular puzzle involves," I ventured.

"I would judge it to be less than twenty-five salient pieces, but there may be only a dozen. How am I to know with only a handful to go on? I need more data. Without data, I'm reduced to pitching pennies pointlessly against an obdurate wall of imponderable granite."

"That is unfortunate." I had availed myself of a cigarette and realized I hadn't examined the mail that had been set on the great table by our landlady, Mrs. Hudson. I corrected this oversight at once.

Taking the pile back to my seat, I went through it and was surprised to find an envelope addressed to Sherlock Holmes.

"Mrs. Hudson has lapsed in her responsibilities to us," said I, standing up and carrying the envelope over to Holmes.

"What is this?"

"A letter addressed to you. This was inadvertently included in my portion of today's post."

Customarily, Holmes might show indifference to his mail when he was otherwise engaged in a problem, but here, he was in need of distraction. I was as happy to provide it as he was to accept it, for he all but snatched the envelope out of my hand.

"Did you notice the return address?" he asked as he took the envelope in hand.

"I confess that I did not. Once I saw that it was addressed to you, it became your business and not mine."

"It reads '*Sir George Dumphry, Dunshire, Bart*'. He writes from Peterborough. I wonder what the baronet could want?"

"Do you know him?"

"Not in the slightest."

Opening one end of the envelope with his letter opener, Holmes extracted the contents, unfolded it, and read quietly for more than a minute.

"Sir George is in dire need of insight," Holmes murmured.

"Really? What is his issue?"

"He has inherited Dunshire Priory from his brother, so called because a priory had previously existed on its foundation, and has become distressed over inexplicable noises that are making nervous wrecks of his family and household staff."

"Noises? Of what character?"

"At certain times on odd days, the sound of footsteps parading in a circle has come down from the storage loft. Dissatisfied with his servants' reports, Sir George has personally investigated his attic, but found no person making the sound."

"An animal, perhaps."

Holmes shook his head gravely. "No, Sir George is quite clear on that point. He has had the attic region searched high and low. There is no indication of squirrels or other such vermin."

"That is rather remarkable," I mused.

"Further, Sir George is inclining in the direction of believing that he has taken up residence in a dwelling that is haunted. Indeed, he has learned that Dunshire Priory has had that reputation for generations."

"I'd rather doubt such things myself," said I.

"You know my opinions on that score. I am with you to the limit. I do not seek ghosts. Nor do I expect to find them."

"I take it by that remark that you intend to decline Sir George's request for assistance."

Holmes was a moment in replying. His cigarette had gone out and he flung it into the cold hearth. Then he again took up his cherry-wood pipe and ignited the black shag remaining in the bowl. Soon, he was pensively smoking once more. He read Sir George's message over again.

"I think that the baronet's improbable problem is worthy of my attention."

"But you don't hold with ghosts."

"And I do not expect to find them, but I require a diversion, for I have found that if I take my mind off one problem by attacking another, when I return to the first problem, it is with a fresh attitude and a cleansed mental palette."

"I cannot argue against your logic. It is sound. I have had the same experience in my medical practice. There is something about letting go of a problem and seizing it again at a later time that alters the perspective."

"Precisely," said Holmes. "Now, Sir George has invited me to be his guest at Dunshire Priory. I will write him back to expect me. I see no reason why you cannot accompany me."

"Am I specifically invited?"

"You are not, but I don't think this is an issue. Sir George appears quite anxious for assistance. As well, he makes a point that Dunshire Priory boasts four bedrooms. I'm certain that you will be as welcome as I am."

"If you're sure, then I'll be happy to accompany you. Peterborough is sure to be quite pleasant this time of year."

"So it is settled," said Holmes. Taking up a pen and writing paper, he fell to inscribing a reply. This he gave to Billy the page boy to post. No more was said about the matter until the following day, when the reply came in the evening mail.

"It is all arranged. Sir George expects us on the morrow. He didn't object to my inviting you along. Let us get a good night's sleep before we take the earliest train to Peterborough that we can engage."

The expected brougham carriage was waiting for us at Peterborough East railway station. Without further ado, the driver conveyed us and our luggage to Dunshire Priory.

A footman took our bags as we made our way to the imposing entrance door of the charming old brick country home surrounded by thickets of hazel and ash trees. It was quite broad, this manor, and boasted but one storey.

Dispensing with the formality of the butler answering the door, Sir George himself greeted us at the entrance.

"Mr. Sherlock Holmes!" he exclaimed. "How very good of you to come! And this, I assume, is Dr. Watson. Pray enter. I'm delighted that you could find the time to visit."

"Thank you, Sir George," said Holmes. "We are eager to hear your tale."

"And it is a remarkable one," said the baronet as we made our way to the great vaulted drawing room with its grand hearth. "I regret that my wife isn't here in residence to greet you. She has gone into town to do a bit of shopping, accompanied by the butler."

Our host waved us toward comfortable chairs. Sir George sat down upon his own seat, facing us.

Sir George was the blustery sort, with a wide, florid face crowned by receding hair so white it scarcely looked natural. There wasn't a trace of grey to be discovered in it. He wore *pince-nez* spectacles, which he removed in order to appraise us with his pale blue orbs.

I immediately took him to be a man without airs, and honest to a fault. My friend has sometimes criticized me for my failure to be as keenly as observant as he, to which I will freely admit, but one cannot make his way through life as a physician without learning to judge a man by his demeanor. And I took the baronet to be of the finest type of Englishman of his class.

"Tea and crumpets will be served momentarily," he announced. "While it is brewing, I would be pleased to tell the story of my unhappy predicament in full."

"Please do so, Sir George," said Holmes. "Your letter offered only the most general of outlines."

"The details of the matter belong to speech and speech alone," said our host, "and I'm not in any way an accomplished writer of letters. I prefer to speak my piece. And I am pleased to host such an illustrious audience to hear my tale of household woe."

"Very good," stated Holmes.

"Now, in order to understand where matters stand, I must speak of ancestral events."

At this, I quite logically assumed that Sir George would be invoking an ancestral ghost. In that, I wasn't far off the mark, yet also precisely correct. I wasn't prepared for the queer turns his story took.

"The issue to hand appears to go back to the Battle of Agincourt, on which I need not dwell overmuch. Suffice it to say that an ancestor of my wife's, James Trussell, the Duke of Grumley, marched under King Henry into France as part of that noble expedition which trounced the French Army. Alas, he perished there, and with him his two sons, which absolutely annihilated the male line in that generation. His wasn't the only noble family to be wiped out at Agincourt, but no matter. While His Grace's body was buried in France, his armor was returned intact to his widow. This array has been passed down through succeeding generations. When I married my present wife, I fell heir to Trussell's armor."

Gesturing with one rather thick hand, Sir George pointed to an impressive steel helmet resting on a pedestal under a long glass dome of the type that would typically serve as a dust cover for a table clock. This display sat beside the arched entrance to the adjoining library.

286

My eyes went to the helmet. I was surprised at how well it had endured the five centuries since Agincourt.

"There reposes the sallet of my wife's forebear," Sir George proclaimed rather proudly. "When I inherited Dunshire Priory last winter, I had the entire suit of armor brought here. It had stood intact, upright in my old library, but here it occupied an inconvenient space, so I consigned the array to the storage loft, but kept the helmet on display here, as you see. All was well until recent weeks."

With a heavy sigh, Sir George placed both hands on his knees, and seemed to gather himself before unleashing his next torrent of words.

"Before I get into that, I must remember to mention an unfortunate fact about the death of James Trussell of Agincourt renown. Regrettably, the Duke was beheaded in battle. When his suit of armor was returned to the widow, it was minus the gorget of mail, which had been ruined by the blade that had decapitated the unfortunate knight. When the armor first came into my former household through marriage, I had the gorget replaced with an example from the same century. Otherwise, the armor is all original plate and mail."

Holmes had been listening patiently, but I could detect a tremor of impatience in the way he looked about the room and studied Sir George. Well did I know his opinion of ghosts. No doubt he was prepared to pounce on any imperfections in Sir George's story that would disprove the notion of an active phantom.

"And here we come to the crux of the matter," continued Sir George. "From time to time, particularly at night, but not always so, the servants have been complaining of recognizable sounds of footsteps in the portion of the loft set aside from their quarters for storage. There stands the suit of armor. Headless, as it were, just like James Trussell."

Having unburdened himself, the baronet sat back and awaited Holmes's response.

Holmes was nearly a minute in speaking.

"I beg your pardon, Sir George," he said quietly, "but I don't yet see what you are driving at."

Our host reached for his *pince-nez* spectacles, set them on his nose, and said, "Is it not obvious?"

"If it is," said Holmes, "it isn't obvious to me."

Sir George blinked several times, and said, "It appears to me that the suit of armor is tramping about the loft in quest of its head."

An uncomfortable silence attended Sir George's announcement.

Speaking for myself, I didn't know what to say, so I kept my own counsel.

Holmes finally spoke up. His voice was polite and respectful, but I, who knew him so well, detected a tincture of disbelief in his tone, which I imagined concealed an abject incredulity.

"Are you suggesting that the suit of armor has animated itself by some means?"

"Oh, no! Not the suit of armor, but its former occupant has seized command of it."

"I take it that you mean, James Trussell, the Duke of Grumley?"

"Well, who else could I mean? No one has worn that armor since he fell in battle."

"Do you proclaim that His Grace has returned to the land of the living in order to don his battle armor of old?" asked Holmes evenly.

"I am surprised, Mr. Holmes. I expected better of you. Is it not logical?"

"I don't think ghosts are logical. As a matter of truth, I confess that I am dubious of their existence, but I would like to know your logic in asserting this remarkable development as fact."

Sir George harumphed in his throat. Once more, he gathered himself together before speaking.

"The Duke of Grumley lost his head in battle. No doubt this continues to grieve him in the afterlife. By whatever means the departed are aware of the living, he undoubtedly noticed that his helmet had been separated from his suit of armor, and is endeavoring to rejoin them. The fact that the loft doors are locked has thwarted his intentions to date."

I was aghast at this theory, offered in such a matter-of-fact manner. I continued to hold my tongue. Let Sherlock Holmes deal with the man. He was defter of wit than was I.

Holmes considered his next words carefully, for he took some moments before speaking again.

"I must ask you, Sir George: Has anyone seen the apparition of the Duke of Grumley himself?"

"No one. There is only the sound of footsteps, walking in circles. I myself have heard these manifestations while standing under the library. Directly above the library stands the suit of armor, you understand."

"No doubt you have investigated the sounds?"

"Yes, but whenever I enter the loft, the suit of armor is as it should be."

"I see," murmured Holmes. "So no one has seen the suit of armor walking about?"

"No. The servants are afraid to pass through the door separating their quarters from the storage portion of the loft. Moreover, they are prevented from doing so, for it is kept locked, but all tell the same story. Through the bolted door, they hear the same peculiar series of sounds, suggestive of an unknown person walking about in a continuous circle."

"Now, I understand," said Holmes. "You have merely surmised that the suit of armor is seeking its head."

Sir George lifted a wise finger, saying, "Just as the Duke of Grumley's ghost would no doubt seek his own head. This is the salient point. These represent parallel actions. Absolutely parallel."

"I take it that you are a firm believer in apparitions," asked Holmes.

"Tales have come down through my family, as well as my wife's family, of such things. Sober gentlemen have sworn to seeing spirits prowling about their own homes. There have been witnesses. Testimony that the same apparition has been seen by more than one person. All witnesses were of the highest character, and therefore unimpeachable."

"But no apparitions have been reported in this domicile?" pressed Holmes.

"No, not as yet, but we haven't yet resided here a year. It is well known that these phantoms take their time before manifesting. I believe that many watch from darkened corners, observing the new occupants before deciding whether to make their presence known or not."

I could see that in his personal opinions, Sir George was firm and fixed. Furthermore, his beliefs were generally of the unshakable sort. His forbears had seen their ancestors coming and going after their deaths, and so this was gospel to him.

Understanding this, and recognizing that we were guests in his home, Holmes was careful to pick his way forward through the disorderly thicket of superstition.

"When was the last time these footsteps were heard?" he inquired.

"Three nights ago."

"And how did you respond to them?"

"I rushed into the loft, but by the time I entered, the suit of armor had returned to its assigned station. I did, however, find that the dust of the floor appeared to have been disturbed, as if by its steely tread."

"Did you discover footprints?"

Sir George shook his head firmly. "I wouldn't call them that. I would call them disturbances amid the dust, and minor detritus of the loft floor.

"I will look at them after we have our tea," said Holmes.

Momentarily, the maid appeared. As she was placing the tea service, Sir George said, "This is Mary. She has heard the queer footsteps many times. Tell them, Mary, would you."

Giving a little curtsy, Mary the maid declared, "I have heard the footsteps five times. They are always the same. Although sometimes they appear to be hasty and at other times they are more deliberate, but I would swear before the Almighty that these are the commotions of a man walking about in the far loft."

"What is the duration of these sounds?" asked Holmes.

The question was addressed to the maid, but Sir George answered for her.

"Sometimes the footsteps come rapidly, and are just as soon no more. At other times, they are prolonged and intermittent. For example, twice I poked my head up into the loft and they ceased, but once I returned to the library, they resumed as before. Only once did I believe that I caught the footsteps in action before I entered the loft, but because it was dark, I could see nothing until I stepped all the way in. When I brought my lantern up, the suit of armor was exactly as it should be. Inert. Isn't that right, Mary?"

"It is just as Sir George says. It is a shivery thing, and has been going on far too long."

"Thank you," said Holmes.

With that, the maid withdrew.

As we drank our tea, absorbed in silence, I looked to Holmes. His expression as seen in profile was impassive to a fault.

At length, he put down his cup and asked, "Sir George, I beg your indulgence, but I must ask an obvious question."

"Go ahead."

"Why have you not returned the helmet to its rightful owner?"

Sir George appeared slightly taken aback by the question. He set down his own teacup and said, "Why, because this is now my house, and I will decorate it as I see fit. The sallet will remain on display and the suit of armor shall continue to be stored in the loft. I just want this infernal stalking about to be brought to an unequivocal halt."

I confess to being flummoxed by this statement. If one were to take Sir George's pronouncements at face value – and I did not. Furthermore, I knew Sherlock Holmes did not! – the solution was obvious, but the man was stubborn. He wanted his own way. And he expected Holmes to resolve it to his satisfaction, and against all common sense. Or so it appeared to me.

In a composed voice, Holmes imparted, "I will endeavor to do my utmost to grant your wish, Sir George."

"Excellent! Once we finish our tea, I will – *introduce* – you to the suit of armor."

I didn't care for that choice of word – *introduce* – but it was to me clear that the baronet perceived the armor as having a personality.

Once we were finished with afternoon tea, Holmes walked over to the helmet on its pedestal and studied it for some minutes. I joined him.

The helmet shone richly, while the perforated visor projected forward like a steel snout, showing no trace of denting or battle damage such as one might expect in a fallen knight's armor. Gilded copper accents provided a touch of artistic distinction.

"The sallet is authentic, as is this visor," he pronounced.

"Yes," said Sir George. "It has come down through my wife's line since the fall of the House of Grumley."

"Shall we venture into the loft?" suggested Holmes.

"Yes. Kindly follow me."

Sir George took up an oil lantern, lighted the wick, escorted us into the library, and then beyond it.

Unlocking a door disclosed a distressingly narrow staircase leading upward. It was one of those frightful passages designed for servants. It was altogether too narrow, the risers too high, and the steps much too narrow.

Stepping carefully, Sir George led the way, all but blocking the light of his upraised lantern.

"Mind that you don't take a tumble," he cautioned.

I found climbing these steps difficult. They were set unnaturally. One had to lift one's foot far more than one was accustomed. Furthermore, the steps were so uncomfortably narrow that it was impossible to place the whole of one's sole on them. It was rather like climbing a steep shale hill.

We came to the broad topmost step and a door, which Sir George opened with a brass key.

The lantern had lit our way, and now we were stepping into the loft itself.

This attic occupied one end of the manor's uppermost floor. As soon as we entered, the smells of dust, and of old odds-and-ends, came to our nostrils. Dusty sheet-draped furniture stood about, as well as trunks and books stacked on rude plank shelves tucked into the broad spaces between the exposed rafters. The shelves appeared to consist of the same rough-hewn spruce planking that comprised the floor, which was fearfully spalled with age, for the wood wasn't varnished. No window pierced the far wall, which was of brick. Sir George's lantern provided the sole illumination.

It was possible to stand upright beneath the roof line comfortably. We walked along the squeaking and groaning floorboards until Sir George brought us to the farther wall, where the suit of armor stood upright, immobile, and obviously mute, against the terminal wall. It was mounted as such armor is so often arranged in museums – as if still occupied. Like the sallet on display in the house proper, it was decorated with copper filigree.

291

The array hadn't been dusted in some time, yet it gleamed dully. In the lantern light, the void where the helmet would normally rest gave me a feeling of abnormality. It was then that I recalled that the original owner had been decapitated. I found the symbolism distasteful.

"This is the suit of armor belonging to the Duke of Grumley," said Sir George with the same note of pride as if he himself had descended from that line.

"So I see," murmured Holmes. "Would you be so good as to hold the lantern a trifle higher?"

Sir George lifted the lantern and Holmes took out his glass, which he used to study the glowing steel plate.

I had to admire the armor, for it seemed to be authentic to the period. My imagination carried me to the Battle of Agincourt in 1415, when the longbowmen of King Henry won the day against the forces of Charles VI, despite being vastly outnumbered. I observed that the first two fingers of the right-hand gauntlet were missing, but the visible chain mail showed no signs of rust or separation.

"According to legends handed down through the generations," advised Sir George, "before he was beheaded so cruelly, two fingers of the Duke's right hand were severed. The French were so angered by the proficiency with which our English longbows penetrated their armor that they made certain any knight who fell under their power lost the ability to ever again draw a bowstring against them."

"I have read stories that this was done," I remarked. "Intriguing to behold evidence of those storied accounts."

After some time, Holmes turned to Sir George. "Kindly show me the spot where the footsteps made disturbances."

Sir George turned, saying, "We have just passed over them."

"I was afraid of that," said Holmes. "For we appear to have trampled these traces."

Sir George laughed a trifle nervously. "Neither fret nor fear. Mr. Holmes. It won't be long before the Duke's suit of armor walks again, and fresh tracks are created. Of that, I assure you."

Holmes walked around, stepped here and there, and noted that the squeaking of the floorboards was most prominent in one spot, and less prominent elsewhere, where the wood merely groaned.

"Are these the sounds you heard, Sir George?" asked Holmes as he pressed the floor planking repeatedly, producing a steady creaking and squeaking.

"Not precisely. Those constituted a continuous circuit of noises. It can be quite unnerving. There is no doubt but that they represent someone stamping in a circle, over and over. At times, they have an impatient note to them. At other times, the footsteps are slower and more methodical."

Returning to the immobile suit of armor, Holmes employed his shoes to make the floorboards groan over and over.

"Did this particular sound attend any of the 'manifestations', as you call them?"

Sir George shook his head. "No, the noises were creaky – not in any way a groaning of distressed wood."

"And you say the servants aren't allowed in this end of the loft?"

"They are strictly forbidden, nor do they have keys to any of the doors."

Holmes turned to the stout door at the other end, which divided the loft into equal halves. "I take it that this door leads to the servants' quarters."

"It does, but it isn't in use."

Holmes paid special attention to the floor planks, after which he knelt down and traced his finger through the accumulation of household dust.

It became obvious to me that no one had stepped through that connecting door in quite a long time. The coating of dust was undisturbed, except for the mark made by Holmes's finger.

"I have seen enough here," he said flatly. "Let us return down."

We repaired to the drawing room and resumed our seats.

"What do you make of it?" asked Sir George.

Holmes took the liberty of lighting his pipe before replying. "I have some preliminary thoughts in that direction, but I need more data. Can you tell me the dates upon which footsteps have been heard?"

Sir George considered, and then said, "I wouldn't recall the exact dates, except for the first incident, which was the 25th of July. Perhaps Lady Dumphry might better recall the rest for you upon her return."

"So the footsteps are heard toward evening most often?" asked Holmes.

"Yes," said Sir George. "But not exclusively so. Once I heard them in the afternoon. On another occasion, the servants claimed to have been roused from sleep early in the morning before I rose from my bed."

"Very good," said Holmes. "And you were certain the footsteps haven't been heard prior to the advent of summer?"

"I have not heard them. And the servants all swear that they hadn't until recent weeks."

"And what do you ascribe this revenant rousing from his well-deserved slumber?"

"I cannot fully explain it, but it may be that the deceased didn't become aware of the separation of his helmet from his armor until recently."

Holmes took the fuming pipe from his mouth. "I must assert to you in all frankness, Sir George, that I'm disinclined to describe this phenomenon to the activity of any sort of ghost."

Sir George looked a bit taken aback. "That is rather premature of you, don't you think? Why, you have barely been here for two hours."

"While this is true, Sir George, having been called to investigate a good number of alleged hauntings before, I have yet to uncover a provable phantom."

Sir George laughed good-naturedly, but also with a touch of polite condescension, I thought.

"Well, there is always a first time, is there not?"

"Undoubtedly," murmured Holmes in a noncommittal tone.

"It is my hope," stated Sir George, "that you gentlemen will spend a few nights here and, I greatly hope, resolve the riddle to the satisfaction of all."

"I have no doubt about that," said Holmes. "The only question is how many days will be required to uncover a definitive answer."

"I don't see that there is any rush," declared Sir George, "so long as the result is satisfactory."

"Then it is settled," decided Holmes. "We shall be your guests until the mystery is resolved."

Later that afternoon, Sir George's wife arrived and we were introduced. Lady Dumphry was a comely woman whose face was dominated by ruddy cheeks and a pair of eyes as bright as silver coins. I quite liked her. Like her husband, she appeared naturally imbued with a spirit of good humor.

Lady Dumphry had evidently been shopping in town, for the butler who accompanied her carried in a cumbersome package wrapped in brown paper and twine. He stepped gingerly, as if his burden was fragile.

"You may set that down on the dining table, Arthur," she directed.

"What is this?" wondered the baronet.

"While you gentlemen go about solving this awkward matter in your own way, I have brought something I pray will assist in the resolution."

With her own hands, Lady Dumphry tore off the wrapping paper after the butler had parted the twine with a knife.

These actions revealed a prodigious carboy bottle of olive-green glass. Within, apparently assembled in the same clever manner as a miniature ship in a bottle, was a colorful construction of which I could make neither heads nor tails. So as not to give the reader the wrong impression. I will note that the bottle stood upright and not horizontally.

"Now, what is this?" asked Holmes curiously.

"It is a spirit house," proclaimed Lady Dumphry proudly.

"So you say," rejoined Holmes. "And what, if I may ask, is its purpose?"

"It is said that if an unwanted spirit enters a dwelling and declines to leave, placing a spirit house in a prominent location will attract its attention," explained the woman.

"I don't recognize the structure within," I ventured. "It suggests the outlines of the battlements of a castle, but only in the most rudimentary way."

"Oh," she exclaimed brightly, "it isn't to be meant to be anything in particular. The idea of a spirit house is to create a folly in miniature within the glass to attract and hold the attention of the annoying spirit. The more elaborate the folly, the more firmly it will hold a phantom's attention."

"So it is a mere snare?" inquired Holmes.

"I imagine one could say so."

"Should the snare capture the spirit in the bottle," continued Holmes, "are the two then removed from the house for disposal?"

"Oh Heavens, no!" returned Lady Dumphry. "That would never do. Especially if the spirit constituted an ancestor. No, it is just something to fascinate the mind of the ghostly wanderer. In this way, they get into considerably less mischief. Or so I'm told by the old woman who sold it to me."

"I am unfamiliar with this folk custom," said Holmes, bending down and studying the interior structure.

I did the same, and saw that resting on a bed of what appeared to be sawdust reared up several columns of differently colored beads. This odd arrangement surrounded and was connected to a central column that consisted of stacked spools of brightly colored thread. This continued into the wide bottle neck, which was plugged by a blackened cork topped by a stopper of clear glass. Interspersed among the colored beads were equally colorful short tubes, although many were the hue of various woods. There seemed to be no purpose to the haphazard arrangement of tubes and beads. None were harmonious. Colors jostled against one another contrary to artistic harmony. It might have been the product of a primitive conjuror, except that the elements were quite English, and readily purchased in millinery shops.

Rather taken aback by the foolishness of it all, I straightened up again, but I of course kept my opinion to myself.

For his own part, Holmes stood back from the glass bottle and remarked, "It is strikingly elaborate. Did the old woman who sold it to you construct it herself?"

"I did not ask, but I doubt it. She had several for sale in her curiosity shop. Some bottles were much smaller and filled with paper corkscrew twists and twirls, but they wouldn't do. I purchased the most elaborate of her wares, for if we are to have results, it is better that they are sooner than later. Furthermore, if this spirit house fascinates the ghost of the long-deceased James Trussell, it must occupy him wholly."

"This is most intriguing," said Holmes, without offering an opinion of the efficacy of such an outlandish contraption, which I thought both wise and prudent of him.

I recognized that his fascination with the spirit-house bottle was in fact genuine. Holmes took a keen interest in all things that might add to his ever-growing fund of knowledge. I was also confident that he placed no special powers in the absurd contrivance.

The Baronet addressed the butler. "Arthur, kindly place this bottle at the library entrance, next to the helm of the Duke of Grumley. Mind that you don't drop it."

"Yes, Sir George," said the Butler, who then carried out his master's instructions with the expression of a man who was long-suffering.

I couldn't resist asking our host a question about the placement of the spirit house.

"Sir George, would it not be more efficacious to set the bottle in the loft, where you believe your ghost wanders about in evident frustration?"

I hasten to inform the reader that I wasn't being mischievous. I genuinely wished to learn the baronet's answer, the better to understand the workings of his mind, which I found remarkable.

Sir George looked somewhat baffled by my inquiry, superficially logical as it appeared to be. He glanced toward his wife, who came to his immediate rescue.

"That wouldn't do," she explained. "The spirit house would simply sit in darkness, and no doubt be overlooked by our visitor. No, it must be visible. Otherwise of what use would it be?"

Nodding in vigorous agreement, Sir George added extemporaneously, "I would prefer to capture the apparition where I can see it in clear light, for I have always wanted to make the acquaintance of a genuine ghost."

Now it came Lady Dumphry's turn to nod in agreement. And there the sticky issue rested, to the satisfaction of everyone except Holmes and myself. Neither one of us could reconcile the idea of an immaterial spirit with an animated suit of armor possessing the substance of steel, but the contradiction didn't bother our hosts, if indeed it chanced to occur to them.

Over dinner, Holmes asked Lady Dumphry many questions, and her answers were much like those of her husband's.

"Would you recall the dates of the prior occasions when the supposed ghost walked?"

Beaming helpfully, Lady Dumphry rattled off a number of dates, although she confessed uncertainty about one of them.

"Ghosts," she asserted, "have always been welcome in the halls of my ancestors, but only so long as they behave. This one must be taught manners. He is making the servants perfect nervous wrecks. I can't have it. I simply won't tolerate it. This ghost must be brought under control or simply banished."

"I have promised Sir George that I will solve the problem for him," stated Holmes. "And you, Madame, may rest assured that I will."

At these words, Sir George and his wife beamed happily.

Speaking strictly for myself, I concentrated on the lamb, for I felt as if I was sharing a meal with two happily deluded people. This made me uncomfortable, but not overly so. I took Sir George and his wife to be a perfect pair of country eccentrics.

We passed the remainder of the evening in the drawing room, where the conversation ranged from the niceties of the Battle of Agincourt to more modern matters.

From time to time, Sir George raised a quieting finger and cocked his head ceilingward, as if hearing the inexplicable footsteps.

However, no sounds reached our ears that matched that peculiar phenomenon.

When it came time to retire, we retreated to the bedroom that had been provided for our comfort. It was quite sumptuous, with two rather elaborate four-poster canopy beds.

The day had been warmish, and the next day promised to be even more so. I considered how many blankets would be sufficient for the night and decided to make do with what the maid had provided.

The household noises soon settled down. After undressing and donning a nightshirt, Holmes got into his bed, while I did the same.

"Have you formed any definite opinion as yet?" I asked him in a quiet voice.

In a subdued tone, Holmes muttered, "As you might imagine, I have dispensed with any notion of ancestral phantoms from the start."

"I quite agree with you. Sir George's thinking is faulty on that subject."

"It borders on being demented," stated Holmes very definitely. "But the fellow is otherwise intelligent."

"Yet he is entirely convinced of his convictions. How will you disabuse him of those?"

"I don't think I will be too harsh on Sir George and Lady Dumphry. He is quite invested in the story of the Duke of Grumley and his wayward suit of armor. Regrettably, and I shall not divulge this, nor should you, but that suit of armor doesn't truly date to the Battle of Agincourt."

"It doesn't?"

"No, it's from a later era. The helmet, however, is unquestionably authentic. That, I can believe was carried back from France, but the idea that an entire suit of armor would be returned to the widow when the body was buried on the battlefield on which the man fell is preposterous. No one would go to such an extraordinary effort – not unless the armor was taken up by another knight, one who survived Agincourt. I'm also skeptical that a mail gorget was part of the original ensemble. A proper bevor is more likely to be worn by a duke, but this assumption can never be proven one way or the other. Furthermore, latter-day accounts of the dismembering of English archer's fingers by vengeful French knights are suspect. More to the point, a knight at Agincourt would never employ such a lowly if effective weapon as the longbow. It would be beneath his station."

"Why yes, of course!" I exclaimed. "You're correct. How foolish of me to overlook that fact. Every schoolboy would know it."

"No doubt someone pawned off the existing armor as the genuine article, and gullible persons accepted it without qualm. It doesn't matter whom. Nevertheless, the armor doesn't belong to the helmet, and Sir George's theory that the shade of His Grace is determined in death to reunite the two sections falls apart on the basis of that fact alone. Even if such a revenant existed, he would scarcely care about armor that never was his."

"I see. Well, there's no reason to disabuse Sir George of his beliefs on that score. They are harmless, but if you are to lay the ghost of his imagination, you will have to be quite strict about it. The baronet will accept nothing less than absolute proof of anything contrary to his beloved fantasy."

"I'm quite confident that I can produce such proof. It's only a question of how many nights we must spend at Dunshire Priory before all parties are in agreement as to the cause of the mysterious circling footfalls."

With that, Holmes put out the light, and we drifted off in the comfort of our beds.

With the dawn, I awoke to spy Holmes pacing the room in his dressing gown.

"You're up early," I commented, throwing off my covers and sitting up.

"Ah! I see that you're awake. I've been eager to share my discovery ever since it came to me while it was still dark."

"You have solved the ghostly mystery?"

"Not yet, but during the night the solution to Inspector Lestrade's official conundrum came to me. One of the pieces of the puzzle is faulty. I had been attempting to incorporate it into possible theories, but I belatedly realized that the inspector had failed to recognize it as superfluous. Having discarded it, I was able to assemble the other pieces in my mind, and extrapolate the rest. The culprit is now known to me. I may write Lestrade after breakfast, for I don't know when we shall be back in London."

"I see," I said, suppressing my disappointment. "Have you given any further thought to Sir George's headless ghost?"

"None whatsoever, but be of good cheer. The solution may soon manifest itself to our satisfaction."

We dressed for breakfast and presented ourselves to the dining room, where Sir George and his wife were enjoying coffee.

Lady Dumphry greeted us warmly, adding, "It promises to be a frightfully hot day."

"I consider that to be welcome news," said Holmes.

"You prefer the heat to more temperate conditions?" asked Sir George.

"In this particular instance, the answer is yes. A hot day may prove to be more satisfying than one might expect."

With that cryptic comment, Holmes and I took our chairs. Before long breakfast was set before us. We dined handsomely, in the manner of country squires.

The morning was spent in idle conversation after a more elaborate tour of the Dunshire Priory than we had previously been given. I was impressed by Sir George's rather extensive library. The man's literary tastes ran the gamut from the erudite to a wide variety of popular novels. I was quite surprised at his eclectic choices. However, I wasn't surprised to discover the works of the Grimm Brothers, Poe, Le Fanu, Mrs. Oliphant, and others who spun tales of the strange and the supernatural. It quite fitted Sir George's far-flung interests.

I fully expected Holmes to expend a great deal of effort in investigating the mystery at hand. Yet beyond taking the household staff aside by turns and speaking to them for a few minutes at odd times, he didn't seem to put forth very much effort in that direction.

As the day wore on, it became exceedingly hot, and perhaps this dampened his enthusiasm for investigation, but I rather thought not. It struck me that he was simply temporizing, awaiting a certain time or a specific event that he was expecting.

I couldn't imagine what that might be. Unless he expected the ghost to walk that very day.

Despite the heat, Sir George went grouse hunting that afternoon. Holmes and I were invited along, but I thought the day too hot to be out of doors for the number of hours required. Lady Dumphry and I passed a pleasant afternoon discussing various illnesses and maladies that had plagued her family in recent years. Here, I found myself on comfortable ground. Thus, the hours passed agreeably in spite of the rapidly climbing temperature.

Holmes did accompany Sir George on his hunt. When they returned, each exhibited two fine-looking red grouse. And thus dinner was decided upon.

With the evening came a welcome cooling. In contrast with the day's heat, it was delightful change, although I must note that it was still warmer than I would have preferred.

Over dinner, Sir George chanced to make a remark that I thought odd, but well in keeping with the man's eccentric nature.

"I suspect that the ghost will pace tonight."

"What leads you to say that?" inquired Holmes.

"He often walks on the nights following a hot day. Or during the day, once the temperature cools after a hot night."

"I thought as much," said Holmes.

"You did?" asked Sir George, blinking his rather innocent-looking eyes.

"That the footfalls come with the cooling of the day or night parallels my expectations."

Lady Dumphry smiled and said, "My own personal theory is that the ghost doesn't care for the heat of day. Don't they often prefer to operate at night and roam moonlit graveyards?"

Holmes asked, "If ghosts don't prefer the heat, why do you suppose this one has remained quiescent during the cooler seasons?"

Lady Dumphry laughed as if the question were impertinent, or perhaps silly.

"Why, you shall have to ask the ghost when you capture him, Mr. Holmes!"

Sir George laughed at what he thought was his wife's witty remark. His mirth was quite jolly.

Holmes smiled in a way I thought to be cryptic.

After dinner, drinks were served along with coffee, and we wiled the evening away in idle conversation.

A bit past nine, the pitter-pattering of a light rain on the roof was heard. With this came a cool breeze through the open windows, vanishing the last vestiges of the uncomfortably sultry day.

As nightfall came on, the butler went around the room, lighting the wall sconces. Lastly, he placed a flickering candlestick beside Sir George, who dismissed the fellow and said, "Should the specter stir, I now have my light at hand."

The hour was past ten o'clock when Sir George suddenly bolted from his chair, crying out, "Hark!"

All talk ceased abruptly.

The maid was in the act of taking away coffee cups when she gasped and ran into the kitchen, plainly in superstitious fear. Arthur the butler appeared, glanced upward and turned pale. He retreated from our sight.

"My word!" I cried out. "That sounds exactly like a man walking about the loft."

"Or a ghost!" countered Sir George.

We all four moved into the library, where we gathered directly beneath the commotion.

There was no question about it. The floorboards above our heads creaked and squeaked disconsolately, but with a definite regularity. It was exactly as if someone were striding in a circle of narrow compass.

"Shall we investigate?" prompted Sir George, producing the key to the loft door.

"By all means," said Holmes.

Eagerly, Sir George took up his candlestick, raced to the back of the house beyond the library and went directly to the door that opened onto the steep servants' stairs. We climbed upward, Holmes directly behind Sir George. Lady Dumphry chose to remain in the library, hovering beside the helmet of her ancestor. There was something about her expectant expression that made me think she considered the idea of a ghost in her loft as thrilling and not frightening. No doubt she had been educated to believe that household ghosts were invariably friendly, and probably of blood relation.

Reaching the top, Sir George opened the upper door and plunged inward.

I, bringing up the rear, arrived last.

Sir George had his candlestick upraised while Holmes struck a Lucifer. These wavering lights showed the headless suit of armor standing precisely where it belonged, at the end of the rafter-buttressed space.

The sound of footsteps was heard no more. They had ceased almost at once.

"Confound you!" Sir George shouted at the suit of armor. "You mock me again! Why do you not let us see you parading about?"

"Because he doesn't parade about," said Holmes quietly.

Sir George turned and demanded, "What makes you say that, Mr. Holmes? You heard the sound of treading feet as clearly as I did."

"But we hear them no more, do we?"

Sir George lowered his candle in defeat.

"No, we do not. Can you explain it?"

"I will attempt to do so," declared Holmes. "But first, let us retreat to the library. It is too stuffy up here and these naked flames put us all in peril."

"Can we not discuss it here, or are you afraid that the ghost will overhear?"

Holmes gave forth a light laugh. "No, I'm not afraid of eavesdropping phantoms, but I will explain fully once we have returned to the library."

Down the stairs we trudged. Holmes took a position in the center of the library.

Putting down his candle, Sir George stood before Holmes and asked, "Well, out with it then. Let us hear your theory."

"If you don't mind," said Holmes, "I prefer that we wait for the next development before speaking."

"Development? Whatever do you mean?"

"I mean the return of the footsteps."

"You expect them to return? How soon?"

"I'm not certain, but I don't think we have to wait long."

Nor did we. Before very many minutes passed, the footsteps resumed in the attic again. They made a circular creaking, as of a man pacing in a nervous circle.

"The ghost has returned!" crowed Sir George.

Holmes shook his head. "The ghost has *not* returned. What has returned are the special conditions that were so often creating the illusion of circular footfalls."

"Illusion! You can hear them, as well as I do!"

"I hear them, but I perceive them differently than you do, Sir George."

"Go on."

"You yourself have said that the footsteps invariably sound in the aftermath of a hot day or evening, such as today. Given that fact, and the additional information that the footsteps didn't begin to be heard until the arrival of summer, forces me to think in terms of a commonplace phenomenon, not supernatural forces."

Above our heads, the creaking and squeaking of active feet seemed to mock Holmes's unequivocal assertion.

"We have all noted that the attic floor planks squeak when stepped upon," Holmes reminded.

"Which is why I insist that the headless suit of armor belonging to the restless knight itself is pressing down on the floorboards, producing the annoying squeaks and creaks we all hear."

"It is clear to the ear," added Lady Dumphry plaintively.

"Quite clear," agreed Holmes. "But I remind you both that when I tested the floor planks earlier, my actions produced not only the familiar creaking, but in certain places the groaning of old softwood under pressure."

"What of it?" countered Sir George. "The ghost walks in a circle at the specific spot directly above our heads."

"A spot in the approximate middle of the loft void," reminded Holmes.

"Yes."

"Assuming for the moment the existence of a striding suit of armor, it must first pass over the section of floor that groans when stepped upon before reaching said spot," Holmes pointed out.

Sir George blinked his bland blue eyes. He seemed slow in responding. I didn't think Holmes's point had quite yet penetrated.

Holmes pressed onward. "The weight of that armor, I submit to you, Sir George, is such that it must make the floorboards groan if it were ambulatory, even if untenanted. For before anyone can reach the middle of the floor, he must first pass over the section of spruce that groans."

"I see," said Sir George. "But that observation doesn't explain the persistent creaking of feet stepping on wood boards."

"It is a fact that in old houses certain wholly natural phenomena manifest," advised Holmes patiently. "Houses settle. They sometimes lean or lurch in one direction if the foundation isn't kept up. Wood, being a natural substance, is subject to stresses and strains that alter it. It is a fact of science that heat rises. And on a hot day, indoor heat will accumulate beneath the ceiling, which is why intelligent architects build rooms with high ceilings. So that the trapped heat will travel upward and not torment the inhabitants.

"Such rising heat invariably seeps into lofts and attics, which are already quite hot as a result of the surrounding atmosphere and the lack of good ventilation. The absence of windows also contributes to this heat.

Recall one of the fundamental practical purposes of the attic void, which is to trap heat so as to keep the timbers of the roof perpetually dry."

"Yes, yes," said Sir George. "This is an absolute necessity in our rainy English climate. I know that."

"I submit to you, Sir George, that the phenomenon taking place overhead is nothing less than the squeaking of floorboards that are shrinking in the cycle of cooling taking place in the void. The unvarnished spruce planks have expanded in the heat and now they are going back to their normal configuration. These contractions are what is producing the suspicious creaking. The fact that they evoke the sound like circular footfalls is simply a freak of the construction of the loft's plank floor. Nothing more. Each hand-sawn board is unique and therefore demonstrates different rates of expansion and contraction, and so produces quite unique noises. Just as unpracticed fingers fumbling for a piano keyboard will accidentally produce fragments of music, your hyperactive loft planking is suggestive of footfalls. I might add that spruce is resinous softwood. Consequently, it is especially prone to such unsettling alterations, owing to its elasticity, as well as its propensity for both absorbing and releasing moisture."

"If that is so," challenged Sir George, "how do you explain the fact that once we enter the attic, all noisy activity ceases?"

"It is quite simple. Once a person enters the loft and steps onto the threshold, his weight transmits itself to the restive floorboards, thus suppressing the noises in progress. You will note that, until you are standing on the attic floor proper with your light, you cannot see far into the interior of the loft. The act of stepping onto the planking serves to settle the phenomenon, which, as I say, is entirely natural."

Sir George regarded Holmes with a lingering degree of skepticism.

Seeing this, Holmes landed the final blow of his argument.

"If you have any doubts on the score, you need only climb those steps, revisit the loft and see for yourself."

"Very well. I shall do exactly that."

Decisively, Sir George went to the servants' stairs, mounted them, and so disappeared into the loft. Remaining below, we followed the progress of his tramping feet, which communicated itself throughout the house.

At once, the squeaky circular footsteps ceased.

The floorboards above now creaked and groaned in a quite different manner, one indicative of a man creeping around rather aimlessly.

Once Sir George returned to the library, the queer squeaking resumed. The Baronet's expression and sunken shoulders shared the aspect of a crestfallen man.

"I am sorry to disappoint you, Sir George," said Holmes gravely. "I know that you wished this matter resolved to your satisfaction, which objectively I believe I have done, but I understand that you have an attachment to your household ghost."

"I will admit it," said Sir George. "I rather liked the idea of the Duke of Grumley once again putting on his famed suit of armor to go in search of his helmeted head. It is the romantic in me, I suppose. I simply abhorred the noisy way he went about it."

Lady Dumphry inserted herself into the exchange.

"But, Mr. Holmes, what about the disturbances in the floor of the loft?"

"I suspect mice. No doubt if you set appropriate traps in the attic, they will no longer be an issue. I will also note that it is impossible to thread one's way through the jumble of bric-a-brac stored in the loft in order to reach the armor without crossing the spot where the dust has been found to be disturbed. Some of those disturbances, Sir George, I submit, were the doing of your purely human explorations.

"As for the persistent creaking," added Holmes, "if you are of a mind to do so, have a mason and window fitter set a window at the end of the loft where the suit of armor stands guard. It should be enough to permit a free flow of air, and release the trapped heat, which should in turn reduce the creaking, if not do away with it altogether."

With an aggrieved sigh, Sir George nodded resigned acceptance of Holmes's recommendations.

"Well then," he said, snapping back to his customary good cheer, "you appear to have resolved the matter to my satisfaction. I will be happy to write you a check. And since the hour is late, you are welcome to stay another night, of course."

"Thank you, Sir George," said Holmes graciously. "But the night isn't so far along that Dr. Watson and I cannot catch a late train back to London. If you will be so good to lend us your brougham, we will be off."

And so the awkward matter was settled.

In parting, I thanked Lady Dumphry for her cheering conversation, but couldn't resist asking, "Whatever will you do with your expensive spirit house now?"

"Why, Dr. Watson, I will keep it, of course. Between my husband and me, we have many notable ancestors. Should one pay us a call, the bottled spirit house should hold him long enough that we might engage in a most intriguing conversation."

"That reasoning is sound enough for me," beamed Sir George. "I will not banish it to the loft. It shall stand in my library for as long as I am master of this household."

Holmes and I were soon at the railway station, where we were able to secure a compartment for the journey homeward. In Holmes's breast pocket was a handsome check, signed by Sir George Dumphry, Bart.

"This was an altogether satisfactory adventure," said Holmes as the train pulled away from the station and he dug into his pockets for his clay pipe and pouch of tobacco.

"I expected a longer stay," I noted.

"As had I. Fortunately, the weather turned in our favor. And I'm eager to return to London and pay a call on Scotland Yard. I have the answer to Lestrade's conundrum, and I am pleased to say that for the first time in my career as a consulting detective, I have solved two mysteries simultaneously."

"I remain interested in this second mystery," said I, "if you care to share it with me."

"Since we have a long journey ahead of us, and the solution is clear, I see no reason why not."

As the train rattled through the evening, Holmes regaled me with the entire story. Taking out my pen and paper, I made copious notes, for although the matter was relatively minor, the way Holmes worked it out was quite ingenious.

I imagine one day I will produce a sketch from those notes. At present, I thought that the puzzle of the restless knight was of far more interest to the English reading public. And now you have it.

NOTE

* For those who would flag the word "hyperactive" as modern, it has been in use since at least the 1850's.

The Six-Thirteen from
Fairfield Junction
by Denis O. Smith

There can be few among my readers who are entirely unfamiliar with the strange mystery connected with the *Marie Celeste*. It will readily be recalled, I am sure, that in 1873 the *Marie Celeste*, a handsome brigantine of some hundred-foot length, was discovered drifting in the Atlantic Ocean, many miles from the nearest land. Her equipment was in good order, she was well provisioned, and her cargo was undisturbed. But, to the astonishment of those who found her, there was not a soul on board, and no clue as to what had become of the captain, the crew, and the passengers. Nor, although a quarter-of-a-century has now passed since her discovery, has any clue to the mystery ever been found.

What is not so generally known, however, is that another, strikingly similar case occurred more recently, which also caused astonishment and mystification in those that first discovered it. Perhaps even more amazingly, this second case took place not on the high seas, hundreds of miles from the nearest human habitation, but on dry land, here in England, in the heart of the countryside. For this case concerned not a ship but a railway train. When the Six-thirteen evening branch line train from Fairfield Junction to Parlingham reached its destination, shortly after quarter-to-seven, all those known to have been aboard when it left Fairfield Junction had vanished without trace, despite the fact that the train had not stopped once on its journey.

News of this strange and sinister occurrence spread round the district like wildfire. What on earth could have happened, people wondered, to bring about such a weird and unprecedented state of affairs? It was too late in the evening for the following day's papers to carry anything but the barest of accounts of the matter, but, taking their lead from the local paper, they almost all described it as "*The* Marie Celeste *of the railways*".

It was certainly an interesting and surprising business, and I was fortunate that, sharing chambers as I did with the noted criminal investigator Sherlock Holmes, I was able to observe the matter at first hand, almost from the beginning.

Our introduction to the case was a dramatic one. It was a cold, wet, and blustery period in early March 1886, and neither Holmes nor I had ventured out of doors all day. As the evening wore on, the wind seemed to pick up yet more savage power and hurl sheets of rain against our window panes. The clock on the mantelpiece was showing nearly ten-to-nine when, above the violent lashing of the wind and the rain, there came the sudden harsh jangling of the front door bell.

"Now, who can this be, out and about in this foul weather?" said Holmes, looking up from where he was pasting newspaper cuttings into a scrap-book.

"Perhaps it is some visitors for Mrs. Hudson," I suggested, "no doubt hoping for a hot cup of tea."

My friend chuckled. "If so," said he, "their desire for tea must certainly be a desperate one, to lead them to brave the elements on such a night as this."

Moments later, however, there came the sound of rapid footsteps on the stair, followed by a sharp *rat-a-tat-tat* on our door. The visitor was evidently not for the landlady but for us, and, equally evidently, someone the maid knew well, as she had clearly not accompanied him up the stair. I sprang to my feet and pulled the door open. There stood our old friend, Inspector Lestrade of Scotland Yard, his overcoat glistening wet.

"Come in, Lestrade, come in!" cried Holmes. "Dry yourself by the fire and tell us what we can do for you!"

Lestrade stepped to the fire, rubbing his hands together vigorously, but shook his head. "I've no time to get dry, Mr. Holmes," said he. "I'm on an urgent errand, which will, I believe, be of great interest to you, and all I wish to know is if you will come with me or not."

"What is it, then?" asked Holmes, evidently struck, as I was, by the policeman's urgent tone.

"A very strange business, from the little I have heard," replied Lestrade. "I don't yet know all the details, but it sounds very much as if a violent crime has been committed."

"Where did this crime take place?"

"Gloucestershire."

"Gloucestershire!" I cried in surprise.

"Yes, I know it's a long way, Dr. Watson. But they have asked for an experienced detective officer to be sent down there – someone reliable, and experienced in interviewing witnesses, they said – and I have been assigned to the case. The facts are simply these: That when the evening train from Fairfield Junction, in Gloucestershire, to somewhere or other, reached its destination, they found that there was no one aboard!"

"Why, that is not so strange!" I cried, laughing. "These rural branch lines are often very lightly used, Lestrade, especially in the evening. I have been on such a train a few times, and on at least one occasion I was the only passenger!"

"No, no, Dr. Watson," Lestrade interrupted, shaking his head vigorously. "You don't understand. It is not simply that there were no passengers on the train – although that is true enough. There were no railway employees, either! The engine-driver had vanished without trace, as had the fireman, and as had the guard of the train! And yet the train had not stopped once on its run from Fairfield!"

"What!" I cried in astonishment. "How is that possible?"

"That is certainly a singular problem," said Holmes, springing to his feet. "When does your train for Gloucestershire leave?"

"Nine-fifteen, from Paddington," replied the policeman, with a glance at the clock. "It is the last train of the evening, and I must leave this minute if I am to catch it! I have a cab waiting downstairs. Will you come?"

"Certainly," said Holmes. "And Watson, too, I am sure. Yes? Then throw some clothes and your razor into a bag, and be ready to leave in ninety seconds!" With that, my colleague dashed from the room.

A minute later, I returned from my bedroom and found Holmes and Lestrade waiting for me on the stairs. Holmes scribbled a note to the landlady explaining our abrupt departure, which he left on the hall table, and a minute later we were in the cab and driving furiously for Paddington Station.

We boarded our train with scarcely a minute to spare, and soon we were slipping in the darkness through the dimly-lit western suburbs of London and into the dark and silent countryside beyond.

Our journey was a long and tedious one. Lestrade knew nothing more about the case than he had already told us and, save the occasional brightly-lit station – through most of which we raced at great speed – the night was such a black one that there was nothing to be seen outside the confines of our small compartment. Having fairly rapidly exhausted our speculations about the mystery which was summoning us to the west of England, we all three lit our pipes and sat in silence for some time. Holmes and Lestrade then fell to discussing the current state of crime and detection in London, but I could not raise any interest in what seemed to me a very generalised discussion, and instead followed my own train of thought about the strange events in Gloucestershire.

How on earth, I wondered, could the locomotive and its train of carriages, several tons in weight, have proceeded from one end of the line to the other with no one aboard to guide it, and no one to stoke the fire in the boiler? What about the signals the train must have passed, and the intermediate stations, if there were any? And what happened at Parlingham, at the end of the line, with no one aboard the train to apply the brakes? And, above all, how and why had everyone on the train vanished without trace? The driver and fireman would, presumably, have been on the footplate of the locomotive, at the front of the train, the guard probably in the last carriage of the train, with any passengers somewhere in between them. How could they all possibly have been affected in the same way? I asked myself many such questions, but could suggest plausible answers to none of them.

At length, after more than two hours of this monotonous journey, I felt the train begin to slow. Sherlock Holmes leaned forward, peering into the darkness outside. "I believe we are approaching Fairfield," said he, with a glance at his watch. "It is to be hoped there will be someone there to meet us."

"There should be," replied Lestrade. "Scotland Yard has sent a message that I am coming."

Even as he spoke, the train abruptly slowed with a jerk, as if a brake had been applied, and, moments later, we drew slowly into the brightly-lit platform at Fairfield Junction. The night air was very chilly. I glanced at the large station clock which was suspended over the platform above our heads, and saw the time was about half-past-eleven.

As we made our way out into the carriage yard, a fine rain was falling. A tall man in a braided uniform and cap stepped forward and introduced himself in a brisk and business-like manner as Superintendent Huggins of the Gloucestershire Constabulary. He and Lestrade shook hands.

"But who are these gentlemen?" the superintendent asked, indicating Holmes and myself.

"This is Mr. Sherlock Holmes," replied Lestrade. "He is a consultant criminologist who has often been of assistance to us in the past. And this is his colleague, Dr. Watson, a medical man. They have a particular interest in unusual cases."

"Ah!" said Huggins. "If so, then they have come to the right place. I've been on the force nigh on thirty years, Mr. Lestrade, and I don't ever recall a case as strange as this one! Well, I'm sure there is no objection to their accompanying us and observing our methods, if you vouch for them, although I don't think we shall have any need to 'consult' anyone about anything. But come, let us get aboard the van, and I'll describe it all to you as we go!"

"One moment," interrupted Holmes. "Where are we going?"

"To Parlingham," replied the superintendent in surprise. "That is where the chief police station for the district is situated. It is also where the train at the centre of this business is now standing."

"The situation of the police station is surely irrelevant to the case," responded Holmes. "I should prefer it if you would give us a brief account

310

of the matter before we leave Fairfield. We may wish to question the staff here."

"But nothing of any consequence happened here."

"One cannot say that with any certainty," said Holmes. "The branch line train departed from here on its singular journey. That is surely sufficient to make it of possible relevance to the case."

"Oh, very well," said Huggins, a trace of annoyance in his voice. He glanced at Lestrade. "But let us at least get out of this rain."

We followed him to the police van, which stood at the side of the carriage yard. "Now," said the policeman, as we clambered aboard. "Where shall I begin? I assume you have been given an outline of the matter," he added.

"Only the bare bones of the business," returned Lestrade. "We know that all those travelling on the train had disappeared by the time it reached the end of the line, but nothing more than that."

"Then you know almost as much as anyone does," said Huggins, with a short, bitter laugh.

"Any obvious clues?" interrupted Holmes. "Any doors on the train left open, for instance, or disorder in any of the compartments?"

Huggins shook his head. "No," said he, "there was no disorder anywhere – that is what is so mysterious about it. As for the doors, the only one which was open was that of the guard's compartment at the rear of the train, and that is not so surprising. As you are no doubt aware, unlike the doors of the passenger compartments, which all open outwards, the guard's door opens inwards and can be pegged back to keep it in that position. This is necessary, of course, as the guard sometimes has to hop on or off the train when it is moving very slowly – in a station, for instance. This open door was on the left side of the train – left, I mean, from the guard's point of view as he looks forward along the train."

"Is that the side that the station platforms are on?" asked Holmes.

"Yes, all the branch line platforms are on that side. All the other doors on the train were closed. One of them – the door to one of the first-class compartments – was not closed very firmly, but I don't think that that is of any significance. You know what train doors are like: If you slam them they close soundly, but if you are a little too delicate with them they do still close, but in a loose, rattling sort of way. Anyhow, as the door in question was on the other side of the train, facing *away* from the platforms, I don't think it can have had anything to do with what happened tonight. It has probably been like that since the last time the carriage was cleaned, I imagine."

"I think we understand," remarked Lestrade. "What I should like to know now," he continued, "before you get into any details, is whether you have made any progress in the matter yet."

"Not exactly," replied Huggins after a moment's hesitation, "but I am hopeful of hearing something soon. I have men out all over the district, making enquiries. I also have men walking the line, one from the Parlingham end, and one from this end, but I have heard nothing back from them yet."

Lestrade nodded his head. "And what is your own opinion of the matter?" he asked.

"My opinion?" returned Huggins in surprise. "I don't really have one, Mr. Lestrade. I've never been a great one for theories and opinions. One fact is worth a thousand theories, eh? In this case, I don't mind admitting that I haven't the faintest idea what has become of the men who have disappeared."

"Does anyone else have an opinion?" persisted Lestrade.

Huggins snorted. "There are several opinions, most of them perfectly ridiculous. If I were to tell you what the opinion is that I have heard the most, you would not believe me!"

"Well?"

"Most folk are saying that it's all the work of The Old Man of the Woods."

"Who is this 'Old Man of the Woods'?" asked Holmes in surprise.

"You gentlemen are from London," returned Huggins after a moment, "and no doubt have a more refined view of things, so you might not understand. But I'd wager there isn't a country district in England that doesn't have its own particular myths and superstitions. In these parts, no doubt because of the dense woodlands round here, our local hobgoblin or bogey is known as 'The Old Man of the Woods'. He is generally supposed to be the fount of all evil and the cause of all troubles. He lives in the dark woods, and his only pleasure is to be wicked and to cause as much misery for everyone as possible. Of course, no one has ever seen The Old Man of the Woods, but, despite that, everyone seems to know enough about him to terrify children with warnings about him, and he is the first explanation on everyone's lips when anything goes wrong."

"I see," said Holmes. "Well, I am sure we shall all give 'The Old Man of the Woods' the attention he deserves. Now, about the case itself: What can you tell us? You had best start at the beginning, and we can question you if anything is not clear to us. If you could tell us something about this branch line, the stations on it, and the train-service it offers, that would be a useful start, for we know nothing whatever about it."

312

"Very well," said the policeman after a moment. "The branch line goes from Fairfield to Parlingham. It's very hilly country, up and down, so that sometimes the railway line is in a deep cutting, and sometimes it is on a high embankment. There are also some very dense woodlands – as I've just mentioned – through which the line passes. It's no great distance from one end of the line to the other, so the train usually does it in about twenty minutes, even though it never goes very fast. Speed has never been much of a requirement in these parts. Much of the traffic is in goods – sheep and other livestock, farm produce, coal – that sort of thing. All in all, it's not a very busy line, especially on the passenger side. It varies from day to day, of course, and the earlier trains are generally busier than the later, but the Six-thirteen, which is usually the last train of the day, often has only a handful of passengers – and, sometimes, none at all. However many passengers there might be, the trains are always the same: Three carriages, the first one all third class compartments, the second one a mixture of third and first class, and the third the guard's van, which of course also carries all the goods and luggage."

"Was there much in the way of goods on this evening's train?" asked Holmes.

Huggins nodded his head. "Yes. There were numerous crates, boxes, and packages in the guard's van, but they don't appear to have been disturbed in any way."

"Which suggests, of course, that attempted theft was not the cause of tonight's strange events," said Holmes. "Are there any other stations on the branch line?"

"Yes, just one – Bellbrook Halt – which lies roughly halfway between the two ends of the line. That consists of just a single platform and a waiting room, and is very little used. Indeed, I doubt it would ever have been built at all but for a generous contribution to its construction made by Viscount Bellbrook, the largest landowner in the district, whose family seat, Bellbrook Castle, is close by. Being a 'halt', as the railway company calls it, trains do not stop at Bellbrook unless there is someone who wishes to board or leave the train there. Anyone already on the train who wishes to alight at Bellbrook must notify the guard in advance – at Fairfield or Parlingham – that they wish to do so, and anyone waiting at Bellbrook hoping to catch the train there must stand on the platform and make a clear signal to the approaching train."

"Do you know if the Six-thirteen stopped at Bellbrook this evening?" queried Holmes.

"We really have no idea," returned Huggins with a shake of the head. "I doubt it, because it very rarely does, so they tell me. But it is possible, I suppose."

"Can you not tell from the tickets issued if anyone intended to alight at Bellbrook?" asked Lestrade.

Superintendent Huggins shook his head. "No one bought a ticket here – Fairfield – to travel to Bellbrook, but someone could have arrived here from London – or anywhere else – on a through ticket from there to Bellbrook. We haven't yet had chance to look into that possibility."

"We have been told," said Holmes, "that there were certainly no passengers on the train when it reached Parlingham this evening. But is it known if there were any passengers aboard when it left Fairfield?"

"There may have been," replied Huggins, "but I'm afraid that that, too, is a question we have not yet been able to answer."

"That seems a singular state of affairs," observed Holmes, raising his eyebrow in surprise.

"Yes, I know it is a strange thing, not to know if there was anyone on the train or not," conceded Huggins. "But come, I believe the rain has stopped. Let us go and see Mr. Thomas, the station-master here. He will explain it to you better than I can."

We therefore left the police van and made our way back to the station building, where Huggins conducted us to the station-master's office. He proved to be an affable man who was clearly astonished by what had happened.

"The three railwaymen who have disappeared," he began, shaking his head vigorously in disbelief, "they are all so respectable and reliable. Who – or what – can have attacked them? For I cannot think for a moment that they would have abandoned their posts voluntarily and left the train to plough on by itself, completely out of control. Someone could easily have been killed by it."

"Perhaps you could give us some details about the men," said Holmes, "which might help us to understand what could have happened to make them leave their train."

"Certainly, certainly," said Thomas. "All three of them have been working on this line for some years, with – as far as I am aware – no blemish of any sort against their names. The guard, James Morris, is the senior man. He has been a faithful servant of the company for more than thirty years, and his record of safety and diligence is as good as any man I have ever known. He would do anything to preserve the safety of his train. The engine-driver, Arthur Milbank, is also a very experienced man. He used to work the London Express, based at Gloucester, and was a real racer in those days. He was disciplined once, I remember, for driving too fast through some station or other – Swindon, I think it was. But he mellowed with age, and some years ago he opted for a quieter life and transferred to the Parlingham branch line.

314

"The fireman, John Turner, is a younger man than the other two, a big strong chap. He was a bit wild in his youth, so everyone says. The usual story, as I understand it: Lost his head over some woman, then lost his head even more when she threw him over. He was working at Bellbrook Castle at the time, as she was. He was employed in the gardens there, I believe, but he's been working for the railway company now for nigh on ten years, and so far as I'm aware there's never been any complaint against him. He lost his father when he was quite young, and that may have unbalanced him in his youth, but since he's been working here, old Milbank has been like a father to him, and that has probably helped him find his feet. So," he continued after a moment's silence, "I'm sorry if that doesn't help you at all, but that's all I know."

"Pardon my ignorance," said Inspector Lestrade, as the station-master fell silent again, "but could you tell us how the train could keep going when no one was aboard, and what would have happened when it reached the end of the line at Parlingham?"

"Certainly," said Thomas. "The branch line is a fairly level one, so it's not difficult to work. They'd have got steam up while they were here, waiting to depart. It's getting going from a standing start that uses most steam up, so they'd have kept the fire stoked up for the first couple of miles, to replace the steam they had used up. After that, they'd close down the regulator a bit, with plenty of steam in the dome to keep them going. By the time they got to Bellbrook, they'd be going pretty slowly, but that's how they'd want it, in case there was anyone waiting on the platform there to board the train. After Bellbrook, the line is level all the way, except for the last half-mile or so, which is a falling gradient, so the fire doesn't need banking up any more. The driver can just let the engine coast along, and it will have enough momentum to take it all the way to the end of the line. So the fact that in this case there was no driver or fireman on the footplate didn't matter from that point of view."

"But what about at the end of the line?" Lestrade persisted. "What usually happens then, and what would be different today?"

"Normally," replied Thomas, "the driver would apply the brake a little way before they reached the station, so that by the time they reached the platform they would be going very slowly. That's a matter of safety. Even at a very slow speed the train will keep rolling – there's so much dead weight pushing it along, you see. Today, who knows what might have happened?" He puffed his cheeks out and shook his head again. "We were very, very fortunate that the station-master at Parlingham, Mr. Williams, happened to be on the platform as the train drew in there. Otherwise there could have been a dreadful tragedy. As it was, Williams saw the train approaching and thought nothing of it, he says, except that it seemed to be travelling more slowly than usual. But as the engine drew closer to where he was standing, he was, he says, astounded to see that there was no footplate crew aboard her. He realised at once the great danger that the uncontrolled train represented, sprang aboard the footplate, closed the regulator completely, screwed down the brake as fast as he could and managed to stop it just before it overran the end of the platform. Had he not acted so promptly, I dread to think what severe damage the train could have done to the railway buildings at the end of the line – and to anyone who was working or standing there."

"How very fortunate that the station-master was on the platform and not in his office," remarked Lestrade. "I remember an occasion when a heavy passenger train overran the platform at one of the big London stations. It was only creeping along, apparently, but it still managed to cause massive damage!"

"I can well believe it," said Mr. Thomas, nodding his head. "Now, is there any other enquiry I can help you with?"

"Yes," said Holmes. "I understand that no one is sure whether there were any passengers on the Six-thirteen tonight or not. Can you shed any light on that, Mr. Thomas?"

"Not really, I'm afraid," replied the station-master in an apologetic tone. "That time of day is one of our busiest, and the platforms are often crowded then. You see, the London express arrives at eight minutes to six, and a lot of people alight here. Apart from those passengers whose destination is Fairfield itself, or Parlingham, there are also those who are travelling to somewhere further down the line. The London express doesn't stop again between here and Gloucester, so anyone wishing to travel to one of the stations between here and there will wait here for the slow train to Gloucester, which stops at every station on the way. This stopping train comes in at three-minutes-past-six, and departs again at eight-minutes-past. After that, the platforms are practically empty again. But between the arrival of the express and the departure of the stopping train the platforms are, as I say, full of passengers.

"Now, the chief porter, Peter Reece, was on the platform all that time, and he says he noticed that at least one man walked over to the other side of the platform, where the branch line train was waiting. The man was standing over there for some time, says Reece, but whether he actually boarded the train in the end, or had just walked over that way to stretch his legs while he waited for the slow train to Gloucester, he cannot say for certain."

"Was he able to describe this man?" asked Holmes.

"Yes," replied the station-master. "He says he was a tall, thin, scholarly-looking gentleman, possibly elderly, wearing a dark overcoat

316

and silk hat, and carrying a small leather travelling-bag and a walking stick. Reece says that, although he didn't really give the man much thought at the time, as he was busy and the platforms were crowded, he had the impression that the man might have been a doctor, or some other sort of professional man."

"Did he recognise him?" asked Lestrade.

"No. He doesn't think he had ever seen him before. I think, from what Reece told me, that the only reason this stranger caught his eye at all was because he looked very different from most of the passengers that Reece is used to seeing on the branch line train, who are, in the main, local, country folk."

"Where was the guard of the Parlingham train at the time the porter saw this stranger?" asked Lestrade.

"Usually," said Thomas, "he would be with his train, preparing it for the journey, stowing away any luggage and so on. But on this occasion, as it happened, he had come to see me about something – nothing very important, but it took several minutes to resolve – so that he was not with his train until just before they were due to leave."

We thanked the station-master for his assistance and made our way out once more to the carriage yard. It had stopped raining, but it was a dark and chilly night, for the clouds were low and heavy.

"Well," said Superintendent Huggins, with a shake of the head, "you now know as much as I know, which is – to put it bluntly – precious little. At least if we now make our way to Parlingham, we shall be in a position to hear any reports that might come in from all the men I have tramping about the district."

"Very well," said Holmes, "but I should like to call at Bellbrook Halt on the way. Of course, we may learn nothing there, but there is a chance we might. The well-dressed man seen by the porter intrigues me, for a number of reasons. In the first place, he appears from what we have heard to be a stranger to these parts, which I imagine is moderately unusual on a line such as the Fairfield to Parlingham branch. His presence is therefore, at the very least, something of an odd coincidence, coming on the same evening as the singular occurrence which has brought us all here. Generally speaking, I have found that when two unusual things occur in close proximity to each other, there is nearly always a connection between the two of them."

"But it is nearly midnight," protested Huggins, "and, from what we know, the man you mention may not even have been on the branch line train."

"That is, of course, true," said Holmes, "but it is equally possible that he was, and I don't think we should neglect the chance to learn something about him. Furthermore, the porter saw that man standing on the platform by the branch line train for some time, and it is possible that he was waiting there in order to inform the guard in advance that he wished to alight at Bellbrook – which you told us is the correct procedure. And, from the description the porter gave of him, he sounds perhaps more likely to have been paying a visit to Viscount Bellbrook than visiting the village of Parlingham."

"Very well, Mr. Holmes," said the superintendent in a tone of resignation. "I can't imagine we are very likely to learn anything at Bellbrook Halt, but as it is not much out of our way we may as well call there, I suppose."

We had been crossing the carriage yard as they were speaking, and just as we reached the police van there came a terrific clatter of hooves and rattle of harness as another police vehicle raced into the yard and drew to a halt beside us. A man in police uniform sprang down whom Huggins identified for us as Sergeant Maldon. "Sir," said this newcomer in a loud, urgent tone, addressing the superintendent, "there has been a development!"

"What is it, Maldon?" returned Huggins.

"One of the missing men has turned up, sir!"

"Who? Where?"

"James Morris, the guard. In the woods, just the other side of Bellbrook Halt, sir."

"Has he been able to explain the matter to you?"

"No, sir. He's not in a position to explain anything to anyone."

"What! Don't tell me the poor fellow is dead!"

"No, sir, but he's unconscious. He appears to have been the victim of a particularly savage attack. The doctor says he has a fractured skull, and has given him a dose of something to numb the pain, which has put him into a deep sleep."

"How was he found?" asked Huggins.

"It was Pickering, sir, the man who attends to the lamps at Bellbrook Halt."

"Ah!" said Huggins. "I know the man you mean. I'll explain, gentlemen," he continued, turning to us. "From what I told you before about the stations on the line, it will not surprise you to learn that there are no permanent staff at Bellbrook. There is, however, a part-time employee, this man Pickering. He is actually employed as a cattle-man at one of the local farms, which is where he lives. But the railway company also employs him to sweep the platform at Bellbrook, keep the place neat and tidy, make sure there is oil in the station lamps, and so on. On dark evenings like the present, he has also to light the lamps at dusk, and extinguish them after the last train has passed. Now, Maldon, what happened this evening, then?"

"Well, sir, this evening, at about half past six, Pickering was coming along the road to fulfil his final duty of the day when he heard the train approaching in the distance. He admits he was a little late in getting there and, by the time he reached the station, the train had already passed through it. He says that by the sound of it, which he could hear quite clearly from a distance, the train had not stopped at the station, but had just passed slowly through. He therefore extinguished the lamps and made his way home. The reason Pickering has come forward to tell us all this is because of something that happened immediately afterwards.

"You may not know, sir, but Pickering has a daughter, Ellie, a plucky girl, about fourteen or fifteen years old, who sometimes accompanies him on his evening walk to Bellbrook Halt. She was with him tonight, and as they left the station, she said she thought it would be quicker to walk home through the woods rather than following the road. Pickering said he thought the road was better, so she proposed a contest: He could go by way of the road, she by way of the woods, and they would see who arrived first at the place the two meet again, where the road passes over the railway line. So that is what they did."

"It seems a little careless of him, I must say," interjected Superintendent Huggins, "to let his young daughter go off alone through the woods in the dark."

Maldon nodded his head. "Yes, I thought the same, sir," said he, "but it's not quite as careless as we might think. Ellie is, as I say, a plucky girl, and she had a lantern with her. In any case, she was really just following the railway line, rather than going into the woods at the side of it. Now, just the other side of the thickest part of the woods, the road that Pickering was following curves round and passes over the railway line on a small stone bridge. When he reached this bridge, he found Ellie was there already, waiting for him, as he had expected. He says he knew that she would run, to make sure she got there first, so he wasn't surprised to find her a little out of breath, but he could also see that she was really frightened about something. He asked her what was the matter, and when she had calmed down a bit she told him that as she was coming along the railway line she had heard someone in the woods, thrashing about and 'moaning and groaning', as she put it. She thought it must be The Old Man of the Woods, and was terrified."

"We have heard about 'The Old Man of the Woods' from Superintendent Huggins," Holmes interrupted, as Maldon cast us an interrogative glance.

Maldon shook his head. "They are superstitious folk in these parts," said he, with a chuckle. "Anyway, Pickering told his daughter, Ellie, not to worry about it. He says he thought it was probably just a drunken tramp, so the two of them went home and forgot about it. It was only later, when news reached the farm where they live, about the incredible arrival of the empty train at Parlingham, that Pickering thought that what Ellie had heard in the woods might be connected to whatever had happened on board the train. He hurried to Parlingham to inform us, and I at once sent some men to Bellbrook Halt to look into it.

"It didn't take them long to find the source of the 'moaning and groaning' that the girl had heard. It was no wonder that it had sounded so loud to her, and had startled her so much, for poor Morris lay only a yard or two into the wood beside the railway line."

"Right," said Huggins. "We'll get off to Bellbrook at once, and see the matter for ourselves. We were just about to go there anyway, even before this discovery."

We set off at a brisk trot down the main road from Fairfield, Sergeant Maldon's van following close behind us. After about three miles on this dark, deserted road, we turned off to the right, down a narrow and twisting lane. A further mile or so and we passed through a small, silent village, and came at length to Bellbrook Halt. Upon the station platform, several bright lamps had been lit, and two uniformed policemen were waiting there, who stood to attention as we approached.

"Any fresh developments, Watkins?" asked Sergeant Maldon. "Any sign of the other missing men?"

"No, sir," one of the constables called back.

"Then I'll show you where Morris was found, sir," said Maldon to Superintendent Huggins. "This way, gentlemen!"

He took a lantern from one of the constables and led the way along the platform to the left, and down onto the railway track. Immediately after passing the station, the line began a long curve round to the left, and we followed our guide along this for perhaps two-hundred yards. The ground on either side of the track had begun to drop away slightly once we were clear of the station, so that by the time Maldon halted, the line on which we stood was on a raised embankment perhaps eight or ten feet up from the gully on either side. On our left, below us, a lamp had been fastened to a tree.

"This is the place, sir," said Maldon. "It's very slippery, sir, with all the rain we've had, so you have to be careful."

"Thank you, Maldon," returned Superintendent Huggins in an ironic tone, as he began to carefully descend the slope from the line. "I think we can all – " Abruptly, the words died on his lips, as his feet slipped from

320

under him. I was standing the nearest to him, and I instinctively reached out my hand to seize his wrist. But his impetus could not be stopped, and the pair of us slid down the slope, and ended up in a muddy heap in the gully at the bottom.

The superintendent muttered a series of oaths under his breath, as Holmes, Lestrade, and Maldon, forewarned by our mishap, made their way with great care down the side of the embankment.

"Are you all right, sir?" asked Sergeant Maldon.

"Yes, I'm all right," returned Huggins in a tone of annoyance. "Are you all right, Dr. Watson? Good. Nothing injured, except our dignity, eh? Now, Maldon," he continued, "show us where Morris was found. Was it very far into the woods?"

"No, sir, not at all, just three or four feet. I'm sure that the girl – Ellie Pickering – who heard Morris groaning would have seen him if she had been walking where we are now standing, but, of course, she wasn't. She was up there on the railway track on top of the embankment, and probably running as she passed this point."

"Anything to be seen here?" asked the superintendent. "Any clue as to what might have happened to Morris, or any sign of where the other men might have got to?"

"No, sir. We've been quite a way into the wood just here, and there's nothing to be seen at all – nothing except mud and scrubby undergrowth."

"That's not quite true," interjected Holmes. "There are also several large rocks and stones on the ground just here."

"Of course, that is true," responded Maldon, a mixture of surprise and annoyance in his voice. "I was not intending to give a full list of every little thing I could see here."

"My observation is not irrelevant," persisted Holmes. "What I mean is that Morris's skull-fracture could have occurred when his head struck one of these large stones, as he slipped down the embankment. We have just had a practical demonstration of how dangerous and unstoppable such a slip can be."

"It is possible, I suppose," said Huggins, "although how that helps us shed any light on the matter in general, I confess I can't see, Mr. Holmes. Even if what you suggest were true, it doesn't explain – or even begin to explain – what Morris was doing out here in the first place, and why he wasn't sitting peacefully on his bench in the guard's van as usual."

"Indeed," returned Holmes in a placid tone. "But it is a capital error to dismiss from consideration some explanation simply because it doesn't provide an answer to every single point of a mystery. One cannot always alight on the right trail straight away, but, like a hound casting about for a promising scent, must consider every single possibility, however unlikely or trivial each of them may seem. Sometimes, little, apparently insignificant details play a large part in a case. In one murder investigation I handled, it turned out that the whole case hinged on the fact that a woman had called in at the local baker's shop to purchase a Bakewell tart. In another case, the fact that a man had cut himself while shaving one morning proved to be the key point in the solution of the mystery."

"That's all very well in theory, Mr. Holmes," said Huggins in an impatient tone, "but how does that help us in practice?"

"In this case, it frees us from wasting our time and mental energies on wondering who it was that attacked the guard so violently, and why on earth he should do so. Instead we can – as you suggest – speculate on the more straightforward question of *how* the guard came to be outside his van."

"Do you have any suggestions on that subject?"

"It may be that the answer lies in the curvature of the line. It has been curving quite sharply to the left since it passed Bellbrook Halt. The train, so I understand, was quite a short one, so it may be that someone looking out of the doorway of the guard's van could quite easily see the footplate of the engine."

"That's probably true," said Sergeant Maldon. "But why should that have made Morris leave his guard's van?"

"Perhaps," replied Holmes, "because he saw something which made him believe the train was headed for disaster unless he acted quickly."

"Such as?" asked Maldon.

"Such as that there was no one there on the footplate, in charge of the engine. Tell me, Sergeant: Would there be any way for the guard to communicate with the engine-driver or fireman?"

"Yes," replied Maldon. "There is a continuous cord which runs along the left side of the carriages, above the doors. One pull on that would ring a bell on the footplate of the engine."

"And how might the driver respond?"

"With a short blast on the engine whistle."

"So it is possible, at least, that Morris could have pulled the bell-cord, received no response from the driver by way of a whistle, looked forward and seen that there was no one on the footplate, and so decided there and then that he would jump down from his carriage – which would not be a dangerous thing to do if the train was travelling as slowly as everyone seems to think it was – run along the side of the line, and spring aboard the engine, where he could quickly bring it to a halt."

"But he would have had no need to do that," objected Sergeant Maldon. "There is a brake in the guard's van. He could have applied the brake from there."

Holmes nodded. "I am aware of that," said he. "But perhaps he could tell from the sound of the engine that it was not simply coasting, but was being actively supplied with steam, in which case the brake in the guard's van would have been fighting against the power of the engine's pistons. If so, he might have judged that the only way to bring the train peacefully to a halt was to get aboard the locomotive, close down the steam pipes, and then apply the brake from there."

"That is possible," conceded Maldon, "but where does that leave us?"

"I don't suppose you have been able to examine the undergrowth at the side of the line yet," remarked Holmes.

"Not very thoroughly," returned the sergeant after a moment, with a shake of the head. "What with the darkness, the heavy rain we had earlier, and the shortage of men, we haven't been able to do much in that respect. Of course, when we were following the directions given to us by Pickering and his daughter as to where the moaning was coming from, we walked along the line from Bellbrook Halt, just as we have done just now, looking keenly to our left. And when we found Morris, we looked all round him in a wide circle, but there was nothing else to be seen there."

"Very well," said Holmes after a moment. "What I propose then is this. That we return now to Bellbrook and examine the *other* side of the line carefully as we go."

"I suppose we might as well," returned Maldon, "but it's nearly all just brambles on that side of the line. I can't imagine there's anything there."

"I don't doubt it," said Holmes. "But one can never be certain about anything until one has examined it for one's self."

"Do you have any particular reason for your interest in the other side of the line, Mr. Holmes?" asked Superintendent Huggins in a dubious tone.

"There is one indication at least, that something may have happened on that side," returned Holmes.

"I can't imagine what that could be."

"One of the passenger doors on that side was not closed properly," said Holmes, "as you yourself mentioned."

"Oh, that!" said Huggins dismissively. "I doubt if that is of any significance at all!"

"Let us see for ourselves," said Holmes, "rather than debating the matter in the abstract, like a group of mediaeval scholars. As you yourself said, Superintendent: One fact is worth a thousand theories. May I?" he continued, taking a lantern from one of the policemen.

Throughout this exchange, my friend's tone had been a pleasant, almost light one, but I who knew him well could tell that he was growing increasingly impatient with all this talk. Now, as he sprang nimbly up the

323

embankment to the railway line, Superintendent Huggins looked queryingly at Lestrade, then at me.

"Mr. Holmes is always keen to examine everything for himself as soon as possible," I said.

"His methods may sometimes seem unorthodox," added Lestrade, "but are generally helpful to us in the end."

"Let's see if he discovers anything, then," said Superintendent Huggins with a shake of his head as we made our way carefully up the embankment. Holmes was already some distance ahead of us, bent over as he walked along, like some strange bird of prey, as he scrutinised the foliage at the side of the line. Now, as if fate were rewarding him for his enterprise and his determination to get on with the task in hand, the clouds, which had previously been uniformly dark and heavy, were beginning to break up a little and reveal a glimmer of moonlight. It was not much, but it was better than no light at all.

We had been walking along the railway track for about a hundred yards, always keeping about fifteen or twenty yards behind Holmes, when I saw my friend abruptly stop. In a few moments we had drawn level with him.

"What is it?" I asked.

"There's something down there," he returned without looking round. "If you would be so good as to hold the lantern, Watson," he continued, passing it to me, "I'll just hop down and have a closer look."

The ground on either side of the railway line had been gradually rising as we walked along, until it was now just three or four feet lower than the line. Holmes jumped down and bent over again to examine what appeared to be a tangle of undergrowth.

"A-ha!" said he after a moment.

"What is it?" asked Superintendent Huggins with heightened interest.

"I can't say for certain yet," replied Holmes. "Some sort of fabric, I should say. Yes, by George! It's the bottom of someone's overalls. And here is a boot – with someone's foot in it!"

We jumped down to join him in the gully at the side of the line, and hold the lanterns nearer.

"Has anyone got a pair of gloves with them?" asked Holmes. "Some of these old brambles are extremely vicious."

"I have," replied Sergeant Maldon. "Here, let me have a look." He pulled on a pair of thick-looking gloves and bent to the brambles, which he lifted up with a grunt of effort. "Does that help at all?" he asked.

"Yes," said Holmes. "Keep it there if you can, and I'll try to pull this man out."

There followed several minutes of pulling and pushing, and, it must be said, not a few oaths, as the brambles, like some strange malevolent creature, seemed determined to do their utmost to thwart all our efforts, refusing to yield up their captive. But at length, as Maldon and I did our best to hold back the wild tangle of vegetation, Holmes and the superintendent managed to drag the still figure of a man free from the brambles and onto the strip of bare earth at the side of the railway embankment. I at once bent to him and examined him as best I could by the weak light of the lanterns. "He is alive," I said, "but is in a state of deep insensibility, and does not respond to any stimulus. We must get him to where he can be properly cared for at once!"

"What do you think has happened to him?" asked Superintendent Huggins.

"Concussion of the brain, by the look of it," I responded. "He has a large bruise and a cut above his brow. I think he must have struck his head on something, like the other man – according to Holmes's suggestion – but in this case, probably not a rock, as I don't think there is any evidence of a fracture."

"Do you have any idea who it is?" the superintendent asked Sergeant Maldon.

The sergeant bent down lower, and scrutinised the unconscious man's face. "I'm pretty certain it's old Milbank, sir – the engine-driver."

Huggins nodded. "I rather thought it must be. Instruct a couple of your men to get the poor devil to the Parlingham infirmary as quickly as they can!"

Sergeant Maldon blew two sharp blasts on a whistle, and a moment later two constables came running from Bellbrook Halt. In a few words he explained the latest development to them and issued his orders.

"Now," said the Superintendent, when the constables had carried the unfortunate engine-driver away, "what next? Do you have any theory to account for this latest discovery, Mr. Holmes?"

"Several."

"Such as?"

Holmes shook his head. "It is too early to decide between different hypotheses," said he, "so there is no point in trying to list them. Some of them may be close to the truth, others may be miles away from it."

"What do you suggest we do then?"

"Continue our examination of this side of the line, back to Bellbrook Halt. I suspect the next 'discovery', as you call it, may be decisive."

"What do you think, Mr. Lestrade?" asked the superintendent.

Lestrade shook his head. "Mr. Holmes has found one of the missing men for us," he returned. "Perhaps he will find another. I have no better alternative suggestion to make."

"I noticed," said Holmes, "when we were at Bellbrook Halt, that there was a large, flat, open area on the other side of the line there. Do you know what purpose that serves?"

"I haven't the faintest idea," replied Superintendent Huggins.

"I believe," interposed Sergeant Maldon, "that the railway company have used it on odd occasions when they were loading some unusually large and heavy items onto a goods wagon there. They have a special wagon for that sort of thing, which has a crane on it."

"I see," said Holmes. "There appeared also – unless I am mistaken – to be a narrow track leading away from that flat area into the wood beyond. Would anyone use that to arrive at or leave the station?"

"I shouldn't think so," replied Maldon. "It's a public footpath, but it doesn't go anywhere very useful, except, eventually, to Bellbrook Castle. Bellbrook Village is in the opposite direction – we passed it on our way here."

"Well, well," said Holmes. "Let us proceed, then, and see what we turn up." With that, my friend resumed his steady pacing along the track, his keen eyes fixed on the ground at the side. Several times he paused and bent to examine some mark more closely before resuming his slow, careful progress. As we drew nearer to Bellbrook Halt, the land on either side of the railway line had continued to rise, until it was now level with the ballast on which the track was laid.

We had almost reached the station when I saw Holmes bend down and examine some mark on the ground very closely.

"What is it, Holmes?" I asked, as I drew level with where he was crouching down.

"A footprint," he replied without looking up.

"There are enough of those to keep us in business all year," remarked Superintendent Huggins in a dismissive tone, "most of them made by my men coming and going all evening."

"This one is not the same as those others," insisted Holmes. "The sole is unusually broad, the heel is a different shape, and the boot is going in the opposite direction to many of the other prints. I have been following it all the way from where we found the unfortunate engine-driver, Milbank. Of course, the fact that these prints first appear at the same place as we found Milbank is highly suggestive."

"Suggestive of what?" asked Sergeant Maldon.

"As they appear at the same place, and both men have almost certainly come from the train, which was moving at the time, then they

326

almost certainly came to that spot at the same time. Either these broad prints are those of a stranger who pushed Milbank from the train – but, then, we must ask 'Where is the fireman, John Turner?' – or they are the prints of Turner himself, who fell from the train with Milbank."

"But why should they both have fallen from the train?" asked Maldon.

"Perhaps because they were having a violent quarrel about something," suggested Holmes. "Anyway, whoever he was, the owner of these boots was in a very great hurry to get back to Bellbrook Halt."

"How do you know he was in a hurry?" asked Lestrade.

"Because the toe-end of the boot is generally more deeply marked than the heel, indicating that the man wearing these boots was running. I wanted you to see these prints now, in case we get any more heavy rain and the prints are obliterated. Now, let us proceed!"

I bent down to examine the footprint in question and saw that what my friend had said was true, then hurried with the others to catch him up, for he was now striding out again ahead of us. Presently, we reached the flat, open area he had referred to earlier.

"Keep back," said he. "I am looking to see if – yes, by George!"

"What is it?" asked Sergeant Maldon.

"The next significant piece of evidence," replied Holmes. "I had wondered if someone had hopped off the train at Bellbrook, and it appears that that was indeed the case."

"But the train did not stop here tonight, from all we have heard," protested Maldon.

"No, but if it was travelling as slowly as everyone seems to think, it would not have been particularly difficult or dangerous for someone to hop off just here, pushing the door shut as he did so. See," he continued, beckoning us to come closer. "That narrow footprint with the pointed toe is the one I mean."

"That certainly appears to be different footwear from all the other prints," remarked the superintendent, "but how can you be so certain that it belongs to someone who alighted from the train?"

"Because the first such narrow footprint occurs here," replied Holmes, turning and pointing to a spot closer to the railway track. "As you can see, his foot slipped a little on the mud as he landed, and he steadied himself with his walking stick before setting off across the open area, towards that footpath over there."

We all followed Holmes's direction. There was no doubt about it: Just to the side of the first, smudged footprint was a small, round indentation which could only have been made by a walking stick.

"From what we heard earlier from the station-master at Fairfield," Holmes continued, "the scholarly-looking gentleman who was seen standing for some time on the platform there was carrying a walking stick."

"I believe you are right," said Huggins, "although we don't, of course, know for certain that that man actually boarded the train."

"No," said Holmes, "but, after all, we don't yet know anything much for certain, do we? Let us now follow these narrow-footed tracks and see where they lead us!"

Holding his lantern low to the ground, Holmes set off across the flat, muddy area, and we followed behind him, keeping to the side, as well as we could, of the footprints we were following. Abruptly, Holmes stopped.

"What now?" queried Inspector Lestrade.

"The other man – broad-foot – has now joined us," returned Holmes. "He has run across this open area, as you can see, and turned up the track, where narrow-foot has already gone. I fear this pursuit will not end well, but follow him we must!"

With that, Holmes turned up the narrow track, the rest of us following behind him. After a short distance, the track entered a very dark belt of trees, but we had gone scarcely twenty yards or so through this when Holmes stopped once more. The undergrowth beside the path where he stood appeared disturbed and flattened, and as Holmes bent over to examine it more closely, I heard him mutter something under his breath, then he turned to us.

"Broad-foot caught up with narrow-foot just here," he announced. "One of them is still here, as I feared. Can one of you help pull him out, onto the path?"

I hurried forward to lend a hand. This man was not so tightly caught in the undergrowth as the engine-driver had been, and we soon had him out on the track. But even the very briefest of examinations was sufficient to tell me that this man had passed beyond all human help.

"This man is dead," I announced to the others, "and has been for some time. Like the other two, he has suffered a severe injury to the head. He has a massive bruise across his forehead and brow."

"Who is it?" asked Superintendent Huggins in a forlorn voice.

"By the look of the size of him, and his thick, coarse overalls and shirt," said Holmes, "I should say it is the locomotive fireman – Turner, I think you said his name was."

The others crowded round to see. Sergeant Maldon nodded his head. "Yes," said he, "that's John Turner all right. But how could such a big, powerful man be struck down so completely by the thin, elderly fellow we have heard about? And where is that man now?"

"'The race is not always to the swift, nor battle to the strong', as it is said," returned Holmes. "I think that what must have happened is that when Turner caught up with the other man, the latter, perhaps terrified by Turner's sudden appearance, must have struck out at hazard with his stick and fortuitously caught Turner a heavy blow across the brow. As to the whereabouts of this other man, I imagine he is at Bellbrook Castle, with Viscount Bellbrook."

"What!" cried Superintendent Huggins. "But that is fantastic! How can you know?"

"According to what I was told earlier, this track doesn't lead anywhere except to Bellbrook Castle, so it is not such a wild speculation. We had wondered earlier if that was perhaps the destination of the man seen on the platform at Fairfield Junction. It may be that he forgot to inform the guard that he wished to alight at Bellbrook Halt, or was unable to do so, owing to the guard's absence, which we heard about earlier. But – however that may be – it is evident that it was always his wish to alight here, from the fact that when the train did not stop he hopped off it as it passed slowly through the station. It also seems very likely that he has been here before, and knows his way about, from the fact that, having alighted, he set off at once up this narrow track through the woods, despite the fact that it must have been already going dark by then."

Superintendent Huggins stood in silence for a few moments, and it was clear that he was struggling to decide what action we should take next. "What do you think we should do, then, Mr. Holmes?" he asked at length.

"I think we must go at once to Bellbrook Castle," returned Holmes.

"But it is well after midnight now," protested Huggins, "and it seems to me utterly inconceivable that Viscount Bellbrook could know anything about this business! We can hardly go banging on his Lordship's door in the middle of the night, just because the path we're on happens to go in the direction of Bellbrook Castle!"

"There is a man lying dead here," said Holmes, "and two more lying seriously injured in the infirmary at Parlingham, and Viscount Bellbrook's visitor is probably responsible – either directly or indirectly – for all that has happened. He may be the only man alive who can shed any light on what exactly has occurred here this evening, and therefore we must speak to him as soon as possible."

"What do you think, Mr. Lestrade?" asked Huggins.

"It may be," replied Lestrade after a moment, "that everyone at Bellbrook Castle is already in bed and fast asleep, but it is also possible that they may not be, in which case I would agree with Mr. Holmes: We should try to interview the man who alighted from the train here, if he is indeed at the Castle."

"As a matter of fact," interjected Sergeant Maldon, "there is a particular reason tonight why they may *not* be already asleep."

"And what is that, pray?" returned the superintendent in surprise.

"Because, sir, there is some special event – a festivity of some sort – taking place there this evening."

"What? Do you mean a ball? I have heard nothing about that."

"No, not exactly a ball, sir. Apparently, Viscount Bellbrook recently celebrated his fiftieth birthday, so he was holding a sort of reception this evening at the castle for all his friends and relations."

"Are you sure about this, Maldon? It's the first I've heard about it!"

"Yes, sir. My wife heard it from someone she knows whose sister works in the kitchens at the Castle."

"Very well, very well," said the superintendent in a tone of resignation. "We'll get up to the Castle, then. But first, let's get this poor devil a more dignified place in which to rest."

We carried the body of the fireman back to the railway station and laid him down on the floor of the waiting room, with one of the constables to stand guard there and notify the others when they returned of where we had gone. Then the five of us – Huggins, Maldon, Lestrade, Holmes, and myself – set off back up the track towards Bellbrook Castle.

As we reached the place where we had found the body of the unfortunate fireman, Holmes cautioned us to avoid walking over the footprints that were already there. "These prints tell the story of what happened here earlier this evening," said he, "so it is important that they are not further disturbed. You will note from the prints, for instance, that the man who struck out at the fireman with his stick was extremely frightened."

"I'm sure he *was* frightened – anyone would be, under the circumstances," interrupted Lestrade, "but how can you tell that from these footprints?"

"Because, having struck out, he did not wait to see what had happened, but dashed off at once. He would probably have known, of course, that his blow had struck home, but not how much damage it had done to his opponent. You can see that he is running here – the heels of his shoes make no mark upon the ground. And now," he continued, pausing for a moment, "he has stopped and looked round, no doubt to see if he is being followed. Now he resumes his hurried progress, and the toe-ends of his shoes are all that touch the ground."

Thus, the five of us proceeded in the pale moonlight for some time, Holmes leading the way with his back bent, holding his lantern close to the ground. After a few minutes, we emerged from the belt of trees, and the track continued between two large, open fields.

"He stopped again here," said Holmes after a moment. "I imagine he was out of breath, as he stood here for some time."

"How can you tell how long he stopped for?" asked Sergeant Maldon.

"Because his footprints are all over the place," explained Holmes, "all pointing in different directions, some of them covering up others, and all in a very small area on the ground. He also put down the bag he was carrying."

"Marvellous!" cried Maldon in an appreciative tone. "You read the roughest and scrappiest of signs as someone else might read a book, Mr. Holmes! You should have been a tracker in the jungle of some far-flung corner of the world!"

"Thank you, Sergeant," responded Holmes with a chuckle. "But this corner of the world is quite enough to keep me occupied!"

As we reached the far end of the large field, I saw that the land beyond it fell away into a broad vale, and as we passed through a gap in the hedge, a very large, ornate-looking building with turrets and towers came into view below us. Even in the dark of the night, its profile was an imposing one.

"That," said Sergeant Maldon, "is Bellbrook Castle."

"I see there are a number of lights still lit there," I observed.

"Indeed," said Superintendent Huggins. "So, we may be in luck after all!"

An easy walk down the hill of seven or eight minutes brought us to a wide, gravel drive which led up to the front of the building, where broad steps rose to the great front door, flanked on either side by bright lamps.

The superintendent banged the heavy door-knocker, and as he did so I heard the sound of gay music from somewhere within the building. Moments later, the door was opened by a tall, dignified-looking man in the livery of a footman.

"Yes, gentlemen?" said he, an impassive expression on his face.

"We have come to see Viscount Bellbrook," said the superintendent.

"His Lordship is engaged at present," said the footman in a firm voice, "and cannot be disturbed."

"This is not a social call," persisted Huggins, "but an official one."

"Yes. sir," responded the footman. "I assumed as much from your uniforms, and from the late hour of your visit. That does not alter the fact that his Lordship is engaged. Might I suggest, sir, that if you call again tomorrow morning – "

"One moment," interrupted Sherlock Holmes in a determined tone. "A man has been killed earlier this evening, near the railway station. Two other men are very seriously injured, and may not survive. We have very good reason to believe that one of Viscount Bellbrook's guests this evening was a witness to what occurred, and we must speak to him at once. I am sure that Viscount Bellbrook would regard this matter as of somewhat greater importance than whatever it is that engages him at present."

The footman hesitated, and it was clear that Holmes's words had plunged him into a state of indecision.

"Indeed," Holmes continued, "I strongly suspect that Viscount Bellbrook would regard it as a positive dereliction of duty were he not to be informed at once of this matter, which is essentially one of life and death."

"Very well, gentlemen," said the footman. "If you will come this way, I will inform his Lordship of your presence."

He stood aside as we passed into a broad marbled hall. From somewhere in the house came the melodious sound of an orchestra playing waltz music. We followed the footman as he led us through a doorway at the side of the hall, into a large ante-chamber containing a long oblong table and half-a-dozen chairs. "Please wait here a moment," said he, as he closed the door.

For several minutes we stood there without speaking, as the muffled sound of the music continued. Then the orchestra ceased playing, and silence reigned. Several more minutes passed and I heard the orchestra strike up again. As it did so, the door of our room abruptly opened, and in strode a tall, erect man in evening dress. His hair was grey, his face was wrinkled, but his voice when he spoke belied these tokens of age, for it was strong, firm and decisive, and it was evident that this was Viscount Bellbrook.

"What is this all about?" said he with a frown, his questioning gaze resting on each of us in turn. "I understand there has been an accident on the railway."

"It's not exactly an accident," responded Holmes. "We believe that one of your guests, who alighted from the train at Bellbrook Halt, encountered someone in the woods between there and here. That is the man we wish to speak to."

Viscount Bellbrook frowned again. "I don't believe anyone came that way," said he. "We twice sent a carriage over to Fairfield Junction in the afternoon, to collect various people who had travelled from London and further afield, but I don't think it called at Bellbrook Halt."

"This particular man did not come in a carriage, but on foot," persisted Holmes. "He is, we believe, a tall, thin man, possibly a little elderly."

"That sounds like Professor Sidgwick," said the viscount, an expression of understanding illuminating his features. "He is something of an eccentric," he added with a chuckle. "I can't think that anyone else I know would have walked all the way from the station on such a dark, wet evening. He is – as you perhaps know – Heppenstall Professor of Moral Philosophy at St. Francis's College, Oxford. We were undergraduates together at 'Frank's', as we called it, many years ago. He used to be a regular visitor here in years gone by, although we haven't seen him here now for nearly ten years – until this evening."

"That would be the man," said Holmes. "We knew that the man we wished to speak to, who alighted at the Halt, must be familiar with how to get from there to here by way of the footpath. May we have a word with him?"

"Yes, yes, by all means," said the viscount. "I'll send someone for him at once." He stepped to the doorway, gave instructions to a servant who was waiting there, then turned once more to us. "Someone was hurt, did you say, on the railway?"

Holmes shook his head. "No. A man has lost his life in the woods, near to the railway. Two other men – railway employees – have been seriously injured in what we believe are related incidents."

"Good Lord!" cried the viscount. "What a dreadful business!" He was about to say more when the door of the room opened again, to admit a tall, elderly man in evening dress. "Ah, Sidgwick!" said the viscount. "These gentlemen are looking into something that took place earlier, near the railway station, and believe that you may have been a witness."

The elderly man turned to us with an inquiring expression on his face.

"You arrived earlier this evening on the branch line train, and alighted at Bellbrook Halt," said Holmes. "Is that correct?"

Sidgwick nodded his head, but did not reply.

"The train did not stop there," continued Holmes, "but was going very slowly, so you dropped down from the carriage onto the flat earth by the line, on the side away from the station platform."

A look of astonishment came over Sidgwick's face. "Were you there?" he asked.

"No," said Holmes.

"Then how on earth do you know what I did?"

"The physical evidence is clear. You then set off up the footpath which ultimately leads here, to the Castle."

"Correct."

"But you had not gone very far when someone sprang at you aggressively – shouting, I imagine."

Professor Sidgwick raised his hands and grasped his head, as he rocked backwards and forwards. He appeared very unsteady, and I feared he might faint.

333

I stepped forward and took his arm. "Here," I said, "sit down on this chair, Professor. It sounds a frightening experience."

"It was terrifying," returned Sidgwick, sitting down heavily, and resting his elbows on the table. "It was so dark, I could hardly see what was happening. It may sound absurd, but, for a brief moment, I thought it must be 'The Old Man of the Woods' that the country folk all speak of in these parts. This person – this brigand or bandit, or whatever he was – lunged at me, shouting loudly, his face all twisted with rage."

"So you struck out with your stick," said Holmes.

"Exactly," said Sidgwick. "I hit something hard, but as I was already trying to run away, I did not know what it was – whether it was my assailant or a low tree-branch – so I made off as fast as I could, and did not stop for breath until I had gone some considerable distance. Even then I did not linger, but set off running again after just a moment. I couldn't hear anything from behind me, and could not be sure that he wasn't still coming after me."

"What an awful experience!" said Viscount Bellbrook with feeling. "You didn't mention any of this when we spoke earlier, Sidgwick, although – to be honest – I thought you didn't look quite yourself."

"I didn't mention it because I didn't want to trouble you on such a festive evening," returned Sidgwick.

The viscount turned to us. "Have you found the villain responsible for this outrage?" he asked Superintendent Huggins.

"Yes, sir."

"I take it you have arrested him, then?"

"No, sir."

"Why ever not?"

"He has not been arrested," interjected Holmes, "because he is dead. It seems tolerably certain that the blow from Professor Sidgwick's stick killed him instantly."

"What!" cried Sidgwick, staggering to his feet once more, his face as white as a sheet. "I didn't know! I couldn't tell! I had to defend myself!"

"Of course," said Viscount Bellbrook. "No one could criticize you for that."

"Something I wish to ask you," said Holmes, when Sidgwick had calmed down a little, and had resumed his seat, "is whether you recognized the man who attacked you."

"It's odd you should ask me that," returned Sidgwick after a moment, "because I was asking myself the exact same question earlier. Although I saw it for only a moment, the man's face did look vaguely familiar. Eventually, I remembered why. When I was changing trains at Fairfield Junction, I approached the branch line train, intending to notify the guard that I wished to alight at Bellbrook Halt, which I remembered from previous visits was the correct thing to do. The guard, however, was not there, so, after waiting some time, I walked to the front of the train, thinking to give the information to the men there. However, the engine-driver was busy doing something 'round the other side of the locomotive and I couldn't attract his attention. His assistant, a somewhat unattractive-looking young man, gave me a very surly look as I approached, and when I told him that I wished to alight at Bellbrook Halt, he just said 'You'd better tell the guard, then', turned his back on me and began shovelling coal noisily. It was this man that my assailant reminded me of."

"Your memory is correct," said Holmes. "The man who attacked you has been positively identified as the locomotive fireman, John Turner. I take it that after your unpleasant encounter with him at Fairfield, you abandoned the idea of notifying anyone of where you wished to alight."

"Eventually, yes. I did wait a little longer for the guard to appear, but gave up as the time for departure approached and took my place in the carriage. I saw the guard run onto the platform a moment or two later, but I could not catch his eye, and thus had no opportunity to speak to him. I thought I would probably have to try to hire a cab at Parlingham Station to bring me here, but when the train reached Bellbrook Halt, it was travelling so slowly that I decided on the spur of the moment that I could jump from the moving train without any risk of injury. I suppose the fireman must have seen me."

"It's a shocking business," said Viscount Bellbrook. "But why should this railwayman have such a grudge against you? You weren't rude to him when you spoke?"

"No, not at all. If anyone was rude, it was he, and I didn't respond to his rudeness in any way."

"The more we learn of the matter, the more inexplicable it becomes!" observed Superintendent Huggins.

"On the contrary," said Holmes, "it is at last becoming clearer. I rather fancy that the grudge, as Viscount Bellbrook called it, goes back somewhat further than this afternoon's railway journey."

"But how could it?" protested Sidgwick. "I had never seen the man before in my life!"

"So you may believe," said Holmes in a thoughtful voice, "but today's events suggest otherwise. You were a visitor here ten years ago – so I understand from something Viscount Bellbrook said earlier."

"Yes," replied Sidgwick. "That was the last time I was ever here."

"Was there any particular reason for this prolonged absence from your old friend's house?"

Sidgwick hesitated. "Not really," he answered after a moment. "It was simply that I was always too busy to accept Viscount Bellbrook's gracious invitations."

Holmes considered the matter for a moment. It was clear there was something on his mind. "Ten years ago," said he at length, "John Turner, the man who attacked you this evening, was not employed by the railway company, but employed here, at the Castle."

"I don't recall the name," interjected the viscount.

"He was not, so I understand, one of the household staff," responded Holmes, "but worked in the gardens. For all I know, he may not have been here very long. At the same time, there was also a young woman here in whom he was interested. I do not know if she and Turner were officially betrothed or not, but there seems to have been some sort of understanding between them – in his mind, at least. Then something happened, and she threw him over, so I was informed. We may not know the name of this woman, but – "

"I think I may know who it was," interrupted Sergeant Maldon abruptly. We all turned to him in surprise. "Rose Hilton was her name, if I am right. 'Rosie', everyone called her. She was some years older than me and seemed almost an adult to me when I was still a boy, but her family lived close to my own parents in Parlingham when I was growing up, and I occasionally saw her in the street."

"Can you remember anything about her?" asked Holmes.

Maldon thought for a moment. "She was uncommonly pretty," he replied at length, "with dark, curly hair. Everyone said she was the prettiest thing in the whole of Gloucestershire. Some people said she was stuck up, but I don't think she was, really. Her manner may have seemed a bit superior, if you know what I mean, but that was just because she *was* superior to most folks, and some people were just jealous of her. I can't really remember anything much else about her, except that I did see her once or twice with John Turner, although I don't think anyone thought he really had much of a chance there. I think she left the district completely when she was still quite young, and – to the best of my knowledge – never came back."

While the sergeant had been speaking, there had come a series of low moans from just behind me. Now I turned, to see Professor Sidgwick's head sunk on the table before him.

"What is it, Sidgwick?" asked Viscount Bellbrook, but before the professor could answer, the door opened and a handsome, middle-aged woman swept into the room. From the elaborate and ornate white-and-gold of her costume, and the sparkling, bejewelled coronet upon her head, I thought she must be the viscount's wife, a conjecture which proved correct when she spoke.

"Charles," said she in an urgent tone, "I don't know what you are all discussing in here, but everyone is wondering where you have disappeared to. Events are coming to an end in the ballroom, and you must come and speak to your guests while they are all still gathered together."

Viscount Bellbrook hesitated. He looked at his wife, at the doorway, at the professor and at us. "Very well," he responded at length. "Gentlemen," he continued, turning to us, "do not go anywhere, and I shall be back in a few minutes!" With that, he and his wife left the room, the door closed firmly behind them.

For several moments we remained in silence, and then Holmes spoke. "I believe," said he to Professor Sidgwick, "that you were about to tell us what you know of Rose Hilton."

Sidgwick raised his head and shot Holmes a penetrating glance. "You, sir," he asked after a moment. "Who are you? You seem to know everything, but I do not think you are a policeman."

"Who I am is irrelevant," responded Holmes. "I am assisting the police in this case. You knew Rose Hilton, I think."

The professor leaned back in his chair, an expression of resignation on his features. "'Rosie'," he said at length, as if correcting what Holmes had said. "Everyone called her 'Rosie' – as your colleague said. Yes, I knew her. She was, at the time, employed here as assistant to the housekeeper, and, as I think you may have surmised, she – or, at least, the memory of her – is what has kept me from visiting Bellbrook Castle these last ten years. When I knew her, about ten years ago, I committed the one folly of my otherwise unexciting and well-regulated existence.

"She was – as your colleague remarked – very pretty, but it wasn't simply that: She was also very attractive in a more general sense, attractive and charming – and I fell under her spell. What – if anything – she saw in me, a man some years older than her, and a dull and dusty scholar of old books, I cannot imagine. But she was always very attentive to my needs while I was staying here. She would come to my room on some trivial errand or other, and would smile and flash her pretty eyes at me. Sometimes, we would chat a little, and she would laugh at my simple little witticisms. As my stay here proceeded, we began to talk more and more, about all sorts of things, and our conversations were always lightened as much by Rosie's humorous remarks as by my own attempts at wit. She was – so it seemed to me – far too intelligent and lively-minded for much of the routine and menial work she was being asked to do here, and I found her very good company in every way. When I left here to return to London – which was where I was living at the time – I felt more cheerful and lighthearted than I had for several years, and I could hardly wait to return here again.

"An opportunity soon arose, as old Viscount Bellbrook, the father of the present viscount, sent me an invitation to a summer garden party he was throwing here. I had attended such events before, and knew what enjoyable occasions they could be. But this time, my over-riding desire was to see Rosie Hilton again. It may sound absurd for a man of my age, but the truth is that I had fallen madly in love with her, in a way I never had with anyone before.

"We ran across each other quite soon after I arrived here, and I was delighted to find that she seemed as pleased to see me as I was to see her. My stay on that occasion was for only a few days, but, despite all the other events which were taking place then, we still managed to spend many enjoyable moments together. I should like to say, incidentally, that it never occurred to me then that she had any other admirer who might perhaps feel he had more claim upon her affections than I did, and she certainly never gave me the slightest reason for thinking that that might be the case. I don't suppose anyone as madly intoxicated as I was ever considers that possibility, or, if they do, they don't give it any heed.

"She told me then – in response to some trivial observation of mine – that she was bored with her current existence here, and yearned for something different and more exciting. When I asked her what she had in mind, she confessed that it had long been an ambition of hers to live in London, and see something of London Society. I suggested that it might be something of a gamble to give up what was a very good post here for the uncertainties of life in London, but she shook her head, and declared her confidence in her own abilities.

"'So long as I could get off to a good start, I'm sure I would do very well,' said she with a sweet smile.

"'If you are sure that that is what you want,' said I, 'then, if you like, you could stay at my house until you got everything sorted out.'

"'That is very kind of you, Dr. Sidgwick,' said she, 'but I couldn't possibly impose upon you in that way. I wouldn't want you to think I come as a beggar.'

"'I wouldn't think that for a moment, Rosie,' said I, laughing, 'but, if it would make you feel better able to accept my offer, you can act as my housekeeper for as long as you wish, and I will pay you accordingly.'

"'Do you not have a housekeeper already?' she asked.

"I shook my head. 'My household is a very modest one. I have a cook and a maid, and that is all. We could accommodate you very easily.'

"Rosie agreed to the proposition then. She seemed very pleased and excited at the prospect of moving to London, and, I don't mind admitting,

I was thrilled at the thought of having her in my household. And so, the die was cast. We exchanged a couple of brief letters, and a month later she moved into my house. This, I must say, was a great success in every way. Rosie had such an easy, unpretentious charm that she got on well with everyone she met, no matter what their station in life, and – I need hardly say – I loved having her there. The whole atmosphere of the house seemed to be lifted by her presence. I felt a little guilty for having poached one of Viscount Bellbrook's senior domestic staff, but I thought that he would probably find a suitable replacement without too much difficulty, whereas to me, of course, Rosie was quite unique and irreplaceable.

"Soon after her arrival in London, Rosie began to make enquiries about employment opportunities, and registered with various agencies. I followed her progress in this respect with great interest, and often discussed it with her, but I admit that in my heart I never really wanted to encourage her too much, for, of course I could not bear the thought of her leaving. Weeks passed, then months, during which my feelings for Rosie did not diminish at all, but, on the contrary, intensified. I took her to the theatre, I took her to concerts, I took her to all sorts of interesting places and events. Sometimes we went for walks on Hampstead Heath and other pretty spots. At length, I resolved to ask her if she would do me the great honour of becoming my wife.

"I remember the day very clearly. Rosie had been out most of the afternoon on various errands, and, my own work for the day being completed, I was sitting with a cup of tea, waiting impatiently for her to return. Each time I heard footsteps on the pavement outside the front of the house, I would look up expectantly, but then sigh with disappointment as they passed by without stopping. Eventually, much later than I had expected, I heard the footsteps pause, and, next moment, heard Rosie turning her key in the lock of the front door. I went out into the hall to greet her. She gave me a beaming smile, and looked, I thought, prettier than ever. I offered her a cup of tea, but she said she would get a fresh pot for us both, so I told her to bring it into the drawing room, when she could tell me all that she had been doing that afternoon. In my mind, this was all just a preamble to my proposing marriage to her, but – Alas! – that part of my plan was never to be fulfilled.

"She came into the drawing room with excitement and happiness on her features and in her voice. I remarked that she looked pleased about something, and asked her what it was. She thereupon described to me how, following a preliminary interview three days previously, of which I was aware, she had now been interviewed for a second time by a nobleman who kept a large household in Belgrave Square. The result of this was that he had offered her the post of housekeeper, to start as soon as she was able.

Rosie was naturally as thrilled at this as she could possibly be, and I congratulated her with as much enthusiasm as I could muster. Inside, though, I felt more forlorn than I have ever felt in my life, as my own private hopes were dashed. I told her to keep in touch with me, and that if she ever found that her new life was not quite so happy as she had hoped, she would always be welcome to return to my humble household at any time.

"Several weeks passed, and, as I had heard nothing from Rosie, I ventured to write her a letter, describing some trivial details of my own daily life and asking how she was getting on in her new circumstances. After a week or two, I received an extremely brief reply, saying that she was too busy to respond in any detail at the moment, but would write again later – although she never did. Many months then passed without a word from her, until, eventually, I wrote again, on some pretext or other, expressing the hope that she was thriving and that things were going successfully for her. To this letter I received a prompt reply, but it was not from Rosie. It was, rather, from someone called George St. John-Wallington, who described himself as secretary to Lord Margrave. In it, he informed me that Lord and Lady Margrave were not at home at present, but were spending some time at their house in the south of France. However, he informed me, he had been authorised to thank all those who had kindly written to express their best wishes on the recent happy occasion of the wedding of David, Lord Margrave, and Rose Hilton.

"After that letter, I made no further attempt to communicate with Rosie. My life continued as before, at least in its external appearances, but with – from my point of view – a permanent shadow of sadness hanging over it. I wrote many essays, I wrote a book. My name became well known in my field and I was, five years ago, offered and accepted the chair in Moral Philosophy at St. Francis's College, Oxford." Professor Sidgwick paused. "But," he continued after a moment, "I would willingly give all of that up this instant if I could have Rosie Hilton back again."

Professor Sidgwick paused for a few moments. "So, gentlemen," he said at length, with a sigh and a shake of the head, "as it seems likely from what you have told me that the man who accosted me earlier – John Turner – wished simply to give me a piece of his mind, as people say, and upbraid me for stealing away his sweetheart, then, if he had been less violent, aggressive, and frightening in his manner, I could have informed him that the exact same fate as he wished to complain about had, in turn, befallen me."

We all remained in silence for some time after the professor had finished speaking. I do not think that any of us could think of anything that would be worth saying after such a very personal and heart-felt account.

Out in the hall, the sound of the viscount's many visitors, talking and laughing, had been growing louder in the last few minutes. Abruptly, the door opened, and Viscount Bellbrook himself entered. He looked enquiringly at our no-doubt solemn faces, and frowned.

"We have just finished going through it all," said Holmes, with a glance at Professor Sidgwick's tired and melancholy features.

"Yes," responded Sidgwick. "I'll give you the gist tomorrow morning," he said, addressing the viscount, "if that is all right. You don't need me to go anywhere tonight do you?" he continued, addressing Superintendent Huggins.

"No, sir," replied the latter. "That won't be necessary. We can take a formal statement tomorrow morning."

As the three policemen, Holmes, and I made our way back down to Bellbrook Halt, where the police vehicle was waiting for us, the clouds in the sky broke up completely, and, by the time we reached the station, the moon was shining brightly.

"What a business!" said Superintendent Huggins with feeling, which brought forth murmurs of agreement from everyone. "I've never known anything like it," he continued. Then he turned to Sherlock Holmes. "Mr. Holmes," said he, "I would just like to say that I had my doubts about you when you first arrived, and didn't think we should need your assistance. But everything that has happened since has proved to me that I was quite wrong. You have led us from darkness to light, from complete ignorance to full knowledge of the case, in a way I have never seen before in my entire police career. It is the finest display of detective-work I have ever witnessed." With that, he put out his hand and shook Holmes's hand vigorously.

"I agree with every word the superintendent has spoken," said Sergeant Maldon, and he, too, shook Holmes's hand.

"Thank you," said Holmes, visibly taken aback by this generous appreciation. "I am grateful for your compliments, gentlemen. But really, I have no special talents. I have simply trained myself to always observe the details of a case, and never to rely merely on general impressions. For it is almost always in the details that the solution of a problem is to be found."

The engine-driver, Arthur Milbank, and the guard, James Morris, both recovered from their injuries after some considerable time, although neither ever worked again. When they had recovered sufficiently to answer questions, their testimony shed light on what had happened on that fateful evening. What was particularly striking about this was that on almost every point, their account confirmed Sherlock Holmes's speculations.

"When we were preparing the engine for the evening run to Parlingham," said Arthur Milbank, "Turner told me that he thought he had just seen the man that he regarded as having ruined his life by luring Rose Hilton away to London. I told him to forget it. 'All that is long gone,' I said, 'and in any case, it's probably not the same man. Don't dwell on it.' But he wouldn't let the matter drop, and told me, five minutes later, that the man had just approached him – 'As bold as brass' said Turner – and asked him about getting off the train at Bellbrook. Turner said he had told the man to let the guard know if he wanted to get off there. 'Well,' says I to Turner, 'if the guard gives us the signal, I'll stop there, and if he doesn't, I won't.'

"When we reached Bellbrook Halt, we hadn't had a signal, so I didn't stop, but I was going slowly in case a signal came late. Turner was bobbing about, looking first out of the nearside, then out of the offside. Then he said 'There he is! He's just jumped out! I'm going to tell him exactly what I think of him!'

"I told Turner not to be such a fool. 'It won't do any good!' I told him. I took hold of him then to stop him jumping off the footplate, but he was driven mad with anger and hatred, and I could hardly hold him. We wrestled like that for a few moments, then with a lunge he tried to pull away from me, but as I was clinging onto him, we went flying off the engine together, and onto the ground. I think I must have banged my head, because I don't remember any more until I woke up in broad daylight in a bed in the infirmary at Parlingham."

The guard of the train, James Morris, gave the following additional testimony: "I was late getting back to the train at Fairfield Junction. No one had told me that they wanted to alight at Bellbrook, but as we were passing slowly through the station there, I thought I heard one of the carriage doors slam. There was no one on the platform, so I quickly looked out of the window on the other side. A tall, thin man was standing there, dusting himself down, and it was clear he had just jumped down from the train.

"As I was standing there, wondering who he was, and why he had adopted such a dangerous course of action, I saw both Milbank and Turner fall together from the engine footplate ahead of me. I had no idea what was happening, but realised that the train was now in a very dangerous state. I started to apply the brake, but it didn't seem to achieve much, so I thought the only thing I could do would be to run along the side of the line and climb aboard the locomotive footplate, and then bring the train to a halt. I opened the door on the onside, jumped down and set off. The train was

342

going so slowly that I made good progress and had almost reached the engine when my feet suddenly slipped from under me. For a second, I was skidding about uncontrollably, then I must have struck my head on something because I remember nothing more but darkness and pain."

When the inquest on John Turner was finally concluded, having been adjourned twice so that the above testimony could be included in the evidence, it was adjudged that the blow from Professor Sidgwick's walking stick was undoubtedly the cause of death. No charges of any kind were laid against Sidgwick, however, the court accepting that he had acted entirely in self-defence while in a state of extreme fear.

As Sherlock Holmes and I travelled back to London the day after the dramatic events I have described above, my friend remained in silent thought for some considerable time. At length I asked him what he was thinking about.

"I was hoping," he replied, "that I never fall in love."

"Why so?" I asked in surprise.

"Just consider, Watson, the misery inflicted upon all concerned in this case by that simple-sounding notion: One man dead before his time, several others whose lives or careers have been adversely affected."

"I don't think falling in love always involves such dire consequences," I remarked.

"Perhaps not," said Sherlock Holmes, "but you cannot be certain of that, Watson, and it is not a risk I would wish to take."

The Most Terrible Murderer
by Alan Dimes

October 1903

*M*y *dear Watson,*

*Can you extricate yourself from the toils of domestic bliss long
enough to join me for dinner at Baker Street on this coming
Thursday evening at half-past seven?*

Holmes

"Who is it from, John?"

I looked up from the brief note and across the breakfast table at my
wife of eleven months. At times I still found it difficult to believe that this
charming and sensitive woman had become a permanent fixture in my life,
and was bound to me in holy matrimony.

"It's from Holmes, my dear. I'm invited to dinner on Thursday."

Emily put her coffee cup down into the saucer and smiled.

"Then you must go, John. You haven't seen each other for such a
while."

It was true. Since the former Emily Manning had accepted my hand
in marriage, and I had resumed my medical practice, this time in Queen
Anne Street, the demands of work and domesticity had drastically reduced
the amount of time I had to spare for my old friend and former fellow-
lodger. I still retained my notes from the many investigations on which I
had accompanied him, and had even given over some of my brief leisure
time to casting one or two of them into narrative form. The last time I had
been in contact with him had been to ask his permission to someday
publish a story which we had previously decided should be suppressed for
an indeterminate period.

"Well, I shall, then, if you don't object."

Emily took my hand and kissed it.

"Ah, my devoted husband! I think I can survive an evening without
you, and you and he are such old friends, how could I object?"

Even as the cab turned into Baker Street that autumn evening, my
mind was flooded with memories. Our first meeting in the laboratory at

344

Barts. The sudden appearance of the giant rat of Sumatra. The awful revelation of the true identity of the Whitechapel killer. The crude stick figures of the dancing men. Merridew, who slit his own throat before our eyes, rather than face trial and an inevitable journey to the gallows. The odious Charles Augustus Milverton and his well-deserved end. And so much else – including, of course, Mary. It is a lucky man who knows such a love but once, and I have known it more often.

So familiar was the door of 221b Baker Street that I almost reached into my pocket for my key, but I caught myself, left the key where it was, and rang the bell.

The door was opened by a familiar figure.

"Mrs. Hudson! How are you?"

"Oh, I'm well enough," replied the housekeeper. "And I can see Mrs. Watson has been taking good care of you!"

"She has indeed. And Holmes?"

"Oh, you know him. The only time he's ever ill is when he's run himself into the ground over some case he's been investigating. He'll be pleased to see you. He has a little surprise for you."

"A surprise?"

"Yes."

She took my hat and coat.

"Go straight up. Dinner will be served in five minutes."

I climbed the steps to our old rooms. As I opened the door, I saw Holmes sitting in his accustomed chair, still his old self, clad in his disreputable dressing gown, his clay pipe clenched between his teeth and his hands steepled in front of him. He was not alone, however. A prosperous-looking man in his mid-forties, with a head of curly brown hair and a full beard speckled with grey, was seated in my old armchair. My first thought was that the man was a client, and about to leave, but he sprang from the chair and seized me by the hand.

"Dr. Watson! It's wonderful to see you once more!"

"Good Heavens!" I cried, in sudden recognition. "It's Murray!"

"How long has it been, Doctor? Twenty-two years? Twenty-three?"

"Since you came to see me in the base hospital in Peshawar. Holmes, you know this man saved my life?"

"I had heard something of the kind."

It was Murray who, after I had been wounded by a Jezail bullet at the Battle of Maiwand, had thrown me across a pack-horse and got me back to the British lines, at no small danger to himself.

"This is indeed a pleasant surprise, "I said. What have you been doing with yourself, old chap? You look as if you've come a good way in this world."

"After I left the army, I stayed in India and got a position managing a tea plantation in Assam. Well, I made a good job of it, if I do say so myself, and pretty soon I was managing a larger one, and made some sound investments with the money I earned."

"What brings you back to England?"

"My wife passed away – "

"My dear fellow, I'm sorry to hear it!"

" – and so I thought I'd come back to the old country. I could have obtained your address from your publisher, but I confess I was eager to meet Mr. Holmes as well as to see you again, so I came to Baker Street, and he was kind enough to arrange this meeting."

At this point, Mrs. Hudson brought up the first course of what proved to be a splendid dinner. Holmes said little while we ate, but smiled once or twice as Murray and I recalled our far-off days in the Jewel in the Crown of the Empire. When the meal was over, however, and we were smoking and taking a glass of brandy, Murray looked over to Holmes and said, "I'd like to ask you something, if I may."

Holmes drew on his cigar and said, "Please do, Mr. Murray."

"Well. I've read all of Dr. Watson's accounts of your cases, and enjoyed them all."

Here he turned to me and said, "I must say, I gained a little fame amongst the expatriate community by being the man who indirectly made your stories possible. But you often mention cases that remain untold. I'm not asking you to break any confidences, of course, but I am curious about them. For example, Mr. Holmes, who would you say was the worst murderer you ever had to deal with?"

"That very much depends on how you are defining 'worst'," said Holmes. "Dr. Grimesby Roylott only did away with one person, but his method of doing so was diabolical. Baron Adelbert Gruner more than once made an unsuspecting woman fall in love with him before it served his turn to kill her. Alfred Tarleton tortured his victims for some time before finally dispatching them, while Dr. Henry Staunton made a habit of killing his elderly patients after ensuring that they had remembered him in their will."

"Then there was Schofield, who murdered the whole Abernetty family," I said, "and Vigor, the so-called 'Hammersmith Wonder', a circus performer who used his powers of contortion to break into people's houses and rob and kill them in their sleep."

I was about to add the notorious Jack the Ripper, but I recalled just in time that we had agreed never to mention our connection to the case, let alone the true identity of the killer.

"And yet, Watson, I think you will agree that the most, shall we say, unsettling murderer we have ever encountered was Bert Stevens."

"Yes, indeed."

"What was it about him that set him apart?" asked Murray.

"It is an axiom of our profession, Mr. Murray, that one should not permit one's judgment to be biased by personal qualities. To do so is to depart from the road of clear reason, which is the only true path to the facts. Elspeth Carson, to give but one example, was a charming young woman, beloved by all who knew her, but she ended on the gallows for murdering three small children.

"Bert Stevens was perhaps the most extreme case of this dichotomy between appearance and reality that I have ever encountered. He was mild-mannered, soft-spoken and gentle in his ways. But beneath that placid surface lay a fiendish, calculating intelligence, untroubled by conscience. But if you would wish to hear the whole story – "

"Yes, I certainly would,"

" – then I hand you over to Watson. He, as you know, is the storyteller." He stood and went over to the bookcase.

"You may need this," he said, taking his casebook for the relevant year from its shelf. He opened it to the date in question, handed it to me, then returned to his seat.

"Thank you, Holmes."

"I shall only interject when I deem it necessary."

I took a moment to light a fresh cigar and gather my thoughts, then I began . . . .

The Events of June 1887

"Inspector Merivale, one of the better Scotland Yard men, and a friend to us both, called on us one evening in late June to discuss a rash of seemingly unconnected killings which had recently taken place in the metropolis. Now, it was unusual to have so many murders committed in such a short space of time – "

"Well," said Holmes, "that statement needs a little modification. It's unusual to have so many *unsolved* murders in such a short span of time. In most cases, it's obvious who the perpetrator is. A man kills his wife in a fit of jealous rage, another bludgeons his mate to death in an outburst of drunken anger – these stories are on the back pages of the newspapers, if they make it into the news at all. They'll be on the front page if the victims or the murderers are known to polite society, but otherwise – Well, there are murders being committed every day, but most of the public are unaware of the majority of them."

"Merivale asked if it were possible that they were all being committed by the same man, and Holmes replied that it was unlikely."

"Indeed," said Holmes. "It is actually quite rare for someone to kill more than one person, and when they do, the victims, if not known to the murderer, are at least usually members of the same profession or social class, and usually killed in the same way. The Polish murderer, Marek Wesolowski, or Thomas Kelly as he was known when he lived in London, killed four of his mistresses by the gradual administration of poison. Then there's the Whitechapel Killer, of course. He did away with at least five East End prostitutes. Perhaps he knew them, perhaps he didn't. He probably strangled them, then cut their throats and disembowelled them. He did more than that to his last victim, but then he killed her in her room, not out on the street."

"So," I continued, "we went through the victims with Merivale, one by one, as we shall now.

"First, Pierre Blanchard, twenty-four, a shopkeeper and a native of Dijon, found strangled in Eldon Street, Stepney, 11:30 p.m. He'd been dead for about two hours. From the marks on the neck, the strangulation appeared to have been carried out by the use of a broad ligature – a cummerbund, perhaps, or a scarf."

"Next was Robert Carver, draper, thirty-four, his wife Sophie, twenty-six, and draper's assistant Martin Ball, seventeen. They were all found in Carver's rooms above his shop in Putney at 7:30 a.m., 15th April. Their heads had been beaten to a pulp by some heavy instrument. They had all been dead between four-and-a-half and five hours. Then, let me see – yes, Jean Dawson, aged only sixteen, found in a dustbin behind Artillery Buildings, Victoria Street, 24th April, at six a.m. Her throat had been slit, her body was naked and completely drained of blood – "

"Oh, God!"

"Are you all right, Murray? Do you want to stop?"

"No, no, I'm fine, it's just – sixteen, for God's sake! And in a damned dustbin! What kind of monster could do such a thing?"

"Merivale suggested a vampire, and I of course said that there were no such things, but he pointed out that there had been killers who drank their victims' blood. Human vampires, you might say. What was the name of that man in Harrogate, in '84?"

"Walter Harvey," said Holmes, "and yes, he did drink some of his victims' blood after he'd killed them, but this would still be a problem: Jean Dawson must have been quite small if she could be stuffed in a dustbin, but even so, she must have had six or seven pints of blood in her body. The police medical examiner determined she'd been dead between two and three hours. The body was completely drained. The killer could have drunk six pints of water in that time, or even six pints of beer, but six pints of blood? He would feel ill after a pint, even if he were really determined to carry it through. No, I came to the conclusions that the body must have been hung upside down and drained somewhere else, then dumped where it was found."

I turned to the following page in the casebook.

"The next was Constable Ernest Romney, thirty-one. He was found in the Edgware Road at 10:25 p.m., May 2nd. He had a bullet wound to the chest, and he'd been dead between one and two hours. Only one of the other victims was shot, and that was in the head."

"Sad to say," observed Holmes, "policemen get killed on duty quite often, so while it certainly counts as an unsolved murder, it might have been even less likely to be connected to any of the others."

"Next we had Mehmed Kartal, secretary to the Turkish ambassador, twenty-seven. He was found in his rooms in Bayswater Road, at seven a.m. on the 15th May. He'd been dead five to six hours, and killed in a most bizarre fashion: A metal spike had been driven through his skull and into his brain."

"It does sound like an odd thing to kill someone with," said Murray.

"It does indeed," said Holmes. "Most murders are unpremeditated, with the killer using the first weapon that comes to hand. Even when a murder is planned, there is still a fairly narrow range of methods employed – poison, strangulation, a gun, a knife, or a blunt object."

"It was at this point, as I recall, Holmes, that you were beginning to suspect that there might, after all, be a connection between these killings, and there was but one perpetrator rather than several."

"Correct. I had, of course, been keeping a weather eye on the progress of the investigations, but it wasn't until we actually sat down with Merivale and began to discuss them together that that connection started to become clear. Now, Mr. Murray, I must tell you that in those little sketches of his, my good friend Watson here habitually exaggerates my abilities. While I own that I have brought the arts of observation and deduction, and of reasoning from cause to effect, to greater heights than any man living, I am still human, and so fall short of perfection. This is particularly true when one considers the fact that I have made it my business to study the crimes of the past, in order to see what light they may throw on the misdeeds of the present.

"The killer, whoever he was, was recreating some of those crimes of bygone days. Let us again take them one by one.

"Pierre Blanchard had been strangled using a ligature. Now, as someone who, like Watson, has served on the Indian sub-continent, you may have heard of the *Thugs*, or the *Phansigars*, as they are sometimes called."

"Yes, indeed."

"The British administration broke the cult in the 1830's. Their most prolific assassin was a man called Behram, who claimed to have had over nine-hundred victims. They worshipped Kali the Destroyer, and the story is that once Kali was fighting a demon, and every time she cut him with her sword, another demon sprang from each drop of blood that the demon shed, until she was fighting an army of them. She defeated them by strangling them, so that no more blood would fall. So her worshippers killed in the same way, using strips of cloth called *rumals*. They mainly killed travellers, and looked on their victims as sacrifices to appease the goddess, who would otherwise destroy the whole human race.

"Robert Carver and his wife, and Carver's unfortunate assistant, were killed in emulation of what are known as the Ratcliff Highway murders, in 1811. There were seven in all, the weapon in each case being a maul, a type of sledgehammer. The probable killer was a sailor called John Williams, who was staying near the Highway at a house in Wapping. He committed suicide before he could be put on trial.

"Now, Mr. Murray, have you heard of Countess Elizabeth Bathory?"

"The name is vaguely familiar."

"She is perhaps better known by her sobriquet, '*The Blood Countess*'. She was a sixteenth-century Hungarian noblewoman who became obsessed with the idea that bathing in the blood of young girls would restore her youth and beauty. She drained hundreds of teenaged girls of their blood over the course of two or three years. The highest estimate is over nine-hundred."

"Surely it would have obvious fairly soon that it wasn't working," said Murray.

"I'm sure you're right," said Holmes, "but it may have been a case of '*The Emperor's New Clothes*'. None of her servants had the courage to tell her that her youth and beauty were not returning, so the killings continued. It must be clear that it was her history which inspired the death of young Jean Dawson."

"What happened to this Bathory woman?"

"She was tried and sentenced to spend the rest of her life in one tiny room with no windows and only a small aperture to pass food and drink through to her. She died after a couple of years.

"The murder of Constable Romney was more difficult to place, because, as I said, policeman are killed with greater frequency than the bulk of the population. But working on the basis that our putative killer was modelling his crimes on those of well-known murderers, I surmised that in this instance he was following in the footsteps of Charles Peace, whose first victim was Constable Nicholas Cock of the Manchester Constabulary, in 1876."

"Which brings us to the case of Mehmed Kartal and the iron spike," I said.

"Yes," said Holmes, "and to explain that we must once again look back through time. In fifteenth-century Wallachia, now part of Romania, there was a *voivode*, or warlord, called Vlad Dracula."

"I've read that book," said Murray." Are we back with vampires?"

"I've met Bram Stoker – " I said.

"Yet another purveyor of fantastical tales."

"Thank you, Holmes. I was about to say, Stoker used the name, but his story has little or no connection to the historical character."

"Dracula was also known as *Vlad Tepes*, which means *Vlad the Impaler*. It was his habit to punish people by pushing long wooden spikes through various parts of their anatomy and leaving them to die a lingering and extremely painful death. Now it was unlikely that our killer, whoever he was, would be carrying a long wooden spike around, by day or by night, but his method fitted another story that was told of Dracula, and perhaps explained the choice of Mehmed Kartal as a victim: Dracula spent most of his life in conflict with the Turks, and on one occasion he was visited by three emissaries from the Turkish sultan, Murad II. He asked them to remove their turbans, and when they refused to do so, he had them nailed to their heads with iron spikes."

"So," I said, "Holmes had established the principle on which the murders were being committed, but how were we to know where the killer would strike next?"

"It seemed odd to me," said Holmes, "that someone who was copying the crimes of previous murderers should choose such an eclectic mix, from a wide range of places and times. We've had enough homegrown killers here in Britain over the last fifty years to supply a variety of motives and methods. This suggested to me either that the culprit was, like myself, a student of the history of crime, or had some other formula for choosing to emulate those particular criminals in that particular sequence. If the former were true, then the order might be completely random, which would make a solution virtually impossible. Clearly, it was not chronological, either backwards or forwards. What little we do know of multiple murderers suggests that their behaviour follows a pattern. We had to find out what that pattern was, and where it came from. I think you can stop there, Watson. There were more victims, but it was at this stage of our investigation that I began to formulate a theory as to what that pattern might be."

351

"Yes," I recalled, "Merivale left us at about half-past ten, and Holmes asked him to call again the following afternoon."

"I must say," said Murray, "this is just like one of your stories, Watson. Better, because it's straight from the horse's mouth. It's pretty grim, though, isn't it?"

"That's one reason why any account of it will stay unpublished for many years after we are gone. After Merivale arrived the following day, we walked together along Baker Street and into Marylebone Road. We visited a particular establishment there that you may have heard of: Madame Tussaud's Waxworks."

"I think I begin to see," said Murray.

"We made our way to the front of the queue, amidst much complaint from the assembled customers, and gained immediate admittance when Merivale displayed his identification. Once we were inside, Holmes led us to a particular part of the museum."

"The Chamber of Horrors!"

"Correct, Mr. Murray," said Holmes.

"We walked past wax *tableaux* of inquisitors torturing heretics, Jacobins guillotining aristocrats, Viking archers riddling Edward the Martyr with arrows, and Romans about to immolate bound Christians during the reign of the Emperor Domitian, until we came to a separate room devoted to representations of individual murderers.

"There were twenty main figures: Marek Wesolowski, Behram the Thug, John Williams, Elizabeth Bathory, Charles Peace, Vlad the Impaler, and the ones I haven't mentioned: Christopher Mills, whose charming habit was to shoot random people through the head, and who was caught when one of his victims unexpectedly survived and identified him – Guiseppe Cardoni, an Italian garrotter whom the Turks employed during the Greek War of Independence, Lu Mei Hua, who killed several of her rivals for the affections of the warlord Zhang Chang by stabbing them through the heart with a long pin, and Michael Bennett, a waterman who cudgelled and robbed some of his passengers and then threw them into the Thames to drown. Each of them, too, had had murders modelled on their crimes, and the killer no doubt intended to emulate the other miscreants represented in this grim tableau.

"'My God!' said Merivale, as we went slowly round the room at Holmes's instigation, weaving through the other visitors and looking at each exhibit.

"'They're all here, in that exact order,' I said.

"'Except for one,' said Merivale, pointing to his left. 'Behram isn't the first.' The figure of Marek Wesolowski, alias Thomas Kelly, was standing closest to the entrance on that side.

"'I believe I have an explanation for that,' said Holmes.

"'Apart from Kelly, the murderer acted in accordance with the order of the wax figures,' said Merivale.

"'Holmes! There are twenty figures in here! Will there be eleven more murders?'

"'No, Watson, nine. And we can prevent them from happening.'

"He turned decisively, and Merivale and I followed him back out to the foyer.

"'We should like to speak to the curator,' Holmes said to the young woman at the cash desk. Having seen Merivale's police card, she left her position, led us down a corridor, and into an area cordoned off by ropes which bore a sign on the wall bearing the message, "*No Entry to the Public*". She indicated a door marked "*R. Pemberton, Curator*" and then left us to return to her position.

"'Best if you identify yourself first, Merivale,' said Holmes. 'The presence of an officer of the law tends to reassure those in a position of authority.'

"Pemberton recognised our names – "

"'Of course,' said Murray. 'Practically everyone has read your stories.'

"I glanced across at Holmes, who made a mock grimace.

"Pemberton was a middle-aged man of about my height," he said. "Very dapper, his moustache waxed and teased into a point at either end, and he had a silver *pince-nez* perched on the end of the bridge of his long nose.

"'So, gentlemen,' he said, 'how may I be of use to you?'

"'How many attendants do you have working for you?' asked Holmes.

"Pemberton went behind his large mahogany writing desk, opened a drawer, and pulled out a brown folder.

"'About thirty,' he said with a smile. 'I try to be methodical. I have to be. I don't have a terribly good memory. They're all in here: Names, ages, pay, shift patterns, prev – '

"'Shift patterns?'

"'Oh, yes. We have to have guards here at night. Would you believe it, people have actually been known to break in and try and steal things from the figures – Napoleon's hat, the arrow in King Harold's eye, Queen Victoria's veil. I don't know if they think they're the real things, but anyway, we had to put a stop to it.'

"'Have any of your attendants been widowed recently?'

"'Yes, one has. What's his name? I told you my memory was bad. Ah, wait a minute – Stevens. Bertram Stevens, that's it.'

"'Can I see his records?'

"'Certainly.'

Pemberton opened the folder and leafed through it until he found Stevens' sheet, then handed it to Holmes.

"'You're on a case,' said Pemberton as Holmes ran his eyes down the page.

"'Well deduced, Mr. Pemberton.'

"'I hope you don't suspect Stevens of anything. I've never met anyone less like a criminal. He's a devout churchgoer. Man wouldn't hurt a fly. Meek and mild. Very quiet – even more so since he lost his wife.'

"'May I take this?'

"'If you bring it back.'

"'Of course.'

"Once we were back in the open air, Holmes suggested that we repair to the nearby Carpenter's Arms.

"'So, Mr. Holmes,' said Merivale as the bartender brought three foaming pints over to our table, 'may we take it that Bertram Stevens is your suspect?'

"'That's correct. Merivale, you pointed out that Kelly was the first of the wax figures, not Behram.'

"The Scotland Yarder took a sip of his beer. "'Yes, and you said you could explain it, that it didn't spoil your theory.'

"'And it doesn't. For what was Kelly executed?'

"'He poisoned four of his common-law wives,' said Merivale.

"'Four of them?" I said. 'How many did he have?'

"'He had a legal wife in Poland, and at least six mistresses in London – all of whom called themselves "Mrs. Kelly" at some point.'

"'All four died of antimony poisoning,' said Holmes, 'given in the form of tartar emetic, a means of inducing vomiting. They all had the same symptoms, but Wesolowski – or Kelly if you prefer – wasn't arrested, or even suspected, until the fourth one died. So, if Stevens killed his wife by tartar emetic, given in gradual doses, the same as Kelly, he might not have been suspected either, particularly since he didn't kill anyone else in that fashion.'

"'Well,' said Merivale, 'we can get an exhumation order for Mrs. Stevens" body, and we can make enquiries at the chemist's in Stevens" immediate area to see if he bought tartar emetic in any of them. It's a poison, so there should be a record.'

"I had been drinking silently, but now I said, 'I can see a couple of problems, Holmes.'

"'Go on."

354

"'Supposing Stevens had his wife cremated? And what if he didn't buy the poison in a chemist in his area? Are the police going to inquire at every chemist shop in London?'

"'Well, that's been done in the past, but I take your point. As for the cremation, that costs more than burial, and Stevens is not in a particularly well-paid job.'

"'Why did you take that sheet of Stevens' shift patterns?'

"'It may at least demonstrate that he was free to carry out the murders at the correct dates and times, though I concede that that is only corroborative if we have more evidence of his guilt.'

"A chemist in Bow Road testified that Stevens had purchased several packets of tartar emetic four months before his wife's death. On this basis, an exhumation order was granted on Mrs. Stevens' corpse in the Roman Catholic cemetery in Leytonstone, and it was found to contain a significant amount of antimony. Stevens was arrested and held in Pentonville Prison pending trial.

"Holmes and I were permitted to sit on the first interrogation carried out by Merivale at Scotland Yard, with a sergeant also in attendance. As soon as Stevens was brought into the room, I understood what Pemberton had said about the unlikelihood of his being a criminal.

"He was short, with wispy, wavy blond hair, a pale, pinched face, and behind wire-rimmed spectacles, large, china-blue eyes that seemed filled with a lasting sadness. His legs were slightly bowed, and I attributed this to rickets, which, along with the general frailty of his physique, suggested that he had suffered malnutrition as a child. Was it possible that this feeble creature had perpetrated such a string of atrocities?

"He sat down and looked from one to the other of us, with a seraphic smile.

"'Now, Stevens,' Merivale began, 'do you know why you are here?'

"'I am afraid I have no idea, but I put my trust in the Lord.'

"The sound of his voice was barely above a whisper, his demeanour modest and self-effacing.

"'Do you deny that you bought eight packets of tartar emetic at Boyson's in Bow Road four months before the death of your wife Sarah?'

"'Is that when it was? No, I don't deny it, if that's what the man at the chemist's says.'

"'Why did you purchase so much?'

"'Sarah had a tapeworm.'

"'But she didn't go to a doctor.'

"'She refused. Her mother died in hospital, which made her suspicious of the medical profession. I read that tartar emetic could be used against parasites, but I did not know how long it would take, so I bought a great deal of it. I talked to our vicar, and he advised me to pray, so I did, every night, but in the end it pleased God to take her.'

"'And that's how you explain the high levels of antimony in her body, is it?'

"Those blue eyes widened and tears welled up in them.

"'I – I don't like to say it, but I am rather afraid that she may have taken her own life. Please, please, don't say anything! I couldn't stand it if she were reburied in unconsecrated ground!'"

"Before Merivale could answer, Holmes interposed. 'You know, Stevens, there's one thing I don't understand.'

"'Wh – what's that?'

"'How someone as intelligent as you could make such a stupid mistake.'

"'I don't know what you mean.'

"'I imagine it was because you were just starting out. You were much more careful with the other killings. They were masterfully done.'

"A strange change gradually came over Stevens' face. The shy, childlike meekness began to recede. His expression held hints of both cunning and pride, but he repeated, though with less conviction, 'I don't know what you mean.'

"'I suppose killing Constable Romney must have been fairly easy, but I'm still trying to work out how you got Jean Dawson's body into that dustbin.'

"Stevens was now looking Holmes in the eye, as if to stare him down, but he said nothing.

"'And as for the iron spike in Kartal's skull – that was a stroke of genius. It took me some time to understand the reference.'

"Stevens' head pulled back until he was looking down his nose at my friend.

"'Do you know who I am?' said the detective. 'I'm Sherlock Holmes. You must have heard the name. And you baffled even me.'

"A self-satisfied smile spread across the murderer's face, which was now utterly transformed from a picture of uncomprehending innocence to one of arrogance, horribly tinged with a hint of glee at his crimes.

"'Even Sherlock Holmes,' he said. 'So, I shall have a special place in the annals of crime.'

"I shuddered. Twelve people had died at this man's hand, in a variety of grisly ways, and here he was, smiling.

"'Do you admit to these killings then, Stevens?' demanded Merivale.

"'My only regret is that I was unable to bring the work to a conclusion. Yes, yes, Mr. Whatever-your-name-is Policeman, I was the artist.'

"Once he had made his admission, Stevens waxed garrulous and began to go into the killings in detail. Holmes and I stood to leave.

"'As it says in *Proverbs*, "*Pride goeth before destruction, and an haughty spirit before a fall*,"'" Holmes remarked as we walked out into the open air . . . .

"That," said Murray, "was a remarkable tale."

"There's a little more," I said. "I see you kept the clipping from *The South London Sentinel*, Holmes. One of the radical newspapers," I explained to Murray. "Let me read it aloud:

> *The public has recently heard much about the shocking series of murders perpetrated by Bertram Stevens, and while it is not our business to condone these actions, we would argue that a little may be said in mitigation. We quote Sir Anthony Brocklebank, the noted alienist:*
>
> *"Bertram Stevens was found abandoned on the steps of the Sacred Heart and cared for by the nuns until the age of seven, when he was placed in the workhouse at Hunslet in the West Riding of Yorkshire. There he was provided with education, and just about learned to read and write, but was generally deemed ineducable and incapable of adopting a trade. He did show the beginnings of an aptitude for music, but this was not encouraged, and there were no instruments available on which he might develop an ability.*
>
> *"Around the age of twelve or thirteen he began to show signs of mental disturbance. He would go into trance states without warning, and when he recovered, earned the scorn of his fellow-inmates by claiming that he had visited far-distant and beautiful lands. He responded to their jibes with uncontrolled violence and invariably received a thorough beating in return. At other times he said that he was really the son of the King of France, or of Italy, and that very soon his father would send a coach for him to take him away, and again, no beating would shake this conviction, whether it was given by his fellows or by the adults in charge. At the age of fifteen, he was sent from the workhouse, devoid of prospects, with no-one in the world who cared a jot about him. He made his way to London.*
>
> *"Somehow, Stevens learned to suppress the problematic aspects of his personality and appear 'normal', I would imagine as a survival mechanism. Indeed, those who*

encountered him described him as meek, soft-spoken, and deeply religious. This assumption of 'normality' is doubtless what enabled him to find a wife and get his job at the wax museum. All this I have gathered from conversations with him and what I have inferred from his records. What I am about to say is speculative, though there is little doubt in my mind that it is the truth: What we have here is a man who has no clear identity. What slender chances he had to form the beginnings of a healthy personality, such as his musical ability, were taken from him or not allowed to develop. He escaped, into oblivion or into fantasy, but these earned him scorn and violence.

"By the time he began work at the museum, he was what we might term a 'Jekyll and Hyde', or multiplex personality, a divided consciousness fitting in with the norms and conventions of society on the surface, but in the deeper recesses of his psyche, full of a repressed need to express anger and violence. Now, the way he explained it to me is that he was 'possessed' – that was the word he used – by the spirits of these murderers, that they took him over one by one and sent him forth to do the same 'work' they had done. I have no doubt that that is what he believed to be the truth. My own interpretation is that on those nights when he was left alone with the wax figures, having few or no inner resources to distract him from brooding upon them, he would read the descriptive passages in front of each figure, and began to admire them – perhaps, for their defiance of the law and conventional human conduct.

"And so, working his way round the room, having no true identity of his own, he took on one persona after another, killing once in each identity, but each time finding it unsatisfying, and moving on to the next in the hope that another murder would bring balm to his soul. What he would have done had he managed to inhabit all twenty and remained unsatisfied, I don't know. Suicide, perhaps."

"Thank you, Watson. I say now, as I said then, that while I can feel compassion for the child he was, I have nothing but contempt for the man he became. To carry out those murders required meticulous planning and cold intelligence, and I have no doubt that what Brocklebank encountered was yet another false persona, geared to appeal to what Stevens must have

358

sensed the alienist wanted to hear. In any event, the jury did not accept this in mitigation, and Stevens went to the gallows."

"I sometimes wonder," I said, "if killers like Stevens, and the Ripper, are not somehow harbingers of the nature of crimes to come."

"Watson! The evening is yet young, and you and Murray have, I fancy, much more to tell each other. Have another cigar, and I'll pour you both another brandy, and we shall forget for a while the dark and evil deeds of which humanity is capable."

Murray and I left at 11:30, and as he saw us to the door, Holmes said, "Let us not forget the words of *Havamal*."

"'*Havamal*'?"

"*The Words of the High One*, an ancient Viking poem: '*Do not let the grass grow on the paths between the houses of friends.*'"

"You remember that terrible murderer, Bert Stevens, who wanted us to get him off in '87? Was there ever a more mild-mannered, Sunday-school young man?"

– Sherlock Holmes
"The Norwood Builder"

Boxing Day, Brother Mine
by Gretchen Altabef

Related to "The Adventure of the Blue Carbuncle", with a nod to Robert Barnard

"The true spirit of Christmas lies, of course, in reconciliation."
– Sir Adrian Tremain

"I had called upon my friend Sherlock Holmes upon the second morning after Christmas, with the intention of wishing him the compliments of the season. He was lounging upon the sofa in a purple dressing-gown...."
– Dr. John H. Watson

26 December, 1887

There is no mystery about Sherlock's purple dressing-gown. It was a holiday gift from me – his brother, Mycroft. I thought a little colour added to his limited black-and-white palette might brighten him up a bit.

Doctor John Watson usually records Sherlock's exploits in his journals, and he recently published their first investigation together – the murder of two Americans nearly seven years ago – but since this affair doesn't concern murder or the Good Doctor, I take my pen in hand. As in most of Sherlock's life, here too there is a certain degree of danger. I rarely partake in these adventures, and they are better told by Watson.

Yes, Sherlock Holmes has a brother. I am the diplomatic one. My life is spent in stately formal, gold-brocaded Royal sitting rooms. Amid changing political environs, I like to think of myself as my country's second Rock of Gibraltar – one with the ability to steer through storms at the elbow of power. This is my *milieu*, where I shine. Clandestine living becomes me. Like Sherlock, I have created my own profession. I work within the highest levels of the British Government, yet no one can pin down exactly what it is I do – also by design.

Omniscience, though quite normal to my way of thinking, is somewhat rare, yet no one can find fault with my sweeping decisions. My wide-ranging views have gained me a special, if completely confidential, position in Her Majesty's government. One might also say that I am Whitehall's central exchange.

Suppose a Minister needs information which involves the Navy, India, Canada, and the bi-metallic question. He could ask his separate advices from various departments upon each, but just imagine how much more efficacious it is to immediately say how each factor affects the other. That is where I come into it. I can humbly admit that time and again, my conclusions have decided the national policy.

My brother Sherlock jokingly refers to me as "the British Government". That may be because of my girth, or a desire to cut me down to size. Where he is active and thin, I am of a more relaxed nature.

Today's December 26th holiday is held in these Isles and colonies immediately after Christmas. Boxing Day, or the Feast of Saint Stephen, is when even the silent gentlemen of the Diogenes Club must do without. This unique holiday has nothing to do with that great British sport, and everything to do with the boxes of gifts that are given to household servants as acknowledgement for their work throughout the year, and it is their designated holiday.

On this day, we acknowledge those who, either through choice or misadventure, serve us. Secretaries, chefs, *maitre' d*'s, porters, barbers, concierges, tailors, doormen, librarians, wait staff, footmen, laundry staff, maids, valets, butlers, and those who carry out their requests. Honour is gratefully paid to an endless stream of deserving caretakers.

While the Diogenes servants were off today celebrating their well-earned holiday, the dearth of their care gave the club a dark and eerie air. The starched brightness of costumes and the deep red velvet of jackets hung ghost-like on hooks. The Oriental carpets, members' stuffed high-backed chairs, and even the gold of the stair railing was lacklustre within the shadows of unlit lamps, undrawn window curtains, and cold fireplaces. The day was even more peaceful because most members had taken refuge elsewhere.

Sherlock calls the servant-class, the "London slavey", and organizes his life without servants. Mrs. Hudson manages the house where he lives, and she has hired a maid to help her with the day-to-day tasks. He hired a boy-in-buttons to answer the door and run up to his floor with clients or messages, thus saving Mrs. Hudson from the constant climb. Billy is given a salary, and his schooling is also paid for by Sherlock. Then there are the Baker Street Irregulars, the street urchin sleuths whom Sherlock hires as needed. Wiggins, their leader, also attends school on Sherlock's shilling.

Nevertheless, it is Sherlock's and my tradition to spend Saint Stephen's Day together. Earlier today, the surrounding library quiet of the club was reminiscent of our Yorkshire upbringing, and neither of us had an interest in the derby football matches played on this day. We typically meet in the Stranger's Room, which is the only room in the club where discourse is allowed. The rule everywhere else in this singular gentlemen's establishment is that one forfeits membership after three noisy infractions. But, as the club was empty today, we soon relocated to the library.

For Sherlock and myself, the deeply shadowed and empty gentleman's club brought back those rare and mysterious days of our childhood when we were completely unsupervised. At Christmastime, our parents, as Lord and Lady of the manor, opened their home with elaborate parties and feasts. It was understandable that on Boxing Day, with the servants gone, they would seek each other's quiet company.

Our only job that day was to deliver the family's gift boxes to our neighbours. In return, we were usually plied with spiked eggnog. On this one day a year, Sherlock and I probed the old Grange inside and out, to its stables and gardens, in order to discover its cold and lamp-less secrets. We created intellectual scavenger hunts and memory games together which ranged further afield each year. Sherlock usually won these contests.

Through the stained-glass windows of the library stood the great city we had both chosen as adults. My fortunate world existed within walking distance of the seats of the British Government: Whitehall and Buckingham Palace, while Sherlock held a map in his mind of every high or low parish and street on either side of the River Thames. Today, we drank fine wine together and shared a most splendid cold repast with Christmas goose, plum pudding, and other delicacies. What my brother gifted me was a rare Tokay wine. Sherlock has never cared for feasts – food is sustenance and fuel for him. Not so for me. My pallet is finely cultivated. Still, he has excellent taste in wine and other spirits. Our parents made sure to raise us as epicures.

When he'd arrived, I was languishing in velvet and plumped pillows in my finest scarlet smoking jacket. Within the complete silence of an empty club, I was sipping a glass of Veuve Clicquot, 1870, the widow's best, and resting after my preparations. He rushed in, dressed in a tattered and rusty black frockcoat and a topper that looked as if a horse had trampled it in the dirt. He entered into the little circle of lamplight and candles I had created. We addressed each other properly by a hearty hand clasping.

"My God, Sherlock. Come – my barber will dispatch that forthwith. Your hair is jarvey length!"

I rang the bell pull.

He laughed. "Thank you, but your bell will not bring a barber today, Brother Mine, and I haven't yet completed the task for which it was grown. You must needs accept me as I am. But hurry, Mycroft: The game is afoot!"

He tugged and insisted me into tweeds.

362

"Into your coat and come!"

"Working on a case during the Holidays?" I laughed. "I admire your fortitude, little brother."

"A Christmas fancy."

"Living undercover in another's shabby suit. If you joined with my Diogenes gentlemen, there would at least be time off."

"Time waits for no gentleman. Mycroft, your laziness is insufferable! Give in, Brother. The daylight is rather limited today."

"Surely you'll share dinner with me?"

He waved it away.

"I require your immediate assistance, if you're open to it."

As he spoke, he stuffed thick slabs of Christmas goose between two slices of bread, wrapped them in a paper, and, with a few strawberry tarts, dropped them into his coat pocket.

"Of course," I answered.

"Splendid! I'll slip out through the servant's entrance. My horse awaits me there."

"Surely this is unnecessary," I said. "A scavenger hunt may be made here in the warmth of the Club. If you can find an open telegraph office and require my assistance further, send a wire."

"The air of your Club is as cold as the icy street! It is crucial that you attend!"

"What have you involved me in?"

"A little Boxing Day cheer," echoed down the stairway with his receding footsteps.

"Complements of the Season!" I called after him.

He swiftly descended the back stairs and was gone. For an instant, I considered the serene day rolling out ahead of me. Then I downed my champagne, moved the feast into the Club's icebox, speedily donned coat, hat, and gloves, and escaped into the December chill through the club members' entrance. When I joined Sherlock minutes later, he was standing beside a cab, all business and sporting an East End accent.

"Oy, where to, Luv?" He showed his perfect set of teeth, the only giveaway to his costume.

With the agility of a youth, he leapt up to his seat and started the horse.

"You have chosen wisely. Ole Jack knows the city like the back of 'is hand! Please kindly 'onour Saint Stephen's Day before you leave me, sir!"

He touched his hat.

My brother's sense of humour was never a favourite of mine. Yet, in a thrice, we had surfaced in Pall Mall and pointed towards Bloomsbury at a swift pace. I was aware that Sherlock's plans would reveal themselves in good time, and happy that between the university and the museum, he had chosen a respectable neighbourhood for his holiday fancy.

We came to a halt at an old pub which lies at the back of Tottenham Court Road. Sherlock hopped down, petted the horse affectionately, and handed the reins to a dirty street urchin. He then dropped the sandwich into the boy's right pocket and the tarts into his left and patted his head.

He quickly scanned my attire and pried from me my stick, hat, and coat, leaving these supreme symbols of a gentleman's attire in the carriage.

In character, he said to me, "Thank ye for yer generosity, Guv."

"If all else fails," I laughed, "you still have a jarvey's occupation to fall back on."

"Keep alert," he said softly in his own voice. "This isn't Pall Mall or the Diogenes Club. Your highborn friends will not help you here."

Sherlock threw the least offensive of the carriage rugs over my shoulders, pinned it with a tarnished rose broach, and crowned me with what looked like one of Doctor Watson's old, discarded caps. Then he put his arm through mine and we entered the pub together as extremely disreputable brothers.

It was indeed a lively place, filled with celebration and holiday cheer. Sherlock lit a soggy cigar and tipped his hat to the landlord. The pub was candlelit, and festive Christmas Holly adorned every fireplace and doorway. Wooden tables with full groaning benches kept grateful men warming at the blazing hearths. It was clear from the expectancy and enthusiasm shown by their audience that the final darts tournament of the year was underway. It was lit by additional candelabra and boisterous with loud concomitant wagering. Sherlock talked for a moment with the landlord. Then he led me to a nearby table and brought over two pints.

"What is this?" I asked.

I pulled out my red silk handkerchief to dust off the bench. But my brother instantly thrust it back into my breast pocket with a growl and a look of fire in his eyes.

"Sit down and be patient, my dear Mycroft!" he hissed. "And leave your snuff box in your pocket!"

"What does this have to do with me?"

"Yesterday, Commissionaire Peterson shared with me his Christmas Eve mystery. In the early hours of Christmas morning, he observed a man carrying a splendid white Christmas goose over his shoulder who was put upon by roughs in this neighbourhood. In the scuffle, the man lost his hat, his goose, and accidentally shattered the window of a local establishment when he raised his stick in self-defence. Peterson rushed to protect the man from his assailants, but they all took to their heels. The Commissionaire retrieved the battered hat and goose and brought them to me to solve the dilemma.

"'*For Mrs. Henry Baker*' was printed upon a small card tied to the bird's left leg, and the initials '*H. B.*' were legible upon the lining of the hat. These were my only clues, but, as there are some thousands of *Bakers* and some hundreds of *Henry Bakers* in this city of ours, it isn't a simple thing to restore lost property to any one of them.'"

"Sherlock, my mind is just as full of essential facts as is yours, yet I haven't memorised the London telephone book!"

"Nor would it help you here. It was only right that the goose should go to Peterson's family dinner, while I retained Henry Baker's hat."

"I will never understand your love of trifles. Where does this lead us?"

"Today, we shall be scouring public houses in search of the roughs who attacked Mr. Baker."

"Whoever may be a tough on Christmas Eve, may be a family man on Christmas Day, eh?"

"Exactly. The holiday changes everything. And I'd rather be led to Henry Baker by someone who was there than search through every street for him."

"I celebrate your choice of a warm inn. So this is why we are here in this garret instead of surrounded by the comforts of my club?"

"It is the game! Your Diogenes Club is deserted. It's highly probable that Watson is at home with his wife, or soaking in the Northumberland Street Baths after his Old-timers football match, so we must advance abroad for our Boxing Day games. You are free of your usual duties, as am I. Since we are united today as family, I thought you might indulge me in the solving of this little mystery."

"I am Watson in this scenario?"

"No, no, no! You are my elder brother, with a brain of greater capacity than mine. And I thought you might enjoy a taste of how lives the common man. Rejoice in your pint. The ale here has a reputation for rich, wine-like flavour, and strength. And since this pub isn't far from the shop where Henry Baker broke a window, he may arrive here at any minute, and this sojourn may soon be concluded."

Sherlock has always been interested in the other classes. He believes in the equality of all. He partnered with a fine middle-class gentleman – a former soldier and a doctor. However, I find Mrs. Hudson's crowded upper floors to be quite beneath a Holmes! We have descended from Squires, so we are gentlemen, nonetheless! While I cannot do my work without this distinction, he frequently finds it a barrier to his.

"Mycroft," my brother whispered, "keep an eye on that darts player – a violent man."

Sherlock was up in a flash. He took the next turn at darts and threw four bullseyes for the team, which was glad to have him. But the man he had indicated was not. That he had a violent nature was apparent in his surly demeanour. He had the stamp of every school bully upon him, though I doubt he ever attended much school.

"Who the hell are you?"

"I'm fillin' in!"

"A ratbag ringer, that's wot!"

"Fair 'n square!"

"Not in my book! Get out of it!"

While Sherlock assessed his man, shouts and threats began to fill my end of the pub. Another row was developing right in front of me. It centred around someone I had recognized, the butler from the Tankerville Club who was discreetly drinking across from me. An observant rough realized the man might be celebrating the Boxing Day holiday and began to taunt him.

"Who the bloody dickens do you think you are? What makes you so different that you deserve a special holiday and gifts?"

He pushed the butler.

"I work like you do. Where's my holiday? Where's my drafted boxes?"

"No different from you, sir. I'm here, as you are, hiding from my good woman on a day of rest."

"Now 'e's telling me fortune! Shut your saucebox and share those gifts! Come on – give us a wee peek."

He laughed loudly and elbowed the butler hard. I had to step in to defend the man.

I addressed him cordially. "My good man, you are mistaken. There is no cause for derision. This man's job is to superbly care for a full club of gentlemen. and he very much deserves his day off."

I patted the first man's back in a friendly way. He moved away from my hand as if it were on fire. Then he turned upon me and knocked off my cap.

"Who're you? I wasn't talking to you, Mr. Jollocks! You sound like you know this mumbling cove, and maybe belong to his almighty club. What's a gentleman doing here in our pub? Or is Mr. High-and-Mighty spying on us? Admit it, gents – Don't 'e look like a spy?"

Sherlock pushed his way through the laughing and jeering crowd that had formed around the butler and myself. He stood next to me in a fighter's stance.

"Gentlemen," Sherlock said, "surely this difference of opinion is not worth a rumbunctious anointing? What will your Misses say to a blooded nose or even a half-mourning blinker?"

"From you? You're as thin as Job's turkey. Better watch that parish pick-axe don't weigh you down. You're off your chump!"

I watched incredulously as the foolish man actually took a swing at Sherlock. I had no fear, for my brother was a semi-professional bare-knuckled boxer. He'd acquired his pugilist skills first at Cambridge, and then in the private clubs, boxing in the ring with those who were far superior to his ability. Yet once he learned the sport, no one could beat him, for my brother's other talents assisted him in predicting his opponent's next move.

I was beginning to enjoy this outing and joined in the betting that had instantly encircled the two men.

"To the blood!" I yelled above the betting.

Sherlock smiled and parried the man's thrown punch, stopping his arm in mid-flight. Then he knocked him down with three rapid-fire lefts to the jaw. From behind, the darts chucker joined in the fray. Sherlock shifted, then addressed the man's wrist with baritsu, forcing him to his knees, and then the floor. When he again gained his feet, my brother threw his signature uppercut. Both men went down. We escorted the butler and the two underdogs outside for questioning. As soon as we gained the pavement, we sent the butler on his way home.

"I don't know no bloody Henry Baker!" the man who began the altercation said, blood streaming from his nose dotted the snow.

My brother gave him a handkerchief.

"Late Christmas Eve," Sherlock said, "you were part of a group of toughs who tormented Mr. Baker. A commissionaire approached you, and he and your gang ran. His sizable white Christmas goose and an old bowler hat were left behind."

"So what if we did? You're no bloody mutton-shunter."

"My name is Sherlock Holmes." He extended his hand. "I'm looking for Mr. Baker. If you can direct me to him, I'll give each of you a half-sovereign."

This changed the energy completely. The air of danger receded, and its opposite expressed itself.

"I'm Barney. And you, sir – Would be Doctor Watson?"

"Forgive me," Sherlock answered. "This is my friend, Mike."

I smiled and tipped my cap. Barney put out his hand. Sherlock elbowed me into action, and I shook it. His grip was surprisingly commanding, reminiscent of Sir James Walter of the Admiralty.

The darts man introduced himself as Tommy. Throughout, he hurried Barney along with cold-related comments and the men quickly brought us to the Goodge Street crime scene.

"We don't know him, but he broke the window of that wine shop." Tommy pointed at the debris. "I'll bet his stick is still around here somewhere, Guv! But none of us knew him," Tommy added.

Sherlock gave each a half-sovereign and released them. I watched as they stomped their way through the snow and headed back towards the pub. My brother was analysing the scene before us. He paced with light, swift steps about the area. I felt it obsessive, especially in the cold weather, yet he called out important points to me.

"Stay where you are, Mycroft! Though this affair had occurred nearly thirty-six hours ago, there are still signs of what occurred. And snow, though damaged easily, is the best substance for foot impressions. The scuffle took place here. Can you see where these footprints overlap? Here's the commissionaire's running tiptoes on top of them! Baker's stick went through the shop window, recently smashed and now boarded up until the glass can be replaced. A shame. I had hoped his stick remained, but it's gone. It would have led me to him."

"Sherlock, are you satisfied, I'm freezing!"

We returned to the borrowed cab, where he paid the street urchin – who immediately ran inside the warm public house. We mounted the carriage and Sherlock, in his cabbie persona, drove me back to the Diogenes Club, where he took the rug from me and swaddled the horse in its warmth.

As the short winter sun began to colour the Stranger's Room windows, I added coal to the fire and handed my brother a warming brandy. Then I went and brought back our cold repast. We pulled chairs up to the blazing fire and talked over the day. Sherlock threw his cigar into the flames, downed his drink, and sat rubbing his hands together for warmth.

"Sherlock, you see importance where no one else can. It was exhilarating, but what was that about?"

"You know my methods."

"Not as well as you do. For instance, how did you single out your suspect? To me, he was the same as all the others."

"That is your blindness. I make a point of never having any prejudices, and of following docilely wherever fact may lead me. The man was wearing a scarf of the green-and-gold Baker Clan plaid knotted around his neck. A simple thing."

"A-ha! He may have been related to Baker, or he had stolen the scarf. Either way, you win, Sherlock."

"Yes, and the fact that as soon as he realised my purpose, he hid this adornment deep inside his coat, underlining my deductions. But surely you noticed this."

"What I did observe was the fact that the shop window was recently boarded up, leaving you no trifles with which to work. Baker's cane was gone, and whatever snow there was has been slushed over by the boots of those passing through Goodge Street."

"That is fine observation for a scavenger hunt. Yet in deduction, it is necessary to sift through clues and keep only the relevant ones. Speculations without facts to back them up can lead to an exhaustive pursuit of an erroneous scent. Are these your only conclusions from this year's Boxing Day game, Brother?"

"Of course not. The majority of the patrons of the pub were humorously enjoying each other's company, while one or two were agitators. I find this same state of affairs can exist in any group of people, even political meetings where the agitators might serve a purpose. Perhaps I ought to offer half-sovereigns the next time I encounter such? Then, there was the fact that you brought me into a dangerous situation. Now, please enjoy some of this splendid goose, dear boy. Where will you go from here?"

Sherlock sighed. "The horse must be returned, and then I'll await further developments. After all, only a goose and a man's hat are at stake. I'll study the hat for clues, and perhaps put out an advertisement or two. That will be the end of it. Mr. Baker is sure to keep an eye on the newspapers, since, to a poor man, the loss was a heavy one."

I thought it the right moment to gift him his pub winnings, which he accepted with a laugh.

"Thank you, Guv!" he said.

We finished the wine and I succeeded in serving him the goose, pudding, mince pie, and the rest.

Following our feast, I poured out two tumblers full of brandy and handed one to my brother. He nodded his thanks and accepted a cigar. I am not a pipe fancier. I prefer the refinement and violet perfume of Royal snuff. But Sherlock revelled in his smoke.

"I wonder," I said, "if Mr. Baker might not give it all up as a loss and just purchase a new hat?"

"Quite possibly. Yet, it's just as possible is that my advertisement will bring him to 221b Baker Street . . . ."

The fire was fed once again. We watched as the flames danced higher, throwing animated shadows on the stone walls of the large hearth.

"What did you think of my Boxing Day game, Mycroft?"

"Somewhat reminiscent of the year the Vicar caught us after one too many eggnogs, and our unforgettable harmonizing during the carols service."

"Yes," he laughed, "that was an excellent Boxing Day diversion."

We then toasted the day and those who served us, our brotherhood, our friends, and the coming New Year, 1888.

The Case of
Colonel Warburton's Madness
by Jane Rubino

I have said elsewhere that, in the course of my friend's long career, I had introduced only two cases to his notice: That of the attack upon young Mr. Hatherley, and that of Colonel Warburton's madness. At the time of the former's publication, I had implied that the young engineer's problem was the more strange and dramatic of the two, while the Warburton matter offered the better display of observation and deduction. In so saying, I did not mean to suggest that the Warburton case was lacking in novelty or intrigue. It may simply have been prevarication on my part, an unwillingness to resurrect a particularly abhorrent case, and one to which I had a personal connection.

The latter half of '88 had subjected all of London to prolonged periods of erratic and unseasonable weather, and the early September day which begins my narrative was particularly intolerable and bleak. The howling winds and unrelenting patter of rain upon our windows, when combined with the moodiness of my companion and the unwholesome fumes raised up by one of his malodorous experiments – (both expressions of his frustration concerning some puzzling atrocities in the vicinity of Whitechapel) – wore upon my nerves, and at last I decided to escape to my club.

I had expected the Windham to be as glum as Baker Street, for many of those who had the means to escape town had done so, and those who took to the club were inclined to hibernate in the library where they would thumb and yawn their way through the newspapers, too dull to engage in conversation. I was surprised, therefore to see a half-dozen fellows in a cluster chattering in hushed tones. "Watson!" called Jim Dunlap – Doctor James Dunlap, who had proposed my membership at the Windham – "You've heard the shocking news about Warburton?"

"Colonel Robert Warburton?"

Dunlap nodded. "A mate of yours, wasn't he? Gone quite off his head. Not two hours ago, he went charging through Lambeth, drew a Baldock from his waist, and began slashing through the crowd, crying out 'Kandahar! Maiwand!' and throwing the crowd into a panic. He wounded a few passers-by and killed one of them, then tried to turn the blade on himself before it was snatched from his grasp."

It would be exaggeration to say that Robert Warburton and I were ever "mates". We two had been in the same regiment, and as we advanced from Bombay to Kandahar, we often came together at muster, as "Watson" followed after "Warburton". Fortune divided us, however, for upon him it bestowed honors and promotion, while I suffered only pain and despair. Not until I was at the base hospital at Peshawar, indulging in gossip with my fellow convalescents, did I understand how far Warburton's good fortune was the result of shrewd, calculating ambition which, combined with handsome exterior and ingratiating manner, allowed him to secure both preferments and exemptions that ought to have gone elsewhere, and to fashion a reputation for courage and honor, though upon strict examination, one would be hard-pressed to distinguish any act of bravery or mark of integrity.

I had little cause for resentment – we had never been on intimate terms, and he had taken no privilege that ought to have gone to me. Still, I was undeniably moved, and bewildered, by the announcement. Had I been told that Warburton had sunk to vice, or even crime, I might have believed it. Our past acquaintance, however slight, had exposed me to his profligate nature, and I have since seen how short a drop it may be from the immoral to the illegal. Still, excess is not madness, and if pressed on the point, I would have sworn that Warburton was as sane a man as I.

"He is the very last fellow I should peg to go off like that!" said one fellow.

"Very few walk away from battle unscathed," said another, who had been, like myself, a military man. "Sometimes its horrors may come upon a fellow years after he returns to civilian life."

They continued to debate Warburton's bizarre conduct for some time, drawing me into the discussion with "What would Mister Sherlock Holmes make of the matter?" and "How do you think your detective friend would approach the case?" until at last I threw up my hands and cried, "He would tell me not to form theories before I have all of the facts."

The facts were too recent and too few for the evening newspapers to get 'hold of them, and so I had to wait until the following day to hunt up any details of the matter. I rose early to collect the morning editions, and when Holmes came to breakfast, he found me as I so often had found him, sitting at the table surrounded by a cloud of morning papers.

"A matter of personal interest, I take it," said Holmes, as he poured out his coffee.

"How can you know that?"

"The advent of war would have you knocking me from my bed, and no commonplace crime would account for this litter," he said, with a wave of his hand toward my papers. "No, it is a matter of some consequence, or

372

you wouldn't have put off your breakfast to run out for the papers – you would have sent the boy – but you wanted to begin going over them straight away. Hence, it is personal."

I nodded. "Yesterday evening a fellow took up a knife and went slashing his way through a crowded street in Lambeth. A few were injured, and one fellow was killed."

"My dear Watson!" Holmes cried. "Was one of the victims an acquaintance?"

"No. The injured were working class fellows, and the dead man was a pantomime performer at Sanger's. But I was once acquainted with the assailant."

"My dear fellow!" Holmes snatched the papers one after another, reading over the reports of the crime, then laid them in a stack upon the hearth. "The reports all seem to agree that it was some past ordeal which brought on this bout of madness."

"At my club, they are of the same opinion, and I know from experience what war-time experiences may do to one's nerves. Yet, I can think of no ordeal that would have sent Warburton off his head. In the past, a heavy loss at cards may have done it, but he is now better able indulge his passion for playing high – or so I have been told."

"What have you been told?"

"I know that he lives in London, though I've seen nothing of him since our military days – fortune has placed us in very different spheres. I am told that he married an heiress, enjoys a life of extravagance and ease, keeps very fast company, plays heavily at cards, and generally lives in a far better style than most of his former comrades. On those rare occasions when his name will crop up, it has always been 'that lucky devil, Warburton'."

"In my experience, devils are deliberate, calculating creatures who rarely rely upon luck."

My response was interrupted by the sound of the bell, which Holmes half-expected to herald the arrival of Lestrade or someone else from the official force, but the card that was sent up was handed to me.

"Why, it's Murray!" I cried, and hurrying to the landing, I called down without ceremony, "Murray! Come up, old fellow!"

Murray, you will recall from my earliest account, had been my orderly at Maiwand. It was he who threw my wounded and near lifeless form across a pack horse and got me to safety. Until I was put on the train to Peshawar, he remained at my side, dividing his attentions equally between the pack-horse and myself, for he had a great fondness for animals, and was known to shed as many tears for a fallen horse as for a fallen comrade. I had heard that when he returned to England, he had entered the Royal Veterinary College and graduated with distinction, and then went up to Scotland to continue his studies.

But for a touch of gray in his brown mop and a slight limp, which called for the assistance of a cane, he was the same tall, rangy fellow I'd known in Maiwand, only the regimentals had been replaced by a seedy frock coat, gaiters, and a flannel traveling cap, and he now sported a stout mustache.

"Watson!" he cried as he clapped me on the shoulder and gripped my hand. "I should know you anywhere!"

"A shabby compliment, Murray! When you last laid eyes upon me, I was limp and bleeding and lying across a pack-horse."

"Old Chance! What a courageous beast he was!"

I laughed at that, and said, "Allow me to introduce you to Mr. Sherlock Holmes. Doctor John Murray."

The two shook hands, and Holmes moved to withdraw, but Murray protested. "If you please, Mr. Holmes – I come to chew over a matter with my old comrade, but some years ago, I read a piece said to be the work of Sherlock Holmes – *The Book of Life*, it was called – and thought it quite smart. I would appreciate your view of the situation as well."

Holmes gave a wry smile at Murray's remark, waved the fellow into a chair, and sat. "You have come up from Surrey?"

"Indeed I have!"

"The spattering of loam and clay upon your gaiters is suggestive of Surrey. There are other regions where that particular mixture might be found, but none near enough to have you arrive at our humble rooms so early in the morning."

"I make my home in Surrey now," said Murray, as he sat and laid his cane on the hearth. "Or return to it, rather as family had long resided there. My father had been a work rider for Lord Singleford, as was his father before him, and when I was a lad of ten, I was put to work in the stables, which nurtured in me a love of animals. When I returned from the wars, I took my degree at the Royal Veterinary College, and over time gained some small reputation for my skill with thoroughbred horses. Little more than a year ago, Lord Singleford wrote to me to ask if I would return to Surrey to work exclusively for his stables and kennels, offering me a handsome salary and a small lodge upon his grounds. I asked only that I be given leave to devote a few days every month to the animal clinics that serve the poor of East London and Lambeth, to which he agreed."

"Now, as I have said, I had worked for Lord Singleford in my younger days, and as such became acquainted with his ward, Lady Alice Ramsay, who was an orphan, the only child of his Lordship's sister. From infancy, she had always been frail, and her doctors believed that regular exercise

374

would improve her health and stamina, so I was given the role of riding master and companion, attending her – always accompanied by her governess or chaperone – when she went for a gallop or for a stroll about the grounds with her dogs. Of course, there was no attachment beyond a mutual love of horses and dogs – our spheres were very different, and I knew my place. If she liked me at all, it was only that she saw so little of anyone else, for her condition kept her from much society – and she was grateful to me, as I once saved the life of her favorite terrier.

"When I joined the regiment, she promised to write to me, and in fact, she did so – that is, when Lord Singleford very kindly wrote to inform me of the death of my good father, she was permitted to enclose a few lines of her own. I expected nothing more, of course – the routes were very poor, and the mails very irregular – and so I had supposed at the time that even if she did write, her letters wouldn't have found their way to me."

"So you had supposed *at the time*," Holmes leaned back in his chair, his finger-tips pressed together. "But afterward you had reason to suppose otherwise. Supposed, perhaps, that the lady *had* written, and that her correspondence had been intercepted on its way to you."

"Well, it is true that I may have mentioned Lord Singleford and Lady Alice in someone's hearing around camp."

"And this man stole your correspondence," I theorized.

"I cannot say that with any certainty, I can say only that to do so wouldn't have been beneath the Warburton I knew."

"Warburton?" I asked with surprise. "Colonel Robert Warburton from our regiment?"

Murray nodded. "That's why I'm here. After his arrest, I'm concerned about Lady Alice. I've long suspected that Warburton read my letters while we were overseas and learned about Lord Singleford and Alice. He hadn't known either of them beforehand, and yet when I returned to England, several months after the Colonel, I heard that he and Alice – Lady Alice – were engaged to be married."

"*She* was the heiress that Warburton married." I understood.

Murray nodded, gravely.

"So," said Holmes, in a languid fashion, "this cunning fellow intercepts your correspondence, ingratiates himself to Lord Singleford, and wins the affection and the hand of his ward. The lady's fortune, I daresay, is considerable."

"The dowry was rumored to be six figures, Mr. Holmes, but that is only a small portion of her fortune. There was a sizeable inheritance from the Earl – her father – which was to be held in trust – the trustee being Lord Singleford – until her thirtieth birthday."

"Pray, what is the lady's age?"

"She will be thirty on the first of December."

"Then in just under three months, she will have full control of her inheritance."

"Yes."

"I understand from Watson that the Warburtons make their home in town."

Murray nodded. "Lady Alice has a property in her own right – a pleasant little villa in the vicinity of Cranleigh – but it is all shut up. After their marriage, I called at Grosvenor Crescent to offer my best wishes, but I was told that Warburton wasn't at home, and that he had instructed the staff to turn away callers, as his wife's poor health didn't allow her to receive visitors. Afterward, I spent some years in Glasgow, and so I neither saw nor heard anything of the Warburtons until Lord Singleford offered me my present situation."

"And, pray, what does his Lordship tell you how?"

"That the Colonel spends a great deal of time at cards or the races – he was always a keen one for a wager – while Lady Alice's health allows her to leave her home only for the occasional turn 'round the park in her carriage, attended by a maid or her nurse, and that she receives no visitors but for his Lordship and the solicitors."

"Solicitors," muttered Holmes. "Who advise her in the matter of her trust, which will end in a few months, and give her sole control of her fortune. And since you don't mention children, that fortune would pass to the Colonel in the event of his wife's demise. A prospect," Holmes added, wryly, "that should motivate a gentleman whose wife is in frail health to keep a firm grip on his wits."

Murray shifted in his chair, uncomfortably. "I am bound to say that he appeared to have a hold on the reins whenever I happened to see him – all but for the most recent occasion."

Holmes sat upright. "You've seen the fellow? When?"

"Last spring, and several times after. Unlike many of our comrades, the Colonel managed to avoid the sort of hardships that coarsen a fellow's features or cripple his frame. I knew him straight off. He was as fit and fine-looking as ever."

"Where did you see him?" I asked.

"As I said, Lord Singleford permits me to continue on at the poor clinics, and so I travel regularly from Surrey, usually at week's end. I first spied him boarding the train at Epsom – he in a first class carriage, and I somewhat behind in second class. I had heard that he was often at Epsom and the Downs during the season, visiting the various stables and wagering on the races, though we never happened to meet. My own journey takes me to Waterloo, but there is a stop at Sutton, and I happened to glance out the window and saw the Colonel spring down and look around at the passengers boarding the train, and then wave to a lady and take her by the hand – "

"So it appeared to you that they were acquainted?" Holmes asked. "And the lady wasn't his wife?"

Murray shook his head. "I got no more than a glimpse before they boarded, and her back was to me, and her face veiled, but her traveling dress was plain dark stuff, nothing that I imagine Lady Alice would wear. She was tall as well, and I saw a suspicion of dark hair above her collar – Lady Alice is small and fair-haired. When we drew into Waterloo, they alighted together and spoke for a minute or two on the platform, her hand in his the whole time. I tried to get a better look at her, but they parted and I lost sight of them both in the crowd. You know what Waterloo is."

Holmes nodded, absently. "And this was some months ago, yet it seemed that they were known to one another."

"Yes."

"Pray, continue."

"Five or six times, over the course of the summer, when I traveled up to town, I witnessed the same scene. At Sutton Station, the Colonel would alight to fetch the lady into his compartment and they would alight together at Waterloo."

"She was always veiled?"

"Yes."

Murray nodded. "It was about five weeks ago when I saw them again, and on this occasion, they didn't part at the station, but went off together in a hansom. It was the last time I saw anything of the lady, but not ten days ago, at Waterloo, I saw Warburton stagger from a compartment alone, stumble onto the platform, gesticulating and muttering, his hair and clothing all in disarray. I would have gone to his aid, but a porter took him by the arm and motioned for a colleague's assistance, and together they managed to get him into the waiting room." Murray paused. "I felt duty-bound to report what I saw to Lord Singleford – "

"You reported only that last incident," said Holmes, "and not any of his rendezvous with the lady."

Murray nodded, uneasily. "I didn't think it was my place to gossip. As for that last episode, his Lordship had set it down to drink or indulgence at the time, but now wonders whether the episode may have been a hint of the Colonel's deterioration, and whether yesterday's tragedy might have been forestalled if his Lordship had looked more closely into the matter. This morning, we came up to town together, for Lord Singleford intends to call upon his solicitors to determine whether anything might be done to defend the Colonel."

"What defense, other than insanity, can be offered for a fellow who charges into a crowd shouting 'Kandahar!' and 'Maiwand!', and then mortally wounds a passer-by?"

"None, I should think. But his Lordship isn't only concerned with the Colonel's motives, but for the effect this will have upon his niece. The Colonel is held where he cannot harm himself or another, but *she* must be quite out of her head with distress. Lord Singleford asked if I would call at Grosvenor Crescent, while he is with his solicitors – he believes that the sight of a familiar face may do some good. I made so bold as to ask if I might bring a trusted friend with me – an excellent physician I had known in my Army days and one whose opinion of Lady Alice's appearance would be of more value than mine. He provided me with a note and his card in case there is any unwillingness on the part of the staff to admit me. Will you come with me, Watson?"

"Of course I will go."

With that, we all rose, and as Murray turned to pick up his stick, he spied the stack of newspapers upon the hearth. Snatching one up, he gave a cry and said, "Why – why – I haven't yet seen the latest newspapers! Is *this* the fellow Warburton killed?"

The newspaper had no photograph of the victim, and so had printed a coarse reproduction of one of the bills from Sanger's Amphitheatre, where he had been a performer.

Holmes and I exchanged a puzzled glance. "Do you know him?" Holmes enquired.

"Yes – that is to say, I exchanged a few words with him, many months ago. Poor Shrewsbury!"

"The papers gave the fellow's name as 'Fleming'."

"Oh, not the fellow. The old mare. Shrewsbury. Last January, Sanger had me look her over, to see if she was long for the ring, and that was when I met Fleming. Hugh Fleming, his name was – he was one of Sanger's pantomimes, but he made a few extra pounds working in the stables. I was compelled to tell Sanger that poor Shrewsbury's best days had passed, and later heard that she'd been brought down by the wolves that had escaped his menagerie, and remember thinking that it had all been a grand stunt, one which allowed Sanger to put poor Shrewsbury out of her misery."

"And as to Mr. Fleming?" Holmes prompted.

"Oh, yes! I only saw him that one time, but I recall thinking what a fine-looking fellow he was – far better suited to the stage than to stables – and so I wasn't surprised when one of the other animal keepers mentioned that Fleming once *had* made a living on the stage, and a good one, but the trade became difficult to keep up, what with so few roles, and so many actors about."

"And so many lunatics as well, it seems," said Holmes, as Murray and I departed. "*My* trade would be difficult to keep up without them."

The Warburtons resided in one of those grand London fortresses that would seem a more suitable prison than mansion. The footman who answered our ring seemed about to turn us away when Murray presented him with Lord Singleford's note. This was carried up, and in a few moments we were ushered to a large suite, that was part-sitting room and part-bedchamber. The apartment was handsomely furnished, but decorated in such heavy fabrics and dark colors its appearance was more oppressive than cheerful.

There were two women in the room when we entered. The slight, fragile blonde reclining upon a tufted satin chaise was Lady Alice Warburton. Her small frame was covered in shawls and her complexion was so pale as to appear translucent. Behind her, a tall, slender woman in a gray frock turned away from a task in which she had been engaged and gave us a nod in greeting. There couldn't have been a greater contrast between the two women, for this lady was a striking brunette whose brilliant dark eyes, sensual mouth, and exquisite coloring could only be described as artistic. Her bearing, too, hinted at a strong character, one capable of great self-control, while Lady Alice fairly quivered with emotion.

"Dear Jack! How kind you are to come!" Tears welled up in Lady Alice's blue eyes, and she held out her hands to my friend. "This is Annie, my nurse. I should be so lost without her!"

Murray gave a "Very pleased to know you," to the nurse, then drew an ottoman beside the chaise and took Lady Alice's small hands in his. The nurse meanwhile resumed her task, removing a small packet from a box upon the sideboard, where a tray of tonics, spoons, and pill bottles were assembled. She poured the powdered contents of the packet into a tumbler of water. "You mustn't work yourself into a state," she said in a soothing tone, as she handed the tumbler to her patient. "You must be strong for your husband's sake."

Lady Alice drank the concoction, obediently as a child, and then handed the tumbler to the nurse. "I will try!" she said. "But I am so frightened, Jack! And yet – I should have seen that it would come to this! What am I to do?"

"You must do as your nurse advises and not work yourself into a state. Think only of your own health, and leave all else to Lord Singleford, and to me, for I am at your service entirely. Lady Alice Warburton, allow me to present an old friend from our army days, Doctor John Watson."

"A doctor?" said the nurse, with a lift of her dark brows. "Lady Alice sees only those specialists engaged by Colonel Warburton."

"I am not here in any professional capacity," I assured the woman. "Only to be of use to my friend. Murray once did me a good turn on the field of battle, and I am in his debt."

"Jack's friends must be mine as well." Lady Alice held out her hand to me, and then turned back to her old acquaintance. "I thought I might see something of you, Jack, after you took a post with my uncle. When you answered none of my letters, I thought you had forgotten about me."

"The mails – there is often difficulty – a foreign post isn't as it is here," stammered Murray. "Lady Alice, if I may ask – I do not mean to pain you, but you said just now that you should have seen that matters would come to this – What did you mean by that?"

A slight flush colored the lady's colorless cheek. "Only that Robert has been – for some weeks – not quite himself. Annie observed it, too. Didn't you?"

"I am sorry to say that the Colonel's conduct has been very erratic of late." The nurse bent down to adjust her patient's shawl and to give the lady a comforting pat on the shoulder. "He could be quite good-humored, and then become absent-minded and forgetful or have a sudden fit of temper. One of the maids confided to me that he worked himself into such a frenzy over a trifle that she was afraid he might become violent."

"He has never been rough with you?" demanded Murray.

"Oh, no!" Lady Alice's lips began to tremble. "Never violent – but Floss! Poor little Floss!" She was then overtaken with a fit of sobbing and the nurse leaned down to comfort her, and gave Murray a look that urged us to bring the interview to an end.

Murray rose and, taking the lady's hand, he urged her once more to think only of her health and leave all else to himself and Lord Singleford. Murray then promised to call again, and we bade the ladies a good morning.

"Your mistress and her nurse tell us that there has lately been a change for the worse in your master's conduct," I said to the footman as he handed us our umbrellas.

The fellow hesitated for a moment, uncertain as to how far he ought to confide in us. At last he said, "The Colonel was an easy-enough master, and she is very quiet and makes few demands of us – her nurse sees to all of her needs. We have been very quiet until some weeks ago."

"What happened?"

"It seemed that a change came upon him. He would be calm one moment and then a terror the next. In a fit of temper, he smashed a porcelain ornament that had been given the Warburtons as a wedding present, and I know that the mistress was quite fond of it, and when her Lady Alice's little terrier snapped at him, he ordered me to take it to the animal refuge at Holloway. If she didn't have Miss Fraser to steady her, I don't know what how we should manage. Not that Miss Thompson was wanting, so far as I could see – "

"Miss Thompson?"

"Lady Alice's last nurse. She had been with us since last year, when the mistress suffered a nervous complaint, but Miss Thompson was a small woman, and fifty if she was a day, and the Colonel believed that Lady Alice needed a stronger arm to help her from the bed and support her when she went about, so last month, he discharged Miss Thompson and engaged Miss Fraser."

"And your mistress didn't object to the change?"

"Perhaps a bit at first, but Miss Fraser seems an excellent nurse, and the mistress has got to where she couldn't bear to do without her."

"The blackguard!" Murray hissed as soon as the door was closed upon us. "To take letters she wrote to me is bad enough. But to take away her dog! And such a dreary house! It would drive me mad to live in such a tomb."

"I must agree. I don't like her color – she would certainly benefit from light and fresh air. If you have any influence with Lord Singleford, have him bring Lady Alice to the country – to his estate if she doesn't want to open her own. Will you come back with me to Baker Street?"

Murray shook his head. "No. I am at the poor clinic for the rest of the day, but first I have an errand at Holloway. Thank you, Watson, you and Mr. Holmes both, for taking an interest in the matter!" And then he limped off to hail a cab.

I returned to Baker Street to find our rooms empty, with the *Bradshaw* spread out upon Holmes's desk, and a terse note left on mine which read: "*Refreshment rooms, Waterloo. Come. Holmes.*"

I set out for Waterloo Station, where I found Holmes drinking coffee in a corner of the refreshment room.

"What have you learned?" he demanded as I sat.

I gave a brief recital of our call at Grosvenor Crescent, and then drew out a small paper packet. "The nurse keeps a box of these packets at hand, and I managed to slip one into my pocket as we were saying our farewells. A powder of some sort that is dissolved in water. I thought you might like to analyze the contents."

"You are coming along nicely, Watson." Holmes poked a finger into the packet and drew out a bit of its white powder, held it to his nose, and brushed it against his tongue. "Offhand, I would say that it powdered opium – an unusually strong concentration, perhaps. Under the circumstances, it wouldn't be uncommon for the lady's physicians to prescribe sedation."

"There were a few dozen of these packets. Do they anticipate keeping Lady Alice sedated for a month or more? My prescription would be to get her out of London and into the fresh air of Surrey. Murray has promised to speak to Lord Singleford about it. What have you been about?"

"I have already been to Surrey."

"In spirit, I surmise. I saw the *Bradshaw*."

"I was tracing out Warburton's trysts with this mysterious lady. Now we know that Warburton's passion for racing often brought him to the area around Epsom, and we know that when he returned to town, he boarded prior to the lady's station, which was at Sutton. So she either lived around Surrey and traveled frequently to town, or she lived in town, but had some matter that brought her regularly to Surrey. They met by coincidence, in the course of traveling from Sutton to Waterloo, and by the time your friend Murray spied them, it seems that a romantic relationship had begun. But," Holmes added, with a frown, "there is another quite separate conundrum. I have just come from the mortuary where they have laid out Warburton's victim. He was, as Murray stated, one Hugh Fleming, late of Sanger's Amphitheatre, where he earned his living as a pantomime performer, and supplemented that wage by helping to tend the animals. He was struck just once, a precise and fatal blow, the knife angled so that it would penetrate the victim's heart." Holmes tapped his breastbone. "The poor fellow was gone, I daresay, before he struck the pavement. Quite unusual."

"Not really, Holmes. Warburton was trained as a military man, and knew how to use a weapon."

"Yet only one fatal blow? If a trained military man goes off his head, believes himself to be in the thick of it at Kandahar and Maiwand, and views the crowd milling about as the enemy hoards, I would expect to see that more had been seriously wounded. Yet there were only three victims other than the Colonel, and all three came away with scarcely a scratch. In one case, it was merely a torn sleeve that never touched the flesh."

"One cannot explain the actions of a madman."

"Then when facts are in short supply, one must imagine," he said. "Not that one should cease to gather data." He rose to don his hat and take up his umbrella. "Will you come?"

"Where?"

"Fleming's residence. He lodged in a house along Mason's Terrace, and it happens that his landlady is a past acquaintance of mine."

A brief cab ride took us to a tributary of Westminster Bridge Road, and then along a narrow street lined with two-and three-story houses.

Holmes stepped up to one, pulled the bell, and in a moment, the door was answered by a most unusual creature. She was nearer fifty than forty, and quite short in a stature that was all the shorter for her stooped bearing, the result, I deduced from her crutches, of some old injury. She was attired in a bright silk blouse and loose trousers, her hair was arranged in brassy ringlets framing a thickly rouged and powdered face. Her eyes were a bright, brilliant blue and they brightened more as they fixed on my companion.

"Why it's young Sherlock Holmes!" she cried. "Don't you look fine!"

"Doctor Watson, allow me to present Signorina Vittoria, the belle of Cooke, Fanque, and Sanger, equestrienne extraordinaire."

"'Belle!'" she snorted. "That's all past! It's just plain Jennie Victor now – Jennie Teasedale," she corrected. "I'm only two years married and not quite used to being a missus."

She waved us into a comfortable parlor, one papered wall covered with framed bills of a young Vittoria standing upright upon a galloping horse. "Our boarders keep me close to the sawdust – they're circus folk for the most part. So," she said, grimly. "I expect you've come about poor Hughie."

"He was one of your boarders."

"He was. Poor chaps, Hughie. And that mad Colonel that was mentioned in the newspapers as well."

"I should think you'd reserve all of your pity for Mr. Fleming," I said.

"Hughie's pain's over an' done with, while the Colonel's lives on with his devils. I'd sooner lose an arm than go off my head like that."

"May I have a look at Mr. Fleming's rooms?" Holmes asked.

"If you like – just go on up the stairs to the landing and a door to the right. I had the door left unlocked, half-expecting a Yarder to come by, but I imagine there's nothing for them to puzzle over, as it's clear who done it."

Holmes nodded grimly, and together we mounted the stairs and opened the door to a handsome sitting room, with a bedroom door to our left. The sitting room was large and carpeted, curtained and furnished in a style more fashionable than I should have imagined a circus performer would choose, or could afford. The walls were decorated in the same style as the hall below with framed bills, these featuring a brief history of Hugh Fleming's career at the Opera Comique, the Adelphi, the Lyceum.

Holmes studied the bills. "Hmm! Romeo in 'sixty-seven, Fabien and Louis in *The Corsican Brothers* in 'seventy, *Penzance* in 'seventy-nine. Come!"

Holmes led me into the bedroom. There was a large double bed with a satin coverlet, a night table on either side, a high, carved oak wardrobe, a dressing table with a gilt-framed mirror above it, and an upholstered chaise set beside a small, lace-covered table.

Holmes looked over the furnishings, opened the wardrobe and a few drawers, and then turned his attention to the stout scrapbook upon the night table. "It ends with his last role on the stage, several years ago. There are no bills from Sanger's."

"I suppose Shakespeare's Romeo may not want mementos of his demotion to circus performer."

"A circus performer," Holmes muttered, absently. He closed the book and ran his eyes around the room once more. "Do you find anything unusual about these rooms, Watson?"

"The furnishings seem unusually fine for a lodging house."

"And unusually fine for a circus performer. Well, well, there is nothing to be learned here to suggest any link at all between Fleming and Warburton."

"Surely you didn't think that there was one!"

"I wasn't prepared to eliminate the possibility," was his reply, and together we descended the stairs to find Fleming's landlady waiting in the parlor.

"Your tenant had quite a career on the stage," he said to her.

"That he did! I saw him in *Penzance*, and he was just grand! Handsome as the Devil, and didn't the girls all fall in love with the Pirate King!" She sighed. "And then, the roles just got smaller and smaller until there were no roles at all, and him scarcely forty years old. It's a tiresome trade, acting is, always trying to please a fickle public. As bad as trying to please his fickle wife."

"A wife!" cried Holmes. "Fleming was married?"

"Oh, yes – or was, at least, when they took up here. They'd fine digs somewhere around Covent Garden, but when Hughie's roles got scarce, they needed to find something that wasn't so dear. The furnishings were those he'd already bought when they were in silver, so he had them carted here. He thought it would please the missus, I expect, though from what little I saw, there was no pleasing her. I expect she longed for the old life – not just the money, but the fawning, and the high company and such. His trade and her beauty put them in a smart set at one time."

"Well, where is Mrs. Fleming now?"

The lady shrugged her shoulders. "I've seen not hide nor hair for – it must be more than four weeks now, and even before that, what I did see of her was on the weekends."

"Weekends?"

The lady nodded. "Hughie was just making ends meet at Sanger's, and so last winter, she decides she must find work – what or where, I cannot say, only from something Hughie dropped, I believe it was somewhere near Reigate. At any rate, she would go off on Monday morning and not return until week's end, and as that's when it's liveliest at Sanger's, so I don't know that even he saw much of her then, and for the past month or so, Hughie's moped about and dined alone, and the maid told me that that the missus' clothes were gone, and at last I got up nerve enough to ask him where she was and he said she'd decided to live nearer her post, as it had got too tedious to rattle back and forth every week."

"Did Mr. Fleming ever mention what that post was?"

"No. Not in service. I expect she would have found that beneath her."

"Had Fleming any family other than his wife?"

"Poor Hughie once told me all his family were gone, and when he lost his fame, most of his friends went as well, save for Breezy Bill. They'd trod the boards together in better days, and whenever he could, Bill brought Hughie brought in as a super, or even got him a line or two. I don't know where Bill hangs his hat, but three o'clock or thereabouts you'll find him taking a late lunch in his dressing room. He's at the Adelphi now in *The Union Jack*. Just give the manager my name, and he'll let you pass through."

Holmes bade the woman farewell, and glanced at his watch as we stepped out into the rain. "Not yet one o'clock. Let us return to Baker Street and our own luncheon and continue our researches at three."

He hailed a cab, directing the cabby to stop at the nearest post office and to wait while he dashed in to dispatch a telegram. "To our Reigate confederate, Inspector Forrester," he said, as he climbed back into the cab. "I asked him to inquire around to any establishments in the district that may have employed our cold-hearted Mrs. Fleming."

"You are hard on her, Holmes. Perhaps she hasn't heard of his death yet."

"Reigate isn't Rome. Such a sensational item must find its way into one of its half-dozen or so editions. If she stays away, it cannot be due to ignorance of the tragedy."

"Perhaps something *keeps* her away."

"Or some*one*."

"Someone who lives in Reigate?"

"Or," Holmes said, pointedly, "someone who traveled regularly by rail from Surrey to Waterloo Station. It may be that Mrs. Fleming is a link between her husband and his murderer."

"That would give even more reason for her to hide herself. She certainly wouldn't want to be known as a woman who drove her lover mad enough to kill her husband."

"But that may come to light whether she comes forward or stays away."

We returned to Baker Street for a lunch and a pipe, and at three o'clock prepared to set out for the Adelphi. As we descended the stair, a wire arrived for Holmes, which he opened in the cab. "'*No data on a Mrs. Fleming. Will continue. Exodus Five.*'" He shoved the paper into his pocket and, to my puzzled expression, chuckled. "*Exodus* Chapter Five – I ask him to make bricks without straw."

As Mrs. Teasedale had said, her name was all the entrée we needed to be admitted to the Adelphi and ushered to the dressing rooms below the stage. Our knock was answered with a stentorian, "Come!" and we entered a small, well-mirrored chamber to find the famed actor, William Terriss, lounging on a velvet chaise, a book in his lap.

"Mr. Terriss, my name is Sherlock Holmes, and this is my friend and associate, Dr. Watson. We've come to ask about your friend, Hugh Fleming. I understand that you have known him for some time."

The fellow nodded, gravely. "Twenty years."

"Had you ever met his wife?"

"Not before they married. Poor fellow! Do sit!" he said, and settled upon the chaise once more. "You must understand, he was handsome as the Devil and, for a time, enjoyed tremendous success on the stage. Every night, women would flock at the stage door and wait for Romeo or the Pirate King to show himself. The marriage came after a whirlwind courtship, and took many of us by surprise – at least until we saw his young wife, for she was one of the most beautiful women I ever laid eyes on. They made a handsome pair, and when he was at his peak, they had entrée to the very best circles. But ours isn't an easy profession, nor a reliable one. Skill doesn't ensure success. I have seen superb performers who fail to please the public, and mediocre ones who tread the boards for a lifetime. When his career began to founder – Ah, well! '*Thus, grief still trods upon the heels of pleasure. Married in haste, we may repent at leisure.*'"

"And Mrs. Fleming began to repent the whirlwind courtship and hasty union."

Terriss nodded. "But of course, it was Mrs. Fraser, not Fleming."

"What?" Holmes roared.

"It is quite common." The actor, pointed toward himself. "William Terriss is William Charles Lewin. My wife was Isabelle Lewis before she adopted 'Amy Fellowes' for the stage. And Hugh? He was Hubert Fraser."

"*Fraser*," Holmes muttered. "Thank you, Mr. Terriss. You have been very helpful."

"A noble soldier has lost his wits, and Hugh is cut down in his prime. How can either of them be helped?"

Holmes only thanked the actor again and took his leave. "You're quite certain," Holmes asked, as we hopped into a cab, "that Lady Alice's nurse was named 'Fraser'?"

"Yes – that is, the footman referred to her as *Miss* Fraser – Lady Alice was on a more familiar footing, and called her 'Annie'. Your suspicions were correct then – Warburton and Mrs. Fleming – or Fraser – met as fellow travelers, a friendship develops between them, and then something more than friendship. But to bring the woman into his home, to engage her as his wife's nurse, so that they may carry on their love affair under the roof that his wife's fortune has paid for! It is insufferable!"

"True, he doesn't shine as a soldier or a husband, but this new information raises a sobering question of whether the Colonel was truly mad when he charged through that crowd, or was it all a performance? Had it been his object all along to get rid of an inconvenient husband by disguising a deliberate murder as the act of a madman?"

"But that makes no sense, Holmes! Such an act must lead to his own arrest. He is in custody now. Even *I* could do a better job getting rid of a rival."

"Watson, remind me to never underestimate you! But recall how the newspapers, and therefore the public, characterized the Colonel's actions. He is the military hero and the horrors of battle have caught up with him. His solicitors will argue for a ruling of insanity, to be detained at Her Majesty's pleasure."

"Detained, perhaps, for years."

Holmes shrugged his shoulders. "And perhaps not. You and Murray both observed that the Colonel was keen to take up a wager, and had a passion for playing high. What higher stake than his own liberty? He wagers that a military hero will not be given less consideration than Dudley and Stephens in eighty-four. In a few weeks, he will feign a slow return to sanity, an absence of any memory of his act, a pitiable display of contrition – a performance that would, I daresay, rival poor Fleming's. By the time his case is brought to the courts – if it is – he will be an excellent candidate for leniency."

"We should go to the police immediately."

"I would prefer to wait until I hear something more from Forrester. In the meantime, let us return to Baker Street. I can occupy myself with an analysis of the powder you so cleverly removed from the nurse's store."

"The nurse," I mused. "You know, she seemed cool enough this morning, but that may have been shock, and remorse as well. However far she may have allowed herself to fall in with Warburton's scheme, once she was introduced to her lover's wife, she may have seen matters in a more compassionate light. Perhaps what drove Warburton to the crime –

whether or not it was a crime of madness – was her decision to end their affair."

"I will leave the finer feelings of that sex to your analysis, Watson. But whether or not she has become genuinely fond of her patient, I think you would do well to redouble your efforts to have Murray to get Lady Alice out of London as soon as she is strong enough to travel."

At Baker Street, Holmes immediately busied himself with an analysis of the powder I had taken from Lady Alice's suite that morning. For some time, he sat before an array of bottles and test tubes, measuring and mixing and heating, no sound but for the clinking of the glass vials.

At last, he sat back and shook his head. "I was correct, it is powdered opium. Now, even dissolved in water, it would by no means be tasteless, but a patient in frail health would have become accustomed to some unpalatable concoctions, and you stated that Lady Alice was a very compliant subject."

"She took the tonic that she was given without question."

"It is the concentration that disturbs me. It is beyond what is generally a sedative dose, and great care would have to be given. It wouldn't take a very large amount to be fatal, particularly when the patient is small and frail."

He was interrupted by a knock at the door, and the page entered, handing a wire to Holmes. "Ah – it is from Forrester," he said and, running his eyes over the words, he leapt to his feet and snatched his coat. "Come, Watson! Come!" he cried, and dashed out of the room before I had risen from my chair. By the time I had reached the street, he was already in a cab and fairly pulled me in beside him, then called out the Warburton's Grosvenor Crescent address.

"What is it, Holmes?"

For an answer, he thrust the paper into my hands. "'*Miss Anne Fraser employed at Banstead Hospital since January,*'" I read. "'*Resigned post four weeks ago.*' This tells us nothing that we didn't already suspect, Banstead is along the branch line that links Epsom Downs to Sutton, which suggests that it was along this route, while the lady was still living with her husband, and Warburton was attending a race day, that she and the Colonel first met."

"It suggests more than that," Holmes muttered, his expression more dark and grave than I had ever seen before. "Cunning, cunning woman!"

At Grosvenor Crescent, Holmes tossed a few coins to the cabby, dashed up the walk, and pulled the bell with such force that he might have broken the wire. When his ring was answered, he thrust his card at the footman, and chafed so impatiently while it was carried up that I half-expected him to spring up the stairs and burst in upon the lady.

At last, we were ushered to the lady's boudoir, and found her sitting alone upon the chaise.

"Where is your nurse?" Holmes demanded without ceremony.

The lady started at his peremptory tone. "She went down just now to see why my tea was late. Was it Miss Fraser you wanted to see, sir?"

"Watson, stay with Lady Alice," Holmes ordered, and I did what little I could to calm the poor woman as we heard the sound of Holmes charging along the corridor and down the back stair.

In ten minutes, he returned, his features set in frustration. "Miss Fraser has gone. The cook saw her pass through the kitchen, dressed in her cloak, hat, and veil, and carrying a Gladstone bag."

"Gone?" Lady Alice began to tremble. "She wouldn't leave – not when I have come to depend upon her so!"

"I daresay you have," Holmes said gravely, and then drawing up a chair to the lady, he took her hand and said in a gentler tone, "I am very sorry for all that you have had to bear, Lady Alice, and all will be explained when you are strong enough to hear it – But there! I hear the bell, and I have no doubt it is someone whose presence will be more welcome than ours."

In a moment, the door was thrown open and Murray entered, carrying a wriggling white terrier under his arm.

"Floss!" the lady cried, and the dog leapt from my friend's grasp and bounded upon his mistress' lap, licking her face with energy.

Murray was surprised to see us. "You must have some news," he said, and then looking around the room, asked, "Where is the nurse?"

Holmes rose and gestured for Murray to take his place beside the lady. "Nurse Fraser has left rather abruptly, Murray, so we I must leave Lady Alice in your care. And I would advise you – I would insist – that you send for Lord Singleford immediately and see that Lady Alice is taken to Surrey. I will call on his Lordship in a day or two to explain all, but I think now the best medicine would be more tranquil surroundings and the company of an old and trusted friend."

Murray had always been quick to take stock of a matter, and to do what needed to be done without question. "You may leave all to me," he said, and Holmes bowed to the pair and led me away.

I had expected Holmes to direct the cabby to the nearest police station or to Scotland Yard, yet it was our Baker Street address that he called out.

"You don't mean to have the official force search for Mrs. Fraser?" I asked.

"We will not find her. I daresay she always anticipated the necessity of an escape if her plan faltered and made her own plans accordingly." He sighed, deeply and muttered, "'*Oh, what a tangled web we weave, when first we practice to deceive.'* Many set the sentiment down to Shakespeare, but it is Scott. *Marmion.* My mother was fond of the piece."

I couldn't recall Holmes ever mentioning his mother.

Holmes said nothing more until we had returned to Baker Street and settled beside the fire. "Even the most rational reasoner is lost without imagination – in the absence of data, it is imagination that will supply the possibilities, just as it will bring on the horrors. For where there is no imagination, there can be no horror."

He studied my puzzled expression. "It was Banstead that did it, Watson. That and the concentration of the drug. You know Banstead Hospital?"

"Not terribly well. It's a sanatorium, I believe."

"An asylum for the insane." He reached for his pipe and lit it. "Now imagine this: A handsome profligate, with a taste for high living and the gift of insinuation, wins the affection and hand of a gentle, passive creature, an heiress. He wanted for nothing – her dowry was considerable, and his docile wife gave him free use of whatever allowance the administrator of her trust deemed reasonable. But it is the way with many who want for nothing – they always want more. When she is thirty, she comes into her full inheritance, but as to its disposition, is it possible that such a submissive creature will submit to whatever her uncle and his solicitor advise? Perhaps they will persuade her to resume a trust arrangement, and Warburton will return to living on the allowance doled out by a trustee – unless, of course, the wife dies, whereupon the fortune must pass to her husband.

"Now, let us leave that happy couple aside for the moment and turn to another pair, whose happiness has suffered a blow. A striking beauty had attracted the notice of a popular stage actor. They wed in haste, and for a time enjoy the blessings of fame, but when his fortunes decline, she finds herself living in a boarding house in Lambeth, wed to a circus clown. A need to supplement their income has her looking for a post, and she finds work as an assistant at Banstead Asylum, traveling from Surrey to Lambeth as infrequently as possible."

"And it is on one of these journeys, the dissatisfied husband and the disappointed wife meet."

Holmes nodded. "He is charming and she is beautiful, and that chance meeting leads to regular rendezvous. They confide in one another. They commiserate. They indulge in that fatal 'What if?' that is so often at the root of crime. What if there were no wearisome wife? No humiliating husband? But of course, when a husband or wife is killed, the first to be suspected is the surviving spouse. So it wouldn't do for Warburton to murder his wife, or for Mrs. Fraser to murder her husband. But what if it might be arranged so that each murdered the spouse of the other?"

"But," I protested, "only Fleming was killed."

"Oh, it wouldn't do to have the one crime come hard upon the other," he said, a bit airily. "That would indeed be an intermingled web! No, Mrs. Fraser laid out the chronology very well – "

"Mrs. Fraser!"

"Oh, yes. And I daresay she might have succeeded if I hadn't sent up my card. I erred there, for no doubt when she saw '*Mr. Sherlock Holmes*', she knew the game was up and fled."

"But you are quite certain that Warburton's madness was a sham?"

"Oh, yes, one laid out by Mrs. Fraser and performed as credibly as poor Hugh Fleming ever could. At Banstead, the lady was able to read the records of the patients and observe their behaviors first-hand, which allowed her to coach Warburton in the role of a fellow who was losing his wits – a performance that began not long after Mrs. Fraser was installed at Grosvenor Crescent."

"Which would explain why Murray saw Warburton stumbling from the train some weeks ago."

"Precisely. They would even have devised a motive for his madness, one calculated to ensure public sympathy – that he was a military hero, bedeviled by the horrors of war. '*Though he be mad, there is method in't.*' I have no doubt that while he feigned his recovery, she would continue on as Lady Alice's nurse, insinuating herself into that poor woman's trust and affection, coached in how it might be done most effectively by the one who knew her best."

"Warburton!"

Holmes nodded. "Mrs. Fraser would keep the patient in a state of compliant sedation until the day came for her to administer the fatal dose. There would be a note, of course, stating that Lady Alice, driven by despair over her husband's plight, had taken her own life."

"Holmes! You horrify me!"

"Horror is the curse of a well-cultivated imagination. Allow me to indulge mine a bit further. The Colonel would have shown every symptom of recovery when the time came near for Mrs. Smith to dispatch Lady Alice, and so his bereavement would further support any petition for clemency. Now, of course, clemency isn't a speedy process. Even Dudley and Stephens weren't tried until two months after their arrest, and not released until six months after that. Still, Warburton had every confidence that a Colonel would warrant the same compassion as a pair of cannibals. I daresay, he quite expected to be released in under a year, unite with his paramour, and claim his wife's fortune. Unless, of course," Holmes added, gravely, "his paramour had another scheme entirely. She might think it would serve her better to make herself so invaluable to Lady Alice that the lady, once she came into her fortune, would be moved to amend her will in order to generously recompense the faithful attendant who had stood by her in crisis, and assign no more than a modest stipend – just enough to satisfy the cost of his care – to her lunatic husband."

"You believe that Mrs. Fraser meant all the while to betray Warburton?"

"When she saw what was at stake – Well, she was something of a gambler herself. Why share when she might have all? I have more than once seen a specialty among the criminal classes of beguiling and obtaining the trust of vulnerable women, and those who practice it, when they aren't women themselves, have an accomplice who is. Women have a decided knack for winning one over, which is why they are never to be entirely trusted – not the best, and certainly not the beautiful."

The sound of the bell cut off my retort.

"That would be Lestrade. I invited him to dine with us, with the promise of a very interesting narrative."

"But Holmes," I said, "when Warburton learns the truth of the matter – that he has been betrayed, that his wife is living, and his conspirator has fled – what will become of him?"

"Oh, I daresay he will go quite mad."

On the day following this wretched episode, I rose in a foul temper. The dismal weather set my wounded leg throbbing, and the disappearance of Mrs. Fraser, whose scheming had put one husband in his grave and another in a madhouse, left me with a cynicism toward both mankind and marriage, and a relief to know that I was not likely to be a candidate for the latter.

Holmes meanwhile indulged in a demonstration of his deductive skills at my expense, and then lamented how dismal, hopeless and prosaic the world was when he had no opportunity for the exercise of his powers. At last, he looked at my glum expression and burst into laughter. "I am as intolerant of idleness as you have become on the prospect of matrimony," he said.

"I think you will find your next client before I find a wife."

Holmes's reply was interrupted by our landlady, who presented him with a card upon a salver, which he took and read aloud, "'*Miss Mary Morstan*'. Hmm. I have no recollection of the name. Ask the lady to step up, Mrs. Hudson. Don't go, Doctor. I should prefer that you remain . . . ."

Of all the problems which have been submitted to my friend, Mr. Sherlock Holmes, for solution during the years of our intimacy, there were only two which I was the means of introducing to his notice – that of Mr. Hatherley's thumb, and that of Colonel Warburton's madness.

– Dr. John H. Watson
"The Engineer's Thumb"

NOTES

The tale incorporates several allusions, both canonical and actual. Murray, is, of course, mentioned in *A Study in Scarlet*, Warburton's name is dropped in "The Engineer's Thumb", Lord Singleford's Rasper raced in the Wessex Plate in "Silver Blaze", Vittoria the Circus Belle is mentioned as one of Holmes's old cases in "The Sussex Vampire", and the "*so-called wife*" and worthy helpmate of Holy Peters in "Lady Frances Carfax" was "*an Englishwoman named Fraser*".

As for the actual references:
- The Windham Club, or Old Windham Club on St. James's Square, was a social club, a mix of medical, professional, and former military gentlemen, and James Dunlap, MD was a member in Watson's day.
- Banstead Hospital, *a.k.a.* Banstead Lunatic Asylum, was renamed Banstead Mental Hospital in the early twentieth century, and later simply Banstead Hospital.
- Sanger's Amphitheatre which was a popular circus. In early 1888, "Lord" George Sanger, a true showman, gave a moving tribute to the past-its-prime mare, Shrewsbury, who had been felled by a pack of wolves that had escaped Sanger's menagerie. There was some evidence afterward that it was all a stunt engineered by Sanger himself.
- William Terriss was among the most popular actors of the day. His athletic, swashbuckling roles earned him the name "Breezy Bill". Sanger and Terriss had in common the fact that they were both murder victims, Sanger by an employee, and Terriss by a deranged actor.
- As for Dudley and Stephens: Following a shipwreck, they, with two others were cast adrift for three weeks. Dudley, Stephens, and a third sailor were rescued, the fourth having been murdered and cannibalized. They were tried in late 1884, and released from imprisonment in the middle of 1885.

The Exploited Assassins
by David Marcum

"**B**ut Mr. Holmes," cried Dr. Clayton Walker-Baird, the noted physician, "what if he actually *did* kill the Queen?"

When the doctor arrived at our Baker Street rooms just fifteen minutes earlier, he'd been the same calm and steady man I'd known for over five years. Now, however, he had worked himself up into something of a frenzy – or as much as someone like him could ever become frenzied.

I was returning from Camberwell, where I'd gone to see my newly intended bride, Miss Mary Morstan, at the home where she was a governess for the Forresters. We had much to discuss regarding our planned marriage, and the time we'd shared had raced by. Mrs. Forrester, much in favor of the match, had made a merry lunch for us, and it had been a most enjoyable mid-day excursion. I have some recollection that the weather that day was actually dark and wet and chill, but after visiting with Mary, my heart was light and had no room for such perceptions. Thus, finding Dr. Walker-Baird on our doorstep had been rather jarring, pulling me back from my pleasant contemplations to that world where men and women of all walks found their way to Holmes's door, seeking solutions to their problems.

Walker-Baird had just arrived and was reaching for the bell, and his waiting carriage was standing nearby. He was a stocky man, around forty, with thinning sandy hair and a forward-pushing curvature at his middle. He had always been typically pleasant, and willing to tease in a friendly manner, yet one sensed he could turn offensive under certain circumstances. I had never seen him behave that way, or heard of it from anyone else, but it was still a feeling that I had about him. He seemed surprised to see me as I joined him at the door, and even more so when I explained that I shared lodgings with Holmes, with whom he was there to consult.

"Ha ha!" he said. "That should serve as a reminder that I ought to consider beyond the surface. After seeing you occasionally at Barts, I solely associate you with the hospital, without considering that you have a life elsewhere." He shook his head. "Ha ha! Education never ends."

He wasn't the first to say so.

As I unlocked the door, I reflected that Walker-Baird had always been a rather scattered fellow, although he was an excellent physician. His duties crossed all aspects of society, and when he was younger he could have locked himself into the finest Harley Street practice, but to his credit, he always made time for some of the hospitals where charitable efforts were most needed and appreciated.

Upstairs, I introduced Walker-Baird to Holmes and then made to excuse myself, but Holmes waved me toward my chair, explaining that, "Watson has been a most useful confidant in many of my cases." He made the statement as if there was no debate as to whether I would remain, and Dr. Walker-Baird nodded abstractedly as I handed him a whisky.

"Sir James Saunders said that I should speak with you," he began. Any calmness he'd carried in with him was starting to fray as the time approached to tell us why he was there.

Holmes nodded politely. "I've been of some assistance to Sir James once or twice in the past."

"So he told me, although he didn't provide any details . . . ." He left it hanging, apparently waiting for Holmes to happily babble forth just how he had been of service, as if he were interviewing for a job, but my friend simply maintained his sphinx-like expression, allowing the silence to uncomfortably grow. It was a technique of his that I've also used in my medical practice, wherein the other person feels compelled to fill the empty quiet. Walker-Baird frowned, shifted in the basket chair, took another sip, and then realized that it was his move.

"I was initially against involving outsiders," he continued, "but I didn't know who to approach. The two policemen acted most suspiciously in the matter, and Sir James – he convinced me that instead of first going to the authorities, you might provide some insight."

Holmes still didn't speak, but rather made a small motion with his fingers, similar to beckoning a wary dog to approach, indicating that the doctor should continue. I could see that he was becoming fractionally impatient with Walker-Baird's rather imprecise approach to the purpose of his visit.

"It's about a patient, you see," explained the doctor. He seemed to stop short, as if recalling something important he'd only now thought to consider. He leaned forward, his voice dropping. "Sir James assures me that your work is confidential," he said tentatively, as if wishing to avoid offense.

Holmes nodded. "You need have no fears on that account. This patient . . . ?"

"Yes, yes. At first, there was nothing special about him, but then – Ah, but there must be something special, or I wouldn't be here, now would I? He was brought in by the police – a pair of constables. He'd been captured by them and had sustained a few superficial injuries. Yet, for some reason, they landed him at Barts, when there were closer hospitals.

396

Then, when the patient finally spoke, and began to explain what had happened – what he said he'd done – "

Holmes raised a hand. "You're telling it out of all order, Doctor. What is the man's name?"

Walker-Baird nodded and cleared his throat, intending to concentrate. He sat upright and looked straight ahead, as if he were a student reciting his lesson. "Fowler. Boyd Fowler. He's a Scotsman – at least he seems to be, based on his accent and his address. He looked to be in his mid-thirties – about your age, I expect. Tall and thin – like you, Mr. Holmes, but with bigger hands, and his features show his Pictish heritage. A rough fellow – callosities upon his hands, very worn clothing, hair a bit ragged, but not too long past his most recent haircut. He seems to be a taciturn fellow – And truth-be-told, he didn't say anything at all when I first examined him, but as I questioned him while treating his wounds, he suddenly began to speak – and that's when he said he'd just killed the Queen."

When Walker-Baird finally got to the point of his visit, mentioned with no more initial emphasis than if had been another feature of Fowler's description, it surprised us both. Holmes and I glanced at one another, his gaze asking me if Walker-Baird might be delusional – an action that didn't go unobserved by the doctor. He nodded, as if he'd achieved the desired effect.

"Yes, that's what he said. It seems that he'd received his various injuries – a deep slice on his inner forearm, as well as other superficial cuts and bruises on his face, hands, and forearms, after shooting Her Majesty while she was on a carriage ride through one of the parks near the Palace earlier today." He stopped speaking, looking from one of us to the other as we considered the terrible news he'd just shared.

I couldn't believe it – that our Queen, who had been on the throne for over half-a-century, and who had celebrated her Golden Jubilee just the previous year, was *dead*! No, I thought. It was impossible. She couldn't be gone. It was too sudden. Too unthinkable.

Holmes was frowning, but he evidently didn't believe the story. Now sitting forward on his chair, looking intently at our visitor, he said, "Again, Doctor – I beg that you begin at the beginning."

Walker-Baird nodded, apparently realizing the shock of what he'd just told us.

"Sometime before lunch – around 11:30 – the patient was brought in for treatment, in the custody of a two constables. I was making rounds in the ward when I looked up and saw one of the nurses directing them and the patient to an empty bed. As I approached, I noticed that the prisoner was wearing manacles, and I asked that they be removed, but the officers refused. They both seemed rather agitated, but I assumed that it was related to the events of the arrest. I asked if the prisoner had been violent, or if I needed to summon a couple of orderlies, but the older constable shook his head. 'He's been quiet ever since we took him.'

"I nodded, uninterested in the details of the arrest. The younger officer took up station facing the greater room, his back to us, while the other, staying with the prisoner, pulled a curtain around the bed to prevent anyone from seeing what was happening during the examination. The ward was quite busy this morning, and I was working alone – which was unfortunate, considering what soon happened. I began to examine the patient, and as I mentioned, he had a deep cut on his forearm, a slice that had opened a small vein, making quite a bloody mess. Additionally, his clothing was torn, and his face, hands, and arms had fresh bruises, cuts, and abrasions."

"Of what sort?" asked Holmes. "As if he had been in a fight? Defending himself? Or possibly of the sort one might get when fleeing?"

"I see what you're saying," nodded Walker-Baird. "I would definitely say that they were of the latter nature, and that fits with his story. I was soon told that he'd run through brush while escaping, and the signs fit his wounds. General scrapes and cuts upon his face, and the front and backs of his hands. His clothing was somewhat torn and roughed as well, and in places his sleeves had apparently been pushed back, leading to additional similar cuts upon his wrist and forearms. Besides that, he winced sometimes as he moved, as if his body was sore as well, but upon examination, there were no wounds or bruises apart from those I've mentioned.

"The patient's name was Boyd Fowler, seemingly confirmed by a letter I found in his coat pocket, addressed to Boyd Fowler at Eunan Farm, in Aboyne. At that point in the examination, he was unaware of his surroundings, and didn't question me when I removed it. Almost immediately, it was snatched from my hand by the older constable."

I saw Holmes nod to himself, and asked why.

"Possibly no reason. But Aboyne is about fifteen or twenty miles east of Balmoral."

I nodded, trying not to show my surprise at this obscure fact stored in my friend's brain attic. I knew that he carried a well-earned and curated encyclopedic knowledge of the capital, but that he also knew a great deal of obscure British and Scottish villages, as well as their spatial location and distance from other sites, was yet another of his gifts that I often neglected to recall.

"You see a significance?" I asked. "You think that is the connection with the Queen?"

He shook his head. "It is simply a factor to keep in mind. Please continue, Doctor."

Walker-Baird nodded. "As I said, when I pulled out the letter, the constable snatched it from me, and he seemed most peeved when I tried using the man's name to get a reaction – without any initial success. He was nearly catatonic.

"Normally I don't see patients very much anymore. My duties have extended in an administrative direction. But I was taking a shift today – to keep my hand in, you understand," he added in an aside to me. I acknowledged it, and he continued. "It was a routine treatment, as I used to see when I was a young doctor working in the clinics and hospitals on Friday and Saturday nights. The cut on his arm had been rudely bandaged with a piece of tied cloth, clearly the missing piece torn from Fowler's shirt, and a tight splint in the form of a stick had been applied. The constable acknowledged that he'd had sense enough to do that. Although the rag was soaked with blood, the bleeding had essentially stopped. After disinfecting and numbing it, I started stitching him up. Fowler had no reaction – he simply faced forward as if nothing were happening, his eyes wide and gazing into the distance. I began to wonder if he'd been medicated before his arrival. I might have suspected that he was drunk, but there were no indications of alcohol use upon him, and he didn't seem as if he were sleepy or disoriented. He sat straight, his eyes focused on the curtain pulled round his bed.

"As I worked, I asked Fowler the typical chatter – questions like 'How did this happen?' and so on – but the patient made no response whatsoever. Then I repeated the same questions to the constable, who was nearly as unforthcoming as the patient.

"'He was fleeing from us,' was his limited response. 'Getting away from us, too, until he cut through a hedge. Got stuck – forced his way out the other side. That's where we were waiting. We got him, but he fought back. He has the cuts from the bushes – including that slice on his arm – and the bruises from where he resisted arrest.'

"'Where did this occur?' I asked, simply making vague conversation at that point while I worked, as the location of the arrest made no difference to the treatment.

"The constable stated, 'Hyde Park.' Then he seemed irritated, as if he'd said more than he meant to.

"I frowned. 'That's quite a distance from Barts. It seems like a bit of extra effort to bring a prisoner this far for such minor injuries. Didn't you consider a closer hospital – Charing Cross, perhaps?'

"The constable shook his head. 'We thought best to keep things discreet – so as not to attract too much interest.'

"'I wonder why,' I said, half to myself, for as yet there was nothing special about this patient or his injuries. 'Well, Barts is certainly out of the way,' I muttered, simply making another comment, but that seemed to finally raise Fowler's interest.

"'Barts?' he asked, his voice dry and raspy, as if he hadn't used it for quite a while. It was then that I heard his marked Scottish accent. 'I've been here before," he muttered, his eyes blinking and now looking around – at me, and the constable, and his surroundings. 'Just a month ago.' Then, after a pause and clearing his throat, he added, 'Late August.' He licked his lips. 'Was it August? What month is it now?'

"'September,' I replied, even as I pondered his words. That he had previously been to Barts interested me, but I also noticed that the constable frowned, significantly this time, his body tensing as if he were concerned. And that was a fact that he wished the prisoner hadn't mentioned. He shifted as if he were coiling in order to physically stop Fowler from speaking. Rather than comment upon it, however, and risking escalating the situation, I simply went about cleaning the patient's wounds for a couple more minutes, asking no questions, before abruptly rising and stepping out of the curtained area, stating that I needed some additional supplies. The nature of this whole encounter was making me more and more suspicious. The older constable squawked some protest, but I stepped past him and went about my business.

"I walked past the younger constable standing guard outside the curtain and on across the ward until I found a nurse helping another patient. I quietly asked that she locate any records from when Boyd Fowler had been treated in August, and to do so without attracting any attention. I'm not sure why, but something didn't feel right about this – the constables weren't acting like officers I've known before. I instructed her to hold onto the documents until I could check them privately – and that she should on no account bring them into the curtained area where the constables could see. Then I turned to a nearby supply drawer and found a roll of wider gauze – to fulfill my excuse for leaving the patient – and returned to finish treating him.

"Dr. Watson can tell you that keeping up a running prattle with a patient is one of the tools of the trade, and despite Fowler's lack of responses after his previous statement, I kept talking to him, even though he didn't answer. His eyes, however, were now more conscious of the treatment space, and he was also watching with interest as I bandaged his arm. My one-sided conversation, dull and innocuous, seemed to lull the constable, who had been so concerned a moment before when Barts was mentioned, and I felt safe to mention the hospital once again.

400

"'What brought you to Barts a month ago?' I asked, as if it were just more of the same clatter. Of course, the constable tensed, and I had to wonder what was so upsetting about Fowler's previous visit. Both the constable and I were surprised when Fowler actually replied.

"'To see the doctor,' he replied.

"'Here now – ' the constable grumbled.

"'Oh?' I asked, ignoring him. 'Which one?'

"'Crewe,' rumbled the patient.

At this point, Walker-Baird paused in his tale, looking at me to see if I caught the significance. I had, and nodded, and I noted that Holmes had seen my confirmation as well.

Walker-Baird continued with his narrative. "'Really?' I asked, aware that the constable was now even more alert, as if he were about to put a stop to all treatment and whisk Fowler back from whence he'd arrived. 'What for?'

"'Dreams. My dreams. Of killing her.'

"I lowered my hands, the bandage half-tied. 'Killing her?' Killing who?'

"'The Queen.' His focus had been upon his arm, but now he looked up, his eyes meeting mine. He seemed to be in terrible pain, and unshed tears were beginning to rim his eyelids. 'I dreamed it so many times, and today I did it. I killed her.' He gave a small shudder and sob. 'I killed her!' he repeated. 'I killed her!'

"With that, the constable stood and rushed forward, pushing me roughly to one side and grabbing Fowler's shoulder as if he should shake the words back into him before they were spoken. But it was too late, and before I could be stopped, I hissed, 'You *killed* her? The *Queen*? How?'

"As you can imagine, I was stunned. Up to that moment, the patient had simply been another of many, more curious than some, but still just more wounds to be treated. They weren't serious, and although there was some mystery in the way he was being handled by the police, I've come across many stranger things. I was curious about his apparent catatonia, and that he'd been seen a month earlier by Dr. Crewe, but none of this was of more than passing interest – just another patient. But now – now this man had just quietly confessed that he'd murdered the Sovereign.

"I became aware that the ward around was still as noisy as before, nothing atypical or unusual. We'd been speaking so softly that nothing beyond the drawn curtain had been overheard. Even the younger constable standing just outside hadn't detected anything to spur him into motion in order to help his companion. But I sensed that some-such action was imminent.

"'She was riding this morning, as she always does,' Fowler said, his words coming more urgently as he seemed to be further waking up from whatever state he'd been in upon arrival. He was trying to talk around the older constable, urgently sharing his story with me while he could. 'I . . . I had dreamed it . . .," he said, quickly, looking into my eyes as if running out of time. "The plan . . . and I was waiting for her. *Them*. At the park – along Rotten Row. I had a pistol . . . I don't know where I found it. I had it, and when she drove by, I stepped forward and shot her. She . . . I *hit* her. She fell back. I *saw* it!'

"Tears were now running down his face. 'I thought she would cry out, but there was nothing – no sound at all . . . as if my ears were plugged. All I could hear was the roar of my own heartbeat. I dropped the gun. I turned and ran – never looked back. I don't know which way that I went, but then someone tried to grab me. I pushed into a hedge, to get away, but they were waiting. The police, on the other side. They arrested me, because I shot her. I shot her. I *killed* her . . . .' He gave a great sob, and then seemed to retreat back inside himself, his eyes losing focus once again.

"By now, the constable had allowed more than he'd ever intended, and he fully pushed me aside, taking custody of his prisoner while calling for his associate, who flung back the curtain and rushed in as if expecting to find that we'd both been overpowered. Instead, he was met with the prisoner being hustled out, and he shifted his emphasis to offering assistance.

"Ignoring the attention that they were receiving from the others in the ward, they hurried the Scotsman through the double doors to the hallway outside. After a few seconds, I regained my balance and followed, but they were already gone, and I couldn't find anyone to tell me in which direction they'd departed – although I'm not sure what my intention would have been had I caught up with them. The entire incident took no more than five minutes or so, and except for the prisoner's fantastic story, I don't know much of anything at all."

"You knew the name of the patient's doctor," corrected Holmes. "'*Crewe*.' You recognized him, Watson."

I nodded. "Dr. Patton Crewe is a specialist in the treatment of different sorts of mania." Then, unable to help myself, I added, "Some of his ideas are considered questionable – quite questionable, as a matter of fact. He dabbles in mesmerism and such."

Walker-Baird cut a glance my way, as if surprised that I was willing to be that candid with my criticism to someone outside the medical profession, but he added, "A minute or so after this all happened, another nurse came into the ward, looking for the two constables. Apparently they

402

had sent her to find Dr. Crewe when they first arrived, but she was there to report that he wasn't in the hospital."

Holmes nodded. "And what of the records that you sent the other nurse to fetch?"

Walker-Baird swallowed and pulled some folded sheets from his coat, handing them to Holmes. "Fowler has been seen at Barts on a number of occasions – not just a month ago, although that was his most recent visit. He first started seeking treatment a full year ago, when he moved to London. The forms showed that he came here from Scotland to '*find work*'. He was having headaches, and – according to the records – he believed that he was having '*bad thoughts*', although nothing about their nature was specified. He visited a dozen times in late 1887, and on each occasion, he was examined the physician-on-call. Then, early this year, he was first examined by Dr. Crewe, who happened to be responsible that day for walk-in patients. Although the records don't indicate way, Fowler was immediately sent down to the Somerset Asylum for three months. Afterwards, he obtained a release, and since then he's resumed making a nuisance of himself at the hospital – walking in at irregular times about his headaches – although never in the company or custody of the police. It was only chance that I happened to be there today. If I worked shifts more often, I might have recognized him."

Walker-Baird paused, and I rose to refill our glasses. Meanwhile, Holmes stood and walked to the open window, where the sounds of the street drifted in. They sounded no different than they had since I had arrived and met Walker-Baird at the front door. A moment passed, and then another, as Holmes looked through the medical notes.

As the silence continued, Walker-Baird seemed to become more worried, fidgeting and looking from my friend to me, and back again. Finally he could no longer keep it to himself. "But Mr. Holmes," he asked, "what if he actually *did* kill the Queen?"

For another moment, Holmes didn't replay. Then, turning back our way, he stated, "If the Queen has been killed, the news hasn't spread yet. No one in the street acts any differently, and the newsboy is still bellowing about the usual tripe. How long can they flog the story that Wilson took two-hundred-fifty wickets?" He took the glass I handed him and resumed his seat. "You mentioned that Sir James referred you to me. Did you discuss this with anyone besides him?"

Walker-Baird shook his head. "After the constables hurried away with the prisoner, I looked around, but everyone in the ward had already returned to their business. The hospital sees a lot of indigent care, particularly from Spitalfields and Whitechapel – people that don't go the London Hospital, for whatever reason – and they had already lost interest in the abrupt departure of Fowler and the constables. Still very much concerned with what I'd just heard, I went looking for Sir James. We talked about it, and he started to seek out a telephone and ask a friend if the story could be true, but then he leaned toward discretion. Even though he was as rattled as I, he had no insight. The best he could do was to advise that I come see you immediately. He would have joined me, but he had a surgery that could not be rescheduled. He only hoped that, following this news, his nerves didn't cause him to botch it. I didn't even take the time to send a message for an appointment."

He turned his hands up. "Now, I don't know what else that I can do, or tell you. Sir James said you were the man for the job. It's far beyond anything of my experience. Can you look into this?"

Holmes rose. "I can – *we* can – and I'll report back to you and Sir James if it turns out to be anything that that I can share."

"Then that's all I can ask," replied the doctor, finishing the last of his whisky and rising to his feet. With a presentation of his card so that we had his home and office address, he departed.

Holmes and I resumed our seats, and he quickly re-read Fowler's medical reports before handing them to me. They appeared to be quite routine – typical physicians' scrawls, quickly written by busy doctors about a forgettable patient. There was nothing of value beyond what Walker-Baird had mentioned. Seeing that I was finished, Holmes asked, "What else can you tell me about this Dr. Crewe?"

I took a moment to gather my thoughts, giving Holmes the opportunity to rise, walk around me, and retrieve one of the scrapbooks kept on the shelves near the door to his bedroom. I heard him muttering as he looked here and there before saying something about "No help" as he returned to his seat, giving me an expectant look.

"I don't know much about him," I began. "He's been a presence at the hospital since not long after my return to England, and after first meeting him, and hearing of some of his ideas, I did a bit of research. He's had several papers published in lesser journals, and I was told by one or two people that his efforts were rejected by *The Lancet* and a few others of similar respectability."

"You mentioned mesmerism."

I nodded. "He advocates the use of such techniques towards pain management. I can't say that I entirely disagree with everything that he espouses. I saw many things in India demonstrating how the mind can fool itself, if only given the chance. And of course, every doctor is aware of the power of the *placebo*. But Crewe seems to be less of a *doctor* and more of a *sideshow attraction*."

"How so?"

404

"On occasion, he has been known to place a susceptible patient under his hypnotic influence and then make the fellow to appear ridiculous – imitating a chicken or a monkey or some such nonsense – for the simple amusement of the staff. I've never seen it happen myself, you understand, but I've heard about it afterwards. A man with such little regard for his patients and their ethical care has no business being a doctor."

The thought of Crewe's actions recalled the anger that I'd initially felt when I'd first heard of his antics. I pulled myself from that vision of mistreated patients to glance at Holmes, expecting to see him amused at my righteous indignation, but I found him nodding in agreement.

"When a doctor goes wrong . . ." he stated, and I was reminded of his long-standing (and well-proven) distrust of many in the medical profession. "One has to wonder," he continued, "what a doctor such as that could be doing with a man who he recommended be treated for three months in an asylum." He stood abruptly. "I believe that a visit to my brother is in order. Can you join me?"

During the hansom cab ride from Baker Street, Holmes related details of the investigations he'd undertaken for Sir James Saunders in the past. One sounded insignificant, while the other was apparently relevant to the nation's most urgent foreign policies – or so it seemed from the vague account that was given to me. I asked Holmes how he had come to Sir James's attention and assistance in the first place, and he indicated that other services he'd provided to different government departments had led to similar work, and so on, until a situation arose in Sir James's bailiwick that required Holmes's special skills. I wanted to ask more, but at that point our short journey was complete.

Normally I found myself quite interested when Holmes was relating his past cases, but on that day I was only partially paying attention as I tried to puzzle out how a visit to his brother might be relevant to what we'd just heard.

It must be remembered that at that moment in time, it had only been one week since I'd first met Mycroft Holmes, during the tragically failed attempt to save a poor Greek who had come to London seeking his sister, only to be murdered in an empty house down Beckenham way. In the days that had followed, I had thought of the elder Holmes in passing a few times, but not with any great interest – and when I did, it was mostly because I'd known Holmes for so long and never before learned that he had a brother – a fact that surprised me, although it shouldn't have. Meeting Mycroft Holmes had certainly been an interesting experience. Of course, the physical differences between the two Holmes brothers was a curiosity. Both were tall, with the same sharp all-seeing eyes and general facial features, but whereas Sherlock Holmes was slim, as if he used up every bit of fuel that he acquired by shoveling it immediately into a hot furnace, Mycroft Holmes was stout – somewhat corpulent really – and like a careful steward of his own resources, he seemed to be hoarding his fuel for burning at some later date that might never arrive.

I had expected that we would be traveling to Pall Mall, as we had just a week before, and to the odd club where Mycroft Holmes apparently held court, but instead we found ourselves in front of one of the many great buildings that line Whitehall, near the Horse Guards. Then I recalled being told that every day, Holmes's brother walked from his lodgings across from the Diogenes Club and around to his employment where he audited the books for some of the Government departments. As it was still mid-afternoon, I expected that was where we would seek him.

We stepped down from the hansom and crossed to the heavy double doors, opened by an expressionless fellow who kept his gaze outward. Holmes seemed to be recognized, for he led me inside with just a wave toward a man at a tall counter who nodded and made no attempt to question us. After passing down a number of interminably long hallways and up and down several flights of stairs, ever more toward the rear of the building to the point that I was thoroughly lost, we reached a plain brown door in a hallway of many similar entrances. Holmes knocked twice, then once more, opened it without response, and led me into a small, workmanlike, and rather dim room with a desk, a few chairs, and a small window looking west toward St. James's Park.

From behind the desk, Mycroft Holmes looked up without surprise. He rose and offered his hand to the two of us. "Sherlock, Doctor. You've come about the supposed assassination of the Queen."

I was taken aback as the elder Holmes waved us toward a pair of chairs, but also relieved at the word "supposed", implying that our fears were unnecessary. Holmes and I had both remarked during our cab ride that the city appeared to be rolling along as normal – a good indicator that Boyd Fowler's assertion had been the merest moonshine.

"Excuse the meagre accommodations, Doctor," Mycroft Holmes said. "I have a more formal office elsewhere, but I tend to avoid it if at all possible. I find that I can accomplish much more here, where I'm left alone." He glanced at his younger brother. "Not that your visit is an intrusion. You knew to seek me here instead of the other office because Preston fled west from Inverness?"

Sherlock Holmes nodded. "When I received word which way he'd bolted, I thought you'd be here, getting your pins lined up."

Mycroft looked back my way, as if measuring my trustworthiness, before returning his attention to his brother. "The situation in

Camastianavaig on the Isle of Skye is rapidly coming to a head, and unless we get things in hand quickly, it may catch fire like dry grass hit by lightning."

My confused expression must have been something to see, for Mycroft Holmes smiled with friendly amusement. "You appear to be all at sea, Doctor. I gather that my brother hasn't explained the full scope of my duties within the Government – at least, as he understands them. You could have, Sherlock. The Doctor has been cleared, as you know. Suffice it to say, I sit in an elevated position where I can see the *inter-relatedness* of things – including how today's event at Barts is part of a larger picture."

"So this Fowler fellow didn't kill the Queen," said Sherlock Holmes, pulling the conversation back to the reason for our visit.

Mycroft shook his head. "But the poor fellow is being used, nonetheless – shamefully manipulated – and we need to get an understanding of what is happening as soon as possible." He glanced my way. "Can I offer you something to drink, Doctor?"

I shook my head, rather dazed, as if I had abruptly fallen into very deep water. No doubt my eyes were wide as I struggled to catch up. Mycroft took a bit of pity on me, poured a generous brandy from a container on his desk, and pushed it in front of me, despite my refusal. Then, as I sipped, he explained.

"Soon after Dr. Walker-Baird went 'round to Baker Street, Sir James decided to postpone his surgical engagement. He thought about following Walker-Baird to your rooms, but instead decided that it would be better to drop in here and tell me what little he knew about this morning's event – not realizing that I already knew a great deal more about it than him. I estimated that you'd be arriving within the next hour or so – and here you are."

He looked back at his brother. "You know, Sherlock," he said, "that I have my fingers in many different pies. A lot of it is a complete waste of my time, but occasionally I'm pointed in a useful direction. Not long ago, word came that Donald Mirehouse, the cabinet minister, was behaving even more . . . *peculiar*, I suppose, is the way to put it. Even more peculiar than usual. His finances have become precarious, and he's been associating with some most-dodgy types – rather on the radical side of things.

"It might have gone unremarked, for he isn't the only one to get himself in that sort of trouble, except for the recent inheritance he received from his uncle, the textile industrialist. A routine – and discreet – evaluation revealed that instead of putting him on more solid ground as one would expect, the funds seemed to immediately be siphoned off . . .

407

somewhere. Furthermore, that curiosity led us to determine that the rest of his affairs are also in a perilous state of near-collapse.

"While we were trying to decide how to address the matter, other inquiries were set in motion – just to get our pins lined up, as you put it. It was then that we learned that Mirehouse has been in close contact with the German, Hans Andernach."

I cleared my throat. "I hate to interrupt," I said, "and I realize that I'm in far over my head, but I'm still trying to gather my wits about a possibly mesmerized man who says that he killed the Queen, and instead we're talking about a man from Inverness and a cabinet minister and the Isle of Skye. Would it be too much trouble to explain the connection?"

Holmes looked my way, his expression kindly, rather than impatient. "I wasn't quite forthcoming last week when I brought you to the Diogenes Club," he explained. "Mycroft holds a unique position within the government – an *elevated* position, as he mentioned, where he can see how different events are connected and affect one another, and then he can set things in motion to nudge them in the way that most benefits England."

"It is also a *secret* position," added Mycroft, "although the Germans and the French each have a man who has somewhat similar gifts, attempting to carry out the same function. The Russians believe that they have someone as well, but he is a fool and will eventually lead them astray."

"A few weeks ago," continued Sherlock Holmes, "Mycroft had me do some preliminary investigation into Donald Mirehouse, as he was beginning to display signs that he's a weak link. It was then that I caught a whiff that there might be a plot to assassinate the Queen – but I was unable to find any other pieces of the puzzle."

"And the man in Inverness? And the Isle of Skye?"

"All part of the larger picture," answered Mycroft, "and unrelated to today's events – at least, it's nothing that need concern us right now."

"You mentioned a German," I said. "Are they behind this plot – whatever it may be?"

"It's possible," explained Holmes. "Hans Andernach, the man who has been in contact with Mirehouse, is a German agent."

"*The* German agent," amended Mycroft. "He was Bismarck's closest proxy when crafting their Triple Alliance Treaty six years ago. A German alliance with Austria-Hungary and Italy changed the balance of power – or at least forced us to respond. Together, those three countries are forming a virtual wall between us and Russia. But Andernach is also something of a rogue who sees the value of chaos to effect the changes he desires – even when the chaos is deadly."

"This is disturbing news," said Holmes. "So Mirehouse is in league with Andernach?"

"It seems more and more apparent," explained Mycroft gravely, "based on Mirehouse's finances, that he has been compromised by the Germans."

"What has been done?"

"Nothing overtly. Not yet. This has only come to our attention within the past couple of days. So far, we've made a further and deeper study of Mirehouse's records and his history. We've seen where he went wrong – a typical case of bad behaviour and blackmail – and how Andernach was able to gain influence over him. Fortunately it only occurred quite recently, so there's a good chance that very little damage has been done. At least, that's our fervent hope."

I looked from one of them to the other. "And you think that this mysterious damaged Scotsman at Barts has something to do with the plot against the Queen you sniffed out a few weeks ago?" I asked. "That he's connected to a compromised minister and a German agent?"

"It was when Dr. Walker-Baird mentioned a plot against the Queen," explained Holmes, "that I knew that we must confer with Mycroft."

"It's more than that," added Mycroft Holmes. "The fact that this Dr. Crewe is connected opens a completely new door."

"How so?"

"Do you both recall MacLean's attempt to kill the Queen in '82?"

We each nodded. In March of that year, Roderick MacLean, then in his late twenties, stood in the entrance of Windsor Station and fired a revolver at the Queen as she walked from her train to a waiting carriage. His shot missed – a nearby Eton schoolboy named Wilson used his umbrella to jostle MacLean's arm. Afterwards, it was learned that MacLean had been certified insane two years earlier, although he'd somehow been allowed to travel about freely and then obtain a gun. He was tried and found "Guilty, but Insane", and he'd spent the years since in Broadmoor.

Mycroft tapped a small stack of telegrams lying upon his desk. "After hearing Sir James's account, I requested some information. Fortunately I have the resources to obtain it quickly. I was interested to learn that MacLean, a Scotsman like Fowler, was also treated for headaches for two years before he was sent away – " He looked from one of us to the other to emphasize his next point. " – to the Somerset Lunatic Asylum."

I leaned forward. "The same hospital where Fowler was treated," I stated, unnecessarily, as both Holmes brothers already understood the significance.

"There's more," added Mycroft. "Do you know who treated MacLean while he was there? None other than Dr. Patton Crewe, our curious mesmerist. A quick review of both MacLean and Fowler's case files by the Somerset Asylum doctors revealed that Crewe's notes identified each as an '*ideal subject*' for his mesmerization studies."

"Good Lord!" I breathed. "Is it possible that MacLean was mesmerized and turned into some sort of sleepwalking weapon aimed at the Queen?"

Sherlock Holmes nodded. "We must re-evaluate what occurred six years ago – and consider today's events in that light as well."

"I already have men doing so," Mycroft stated.

"But Fowler is in custody," I said. "Surely he can explain what has happened. He simply needs to be properly interviewed by a medical professional with experience in this area."

"I suspect," interjected Sherlock Holmes, "that it won't be that easy. I believe that Mycroft is about to tell us that the two constables who brought Fowler to Barts are not legitimately employed policemen."

"That is correct," the elder Holmes confirmed. "Both the City of London and the Metropolitan Police have confirmed that neither organization has officers who took a supposed assassin into custody this morning along Rotten Row, and likewise neither has men who took a patient to Barts. Whoever these men were, they have gone into hiding with Boyd Fowler after he came to himself while being treated and spoke to the wrong person."

"We need to find out who they are," I said with enthusiasm, not realizing that both Holmes brothers already knew this. "And it's also of interest to know why they brought Fowler to Barts, as it sounds as if his wound wasn't too serious."

"Clearly," said Sherlock Holmes, "they brought him there to see Crewe, probably because he *didn't* actually shoot the Queen as he'd been trained to do while in a mesmerized state. He ended up being accidentally treated by Walker-Baird, and then, when he began to wake up and relate what he thought he'd done, they had to hurry him out without being able to consult with the mesmerist."

"It's a working hypothesis," agreed Mycroft. "As you will understand, this must remain most secret, and even many of my own agents aren't cleared to investigate it. I'll leave it to you, Sherlock, and you as well, Doctor, to see where the thread leads."

Sherlock Holmes stood. "Of course, Dr. Walker-Baird has been taken into protective custody," he said.

Mycroft nodded. "Not long after he left Baker Street."

"You don't think he's in danger?" I asked.

"It's possible," said Holmes. "He was unwittingly brought into this business when Fowler unexpectedly spoke with him. Whoever is responsible may try to keep these news from spreading – by whatever means necessary."

And with that, the meeting was abruptly complete. We had been dismissed, for there was nothing else to discuss. Mycroft stood as we departed, and it wasn't long before we were back outside, in front of the vast building.

Holmes preferred to walk for a bit, so we turned north toward Trafalgar Square before heading west along The Mall. As we progressed, I finally had no choice but to ask Holmes about his brother.

"You must forgive me for not immediately telling you of Mycroft's unique position," he replied. I held my tongue, suppressing the comment that he hadn't even told me of his brother's existence for nearly eight years. "It's something that he made for himself, unlike any other. He mentioned equivalent men on the Continent, but I don't believe it. No man alive has a more orderly brain than Mycroft. Every branch of Government funnels its questions through him and he sees their interconnections, and how one relates to the other. He specializes in *omniscience*. In this alone, he would be indispensable, but in fact he is also in charge the Government's various agents who work in secret, both at home and abroad. As their leader, and based on what they learn and also do at his bidding, many is the time that '*M*', as he's called, has decided national policy.

"But not a word of it must be hinted," Holmes added, glancing at me as we walked. The rains from earlier in the day had ceased, but there were puddles along the pavement which we dodged as necessary. "Should you ever publish anything else, as you did late last year when relating that little Mormon diversion, you must make no mention of Mycroft."

I nodded in agreement and we continued on for a good way, maintaining a companionable silence while Holmes was deep in thought. Finally, when we had circumnavigated around the Palace and then up Constitution Hill, I realized that he was heading for Rotten Row, where Boyd Fowler claimed to have shot the Queen. What we found were a vast number of our fellow Londoners, walking and standing and talking and living, all acting as if it were simply another normal day.

"It would appear," he said, "that that we might be tempted into overthinking this affair."

"How so?" I asked.

"Well, leaving compromised cabinet ministers and German agents to Mycroft's attention, we're left with Boyd Fowler and Dr. Crewe – the latter of which, I suspect, isn't too hard to locate. If I can get an idea of

411

what he's up to, we can attack this tangled skein from his direction and let the rest sort itself out."

He turned my way. "If you don't mind, return to Baker Street and await developments. I have one or two lines to cast before I meet you there."

"Isn't there something that I can do?" I asked.

He thought and then nodded. "Yes. See what more you find out about Dr. Patton Crewe." He smiled. "With discretion, of course." Then he nodded and set off with typical briskness back in the direction from which we'd come. Within a moment, he was well out of site.

My own pace being less energetic and, already weary by our walk from Whitehall, I hailed a hansom and was soon deposited at our Baker Street doorstep. It was certain that Holmes had noticed my weary condition, leading him to suggest my more docile alternative service.

Upstairs, I divested myself of my overcoat and turned toward my armchair. However, instead of sitting down and likely falling asleep, I diverted myself to Holmes's scrapbooks, where – with a bit of luck and also some diligent searching using what little I had learned about his peculiar filing system – I confirmed that there was nothing there about Dr. Patton Crewe. I'm not sure why I had thought otherwise, but I had the nagging sense that I ought to check further. Then, I looked once again at the only Crewe that I'd run across – Pencombe Crewe, a fellow who had lost his place in society because of some gambling scandal. Thinking that there couldn't be all that many Crewes in the capital, and with a wistful glance toward my chair where the prospect of an afternoon nap awaited, I instead returned to my coat and hat and departed once again, on my way to several locations where I hoped to find further information.

My search was not without success. As the afternoon waned, I visited Barts, as well as a couple of other hospitals where I'd learned that Dr. Patton Crewe also attended patients. I also looked up his biographical information in the Barts Medical Library, with the aid of a most-helpful medical librarian, confirming that Crewe's father was indeed the ill-fated Pencombe Crewe briefly mentioned in Holmes's scrapbooks. I realized that while Holmes knew many things, he didn't know them all, and that it was possible, even likely, that he hadn't made this connection. Like Holmes, I have cultivated certain useful contacts over the years that seem to know a little bit of everything within their limited circles, and from one such, Dr. Johnny "One-Eye" Wingrave, I obtained the following story about Crewe's father.

There are those who somehow seem to be above the law, forever escaping whatever justice that is due to them, but Pencombe Crewe wasn't someone who was part of that lucky group. In the mid-1870's, he was a close pal of Bertie, the Queen's eldest son and heir to throne, and well-known for his notorious and scandalous behavior. Pencombe Crewe, a former soldier and sole heir to his late father's fortune, was often right there with him. In 1878, Crewe and the Prince had been gambling while on a trip to Paris, as was their wont, and heavy losses were incurred. There was some whiff of Royal cheating, and the Prince happily pinned the accusation on Crewe, whose reputation was not only destroyed immediately, but the shaken man was also left with an immense debt to repay – both his share and the Prince's. As if that weren't enough, over the previous few years he'd made enough enemies by way of the Prince's supposed friendship that is was easy for Bertie to go ahead and cut all ties, essentially ruining him and striking him from society, almost overnight.

Almost twelve months to the day after his association with the Prince ended, a year in which he became a pariah amongst the group that had formerly accepted him as one of their own, Pencombe Crewe hanged himself, leaving his motherless son, Patton, shamed and on the verge of destitution. Patton Crewe had been pursuing his medical degree at the time, and his studies had been nearly permanently derailed before he found a patron to support him. However, after receiving his degree (about the same time as me, and also from the University of London, although I had no recollection of him), he had started down the path to where he now professionally resided – a supporter of the dubious fringe treatments and benefits of mesmerism.

I returned to Baker Street about an hour before our evening meal, and Holmes joined me not long after. He was a good mood, standing before the fire and rubbing his hands energetically, and my report seemed to line up with whatever he had learned.

"Did your source of information indicate the name of the man who served as Dr. Patton Crewe's lifeline?" he asked.

I shook my head.

"It was Donald Mirehouse," Holmes said, now seated and smiling around his pipe.

"The compromised Cabinet Minister?" I asked.

Holmes nodded. "Mirehouse stepped forward and supplied the funds that Crewe needed to complete his studies, and then set him up in practice, in some ways similar to how Trevelyan was funded by Blessington in that Brook Street house back in '81. If he'd simply buckled down and gone to work, Crewe could have made a success of that life, but instead, he became rather vocal regarding the shabby way in which his father was treated by the Royals. He now has something of a reputation for expressing revolutionary thoughts, which can be verified with just the shallowest scratching of the surface."

"And he's tied up with this man Mirehouse, who is suspected of possible treason."

"And," added Holmes, "Crewe found a pair of 'ideal subjects', one of whom tried to kill the Queen six years ago – "

" – and the other who thinks that he did so today, even if it's all in his mind." When Holmes didn't immediately respond, I asked, "What are we going to do about it?"

"We are going to eat a bit of supper, and then join Gregson, Lestrade, and a few other policemen, along with the Irregulars, at Mirehouse's home in St. John's Wood."

He offered nothing further, and my anticipation of the coming confrontation didn't lessen my enjoyment of Mrs. Hudson's curried chicken.

Mirehouse lived in Eamont Street, just north of Regent's Park, and when we finished eating, Holmes suggested the idea of walking there before then shaking his head. "No, Lestrade and the rest are waiting for us. We shouldn't delay any longer." In any case, we ended up walking there anyway in a fruitless search for a cab, and in a short time we were at the Park end of the Eamont Street, where Gregson and Lestrade stepped out of the shadows.

"If your brother hadn't authorized this," began Gregson as they joined us, "I'm not sure that we'd be very comfortable serving a warrant to search a Cabinet Minister's house."

"Not to worry," said Holmes. "As my investigation progressed this afternoon, I put the Irregulars in place in several important locations. According to their reports, Crewe's home has been empty, while a man of his description was seen entering Mirehouse's residence late this afternoon, and he hasn't come out. However, a couple of men dressed as constables have been in and out several times. None of the lads recognize them – and you know that they have rather full knowledge of most of the London constables' identities. There is a window on the first floor front with closed drapes, but someone regularly pulls back the curtains, watching the street through a narrow gap. Likewise, there's a room at the rear of the second floor, overlooking the mews, that has closed drapes, but a light is lit there, and occasionally someone peeps from there as well. That will be where we'll find the prisoner."

"Prisoner?" asked Lestrade.

"Indeed. Boyd Fowler, the poor man who has been mesmerized in an attempt to turn him into an assassin. It was no fault of his that he was used in this way while simply seeking treatment for his headaches." He looked around and then waved his stick back and forth over his head. In just a moment, we were joined by Wiggins, the leader of his Irregulars, that band

414

of lads and lasses who were able to go everywhere and see everything, remaining unnoticed while they gathered vital information. I hadn't encountered Wiggins for a few weeks, since he and his troops had been looking for Jonathan Small along the Thames.

"Any changes since your last report?" Holmes asked him.

"None at all," was Wiggins' confident reply. He had walked up and situated himself between the two inspectors, taking his place without any doubt that he deserved the spot. I was amused to see that he was now taller than Lestrade. Both men gave him rather sour looks, but neither could deny how useful he and the other Irregulars had been over the years.

"Excellent," said Holmes. "Then I see no reason to delay."

Though a police operation, Holmes was clearly in charge. There were no loud whistles or yelling. Rather, at a subtle gesture from Gregson, men slid from the shadows toward the house like darker shadows, and one would have been hard-pressed to hear even a brushed footstep. Gregson's work with the Special Branch, formed just five years earlier, had led to a number of useful advances, as these very effective agents demonstrated.

On the front step, Holmes quietly leaned forward to examine the lock. Then, as both inspectors pointedly looked elsewhere, he quickly pulled a wiry piece of metal from his pocket, made a quick manipulation with his hands, and softly unlocked the door. We could barely hear him as he counted to three before throwing open the door and stepping aside, allowing the various policemen to flood past him, suddenly moving from silence to deafening confusion and cacophony as their shouts and yelling filled the house.

A stunned butler appeared at the rear of the hall, and Lestrade tucked a folded warrant into his coat pocket without explanation before joining the sweep of men surging through the building. One of the officers had unlocked the back door, and more of them came in that way, adding to the number who had overwhelmed from the front. The surprise attack was complete and successful, and in less than three minutes, five men were assembled in the dining room, while the confused servants were being kept in the kitchen.

Donald Mirehouse was a blustering figure, wearing a much-too-tight smoking jacket belted across his barrel-like corporation. He had too-little hair on top, and what was on the back of his head was grown too long and combed forward over his fat orange face, held down with shiny Macassar oil across his too-great dome-of-a-forehead. Through his pursed mouth, he sang the old songs of "Do we know who I am?" and "I'll have you jailed!", with a chorus of "This will mean your jobs!" and all the other verses. The Yarders didn't care, instead focusing on Crewe, the two false constables, still in uniforms that were easily identifiable as rag-bag cast-offs from some old clothing shop, and the fifth man, sitting at the other end of the table, apparently trying to wake up and figure out just what was happening.

I stepped across to examine him and found that, except for having been drugged with some sort of sedative, he appeared to be in good physical condition. I reported that the wounds that Dr. Walker-Baird had treated that morning didn't require attention, and the bandages he'd applied, while needing changing soon, would do for the present.

Holmes took the lead in questioning the four others. Mirehouse tried to talk over him, but he soon shut up when one of the darkly clothed policemen took up station beside him in an intimidating way.

"There is much to be sorted over the coming days," Holmes began, "but suffice it to say, Mr. Mirehouse, you are going to be questioned at length by Government agents about this incident, and a number of others as well. What remains to be determined is if you will become the Government's tool, 'turned' as they say, to be useful in some way working against our enemies, particularly at feeding false information to Germany through your contact, Herr Andernach, or whether, if he doesn't take the bait, you finish your remaining days, however many or few there may be, in The Tower." He glanced toward Gregson. "He can be removed now. We don't need him for the rest of our discussion, and others are waiting to speak with him."

Mirehouse's face had been livid and angry when Holmes began, but within seconds it had blanched to a sickly dead orangish-white. As he was pulled upright and marched out of the room, he tried to turn and get Holmes's attention, whining of false accusataions and conspiracies and a mistake being made before finally raising his voice about working something out with money. When the door was shut behind him, Holmes turned to Crewe.

"You'll follow him in a moment," he said. "Over the next few days, we will uncover a great deal more than we already know about your involvement with MacLean's failed attempt to kill the Queen in 1882, but for now, I expect a few answers regarding Mr. Fowler."

Crewe was about my age, but he looked at least ten years older. He was a small and twitchy fellow, with the broken facial capillaries and the coloring of a drunkard. Unlike Mirehouse, who had started angry and then collapsed, Crewe was already broken, slumped in his chair, a shaking hand covering his eyes, and small sobs continually rolling forth while Holmes spoke.

For nearly ten minutes, Holmes questioned the little doctor, and gradually the story was pieced together. After MacLean was chosen in '82, trained for his task by way of mesmerization, and then arrested when the assassination failed, Crewe spent the following years in fear, aware that any moment MacLean's mind might clear long enough to implicate the doctor that had found and used him in such a terrible way. But that never happened, and gradually, and particularly after "Bloody Sunday" the previous November, Crewe's hatred of The Crown had reasserted itself, overwhelming any common sense that might have prevented him from taking another chance when he'd managed to avoid disaster the first time. When Fowler, having many of the same symptoms as MacLean, had presented himself for treatment, it had seemed like too good of an opportunity to miss, and Crewe had started laying the groundwork for Fowler to make his own attempt on the Queen's life.

That morning, feeling that the patient was nearly ready, two of Crewe's cohorts, the false constables later identified as Abraham Fields and Curtis Wigham, had taken him to Rotten Row for a rehearsal. It had not gone as expected. Instead of going through the motions in the way he'd been trained, Fowler had instead become agitated to the point where he attempted to flee, injuring himself in the process.

Mistakenly thinking that Crewe was working at Barts that day, the two false constables had carried him across town for treatment, and to discuss what went wrong, but when they arrived, a misunderstanding on the part of a staff member had ended up placing them directly into the ward for treatment of Fowler's injuries. This was all right, they thought, as he did need to be seen by a doctor, and afterwards they could still find and meet with Crewe. But then Fowler had started talking about how he believed he'd just killed the Queen in front of a stranger, the doctor who was binding his wounds, and they had panicked and chosen to depart immediately in order to seek Crewe elsewhere.

They found him at his home, and from there all four shifted to Mirehouse's residence, where they had waited through the day to see if Fowler's wild statement at the hospital had caused any problems.

Meanwhile, Fowler seemed to become more self-aware as Crewe spoke, and I noticed that he was nodding in agreement.

"That's right," he finally said, his Scottish accent strong and his voice raspy. He squeezed his eyes shut as if the light suddenly hurt his eyes "I remember . . . I remember some of it. What day is it?"

"September 19th," I replied.

"And the year?"

"1888."

"Thank goodness for that. I had no idea just how long these -------- have held me." He smiled then and shook his head, although that seemed to hurt him, and I thought of the problems he'd had with headaches. I would see about getting him some proper treatment.

Later, after Fowler was taken back to Barts, where I would examine him on the morrow, and Crewe and the false constables were removed to the Yard, Holmes had a word with Wiggins in order to dismiss him, and then we decided to walk back to Baker Street, this time through the Park. It was a pleasant evening, and not too late, the entire affair having been concluded in less than an hour.

"Do you suppose Andernach will be fooled into believing whatever Mirehouse is instructed to tell him?" I asked.

"I expect so. Mycroft is very capable at this sort of thing, and there are a number of similar fish already caught on his hook and dancing to his tune, if I mix a metaphor. I even know who some of them are." His voice saddened. "I suppose it's too soon to make a prognosis for Fowler's recovery," he added.

I nodded. "Until I've had a chance to speak with him, and for the specialists to have a look, it is. Crewe has been meddling with him for a year. Who knows how deeply his manipulations and suggestions have rooted themselves? But the fact that he was able to resist when taken for a practice run, and then to speak as himself tonight and have some understanding of his situation, is most promising."

We had entered the Park by way of the small bridge across the canal across from Charles Street, and were now walking south along the Outer Circle, in the stretch between St. Dunstan's Villa and North Villa. I could tell that Holmes, rather than being pleased at the outcome, was rather concerned and distracted.

"It's too easy," he finally said. "For men like Crewe to identify the weak links and turn them into weapons. How many others are out there, all of them living infernal devices, primed for explosion and waiting for the right opportunity? And all of them aren't all aimed at those in power, and they haven't been singled out by a mesmerist and turned into a weapon. Some are already madmen, all on their own, who could not care less who they hurt or kill – the powerful, or the weak and innocent and helpless. We've both seen that far too many times. The Irish dynamiters. Loudon, Baron Maupertuis' strong-arm man. That fellow who faked his death and then nearly made a pitchblende bomb."

Having observed the signs before, I could see that Holmes was on the way to working himself downward and into a brown study. "What you need," I said, "is a challenge." I should have remembered to be careful what you wish for. "Something that will keep you occupied. This was no more than a one-day distraction – moving about and asking some questions. Didn't you mention just this morning at breakfast that Abberline wants to further confer with you tomorrow about the Whitechapel killings?"

He nodded. "It's been eleven days since the last murder, and he has new information, based on what I told him that night. Apparently he's now seen as the lead man in the investigation."

"Well, then, that ought to keep you busy for a little while."

"I suppose, although I suspect it will turn out to be nothing more than some shabby little fellow with a grudge against street women. He's probably thrown himself into the Thames by now, never to be heard from again."

Sherlock Holmes was not often incorrect, but in this case, he could not have been more wrong. Those were still early days in our attempts to stop the Rippers and their Reign of Terror, and walking home that night, we had no idea of just what what was still to be faced, and almost immediately. I'd told Holmes that he needed a challenge. What foolishness, for he was about to face one of his most dangerous and taxing challenges of his life – and me along with him. Never announce that you have plans, goes the old maxim, for the gods will disabuse you of that notion. Do you pray for patience? Beware, for you'll have the opportunity to learn patience. Do you think that life has never tested you? Be careful what you utter, for you *will* be tested.

Years after that night, I would remember our quiet walk home through the Park as one of the calm places before the mighty tempest, when preventing one man from killing the Queen amazingly seemed like a small case when compared to the evil we were about to face.

But on that night, I was pleased with what we had accomplished, and that was enough then to be going on with.

419

The Case of the
Missing Docker
by Jonathan Schneer

We were idling listlessly in our sitting room one chilly and intermittently wet Sunday afternoon in November '88 when I finally broke a long silence.

"Don't do it," I said.

For days, no case had occupied the active and fertile mind of the man who sat across from me, the man with whom I shared lodgings, and whom I esteemed as no other. Having recovered the Indian Maharajah's infamous giant "Blue Diamond" against all odds seven days previously, Sherlock Holmes, the world's only private consulting detective, had been cock-a-hoop, effervescent as champagne – for a day or two. Now, a week later, the apathetic mood I had learned to hate and fear was hard upon him. He had no pressing business, and he was consumed by lethargy. For four days, neither his chemical experiments, nor his voluminous files charting the criminal world past and present, nor even his violin, drew him. When alone, he sat motionless and silent. When with me, he rarely uttered more than a word. That day, he hadn't spoken for many minutes. The teapot brought to us by our ever-solicitous landlady, Mrs. Hudson, remained full, as did the tin of biscuits. "Your favorite assortment, Mr. Holmes," she had reminded him, to no avail. The morning papers, which he had barely skimmed, littered the carpet at our feet. The coal fire flickered noiselessly and cheerlessly. He had been sitting like a statue, but I knew he was about to reach from his armchair for the side table drawer in which he kept the loaded syringe.

When I spoke to him, he raised an eyebrow, but did not stay his hand. "You are learning, Watson," he observed mildly. "You appear to have read my mind."

"Don't do it," I repeated as he stretched for the drawer.

He looked at me with something like amusement: "But my seven-per-cent solution is also my hundred-per-cent solution."

"Holmes, please. I speak not only as your friend, but as a medical man."

He yawned. "You may be a doctor, but even so, what can you know of boredom as I experience it? Can you even begin to measure my *ennui*? I have borne it long enough. It will be terminal, I assure you – unless promptly treated. That is what *this* will do." And his hand closed round the hypodermic.

I was about to protest again, but footsteps ascending the stairs outside our little set of rooms distracted me. Holmes heard them also. "Mrs. Hudson again," he judged. "I recognize the tread. And she is bringing us a visitor – a woman of the working class, or I miss my guess."

I raised my eyebrows.

"Her step is light and she wears wooden shoes." He put down the needle, closed the drawer, inclined his head towards the door and, in a more cheerful voice than I had heard for several days, commanded those outside to "Come!" – even before the knock had sounded.

Mrs. Hudson entered first, looking somewhat bemused. She was accustomed to introducing more respectable representatives of the British public than the slight and shabby figure trailing in her wake. Holmes and I both stood as Mrs. Hudson announced, "Mrs. Elizabeth McCaskell."

As she left the room, I covertly examined the woman who stood warming by the fire. She could not have been much more thirty years of age, but they had been hard years. She might have been pretty when she was younger, but now her face was lined and pale. She was thin. Her brown hair hung to her shoulders in tangled strings. She wore, unbuttoned, a threadbare coat that might once have been red, and beneath it a ragged, faded dress that might once have been blue. She had on her feet wooden clogs, much scuffed. She was wringing her hands in curious fashion. I noticed a red ribband wound 'round her wrist, and employing methods taught me by my friend, deduced that she was a seamstress. Her jaw was swollen, no doubt the result of a blow to the face. I surmised that her husband beat her. Her fingers were stained yellow. I inferred that she smoked heavily. Careworn, toilworn, she looked to me a sadly typical example of the million unsung working women who inhabit our imperial metropolis. My heart sank, for I could not imagine my friend finding anything to interest him in this forlorn and bedraggled female representative of the British laboring class.

But . . . "Mrs. McCaskell, please sit down," he urged her politely, pointing to the settee. "It is a long walk from Bow and, in addition to being somewhat damp, you are no doubt much fatigued."

"Yes, I am tired," the lady agreed, gratefully taking a seat. "But how did you know I walked all the way when, aside from an excellent omnibus service, there is also the underground to Baker Street? And how did you know I came from Bow?"

Holmes did not so much as smile. "You are a match girl," he told her, "Your discolored fingers betray you. You belong to the union currently striking at Bryant and May's Match Works. Your red ribband betrays you.

The factory is located in Bow. That betrays your proximate address. You earn no more than a pound a week in good times, as the newspapers have taken care to advertise, and now you receive only meager strike benefit. That betrays your mode of locomotion – as does your muddy foot-ware." His face clouded. "And," indicating her swollen mouth, "you have early signs of 'phossy jaw', the bane of all who labor for Messrs. Bryant and May. I advise you to find a different occupation."

Our guest, who had been taken aback as Holmes ticked aspects of her life story, almost smiled: "That last betrays *you*, Mr. Holmes," she said, "although everything else you said was very clever. But you know little of my world if you think I can so easily change the way I earn my bread."

"It is true," Holmes acknowledged, "that I have little personal acquaintance with men and women of your class, and, although I would wager that I know the streets of East London as well as you, I know little of life within that quarter. And yet, I do suspect that you fear for your husband."

She started. "How so?"

"You have not ceased to play with your wedding ring since entering this room," Holmes explained. "That means you are worried about something. The ring is a memento of your marriage. You are still married, or you would not wear it. That suggests that you are worried about the man who married you." And, in a kindlier tone: "I will ring Mrs. Hudson to refresh our teapot. And then please, you will tell us all about it."

Once the lady held a steaming cup of tea in her hands, she seemed to gain confidence, although whenever she put the cup down, she would twist the inexpensive band that circled the fourth finger of her left hand.

"You are right, Mr. Holmes," she began, "I am most worried for my husband. There is not a better, more honest, man in all London. He works regular at the docks, and he brings me his earnings on the Friday, scant though they may be. He will neither smoke nor gamble, nor has he time for those who do. I pack his lunch for him every morning, and his flask of tea, and that is enough for him. He will not stop at the pub after work, as other husbands do. He has joined the union," she added proudly, "although as of yet it has few members, much like our union at Bryant and May. But he vows that it will grow, as ours surely will too. We are both at the chapel on Sundays, and he attends the Workman's Hall most nights after work, where he is learning to write in Latin."

Holmes's face had clouded at mention of the union, but now brightened. "Indeed?" said he. "He sounds a most estimable working man."

"But," she continued, "our Mick did not come home after work yesterday, Saturday, nor has he sent me any word. I begin to fear . . . ."

She put her hand to her mouth before collecting herself. "I bumped into one of his mates on the Whitechapel Road this morning, Francis Cronin as he is called. I asked Francis if he knew where our Mick might have got. He said they worked a schooner carrying rum from Jamaica yesterday, but he did not know what Francis did after, and I believe him. But then . . . ." She trailed off.

"Which dock employs your husband?" Holmes asked sympathetically. "And what is his trade there?"

"Ah," said Mrs. McCaskell, collecting herself, "that is a common enough story in these hard times. Our Mick apprenticed as a shoemaker when he were a lad in Norwich. Only, as you will know, there is little chance for a skilled shoemaker these days. The factory killed the trade, and our Mick could not abide a factory."

Holmes was studying her intently. "But you do," he observed.

"I am a woman," she answered simply. "I have no recourse." Then: "So, our Mick took ship, though he were but a lad at the time. He sailed the world. But once, when his ship put into London . . . ." She pointed at herself. "Well, that were that. And an able-bodied seaman always has a chance at the docks. Now our Mick has an understanding at the West India Dock with a contractor, Jock Jones by name. Mick will take any kind of work from Jock."

"That is enough to be going on with," Holmes said, rising. "I will be in touch."

"So fast?" whispered Mrs. McCaskell. "Just like that? You will look for my husband?" She put down the teacup in surprise and rose as well. "You are so famous – I hardly dared hope." Then, reaching for her purse: "I am very much obliged to you, Mr. Holmes. I cannot pay much, but I will pay all I have for news of our Mick."

"My good woman," Holmes told her, "put that away until Messrs. Bryant and May come to their senses and increase your pittance. I charge my clients as I choose, meaning in this case, according to their ability to pay."

She was taken aback again. "We will make a socialist of you yet, Mr. Holmes," she said, gathering herself and turning towards the door.

"Stay a moment," Holmes commanded, growing serious. "You realize that you may not like what I discover?"

She nodded soberly. "I know what you are thinking. But our Mick would never desert me. And I must learn what has happened." Then, with her hand on the door another thought struck her: "As you conduct your search, Mr. Holmes, beware of Jock Jones. He favors Mick with work, so Mick stands him. But Jock's a proper villain. He hates the union. He hates anything that is good and true." Then she was gone. We

423

heard her going downstairs, and then the sound of the outside door opening and shutting.

"Holmes," I expostulated as soon as I knew she had reached the street, "surely you must reconsider! A dock laborer has deserted his wife. It happens every day. He will not thank you when you find him. And a more suitable case is bound to come along soon."

"I doubt such a paragon as Mrs. McCaskell has just described to us would desert his wife," he replied, "Moreover, I am deathly bored. This will do for the moment." Then, after a brief pause: "But she is a brave girl, is she not?" He was headed for his room. "I must pack a bag."

That was Sunday afternoon. Holmes rushed out and did not return before I went to my bed, nor was he there when I breakfasted the next morning. I did my rounds at Barts Hospital and returned at the end of the day to find him in his dressing gown, dozing by the fire. He roused when Mrs. Hudson brought us two of her excellent veal chops. While eating, he told me where he had been and what he had been doing that day.

"I went looking for work at the West India Docks this morning – suitably disguised. It is an astonishing business. It was not yet light when I arrived at the dock gate, but hundreds of men already had assembled, waiting for the 'call on'."

"And what may that be?"

"Outside the gate there are a dozen small platforms. They look like church pulpits. On each of them stands a man. A hundred dockers cluster before him, and at a signal he begins calling out names. Those he calls will work that day. Of course, he favors men he knows. As for the rest – ?" Holmes shrugged. "Some call to him their surnames, others their Christian names, to remind him who they are. Some call out *his* name to attract his attention. And he tosses little brass tickets into the crowd. Whoever catches one has a job for the day. The men fight for them like wild beasts. It is an awful scrum, and it is repeated before the wharves and gates of every dock up and down the Thames daily. And the number of jobs depends on how many ships need to be worked. That varies from day to day. Many thousands sought work this morning and did not find it.

"I knew from Mrs. McCaskell to look for the contractor called Jock Jones. He wasn't hard to find. He's a great brute of a man, several inches taller than me, and at least two stones heavier. He has the bearing of a soldier, and he served in India or I miss my guess, but also, he may once have been a docker, for he carries a docker's hook, a ferocious-looking instrument meant, in his hands I am sure, to intimidate the men who depend upon him for their livelihoods. I realized immediately there was only one way to acquire a brass ticket from a man like that, which was to

424

signal that I would give him half my earnings in return for a job. When he got my meaning, he tossed a ticket in my direction, but I had to fight for it.

"The ticket was my *laissez passer* through the dock gate. Imagine something resembling a Roman arch, with uniformed guards on either side. Anyone who wishes to enter the West India Docks must pass through. And just before the entrance, standing to one side on a makeshift soapbox, a little man with a big voice was exhorting all within earshot to join a union of dock laborers. Not one in ten paused to listen, for each is grateful to have work at all, and each fears to lose it – which would surely be the result if Jock Jones or one like him noticed.

Holmes put down his knife and fork and pulled out his pipe. Soon the room was enveloped in the pleasant scent of his blend of tobacco.

"I spent the day on the quay, manhandling enormous barrels of rum. They are dropped there by a great winch that is stationed on the ship's deck, and that reaches for them into the ship's hold. The barrels are so unwieldy and so heavy that it takes four men to lift a barrel from quayside onto a trolley, and the same four to keep the trolley straight and wheel it into the warehouse, and the same number to unload it. We brought them all into an enormous room lined with hundreds more, each taller and broader by far than I am. You could hide an army in that room. It seems to stretch the length of the warehouse. Jock Jones showed up at one point, swinging that evil hook of his. He made certain to remind me of our bargain at day's end. At five-pence-an-hour, I earned a little more than four shillings and tuppence. If I work the week, I will earn a little more than two pounds, of which I am to give him half. It is a coolie wage, but most men pay him something."

"Holmes," I interrupted, "all this to find a man who has done a runner? You know that he probably has tired of his mouse of a wife and flitted back to Norwich."

Holmes pulled from the folds of his dressing gown his .450 British Bull Dog pocket revolver. "I returned to Baker Street for this." He had a glint in his eye. "I suspect that there is more to this little affair than you may think, and what's more, I am enjoying myself."

He was gone the next morning, but had left a message for me with Mrs. Hudson: "*Expect me Wednesday.*" I wasn't surprised. My friend often disappeared when working on a case, sometimes for as much as a week. I supposed that he had returned to some little room he had taken in dockland on Sunday afternoon. He would live the life of an East End docker until he picked up Mick McCaskell's trail. I had no doubt that he would do soon. I only wished, on his behalf, that he had a larger problem to distract him.

November in London can be dreary, and that year it most certainly was: Grey when not raining, always cold, and the London fog thick enough to taste, and to drive the cabbies to despair. I did my rounds at the hospital those days while Holmes was gone, wondering whether, after all, the life of a country doctor would not have suited me better than this quotidian grind in a vast and soulless metropolis. I longed for my friend's company.

On Wednesday morning, I entered the sitting room, made for the table – and there he was, tucking into the eggs and bacon. But he did not look happy.

"Ah, Watson," he greeted me. "I was wondering what great dissipation last night kept you in bed so late this fine day." It was raining again.

"It isn't yet eight o'clock," I pointed out.

"Time is of the essence," he said.

"You have found McCaskell!" I cried. "Must we catch an early train to Norwich then?"

"No. I was in touch with the Norwich authorities right off. They instituted inquiries. McCaskell is not there. I am sure of it. But I expect that I know his proximate whereabouts in any case."

"He has taken ship, has he?"

"I've had that looked into as well. No one of his name or description has done so these past three days."

"At least tell me you have tracked down his friend, the docker, Francis Cronin."

"Of course, I have," Holmes replied. "Jock Jones put me on the crew with Cronin my first day of work, as I expected he would. The crew was one man short, with McCaskell gone."

"And Cronin has told you where McCaskell is," I reasoned.

"In a manner of fashion."

I was growing impatient. "Holmes – " I began.

He raised a hand. "It was important, first, to gain Cronin's trust, and that of his gang, of which I am now the fourth member. I succeeded. Yesterday, the group initiated me into a most nefarious practice."

"They dunked you into the Thames?" I had read that dockers employed that practical joke on unsuspecting, inexperienced, colleagues.

He smiled for the first time that morning. "Something far more reprehensible. After swearing me to absolute secrecy, they taught me to 'Suck the Monkey'."

I looked my dismay.

"Oh, it's not so bad. While Jock Jones was making the rounds, checking on other crews and waving his hook, we four slipped into the hold of the ship we had been working Monday. It still contained many

426

dozens of barrels of wine and spirits. In one of them, at the rear, there was a small plug, invisible to anyone who did not know of it already. Francis had drilled the hole and installed the plug last week. Yesterday, he pulled it out and inserted a rubber tube. 'Go on, then,' he urged me, and I did. It was most excellent dark Jamaican rum.

"Each of us took a turn. Several of us took more than one. Francis suggested we toast the absent Mick McCaskell. We did so, but only once. I don't think the gang misses him much. That nonpareil is too saintly for so lusty a crew.

"After we drank our fill, Cronin bunged the plug back into the barrel, we climbed up the ladder onto the deck, walked down the board onto the quay, resumed work, and no one was any the wiser. You would not credit how many barrels they have drilled between them. It is extraordinary, but they insist on sampling all varieties and vintages. It is not a bad revenge," Holmes judged, "given a wage of five-pence-per-hour."

"The wage is small," I acknowledged, "but that hardly justifies robbery."

"I expect James Eastman, Importer and Purveyor of Fine Wines and Spirits, and owner of that cavernous warehouse, would agree with you," Holmes replied. "But, in fact, the crew has additional, more substantial, means of augmenting its income."

I looked my incomprehension.

"We finished the rum barrels mid-afternoon yesterday, not long after our little escapade," Holmes explained, "by which time another clipper had arrived with a cargo of oranges in crates. Jock Jones immediately put us to work unloading it. We were no more than two hours on that job when he appeared. He really is a Goliath in a ship's hold, and always with that diabolical hook in his hand. I can see why the men fear him. He cracked open a crate with a single blow of the hook. 'Pull one out,' he directed, and Francis Cronin chose an orange to quarter with a little knife. 'This will do,' said Jock Jones, who tasted first. 'Now get back to work.'

"When Jones was gone, I asked Cronin what that had been about. He did not want to tell me at first, but eventually he did. The gang depends upon Jock Jones for daily hire. Its members, and not only they, are in his power. By day, Jones is a contractor of dock labor, as I well know – and by night, as Francis informed me, he is a thief on a large scale. He keeps watch for cargo that can be transported easily – and that will not be easily be missed. A dozen crates of oranges will not be missed from a cargo of five-hundred crates. Jock Jones intended to revisit the warehouse last night with Francis Cronin, who dares not refuse him.

"They would load a dozen crates onto a little skiff that Jones keeps on a rope out of sight in one of the pools behind a warehouse. He knows how to smuggle contraband out of the docks, and who will pay him for it. Sometimes he presses Cronin to help him, sometimes he presses others in the gang, or all of them at once, and not one of them happy about it – or prepared to defy him. Under his direction, they once stole an entire pallet of bearskins. Jones gives the men a little money from his profits and they keep silent, not out of gratitude, but from fear.

"After learning this, I managed to bump into the villain himself at The Duck and Parrot in the Commercial Road, a pub he frequents after work. A labor contractor will rarely condescend to talk with a mere docker at a pub, but as we stood side-by-side at the bar (as I had arranged we should), I borrowed from your own past and told him I had served in India with the Fifth Northumberland Fusiliers. That opened him up a little, for he told me that he too had served in India – as I surmised, you will recall – and then he could not help warning me against Lascar seamen. He says they are 'adept with the knife'.

"He brought up the little trade unionist who stands every morning and afternoon at the dock gates, and whom he claims to have beaten more than once. 'I failed to discourage him, but I am not done,' he told me, '"and I trust that I have now discouraged you.' I told him he had no need to discourage me where the union is concerned. A man must rely upon himself, not upon a workers' combination – upon which he clapped me on the back, called me a fine fellow, and reckoned he might 'steer something good my way'. Jock Jones, is not merely a thief, Watson. He is a dangerous man, if unimaginative."

I was growing impatient. "And what light does this shed upon the disappearance of Mick McCaskell?"

"Mr. Jones set me thinking. But first, let me acquaint you with another aspect of this modest adventure. My next step was to also stand the little trade-union orator to drinks at The Duck and Parrot. He wasn't at the bar with Jones, but I tracked him down to the snuggery. I gave him two beers, and he could have done with more, as he has a tremendous thirst. He told me he is a tea cooper, so we were able to discuss barrels."

"Whatever was the point of that?"

Holmes merely smiled. He put down his pipe and steepled his fingers. "That little man loves to talk. Once he starts, it's as if you have opened a tap. He told me about the risks he faces – the dangers, the beatings – all for preaching the gospel of trade unionism. I asked him why he didn't stop, but he only laughed. He was trying to recruit me! Then I asked about Jock Jones. 'He is our sworn enemy,' the little man said, 'for he well knows that if the union controls hiring, which one day it shall do, then he will be out of a job.' The little man also knows Mick McCaskell. He told me that McCaskell is a socialist like himself, a follower of Hyndman – and a rival.

You may not credit it, but McCaskell is studying Cicero at the Workman's Institute in order to become an orator!"

"Good Lord!" I was astonished. "That was what his wife meant when she said he was learning to write Latin."

"And the little man resents him – despises him, in fact. He wants deputies, perhaps, and followers – not competitors for leadership of his blessed trade union. I asked him if he knew where McCaskell might have gone. He claimed not to know that he has gone at all."

At that moment, there was a scuffling sound in the hallway. It took me a moment to identify, though I had heard it often enough in the past. It was young Wiggins rushing up the stairs. He was captain of Holmes's "Baker Street Irregulars", that band of half-a-dozen street urchins that my friend sometimes employed to spy out places he could not go, and to gather information he could not readily obtain. The lad knocked at the door and entered without being summoned. A flustered Mrs. Hudson soon followed. Holmes calmed her with a motion of his hand and gestured for her to leave.

The boy pulled off his cap. His clothing was ragged. His oft-patched trousers ended well above his ankles. Although it was November, his feet were bare. He was grinning widely. "We got it for you, Mr. Holmes, sir," he announced with obvious satisfaction, while handing his employer a scrap of paper. "It took some doing, it did, for it ain't the kind of thing a man is likely to tell – or sell. I sent one of the lads to Whitechapel lookin' for it. Another to Bethnal Green, and two more to Stepney. But it was me who got it – last night, off a man in Blackwall who were desperate for a few pennies to buy some beer."

"Well done, Wiggins!" Holmes congratulated the youngster. He glanced at the piece of paper before throwing it into the fire. Then he reached into his pocket and pulled out a change purse. "You have outdone yourself, and it is not impossible that you have helped to save a life. Give each of your lads half-a-crown for me. And keep this for yourself."

Wiggins carefully placed the half-crowns in one pocket and inspected the coin Holmes meant for him. "A crown!" he whispered. "Five shillings." That coin he placed even more carefully in his other pocket. "Thank you, Mr. Holmes, sir." Already, he was returning the cap to his head and backing out of the room. "You know how to find me if you have need." Then he scampered downstairs. As I heard the front door slam, I rose to watch him from the window – and could not find him. He had disappeared. Holmes chuckled. "He is invisible – and that is why he is a most invaluable ally."

"What was on that slip of paper? What do you mean 'helped to save a life'?"

"All in good time. Now I must set my trap. In the meantime, I suggest that you oil your service revolver. Also, you will need warm and sturdy clothing tonight." He too peered out the window: "A waterproof as well, I should think. I pray we are not too late." Then he rose, donned his mackinaw, and clattered downstairs.

"Now for the West India Docks," he announced that evening, after we had finished our dinner. I patted the eleven-inch Webley in my coat pocket.

A hansom cab was waiting for us outside our front door. "East India Dock Road," Holmes told the driver, who flicked his whip just above the hindquarters of the stolid bay that would bring us there. We traveled east on the Marylebone Road towards Holborn, and east again to Cheapside and then east some more, along the Whitechapel Road. Every mile the streets grew darker and dirtier, and the long lines of two-story dwellings on either side turned grimier and more monotonous. A light rain was falling yet again.

"Imagine living here," I murmured to Holmes, as I peered from the cab. "Never to read a book, or to have an interesting conversation, or even to think, except about your next meal."

"It would be difficult," he replied.

By the time we reached the East India Dock Road, the rain had stopped, but the air remained chill and damp. "Pull up," Holmes directed the cabby just where the East and West India Dock Roads diverged. Holmes paid the man. "Don't bother to wait," he instructed. And to me: "We go this way."

We walked south along Bridge Road, just at Limehouse Reach, where the river makes a great bend to trace the Isle of Dogs. It was a black night and silent in that desolate no-man's land, with the river to our right and the Surrey Commercial Docks behind it, and the West India Docks to our left, and great gloomy warehouses looming above on either side. Holmes pulled me off the road just before Cuba Street.

We stood on a patch of scrubby grass, facing a fence, ten feet high, running along the west side of the West India Docks. "It will be somewhere here," he muttered, and struck a match. "There!" he exclaimed in triumph as the little flame died. I could see nothing, but I felt on my face another spatter of rain, and I could hear the creaking of masts, and the wind moaning through ships' rigging nearby. Three men were approaching. "Ah, Lestrade," Holmes greeted their leader, "and two stout assistants. This augurs well. I presume that you are armed?"

430

"We all are, Mr. Holmes," replied Detective Inspector G. Lestrade of Scotland Yard. "And I have repeated to these men all you conveyed to me this afternoon."

"Well then," said Holmes. "It is time, and we are ready to begin. Pull out your watches. We must synchronize them." And when we had: "There is a hole under the fence, just there," and he pointed one way. "Young Wiggins found it for me. It is one of several used by dockers who pilfer from the warehouses at night. There is another hole, further along, out of sight from here," and he pointed in the other direction, "where I will be meeting Jock Jones and the rest of our little gang. We will enter the docks through it. He plans for us to steal a half-dozen barrels of rum from the warehouse of James Eastman. But I think he has something else on his mind as well.

"You must wait here precisely half-an-hour. Then you must crawl through the hole I've indicated," and he pointed again. "When you get through, you will see before you a narrow channel of water. This afternoon, I left a dinghy there tied to a piling almost opposite the hole. Paddle the dinghy north, towards the West India Dock Road, until you see the main entrance to the Eastman warehouse on your right. There are plenty of rings set in the quay where you may tie up. Then the warehouse. Around the corner there is a side door, unlocked. Enter, and you'll find yourselves in that great hall of barrels. Take care not to be seen or heard, for I do believe a man's life is at stake. I will be there with the others, pretending to commit burglary. Show yourselves at my signal. You will know what to do."

He looked searchingly at each of us, gripped my hand, and was gone.

We spoke little for the next half-hour, but stoically bore the increasingly unpleasant night: Drizzle, wind, fog, cold. I was glad when it was time to move, but Lestrade insisted on crawling through the hole first. In fact, it was more a short tunnel than a hole. We had to slither underground like snakes to gain the other side, but then we were through, and the little craft, dark against the black water, indeed almost invisible, was waiting as Holmes had promised it would be. We clambered aboard and cast off. The rest also went as Holmes had foretold. We tied up not far down the channel, climbed up onto the quay, crept around the warehouse to the side door, and entered.

It was an immense chamber – but unlit, so that I sensed its size rather than saw it. At first, I thought we were alone in all that vastness, but as my eyes adjusted, I discerned far off, at the other end, a flickering oil lantern.

"There," I whispered to Lestrade. He squinted, nodded, and touched the others, signing for us to follow. We stole forward, stopped, listened, crept on, and now I could hear men grunting as they struggled to lift what I presumed to be a giant barrel onto a trolley. And then I heard a deep voice full of menace, although at that distance the words were unintelligible.

There were so many rows of barrels, we soon realized we could enter a parallel alley of them and, so long as we were cautious, advance without danger of detection. Within minutes, we were near enough to hear the men speak and, peering round from where we had halted, to see them in the uneven yellow light of the lantern. It cast their giant black shadows against the far wall, which was painted white, and I was reminded of a magic lantern projecting pantomime figures onto a screen. But Lestrade was gesturing, directing. He pointed us each to crouch behind a different barrel, and thus to surround the little group.

I heard that deep bass voice rumble a curse. "Lift it, you bloody Molly, or you'll feel my hook!" That was enough, I thought, and reached for my service revolver, but Lestrade shook his head and put his finger to his lips, and I remembered that Holmes had promised to signal. So we watched and waited. I soon could distinguish the owner of that terrible voice, Jock Jones, from the others. Except for Holmes, he was a full head taller than the rest. He took no part in their strenuous work, and he played incessantly with that ugly hook, as if he hated not to be cracking someone's head with it. His men were maneuvering the barrels, one at a time and with great difficulty, onto a trolley, which then they guided down a ramp that let them outside onto the quay. I couldn't see, but I imagined them lowering the barrels with ropes onto a lighter. I wondered how Jones had procured such a craft. He was no simple thief.

For nearly an hour we watched the men toiling: Four enormous barrels they conveyed to the waiting lighter. Then, "In there," rumbled the man with the awful voice. He was pointing to a door at the far end of the great chamber, and I realized it must open upon a smaller room, perhaps an alcove containing rare vintages. "There is a barrel standing alone, against the side wall. It will be the last tonight."

The little crew disappeared for a few minutes, then reappeared with an enormous barrel they had maneuvered onto their trolley.

Holmes spoke in his normal voice: "This is the barrel you have wanted all night, Jock, is it not?" And he raised a hand in our direction. Somehow, he knew we were there, although none of the others did.

The giant blinked once, twice, then stepped threateningly in my friend's direction, brandishing the hook. "I thought I smelled something wrong about you."

"No," said Holmes coolly, a revolver had appeared in his hand. The three other dockers were standing stupefied around the trolley. I stepped from behind the barrel that had hidden me, my gun aimed at Jock Jones

432

too. North, south and east – so did Lestrade and his men. Each of them held a revolver.

"You are under arrest," Lestrade informed the giant.

"Drop the hook," Holmes ordered.

Jock Jones looked in every direction, but there was no escape.

"The irons," Lestrade said, and one of his assistants cuffed the big man's hands behind his back.

I breathed a sigh of relief. Holmes picked up the hook.

"Look at this." He was pointing with the hook to the top of the barrel that he and the three other men had just brought in. I saw that some sharp instrument had scored it fiercely. Holmes matched the claws of the hook to the marks. They fitted perfectly.

Holmes's face was grim. He grasped the hook firmly and began trying to pry the lid from the top of the barrel with it.

"Who are you?" one of the gang wanted to know. "What are you doing? Are you a policeman? You know we wanted no part of this."

"Ah, Francis," Holmes replied. "Do not be alarmed. But help me with this lid. We must hurry."

With difficulty, the two men finally managed to pry it off and set it on the floor. They peered into the container – and recoiled as if they had been struck. A terrible stench rose from the barrel. Francis Cronin gagged. Holmes made a face, but he was undeterred.

"Help me," he commanded. "He has been in there for four days now." Then, he and Francis Cronin reached into the barrel and, with much effort, managed to pull the inert figure of a man from it. An indescribable odor accompanied the figure. They laid it on the floor, face up.

"It's Mick!" exclaimed a member of the gang in wonderment. "And with the start of a beard!"

Holmes, kneeling, had the man's wrist in his hand. "He's alive, by God."

The big man couldn't help snorting a disbelieving curse.

"Barely alive," said I, kneeling beside him as well, "and lucky to be. Look at that!"

The unconscious McCaskell had reflexively tried to pull away from Holmes and, in doing so, had turned his head, to reveal a horrible gash, scabbed over and nearly black. "We must get him to a hospital immediately."

Lestrade spoke. "There will be a police van on the East India Dock Road waiting to take him," pointing at Jock Jones, "to Scotland Yard. But we will stop at Barts along the way."

"He must have water now," I broke in.

"Here is hot tea," said Francis Cronin, offering his own flask.

433

"Only a little," I cautioned.

Gently, Holmes brought the flask to McCaskell's cracked and swollen lips. The man on the floor swallowed a few drops reflexively. His eyes fluttered. He groaned, but he did not move again.

"Look here," whispered one of the dockers incredulously, peering into the barrel despite the reek: "There is no rum inside."

"Aye," answered Holmes. "Jock found an empty one to suit his purpose."

I stood, walked over to the barrel, and ran my hands over it, for something else was bothering me: "This must have been a barrel with a hole in it for 'sucking the monkey'," I said, "and McCaskell must have punched out the plug, else he would have suffocated." And then, indeed, I found the hole, about waist high.

"And down at the bottom," said the same docker wonderingly, still peering into the barrel, despite the stench. "There is Mick's flask."

Jock Jones cursed again.

"You left him for dead, or dying, did you not, Jock?" Holmes accused, "and in a side room where no one could hear him cry if he lingered. But he had a little to drink from the flask, and air to breathe through the hole he punched. He was tougher than you thought."

"You will not charge me with murder," the big man growled, "for he is not dead."

"You may not swing for what you have done," Holmes answered him, "but you will go down for it." He turned to the three dockers. "It's time for you to disappear. Count yourselves lucky. I realize none of you had anything to do with this," indicating the man on the floor. "And I know you would not be here at all, if not for him," pointing now at the man in handcuffs. "But say nothing about any of this. What the police do not know about recent larcenies at West India Docks will not hurt them," and he winked at Lestrade. Then, turning to the gang, he added with a little smile, "You had better exit the dock as you came into it, under the fence. Do not let anyone see you."

The next morning after breakfast, we took another hansom cab, this time to Barts. But I did no rounds that day. Rather, upon arriving, I consulted with a colleague who then showed us to the room in which Mick McCaskell lay sleeping. An enormous bandage covered most of his head. Someone had shaved his incipient beard. A slim figure was bending over him. It was Elizabeth McCaskell.

She rose as we entered. "Mr. Holmes," she began in a broken voice. My friend made a shushing motion. I went over to the bed. McCaskell's pulse was still weak, but it was steady now.

434

"He took a nasty blow to the head," said I. "After four days in that barrel, he has lost strength. He is malnourished. We must nurture him with fluids first. Food will come later. It will take time to rehabilitate him. It was a near run thing, but he will recover."

"I cannot thank you enough," Mrs. McCaskell struggled to say. "But I don't know how I will pay for his care."

"That is my responsibility, I think." A tall, distinguished-looking gentleman, with silver hair and a trim silver goatee, had entered the room, his top hat in his hands.

"Mr. Sidney Holland, the dock director," Holmes introduced him. "I am gratified by your presence."

"Your fame proceeds you, Mr. Holmes," the dock director enunciated in an accent that could have cut glass. "I was pleased to make your acquaintance yesterday." And, turning to Elizabeth McCaskill, "I can do no other."

"What?" said Mrs. McCaskell, and began to weep unashamedly.

Sidney Holland looked enquiringly at Holmes, who was standing with his back to the window through which a shaft of light was pouring. Finally, the weather had turned.

"Yes," Holmes said. "It's time for me to explain." He looked at the careworn young woman, who was wiping tears from her face. "You came to me with a little puzzle," he began, "but I recognized from the first that it might have deadly implications."

"How so?" I asked, for now he had puzzled me.

"The union. Mrs. McCaskell mentioned from the first that her husband was interested in the union, and it occurred to me that an aspiring trade unionist at the docks might run risks. That little fellow with the big voice confirmed as much when we spoke at the pub. If he succeeded, the union would put Jock Jones out of business. That outlaw would do much to protect his own livelihood."

"Which is why he beat the little man, of course," I interjected. "And McCaskell was a trade unionist as well." A thought struck me: "But Holmes, the little man hated McCaskell as much as Jock Jones did."

"Yes, that muddied the waters for a moment," Holmes conceded. "But I soon realized that McCaskell's absolute probity was the real problem, not the trade unionism." He turned towards Mrs. McCaskell: "He is an excellent husband, no doubt, but a perfect man in an imperfect world will have few friends. I think his mates among the crew resented him too."

In response, Mrs. McCaskell raised her husband's hand to her lips.

"But the members of the crew would never have hurt him," Holmes reassured her. "Their conduct last night proved that. They know he is an honest and a good man before he is anything else. How would such a man have regarded Jock Jones's villainy? I have no doubt that he intended to go to the police about it. Surely Jones himself had the same intuition – with results we have before us." And he gestured towards the bed.

"How did it come to you that Jones would hide McCaskell's body in a barrel?"

"At first I didn't think of barrels. I thought I confronted a simple case of murder, and my task would be to prove it. Then Jock Jones told me at The Duck and Parrot about beating the man who stands every day on the soapbox at the dock gate. Such a little fellow, he is. You could beat him to death and fit him in a barrel and none the wiser. And then I remembered how enormous those barrels of rum are. You could fit a bigger man into one of those. That was the key."

"Mick McCaskell would fit!"

"Precisely. He would have been fished out of the water. He would have been discovered sooner or later in a back alley. Where better to hide a body than in a barrel in the backroom of a warehouse in the West India Dock? Jones lured McCaskell into Eastman's warehouse on some pretext at the end of work Saturday. Earlier he had loosened the top of that empty barrel with his hook. You saw the scratch marks. Then he raked that diabolical claw right across his victim's scalp, picked him up, and threw him in, thinking he was dead, or soon would be, with no air or water in there, and a vicious head wound. Of course, he knew nothing of 'sucking the monkey', so he didn't think to check for a bung hole. He didn't remember that McCaskell customarily carried a flask of tea in his pocket. Jones replaced the top of the barrel and left the warehouse. No corpse to dispose of. No police nosing round the docks after the corpse was discovered.

"I knew about the tea, and I knew there might be a hole in the barrel from the crew, if only McCaskell was able to punch it out," Holmes continued, "but I didn't know which barrel he was in, or how to find it. Which is why I jumped when Francis Cronin told me that we were going into Eastman's warehouse to steal barrels of rum last night."

"But how did you know they would take the barrel with McCaskell in it?"

"I didn't. But they would have to, if McCaskell really was in one. Jock Jones needed that barrel out of the warehouse, and out of the docks entirely. Much better to dispose of McCaskell's body far from home. When we came to the fifth barrel last night, I realized immediately that it had a different weight and feel than all the others. It had to be the one with McCaskell in it."

"And if it had weighed and felt like all the rest?"

436

"Then I would have known I was mistaken, and that barrels had nothing to do with the disappearance of Mick McCaskell. In that case, we would merely have arrested Jock Jones for robbery."

He turned toward the dock director, Sidney Holland. "But you're sitting on a powder keg with your 'call-ons' and five-pence-an-hour at the docks."

"We will keep the union out," that gentleman replied, "for we must. Our country is great because it is free. Any workman's combination will jeopardize that. It will dictate to the employer whom he can hire, and for how long, and for how much. A workman must stand on his own two feet. He must negotiate his terms of engagement with his employer man-to-man. He must not delegate that task to a union boss. It is not the British way.

"But I listened carefully to what you told me yesterday, when you called," he continued, addressing Holmes. "I would not object to raising the dockers' rate from five- to six-pence-an-hour, if it keeps the union out. I will have to convince my colleagues on the board, which will not be easy." He turned to regard Mrs. McCaskell. "And I will take care of her husband – and of her too, if she will let me."

Elizabeth McCaskell let out a little cry.

"One of our maids has returned to her family in Devon," the dock director continued. "I would be glad for this good woman to take her place at eight-pounds-per-month, room and board included." He was looking at her jaw. "It will get you away from those damnable matches."

"Come, Watson," said Holmes to me. "I think we are done here."

We were strolling in brilliant sunshine down Cock Lane.

"They will not do it," Holmes stated abruptly. "The dock directors will not agree to pay six-pence every hour unless they are forced."

"Can the dockers force them?" I asked.

"I doubt it," said Holmes. "A more ignorant rabble I have rarely encountered. On the other hand, if the dockers can organize, then anyone can."

"Do not frighten me," I joked.

"It is no joke. They are ignorant. They are accustomed to doing as they are told, and to being poor. But they are desperate."

"Then," said I, "take heart from what you have just witnessed. A more generous offer than the one just made by Sidney Holland to the McCaskells I have rarely known."

"Charity," Holmes mused, "but on a much larger scale of course, organized through the churches, perhaps." He smiled, and then the smile disappeared. "It may be the solution. But, if it is merely a seven-per-cent solution, it will never be enough."

About the Contributors

The following contributors appear in this volume:
The MX Book of New Sherlock Holmes Stories
Part XLIII – 2024 Annual (1874-1888)

Mike Adamson holds a Doctoral degree from Flinders University of South Australia. After early aspirations in art and writing, Mike secured qualifications in both marine biology and archaeology. Mike has been a university educator since 2006, has worked in the replication of convincing ancient fossils, is a passionate photographer, master-level hobbyist, and journalist for international magazines. Short fiction sales include to *Metastellar*, *Strand Magazine*, *Little Blue Marble*, *Abyss*, and *Apex*, *Daily Science Fiction*, *Compelling Science Fiction*, and *Nature Futures*. Mike has placed some two-hundred stories to date, totaling over a million words. Mike has completed his first Sherlock Holmes novel with Belanger Books, and will be appearing in translation in European magazines. You can catch up with his journey at his blog "The View From the Keyboard"
http://mike-adamson.blogspot.com

Gretchen Altabef has authored five Sherlock Holmes novels. Her stories, though murder mysteries, are full of hope and the bonhomie of friendship. Her fictional journeys grow out of her historical research. She shares with her main character a half-humorous perspective on the world and the creative application of imagination, and intuition. She is a member of *The Sherlock Holmes Society of London*, *The Adventuresses of Sherlock Holmes*, *The ACD Society, The John H. Watson Society*, and *The Sherlock Holmes Society of India*.

Brian Belanger, PSI, is a publisher, illustrator, graphic designer, editor, and author. In 2015, he co-founded Belanger Books publishing company along with his brother, author Derrick Belanger. His illustrations have appeared in *The Essential Sherlock Holmes* and *Sherlock Holmes: A Three-Pipe Christmas*, and in children's books such as *The MacDougall Twins with Sherlock Holmes* series, *Dragonella*, and *Scones and Bones on Baker Street*. Brian has published a number of Sherlock Holmes anthologies and novels through Belanger Books, as well as new editions of August Derleth's classic Solar Pons mysteries. Brian continues to design all of the covers for Belanger Books, and since 2016 he has designed the majority of book covers for MX Publishing. In 2019, Brian received his investiture in the PSI as "Sir Ronald Duveen." More recently, he illustrated a comic book featuring the band The Moonlight Initiative, created the logo for the Arthur Conan Doyle Society and designed *The Great Game of Sherlock Holmes* card game. Find him online at:
www.belangerbooks.com and
www.redbubble.com/people/zhahadun and
zhahadun.wixsite.com/221b

Alan Dimes was born in Northwest London and graduated from Sussex University with a BA in English Literature. He has spent most of his working life teaching English. Living in the Czech Republic since 2003, he is now semi-retired and divides his time between Prague and his country cottage. He has also written some fifty stories of horror and fantasy and thirty stories about his husband-and-wife detectives, Peter and Deirdre Creighton, set in the 1930's.

Sir Arthur Conan Doyle (1859-1930) *Holmes Chronicler Emeritus*. If not for him, this anthology would not exist. Author, physician, patriot, sportsman, spiritualist, husband and father, and advocate for the oppressed. He is remembered and honored for the purposes of this collection by being the man who introduced Sherlock Holmes to the world. Through fifty-six Holmes short stories, four novels, and additional Apocryphal entries, Doyle revolutionized mystery stories and also greatly influenced and improved police forensic methods and techniques for the betterment of all. *Steel True Blade Straight.*

Steve Emecz's main field is technology, in which he has been working for about twenty-five years. Steve is a regular speaker at trade shows and his tech career has taken him to more than fifty countries – so he's no stranger to planes and airports. In 2008, MX published its first Sherlock Holmes book, and MX has gone on to become the largest specialist Holmes publisher in the world with over 500 books. MX is a social enterprise and supports three main causes. The first is Happy Life, a children's rescue project in Nairobi, Kenya, where he and his wife, Sharon, spend every Christmas at the rescue centre in Kasarani. They have written two editions of a short book about the project, *The Happy Life Story*. The second is Undershaw, Sir Arthur Conan Doyle's former home, which is a school for children with learning disabilities for which Steve is a patron. Steve has been a mentor for the World Food Programme for several years, and was part of the Nobel Peace Prize winning team in 2020.

Mark A. Gagen BSI is co-founder of Wessex Press, sponsor of the popular *From Gillette to Brett* conferences, and publisher of *The Sherlock Holmes Reference Library* and many other fine Sherlockian titles. A life-long Holmes enthusiast, he is a member of *The Baker Street Irregulars* and *The Illustrious Clients of Indianapolis*. A graphic artist by profession, his work is often seen on the covers of *The Baker Street Journal* and various BSI books.

John Atkinson Grimshaw (1836-1893) was born in Leeds, England. His amazing paintings, usually featuring twilight or night scenes illuminated by gas-lamps or moonlight, are easily recognizable, and are often used on the covers of books about The Great Detective to set the mood, as shadowy figures move in the distance through misty mysterious settings and over rain-slicked streets.

Arthur Hall was born in Aston, Birmingham, UK, in 1944. He discovered his interest in writing during his schooldays, along with a love of fictional adventure and suspense. His first novel, *Sole Contact*, was an espionage story about an ultra-secret government department known as "Sector Three", and was followed, to date, by three sequels. Other works include seven Sherlock Holmes novels, *The Demon of the Dusk*, *The One Hundred Percent Society*, *The Secret Assassin*, *The Phantom Killer*, *In Pursuit of the Dead*, *The Justice Master*, and *The Experience Club* as well as three collections of Holmes *Further Little-Known Cases of Sherlock* Holmes, *Tales from the Annals of Sherlock* Holmes, and *The Additional Investigations of Sherlock Holmes.* He has also written other short stories and a modern detective novel. He lives in the West Midlands, United Kingdom.

Paula Hammond has written over sixty fiction and non-fiction books, as well as short stories, comics, poetry, and scripts for educational DVD's. When not glued to the keyboard, she can usually be found prowling round second-hand books shops or hunkered down in a hide, soaking up the joys of the natural world.

Kelvin I. Jones is the author of six books about Sherlock Holmes and the definitive biography of Conan Doyle as a spiritualist, *Conan Doyle and The Spirits*. A member of

The Sherlock Holmes Society of London, he has published numerous short occult and ghost stories in British anthologies over the last thirty years. His work has appeared on BBC Radio, and in 1984 he won the Mason Hall Literary Award for his poem cycle about the survivors of Hiroshima and Nagasaki, recently reprinted as "Omega". (Oakmagic Publications) A one-time teacher of creative writing at the University of East Anglia, he is also the author of four crime novels featuring his ex-met sleuth John Bottrell, who first appeared in *Stone Dead*. He has over fifty titles on Kindle, and is also the author of several novellas and short story collections featuring a Norwich based detective, DCI Ketch, an intrepid sleuth who investigates East Anglian murder cases. He also published a series of short stories about an Edwardian psychic detective, Dr. John Carter (*Carter's Occult Casebook*). Ramsey Campbell, the British horror writer, and Francis King, the renowned novelist, have both compared his supernatural stories to those of M. R. James. He has also published children's fiction, namely *Odin's Eye*, and, in collaboration with his wife Debbie, *The Dark Entry*. Since 1995, he has been the proprietor of Oakmagic Publications, publishers of British folklore and of his fiction titles.

Roger Johnson, BSI, ASH, PSI, etc, is a member of more Holmesian societies than he can remember, thanks to his (so far) 16 years as editor of *The Sherlock Holmes Journal*, and thirty-two years as editor of *The District Messenger*. The latter, the newsletter of *The Sherlock Holmes Society of London*, is now in the safe hands of Jean Upton, with whom he collaborated on the well-received book, *The Sherlock Holmes Miscellany*. Roger is resigned to the fact that he will never match the Duke of Holdernesse, whose name was followed by "*half the alphabet*".

Daniel Lenois graduated with a Bachelor of Arts in English Literature from Central Connecticut State University in 2023. A lifelong appreciator of Sherlock Holmes since reading the original stories as a child with his father, Daniel currently moonlights as a graduate student while also pursuing his real passion in the area of literary achievement. Prior and forthcoming publications include *The Helix*, *Blue Muse*, *Unleash Lit*, *Savage Planets*, and *Shacklebound Books*.

David Marcum plays *The Game* with deadly seriousness. He first discovered Sherlock Holmes in 1975 at the age of ten, and since that time, he has collected, read, and chronologicized literally thousands of traditional Holmes pastiches in the form of novels, short stories, radio and television episodes, movies and scripts, comics, fan-fiction, and unpublished manuscripts. He is the author of over one-hundred-twenty Sherlockian pastiches, some published in anthologies and magazines such as *The Best Mystery Stories of the Year 2021* and *The Strand*, and others collected in his own books, *The Papers of Sherlock Holmes*, *Sherlock Holmes and A Quantity of Debt*, *Sherlock Holmes – Tangled Skeins*, *Sherlock Holmes and The Eye of Heka*, and *The Collected Papers of Sherlock Holmes* – six volumes and more to come. He has won back-to-back first place fiction awards from *The Arthur Conan Doyle Society* (2023 and 2024) and the Nero Wolfe *Wolfe Pack*. He has edited over 1,100 Holmes adventures and eighty books, including dozens of traditional Sherlockian anthologies, such as the ongoing series *The MX Book of New Sherlock Holmes Stories*, which he created in 2015 to promote traditional Canonical Holmes. This collection is now at forty-five volumes, with more in preparation. He was responsible for bringing back August Derleth's Solar Pons for a new generation with his collections of authorized Pons stories, *The Papers of Solar Pons* and *The Further Papers of Solar Pons*. Pons's return was further assisted by his editing of the reissued authorized versions of the original Pons books, and then several volumes of new Pons adventures. He has done the same for the adventures of Dr. Thorndyke, and has plans for similar projects in the future. He has contributed numerous essays to various publications, and is a member of a number of Sherlockian groups and Scions, as well as *The Mystery Writers of America*. His irregular Sherlockian blog, *A Seventeen Step Program*, addresses various topics related to his favorite book friends (as his son used to call them when he was small), and can be found at *http://17stepprogram.blogspot.com/* He is a licensed Civil Engineer, living in Tennessee with his wife and son. Since the age of nineteen, he has worn a deerstalker as his regular-and-only hat. In 2013, he and his deerstalker were finally able make his first trip-of-a-lifetime Holmes Pilgrimage to England, with return Pilgrimages in 2015 and 2016, where you may have spotted him. Another is planned in mid-2024. If you ever run into him and his deerstalker out and about, feel free to say hello!

Will Murray is the author of some 75 novels, including some 20 posthumous Doc Savage collaborations with Lester Dent, and 40 books in the long-running Destroyer series. Other Murray novels star the Executioner, Tarzan of the Apes, The Spider, Pat Savage and the Mars Attacks characters. His book, *Nick Fury, Agent of S.H.I.E.L.D.: Empyre* (2000) foreshadowed the 9/11 terrorist attacks. Murray has penned more than 45 Sherlock Holmes short stories. Twenty of Murray's Holmes short stories have been collected as *The Wild Adventures of Sherlock Holmes*, Vols 1 and 2. His novelette, "The Adventure of the Vengeful Viscount", in which Tarzan of the Apes, otherwise Lord Greystoke, hires Sherlock Holmes to solve a mystery, was approved by both the Estate of Sir Arthur Conan Doyle and Edgar Rice Burroughs, Inc. Murray is the author of the non-fiction book, *Master of Mystery: The Rise of The Shadow*, which is an exploration of the famous radio and magazine character, and a sequel, *Dark Avenger: The Strange Saga of The Shadow*. *The Wild Adventures of Cthulhu* Vols 1 & 2 collect Murray's Lovecraftan short stories. For Marvel Comics, Murray created the Unbeatable Squirrel Girl with legendary artist Steve Ditko. Website: *www.adventuresinbronze.com*

Sidney Paget (1860-1908), a few of whose illustrations are used within this anthology, was born in London, and like his two older brothers, became a famed illustrator and painter. He completed over three-hundred-and-fifty drawings for the Sherlock Holmes stories that were first published in *The Strand* magazine, defining Holmes's image forever after in the public mind.

Ember Pepper was born and raised in San Diego, CA. She has an M.F.A. degree in Creative Fiction Writing. She has been a fan of The Great Detective since she was a pre-teen and her greatest artistic enjoyment is challenging herself to write quality pastiches of Sherlock Holmes and his stalwart biographer and friend, John Watson.

Tracy J. Revels, BSI, a Sherlockian from the age of eleven, is a professor of history at Wofford College in Spartanburg, South Carolina. She is a member of *The Survivors of the Gloria Scott* and *The Studious Scarlets Society*, and is a past recipient of the Beacon Society Award. Almost every semester, she teaches a class that covers The Canon, either to college students or to senior citizens. She is also the author of three supernatural Sherlockian pastiches with MX (*Shadowfall*, *Shadowblood*, and *Shadowwraith*), and a regular contributor to her scion's newsletter. She also has some notoriety as an author of very silly skits: For proof, see "The Adventure of the Adversarial Adventuress" and "Occupy Baker Street" on YouTube. When not studying Sherlock, she can be found researching the history of her native state, and has written books on Florida in the Civil War and on the development of Florida's tourism industry.

Jane Rubino is the author of *A Jersey Shore* mystery series, featuring a Jane Austen-loving amateur sleuth and a Sherlock Holmes-quoting detective, *Knight Errant*, *Lady Vernon and Her Daughter*, (a novel-length adaptation of Jane Austen's novella *Lady Susan*, co-authored with her daughter Caitlen Rubino-Bradway, *What Would Austen Do?*, also co-authored with her daughter, a short story in the anthology *Jane Austen Made Me Do It*, *The Rucastles' Pawn*, *The Copper Beeches from Violet Turner's POV*, and, of course, there's the Sherlockian novel in the drawer – who doesn't have one? Jane lives on a barrier island at the New Jersey shore.

Jonathan Schneer is an *emeritus* professor at the Georgia Institute of Technology, where he taught modern British history for thirty years. He has written nine history books published by university and commercial presses. His work has been translated into Russian, Chinese, Turkish, Estonian, French, and German. He has held many visiting fellowships at Oxford and Cambridge Universities, and elsewhere, has spoken about his books on radio, television, and podcasts, at seminars, conferences, meetings, book fairs, community centers, museums, libraries, book stores, etc. Now that he is retired, he divides his time between Williamstown, MA, and Decatur, GA. He certainly enjoys writing about Sherlock Holmes.

Fifteen of **Brenda Seabrooke**'s Sherlock Holmes pastiches have been anthologized in MX Publishing and Belanger Books, six in *Best Crime Stories of New England*, one in *Destination: Mystery* and *Mystery Tribune*, and twelve in literary reviews such as *Yemassee*, *Confrontation*, and one in *Redbook*. Twenty-two of her books for young readers have been published at Penguin, Clarion, etc., and won awards such as a Notable from the National Council of Social Studies, Junior Literary Guild, Hornbook Honor, an Edgar finalist, etc. She received a grant from the National Endowment for the Arts, and The Robie Macauley Award from Emerson College. In 2022, MX published her collection, *Sherlock Holmes: The Persian Slipper and Other Stories*.

Peter Shumway is a retired computer professional residing in Pennsylvania with his wife, Patty. They have been married forty-one years and have two daughters and four grandchildren. In the early 1970's, Peter performed magic with Bill Baker's World of Magic, John Bundy's Magic Concert, and traded secrets with David Copperfield when they were teenagers. Peter read the original Sherlock Holmes stories while in college in 1979, and has enjoyed rereading them many times since. He published his pastiche *Sherlock Holmes and The Kiss of Death in* 2005 and *Gullible's Journey* in 2023. When he was offered the opportunity to write a short story for the MX Series, he picked up his pen one more time.

Hailing from Bedford in the South East of England, **Matthew Simmonds** has been a confirmed devotee of Sir Arthur Conan Doyle's most famous creation since first watching Jeremy Brett's incomparable portrayal of the world's first consulting detective, on a Tuesday evening in April 1984, while curled up on the sofa with his father. He has written numerous short stories and his first novel, *Sherlock Holmes: The Adventure of The Pigtail Twist* was published in 2018. A sequel, *Sherlock Holmes: The Adventure of The Found Note* was published in November 2023. Matthew currently co-owns Harrison & Simmonds, the fifth-generation family business, a renowned County tobacconist, pipe and gift shop on Bedford High Street.

Denis O. Smith's first published story of Sherlock Holmes and Doctor Watson, "The Adventure of The Purple Hand", appeared in 1982. Since then, numerous other such accounts have been published in magazines and anthologies both in the U.K. and the U.S. In the 1990's, four volumes of his stories were published under the general title of *The Chronicles of Sherlock Holmes*, and, more recently his stories have been collected as *The Lost Chronicles of Sherlock Holmes* (2014), *The Lost Chronicles of Sherlock Holmes Volume II* (2016), *The Further Chronicles of Sherlock Holmes* (2018). He also wrote a Holmes novel, *The Riddle of Foxwood Grange* (2017). Born in Yorkshire, in the north of England, Denis Smith has lived and worked in various parts of the country, including London, and has now been resident in Norfolk for many years. His interests range widely, but apart from his dedication to the career of Sherlock Holmes, he has a passion for historical mysteries of all kinds, the railways of Britain and the history of London.

Robert V. Stapleton was born and brought up in Leeds, Yorkshire, England, and studied at Durham University. After working in various parts of the country as an Anglican parish priest, he is now retired and lives with his wife in North Yorkshire. As a member of his local writing group, he now has time to develop his other life as a writer of adventure stories. He has published a number of short stories, and he is hoping to have a couple of completed novels published at some time in the future.

Daniel Stashower , BSI, s an acclaimed biographer and narrative historian and winner of the Edgar, Agatha, and Anthony awards, as well as the Raymond Chandler Fulbright Fellowship in Detective Fiction. His work has appeared in *The New York Times*, *The Washington Post*, *Smithsonian Magazine*, *AARP: The Magazine*, *National Geographic Traveler*, and *American History*, as well as other publications. His books include *The Ectoplasmic Man*, *The Hour of Peril*, *Teller of Tales*, and *The Beautiful Cigar Girl*.

Kevin P. Thornton has had a varied career. He has been a soldier, a military contractor, a logistics consultant and, at various times, a forklift driver and a barman. It was not a well-thought-out path. He has played rugby, cricket, and other games of violence with virtually no success but plenty of gusto, and has the aches and scars to prove so. He has also had a varied writing career. In his time, he has written for *The New York Times* on the wildfires in Alberta, as well as a long running column in the *Fort McMurray Today*. He has had poetry published in more than a dozen collections, some of which have even sold commercially. He has also edited a journal on a military base in Afghanistan, and is currently the chief and only writer of a magazine for a Dene and Cree First Nation in Canada. He has written about half-a-dozen books, all of which were shortlisted in the *Crime Writers of Canada* unpublished awards, all of which are still unpublished. He has had rather more success with short stories, with somewhere around thirty anthologized. Many of these involve Sherlock Holmes and, while he would hesitate to call himself a Sherlockian – just as he hesitates over such titles as author, poet, journalist, columnist, editor – he is quite fond of the gentlemen of 221b. "They allow me to write crime stories succinctly, and if I were to title myself, I would take that as a starting point; if forced to take a stand I would describe myself as a storyteller." Kevin is one of the founding members of the *Northwords Literary Mag*azine of Fort McMurray, Alta. and a current or former member of the CWG, WGA, CWC, CWA, MWA, ITW, S-in-C, MofM, and the IACW. Decoding available on request. In 2015, he was accepted as a member of *The Keys*, the London based organization of writers founded by G.K. Chesterton and Ronald Knox. He has two sons of whom he is enormously proud, and a wife he adores, and who in turn seems to love and tolerate him, depending on the mood and the moment.

Emma West joined Undershaw in April 2021 as the Director of Education with a brief to ensure that qualifications formed the bedrock of our provision, whilst facilitating a positive balance between academia, pastoral care, and well-being. She quickly took on the role of Acting Headteacher from early summer 2021. Under her leadership, Undershaw has embraced its new name, new vision, and consequently we have seen an exponential increase in demand for places. There is a buzz in the air as we invite prospective students and families through the doors. Emma has overseen a strategic review, re-cemented relationships with Local Authorities, and positioned Undershaw at the helm of SEND education in Surrey and beyond. Undershaw has a wide appeal: Our students present to us with mild to moderate learning needs and therefore may have some very recent memories of poor experiences in their previous schools. Emma's background as a senior leader within the independent school sector has meant she is well-versed in brokering relationships between the key stakeholders, our many interdependences, local businesses, families, and staff, and all this while ensuring Undershaw remains relentlessly child-centric in its approach. Emma's energetic smile and boundless enthusiasm for Undershaw is inspiring.

Marcia Wilson is a freelance researcher and illustrator who likes to work in a style compatible for the color blind and visually impaired. She is Canon-centric, and her first MX offering, *You Buy Bones*, uses the point-of-view of Scotland Yard to show the unique talents of Dr. Watson. This continued with the publication of *Test of the Professionals: The Adventure of the Flying Blue Pidgeon* and *The Peaceful Night Poisonings*. She can be contacted at: *gravelgirty.deviantart.com*

The following contributors appear in these companion volumes:
Part XLIV– 2024 Annual (1889-1897)
Part XLV – 2024 Annual (1898-1917)

Ian Ableson is an ecologist by training and a writer by choice. When not reading or writing, he can reliably be found scowling at a clipboard while ankle-deep in a marsh somewhere in Michigan. His love for the stories of Arthur Conan Doyle started when his grandfather gave him a copy of *The Original Illustrated Sherlock Holmes* when he was in high school, and he's proud to have been able to contribute to the continuation of the tales of Sherlock Holmes and Dr. Watson.

Mike Adamson also has a story in Part XLV

Tim Newton Anderson is a former senior daily newspaper journalist and PR manager who has recently started writing fiction. In the past six months, he has placed fourteen stories in publications including *Parsec Magazine*, *Tales of the Shadowmen*, *SF Writers Guild*, *Zoetic Press*, *Dark Lane Books*, *Dark Horses Magazine*, *Emanations*, and *Planet Bizarro*.

Donald I. Baxter has practiced medicine for over forty years. He resides in Erie Pennsylvania with his wife and their dog. His family and his friends are for the most part lawyers who have given him the ability to make stuff up just as they do.

Chris Chan is a writer, educator, and historian. He works as a researcher and "International Goodwill Ambassador" for Agatha Christie Ltd. His true crime articles, reviews, and short fiction have appeared (or will soon appear) in *The Strand*, *The Wisconsin Magazine of History*, *Mystery Weekly*, *Gilbert!*, *Nerd HQ*, Akashic Books' *Mondays are Murder* web series, *The Baker Street Journal*, *The MX Book of New Sherlock Holmes Stories*, *Masthead: The Best New England Crime Stories*, *Sherlock Holmes Mystery Magazine*, and multiple Belanger Books anthologies. He is the creator of the Funderburke mysteries, a series featuring a private investigator who works for a school and helps students during times of crisis. The Funderburke short story "The Six-Year-Old Serial Killer" was nominated for a Derringer Award. His books include *Sherlock & Irene: The Secret Truth Behind "A Scandal in Bohemia"*, *Murder Most Grotesque: The Comedic Crime Fiction of Joyce Porter*, *Sherlock's Secretary*, *Of Course He Pushed Him*, *Nessie's Nemesis*, *Ghosting My Friend*, She *Ruined Our Lives*, and *The Autistic Sleuth*.

Mike Chinn's first-ever Sherlock Holmes fiction was a steampunk mashup of *The Valley of Fear*, entitled *Vallis Timoris* (Fringeworks 2015). Since then he has written about Holmes's archenemy in *The Mammoth Book of the Adventures of Moriarty* (Robinson 2015), appeared in several volumes of *The MX Book of New Sherlock Holmes Stories*, and faced the retired detective with cross-dimensional magic in the second volume of *Sherlock Holmes and the Occult Detectives* (Belanger Books 2020).

Craig Stephen Copland confesses that he discovered Sherlock Holmes when, sometime in the muddled early 1960's, he pinched his older brother's copy of the immortal stories and was forever afterward thoroughly hooked. He is very grateful to his high school English teachers in Toronto who inculcated in him a love of literature and writing, and even inspired him to be an English major at the University of Toronto. There he was blessed to sit at the feet of both Northrup Frye and Marshall McLuhan, and other great literary professors, who led him to believe that he was called to be a high school English teacher. It was his good fortune to come to his pecuniary senses, abandon that goal, and pursue a varied professional career that took him to over one-hundred countries and endless adventures. He considers himself to have been and to continue to be one of the luckiest men on God's good earth. A few years back he took a step in the direction of Sherlockian studies and joined *The Sherlock Holmes Society of Canada* – also known as *The Toronto Bootmakers*. In May of 2014, this esteemed group of scholars announced a contest for the writing of a new Sherlock Holmes mystery. Although he had never tried his hand at fiction before, Craig entered and was pleasantly surprised to be selected as one of the winners. Having enjoyed the experience, he decided to write more of the same, and he has now written new Sherlock Holmes mysteries related to and inspired by each of the sixty stories in the original Canon, along with a number of others.

Martin Daley was born in Carlisle, Cumbria in 1964. His thirty-year writing career has seen over twenty books and numerous short stories published. Inevitably, Holmes and Watson remain his favourite literary characters, and they continue to inspire his own detective writing. In 2010, Martin created Inspector Cornelius Armstrong, who carries out his police work against the backdrop of Edwardian Carlisle. With the publication of the first *Inspector Armstrong Casebook* (published by MX Publishing), Martin became a member of the Crime Writers' Association. Most recently, he published *The Selected Cases of Sherlock Holmes.* He lives with his wife Wendy, in Kirkcudbrightshire, in Southwest.

Alan Dimes also has stories in Parts XLIV and XLV

Brett Fawcett is a humanities and Latin teacher at the Chesterton Academy of St. Isidore in Sherwood Park, Alberta. He lives with his wife and son in Edmonton, where he is a member of The Wisteria Lodgers (The Sherlock Holmes Society of Edmonton). He vividly remembers the first time he finished reading the Sherlock Holmes stories in Grade 6, and has been a student of Holmesian literature and scholarship since then. He is also a frequent author of columns and articles on topics like theology, education, and mental health, as well as the occasional mystery story.

Paul A. Freeman is an English language teacher. He is the author of *Rumours of Ophir*, a crime novel which was taught at 'O' level in Zimbabwean high schools and has been translated into German. In addition to having two novels, a children's book and an 18,000-word narrative poem (*Robin Hood and Friar Tuck: Zombie Killers!*) commercially published, Paul is the author of scores of published short stories, poems and articles. He is a member of the *Society of Authors* and of the *Crime Writers' Association.* He lives and works in Mauritania.

Arthur Hall also has stories in Parts XLIV and XLV

Paula Hammond also has a story in Part XLIV

Stephen Herczeg is an IT Geek, writer, actor, and film-maker based in Canberra Australia. He has been writing for over twenty years and has completed a couple of dodgy novels, sixteen feature-length screenplays, and numerous short stories and scripts. Stephen was very successful in 2017's International Horror Hotel screenplay competition, with his scripts *TITAN* winning the Sci-Fi category and *Dark are the Woods* placing second in the horror category. His three-volume short story collection, *The Curious Cases of Sherlock Holmes*, will be published in 2021. His work has featured in *Sproutlings – A Compendium of Little Fictions* from Hunter Anthologies, the *Hells Bells* Christmas horror anthology published by the Australasian Horror Writers Association, and the *Below the Stairs*, *Trickster's Treats*, *Shades of Santa*, *Behind the Mask*, and *Beyond the Infinite* anthologies from OzHorror.Con, *The Body Horror Book*, *Anemone Enemy*, and *Petrified Punks* from Oscillate Wildly Press, and *Sherlock Holmes In the Realms of H.G. Wells* and *Sherlock Holmes: Adventures Beyond the Canon* from Belanger Books.

Paul Hiscock is an author of crime, fantasy, horror, and science fiction tales. His short stories have appeared in a variety of anthologies, and include a seventeenth-century whodunnit, a science fiction western, a clockpunk fairytale, and numerous Sherlock Holmes pastiches. He lives with his family in Kent (England) and spends his days taking care of his two children. You can find out more about Paul's writing at: *www.detectivesanddragons.uk.*

Naching T. Kassa is a wife, mother, and writer. She's created short stories, novellas, poems, and co-created three children. She resides in Eastern Washington State with her husband, Dan Kassa. Naching is a member of *The Horror Writers Association*, *Mystery Writers of America*, *The Sound of the Baskervilles*, *The ACD Society*, *The Crew of the Barque Lone Star*, and *The Sherlock Holmes Society of London*. She works in Talent Relations at Crystal Lake Publishing and was a recipient of the 2022 HWA Diversity Grant. You can find her work on Amazon.
https://www.amazon.com/Naching-T-Kassa/e/B005ZGHTI0

Susan Knight's newest novel, *Mrs. Hudson Goes to Paris* (2022) from MX publishing, is the latest in a series which began with her collection of stories, *Mrs. Hudson Investigates* (2019), the novel *Mrs. Hudson goes to Ireland* (2020), and *Mrs. Hudson Goes to Paris* (2022), and *Death in the Garden of England* (2023) She has contributed to many recent MX anthologies of new Sherlock Holmes short stories and enjoys writing as Dr. Watson as much as she does Mrs. Hudson. Nine of these stories comprised *The Strange Case of the Pale Boy and Other Mysteries* (2023). Susan is the author of two other non-Sherlockian story collections, as well as three novels, a book of non-fiction, and several plays, and has won several prizes for her writing. Susan lives in Dublin.

449

Daniel Lenois also has stories in Parts XLIV and XLV

Jeffrey Lockwood spent youthful afternoons darkly enchanted by feeding grasshoppers to black widows in his New Mexican backyard, which accounts for his scientific and literary affinities. He earned a doctorate in entomology, and worked as an ecologist at the University of Wyoming before metamorphosing into a Professor of Natural Sciences & Humanities in the departments of philosophy and creative writing. He considers Sherlock Holmes a model of scientific prowess, integrating exquisite observational skills with incisive abductive (not deductive) reasoning.

David MacGregor is a playwright, screenwriter, novelist, and nonfiction writer. He is a resident artist at The Purple Rose Theatre in Michigan, where a number of his plays have been produced. His plays have been performed from New York to Tasmania, and his work has been published by Dramatic Publishing, Playscripts, Smith & Kraus, Applause, Heuer Publishing, and Theatrical Rights Worldwide (TRW). He adapted his dark comedy, *Vino Veritas*, for the silver screen, and it stars Carrie Preston (Emmy-winner for *The Good Wife*). Several of his short plays have also been adapted into films. He is the author of three Sherlock Holmes plays: *Sherlock Holmes and the Adventure of the Elusive Ear*, *Sherlock Holmes and the Adventure of the Fallen Soufflé*, and *Sherlock Holmes and the Adventure of the Ghost Machine*. He adapted all three plays into novels for Orange Pip Books, and also wrote the two-volume nonfiction *Sherlock Holmes: The Hero with a Thousand Faces* for MX Publishing. He teaches writing at Wayne State University in Detroit and is inordinately fond of cheese and terriers.

David Marcum also has stories in Parts XLIV and XLV

Kevin Patrick McCann has published eight collections of poems for adults, one for children (*Diary of a Shapeshifter*, Beul Aithris), a book of ghost stories (*It's Gone Dark*, The Otherside Books), *Teach Yourself Self-Publishing* (Hodder) co-written with the playwright Tom Green, and *Ov* (Beul Aithris Publications) a fantasy novel for children.

Mark Mower is a long-standing member of the *Crime Writers' Association, The Sherlock Holmes Society of London*, and *The Solar Pons Society of London*. His pastiche collections include *Sherlock Holmes: The Baker Street Case-Files, Sherlock Holmes: The Baker Street Legacy, Sherlock Holmes: The Baker Street Epilogue*, and *Sherlock Holmes: The Baker Street Archive* (all with MX Publishing). His non-fiction works include the bestselling book *Zeppelin Over Suffolk: The Final Raid of the L48* (Pen & Sword Books). Alongside his writing, Mark maintains a sizeable collection of pastiches, and never tires of discovering new stories about Sherlock Holmes and Dr. Watson.

Tracy J. Revels also has stories in Parts XLIV and XLV

Roger Riccard's family history has Scottish roots, which trace his lineage back to Highland Scotland. This British Isles ancestry encouraged his interest in the writings of Sir Arthur Conan Doyle at an early age. He has authored the novels, *Sherlock Holmes & The Case of the Poisoned Lilly*, and *Sherlock Holmes & The Case of the Twain Papers*. In addition he has produced several short stories in *Sherlock Holmes Adventures for the Twelve Days of Christmas* and the series *A Sherlock Holmes Alphabet of Cases*. A new series will begin publishing in the Autumn of 2022, and his has another novel in the works. All of his books have been published by Baker Street Studios. His Bachelor of Arts Degrees in both Journalism and History from California State University, Northridge, have proven valuable to his writing historical fiction, as well as the encouragement of his wife/editor/inspiration and Sherlock Holmes fan, Rosilyn. She passed in 2021, and it is in her memory that he continues to contribute to the legacy of the "*man who never lived and will never die*".

Dan Rowley practiced law for over forty years in private practice and with a large international corporation. He is retired and lives in Erie, Pennsylvania, with his wife Judy, who puts her artistic eye to his transcription of Watson's manuscripts. He inherited his writing ability and creativity from his children, Jim and Katy, and his love of mysteries from his parents, Jim and Ruth.

Jonathan Schneer also has a story in Part XLIV

Alisha Shea has resided near Saint Louis, Missouri for over thirty years. The eldest of six children, she found reading to be a genuine escape from the chaotic drudgery of life. She grew to love not only Sherlock Holmes, but the time period from which he emerged. In her spare time, she indulges in creating music via piano, violin, and Native American flute. Sometimes she thinks she might even be getting good at it. She also produces a wide variety of fiber arts which are typically given away or auctioned off for various fundraisers.

Shane Simmons is the author of the occult detective novels *necropolis* and *Epitaph*, and the crime collection *Raw and Other Stories.* An award-winning screenwriter and graphic novelist, his work has appeared in international film festivals, museums, and lectures about design and structure. He was born in Lachine, a suburb of Montreal best known for being massacred in 1689 and having a joke name. Visit Shane's homepage at *eyestrainproductions.com* for more information.

Robert V. Stapleton also has a story in Part XLV

Thomas A. (Tom) Turley has been "hooked on Holmes" since finishing *The Hound of the Baskervilles* at about the age of twelve. However, his interest in Sherlockian pastiches didn't take off until he wrote one. *Sherlock Holmes and the Adventure of the Tainted Canister* (2014) is available as an e-book and an audiobook from MX Publishing. It also appeared in *The Art of Sherlock Holmes – USA Edition 1*. In 2017, two of Tom's stories, "A Scandal in Serbia" and "A Ghost from Christmas Past" were published in Parts VI and VII of this anthology. "Ghost" was also included in *The Art of Sherlock Holmes – West Palm Beach Edition*. Meanwhile, Tom published two collection of historical pastiches entitled *Sherlock Holmes and the Crowned Heads of Europe* (2021) and *Watson's Wives and Other Tales of Sherlock Holmes* (2024). Although he has a Ph.D. in British history, Tom spent most of his professional career as an archivist with the State of Alabama. He and his wife Paula (an aspiring science fiction novelist) live in Montgomery, Alabama. Interested readers may contact Tom through MX Publishing or his Goodreads author's page.

DJ Tyrer is the person behind Atlantean Publishing and has had fiction featuring Sherlock Holmes published in volumes from MX Publishing and Belanger Books, and an issue of *Awesome Tales*, and has a forthcoming story in *Sherlock Holmes Mystery Magazine*. DJ's non-Sherlockian mysteries can be found in anthologies such as *Mardi Gras Mysteries* (Mystery and Horror LLC) and *The Trench Coat Chronicles* (Celestial Echo Press), and on *Mystery Tribune*.

DJ Tyrer's website is at *https://djtyrer.blogspot.co.uk/*
DJ's Facebook page is at *https://www.facebook.com/DJTyrerwriter/*
The Atlantean Publishing website is at *https://atlanteanpublishing.wordpress.com/*

Daniel D. Victor is a retired high school English teacher who lives with his wife in his native Los Angeles, California. His doctoral dissertation on the assassinated American writer David Graham Phillips led to Victor's first Sherlock Holmes pastiche, *The Seventh Bullet* (St. Martin's Press) and ultimately to his ongoing series, *Sherlock Holmes and the American Literati*. Each novel in the series introduces Holmes to an American author who was writing during the period Holmes was detecting. Victor has also recently published *Cruel September*, a novel based on his many years of teaching in Los Angeles.

I.A. Watson's first professional publishing credit was with a Sherlock Holmes story. The tale in this book will be his 50th (counting his novel *Holmes and Houdini*, and one or two short stories in publishers' queues). He is constantly surprised at how many ways there are to tell Sherlock Holmes adventures, which he holds to be a sign of Sir Arthur Conan Doyle's genius in developing so flexible and resilient a format for such a compelling cast of characters. A full list of I.A. Watson's 100+ published works including twenty or so novels is available at:
http://www.chillwater.org.uk/writing/iawatsonhome.htm

Marcia Wilson also has stories in Parts XLIV and XLV

The MX Book of New Sherlock Holmes Stories
Edited by David Marcum
(MX Publishing, 2015-   )

"This is the finest volume of Sherlockian fiction I have ever read, and I have read, literally, thousands." – Philip K. Jones

"Beyond Impressive . . . This is a splendid venture for a great cause!"
– Roger Johnson, Editor, *The Sherlock Holmes Journal*,
The Sherlock Holmes Society of London

Part I: 1881-1889; Part II: 1890-1895; Part III: 1896-1929

Part IV: 2016 Annual

Part V: Christmas Adventures

Part VI: 2017 Annual

Eliminate the Impossible
Part VII: (1880-1891); Part VIII: (1892-1905)

2018 Annual
Part IX: (1879-1895); Part X: (1896-1916)

Some Untold Cases
Part XI: (1880-1891); Part XII: (1894-1902)

2019 Annual
Part XIII: (1881-1890); Part XIV: (1891-1897); Part XV: (1898-1917)

Whatever Remains . . . Must be the Truth
Part XVI: (1881-1890); Part XVII: (1891-1898); Part XVIII: (1898-1925)

2020 Annual
Part XIX: (1882-1890); Part XX: (1891-1897); Part XXI: (1898-1923)·

Some More Untold Cases
Part XXII: (1877-1887); Part XXIII: (1888-1894); Part XXIV: (1895-1903)

2021 Annual
Part XXV: (1881-1888); Part XXVI: (1889-1897); Part XXVII: (1898-1928)

More Christmas Adventures
Part XXVIII: (1869-1888); Part XXIX: (1889-1896); Part XXX: (1897-1928)

2022 Annual
Part XXXI: (1875-1887); Part XXXII: (1888-1895); Part XXXIII: (1896-1919)

"However Improbable . . . ."
Part XXXIV: (1878-1888); Part XXXV: (1889-1896); Part XXXVI: (1897-1919)

2023 Annual
Parts XXXVII (1875-1889), XXXVIII (1889-1896), and XXXIX (1897-1923)

Further Untold Cases
Part XL: (1879-1886), Part XLI: (1887-1892) and Part XLII: (1894-1922)

2024 Annual
Parts XLIII (1874-1888), XLIV (1889-1897), and XLV (1898-1917)

In Preparation . . . *Part XLVI (and XLVII and XLVIII as well?)*
and more to come!

The MX Book of New Sherlock Holmes Stories
Edited by David Marcum
(MX Publishing, 2015-   )

Publishers Weekly says:

Part VI: *The traditional pastiche is alive and well . . . .*

Part VII: *Sherlockians eager for faithful-to-the-canon plots and characters will be delighted.*

Part VIII: *The imagination of the contributors in coming up
with variations on the volume's theme is matched by their ingenious resolutions.*

Part IX: *The 18 stories . . . will satisfy fans of Conan Doyle's
originals. Sherlockians will rejoice that more volumes are on the way.*

Part X: *. . . new Sherlock Holmes adventures of consistently high quality.*

Part XI: *. . . an essential volume for Sherlock Holmes fans.*

Part XII: *. . . continues to amaze with the number of high-quality pastiches.*

Part XIII: *. . . Amazingly, Marcum has found 22 superb pastiches . . .
his is more catnip for fans of stories faithful to Conan Doyle's original*

Part XIV: *. . . this standout anthology of 21 short stories written
in the spirit of Conan Doyle's originals.*

Part XV: *Stories pitting Sherlock Holmes against seemingly supernatural phenomena highlight
Marcum's 15ᵗʰ anthology of superior short pastiches.*

Part XVI: *Marcum has once again done fans of Conan Doyle's originals a service.*

Part XVII: *This is yet another impressive array of new but traditional Holmes stories.*

Part XVIII: *Sherlockians will again be grateful to Marcum and
MX for high-quality new Holmes tales.*

Part XIX: *Inventive plots and intriguing explorations of aspects of Dr. Watson's
life and beliefs lift the 24 pastiches in Marcum's impressive 19ᵗʰ Sherlock Holmes anthology*

Part XX: *Marcum's reserve of high-quality new Holmes exploits seems endless.*

Part XXI: *This is another must-have for Sherlockians.*

Part XXII: *Marcum's superlative 22ⁿᵈ Sherlock Holmes pastiche anthology features 21 short stories
that successfully emulate the spirit of Conan Doyle's originals while expanding on the canon's
tantalizing references to mysteries Dr. Watson never got around to chronicling.*

Part XXIII: *Marcum's well of talented authors able to mimic the
feel of The Canon seems bottomless.*

Part XXIV: *Marcum's expertise at selecting high-quality pastiches remains impressive.*

Part XXVIII: *All entries adhere to the spirit, language, and characterizations of
Conan Doyle's originals, evincing the deep pool of talent Marcum has access to.
Against the odds, this series remains strong, hundreds of stories in.*

Part XXXI: *. . . yet another stellar anthology of 21 short pastiches that
effectively mimic the originals . . . Marcum's diligent searches for high-quality
stories has again paid off for Sherlockians.*

Part XXXIV: *Mind-bending puzzles are the highlight of Marcum's fully satisfying 34ᵗʰ anthology,
which again demonstrates that multiple authors are capable of giving Sherlock Holmes and
Watson innovative mysteries to tackle while staying in character. Marcum's inventory of canonical
pastiches shows no signs of being exhausted any time soon.*

The MX Book of New Sherlock Holmes Stories
Edited by David Marcum
(MX Publishing, 2015-   )

An Investees' Anthology
Edited by David Marcum
(MX Publishing, 2022)

Selected Contributions to
The MX Book of New Sherlock Holmes Stories
by Members of
The Baker Street Irregulars

*All royalties from this collection are being donated
for the benefit of the preservation of Undershaw,
a school for special needs students located at
one of the former homes of Sir Arthur Conan Doyle*

Stories, Forewords, and Poems in this volume
have previously appeared in Parts I – XXXVI of
The MX Book of New Sherlock Holmes Stories

Featuring Contributions by:

Mark Alberstat, Marino C. Alvarez, Peter Calamai, Catherine Cooke, Carla Coupe, David Stuart Davies, John Farrell, Lyndsay Faye, Sonia Fetherston, Jayantika Ganguly, Jeffrey Hatcher, Roger Johnson, Leslie S. Klinger, Ann Margaret Lewis, Bonnie MacBird, Stephen Mason, Julie McKuras Nicholas Meyer, Jacquelynn Morris, Otto Penzler, Christopher Redmond, Tracy J. Revels, Steven Rothman, Nancy Holder, Mark Levy (and Arlene Mantin Levy), Nicholas Utechin, and Sean M. Wright (and DeForeest B. Wright, III)

MX Publishing

MX Publishing is the world's largest specialist Sherlock Holmes publisher, with over five-hundred titles and over two-hundred authors creating the latest in Sherlock Holmes fiction and non-fiction

The catalogue includes several award winning books, and over two-hundred-and-fifty have been converted into audio.

MX Publishing also has one of the largest communities of Holmes fans on Facebook, with regular contributions from dozens of authors.

www.mxpublishing.com

@mxpublishing on Facebook, Twitter, and Instagram

www.ingramcontent.com/pod-product-compliance
Lightning Source LLC
Chambersburg PA
CBHW032302020726
47495CB00001B/207